# THE FOUR WORLDS - SUBVERSION

## THE FOUR WORLDS
### BOOK 2

SKYLER RAMIREZ

Copyright © 2023 Skyler S. Ramirez

All rights reserved

The characters and events portrayed in this book are fictitious. Any similarity to real persons, living or dead, is coincidental and not intended by the author.

No part of this book may be reproduced, or stored in a retrieval system, or transmitted in any form or by any means, electronic, mechanical, photocopying, recording, or otherwise, without express written permission of the publisher.

Paperback ISBN: 978-1-964457-73-4

Printed in the United States of America

Published by Persephone Entertainment Inc.

Texas, USA

*To my four children, for keeping me on my toes and being my sounding board for all my story ideas.*

Don't ever miss a new release!

Sign up now for Skyler's newsletter and get access to new release updates, free content, and great deals.

Just go to
**www.skylerramirez.com**

# THE FOUR WORLDS

Earth
Luna
Mars
Europa

# Map of Human Space, Circa 700 P.D.

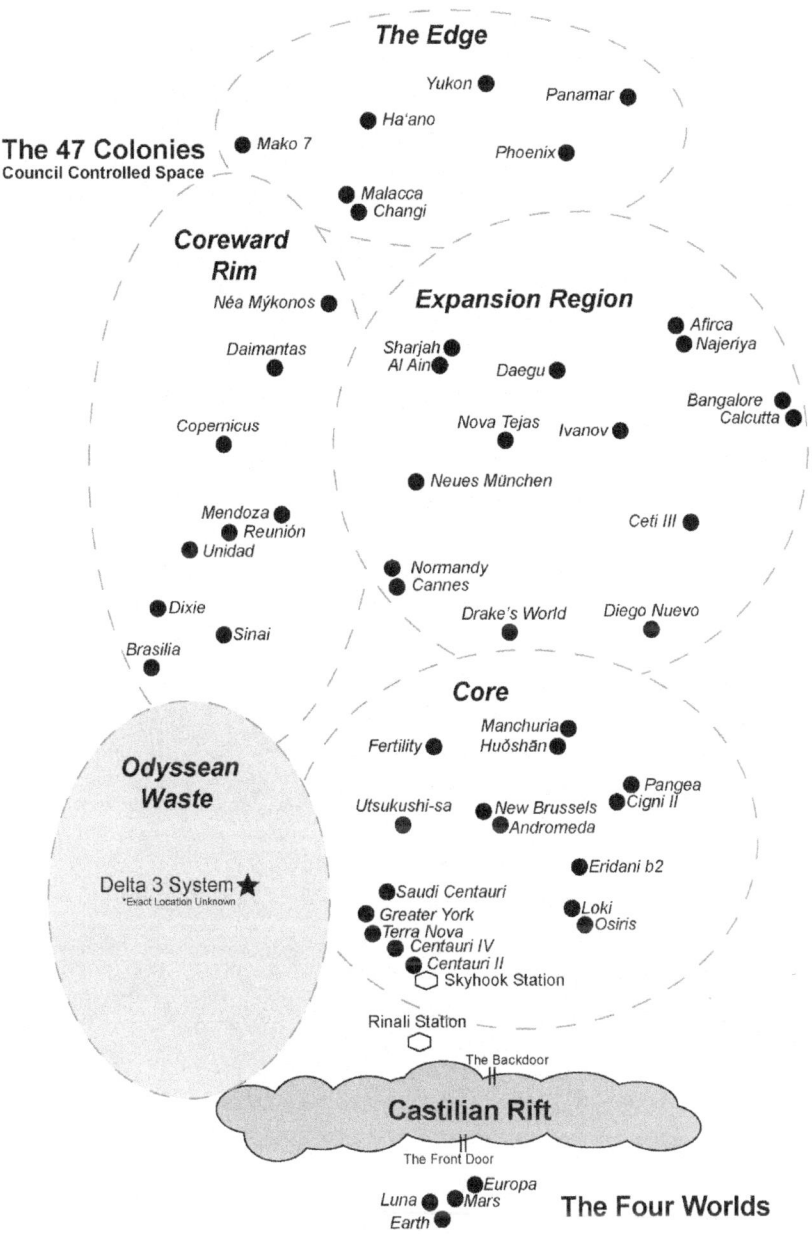

# PROLOGUE

### JUNE 1, 731 P.D. (POST DIASPORA); THREE MONTHS AFTER THE REVELATIONS

The bullet bounced off the side of Sarah Nowak's head with a metallic clang. She shook her head briefly to clear the ringing in her ears, her heads-up display flickering madly as it tried to interpret the rapid head movement as a command.

Sarah ignored the light show in her HUD and turned to raise her right arm toward the man who had shot her. For a moment, she stared at him through the washed-out crimson light cast by the planet's dim red sun. He was short, about on par for denizens of Panamar, but looked even shorter next to the three-meter tall mech suit Sarah wore, or more accurately rode.

The man snarled at her, screaming something she couldn't hear, and held down the trigger of his old-generation assault rifle. Rounds, propelled to supersonic speeds by the rifle's integrated rail gun, violently impacted on the chest of Sarah's mech but had no other effect than to scratch the paint scheme that bore the colors of her Guard mechanized unit.

Her HUD finally stabilizing, a target reticle appeared on the man's chest, and Sarah flicked the ring finger on her right hand to select lethal anti-personnel rounds. Then she flicked her index finger once to simulate pulling a trigger. Instantly, a spot of red—brighter than the sunlight of this Council-forsaken world—appeared where Sarah had been aiming, and the man's corpse dropped the rifle and unceremoniously collapsed to the ground.

She stared at the dead body for a moment, lightly mesmerized by the interplay of red on red, as if the entire planet was painted in a bloody monochrome. She so missed the yellow star primary of her own world, but when the Guard said it was time to go waste some rebels on Panamar, she jumped on the nearest troop transport and…

"Nowak, report!" barked a voice in her comm, and the image of Lieutenant Jose Sandoval's face popped up in her HUD. By his well-groomed appearance, it was clear to anyone who saw him that the man rode a desk for a living. Of course, most Guard paramilitary officers Sarah had worked with hadn't seen combat since their early days, if at all. They left that to the grunts like her.

"Hostile engaged and dispatched, Lieutenant," she replied calmly. "They're using standard anti-personnel ammo; it's not powerful enough to do more than scratch the suit."

"Roger that. Stay frosty. Even AP rounds can weaken your dome if there are enough of them. I don't want these guys getting lucky, Sergeant!"

"Yes, sir!" As if he needed to tell her that. *No sir! This momma is going home to her little girl when this is over.*

A line of red arrows—red to draw her attention, though clearly designed by an engineer who had never been to the red hellscape of Panamar—pointed to the left on the periphery of her HUD, alerting her to the next threat. She turned her head, the torso of the mech suit pivoting to follow, and saw the red outlines of three hostiles crouching beneath the windows of a café less than fifty meters away.

"Engaging three hostiles at marked coordinates," she said to her comm, knowing her suit would automatically transmit the exact location of her targets to the command post overseeing the Guard $4^{th}$ Light Mechanized Division, where Lieutenant Sandoval was coordinating the movements of Sarah's Bravo Company, $17^{th}$ Platoon, $2^{nd}$ Squad.

"Walker, Feng, get up here!" she called out next, the comm automatically redirecting her message to Corporal Harrison Walker and Private Feng Chu Hua, the other two members of 2$^{nd}$ Squad that were on patrol with her today.

Walker let his suit acknowledge the order as he cut across from a parallel side street, but Feng's soprano and far-too-young voice chimed in, "Coming, Sarge!" in gross contrast to the two metric tons of armored mech that the young woman drove with the confidence of a veteran, and—most of the time—the skill to match.

Sarah waited while her two subordinates made their way over to her, watching the relatively motionless red icons of the hostiles and idly wondering what type of food the café served on better days, when it wasn't being used to fight some idiot's war against the legitimate government of the 47 Colonies.

When Feng and Walker arrived and took up position on either side of her, spaced out in case the hostiles had any heavy anti-armor weaponry, Sarah wordlessly twitched her nose twice to turn on squad targeting mode and stuck out her tongue to designate the targets for Walker and Feng.

Once, while she'd been a student at the Guard Mechanized Warfare School on Greater York, one of Sarah's instructors had shared videos taken inside the cockpits of training mechs. Unfortunately, he'd chosen Sarah's mech first, and the entire class laughed uproariously at the images of her making the outrageous combinations of grotesque facial expressions and head movements that were required to control one of the Guard light mech units. After that, the instructor randomly chose a few more students' vids to show them that they *all* looked ridiculous controlling their massive suits. But for months afterward, a few less mature students called her 'Grimace' behind her back. Until she'd pinned one of the ringleaders and nearly broken his arm in hand-to-hand combat training. Then they'd just avoided her.

Now, how she looked making faces inside her mech was the furthest thing from Sarah's mind as the suit screamed an alarm at her. "Anti-matter detected!" she cried into her comm. "Take 'em. Now!"

In concert, all three Guard mechs raised their left arms, and three small rockets sped out of the launchers slung there in place of mechanized hands. Sarah barely had time to register the launch as the three projectiles simultaneously bored into the concrete wall of the café, directly in front of each of the three hidden hostiles. In a fraction of a second, they'd burrowed in far enough, and then in near-perfect unison, each projectile's little brain detonated the shaped charge in its nose.

The effect would have been horrifically gruesome for anyone unfortunate enough to be watching from inside the café. The shaped charges turned the walls themselves into shotgun blasts as they blew inward and pulverized the concrete into gravel—bits of the building that traveled at close to the speed of sound and impacted center mass of the three rebels who had been hiding inside.

By the time Sarah's mech crashed through the café wall and what was left of the window and surveyed the damage, all that remained of the three hostiles were bloody masses of flesh and what might have once been faces under all the gore.

Hunched over in her mech—the café's designers hadn't considered three-meter-tall armored clientele in their discussions with their architect—Sarah's HUD quickly led her to the source of the anti-matter signature. She looked down at the object, which was half hidden under the gore of its former owner. It so captured her attention that she barely noticed as the two other mechs entered the café behind her.

"Blast, Sarge! An AM launcher?" Walker's voice intruded into her thoughts. "How did the rebs get their hands on Guard tech?"

Sarah resisted the human urge to shake her head—the result would have been a pivoting back and forth of her mech, possibly enough to make her sick given the abattoir surrounding them in the small café—and just stayed silent, studying the weapon.

"I heard it's like this all over the city," Feng's sprightly voice somehow managed to sound cheerful even when delivering bad news. "These are more than just rebels with home-printed ARs. I mean, an anti-matter launcher in the middle of the slums of Panamar? The tech level on the Edge isn't close to advanced enough to make that."

"Someone's running arms in from the Core worlds or stealing from the Guard depots here on planet," Walker agreed. "Hey, Sarge, you think they're connected to—"

"Can the chatter, 2nd Squad!" interrupted the voice of Lieutenant Sandoval on all of their comms. "Nowak, Feng, survey the site for further intel and report anything you find to the command post. Walker! You bring that AP launcher back to the CP now. Nowak and Feng can finish up there."

"Roger that!" Walker and Feng chorused, while Sarah just responded, "Sir!" All three of them were enacters: part of the small population of humans who were genetically programmed with perfect obedience to the authority of the Council government, of which Sandoval was the closest representative. Otherwise, Sarah might have muttered something about how would *he* like to spend the next fifteen minutes hunched over, painfully searching the bloody mess of the café. But she knew from experience that even a snarky but harmless remark like that would border just enough on disobedience to trigger her subconscious pain response. And she wasn't looking for a genetically induced headache today.

With Sandoval's orders, all out-loud speculation as to the source of the AM launcher, a weapon powerful enough to have taken out all three of their mechs *and* the surrounding city block, obediently ceased. Every member of the 4th Light Mechanized Division was an enacter. A two-ton tank on legs with enough firepower to level a small town wasn't something you trusted to the chance compliance of a reg. Only enacters, perfectly obedient in every way, were entrusted with that kind of destructive force.

*But there are whispers about enacters who...* Sarah mentally shook off the thought before it could trigger her pain response and focused on the task at hand. She watched as Walker gingerly grasped the AM launcher in his suit's right hand and cradled it like a baby in the giant mech's arms. No one wanted that thing going off by accident, though AM launchers had enough failsafes to prevent an accidental discharge even if he'd *stepped* on it with the massive mech.

"Sarge, you may want to look at this," Feng called from the other side of the café, followed by the incongruous sound of her high-pitched voice swearing as the small woman stood up too quickly and put her mech's dome through the ceiling. Sarah would have laughed had they not been surrounded by so much blood. At least the café had some still-working light fixtures, which cast a bright and cheerful yellow glow at odds with the grisly scene but still felt better than the red gloom outside.

After watching Walker safely depart the café with the AM launcher, Sarah worked her way over to stand, or rather crouch, her mech next to Feng's and looked down at the surface of the table the private had fixated on. *Flyers of some sort,* she thought, and made the various facial movements to make her HUD magnify one of them for her to examine more closely.

'The Revelations are True!' read the headline, and Sarah winced. *Not this scud again.* But she read on, out of morbid curiosity, skimming the words and pulling out the highlights she knew she'd find there.

'The Assembly is lying to you.... there is no Council.... the government is turning everyone into enacters... secret navy... invasion of the Four Worlds and the ancient homeworld....'

Then she read the first two lines of the last paragraph on the page, the ones she knew were coming—that she *wanted* to find—even though she knew it was likely to give her a royal headache.

'An enacter, a servant of the Council itself, has defied the government's orders! This proves enacters can choose for themselves! There is no—'

"Second Squad, no one can see those lying pamphlets." Sandoval's words again broke her concentration; her HUD showed Feng had obediently streamed video of the finding back to the CP. "Torch the whole place and then continue your sweep of that sector."

Again, had Sarah not been earnestly trying to avoid the pain of even borderline disobedience, she might have murmured about rear-echelon micro-managers; instead, she held her peace. But for a moment, that's all she did. She didn't immediately follow the lieutenant's orders. Instead, she kept staring at the flyers, trying to pick out more of the message they contained.

Then, the pain came.

At first, it was just a dull ache behind her eyes. She wasn't really going to *disobey* a direct order, was she? Then, when her hesitation continued as she tried to read further, the pain hit like an avalanche, drawing a grunt as her vision broke into bright flashes, this time *not* from her HUD.

"Sarge, you OK?" asked Feng through the suit comms. The other woman had already ignited the flamethrower housed alongside her left arm's launcher and was dutifully incinerating the side of the café away from Sarah, but had turned her mech's dome back to study her boss.

Sarah felt herself give up on the mental tug-o-war in her head and —almost without conscious thought—felt her left hand twitch in the pattern that called up and ignited her own flamethrower.

"Sure, Feng. I'm fine. Just a cramp." The sharp pain in her head that belied her lie faded slowly as she watched the blue and orange flames curl the edges of the fire-resistant paper until nothing remained but black char.

---

## THREE WEEKS AGO

Sarah Nowak laughed and smiled at the gurgling little girl bouncing on her knee. "Mommy loves you," she said as she scrunched up her nose and shook her head playfully at her six-month-old daughter, Geneva, as the baby laughed and clapped her chubby hands at her mother's silly antics. "Mommy is going to miss you *so* much."

"I just don't understand why they'd send you into combat so soon!" a male voice complained behind her, the tone loaded with anger and frustration. It was the argument Sarah had hoped to escape by playing with her little girl.

Instead, she sighed and looked away from her cheerful daughter and up and over her shoulder at her less-than-happy husband, Octavio, who stood behind the cheap faux-leather couch in their small two-bedroom apartment and looked down at his wife and daughter with a frown on his face.

"I told you, Love," Sarah said with a sad smile of her own, biting back the sharper response that had first leapt to her mind at the unwelcome interruption—the marriage book she'd read last year had convinced her to seldom say the first thing she thought of. "The Guard needs everyone right now. Those blasted lies that traitor Siefred told have thrown a half-dozen worlds into chaos. Besides, I can't let my squad go without me."

Octavio Nowak shook his head and pressed his mouth into a thin line before responding. When he answered, the anger in his voice was even sharper. "Come on, Sarah. They're supposed to excuse you from combat for at least a *year* after you've had a kid. And your squad will be fine without you. Aren't you always saying you've trained them well enough that they barely even need you anymore?"

Now it was Sarah's turn to frown. She felt her hackles rising at her husband's tone but calmly reminded herself he was mad at the situation, really, not at her. She was proud of herself for maintaining her cool when she really wanted to unload on him for ruining her last night before deployment.

"Come on, Tavi," she said with overemphasized patience. "What kind of world would it be if people like me shirked their duty when the Council needs us the most? Besides, you knew what you were getting into when you married me, right? I'm a guardswoman *and* an enacter. I can't exactly say no."

Octavio's frown deepened as he moved around the couch and plopped down next to his wife and daughter, refusing to meet the former's steady gaze. He sat there for a long moment, studying his hands silently, eyes tracing the deep lines from manual labor that he so hated but that to Sarah stood for all the love and devotion he put into making a living for her and Geneva by augmenting her anemic Guard Paramilitary Force salary.

Sarah and Octavio Nowak had been married for only two years, but she knew her husband well enough to know he was working up to something… and that she wasn't going to like it. But she tried with all of her might to ignore what was coming and just be content to be with her family the day before she had to ship out for one of the seemingly endless peacekeeping missions the Guard Paramilitary Forces were being called to perform in the wake of the so-called 'Revelations', a set of damning but obviously false allegations against the Council government by one of its own former Assembly speakers.

Finally, after a long pause, during which Sarah tried unsuccessfully to re-immerse herself in playing with little Geneva, Octavio looked at her and spoke.

"Come on, Sarah." There was a note of pleading now in his voice. "Aren't you the *least* bit curious if the things the Revelations say are true?"

Sarah shook her head at him violently before he even finished speaking, a warning and pleading of her own in her voice. "Tavi, don't. Don't go there."

But her husband was nothing if not stubborn, and he pressed on anyway, the firm line of his tightened jaw broadcasting to Sarah that she wouldn't be successful in turning aside the dreaded conversation *this* time. "What if..." he continued, "Well, what if that enacter we read about actually *did* disobey the Council. Blast, assuming there really *is* a Council to begin with!" He stood abruptly and threw up his hands. "Don't you wonder, Sarah? If *he* did it, maybe *you* could too."

He turned, looking down at her again, and she felt the blood rush to her face as the anger flowed through her, instantly causing her to forget everything she'd read in the blasted marriage book. Standing abruptly herself, startling Geneva into a cry of displeasure at the sudden change in elevation, Sarah glared at her husband. "Tavi, how could you even say that?" she half-growled when what she truly wanted to do was scream. "That's borderline treason, and if the Injunctions of 342 didn't protect me from turning in my own husband, I'd have to follow my orders and arrest you *right now*!" She punctuated her last two words by shifting Geneva to one arm and jamming the forefinger of her free hand into her husband's chest through his threadbare shirt.

Octavio frowned and looked hurt for an instant, but then his face hardened again with his resolve. He gently but firmly reached down, grabbed the hand she'd poked him with, and cradled it between the calloused hands whose touch she usually loved so much. "Sarah, please, honey, just *think*. If one enacter did it, couldn't another one do it too? It's not disobedience, really; it's just calling them and telling them you're not ready—that you need your full year off from combat to be with our child. That's all. It's not disobeying, just pushing back a little."

"It's the *same thing* for an enacter!" Sarah yelled back now, though her eyes betrayed her and were watering up at her husband's stubborn refusal to back off the point. Geneva started crying in earnest, and Sarah absently and gently bounced the red-haired baby in the crook of her arm. *Why can't he understand?* she asked herself for surely the thousandth time in her short but otherwise happy marriage to the headstrong oldest son of a dry cleaner and a pharmacist on Greater York.

"I don't know how many times I have to explain this to you," she said, forcing as much calm as she could back into her voice, though she could hear it was heavy with frustration as she pulled her hand out of Tavi's grasp and poked him again in the chest. Given her own diminutive height, she had to reach up a bit to poke him like that. "There's *no* flexibility"—poke—"*no* wiggle room"—poke—"*no* loopholes"—poke—"not for someone like *me!*" Now she turned the finger to poke her own chest, her voice continuing to rise to drown out Geneva's wails.

"If the Council says jump, I jump. Even if it wasn't the right thing to do, it's just not *optional* for me. I can't wish away a millennium of genetic programming just because *you* don't like what it means for our family!"

She saw from Tavi's face that he knew he'd gone too far and that she had as well. Tears had sprung to the dark eyes that she'd only seen cry on less than a handful of occasions, *including* their wedding day and the day of Geneva's birth. The sight of those nascent tears startled Sarah out of the worst of her anger, and her voice softened with her next words.

"Besides, you know that mech drivers are some of the safest guardmembers in a skirmish, especially against the pop guns that those poor idiots on Panamar can cobble together. I won't even get a scratch. But if I didn't go... Well, even if I could somehow cope with the pain, the agony would make me as useless as a puddle in the corner to you and Geneva. You *know* that. It will only be for a few weeks, and then I'll be back with you two here for the rest of my maternity leave. I promise."

She instantly regretted her last two words. She knew, and Tavi knew, that it was a promise she simply couldn't keep. Not if the Guard ordered her back into combat again after she returned.

Still, Octavio seemed willing to play along with the fiction and the intent behind her words. He tentatively reached down again and gently clasped the hand she'd been using to poke him in the chest. A single tear rolled down his face as he regarded his wife with sad understanding. He sat back down on the couch and pulled her down after him and into a wordless embrace, their daughter's body between them. They stayed that way for a long time, listening together as their little girl's sobs softened and her small flailing hands calmed from the warmth of the tiny family's hug.

Sarah wished not for the first or even hundredth time that she could somehow put her husband first—that she could ignore the biological imperatives that demanded absolute and unwavering obedience to her superiors' orders—but even that fleeting thought brought the instant beginnings of a headache as her subconscious punished her for merely *contemplating* disobedience. So, she quickly squashed the thought and mentally squared her shoulders as the pain slowly receded.

Sarah Nowak knew what she was—had known since the age of five, when the smiling men took her from her parents' home on Pangea and told her she was special. She was an enacter. It was a great privilege, they'd told her. She, and those small few like her, were the only thing standing between the citizens of the 47 Colonies and total anarchy. They were the 'thin line', even more so than the regs—the ordinary guardmembers who weren't enacters—who kept the darkness of chaos at bay and helped the Council maintain order and peace in the colonies for the last 600 years.

Never mind that, just like every other enacter in the history of humanity, the privilege came with the awful burden of not having a choice. Sarah hadn't chosen to become an enacter or join the Guard. When she *had* chosen to marry Octavio, a non-enacter, her peers and her superiors told her it would never work. But they stopped short of ordering her not to do it. The Council's laws strictly prohibited them from meddling in her choice of marriage partners.

Even so, deep down, Sarah had known the sad truth at the time:

they were right. She and Tavi had no business being married. As an enacter, she could *never* give him her entire self. Her first obligation would always be to the Council, never to the man she loved or even to their precious daughter. And as a reg, he could never really understand that. In his mind, there would always be the tiniest sliver of doubt. *Maybe if she loved me enough, she could make the choice...* That sliver had grown of late to a wedge because of those blasted Revelations: that scud full of lies from an ex-Assembly speaker and a disgruntled reporter about a mythical enacter who had somehow chosen his own path, albeit the way of a traitor.

The tears flowed freely now from her eyes as she buried her face into Octavio's broad chest, feeling his thin shirt getting damp but not caring and lacking the motivation to break the embrace. Because when she did, she would have to return to the reality of her situation and go pack her bags for the next day's deployment.

*Stupid Panamarians!* she thought angrily to herself. *Why can't those malcontents just be happy with everything the Council gives them? Why do they have to tear me away from my family because they don't like paying taxes, or listening to Council edicts on farm production, or whatever stupid reason they have for rebelling this time? Don't they know that they're ruining my life, too?*

Octavio held her like that for a long time, letting her work through her frustrations in silence as he worked through his. In moments like this, Sarah remembered why she'd ignored the counsel of so many and married Tavi anyway. And why she'd stubbornly refused to consider divorce, even when it was clear early on that their differences might be too great to reconcile. And why even now, she clung to him as the only rock in a world that often made no sense.

Because he was *her* choice. No one had chosen him for her or commanded her to marry him. Next to birthing Geneva, he was quite literally the *only* major thing she could remember choosing for herself in life. And that made him more precious than all the riches in the colonies.

After what felt like a very long time but still not nearly long enough, Sarah lightly disengaged herself from her husband's arms and quietly handed him their daughter so that she could go into their small bedroom and start packing her bag for the long cold trip through the void to *Panamar*.

*Those rebels are in for a shock when I get there,* she thought grimly. *They're pulling this mama away from her family, and I'll make them regret it.*

---

## PRESENT DAY; JUNE 1, 731 P.D.

Sarah sat alone on her drab green cot in her squad's temporary barracks, staring down at her hands, tracing the lines in them, thinking of her husband's powerful hands, and wishing vainly that he was there with her.

It had been a long day. They'd torched the café around noon, and the rest of the afternoon's engagement was a blur of muddled memories tinged with the sick crimson light of a sun that was never meant to support human life. *Everything* about this backwater Edge planet frustrated her, but most of all, the fact that the 'isolated insurrection' she and her unit had come to put down was proving to be a full-blown rebel force. And the scattered success the rebels were having, even against the mechs, was threatening to extend their engagement and Sarah's deployment by several weeks, if not longer.

The rest of her squad was at dinner, including the fourth member, Private Samuel Jennings, who had stayed out of combat for the day with a stomach bug that so often plagued travelers to this jungle hell, even against the broad-spectrum antibiotics the Guard had shoved down their throats on the voyage here. Sarah had begged off joining them for the meal, giving the excuse that she would rather use the time to debrief herself on the squad's performance and look for ways to improve for the next day. She wryly reflected on how easy it was to lie *downward* to her subordinates. They didn't represent the Council's authority to her—though *she* certainly did to them—so she could lie to them all she wanted. It just didn't work in the other direction.

She had been afraid that Lt. Sandoval would confront her when the squad returned and question her about her hesitation to burn the pamphlets. The fear had faded when he'd only crinkled up his nose at the smell of the squad out of their mechs and told them to hit the showers and the chow line. It wasn't surprising. Sarah had learned that the officers didn't care if she liked or even agreed with her orders; they knew she had no choice but to ultimately follow them.

Still, there were minor rebellions. Sandoval's order to hit the chow line hadn't specified when, so Sarah reveled in the brief time alone with her thoughts. She'd go eat when the squad got back.

She stopped studying her hands and lifted her left wrist, calling up her watch's holo display. Poking commands that came as naturally as breathing, she pulled up her messages and saw the note from Tavi that she'd read ten times already in the past 24 hours since the most recent Guard courier ship had delivered their mail.

Numbly, she read her husband's words again as they hovered in the air before her.

*Sarah,*

*We love you and miss you. Geneva has been looking for you everywhere. You're the first thing she looks for when she wakes up, and she fights going to sleep, trying to catch a glimpse of you at night. She laughs and smiles whenever I show her your picture or one of your vids. You mean the world to our daughter and to me. I hope you're still safe and that your squad is, too. I know how important they are to you, but I know you've trained them well. Say hi to Chu Hua for me and remind her of her promise to watch your back.*

*I'm sorry again for arguing with you before you left. I just wish you were here and that things could somehow be different. I know you have no choice, no matter how much you want to stay with us, but I hope you've given some thought to the conversation we had on your last night at home.*

*I saw on the news that the situation in Panamar is contained and that the insurrection was a small one. Does that mean you'll be coming home soon? Let me know if you can. Geneva and I will be waiting.*

*Love,*

*Tavi*

*Contained,* she thought yet again, shaking her head. *Is that what the newsies are saying? It certainly didn't look contained today, especially if there are more of those blasted AM launchers scattered about.*

She felt a pang in her head at the thought of the deadly weapon. Lieutenant Sandoval had ordered her and her squad to say nothing about it and to do their best to forget they'd ever seen it. Unfortunately, that meant that every time she thought about it, her enacter gene hit her for being disobedient to orders. Luckily, it was a minor disobedience; 'do your best' left a lot of latitude in the order, so the pain was relatively light. Still, it had been a jerk move for Sandoval even to issue an order like that. Typical for the man.

Regardless of the source of the pain, Sarah wanted nothing to do with it. So, instead of dwelling on the scary thought of leveled city blocks from a much-too-well-armed group of rebels, she thought back to her last night at home.

## THREE WEEKS AGO

Sarah lay awake, as she did most nights immediately before a deployment. It would be a ten-day submerged voyage on the Guard troop transport from Greater York in the Core colonies to Panamar on the Edge, but that didn't change the fact that she felt like she was going into combat as soon as she woke up the next morning. It never did.

She felt the warmth of Tavi pressed against her back with his arm slung limply across her waist. His breathing had been even for a while now, so it surprised her to hear him whisper in her ear.

"Can't sleep again?"

"You know it," she replied, keeping her voice just as low so as not to disturb the baby sleeping in the bassinet next to their bed. Tavi kept making noises about moving Geneva into the nursery in the apartment's other bedroom. Still, she knew it was all talk and that he enjoyed having the baby so close, especially now that Sarah was leaving. She smiled at the thought that no matter how long her deployment lasted, she would likely return home to find the little girl's bassinet still in the same spot.

Oblivious to her inner thoughts, her husband continued, "It's like you said, though, right? Nothing those rebels have can even hurt those mechs of yours, right?" She heard the hope in his voice and knew he was trying to both soothe her and convince *himself* that there was nothing to worry about.

"Right, Love," she responded as she rolled over and faced him in the queen-size bed. "Those terrorists won't know what hit them when *we* stomp in." She put more conviction into her whispered voice than she felt. There was scuttlebutt about some of the non-enacter Guard regs stationed on Panamar having possibly joined the rebellion… but she mentally thrust that unlikely worry aside.

Tavi raised himself onto one elbow, looking deeply into her eyes, clearly building up to something, and she felt her breath catch a little. She didn't want another argument, not now, with only a few hours left before she headed to the port and a multi-week deployment.

But she'd learned that Tavi was the type of man who just had to say his piece, even when keeping it inside was better for all involved.

"Sarah, I…" He didn't finish the sentence and lowered himself back to cuddle up to her as if he'd decided to keep quiet.

But Sarah also knew that if he didn't get out what he was thinking now, it would fester until she got back and put him in a sour mood. That wouldn't do; she *needed* him to be there for little Geneva. "What is it, Tavi?" she asked, dreading the answer.

"Nothing, sweetheart. Just try to get some sleep."

Now it was her turn to raise herself up on her elbow and look down at him.

"Seriously, Tavi, what is it?"

Even in the dark room, she could see him scrunching up his face in thought. When he finally spoke, his words came haltingly. "Well, it's just that… Well, have they ever ordered you to do something you *knew* was wrong?"

The question surprised her. She'd been expecting him to resume the argument they'd had earlier and ask her again if she could somehow push back on her deployment orders. Sarah took a minute to reflect carefully on her answer.

"Well, you have to understand something," she said slowly, buying herself time to think. To his credit, he waited out her long pause without jumping in to qualify his question or ask any follow-ups, which showed just how serious he was about this conversation. "Me even thinking that an order from the Council is wrong triggers the pain. It's like... Well, it's like those religious nuts my squad ran into a few years back. You know, the ones who said that some god commanded them to blow up that school on Ceti III. They were so *sure* that what they'd done had been commanded by their so-called deity that they couldn't compute that it might have been wrong. Because for them, *anything* their god told them to do *was* the right thing to do."

"Sarah," Tavi said, the frown in his voice clear, "that's a *really* scary comparison."

"Just let me finish," she admonished gently. "The Council is a benevolent and just government. Sometimes they may give me an order that I wouldn't necessarily agree with, given the information I have. But I *have* to assume that they know more than I do, so even if the order doesn't make sense to me at the time, I have to trust that it's the right thing to do.

"The difference between me and those religious nuts is the source of the orders. They obeyed a false god invented by their leaders to exert power over them. *I* obey the rightful government of humanity, which has proved over more than a thousand years that they have our best interests at heart."

"But what if they're wrong?" Tavi asked, his whisper so small that Sarah had to strain to hear him. "What if the Revelations are right? What if the Council is just like that false god?"

She shook her head emphatically, her frustration growing just like it had earlier in the day. "I don't want to hear anything about the Council not existing because of what those *cursed* Revelations say," she replied sharply, the volume of her voice raising well over that of a whisper. Then she softened her tone. "Still, I suppose even the Council could be wrong occasionally; they are only human, even if they're the smartest and most capable among us."

Even that simple acknowledgment of Council fallibility put a dull ache behind Sarah's eyes, and she vainly shook her head to clear it, to no avail. Still, she pressed forward. She owed it to her husband to finish this conversation, and she resolved not to let him see how much it hurt her to do so.

"But the Council comes a lot closer to perfection than most," she continued, "so even if they did order me to do something wrong, I *have* to believe that *they* believed it was the right thing to do in the moment. I also have to believe that they're going to be right a *lot* more often than they're not.

"That's especially important because the Council isn't on the ground with me on my missions, so I'm getting their orders through the officers in my chain of command. They are doing their best to interpret and pass along the Council's will—taking their superiors' strategic direction and turning it into tactical orders—but they're not perfect either, so they may make mistakes in the orders they give me."

The dull ache had sharpened a bit with this line of thought, so she quickly added, "…however unlikely that may be," and the pain lessened slightly.

Tavi stayed silent for a moment, clearly fighting his male instincts to argue every point and genuinely considering her answer. When he replied, he spoke slowly, as if he was tasting each word as it rolled off his tongue to make sure it was right. "But if you ever felt that your officers, for example, were ordering you to do something that was just plain *wrong*, maybe not even intentionally, but just because they *did* interpret the Council's orders or the situation incorrectly… would you still have to follow that order?"

The pain came sharper now as Sarah considered her answer to his question, and her breathing quickened despite herself. Normally, when that happened, Tavi was quick to change the topic and let her be, and now a feeling of anger flashed through her. *How can he even ask me that when he knows how much the answer could hurt me?*

She quashed the anger quickly. It was just a question, and a question couldn't hurt her. Only the answer she'd briefly considered giving had, and that wasn't her husband's fault. Once again, she felt sadness encroaching on her heart, knowing that he could *never* fully understand one of the most important aspects of her life. Worse, little Geneva might have also gotten the enacter gene from her. That would leave Tavi alone in a family of enacters, at least until the girl's fifth birthday, when she would have to leave them to attend the Enacter Academy just as Sarah had.

She sighed and answered her husband's question, not in the way she wanted, but in the best way she could that wouldn't bring more of the pain. "That's not how combat works, Tavi. You can't have grunts on the ground questioning or even stopping to think critically about every order we get from our officers. That's how people die. It's even that way for the non-enacters in the Guard. You get an order, you follow it, trusting that, right or wrong, it needs to be done. There's no wiggle room. If there was, it would be chaos. And I have to think that more innocent people would die in that chaos, including possibly me."

Tavi considered her answer for a moment. Then he went back to a variation of his original question. "But have you ever had to do something you felt afterward was wrong?"

Sarah sighed again. "Not yet, and I hope I never do." Even her acknowledgment that it was *possible* drove a spike through her temple and brought the pain on stronger than before. But, deep down, she knew it was still the right response.

Later, when she was sure that Tavi was finally asleep and the pain remained unabated, Sarah did what she always did in these situations. In the barest of whispers, she chanted the refrain taught to her the first week in the Enacter Academy: "The Council is good. I obey the Council. The Council is good. I obey the Council."

After several minutes of repeating the refrain and doing her best to believe it, the pain lessened until it was only a dull ache in the back of her mind, and sleep finally took her.

## PRESENT DAY

"Second Squad will go down four parallel avenues with one mech per street. Since the separation is only a short block, less than a hundred meters between them, you'll be able to quickly provide support to your squad mates if they run into something they can't handle alone." The monotone voice of Lt. Jose Sandoval droned on in the morning briefing, and Sarah silently thanked the inventor of Guard stim pills for the hundredth time that week.

"First Squad and 3rd Squad will follow behind 2nd, mopping up anything they miss. Fourth and 5th Squads will ride the dropships above as a quick reaction force if any of you run into anything particularly heavy, though we're not expecting that."

Were Sarah not an obedient enacter, she would have interrupted the briefing at that point to ask about the anti-matter launcher they'd found the day before. But even thinking about it once again gave her a headache, so she kept her mouth shut. Nonetheless, even the pain couldn't mask her internal worry about her squad.

"The goal today is to clear the southern sector of the city of the last bits of resistance," the lieutenant continued, happily oblivious to his sergeant's inner worries. "Guard regulars will take over this portion of the city after today, so we can get started on the western sector while 5th Platoon takes the east. Hopefully, in about 48 hours, we can meet in the middle and then tackle the northern part of the city together. Be out of here by the end of next week if we're lucky."

*Yeah, right,* Sarah thought, despite the pain. *We were supposed to have taken the entire southern sector in two days. But these rebels are much better armed and trained than they should be.*

"Questions?"

There were a few from the other non-commissioned officers in the platoon, but they were strictly tactical. No one argued the orders or questioned the reasons or the logic, no matter their inner thoughts. Typical for a room where everyone shared a genetic predisposition to obey.

Fifteen minutes later, Sarah and the rest of 2nd Squad boarded the armored dropship that would deposit them at their starting location in the sprawling cityscape. The mechs had more than enough power to make it there and back on their own, but the dropship was the one subtle nod the Guard made to the sheer exhaustion of its troops after driving the mechs for twelve hours a day for a solid week.

The four avenues Sarah's squad was assigned to clear threaded between two hills. Sandoval's briefing had specified that the hills were full of residential neighborhoods populated by some of the wealthier people in the city, which supposedly made them less likely to be abetting the rebels. Guard regulars, derisively called 'softies' by some of the mech drivers, would still patrol those neighborhoods in case any of the rebels tried to flee uphill to escape the mechs. Still, they expected the heaviest resistance to be along those four urban thoroughfares. That's why they were sending in the big boys and girls to handle it.

After a short five-minute ride, the dropship deposited Sarah and her soldiers at the starting grid, and they quickly fanned out across the four avenues. They plodded slowly down the roads, using their suits' built-in scanners to detect any weaponry on the streets or even in the nearby buildings. While the scanners weren't foolproof, they were tuned to pick up the power signature of anything bigger than a sidearm at a range of 50 meters, even through light shielding, and could see a small pistol within 20 meters. Of course, they wouldn't always pick up a high-tech shielded weapon, like another AM launcher, but Sarah consciously abandoned that worry before thinking about the taboo subject brought back the pain.

As they went, loudspeakers mounted on the shoulders of their mechs rotated a series of brief messages in multiple languages, including the local patois mix of Italian and Portuguese, instructing the citizenry to stay inside their homes and to comm the Guard immediately if they knew the locations of any terrorists. No one called, of course. Few ever did unless they were enacters themselves, and since something like 98 percent of known enacters in the galaxy worked for the government—*After all, why let that perfect obedience go to waste in a civilian occupation?*—they'd already been evacuated from the city. Not that a backwater planet like Panamar had many enacters to begin with. Even most of the Guard assigned to the jungle hell were non-enacters who had upset someone in their chain of command at some point.

After about an hour, during which Sarah had covered just six kilometers, moving slowly to give her scanners time to find anything around her, her suit sounded an alarm, and a series of red indicators lit up her HUD. Even a disciplined guardswoman like Sarah found an hour of slow plodding down an empty street monotonous beyond description (and frankly a little depressing in the melancholy red glare that passed for daylight on this rock), so she had to shake off her malaise quickly when the alarm sounded. Then she checked her HUD to see just what it was the suit had found.

It surprised her to see the data coming not from her suit's sensors but from an overwatch drone hovering several hundred meters in the sky above her and scanning for hostiles out in the open. While fairly common in Guard engagements, Sandoval hadn't mentioned the deployment of the drones in his briefing, and they were fairly ineffective in urban settings where the narrow avenues and tall buildings blocked their view of pretty much everything that wasn't directly below their flight path.

"What're you seeing, Nowak?" The voice of Sandoval intruded on Sarah's comm. He could see the same picture she could, so the question was more about talking things through with his sergeant—and micromanaging from his comfortable seat at the CP—than getting any information he didn't already have.

"I show three hostiles a block forward of my position. Moving to engage," she replied.

"Want to wait for backup?"

"Negative. Drone shows they're armed with light railguns and a few sidearms. Should be quick work as long as they stay in the open." Sarah knew better than the armchair lieutenant that such a small force was just as likely to be a purposeful distraction meant to draw her entire squad off their assigned search patterns than an actual threat. At least Sandoval was smart enough to let *her* make the call.

"Roger. Keep me posted."

The comm channel closed, and Sarah picked up the pace to a brisk walk in the suit. While she moved toward the target, she idly scanned the skies for the deployed drones. Surprisingly, she only saw one on her scanner, the one directly above her. For a fleeting moment, she thought that perhaps the drone was there to watch *her*; that Sandoval *had* picked up on her hesitation in the café the previous day. Then she put the ridiculous thought aside. Surely, she just couldn't see the other drones because of the height of the buildings surrounding her.

As she drew closer to the enemy position, she effortlessly started running, the suit's servos assisting her, adopting a space-eating gait that would have surprised anyone who'd watched her plod slowly along for the past hour. She knew the mech was heavy enough that anyone nearby would feel the ground shake as she dashed down the avenue toward the three targets the drone had identified. She also knew she was leaving cracked and buckled pavement in her path as the poor-quality concrete of Panamar's streets met the hard metal of the massive machine's feet at a run.

She stopped her forward progress in the middle of the street and turned to face where the map showed the enemy. There she saw two men and one woman standing behind a parked hovercar, with their guns pointed in her direction in what they surely thought was a well-planned ambush. They hadn't fired yet; perhaps the speed of the mech's approach had surprised them.

Sarah twitched her nose just so, and the suit picked up on her intent. "Halt!" said a loud, prerecorded male voice from the suit's speakers. "This is the Guard. Lay down your weapons. You are under arrest. Deadly force is authorized."

For a brief second, as Sarah watched the faces of the three rebels magnified in her HUD, she thought and hoped they might actually surrender. But then the woman's face hardened, and Sarah saw her pull the trigger of her assault rifle.

The impacts of multiple railgun rounds hit Sarah in the suit's chest hard enough that the mech shook around her.

"Warning," came another disembodied voice—female this time—in her ear. "Armor-piercing rounds detected. Suit integrity at low-to-moderate risk." An image popped up in the corner of her HUD, an outline of the suit with multiple yellow circles flashing on the chest region where the bullets had hit. *Well, this is unexpected,* she thought grimly.

Sarah brought up her left arm and twitched her pinky finger and then her index finger. A small grenade shot out from the suit's embedded launcher and arced toward the hovercar shielding the three assailants. The rebels saw it coming and tried to react. Two of them, including the woman, ducked back behind the hovercar. The other man dove away from the car toward the doorway of a nearby building.

The grenade hit the car and exploded on impact. A high-explosive round, it was designed to create a pressure wave, not spread shrapnel like a standard anti-personnel grenade. In this case, the shockwave was enough to flip the car over, crushing the two rebels who had tried to hide behind it.

Sarah walked the suit calmly toward the overturned car. Two of the blips on her map now showed flashing red, indicating their vitals were well on their way to ceasing. The third blip, the man who had leapt away from the car, showed flashing yellow. That meant he was injured but still likely combat effective.

"Halt!" came the loud male voice again from the mech's external speakers. "This is the Guard. Lay down your weapons. You are under arrest."

Sarah saw through the HUD's magnification that the man—now that she was closer, she could see he was a boy, just a teenager—was stirring, though his gun was several meters from his body. She saw him slowly get up, his hands raised as he shook his head groggily, the pain clear on his face; no doubt the explosion had burst his eardrums. This close to him, she could also see that his clothes hung loose on his overly slim body in a sure sign of malnutrition. She relaxed marginally; this boy was no threat to her mech.

But as he rose, the suit flagged a metallic reading on the hip away from Sarah: likely a pistol in a holster. She readied to fire the assault rifle in her suit's right arm, just in case the boy decided to draw down on her, though a small arm like that would be completely ineffective against her mech.

Instead of drawing his weapon, the boy bolted the remaining two meters toward the doorway he'd been trying to reach, bursting into the apartment building and out of Sarah's direct line of sight.

She would have shaken her head in frustration, but the suit would have interpreted that as a command. So, she just grunted instead.

"Lieutenant," she said, and the mech automatically opened a comm channel to Sandoval. "Two targets down, but a third escaped into an apartment building. Request a squad of regs to clear it."

There was a brief silence on the line as Sandoval considered the ask. While she waited, Sarah studied the building in front of her. It was built from simple concrete blocks fused together, like so much of the drab architecture in Panamar. But unlike the towering buildings around it, it was only five stories and probably didn't even have a lift, just stairs to reach the highest levels. Cheap all around, just like the depressing planet it was built on.

"Negative, Nowak," came Sandoval's voice. "All regulars engaged on the hill east of your position. Can you do a surgical strike?"

Sarah blinked her right eye twice and then her left eye once. The transparent dome around her head darkened, and her HUD switched to thermal imaging, allowing her to see through the building's thin walls, showing her the yellow, orange, and red shapes of the people inside. One of those shapes, now on the second floor, was outlined in a flashing dotted yellow line as the mech's onboard AI made its best guess as to the identity of the injured rebel boy based on his thermal signature. Unfortunately, his image was close to several others, no doubt residents of the apartment he'd chosen to hide in.

Some numbers popped up next to the boy's outline, dominated by a percentage at the top.

"LT, my suit estimates only a 16 percent chance of successful surgical strike through the building walls. Eighty-four percent chance of civilian collateral. Strongly recommend tagging for the regs once they're available." She said the words in a calm, dispassionate voice, but she could feel a surge of something akin to panic inside her and threatening to creep into her tone. She quickly quashed it down.

"Negative again, Nowak." The lieutenant's words hit her like a death sentence delivered by a judge, and Sarah choked down a gasp of surprise, hoping Sandoval hadn't heard it.

*He's just a boy, and the others with him might even be his family*, she thought.

"Standing orders are to assume any civilians in the vicinity are harboring the fugitives and are with the rebels," Sandoval continued. "You are ordered to engage with HE penetrators."

"Yes, sir," Sarah answered reluctantly, after only a small outward hesitation. But her mind instantly flashed back to the conversation with Octavio, their last night together at home. His voice echoed in her head: *Have they ever ordered you to do something you knew was wrong?*

The pain hit her then. Even her merest hesitation was being interpreted as disobedience by the subconscious part of her brain activated by her enacter gene. It sent a surge of agony through her head that grew by the millisecond as she continued to delay her obedience to the order.

Slowly, Sarah raised her left arm to point it toward the target heat signature, and the pain abated. She twitched her pinky finger on that hand twice to cycle to the high-explosive penetrating rounds—charges designed to burrow their way through the building walls and then explode only when within at most two meters of the target. Unlike the shaped penetration rockets she and her squad had used at the café the day before, these were wide area effect rounds that used their own shrapnel instead of just a shaped charge to doubly ensure the target's death.

Unfortunately, the tiny computer brain in each round simply didn't care about the innocent civilians standing around the target, and they would be just as dead from the blast. On top of that, a single HE round used on a building this small and poorly constructed was overkill, and would likely to take out everyone on the same floor as the target and possibly some of those on the floors immediately above and below.

Sarah took a deep breath, steeling herself against the pain that resurfaced as she continued to hesitate; the agony quickly built to the level of someone shoving an ice pick through her temple. She was about to twitch her index finger and send the round to its destination (and to her blessed relief) when she noticed something in her HUD. *One of the thermal readings... Is that a...?*

She relaxed her index finger and started to lower her arm, but instantly the pain in her head doubled, and she slumped in the suit's embrace, this time with an audible choking gasp. She couldn't remember the last time she'd felt the pain this badly, and it threatened to overwhelm her senses at the same time her subconscious obedience response tried to take over and lift her arm back to discharge the missile. She fought the unbearable urge and physically forced her arm down lower and off target.

"Sir," she practically whimpered through teeth gritted against the pain. "One of the civilians is an infant. The suit calculates a 91 percent probability of the child's death given its proximity to the target."

There was silence on her comm for a long moment as the pain

continued to build and sharpen beyond what Sarah had even imagined was possible. Without conscious thought, she screamed, not caring if Sandoval heard her. The sound reverberated inside the small cockpit dome, assaulting senses already overloaded by her physical anguish. But over and over again, she heard Tavi's voice: *If you knew it was wrong, would you still do it?*

"Tavi, no. I can't," she sputtered through the tears streaming down her face. "Geneva, I can't. I just can't!" She didn't care that Sandoval and anyone else in the CP could hear her desperate pleas; she wasn't even thinking about her officers anymore.

The pain continued to strengthen measure by agonizing measure, and Sarah felt consciousness slipping away from her. From stories at the Academy, she knew there was a point beyond consciousness where her subconscious brain would take complete control and enact her orders just to make the pain stop. She couldn't let that happen, so she shook her head violently to keep herself awake. Lights flashed through lids closed tightly as her suit and HUD desperately tried to make sense of her head movement and panicked facial expressions.

Finally, after what seemed like an eternity in the throes of agony, Sandoval spoke, and even through the pain, Sarah registered the frustration in his voice. "Nowak, you have your orders. Execute now!"

Sarah felt the pain double again, then triple, though those concepts had lost all meaning in the desperate fight with her own mind. Images flashed through her head of her baby girl at home, and she saw in her mind's eye the look of horror on Tavi's face if she ever told him she'd killed an *infant*, even under strict orders. But now, it wasn't some nameless, faceless Panamarian baby she imagined in that doomed building; it *was* her daughter Geneva!

She fell to one knee, the suit shaking the surrounding ground with the impact. "Nowak, report!" yelled Sandoval through the comm, but she ignored him. Her teeth were grinding, and she squeezed her eyes more tightly shut, but tears still streamed unabated down her face. She screamed again, and the noise rebounded around the enclosed bubble of the suit. It felt now like a dozen knives were being thrust into her skull and twisted and moved around to turn her brain into goulash. The pain had spread from her head, and she felt the muscles in her back and legs spasm as her entire body writhed in the confines of the suit.

Sarah kept seeing the rotating images of Geneva playing on her lap and Tavi asking her if she'd ever had to do something she *knew* was wrong to follow orders. The images and words rotated faster and faster through her mind while the voice of Lieutenant Sandoval called out in impotent frustration to her through the horror of the pain.

Slowly, inexorably, her left arm raised back up, and her left eye twitched open as she felt her consciousness fade and her subconscious brain took control of her body for the simple expedient of reducing the pain. "No!" she screamed. "I won't!"

Miraculously through the confusion of her face's agony-driven convulsions, her HUD had cycled back to the thermal view. Now she could see again the baby outlined in the blue designating it as a civilian, held by a larger thermal image of an adult, probably its mother. Less than two meters away was the yellow-outlined, flashing image of Sarah's target.

Her left arm raised higher, and Sarah knew with a terror apart from the physical pain she felt, that in mere fractions of a second, she would follow her orders regardless of her battle against them.

Forcing down the pain into a small place in her mind she hadn't known existed and summoning the last of her strength, she barely managed to twitch the fingers of her right hand in a moderately complicated sequence that overrode one of the suit's core programming imperatives. Her left arm continued to rise of its own volition, but she fought hard enough to alter its trajectory just so.

"Geneva," she cried, "Tavi, forgive me." Then Sarah's left index finger twitched once.

---

Private Feng Chu Hua rounded the corner at a dead run. She'd started sprinting her mech the second Sergeant Nowak's status symbol changed from green to black—signifying KIA—in her HUD, not waiting for orders, just knowing both that her sergeant and friend needed her… and that she would be too late to help.

Chu Hua had been in the Guard Paramilitary Force for only two years after graduating from the Greater York Guard Academy, and she had been a mech driver for only the last ten months after an intensive graduate course to prepare her for the elite role. Despite the enormous size of the mechs, drivers tended to be short and slight; larger people simply didn't fit. It was the same for fighter pilots. It was a lot more expensive to build a bigger mech or fighter cockpit than it was to find someone small enough to fit in whatever the budget provided.

Even amongst mech drivers, Feng was small. At only a hair above 1.4 meters tall, she was a full two heads shorter than most people she met and one head shorter than even most mech pilots. Her stature, coupled with a voice reminiscent of an adolescent girl, had made her the butt of many, many jokes from her fellow mech drivers at the Guard Mechanized Warfare School and earned her the semi-derisive nickname of 'Sprite'.

The jokes normally stopped during simulated combat drills. Feng *loved* driving her mech. It felt like an extension of her body, and better yet, one that made her just as big and just as mean as anyone else in her class. That love was fortunately coupled with no small degree of skill; driving a mech just came naturally to her. She could make her suit move faster, hit harder, and jump higher than anyone else in her training cadre.

But she was still the new kid on the squad and knew she had much to learn. Even in rushing to reach Sarah Nowak's downed mech, she'd run down the alleyway connecting her assigned avenue with the sergeant's too quickly, busting through a brick wall that bisected the alley before she'd even had a chance to check what was on the other side. The result was a ringing in her head and a nice scratch on the front paint of her mech from running headlong into a large metal dumpster parked just beyond the wall.

That had delayed her in getting to her friend. She was frantic with worry and no small amount of guilt at being so slow to respond— though the rational part of her brain knew it wouldn't matter—as she dug in her heels and almost lost control of the mech again as she tried to go from a 30km/h sprint to a dead stop in less than three meters and ended up overshooting the sergeant's downed suit.

When she turned back around and backtracked to her friend, she instantly knew it was indeed too late and that no amount of rushing on her part would have changed that. Inside the shattered dome of the mech, half of Sarah's head was just *gone*. The one remaining eye stared up vacantly at a spot in the sky. Chu Hua stopped, holding her breath in stunned disbelief.

Sarah Nowak had been a giant to Feng Chu Hua from the first day she'd looked down at the diminutive fresh addition to her squad. "I hear you drive that mech like you're three meters tall and have a death wish," Sarah had said calmly to the newly trained driver. Feng had smiled in response, her eyes barely reaching Sarah's chin but feeling a sense of pride that her reputation had preceded her. Sergeant Nowak had quickly disabused her of that pride. Shaking her head at Feng, she had continued: "I've seen your training videos. You move fast and pack a wallop in that suit, but you're sloppy and uncoordinated, and you're going to get yourself or someone else killed real fast."

Nowak had paused then as if giving Private Feng time to argue the point. Chu Hua wisely stayed silent and focused all her energy on stopping the tears she felt building at the stinging rebuke delivered so calmly and matter-of-factly that it somehow made it far worse than if Nowak had screamed in her face. She would soon learn that screaming just wasn't Sergeant Nowak's style, but also that her squad didn't suffer a lick of effectiveness or efficiency for it.

Sarah had drilled Chu Hua mercilessly for the next three months. After each day's maneuvers, when the rest of the platoon, including Nowak's squad, headed home to the barracks or their small off-base apartments (for the married guardmembers), Sarah would upload a set of drills into Chu Hua's HUD that she was expected to complete in *addition* to the day's normal workload. It usually took Feng at least two extra hours to get through the bonus drills, making her miss dinner in the mess hall most nights and forcing her to bribe one of the cooks to keep a plate back for her each day.

Sergeant Nowak would stay most nights and watch Feng do her drills, sometimes suiting up herself and doing them silently next to Chu Hua's mech until her pregnancy showed too much for her to fit in her suit's cockpit. From then on, Nowak would typically sit in a chair on the edge of the training field and watch Feng critically as she went through every drill the sergeant's twisted imagination could come up with.

On the last day of the third month, the drills had been particularly brutal. Though Sarah never raised her voice at Chu Hua and provided only the necessary critiques to help her do the exercises properly, nor did she provide any words of praise. For the last several weeks, Chu Hua had been debating her place in the mechanized division—wondering if she really had what it took.

Every day, she'd enter the training field half convinced it would be her last—that she'd hand her resignation to Nowak and slip off to take a role in the Department of Sanitation or wherever else Guard enacter washouts were sent to languish—but then she'd get in her mech. And how she *loved* being in her mech! Even on the worst, most tiring days, she relished every second of piloting that massive extension of her body.

But today, Chu Hua was utterly exhausted. She finished up the last set of drills that Nowak had devised, a brutal set of sprints with quick pivots around obstacles that moved randomly across the training field —with her mech setup to provide resistance to simulate roughly half of its muscle-assisting servos damaged—and stopped, panting in front of the sergeant's chair.

Sarah looked up from her watch's holo display as if noticing Feng on the training field for the first time. She nodded once, signifying that Chu Hua could hit the showers. The diminutive mech driver did so with a dejected feeling. Now that the thrill of driving her mech was over and she had yet to gain a word of genuine praise from Nowak in the three months of brutal extra training, thoughts of quitting encroached again on her mind.

After getting out of her mech and after her brief shower, she was utterly convinced she'd quit the next morning, but was surprised to find Nowak waiting for her at the women's locker room door.

"Sarge," she said, standing at attention as if ready for inspection.

Sarah Nowak looked at her and smiled slightly and then started walking away down the hall. A few steps away, she turned and looked back at Chu Hua. "Coming?" she asked.

Confused, Feng sprang to follow her sergeant. After walking through the corridors of the Guard Mechanized Operations Base for several minutes, it surprised Chu Hua when they reached the exit to the facility. In her three months in 2nd Squad, she'd only left the base once for a rare weekend pass. Then the realization hit her, and she stopped abruptly just short of the threshold to the outside world. The two reg guardsmen flanking the gate looked at her in puzzlement, but Sarah Nowak kept walking as if she hadn't noticed Feng was no longer following.

*This is it,* Chu Hua thought in despair. *I'm literally being shown the door. I won't be driving mechs anymore. They're washing me out!* Then, quickly, her despair was replaced by anger. *How dare they! How dare she! I've done everything she's asked every day and never complained, and she's kicking me out without a word of explanation! No! I won't go!* But she also knew that, as an enacter, she wouldn't have a choice but to do whatever she was commanded to do.

"This isn't right." The words escaped her mouth so abruptly that Chu Hua was surprised to hear them formed by her own voice. They even sent a sharp little pain into her head as she contemplated arguing her discharge. Still, she stubbornly set her jaw as Sarah turned and regarded her coolly, one hand resting on her swollen abdomen and fleetingly reminding Feng of her mother—what little memories she had of the woman before being taken at an early age to attend the Enacter Academy.

"What's not right?" Nowak asked softly, cocking an eyebrow and waiting for a response.

"K-kicking me out like this," Feng stuttered, then nodded once to add some semblance of strength and resolve to her words.

Sarah's eyebrow hitched higher, and the corner of her mouth twitched up in half a smile. "Kicking you out?" she questioned. "I thought you were brighter than that. You're doing an outstanding job in your training. You'll make one terrific mech driver if you keep at it. Possibly the best I've ever seen."

Chu Hua was stunned, and her mouth dropped open. For a protracted moment, she tried to find the words to respond to the unexpected praise from her superior—the words she'd hungered for since the first day she'd stood at attention in front of Sergeant Sarah Nowak.

Finally, she found her voice. "But why are we leaving the base?"

Now Sarah's smile widened, and she shrugged her shoulders ever so slightly. "Dinner."

Fifteen minutes later, Feng Chu Hua found herself sitting at the small kitchen table in the Nowak's off-base apartment, listening in stunned silence to the gentle but playful banter between Octavio and Sarah Nowak as they casually discussed the furniture they'd need for the new baby's nursery.

When they'd entered the apartment, Sarah had introduced Feng to her husband as "*My* promising young mech driver I've told you about."

From that day forward, Feng Chu Hua had indeed been one of *Sarah's* mech drivers. She may have been born an enacter and disposed by genetics to follow any order from any superior who represented the Council. But there was absolutely no doubt that, enacter gene or no, she would have followed Sergeant Nowak into the fires of Mako 7 with naught but a cup of water if the woman had but asked.

Now, nine months later, she stood looking down at the shattered mech that housed the forever-still body of her mentor, leader, and friend, and Chu Hua felt the tears rush to her eyes and stream down her face.

"Sarah, no," she whispered in despair, and she fell forward, allowing her mech to crash to its knees in front of the prone form of its destroyed twin.

Thinking far quicker than she would have expected in her state of shock, she twitched her nose and stuck out her tongue in a pattern that her suit recognized and then watched as the words she hoped for flashed onto her HUD.

***Suit connection established. Terminal sequence download initiated.***

She knew she had to move fast before Sandoval or anyone else thought to issue her a direct order that she couldn't help but obey. But Feng *had* to know exactly what had happened to her friend. It might be Sandoval's or even Captain Ullen's duty to inform Octavio of his wife's death—her breath caught again at the thought of how that would shatter Sarah's husband, who had become like an older brother to his wife's youngest squad member—but there was no way Chu Hua could avoid facing the man and telling him what she saw. She owed it to him and to Sarah and to little Geneva.

When her HUD played the last two minutes of the wrecked suit's video, what she saw rocked her to her core.

*She disobeyed a direct order! That's not supposed to be possible.*

That thought was quickly chased by the terrible realization that her friend had killed *herself* to keep from following an order that was patently wrong. *A baby! How could they order her to kill a baby?*

In that moment, facing the horrible truth, Private Feng Chu Hua changed forever in a fundamental way that she'd never imagined was possible.

---

Lieutenant Jose Sandoval shook his head grimly as he pressed send on the official report on Sergeant Nowak's death. According to the bit of fiction he'd just transmitted to the waiting Guard ships in orbit—fiction written under direct orders from his superiors no less—Sarah Nowak had died when an unseen sniper hit her mech with an armor-piercing round that drilled through the transparent dome around her head and then through her left temple. Death was instantaneous, and she didn't suffer.

The first part of that was true, at least; death had been instantaneous. But she *had* suffered.

*The pain must have been excruciating,* he thought with a physical shiver down his spine. *How could she have endured it? This is* not *supposed to be possible.*

He'd been stunned when he'd watched the drone footage of the incident—how Sarah had fought the orders with visible effort. He'd been even more chilled living through it again when he'd watched her mech's logs, listening to her scream in agony as she fought against a thousand years of ingrained genetic programming. He would never forget her last words, begging forgiveness from her daughter and husband before she pulled the trigger and ended her own life.

Jose Sandoval still didn't know how or why this had happened, but he knew it was big. There was no going back to the way things were. For an officer who had done his best for years to simply follow orders and keep his head down, that thought was extremely disconcerting.

After sending the report, he sat at his small desk in the Bravo Company command post, inside the perimeter of the Guard's forward operating base in a cleared piece of jungle just south of the city of San Sebastian. He cradled his head in his hands as he tried hard not to think of his entire paradigm shattering around him because of one blasted stubborn sergeant whom he couldn't help but both hate and admire for her sheer strength of will.

He was like that, head in hands and thinking through painful things he'd never been forced to consider before, when Corporal Walker cleared his throat at the door to the small compartment.

Jose looked up to see the young guardsman standing there with a distressed look on his face.

"Yes, Corporal?" he asked softly, intrinsically dreading whatever the man had come to say.

"Um, sir..." Walker hesitated.

"Spit it out, son!" Sandoval barked a little more harshly than he'd intended. But it had the right effect.

"Yes, sir!" Walker straightened and stood at attention. "It's Private Feng, sir. She hasn't checked in for reverie."

Sandoval looked at the man in confusion. Feng was the first on the scene at Nowak's suicide but hadn't openly questioned the story her superiors had told her and the rest of the squad—the same story he'd just submitted in his official report. So surely there wasn't a connection...

"Did you comm her?" he asked the corporal, drawing out his voice in feigned patience that would signal to the man that he'd be in trouble if he was bothering his lieutenant for something so trivial as a soldier missing a simple evening check-in. For all Sandoval knew, she was simply late coming back from the mess hall.

"Yes, sir," answered Walker. "That's when I found this." He put his hand into the pocket of his fatigue pants and drew out a watch. "It's Feng's, sir. She left it on her bunk. I checked the mess. She's not there or in any of the normal spots she hangs out in. She's just gone, sir."

Now Sandoval grimaced, and his first thought genuinely scared him. *Two in one day? It's impossible! Even one shouldn't be possible.*

The light mechanized divisions, to Jose Sandoval's knowledge, had never once had a desertion. Unlike Guard Paramilitary Force infantry divisions, which had the occasional reg who missed his girlfriend or couldn't take the pressure, mechanized divisions were made up one hundred percent by enacters. The idea that they could disobey a single order, much less abandon their duty completely, was anathema to everything the Guard knew about enacters from a thousand years of firsthand experience.

However, an hour later, after a thorough search of the camp turned up no trace of Private Feng Chu Hua, even Jose Sandoval was forced to briefly consider that perhaps everything he'd ever known was simply wrong. But unlike Nowak and Feng, he still found it marginally easy to sweep the inconvenience of reality under the rug and nod with genuine conviction when his superiors told him that 'factors beyond his understanding' were responsible for the anomalous events of the day. It was far easier to believe that than to believe the alternative, and he grasped at the lie like a lifebuoy in a choppy ocean.

Because enacters were supposed to follow orders, not terminate their own lives or desert their units to avoid doing so. Any evidence to the contrary could never *really* be true and could certainly never reach public view. So, Jose thrust down the nagging thoughts in the back of his mind and did his best to believe what he was told.

In the chaos of a sergeant's death and a private's desertion, no one thought to check the root logs in either Nowak's destroyed suit or Feng's abandoned one. If they had, they would have searched even harder for Private Feng Chu Hua when they realized she had downloaded a copy of the suit's final moments, and had taken with her ironclad proof an enacter could indeed make her own terrible choice.

# THE FOUR WORLDS - SUBVERSION

Senior Assembly Speaker Nancy Farnsworth glared around the authentic cherry oak table at her fellow members of the Committee on Truth in Media. When she'd first been appointed to the Assembly over 40 years ago, she'd been impressed by the trappings of power: authentic wood furniture, ornately paneled walls, and gold fixtures in the washrooms. But the novelty of these extravagances quickly wore off and did absolutely nothing to assuage her mood at this particular juncture.

"Well?" she asked impatiently, spearing one of the junior Assembly speakers with her eyes as the man squirmed just enough to give her a sense of smug satisfaction.

"We have all the major news services running stories to counter the so-called Revelations, Ma'am," the man said; he was a speaker, like her, so he didn't let his nervousness show through his voice, but there were other signs in the way he continued to fidget. "But it just doesn't seem to be having the desired impact with the public." As soon as he was done with his answer, he ducked his head down into his raised shoulders, looking like a turtle trying to withdraw into its shell, preparing himself for the inevitable blowup.

Farnsworth felt her face warm and was sure she was turning red. When she replied, she emphasized the consonants and bit off the end of every word. "And. Why. Not?!"

The man who'd been speaking sunk even lower in his seat, clearly wishing he could disappear but maintaining just enough self-composure to at least meet her eyes for one brief moment as he shrugged in futility.

"Come on, Nancy," drawled a man's voice from the other side of the table, breaking the standoff between predator and prey. Farnsworth turned her steely gaze to Creighton Horvath, a tall octogenarian who looked far younger but maintained a shock of white hair to lend himself a look of aged wisdom. It didn't help Nancy's loathing of the man to remember that she'd once considered him attractive, with his rakish good looks and chiseled jaw, and had even entertained the idea of a liaison. Now she did everything in her power to make him shrink from her deadly gaze. But unlike the junior members in the room, he met her stare calmly with his own, the corner of his mouth even quirking up into the momentary but impossible-to-miss beginnings of a smile.

"You know," he continued in his annoying affectation of a Nova Tejas rancher's drawl, even though she knew he'd been born and raised in metropolitan San Antonia and had probably never stepped foot on a ranch, "that the best lies contain a measure of the truth, and that gives them legs to run." He cocked an eyebrow at her in a knowing way that emphasized his words and made clear their personal meaning.

She felt her face grow even redder with rage, and she sucked in a breath and bit her lower lip hard enough to taste blood. She would *not* give Horvath the satisfaction of her blowing up verbally. Creighton was her most vocal opponent in the Twenty—the elite but secret group of the most senior Assembly speakers and the true power in the 47 Colonies—and she and the man had been cultivating their hatred of each other for the better part of two decades since Nancy herself had been appointed to the Twenty by the previous Keeper, just a year after Creighton had joined the elite group.

From day one, she and the man had been at odds. They were both ambitious; each felt that they were the natural choice to succeed the current Keeper, Ian Petrov, when the man ultimately died or retired. The former was much more likely than the latter—Petrov was not the type to voluntarily give up the absolute power that came with the Keeper's seat. Either way, Farnsworth and Horvath both viewed the other as a threat to their eventual ascendance to that lofty title, and neither did a good job of hiding their animosity for the other.

Like now, in front of a large group of junior Assembly members, Creighton had the nerve to not-so-subtly allude to the portion of the Revelations that disclosed Farnsworth's illicit relationship with two interns followed by their mysterious deaths. Nancy had believed she couldn't possibly hate anyone more than she'd already hated Creighton, but the man constantly found new ways to get under her skin.

That all the accusations against her were *true* was beside the point, though she bristled at the semantics used in the Revelations. She had *not* 'raped'—that was such a crude word—either Xander or Peter

Nakamura; she had simply made it clear to both of them that their jobs included certain obligations to her, which they were welcome to decline as long as they were also willing to give up their dreams of working as Assembly staffers.

The whole arrangement was so *normal* for the Assembly that she'd barely given it a moment's consideration. There was zero doubt in her mind that Creighton had similar arrangements with the gaggle of pretty young women who always seemed to inhabit his staff offices. And just like she'd been forced to do when those two stupid interns attempted to go public with their trumped-up accusations, she was sure Creighton had occasionally found the need to dispose of potential accusers in creative but less savory ways.

However, his words and his knowing look made it clear he was reveling in the one simple difference between them: *she* had let herself get caught with her hand in the cookie jar. That stupid reporter, Todd what's-his-name, hadn't stopped digging even when Nancy had quietly arranged to have his story killed and his evidence conveniently lost, and he'd made known his accusations to the entire galaxy when that blasted traitor Kendra Siefred—another member of the Twenty no less!—had given the man a bully pulpit to speak from.

That both the reporter and the traitorous Assembly speaker had died within minutes of broadcasting their cursed 'Revelations' didn't stop the fact that virtually everyone in the 47 Colonies had seen them and were abuzz with speculations on which parts might be truth versus fiction. Moreover, the illegal blogs had picked up the story and rebroadcast it so many times—they'd even distributed anachronistic *paper* pamphlets on some worlds—that the story just refused to die.

That's what this meeting was about. As a senior member of the Committee on Truth in Media, which was really the chief propaganda arm of the Council government, Nancy was the person in charge of both quashing the treasonous Revelations and building and disseminating the counter-narrative. But she'd been hamstrung in the effort from the start, both because the Revelations specifically called her out *and* because the smug rival sitting across from her was taking every opportunity to undermine her in front of any audience he could arrange.

"Perhaps, Creighton, you'd like to elaborate?" she sneered, calling his bluff. While the man could insinuate all he wanted, it was an unwritten but no-less-ironclad rule of the Twenty that they did not *openly* disparage each other in public settings. It might undermine their power and, by extension, the power of the Keeper, the true ruler of the 47 Colonies in the centuries since the extermination of the real Council.

Of course, before the Revelations, everyone else in the colonies, including most of the Assembly, *knew* that the Keeper was simply the mouthpiece for the Council—a group of anonymous and supposedly brilliant and benevolent rulers. That fiction had helped Petrov and the other members of the Twenty rule with more authority and a tighter fist than would have been possible if forced to use only their own authority. Maintaining that lie, even in the face of the Revelations, was one of Nancy's and this committee's primary responsibilities, though few others in the room knew it.

Horvath smiled in response to Farnsworth's taunt, but the smile didn't reach his eyes. "Why Nancy," he drawled, "don't take it personally. I'm just pointing out that more than a few of the tidbits shared by Kendra Siefred and Todd Crowley were true. So, trying to make it all sound false with counter-news reports just makes us sound desperate."

Of course, of all those in the room, only she and Horvath knew just how many of the Revelations were really factual. Essentially, all of what Siefred and Crowley had said in their broadcast was the truth— or some version of it. The scariest part had been the disclosure of Tyrus Tyne's disobedience. The thought of any enacter, especially one of the fanatically loyal and deadly alphas, turning traitor was enough to make even the Keeper genuinely afraid. Worse, they had confirmed that Tyne and the rogue reader, Jinny Ambrosa, had both been on the single ship that had escaped the Council Navy's trap at Rinali and that had later gotten through the Castilian Rift to the Four Worlds. The implications were terrifying. *Everything* depended on the Twenty's planned invasion of Earth and her sisters; that they'd almost certainly been warned of the impending attack was a catastrophe.

Just as inconvenient was having the entire galaxy know about the plot to turn ordinary citizens into enacters or about the secret navy the Twenty had raised to enable the invasion of the Four Worlds. Especially since the government had been claiming for six centuries that the Sol system was unlivable because of a plague. Now they'd had seven different ships, mostly smugglers but also a couple of suspected rebels, try to bypass the naval blockade to travel to the Four Worlds just since the Revelations had come out. None had succeeded, but things were getting out of hand!

It was sad, really. Before the Revelations, the Twenty had done such an efficient job of controlling the flow of information in the galaxy that few in the public had ever suspected just how many secrets their leaders were keeping from them. Well, except for a small number of crackpot conspiracy theorists spouting scud in underground blogs that few took seriously. However, now that the proverbial cat was out of the bag, they were expending an incredible amount of effort on simple damage control, undermining the glorious future they had planned for humanity.

"All I'm saying," continued Horvath, "is that if we acknowledge a few parts of the Revelations that *are* true, or that *may* be true, we'll rebuild a lot more credibility with the public for the parts that we tell them are false."

*Clever use of words, Creighton,* Farnsworth thought with sarcasm dripping from her inner voice. *It's not what's really false, but what we tell the public is false, even if it's true. I just wish you'd be a little more subtle about it because even some of the idiots in this room might pick up on your double-speak if you're not more careful.*

She smiled in a not-so-friendly way at Horvath but was frustrated that he didn't even flinch. "And just what do you propose we acknowledge as truth first, Creighton?"

The man's smile grew larger, and his eyes took on a predatory gleam. For a fleeting moment, Nancy worried he was going to call her out directly in front of the entire committee. But, to her relief, he went in a different direction.

"I was thinking we make public the results of the investigation into Frank Ambrosa—edited, of course. We know he did what the Revelations accuse him of, turning that daughter of his into some kind of super reader, though we still don't know the full extent of whatever abilities he gave her. He did it without the knowledge or consent of the

Council, so there was no wrongdoing on the government's part in any of it. Ambrosa acted alone. So far, we've been handling it internally. Let's make the findings public and even hold a public trial. Show people we're taking the Revelations seriously. Then we can spoon-feed them the truth from a position of authority again."

Farnsworth shook her head with a frown. The man was being awfully open in front of so many junior Assembly speakers who still didn't fully grasp how power and politics in the galaxy truly worked. "Ambrosa knows things," she disagreed. "If he gets on the stand to testify, a lot of other... inconvenient information could come out; things we're telling the populace are lies." *Two can play at the doublespeak game, Creighton.*

Horvath's smile disappeared, but the predatory gleam was still in his eyes as his voice took on a condescending tone. "Come on, Nancy, do I have to spell it out for you? Ambrosa never needs to even be in the courtroom for us to make our point. Besides, we still haven't been able to find him; releasing the details of what he did may get the citizenry to help us keep an eye out for him. And when we inevitably do find him... Well, accidents happen, especially to those who resist Guard arrest."

At this, some of the junior speakers in the room looked shocked, and a few whispered conversations broke out around the large table.

Nancy smashed her gavel onto the wooden table hard enough to leave a mark. "Silence!" Now everyone but her and Horvath took on the look of turtles desperately trying to hide.

She nodded slowly. "It just might work, Creighton." *And it just might. If nothing else, it will take some attention off me.* "I will tell the Keeper about our plan."

Horvath smiled widely again. "Don't you worry about it, Nancy. I've already cleared it with him."

Now he was rubbing her face in it. In the 13 weeks since the Revelations had come out, Farnsworth had been unable to get a one-on-one audience with Petrov, where before, she'd usually had a meeting with the man at least once a month. He'd also refused to meet her gaze directly in the last meeting of the Twenty, and Nancy was starting to think she was being left out of other meetings that normally would have included her. It had gotten bad enough that she'd hired extra security and even commanded one of the vaunted alphas to join her protective detail just in case the Keeper or anyone else got it in their heads to make her and the problems she now represented go away.

"Fine, then this meeting is over," she said, casting a glare around the room, daring anyone to bring up any additional topics.

The junior members of the committee made their way hastily out of the room's two exits. Creighton Horvath stayed seated, and Farnsworth took this as a sign he wanted to talk with her alone and off-the-record. When the room was otherwise empty, she looked at him questioningly, her lips pressed into a tight frown. He grinned and held up a single finger to tell her to wait a moment. Nancy seethed and was about to demand he get to it when she heard the door open behind her.

Thinking that one of the junior members must have lingered in the room, and that had prompted Creighton's reticence to start the private conversation, she turned with an annoyed look. But the sound had not been anyone leaving, but rather someone coming in. In front of the now-closed door stood a tall, square-jawed, blond man with piercing blue eyes—eyes that were fixed squarely on Farnsworth like daggers.

At first, she was shocked at the newcomer's appearance, but then she relaxed. It was only the alpha she'd enlisted as a personal bodyguard, probably worried that she hadn't left the room with the rest of the committee and come to check on her to make sure she was safe.

Nancy turned from looking at the alpha and fixed her gaze back on Horvath, a small smile forming on her lips as she imagined that the appearance of one of the deadliest killers in human space would finally wipe the smug grin off the older man's face.

But to her uncomfortable surprise, Creighton's grin had only gotten wider, and he looked at her like a shark eying a small fish with nowhere to hide. Nancy sat in confused silence, desperately trying to figure out what angle the man was working. Then she heard the footsteps behind her.

Hastily, she turned and regarded the tall blond alpha as he strolled toward her, the heels of his shoes clicking against the real marble floors of the committee room. The man's cold dead eyes hadn't left her, and she felt the blood drain from her face, and her entire body go chill as realization hit her.

"What is the meaning of this?" she croaked out through a throat suddenly dry and hoarse. When the man didn't respond, she desperately looked back at Horvath. "Creighton, what is this?"

Horvath's smile turned even colder. "Nancy, the Keeper and the rest of the Twenty feel that you've become... a liability. The vote was unanimous."

She opened her mouth to demand an explanation, but he held up his hand to forestall her. To her own surprise, she shut her mouth and glanced nervously back at the blond alpha, who was now standing behind her chair, incongruously smiling down at her.

"Alpha, I command you in the name of the Council to back off," she forced out, but the deadly man's smile and gaze didn't even waiver. "I command you! I speak for the Council!" she yelled now, though her voice was still raspy.

"Tut, tut, tut," she heard from across the table and whipped around to look back at Horvath.

"You see, Nancy," the octogenarian said in a soft voice, "you and I both know that there was quite a *lot* of truth in the Revelations: the fleet; the Four Worlds; Project Epsilon, Ambrosa; and *you*."

"That's a lie," Farnsworth forced out, immediately ashamed at how small and pleading her voice was and at how obvious her untruth must sound.

Horvath just shook his head in disappointment, the smile never leaving his face. "The Keeper was willing to overlook your—shall we say indiscretions—as long as they stayed hidden and didn't interfere with the Twenty's ability to govern. But unfortunately, that is no longer the case. As you so helpfully pointed out, just like Frank Ambrosa, you have *far* too much knowledge to testify at your own trial. So, this is just how it *has* to be."

"What?!" she cried. "How *what* has to be?" Though she knew exactly what he meant. It was what she would have done without a moment's hesitation if their situations were reversed.

In response, Horvath simply nodded toward the tall blond alpha, and Nancy turned in her seat once again and looked back up at the interloper.

The man spoke for the first time, his voice hard and arrogant. "Ms. Farnsworth. Since you've never called me anything but Alpha, I'd like you to know my name is Collins. And I've been *very* much looking forward to this moment."

"B—but you're an enacter, and I've given you a command. I speak for the Council!" Nancy managed to force out in one last desperate attempt to save herself, but even she could hear how small her normally authoritative speaker's voice had become.

"Not anymore, you don't," came Creighton's cold reply from farther away this time.

Nancy heard the room's other door shut and looked up frantically to see that Horvath had left her alone with the assassin. She looked back toward the man called Collins to see that he hadn't moved a muscle. Abruptly, she stood up in the small space between her chair and the table and turned fully to face the man.

"No!" she cried. "I'll give you whatever you want. Money, power, anything."

The man called Collins leaned forward so that his face was centimeters from hers, so close she could smell his breath from behind sneering lips. "Why Madam Speaker, I want nothing from you. I'm an enacter, so I obey the Council—or shall we be honest with each other and say the Keeper—and the Keeper wants you dead."

Nancy screamed, but the soundproof room ensured that no one else heard.

# ACT I

Extensive analysis by the Council Committee on Science has revealed some worrying trends in the creation and effectiveness of enhanced individuals throughout the 47 Colonies. We have long known that the genetic mutations have generally declined in potency the further away our subjects have gotten from Generation Zero, the first generation of enhanced individuals to have been engineered by the Second Council circa 250 B.D. However, what we did not expect was for the degradation of abilities to accelerate as it has in the last three generations.

For example, according to internal Council historical records (not shared with the public), the average reading time of a Generation Zero reader was 20.5 hours. By Generation 14, it had reduced modestly to 19.25 hours. And by Generation 28, to 18.1 hours. But in just the three generations since (Generation 31), we have seen a drastic decline to just 15.2 hours, and the rising generation (32) is projected to have an average of just 11.8 hours. From there, AI models project the decline will continue to progress exponentially with each new generation, assuming no newly enhanced individuals are integrated into the bloodlines.

We see the same trend in blenders. A Generation Zero blender could entirely mimic an individual's appearance and body structure within an average of 5.8 days. As of Generation 28, it was 6.4 days. In the rising generation (32), it is projected to be 8.8 days and even longer if the blender chooses to change their DNA to match their subject.

We cannot express in the same terms the decline in speakers or enacters; it is impossible to find the same objective quantitative metrics to describe the strength of their mutations, but using qualitative measures versus historical records, we see the same accelerating decline there as well. For example, the Enacter Academy has reported, anecdotally, that the new generations of enacters are slower to respond to commands before their full indoctrination is complete. If true, this is extremely concerning.

What's more, across all enhancements, these weaker mutations are leading to fewer new enhanced individuals than expected in each new generation. A hundred years ago, if just one grandparent of a newborn baby had a genetic enhancement, the likelihood of that newborn carrying the mutated gene was 28%. Now it is only 8.5%. Effectively, newborn children must now have at least two grandparents carrying the mutation to have a 32% chance of carrying the mutated gene themselves.

This means each new generation will have fewer enhanced individuals as a percentage of the total population, and those that inherit the enhancements will be less effective than their predecessor generations. Within just two more generations, we estimate that 67% of new readers will not be suitable for the current minimum requirements of the Reader Corps. We expect to see similar declines in blenders, speakers, and even enacters.

Perhaps most concerning, we believe that in this rising generation we are likely to see enacters who imprint on the Council but can, in periods of extreme emotional stress, override their subconscious impulses and disobey direct orders. We may even eventually see enacters who can entirely override their genetic programming and break their conditioning, possibly imprinting on new authority figures outside the Council. We do not have to explain to this body the disastrous results if such were to occur.

In summary, in less than 50 years, the Council will no longer have any measurable benefit from the enhanced in any of the four Corps, which will be catastrophic for the Council's ability to effectively govern the 47 Colonies.

To combat these trends, we first recommend Project Epsilon, outlined on pages 17-46, which will allow us to create new enacters from the population of non-enhanced individuals across the colonies. We also recommend similar efforts to create new readers (pp. 48-64), speakers (pp. 65-70), and blenders (pp. 72-94). It is our belief that...

-Excerpt from the *Proposal to Relaunch Research into Genetic Enhancements;* Dr. Julian Pierce, Dr. Amanda Kipling, Dr. Yui Ito; January 27, 675 P.D.

# CHAPTER 1

JUNE 4, 731 P.D.; THREE MONTHS AFTER THE REVELATIONS

Riggs opened his eyes to the mottled sunlight filtering through the leaves outside his window. On the other side of the glass, birds chirped, and the occasional honeybee flitted by on its way to pollinate the spring flowers that covered the idyllic backyard of the modest but comfortable home on Bainbridge Island, in a place called the Pacific Northwest, that the government of Earth had so graciously lent him for the duration of his stay on the homeworld.

The springtime sun warmed his bed and well-appointed bedroom, while dust motes drifted lazily in the beams of sunlight, and the occasional breeze moved the leaves outside and created playful light shows across the room.

Riggs hated absolutely everything about it.

He sat up abruptly and flung the covers off of himself, scratching the stubble on his chin and looking forlornly out the window at his own personal hell.

"Good morning, Mr. Riggs," piped a cheerful male voice. "The temperature today will be a comfortable 26 degrees Celsius. I have taken the liberty of rotating appropriate attire to the front of your—"

"Shut up!" Riggs growled, and the smart AI that managed the house immediately stopped its inane chatter. At least it called him 'Mr. Riggs' now. The one and only time it had used his first name, he had threatened to rewire it with the memory board of a toaster. In the weeks that had followed that incident, Riggs had gotten pretty creative in threatening the AI with all sorts of terrible fates if it didn't leave him alone and stop sounding so blasted cheerful. Then even his vaunted creativity had been exhausted, and now he just simply told the thing to 'switch off' or 'shut up' every time it spoke to him.

He was convinced the Earthlings had installed it into the house with the express purpose of torturing him. Just like that unnatural yellow sun that plagued the sky on this cursed planet.

In his more honest moments, Riggs would almost admit to himself that Earth wasn't really all that bad. It was sure better than Panamar, Phoenix, or Daegu, and not nearly as bad as the titanium mines on Krampus, a large asteroid in the Mako system he'd once had the misfortune to spend a few weeks on.

But, regardless of Earth's charms, of the roughly one total year of his lifetime that he calculated he'd spent actually *on* the surface of a planet, the last three months on Earth were by far the worst he'd ever experienced.

The reason for that was simple. He couldn't leave. His ship, the *Blind Monk*, was supposedly fully repaired from its misadventures in fleeing from the Council Navy through the Castilian Rift with half its atmo blown into space. It was now sitting ready to fly somewhere on Luna—he wasn't sure *which* lunar base or settlement—but Riggs had no way to get to it. He was a veritable prisoner here in paradise, and it grated at him like nothing else ever had.

He heard a bang and a crash coming from the living areas of the house, followed by the sound of a not-so-feminine voice swearing loudly. Shaking his head, he pulled on the pants he'd left on the floor next to the bed, ignoring whatever clean clothes the AI had arranged in his closet, and picked up a shirt from the pile on the armchair a few paces away. Smelling the shirt to make sure it wasn't too offensive, he put it over his head and pulled it down while he walked out of the bedroom door toward the sound of muttered curses coming from the kitchen.

"Jynx, what are you doing here so scudding early?" he asked his co-pilot and companion of the last several years.

Jynx—if she even had a last name, she'd never shared it with him—turned and glared at him from over her shoulder. Taller than his own 1.8 meters, trim, and brunette, with striking features that were just a little too sharp, she'd be attractive to any man who hadn't spent at least five seconds with her. That was usually about how long it took for her personality to show through and ruin the effect of her good looks. She and Riggs got along famously.

"I was out of pancake mix," she explained brusquely and returned to ignoring him and making a terrible mess of his kitchen.

Riggs took a seat on a stool at the kitchen counter and regarded her skeptically. "No, you're not. Because the Earthlings send some annoyingly cheerful girl scout to check my pantry every other day, and she doesn't let me come *close* to running out of *anything*. I'm sure they do the same for you, but they probably send a male model instead."

"Well, maybe." Jynx seemed to think for a beat, possibly reviewing a mental picture of the pantry in her equally comfortable house right next door or possibly considering his poor attempt at humor and whether it deserved the courtesy of a laugh or even a snort. Then she shook her head. "Anyway, I couldn't find any, so I came over to use yours."

"Sure, you did," Riggs said, shrugging and pouring himself a cup of coffee from the automated urn on the counter. At least the stupid AI was good for *something*. He could see Jynx had already had at least one cup of the stuff—probably more—judging by the empty used mug next to the clean one for him.

"Any word on the *Monk*?" she asked in what she probably thought was a casual tone as she continued making way more noise than any normal human making something as simple as pancakes.

"Jynx, every day you ask me that same question, and every day I give you the same answer…."

"You'll know when I know," she said in unison with him.

"I know that," she continued, pointing her spatula at his face for emphasis, "but it's just not natural to be tied down like this for so long. I've broken and fixed just about every gadget in my stupid house...."

"And half of the ones in mine," Riggs muttered into his coffee, but she ignored him and continued, still using the spatula to spar with the air in front of him.

"...but I just miss getting my hands on a proper star drive and fusion reactor. I need to do *something*. I'm going crazy over in that hovel."

*Only Jynx would call a house bigger than any she's ever been in a hovel,* thought Riggs wryly, but he also agreed with her.

"Let me make a few calls," he said, pretending to do so grudgingly, even though he was just as stir-crazy as she was. And the Earthies' empty promises that they would see their ship 'soon' were wearing thin after three full months.

"Have you heard from the hijackers lately?" Jynx asked as she picked up a fully burned crisp of a pancake from off the stove and pretended to examine it before flinging it off the spatula and into the kitchen sink.

"They have names, Jynx."

"Sure, they do. What's-Her-Face and Alpha Boy."

"Jinny and Tyrus."

"Whatever. Pretty sure that's what I said. Any word on them? Did the Earthies finally decide Alpha Boy is too much of a security risk and kill him?"

"Not as far as I know," Riggs replied, ignoring the hopeful tone in her voice. "I saw Jinny a couple of days ago, though, and she seemed fine. Says that the Earthies, Earthlings, Earthers, whatever, are all hot and bothered still about the Council fleet that's coming. And that Tyrus is supposedly working with their military as a consultant on Council tech and tactics."

Jynx turned from her third burned pancake and regarded him with a pained expression. "Two days ago? Really? Don't you mean two *nights* ago? What you see in that little reader, I'll never understand."

Riggs set his mug down and shook his head at her. "She's not that kind of girl, Jynx. We had lunch. That's all. It's... nice to talk to someone who—I don't know—is normal."

Jynx let out a guffaw. "Normal? She's a blasted reader *and* an abnorm, Riggs. She's about as far from normal as you can get. Not to mention a rebel, a traitor, and the best and only friend of a murderer."

Riggs slammed his open palm on the countertop, surprising even himself and causing Jynx to jump more than she had when they'd been ambushed on one of the moons of Ha'ano by a bounty hunter a year and a half ago. Through gritted teeth, he hissed at her. "Stop. It. Right. Now. Or did you forget that *we're* rebels and traitors too now by default, or that the *murderer* saved all of our lives when he took a zero-g walk through hard vac to fix the *Monk* so we could escape being as crispy as those pancakes you keep burning?"

She frowned at his outburst. "You know what I mean, Riggs. None of us are normal right now. We're... here." She waved her hands, including the one holding the spatula, around her as if to encompass all of Earth.

He replied calmly now. "I get it, Jynx. I do. I'm bored and frustrated, just like you. But we need to stick close to Jinny and Tyrus. They're our only lifeline here and probably the only chance we have of ever getting back to the *Monk*. And they're not so bad."

Jynx pretended to focus intently on her fifth pancake attempt and shook her head. When she spoke again, her voice caught just enough for Riggs to hear it. "We should have left them on Rinali Station."

Now he was genuinely upset. "Jynx, *we* decided to bring them here after they told us what was going on: all the Council's lies and that fleet. If we hadn't been with them, we probably would have died on Rinali with everyone else."

She spun and threw the spatula at him. He ducked it, barely, and looked back up to see her fuming and her face turning visibly red. "No, Riggs! *You* decided to help them, and I was just along for the ride." With that, she stormed from the kitchen and out the front door, slamming it behind her.

He sighed and poured himself another cup of coffee. Almost 13 weeks on Earth, and Jynx just wasn't coming around at all. She was still just as angry—with him and everyone else—as she had been when she'd first seen Tyrus Tyne, her sister's killer, in the cockpit of the *Blind Monk* just over three months ago on Rinali Station. Before they'd narrowly escaped both the Jaguari Pirates and a massive Council attack fleet to make their way through the Back Door of the Castilian Rift on the one known path to the Four Worlds. And to Earth.

"Never should have come?" he muttered to himself. "Sometimes, I wonder." Then the smoke alarm went off as Jynx's abandoned pancake burned on the stove.

---

Jinny Ambrosa stuck out her lower lip and blew upward to move her blond bangs out of her eyes while she scrutinized her opponent across the court. The trim older woman with black hair streaked with gray eyed her in return from the other side of the net and then tossed the green ball up in the air before bringing her racket up in one fluid motion, sending the ball zooming toward Jinny, but about a meter to her left, requiring the short blond reader to move in that direction and then hit a backhand return.

Jinny stretched out her lithe body and returned the ball smoothly, targeting the far-right corner of her opponent's end of the court, on the opposite side from where the older woman had served. Her opponent was just barely too slow in making her way across the court, and Jinny's return landed the ball just centimeters inside the out-of-bounds line.

"Luv-15," the other woman shouted at Jinny with a wry smile. "You're getting better at this."

"It would help if I could read another player; get some quick tips," Jinny replied with a smile of her own.

The other woman grimaced good-naturedly, knowing that Jinny was at least half kidding. But centuries of suspicion and fear didn't go away after just a few weeks. Still, she responded in the same playful tone Jinny had used. "Heaven forbid. You might see a memory of my husband in his birthday suit, and then you'd be forever ruined for other men."

Jinny laughed aloud. The woman's husband was an elderly

# THE FOUR WORLDS - SUBVERSION

member of the United Earth Congress and probably hadn't exercised for more than five minutes at a time since before Jinny was born. He was *not* the image of a man to whom fitness mattered. Regardless, his wife loved him for who he was, though she often tried and failed to get him to join her out on the tennis court for his health.

"You're absolutely right. That's *not* something I want to see," she replied with a fake grimace of her own.

To which the other woman, Debra O'Leary, replied with a laugh. "You're right; you simply couldn't handle it."

"I heard that, you two!" a male voice shouted from the direction of the house with mock anger. Congressman Corey O'Leary, who always seemed to be heralded by his shock of red hair, appeared carrying a tray laden with drinks and finger sandwiches, which he set on a table to the side of the tennis court. "Ms. Ambrosa, Jinny, I simply must insist you stop trying to read my wife. I shudder to think of the mental damage you would sustain from venturing to a place so dark and dangerous."

The wide grin on his face belied the sober tone of his words and admonition, even as he dodged the tennis ball his wife threw at him from five meters away.

Jinny was quite fond of the O'Learys and had spent the last month staying in a guest house on their property in San Diego, on the Pacific coast of the North American continent. Prior to that, she had stayed in the palatial home of another older man, Harold Tichner, who called himself a professor but was clearly a power broker in the governments of both Earth and Europa. He had introduced Jinny to Corey O'Leary after one of the endless committee meetings she'd been invited to attend when she'd first arrived and had later asked if she'd be comfortable moving in with the O'Learys while he made a trip 'whose details would only bore you, my dear'. She hadn't seen the man in the month since.

"Fine, I'll stop if I must," Jinny said with feigned disappointment. She was quite happy to have not read *anyone* since she'd arrived in the Four Worlds and on Earth. At first, she'd held off reading them because they knew well what readers were, and she didn't want to overstep her bounds. Then she'd continued to hold off when it became apparent just how much cultural stigma there still was in the Four Worlds against those with genetic mutations, even centuries after the Council government had fled the Four Worlds and taken with it most of the enacters, readers, speakers, and blenders it used to keep the populace in line. For some reason, that stigma was strongest against readers and enacters in particular.

But now, Jinny was simply happy not to *have* to read anyone. She had enough already in her head without adding more of the memories of others to it.

Of course, she still was uncomfortable with just how poorly the citizens of the Four Worlds viewed people like her. On Earth, anyone with a detectable mutation, no matter which one, was required to live on the continent of Australia, separate from 'normal' human beings elsewhere on the planet. They could occasionally travel to other locales but had to wear bright badges on their clothing proclaiming their genetic enhancement so that it was apparent to all they might come in contact with. It was like Jinny's reader pin back in the colonies but taken to an extreme.

Debra O'Leary had explained it to her as a necessary evil one evening. "Without the separation, my dear, we'd never know if someone was stealing our deepest, darkest secrets. Having a democracy means we *must* be allowed to have privacy as well, don't you agree?"

Jinny was quite sure she *didn't* agree. And she was still grasping to understand what a democracy actually was, but her angst was somewhat tempered by how openly the O'Learys and some others in the United Earth government had embraced her and Tyrus Tyne despite their mutations. As long as Tyrus continued to resist his enacter programming and Jinny promised not to read anyone, there seemed to be little concern at their presence amongst the normal folk, most of the time—there were exceptions. But still…

She was broken from her reverie by Corey loudly smacking his lips, waving with a flourish to the tray he'd placed on the small table, and proclaiming: "Ladies, brunch is served."

As they ate, they chatted about innocuous topics: the weather; Jinny's fast-improving tennis game; Corey and Debra's grandchildren;

## THE FOUR WORLDS - SUBVERSION

and even a bit of local gossip. When they were done eating, Corey cleared his throat and gave Jinny a serious look.

"I'm afraid they need us at the Capitol this afternoon, my dear."

Jinny smiled and nodded, though she was thoroughly sick of their frequent trips to Houston, the seat of the United Earth government, and all the talking and talking there that never seemed to lead to any action. It had been *three months* since she, Tyrus, and their companions had arrived to warn the governments of the Four Worlds that the Council was planning an imminent invasion. In that time, they'd only spoken formally to the government of United Earth, which included Earth and its moon, Luna. They'd had indirect contact with the Republic of Europa via UE ambassadors. And they had gotten zero access to Mars.

Even in those three months on Earth, little to nothing had been done that she could see to prepare in any meaningful way for the inevitable war, aside from stationing a few UE and Europan Navy task forces at the Front Door, the one known entrance and exit from the Castilian Rift on the Sol side.

Beyond that, many of the political leaders she'd encountered on Earth seemed to either outright disbelieve the warnings or were intent on downplaying the danger. Every night, she went to bed wondering if the next morning she'd wake up to find the Council Navy demanding the surrender of a decimated homeworld.

Tyrus was closer to the military side of things and probably... hopefully saw preparations she didn't, but in the month since he'd been released from the hospital after recovering from his unprotected spacewalk, they'd both been so busy that she had seen him only a few times. She *had* spent some more time with Riggs, but he knew even less than she did. Jynx, she avoided unless absolutely necessary.

However, despite the apparent lack of progress, she continued to accompany Corey O'Leary to committee meetings, congressional sessions, and occasional discussions with other civic and corporate leaders, all in the hope that someday soon, the talk would turn to action.

"Of course," she said to him. "Anything you need."

## ELEVEN YEARS AGO; 720 P.D.

Jinny was nervous. She had just turned 14 a few days before, which made her eligible to do her first 'real' readings outside of the confines of the Reader Academy on New Brussels. And while she'd read *many* people during her instruction so far, it had always been either her classmates or individuals brought specially to the Academy for training purposes. More importantly, the structured environment the Academy provided made it relatively easy for Jinny to hide her unusual abilities from the instructors.

However, reading someone out 'in the wild' gave her no such assurances; she was going to be exposed for the first time to people who did not *want* to be read. The consequences could be disastrous if, in the emotion or confusion of the moment, she let slip even the tiniest hint of her true capabilities.

Luckily, her first extra-academy readings were still taking place in a semi-controlled environment; there would be no expectation for trainees like Jinny to read criminals. Instead, she accompanied a senior reader by the name of Clarissa Lowry to the local prefecture, where they were to conduct the annual loyalty readings for government employees.

Clarissa, as she insisted Jinny call her, immediately put her young trainee at ease. She was a kindly woman in her thirties who took the time to carefully explain to the 14-year-old girl exactly what to expect and what to do in the loyalty readings. "I will read each person first," she told Jinny, "in case they have committed or witnessed a crime or other traumatic event in the last 15 and 1/2 hours."

Fifteen-and-a-half hours was Jinny's official reading period, at least the one she pretended to have with her Academy instructors. It was long enough to be impressive and make her eligible for more assignments post-graduation but wasn't long enough to draw too much attention and risk the discovery of her *actual* much longer reading time. She had been paired with Clarissa specifically because the older woman had a reading time of 17 hours, making her officially one of the most capable readers on New Brussels.

Given Jinny's full abilities, Clarissa's attempt to spare her charge's tender sensitivities would be a vain effort, but it warmed Jinny nonetheless to see that the older woman cared enough to make it. The senior reader was so different from the cold and dictatorial instructors at the Academy, and for the first time in quite a while, Jinny felt that there might be good people in the Reader Corps after all.

Everything went fine for the first several readings. Each one would start with a guardsman bringing a government employee into a small interrogation chamber. The walls, floor, and even table in the room were a dark uniform gray that made Jinny's young mind associate it with despair. Once the subject had been seated on one side of the metal table, Clarissa would read them a brief paragraph on what to expect. Then, with no further explanation or small talk—Clarissa's tender care for Jinny's feelings did not extend to the subjects of her readings; the Reader Corps taught them that their subjects had no rights and could be hiding *anything* from the Corps—Clarissa would grasp the person's hand and hold it for about five seconds. Then she would nod to Jinny to do the same.

Jinny had read five people thus far—Clarissa had only stopped her from reading one woman, who was quickly removed from the room in handcuffs at a signal to the sentinel guardsmen at the doors—when the short brunette man was escorted into the room. As she had with each other subject, Clarissa grasped the man's hand first. Satisfied, she nodded to Jinny.

Jinny held the man's hand for eight seconds, even though she'd read his entire life within the first five. She'd found that senior readers didn't react well if they thought the trainee was showing off or had the potential to surpass the teacher. Even the kind-seeming Clarissa might change her attitude if she felt her own abilities threatened. Besides, Jinny *really* didn't want anyone finding out about her gift.

So, after eight full seconds, she released the man's hand with a smile. He was a lowly maintenance worker for the New Brussels Department of Sanitation, and she had seen nothing in his life, present or past, that she thought would cause him to fail his annual

61

reading. By smiling, she felt she could let him know in her own small way that he had nothing to worry about. Jinny had done that with each of the subjects she read, and Clarissa had at least pretended not to notice her underling's telegraphing facial expressions.

After the man had been escorted from the room, the two readers sat down and compared notes. Despite her friendly disposition, Clarissa quizzed Jinny relentlessly on everything she would have seen in the last 15.5 hours. Throughout, Jinny paused before answering each question, not to think through her wording, as Clarissa no doubt assumed, but to be one hundred percent sure she was not revealing anything from *before* that period.

After about ten minutes of interrogation, Clarissa Lowry gave Jinny a smile and a nod. "You did well, once again, Trainee Reader Ambrosa. And this man has passed his reading." It was the most praise Jinny had received from any of the adult readers at the Academy, and she was feeling very warm and appreciative to Senior Reader Lowry.

The woman poked at the air above her watch and then spoke aloud. "Guardsman Yost, subject 442 has passed. Please escort him back to his assigned work area." She closed the connection before the man responded, confident—as all readers were—that her orders would be obeyed.

Then she turned back to Jinny with a smile. "Now, Jinny, do you have any questions for me?"

Jinny thought for a moment. She hated this part. The woman across the table from her could have no inkling of just how much better Jinny's skills were than her own, and Jinny had to ask *something* to keep her from suspecting. So, she seized on a random memory from the man's bedtime routine the night before, making sure it was within the 15-hour time window.

"Senior Reader Lowry, Clarissa, what's 'The Bible'?"

Clarissa Lowry's face showed momentary surprise, almost instantly replaced by a hard look of suspicion. "Where did you see or hear about that?" she snapped, startling Jinny with the sharpness of her voice, in such contrast to the almost maternal tone she'd adopted toward the young girl up to this point.

"I... uh... The man we just read was reading a book last night before bed. That was the title. I was... just wondering what it was."

She saw Lowry's eyes go out of focus, as many readers did when they were accessing memories that weren't their own. A full minute later, the woman's gaze focused again on Jinny, her expression stony. "*That* book, Trainee Reader Ambrosa, is an extremely dangerous banned text. I admit I missed it, but I am glad and impressed you caught it." The woman's words of praise did not match her demeanor, and Jinny wondered if Clarissa was angry at her for showing her up or at herself for missing the book in her initial reading.

Lowry turned away from Jinny and poked the air above her watch again. "Guardsman Yost, correction on subject 442. Please ask Directorate K to engage with him. I am forwarding my notes to them. That is all."

This time, she waited for the man's acknowledgment before cutting the comm line. Then she looked back at Jinny, a frown on her face. But after a moment's thought, she smiled at the girl again, and all sense of hostility was gone. "Trainee Reader Ambrosa, let's move on to our next subject, shall we?"

---

## PRESENT DAY; JUNE 4, 731 P.D.

"Ladies and Gentlemen, for those who don't yet know me, I am Commander Tyrus Tyne." The title still felt strange and unnatural to Tyrus. He'd never held any formal title with the Council government other than the ambiguous 'Special Emissary' moniker that had opened any doors that occasionally needed opening. And his semi-official title of 'Alpha' was one he never shared openly for obvious reasons. He'd never been a commissioned officer in any naval force, particularly not the Free Colonies Navy, in which he now purported to be a commander.

But the top brass of the United Earth military had felt in all their wisdom that the crowd he now addressed, among many others, would be far more likely to listen to a fellow naval officer than an ex-assassin, so they'd concocted the title, and pressured Tyrus to go along with it and hold to the pretense of being an officer of the rebel navy of which he'd only briefly even been *aware*. They seemed to want to ignore the fact that his story and Jinny's—both with a few strategic omissions—had been published openly for everyone on Earth and Luna to read, first as a series of news articles, then in a quickly released book, and then as a documentary vid, all orchestrated by Professor Tichner and Corey O'Leary while Tyrus still convalesced in his hospital bed. He doubted anyone in the room today would be fooled by a fake military title.

Of course, he also dreaded the day when he had to stand in front of Gerald Williams, Admiral and leader of the Free Colonies rebel military forces, and explain how he'd contrived to promote himself to such a lofty title in *that* man's Navy. Still, that was a problem for *after* they'd somehow managed to save the Four Worlds.

"The Joint Chiefs have asked me to brief you all on the makeup of the Council Navy forces you are likely to face in the upcoming invasion. If you would please direct your attention to page two of your briefing packet."

Tyrus had been released from the Naval Hospital in Houston just a month before, after two months of recovery from his near-deadly spacewalk to save the *Blind Monk* from destruction when the massive Council Navy dreadnought had exploded right next to them at the Back Door, the colonies-side entrance to the Castilian Rift. His doctors had told him he'd died three times before fully recovering: once in the engine room of the *Monk* itself—they had the record of the event from his watch but no explanation for how he'd miraculously revived himself—once on the operating table while Earth doctors fought to save his life, and a third time a week later when some of his overtaxed organs had begun to fail.

That he was still alive now was a minor miracle, but it also meant that he had wasted two entire months recovering when there was quite literally not a moment to lose in helping Earth and the rest of the Four Worlds prepare for what was coming. Even after his release, it had taken an entire *month* for the United Earth government to finally let him brief even the most senior officers in their Navy, which was a testament to how frustratingly slow things were moving in his and Jinny's quest to save the Sol system and its inhabitants.

From the front row, a man wearing a chest full of subtle yet no less impressive ribbons cleared his throat loudly. "Before we proceed, Mr. Tyne, can you please explain why an ex-spy with no naval experience beyond a few skirmishes with pirates is leading a naval briefing? Also, perhaps you can explain exactly *what* navy you happen to be a commander in?"

Tyrus sighed mentally. So much for the Joint Chiefs' hope that a mere military title would help. As he had feared, the crowd had seen straight through the ruse. Still, he'd at least expected to get through his introduction before he was challenged openly.

He let none of his exasperation show. Instead, he fixed a steely gaze on the man who had interrupted his briefing. Admiral Hank Showalker was the commander of First Fleet and one of the most tenured and senior flag officers in the United Earth Navy. He had a reputation for speaking his mind and leaving a trail of dead bodies, both literal and figurative, in his wake. He was also one of exceedingly few active-duty officers old enough to have seen combat in the last true war with Mars, just under 50 years before.

The hardened expression on Tyrus' face was the same one that had caused planetary leaders in the Council government to cower when he'd turned it upon them, but to Showalker's credit, the man didn't even flinch. To the contrary, the corner of his mouth even twitched up as he recognized exactly what Tyrus was attempting to do with the gaze, and it was Tyrus who almost flinched. But only almost.

"Of course, Admiral," he said calmly instead. "The truth is, I'm *not* really a naval officer."

Showalker's lips twitched again at the admission like he'd caught a child with his face covered in cookie crumbs, but Tyrus continued without pause. "But I do happen to be one of only four people in the Sol system with any experience in facing the enemy that was built with the sole purpose of subjugating this world and the other polities in this system."

Showalker smirked. "An enemy that has no concept of what it means to fight a naval war in space if your own history of the colonies is to be believed. There hasn't been a major interplanetary conflict there since they broke off from Earth—nothing but small-scale policing actions and anti-piracy work." The disdain was clear in the admiral's voice, and a murmur rose through the crowd of assembled officers in the large briefing room. Tyrus had expected this reaction and planned for it, and did his best now to suppress a smile.

"Admiral, if you would indulge me, please, how large is the United Earth Navy's order of battle?"

The admiral smiled fully this time. He clearly thought Tyrus was trying to catch him in his ignorance, but Showalker had a reputation for being a walking encyclopedia of all things related to *his* Navy. Earth had only two named fleets, which meant that roughly half of the planet's entire naval force, aside from a few patrol and customs task forces, was under the belligerent admiral's personal command.

"Forty-two capital ships, not counting battlecruisers. Three hundred and sixty-six total warships. That excludes pinnaces, cutters, and support craft. Would you also like a count of active fighters? Because that often changes by the hour."

A soft laughter rippled through the crowd at Tyrus' expense. But now the tall, dark-skinned ex-alpha smiled widely back, and he heard the laughter falter as the assembled crowd took in his reaction.

"Thank you, Admiral, though your numbers are a bit off. There are, in reality, 48 capital ships, but I wouldn't expect most others in the room to know that, as the difference comprises new classes of experimental craft that few here are cleared for."

The remaining laughter stopped altogether, and Showalker's smile faded as his face reddened.

Tyrus continued before the man could interrupt. "Still, the difference is immaterial. Kendra Siefred, who was not only a member of the Twenty—the secret cabal of Assembly speakers who truly rule the colonies—but also the leader of the rebellion and Free Colonies Navy, provided me with files that suggest the enemy forces arrayed against you are likely much, much larger.

"Even our most optimistic estimates, blessed by your own Naval Intelligence, put the Council Navy's order of battle somewhere between 125 and 175 capital ships with proportional counts of escorts and fighters. It is likely that their full order of battle, excluding anything smaller than a frigate, numbers somewhere above a thousand. In other words, they have more ships than *all* the combined fleets of the Sol system."

A new murmur echoed through the room now, one of dismay rather than mockery, with a few officers shaking their heads in disbelief.

"That's not all." Tyrus manipulated the touchscreen on the dais in front of him, and a hologram appeared in the air between him and the assembled crowd. The Four Worlds had decent enough holographic display technology, even if they didn't have the interactive functionality the colonies had developed—Tyrus knew that somewhere on Luna, United Earth scientists were busy tearing apart and studying one of the interactive holographic displays from the *Blind Monk*, though he was sure they'd neglected to tell Cal Riggs about it, much less ask the ship captain his permission.

The image that was now projected in the air was that of a United Earth Navy battleship. Just over a kilometer long and bristling with weaponry, Earth's 36 battleships were the pride of UE Navy. Below the ship, the words '*UENS Congo*' floated in the air, followed by smaller text giving its base specifications, which no one in the room needed any reminder of.

Apart from being a sterling representative of Earth's engineering ingenuity, the *Congo* was also the flagship of Admiral Hank Showalker. Tyrus could see the older man's mixed look of pride and suspicion as he instantly recognized his home in space, where he was truly lord and master of all he surveyed.

"Admiral, the *Congo* is a beautiful ship. I haven't been aboard her, but I have been aboard the *Nevada*, and the Missouri-class battleships are stunning examples of Earth's engineering and war-making prowess. Showalker nodded a silent acknowledgment of the compliment to his ship, but his suspicious glare didn't soften an iota. He knew Tyrus was going somewhere with this that he was unlikely to appreciate.

"But if you'll indulge me a bit further, *this* is the *CNS Intrepid*." At Tyrus' command, a new holo image appeared next to the *Congo* of a ship more than half again its size. At 1600 meters long with a beam of

350 meters, versus the *Congo's* 1100-meter length *and* 200-meter beam, the *Intrepid* was of an obviously foreign design. Where the *Congo* had a sleek aesthetic that was reminiscent of one of Earth's sharks, the *Intrepid* was boxy by comparison, with hard angles and an obvious design for functionality over form. In that regard, it more closely resembled, albeit by complete accident, the more severe design of Martian battleships, but much larger.

"The *Intrepid*," Tyrus continued, "masses out at just under twelve million tons, almost double that of *Congo* and her sister ships, and 30 percent larger even than your Essex-class fleet carriers. Or rather did, before she was destroyed. Still, we know she had several sister ships; at least two more were captured in the sensor records from the *Blind Monk* at Rinali Station. They carry an unknown assortment of weaponry, but close imaging suggests that it is a mix of heavy lasers, rail guns, ship-to-ship missiles, planetary bombardment missiles, and multiple types of disabling weapons."

He was interrupted by a harrumph from the front row where Showalker sat. "Disabling weapons," the old admiral scoffed. "You refer to those weak energy weapons you call shockers. I've seen the sensor readings from your *Blind Monk*, and there is no way one of those things is slowing down a Missouri class."

There were murmurs of agreement from the other officers in the room, many heads nodding up and down in unison so that the assembled crowd took on the look of an ocean with choppy and confused waves in a storm. They were all happy to hear the aged admiral say *something* positive in their favor after Tyrus' words about the superiority in size and numbers of the Council fleet.

Tyrus smiled. "You're largely correct, Admiral." The old man smiled in return, but the smile disappeared instantly at Tyrus' next words. "However, you are also very wrong."

The room went abruptly silent, and the redness returned to Showalker's face. Once again, Tyrus continued before the man could interject. "United Earth intelligence services have run thousands of simulations based on the data brought back on the *Intrepid* and its weapons from the *Blind Monk's* sensors; the same data you've seen. Unfortunately for us, but fortunately for you, the *Monk* and its crew and passengers got an uncomfortably close look at *Intrepid* and gathered a lot of data on her before she used two of those disabling weapons—a shocker followed by a shock cable, to be precise—on our ship ahead of the timely intervention of the Guard.

"What we learned was not encouraging. While it's true that simulations suggest that a good 87 percent of the *Congo's* hull would be thick and insulated enough for even a full-power shock cable to do little more than scramble a few local sensors, there are some glaring vulnerabilities."

He tapped another button on his touchscreen, and a dozen yellow arrows appeared, pointing at various places on the Congo's exterior. "If a shock missile, a 'shocker', were to hit in *any* of these twelve places, within a roughly three-meter radius, it would find itself close enough to key power conduits to entirely disable the *Congo's* systems for at least five minutes—and the enemy would stretch that out indefinitely if they followed it up by attaching a shock cable in one of the same areas."

Before the crowd could process his words, Tyrus tapped yet another button. In addition to the dozen yellow arrows, four red arrows now appeared, pointing to locations on the *Congo's* dorsal and ventral hulls. "And if a shot from *any* shock weapon were to hit one of these four places… Well, let me show you what your own simulations suggest would happen."

He pressed another button, and a dazzling blue missile came from a launcher on the *Intrepid* and darted toward the *Congo,* hitting the red arrow closest to the Council Navy ship. At first, nothing happened other than a play of electrical charge over a small portion of the Earth battleship's hull. Then, with no warning, the image of the *Congo* exploded from within, the dazzling flash of the catastrophic destruction enough to light up the stunned faces of every officer in the room.

"The result is the same if a shocker hits *any* of those four points," Tyrus said solemnly into the dead silence.

Showalker, though, had had enough. He stood up defiantly. "That's impossible!" His voice carried all the authority of his almost six decades of command experience. Even Tyrus had to admit it was impressive. "There's no way a little electrical charge like that could take out a Missouri. Your simulations are wrong, Mr. Tyne!"

Tyrus gave the man a sympathetic smile. "I wish that were the case, Admiral," he said calmly. "But they're not *my* simulations. Your own Office of Naval Intelligence ran them without my input. The Naval Advanced Tactics Academy on Luna corroborated their results and found the fourth point of vulnerability that Naval Intelligence had missed in their review. Finally, the simulation results were confirmed via independent review by the Naval Warfare College right here in Houston.

"I'm afraid that, having never faced shockers or similar weapons in battle before, Earth ships are not designed with that type of combat in mind. Even in the Missouri class, neither the hull nor the internal electrical systems have even the basic failsafes that the lowliest colonial tramp freighter has by simple design, because you've never had to deal with these types of weapons before. It so happens that these four places represent areas where the type of sudden electrical charge introduced to the hull by a shocker would reach a main trunk conduit and cascade into the battleship's reactor. It would happen too quickly and with too much amperage for your normal safeguards to stop and would cause a feedback loop that would destroy the reactor before anyone could do anything to stop it —within 14 seconds, to be exact."

He stopped talking and let his words hang over the audience's heads for several moments. He was half expecting Showalker or someone else to raise a seemingly obvious objection, which he was ready to rebut. That they didn't, increased Tyrus' estimation of their collective intelligence. He was about to bring up the point himself when Showalker, still standing, interrupted him.

In a wondering voice completely at odds with his stern tone of command earlier, the admiral voiced the very point—*and* the rebuttal —that Tyrus was about to. "It would be sheer luck for them to find these spots." He looked Tyrus in the eyes knowingly. "But it would only take *one* lucky shot amongst thousands; then the rest of the devils would know exactly where to aim their shockers to take down our largest and toughest ships with a single shot. It would turn what are arguably the Council Navy's weakest weapons into their most effective against us."

Tyrus nodded, keeping his eyes on Showalker's and conveying more sympathy than his smile had earlier.

"So, what do we do about it?" the admiral demanded, the command authority creeping back into his voice as he lowered himself back into his seat. "You didn't call us in here just to tell us we have no chance against these monsters, I presume, Mr. Tyne?"

Grateful that the old admiral had given him the exact opening he'd been trying to create, Tyrus hit a key that immediately shut off the holo of the enormous Council Navy ship and the wreckage of the United Earth Navy ship beside it.

"That's exactly what we're going to discuss today, ladies and gentlemen. Now, if you'll kindly turn to page sixteen of your briefing packets, we'll discuss some proposed upgrades to both your ships and your tactics that we believe will mitigate the advantages in tonnage and weaponry that the Council Navy has over yours. If I can specifically draw your attention to paragraph three...."

Three hours later, after a firm and not unfriendly handshake from Showalker himself, Tyrus slumped into a chair on the stage in exhaustion after checking to make sure that the last of the officers in attendance had left the room. As an agent and assassin of the shadows, being the center of attention was more draining than he'd expected, not to mention that public speaking skills were *not* part of his enacter or alpha training. Such things were better left to speakers in the colonies.

Still, despite his exhaustion, he shot back to his feet when he heard the soft sound of clapping from the shadows in the upper heights of the room.

"Bravo, my boy," came a grandfatherly voice that Tyrus instantly recognized. After a long moment, a figure stepped gingerly into the light, supported by a cane that was for more than show. Wispy white hair framed a strong face despite its many wrinkles above a blue uniform festooned with enough ribbonry to put even Showalker to shame.

Fleet Admiral Horatio Krishna Lopez, who had once joked to Tyrus that his name alone represented the melting pot of cultures that was Old Earth, smiled down like an elderly teacher praising his favorite student. His olive complexion belied his father's South American ancestry, and Tyrus had seen enough pictures to know that his now-white hair had once been the jet black so common to his mother's Asian ancestors. Disconcertingly, he spoke in a clipped British accent, indicative of the part of Old Earth he'd been raised on.

"You know that little stunt of blowing up Admiral Showalker's ship could have backfired spectacularly," the old man said in a mildly reproving tone.

Tyrus would have shrugged if doing so in the presence of Earth's oldest and most decorated active soldier was even marginally acceptable. Instead, he stood almost at attention and looked up at the old man and nodded. "It was a risk, sir. No question of that. However, I'd guessed that someone of Showalker's reputation with his crews wasn't prone to outbursts or tantrums when cold, hard facts were staring him in the face." He started as if to move off the stage and up the steps toward Lopez, but the old admiral waved him back and started making his way slowly down the steps toward the front of the room.

He laughed, the warm sound filling even the chilly space of the briefing hall. "Sure. You read Showalker right. But please give an old spacer his due and at least admit to me you wanted to have a *little* fun after he tried to put you in your place."

Tyrus couldn't suppress the smile that came at the old man's words. "Sir, I assure you, I did not come into this briefing with the intent of specifically tweaking Admiral Showalker."

Lopez laughed again. "Leave it to a spy to twist words. I have *no* doubt, Tyrus, that you didn't come into the room today *specifically* looking to tweak Showalker. In fact, if I was to gain access to your tablet, I imagine I'd see programmed similar scenarios for *every* UEN ship that had its commander or flag officer present. You didn't come ready to *just* tweak Showalker; you were ready to tweak *any* of them who needed it out of the gate. Am I right?" His smile widened as he peered down at the stage and Tyrus.

"Sir, I can neither confirm nor deny your assertion," Tyrus said, now grinning widely back. Even in his limited interactions with

Lopez, the man always put him at ease. Unlike some of the younger admirals—even Showalker—Lopez seemed so secure in his own experience and authority that he treated everyone as an equal, down to the lowliest spacer recruit, at least outside the confines of formal situations.

The old man laughed a third time. "Well, while I might have chosen different methods, it certainly got their attention and turned a potential disaster of a briefing into probably the one that will stick in their heads the most in this whole sordid affair." The smile disappeared from the admiral's face. "Still, even if we do everything you recommended, we'll be hard-pressed to fight off the entire might of the Council Navy."

Tyrus stopped smiling as well and nodded grimly. "Even our most optimistic projections of the time we have before the Council invades suggest we won't be able to refit even a quarter of UEN capital ships against the shocker vulnerabilities; that doesn't even mention the escorts. Of course, that assumes that Congress and the president even give you the funding you need. And that only scratches the surface of the preparations United Earth needs to make against the invasion. You need more ships, period.

"No sir, we needed the men in this room to leave with *some* hope so that they can continue to do their jobs, believing that it will make a difference. But—"

"But it will," the admiral interrupted him. "Perhaps not enough of a difference, but wars have been won on smaller things. You may not know this from Earth's history, but it isn't always the biggest and most well-equipped dog in the fight that automatically wins, Tyrus. When you have a moment, read up on the Korean and Vietnam wars of the 20$^{th}$ century or the Silent War between the Council and Mars in the 22$^{nd}$ century. In those and many other cases, the big dog was brought to its knees by a drastically inferior force—inferior in size, weaponry, and even training."

"I hope you're right, sir," Tyrus said with a frown, doing the math in his head; he was still getting used to the way Earth counted its years and centuries, so different from the simple post-diaspora count used in the Colonies. "Because the Council is sending an *enormous* dog against

Earth and its sisters. If it's just the UEN standing against them alone, it's more than a long shot."

Lopez nodded and frowned. "Unfortunately, Mars still hasn't responded to a single one of our requests for a discussion of mutual defense. That's not unusual, mind you. They cut diplomatic ties with us over thirty years ago, and we *still* don't even know who's in charge over there since that little coup two years ago. Regardless, they haven't responded to a *single* message from us on *any* topic since, though the vaguely worded requests that the Pereira administration has let us send probably don't sound all that compelling to them."

"Any luck with Europa?" Tyrus asked heavily.

The old admiral shrugged as he navigated the last few steps, and Tyrus moved down from the stage to join him in front of the first row of seats. "They're talking to us and will honor the terms of our mutual defense pact. There was never much doubt of that. Even so, their order of battle is small compared to ours and won't be a game-changer in a conflict of this size. I do believe they will come to our aid when the invasion starts, but without Mars, it still won't be enough."

Tyrus nodded slowly, feeling his shoulders visibly slump despite himself.

"Chin up, my friend," Lopez said with a small smile as he reached the front row of seats and met Tyrus's eyes. "I saw that interview your friend, the reader, gave last week. She's extremely convincing, mostly because she doesn't seem to have a dishonest bone in her body. And it may be sexist of me to say, but the public responds well to pretty young women—far more so than to ugly old admirals or giant looming ex-assassins. If she can get the average Joe on our side, we just might be able to convince the rest of the government to take this threat seriously."

Tyrus didn't know why the average person was supposedly named Joe, but nodded his agreement. Jinny had a way of coming across as innocent, earnest, and just vulnerable enough to stoke feelings of protectiveness from any man, and even many of the women, who watched her on the vids. It wasn't an act either; she really was all those things, but also strong, full of conviction, and surprisingly capable.

Each time he thought of her, it brought to the surface complex feelings that he hadn't had the time to fully explore in his brief time on Earth.

"In the meantime," Lopez continued, oblivious to Tyrus' internal musings, "I have a few ideas of my own that might just help us better prepare ourselves."

"And what, do you mind me asking, are those ideas?"

The admiral shook his head. "Not here." He lifted his cane and swept it around to encompass the briefing room. "The walls here have eyes *and* ears. Let's take a walk.

They moved toward the exterior exit of the room that emptied into a small garden on the grounds of the United Earth Naval Headquarters campus. The humid Houston summer air seemed to swallow Tyrus as soon as he stepped out of the air-conditioned room, and he started sweating immediately. The weather here reminded him of Panamar, of all places. Though at least the sun was the right color.

"First off," Lopez said as he stopped to take in the bright sunlight, apparently oblivious to the humidity, "you mentioned a few top-secret ships—you know, doing that really upset Showalker—but you really don't know what they are or how they can help us. I want to get your opinion on…."

## CHAPTER 2

The first time Jinny had traveled in the Loop, she'd been terrified. She'd ridden the subway before on New Brussels and the lev trains on Nova Tejas, but the Loop was different. First, it was claustrophobic. Instead of the comparatively spacious subway and lev train cars, the car that 'rode' the Loop reminded her of a pill capsule. When she and Corey were enclosed in it, they took up two of the only four seats available, with the remaining dedicated to Corey's aide and bodyguard.

Second, the car had to be as small as it was because the tunnel *itself* was so small. The Loop used electromagnetic pulses to send the cars quickly from point A to point B in the airless tunnels at speeds up to Mach three. It was basically a giant, enclosed rail gun. Cory had explained to her once that the amount of energy required to push the capsules along at their incredibly high speeds increased exponentially in proportion to the diameter of the tunnel.

Third, even though the capsules traveled as fast as they did, there was *no* sense of movement for the occupants. The inertial compensators were dialed up so high to protect a capsule's occupants that *none* of the g-forces got through, and there weren't even lights or anything else along the way to give their movement a visual reference.

## THE FOUR WORLDS - SUBVERSION

That meant for the 42-minute ride from the La Costa substation nearest Corey and Debra's home to the Houston government terminal directly underneath the United Earth Congressional Hall, it felt to Jinny like they were simply sitting still in a closed and too-small capsule, surrounded by darkness.

It was eerie, but she'd slowly gotten used to it. The trick, she found, was to not look out the capsule's front or rear windows at the pitch dark of the tunnel but to focus on something right in front of her inside the capsule. Today, that was a research paper published by the University of Sydney on an experimental method for reversing the effect of the blender gene. Never in the millennium since the Council had genetically engineered readers, speakers, enacters, and blenders—on Earth, as in the colonies, they collectively called all the mutations the 'enhanced'—had there been a successful attempt to *reverse* the genetic engineering without killing the patient. Likewise, gene editing in utero to remove the engineered genes always, for reasons no one could adequately explain, resulted in stillbirth. To Jinny's knowledge, no one aside from her father had been able to alter the mutations in an already-enhanced person.

So, in the Four Worlds, the efforts of scientists to 'cure' the enhanced had, for the last four centuries or so, focused almost entirely on controlling the *symptoms* of their genetic mutations. The paper Jinny was reading now talked about bombarding the cells of blenders with extremely low levels of radiation once a week. In 64 percent of case study participants, this had slowed, just barely, their body's ability to alter its cells to change the blender's appearance and voice.

The scientists running the study felt that they'd only scratched the surface, and while the treatment was not yet practical to administer broadly, that further study down this route could lead them to a place where blenders could retain their natural appearances.

Of course, no adult blender actually knew what his or her natural appearance was. They started blending—changing their skin color, hair color, vocal tones, and even height and weight—typically between the ages of four and six. From that time forward, their body was in a near-constant state of change down to even the level of their DNA. The only thing they *couldn't* change was their gender. Jinny knew from her lessons at the Reader Academy and from her own limited experience (she choked up still when she recalled her friends John and Joan, blenders and fellow rebels who had given their lives to the cause) that blenders changed their appearance with no conscious thought to mirror the appearances of the people they spent the most time with.

At one point, someone on Earth had experimented by putting a group of blenders into isolation for several weeks, not letting them near any other human beings, or providing them with any pictures, videos, or even recordings of other humans—the blender enhancement required actual physical proximity to their subject to change, so withholding pictures and videos was an extreme but unnecessary precaution in the study. They wanted to see if the blenders would then revert to their natural state, to what they would look like without their enhancement.

The experiment was a failure. In every case, the blender simply stopped changing and kept whatever physical characteristics they'd had at the exact moment they'd been locked in the room alone. In the absence of external stimuli, their bodies simply didn't change; there was no genetic memory of their original/natural appearance.

Jinny found papers on this and other enhanced-centric topics fascinating; there had been nothing like them in the 47 Colonies, where the Council—the Twenty really—controlled all science and information and had strictly outlawed research into genetic enhancements, probably to prevent anyone from competing with its control of genetically enhanced individuals. What worried her, however, was that all such studies in the Four Worlds seemed to treat the genetic enhancements like some kind of disease to be cured or a problem to be solved. In fact, many of the papers she'd read blatantly stated that the purpose of their experimentation was to see if the enhanced could be reintegrated into society but only by somehow shutting down their enhancement.

Even in the 47 Colonies, where readers, speakers, blenders, and enacters were relatively common, non-enhanced people were still wary of them, especially readers, due to the invasion of privacy they represented. But given that the enhanced in the colonies represented the Council and the government, there was no open persecution or shunning, just whispers in the dark corners and illegal underground blogs.

## THE FOUR WORLDS - SUBVERSION

Here in the Four Worlds—at least in United Earth and Europa—the discrimination was far more blatant, and it was government sanctioned. Even had the enhanced not been relegated to live apart from the rest of humanity on an island continent, non-enhanced peoples expressed open and frequent sympathy for them, which to Jinny felt even more discriminatory in its condescending tone than the fear that had been directed toward her as a member of the Reader Corps in the colonies.

She knew that one of the major reasons for this discrimination in the Four Worlds was that, even almost six centuries after the Council had left the Sol system, the enhanced were still thought of in connection with the Council government, which was anathema to the principles of open democracy espoused on every planet in the Sol system with the notable exception of Mars. However, there was little contact between Mars and the other worlds in the Sol system, so no one knew the current status of the enhanced on the red planet.

"What has you in such a contemplative state this morning, Jinny?" the voice of Corey O'Leary broke into her thoughts.

Having had many discussions already on the topic of enhanced discrimination with both of the O'Learys—which always resulted in an impasse as each side clung to over 550 years of ingrained dogma—she didn't want to reopen the same conversation again. So instead, she answered with something only slightly less controversial: "Just wondering how much time we have until the Council fleet shows up."

Corey frowned. This was another oft-discussed topic between Jinny and her hosts. The difference here was that they were all three of the same mind, that it was bound to happen sooner rather than later. But thus far, they'd had little success moving the wheels of politics and bureaucracy in Houston to make any real headway toward getting the Four Worlds, or even United Earth alone, onto a war footing to prepare for an earnest defense.

"Well, let's hope today's discussions go better," he replied, throwing her a knowing smile. He said that before *every* session in the capitol, and it had become almost a running joke between them, given how things *never* seemed to go better.

Suddenly, external light invaded their Loop capsule as it pulled into the open air of Government Station in Houston. When the capsule came to a complete stop, the doors opened, and Jinny dutifully followed Corey—who in turn was preceded by his bodyguard—out onto the platform, with O'Leary's aide bringing up the rear.

As they walked, Jinny squared her shoulders and prepared for yet another day of boring sessions that still managed to feel to her like a battlefield.

---

## TWO YEARS AGO; 729 P.D.

Jinny watched the man leave for work at the same time he'd done every morning for the last two weeks. He was a young man, only 24 years of age, with sandy blond hair and a ready smile. As far as anyone could tell, he was a good man, always ready with a compliment and always willing to give to whatever charity came knocking on his door in this suburban neighborhood.

Jinny knew the truth: he may be a good man, but he had made a terrible decision when he married *that* woman. And there *she* was now, standing at the open front door and waving with false cheer to her husband as he got into his hovercar. The pretty young woman with shiny black hair wore a white bathrobe and sandals on her feet and held a cup of coffee as she smiled and bid her husband farewell.

It was all an act. She wasn't faithful to her man; women like her never were. It was always the young and pretty ones who cheated. And especially the ones with black hair. Jinny knew that from personal experience. But luckily for the blissfully unaware and ignorant husband, she was here to make things right.

Every morning she had watched while the pretty young woman waved goodbye to her husband, and every morning she had watched the same young woman go back inside the house, forgetting to lock the front door behind her. Today she would no doubt do the same, and it would be her *last* mistake out of so many.

After the young man had driven away toward his meaningless job in a cold and unforgiving office building, Jinny made her move. She exited the white hovervan she had parked across the street from the couple's home. The logo painted on the van's side, along with the uniform she wore, would belay the suspicions of any nosy neighbors. She walked casually up the short walkway to the home's front door and pretended to knock, just in case anyone was watching.

Taking a quick glance around, she reached down and slowly turned the doorknob. Five seconds later, she was inside the home, silently closing the door behind her. *She* remembered to lock the door; it wouldn't do to have anyone stumble into the house to interrupt her work.

She stood there for a moment, listening. The home's single staircase was right inside the entryway. From the top of the stairs, Jinny could hear water running, just a faucet by the sound, not a shower or tub.

Slowly, she made her way up the stairs, carefully placing her feet on the edge closest to the wall, where it was less likely a worn stair might creak and betray her presence. Her soft, rubber-soled shoes made no sound on the carpeted stairs, and Jinny smiled in anticipation of the surprise on her quarry's face. Reaching the second floor, she stopped and listened again. The sound of water running continued from the open doorway at the end of a short hall, and Jinny made her way gingerly toward it, fighting the overwhelming urge to run toward her victim and satisfy her urge for vengeance.

Because that's what she was today: she was vengeance. She was here to avenge all the poor young husbands whose wives, like this raven-haired vixen, betrayed their trust regularly. Just like her Lilith had done to her. Lilith's hair had been black, just like the young wife in this house, but that wasn't what reminded Jinny most about her ex-wife—it was the eyes. You could always tell by the eyes if a woman was faithful or not. Jinny had missed the signs in Lilith's eyes until it had been too late, but she could see the same signs in the eyes of this young woman, even from her usual spot across the suburban street.

Her heart beat faster as she entered the doorway from which she still heard the sound of running water. It was a bedroom, the white sheets on the large king-size bed unmade, pillows strewn across the carpeted floor. The woman was even a slob like Lilith had been. Jinny smiled in anticipation, savoring the feeling of her vengeance so close.

She turned and proceeded toward the only other door that led out of the bedroom. The sound of running water came from there. She moved even slower now, forcing herself to delay the gratification she knew was coming. Slowly, carefully so as not to make a sound, she reached down to her belt and drew the knife she kept there, hidden in a cleverly designed sheath that blended in with the fake uniform jumpsuit she wore. The feeling of the knife's cool hilt in her hand sent anticipation coursing through her and almost made her leap too quickly into the small bathroom to finish what she had come here to do.

Again, she forced herself to wait, to savor the moment and build the anticipation. Besides, if she moved too quickly, she might miss her favorite part. So instead of leaping into the room, she stepped slowly around the corner of the doorway. She could now see the young woman's robed back as she stood in front of the vanity mirror and brushed her teeth. At first, nothing happened. The raven-haired beauty was staring at a holo from her watch, not even looking in the mirror.

Then, she glanced up, and in the reflection, she saw Jinny. Only it wasn't Jinny's face behind her in the mirror; it was a rugged masculine face framed by bleach blond hair above green eyes. But somehow, that felt right to Jinny. She grinned at the woman, and the man's face in the mirror grinned with her.

The woman's eyes went wide in surprise first and then fear. Then quickly, fear became terror as she saw the knife, and Jinny's favorite moment came. She relished the look of panic when her quarry realized what she had come to do and that there would be no stopping her—that it was time to die for her sins.

Moving quickly now, before the stunned woman could even scream, Jinny stepped forward, grabbing her from behind, and with a single smooth motion of the knife that had become an extension of her avenging arm, slit the—

Jinny woke up screaming, her thin clothing drenched with sweat and sticking to her skin despite the busy air conditioning that kept the bedroom cool in the warm climate of Copernicus' southern hemisphere.

Horrified, she looked down at her hands, *knowing* she would see the young woman's blood on them…

But there was nothing: no blood, no red staining, and no knife. In a fit of mixed horror and relief, she brought her knees up to her chest and rocked back and forth, weeping uncontrollably.

The dream had been so *real* because it wasn't just a dream; it was a memory. Not hers, but the memory of a man named Hendrix, who had murdered 12 young wives, all black-haired beauties like his own ex-wife Lilith, who had left him for another man just three years into their marriage.

The man Lilith had left Hendrix for was a member of the Guard, so the scorned and psychotic ex-husband could never get to her to make his ex-wife pay for what she'd done to him. Instead, he had stalked and murdered 12 young married women who reminded him of Lilith, taking out his rage and frustration on them over and over until he had finally been caught.

Ironically, the guardmembers who caught him near his home on Copernicus had no idea he was connected to the murders that had terrorized the planet for the last year: one murder a month, just like clockwork. Instead, they had arrested him as a suspect in the simple killing of a shopkeeper during a robbery gone bad. A masked man who had a nearly identical build and hair color to Hendrix killed the shopkeeper when he'd realized the man had called the Guard using the shop's silent alarm. Then he had fled into the night with only a few items of little-to-no monetary value.

Hendrix had happened to be driving by the shop shortly after the robbery. His similar appearance to the masked robber-turned-murderer, along with the street network's record of his car being in the vicinity, was enough for the Guard to bring him in for questioning. When he'd resisted telling them anything, they had called in a reader.

Officially, it had been only Jinny's fourth or fifth assignment to read a suspected murderer solo. Junior readers like her rarely read killers and definitely were never sent to read anyone who was suspected of premeditated murder. So, she had trembled as she reached out and grabbed the man's shackled hand in the small Guard interrogation room.

What she had seen shocked her so badly that she screamed during the reading and then collapsed sobbing back in her chair afterward.

The stunned guardsman who had accompanied her into the room had rushed to her side to inquire what the matter was, careful not to touch her himself.

Jinny *couldn't* tell the guardsman about the man's twelve serial murders; doing so would give away her deepest-held secret. So, she'd done the next best thing.

She'd lied.

She told the guardsman that, in reading Hendrix, she had seen him kill the shopkeeper and that it *had* been premeditated. She falsely stated that the man had owed Hendrix money and the robbery had been a ruse to get revenge.

Hendrix had gone to prison for life; it was that simple, given the circumstantial evidence plus the testimony of a reader. Nothing more was needed, and the man's trial had been short, and his guilt essentially predetermined. The serial murders stopped, though that case was never officially solved. Nor did the Guard ever catch the shopkeeper's *real* killer, but Jinny had considered that a fair trade to put a monster like Hendrix behind bars.

But now, something strange was happening. Jinny was *living* the man's memories in her nightmares. Over the three months since she'd read him, she had dreamed of nine of Hendrix's murders, always from his point of view, as if Jinny herself was the one slitting the women's throats. Each time she had awoken in a terrified fugue, believing for several moments that she *had* killed those women; that Hendrix's memories were her own.

And it wasn't just Hendrix's crimes she was reliving. The night before, she had smothered her elderly mother in the nursing home, reliving the memory of a woman called Ursula who had been upset with her mother for cutting her out of a meager inheritance. The night before that, she had assaulted a young woman in a gym locker room, reliving the memory of a scumbag named Nicolai, whom she had read as part of a regular government employee loyalty screening. In the case of Ursula, she'd had to let the woman walk; she was reading her as part of a civil case, something readers did from time to time, and couldn't come up with a way to work the murder of the woman's mother into the reading without revealing her own secret. With Nicolai, she had lied and said he had bragged to his friend about the rape inside of the 15-and-1/2-hour window she could officially read.

But none of that mattered now. Because now she was reliving the violent memories of dozens of people she'd read—criminals and victims—as if they were her own. And it was driving her slowly mad.

She lay awake, drenched in sweat and trembling, exhausted but afraid to close her eyes and embark on another horrific crime. She started weeping again, burying her face into the pillow of the twin-size bed in her small apartment, great sobs wracking her body. She was terrified and had no idea where to go for help. She didn't know if the dreams were a result of her abnormal genetic mutation. If they were, then going to the wrong person for help could easily mean her death.

---

## PRESENT DAY; JUNE 4, 731 P.D.

Jinny resisted the urge to bang her head on the table in front of her for the tenth time in the last two hours.

"Miss Ambrosa, if I may." The man speaking was the source of all her current frustration, and he wasn't actually asking her if he could do anything. 'If I may' was just something he liked to say before he said something offensive or demeaning to her—sometimes both.

"Wouldn't you say," he continued, "that you never personally *saw* direct evidence of the Council Navy?"

She tried not to grimace but kept her expression neutral and leaned forward to reply into the committee room's witness table microphone. "With respect, that's entirely inaccurate, Congressman. I *did* see the Council Navy attacking Rinali Station and the Guard fleet there in an effort to—"

"No, Miss Ambrosa, you did not!" he interrupted her. "You saw *a* fleet attacking Rinali Station and the Guard there, but none of those ships had any markings on them, at least from the sensor records of your ship, that indicated the Council owned or sponsored them in any way."

"Mr. Chairman, I must object to the tone of this inquiry. The witness has been nothing but cooperative, and badgering her is counterproductive to these proceedings." This came from Corey O'Leary, who was the ranking member of the opposition party in the UEN Congressional Committee on Foreign Affairs.

The chairman of said committee was Congressman Dorian Hastings, Jinny's current interrogator and a member of the Blue Party, which happened to be the same party as the sitting United Earth president.

"With all due respect, Congressman O'Leary," Hastings said, again in a tone that was anything but respectful, "we don't truly know that the witness has been cooperative. In point of fact, we cannot verify *any* of the testimony she has brought before this committee. For all we know, every word she's told us is a lie."

"That is outrageous, Mr. Chairman, and while you may say that there is no evidence that she is telling the truth—which I dispute in the strongest terms possible—there is, in fact, no evidence that she is lying. Nor would she benefit in any way from lying to us on these topics. What could possibly be her motive for doing so?"

"Agree to disagree, Congressman O'Leary," Hastings said in a long-suffering tone, pointedly ignoring the other man's question, "but I ask you to please respect that I have not yielded my time to you. And the simple fact is that while we may not understand the witnesses' potential motives for lying to us, she also hasn't been able to adequately explain what conceivable motive the Council could have for invading us!"

He turned back to look at Jinny. "As I was saying, you have *no* evidence that these ships that attacked Rinali Station and the Guard fleet were tied to the Council, the Twenty, or whatever government body you claim holds power in the 47 Colonies.

"In fact, what you have is a sensor picture that shows the logo of the Four Worlds, an old logo from pre-schism times. Is that not correct?"

Jinny leaned forward to the microphone, seeing the verbal trap. "It is true that the *Blind Monk's* sensors captured a Four Worlds logo on the attackers, but that was simply a ploy by the *Twenty* to turn the populace against Earth and its sisters so that they could build and recruit for their Navy openly. Also, the reason the Twenty wants to invade—"

"That's quite enough, Ms. Ambrosa," Hastings interrupted her. "All you've just said is meaningless speculation. The only incontrovertible *fact* is that the ships bore an outdated Four Worlds insignia."

"Wait!" interrupted Corey again. "Are you implying that *we* were somehow behind the attack? That's ridiculous." Left unspoken was the rest of his thought: *Ridiculous even for you, Mr. Chairman.*

"Is it?" asked Hastings with a smile. "I admit Earth had no part in the attack, but that doesn't mean Europa didn't. Or, more likely, Mars."

The committee chamber, which had been growing increasingly loud with the murmurings of the other Congress members at the argument between Hastings and O'Leary, was suddenly silent. Corey was the first to break the silence.

"I don't believe this. You think *Mars* sent that fleet? I refuse to believe, Mr. Chairman, that even *you* could be that foolish. Even if they could get the fleet past our forces at the Front Door and through the Rift, since we're speaking of motives, *why* would Mars even do such a thing?"

Ignoring the insult and the question, Hastings smiled wider. "All I am saying, Congressman, esteemed colleagues, is that we don't *know* anything. So instead of jumping at shadows and increasing our military spending wantonly, we should be engaging in *talks* with the Council government." He purposefully looked at Jinny as he refused to reference the Twenty as she had. "Who knows, perhaps all of this is just the imaginations of Ms. Ambrosa, Mr. Tyne, and a few other conspiracy theorists in the colonies.

"I move that we vote on a recommendation to the broader Congress and our esteemed President Pereira to reject calls for additional military spending—funding that we would have to pull from vital domestic initiatives—and instead create an exploratory committee to discuss sending an emissary of peace through the Rift to the 47 Colonies. Furthermore, I move that...."

He rambled on for five more minutes, fending off a few more objections from Corey before finishing and calling for the vote. The outcome of the vote was never in doubt. The Blue Party, Hastings' and President

Luiz Pereira's party, led a coalition that held a 62 percent majority in the Congress and, therefore, also in the Committee on Foreign Affairs.

When Jinny allowed Corey to escort her out of the chamber, it was in solemn and frustrated silence.

---

"Dave, can you double-check these numbers for me one more time?"

"Sure thing," the man called Dave pecked on his pad a few times, head cocked to the side as was his habit when deep in thought. "They look right to me, or, well, as right as we want them to look. I don't think anyone will notice what we're trying to do."

"Good. Good. We just need this to buy us some time." Marianne Hiltunen, CEO of Wanderlust Interstellar, sat back in her leather cushioned chair—one that would have cost the average person in her company's employ a full month's salary—and sighed contentedly. "All we need is a little more time. We're doing this for the company. And all its employees."

Wanderlust Interstellar specialized in the resurgent field of space tourism in the Sol system. The industry had always existed, of course—there were always people with the desire and, more importantly, the money required to see the wonders of the Sol system in person—but had waned in the decades following the Six-Month War between Earth and Mars 49 years ago. It had momentarily slowed again two years ago when the then Martian dictator—a religious extremist—had launched planet-killer missiles toward Luna.

Luckily, tourists had short memories, and with two years of relative peace, the demand for space tourism was at an all-time high. Eight years before, Marianne Hiltunen had adroitly gained the backing of deep-pocket investors on Earth and Europa to finance turning a failing interplanetary freight shipping company into the now second-largest space tourism line. By doing so, she had earned herself and her investors trillions of dollars in profit with no outward signs of slowing down.

Then she had gotten greedy. Last year Wanderlust had finished building five new passenger liners, each roughly the size of a United

Earth Navy battleship and capable of supporting 2000 tourists in luxury along with 500 crew members. They had launched these ships to great fanfare, more than doubling the size of their existing fleet and heralding the way for unprecedented growth.

Only the growth hadn't come. The cost of constructing the new ships had been exorbitant, and even with full bookings, it would have taken five years just to break even on the investment. But the bookings hadn't been full; rather, they were filling only a third of the cabins on the average voyage. With those poor numbers, they weren't even covering the operating expenses of the massive star liners, and breaking even on the investment had become highly improbable.

The reasons varied: from prices set too high to the entry of a new competitor into the market, Fortune Holidays operating out of Europa, which had used cheaper and smaller refurbished ships but done a terrific job of making them *look* more expensive than they were with fancy paint jobs and slick marketing campaigns. The ruse probably wouldn't last forever, but it was lasting long enough to seriously hurt established competitors like Wanderlust.

The biggest problem, however, wasn't Hiltunen's poorly timed decision to build her new fleet, but rather her stubborn refusal to admit that she'd been wrong to do so. She had, in fact, not admitted it once in the hearing of anyone, including any of the company's investors. Her solution, rather than owning up to the problem and potentially selling the new ships to recoup her losses, had been to hide it all. She had hired an independent accountant, Dave Watts, who had a reputation for creative problem solving with company balance sheets. Then she had tasked him to help her disguise the losses.

So, Dave had gotten to work, operating independently of Wanderlust's accounting department, and using a variety of shell companies and false fronts to make it look like the voyages were almost 80 percent full and that the money was rolling in. Hiltunen's stated goal in the subterfuge was to buy herself enough time to figure out how to recoup the losses. Now they were going over the final quarterly report for the investors in her office, with just her, Dave, and the Wanderlust CFO in the room.

Wendel Piras, the CFO, a smarmy little man who was constantly licking his lips and squinting in a way that reminded Dave of a gopher, nodded enthusiastically at his CEO's claim to be committing fraud for the righteous reasons of saving the company and its employees. Everyone in the room knew that was a lie—that she was really just hoping to stay in her role long enough to hit the nine-year mark, when firing her would cost the board a massive golden parachute payment—but none of them would say it out loud.

"I'll send it to the investors," Piras said in his surprisingly high-pitched voice. "But first, I'll bury the numbers in so many charts and graphs that most of them won't get past the first two hundred pages. No one will know we're fixing things. It should buy us all the time we need."

Hiltunen nodded her approval. "Just a little more time. For the company and its employees," she repeated the fiction.

The meeting ended, and Dave left Hiltunen's office with a slight smile on his face. He'd played his role perfectly. There had been a few times during the meeting where he'd caught Piras looking at him a little too closely, but the weasel had seemed less suspicious and more threatened by his presence. Or so Dave hoped.

Trying not to look rushed, he took the elevator down from Hiltunen's 124th-floor penthouse office to the building's ornate and spacious lobby, which was dominated by Wanderlust's logo—a giant W inside the rings of Saturn; not terribly original—everywhere one looked. Ignoring the guards and receptionists working the front desk, he continued out one of the many lobby doors and found himself on the streets of New Manhattan, which he'd read had once been called Trenton, New Jersey, back when the actual island of Manhattan hadn't been a nuclear crater under the waters of the Lower Hudson Bay.

Dave quickly walked to a black aircar that had pulled up in front of the building just as he'd left the lobby. He opened the car's rear passenger door and slid inside, closing it after him. The instant it latched shut, the car's driver merged back into the city's moving traffic.

The implant in Dave's left hand vibrated, and he looked down at the message displayed on the small screen integrated into the skin of his palm.

*Iasonas: Did you get it?*

He'd looked up the code name of his employer once. Iasonas was the Greek form of Jason and referred to the mythical Jason who had quested for the golden fleece. He had no idea who the man—or woman—who employed him really was, except that they seemed to have a flair for Greek mythology, which made Dave suspect he or she might have been Europan. Either way, the obsession with mythology hadn't just influenced his employer's code name but also the one they had chosen for 'Dave' to use in their communications: Castor, one of Jason's Argonauts. He typed back a one-word response.

**Castor: Yes.**

Then he settled back and sighed contentedly, unconsciously mirroring the same move that he'd seen Marianne Hiltunen make just minutes before. He had to watch out for that. Mirroring another's mannerisms was vital to his identity and trade, but it could also give him away. Not only was what he was doing patently illegal, but his presence alone in New Manhattan was enough to land him in prison for several years.

Blenders weren't allowed to leave Australia without an escort, after all.

The man called Dave sighed again, mindfully shedding the persona of Dave Watts and becoming himself again. Whatever that meant.

Jordan Archer, blender and professional fixer, set his palm implant to mirror mode and looked at himself carefully. He still looked almost exactly like Dave Watts; the past two days of closed-door sessions with Hiltunen and Piras had made some of his features start to subtly change, but returning each evening to the place where the real Dave Watts was being held—allowing him to spend time with the man and reset his appearance—had kept him close enough that he was fairly certain neither the Wanderlust CEO nor CFO had noticed. Jordan, however, noticed the trivial things. It was what had kept him alive and out of prison for his 15 years operating illegally outside of Australia.

The United Earth Federal Police sometimes contracted with blenders out of the southern island continent to do what Archer had just done: impersonate a criminal to capture and record the confessions of real criminals. But Archer wasn't working for the Federal Police or any other law enforcement agency on this one. His employer was a private client. Based on past jobs, he assumed that the information and recordings he'd gotten would be used to extort Hiltunen and convince her to lend her considerable financial support to specific political candidates whom Archer's employer also supported.

This was the 21st job Archer had done for the mysterious Iasonas in just the last two years; during that period, he had worked almost exclusively for the man or woman. He had tried, repeatedly, to discover the identity of his employer by watching carefully to see which political party or candidate seemed to benefit the most from the support of those Archer was used to blackmail and extort. However, there seemed to be little pattern to it; sometimes the candidates supported were from the Blue Party, sometimes the Red Party, and even occasionally the Green Party, the Centrists, the Progressives, or one of the other smaller parties.

The only pattern Archer could detect was that the candidates supported were often the ones most critical of the current president, Luiz Pereira, either in directly opposing his platform, as in the case of the opposition Red Party, or in criticizing it for not going far enough, as with the fringes of the man's own Blue Party. So, whomever Iasonas was, he or she had *something* against Pereira.

Which was fine with Archer. He had worked in the shadowy underbelly of Houston politics long enough to know that many outwardly principled politicians were quite corrupt, selling their influence and votes to the highest bidder. So, whether the Blue Party or the Red Party or one of the others inhabited Government House didn't matter, so long as they were willing to pay Jordan Archer to help them get there and stay there.

He pressed a virtual button on his implant's palm display and sent the two days' worth of recordings he'd taken of Hiltunen and Piras to his employer. And with that, his job was done. The real Dave Watts would be released with a dire warning of his criminal actions being revealed if he ever told anyone what had happened, and Archer could move on to the next job.

*And hopefully, the next body*, he thought with a frown. Watts could have been the poster child for accountant stereotypes. He was pale, pudgy, and badly needed glasses or eye surgery but had never gotten around to getting either. Archer had needed a full week to convert into an exact facsimile of the man, who luckily worked remotely and had only agreed to meet with Hiltunen and Piras in person for the last two days of each quarter's close. And because even Watts hadn't been sure of all of Hiltunen's security measures, Archer had had to 'go all the way' in blender parlance.

Put a blender in a room for a day with someone, and by the end of the day, he would change some of his outward characteristics to match that person. It typically started with hair and eye color. After two days, facial features noticeably changed. After three days, muscle definition either improved or softened to match the subject. After five or six days, the visual transformation was typically complete, including changes to weight and height within reasonable limitations. If the blender had to gain or lose significant weight and/or height, it could take up a day or two longer.

The reason that it took Archer the full week to change into Watts had nothing to do with the man's weight and height, which were fairly average if a bit on the short and pudgy side. Rather, it was changing his *DNA* that took so long.

Archer's employer had suspected correctly that Hiltunen would use biometrics to verify Watt's identity each time he came to the office. This would dissuade most spies and even some blenders from trying to usurp and use the man's identity. But few people outside of Australia understood a blender could and would almost completely change their DNA to match up to the person they were mimicking. The only limitation was that it required an exchange of bodily fluids to do so.

In this case, that meant a blood transfusion from Watts to Archer. They had started small. A small transfusion each of the first two days had altered Archer's blood type, which had then allowed him to start taking larger transfusions from Watts without risking his health. By the end of day seven, it would have taken an extremely deep DNA scan—well beyond the capabilities of even most large corporations—to detect the subtle differences between Archer's DNA and Watts'.

That also meant he had changed not just his appearance but also his internal attributes to match up with the man. That included the Watts' failing eyesight and receding hairline, as well as his food allergies and irritable bowel syndrome. Not fun. Archer was very much looking forward to changing into someone else as soon as possible, though the fact that he'd gone so far into replicating Watts' DNA meant that it would take him longer to shed the man's appearance.

The black aircar, whose driver had never said a single word to him, dropped Archer off in front of a large apartment building in New Manhattan's pricey Yorkville district. Here, Archer kept an apartment he could stay in whenever he was on a job in this part of North America.

As he rode the elevator up to his $47^{th}$-floor apartment overlooking Central Park, his palm implant pinged him again.

*Iasonas: Goods received. The final portion of payment has been delivered to the agreed-upon account.*

Archer smiled and quickly pulled up his banking app to see the 500-thousand-dollar final installment of his fee was indeed already in his account.

*Iasonas: I have another job for you. Longer play. At least 3-4 months. Normal long-term rate plus a 30% bonus if successful in meeting objectives. Interested?*

Archer would answer later. It never paid to seem too eager, even though a 30 percent bump on top of his normal rates would give him enough to go spend the rest of the year on a beach in South America or possibly even across the system on the Europan Riviera. But better to wait and make the man doubt his interest. Then he might be able to ask for 35 percent.

Now, as the elevator reached his stop, he walked off and directly into the spacious apartment that covered the entire $47^{th}$ floor. Most blenders—not that there were many outside of Australia, but enough—after a job like this, hired the services of a 'cleaner', a plain-looking person, to stay with them for several days to reset their appearance and remove any trace of the person they'd been impersonating on the job. Some cleaners, for an additional fee, even allowed blenders to take their blood to reset their DNA.

Archer didn't like the loose ends that came with anonymous cleaners. In at least one instance he knew of, a cleaner had been turned by the Federal Police, which had led to the capture of two blenders the man had worked for over the years.

Instead, and for other reasons as well, Archer *far* preferred the person waiting for him in his apartment now.

When he walked into the living room, the tall blond woman with Nordic features and porcelain-smooth skin unfolded herself from the couch and rushed to throw her arms around him. She held him for a long moment as he returned the embrace and then pushed herself back and studied him, wrinkling her nose as she took in his full appearance.

"Wow," Cecily Johansen said playfully. "This one is ugly."

Archer laughed and held up his pudgy hands like a monster and wiggled the fingers in mock threat at his girlfriend of six years and live-in cleaner of the last five. He had met Cecily on a job very early in his career. She had been the barely adult-age daughter of one of his employers, and the man had used her as a go-between with Archer on several occasions. She'd been fascinated by his life as a blender and had shown him none of the barely concealed disgust that even most of his employers regularly displayed when interacting with him.

Almost a decade later, they'd met again when another potential employer had tried to hire Archer to work against Cecily's father. Normally, that would not have given him pause; money was money, and he hadn't particularly liked the elder Johansen when he'd worked for him. But he *had* liked Cecily, so he not only turned down the job, but he then reached out to her to warn her of the plot against her father.

Cecily, whom he discovered had never actually liked her dad all that much anyway, had surprised him by encouraging him to take the job and then partnering with him to pull it off. It had destroyed her father, who had been forced to flee to Europa ahead of the Federal Police—he was living under an assumed name on Ganymede last they'd heard—and had left Cecily quite wealthy and free from the man's control. She used a modest chunk of that windfall to finance Archer's operations, almost instantly moving him from a mid-tier fixer to one of the best-funded top-tier fixers in Houston and in all of United Earth.

They'd fallen in love quickly after that and had been virtually inseparable ever since. The only reason they hadn't married was that doing so would require paperwork that could expose who Archer was, which would land both of them in prison. It was the same reason they could never have children; the risk of them inheriting the blender gene was far too high.

"Tell me about it," he replied to her complaint. "And you have no idea how gassy this guy is."

She grimaced. "I think I'm going to need you to sleep on the couch until you start to change a bit."

He smirked and reached around her waist to pull her into him. "Not on your life."

She giggled and wormed free of his embrace and plopped herself back on the couch, looking up at him with a genuine smile. Despite her joking around, the thing Archer thought he loved most about her was her ability to see him for who he was, beyond the appearances he wore and discarded like masks.

"There's some of my blood in the fridge if you want to get the change started," she told him. That would help speed the process up. In a few days, he would look like her twin brother, which she never seemed to find as strange as he initially did.

He shrugged and sat down on the couch next to her, reaching an arm around her shoulders and pulling her close. "I don't know. This body is kind of growing on me now that I've seen your reaction to it," he said and then laughed as she poked him hard in the ribs.

# CHAPTER 3

## TWO YEARS AGO; 729 P.D.

Clarissa Lowry looked up from her desk holo with a wide smile. "Jinny! How wonderful to see you. How long has it been?"

Jinny couldn't help but grin back, despite the grim topic she had come to discuss. Clarissa had remained a part of her life since the first time Jinny had shadowed the older woman for loyalty readings and had been a sort of unofficial mentor to the young, timid reader all the way up to and after her graduation from the Academy.

"It's been about a year and a half, Clarissa," she replied, responding to the woman's gesture to step into the office and take a seat across the desk from her.

Clarissa sat back and regarded her thoughtfully. "So long? You're still on Copernicus?"

"Still there. Though I made full reader about a month and a half ago."

Clarissa grinned. "Feels good to have the 'junior' dropped from your title, doesn't it?"

"Feels a lot better than I'd even expected. A lot of the busywork seemed to dry up overnight. It's been a few weeks since I've had to fetch coffee for anyone."

They laughed together at that. The Reader Corps was legendary for its sense of hierarchy. Junior readers were often treated as little more than glorified interns until they made the rank of full reader, which usually took anywhere from four-to-six years. For Jinny, it had taken almost five and had only happened that quickly because she'd been transferred to the smaller Corps office on Copernicus; had she stayed on New Brussels where competition was fierce, she would probably still be waiting another couple of years for her promotion.

Not that Jinny wasn't good at her job. Her abilities literally made her better at it than her supervisors could possibly know. It was more that she had eschewed playing politics, though she also suspected the hand of her father in delaying her career on New Brussels, where he had the most influence. It was yet another reason she had been glad to leave the Core worlds for the more sedate and practical pace of a Coreward Rim world.

"I bet it's a pleasant change of pace for you," Clarissa was saying. "I also bet that you're still not being used to your full potential."

*If only you knew how true that statement is,* Jinny thought. But even her mentor couldn't be trusted with her secret. "It's nice. I love it there," Jinny lied. In truth, she didn't really like being a part of the Corps that much at all, but even with close mentors and friends, one had to be circumspect in how they talked about such things. "It's a much more merit-based culture than what I experienced here on New Brussels."

"I've heard that's the case." Clarissa stopped and looked at her hard, an eyebrow raised. "But you didn't come all the way to New Brussels to simply tell me how much you enjoy *not* being here. Are you here to see your father? Perhaps to reconcile?"

Jinny frowned. "No, Frank doesn't know I'm here. Well, he almost certainly knows by now, but I have no intention of seeing him while I'm on planet. I actually came to see *you.*"

It was Clarissa's turn to frown. "That sounds ominous. I rarely have people travel across half the known galaxy *without* calling ahead, no less, just to see me and catch up on things. There must be a very serious reason you wanted to chat with me."

Jinny nodded solemnly. "There is. But I was hoping we could talk about it somewhere a little less formal." She gestured to encompass Clarissa's office on the Reader Academy grounds. About the same time Jinny had left for Copernicus, Clarissa Lowry had traded her title and office of Senior Reader for that of Reader Instructor. She was now a full-time faculty member at the Academy, teaching Reader Ethics.

It was an interesting topic; most readers considered nearly anything they did in the Council's name to be ethical. And since essentially everything a reader did could be twisted to meet that definition, it restricted little. Clarissa had taught Jinny differently. Readers could fulfill their duties to the Council without abusing their power. A big part of that, the woman had always argued, was to never read someone outside of official duties without their consent.

Jinny believed wholeheartedly in the things Clarissa taught, and she was glad to see the woman get a bigger stage within the Academy itself. But a part of her also blushed every time she considered what her mentor might say if she ever learned that Jinny herself was guilty of going out for the occasional drink without her reader pin on. It wasn't something she did often, but sometimes she just felt an overwhelming need to feel *normal* for even just one evening. So far, it hadn't gotten her into any real trouble; it might be considered a technically illegal practice, but no guardmember would ever dare to arrest a reader for it. So almost every reader did it on occasion. Jinny consoled herself in the fact that she had used some of her surreptitious readings while out for a night on the town to later call in anonymous tips to the Guard about crimes committed. At least two dangerous men on Copernicus now found themselves in prison because of Jinny's covert readings of them when they had approached her at the bar or the club.

Clarissa regarded her carefully, digesting her implied request to meet somewhere off campus. Then she shrugged. "I'll be done grading this stack of assignments in about an hour. Why don't we meet at the Le Madelaine in two hours? You know it?"

"Of course."

"Terrific. I'll meet you then. It's good to see you, Jinny."

Two hours later, Jinny sat nervously at a table for two at Le Madelaine, a French-inspired restaurant on the opposite side of Ivanov City from both the Reader Academy and the galactic headquarters of the Reader Corps. She was grateful to Clarissa for suggesting the restaurant; its location made it unlikely they would run into any other readers while here. It was farther than most of the readers assigned to the headquarters building were likely to travel for a weeknight dinner, and its price tag discouraged the patronage of even those Academy students old enough to be granted off-campus dining privileges.

She had taken a seat in a booth near the rear of the restaurant, purposefully asking the host to place her away from other diners. Her reader pin was enough to persuade the man to accommodate her need for privacy, especially since that same pin might dissuade other potential customers if it was too visible. It was a minor breach of the ethics Clarissa taught, but since it was for Jinny's good *as well* as the good of the restaurant's business, she felt justified in the indulgence.

The other advantage of the booth was that Jinny could see the front door, so when Clarissa walked in, she waved to the older woman and saved the harried host another trip.

Clarissa smiled as she approached the table. She had changed out of the conservative slacks and blouse she wore while teaching and was instead wearing a comfortable pair of jeans and a light sweater against the chillness of New Brussel's northern continent in fall.

"Jinny," she said simply as she arrived at the table, and the younger reader stood so the two women could lightly embrace, careful not to allow any skin-to-skin contact. Outside the confines of the Academy grounds, both felt they could afford a more casual manner, which was one of the secondary reasons Jinny had insisted on meeting somewhere off campus.

Clarissa broke the hug and sat down first, grabbing her menu and perusing the offerings. Jinny did the same, saving the discussion for after they ordered. When the waitress approached, Clarissa ordered a bottle of red wine to start. Both women gave their food orders, and the young server set off to the kitchen to get their meals started. A few minutes later, the sommelier brought their wine selection, and both women took an appreciative sip before they were again left alone.

"So, you travel at least a week in the void, at no small expense, and with no advance notice, and ask to meet me somewhere private so we can talk. You've piqued my interest. Just what is going on, Jinny?" Clarissa's voice was friendly, but her message was clear: *it's time to get down to business*.

Jinny took a deep breath and another sip of wine and then set the glass down and leaned forward to meet her mentor's gaze. "I admit, I surprised you. I knew if I sent you a message first, Frank would intercept it and would know I was coming."

Clarissa raised an eyebrow. "Someday, I hope to hear just what happened between you and your father that makes you hate him so." She waved her hand dismissively as Jinny grimaced. "Oh, don't worry, dear. I won't ask you to tell me until you're ready, and I trust you that it's perfectly justified. You are many things, Jinny, but vindictive isn't one of them. If you're not willing to talk to your own father, I'm sure there is a perfectly good reason."

"Thank you." Jinny smiled. Clarissa, as always, showed her a trust that was rare for a senior reader to display to someone so junior. Jinny would need that trust for what she had come to discuss tonight.

"Now, you were saying about your reason for coming all the way here to see me?"

Jinny took another nervous sip of wine, then looked her mentor in the eyes again. "Have you ever heard of a case of a reader having… dreams, specifically dreams about the memories they've read from others?"

The older reader considered this for a moment. "Yes," she answered slowly, drawing out the word. "It's not all that uncommon, especially within the first 15 days. You would have been taught that in the Academy, I believe."

The '15-day rule' was a secret taught to readers but never allowed to be shared with the public or anyone outside the Corps. It referred to the rough but typical time period in which memories read by a reader persisted in their own memory. Contrary to widely held belief, readers didn't keep all the information they read from others; it started to fade almost immediately, just like their own formed memories. The inconsequential details faded first, followed by the more impactful experiences and observations read, just like a person who leaves a restaurant may remember what they ate and how it tasted for much longer than they might remember the name of their server.

There was something about other people's memories that made them fade much faster from a reader's consciousness than the reader's own formed memories. In the same way that listening to your friend describe the meal they had would typically stick in your memory for less time than the memory of the meal *you* had, anything a reader read from another's mind typically faded altogether within 15 days. The exceptions were particularly traumatic or vivid memories, like murders, rapes, or assaults. Those could last far longer and, sometimes, could even become a permanent memory for the reader.

The 15-day rule was also the main reason readers did not testify in court; rather, they recorded the observations of their readings within 24 hours of the actual reading, and prosecutors used those recordings in trials instead of a live reader. Otherwise, it was highly likely the reader would no longer even remember what they read by the time they were called to testify. Though the official reason was that readers were simply too busy to attend trials when a recording would be just as effective.

Jinny, of course, was the exception to the 15-day rule. Like most readers, she forgot most of what she read fairly quickly—that she read a person's *entire* memory made it an absolute necessity for her brain to release the inconsequential memories as fast as it could after a reading —but she tended to hold on to the more vivid and consequential memories in perpetuity. It meant that one of the most important inherited mechanisms to keep readers sane—the brain allowing them to shed the traumatic memories of the criminals and victims they read—wasn't working for her. She couldn't tell Clarissa that, of course, so she carefully phrased her next question.

"What about after the 15-day period? Perhaps even a month or two later?"

Clarissa chewed on her lower lip as she considered the unusual question. "Well. It's not unheard of, but the memories would have to be highly traumatic. Why? Are *you* having dreams outside the 15-day period?"

Jinny hesitated. She was putting a lot of trust in her mentor to say this out loud, and if she had misjudged Clarissa, then it could mean the end of her life. But she hadn't flown halfway across human space to turn back now. "I'm having nightmares: vivid recollections of crimes from the perspective of the people I've read. Sometimes I'm the perpetrator, and sometimes the victim, but always from their perspective. It's like I'm *living* it—like it's happening to me and not them. And it's happening months after the readings.

Clarissa knit her brow and frowned deeply. Jinny held her breath, waiting for the older woman's response.

"Jinny, this *is* serious," her mentor finally said. "Have you told anyone *else* about this?" There was an urgency in her voice that doubled Jinny's already acute anxiety.

"No. Just you."

Clarissa breathed a sigh of relief that surprised the younger reader. "Good. Make sure you tell *no one* else. The Corps doesn't like *anything* out of the ordinary, as I'm sure you're aware. Even coming to me was a risk, but your secret is safe with me."

"Thank you." Jinny let the relief she was feeling color her voice, though her mentor's tone still made her nervous. *Is there something terribly wrong with me?*

As if sensing her thoughts, Clarissa reached out and placed her gloved hand gently on top of Jinny's. "The good news is that there *are* other records of this happening, though they don't teach about it in the Academy. It's rare, and I'm afraid there has never been any real research into how to make it stop."

Jinny's heart fell further. "What usually happens to the readers who have these nightmares?"

Clarissa looked away, her eyes moistening, and a terror built inside Jinny. The woman looked back at her and spoke in a low tone. "Those that aren't tucked away by the Corps and never heard from again... they usually go insane."

And there it was. Two options for Jinny's future. Capture, which would lead to certain death once the Corps discovered her other abnormalities, or insanity. She felt hot tears well in her own eyes, and she reached up with her free hand to quickly wipe them away.

Clarissa saw and patted her hand again. "Don't give up hope, Jinny. As we would say in academic circles, the sample size is too small to represent the entire population. Especially with the stigmas inside the Corps, it's almost certain that there are other readers this has happened to that have never stepped forward and that possibly went on to lead perfectly normal lives, all things considered."

"But you don't believe that, do you?"

Clarissa shook her head slowly and blew out a long breath. "I wish I did, and I'm sure there *are* some outliers. I just have a hard time imagining the mental toll it would take on any reader to continuously relive such horrible moments from memories not their own. In a few of the documented cases, the effect was powerful enough that the reader started to think and act like the memories *were* their own, like they *became* the other person, even when awake. There's power in repetition. In the classroom, we often teach the same things over and over again to make sure our students remember them. Memories can behave the same way; the more often you recall something, the less likely you are to forget it, though you may change the details over time as the memory fades and your brain fills in the missing pieces: the proverbial fish story.

"So, if you dream something repeatedly, it forces you to recall the memory, which can make it even more solid. And as it solidifies, the theory is that your brain stops recognizing the memory as a foreign one and begins to think of it as your own. If that happens with enough memories, it can manifest as multiple personalities, eventually leading to a complete psychotic break."

Jinny had no words to respond for several moments. It was as if she were looking down the barrel of a gun, an experience that sadly factored into more than one of her remembered nightmares. "So, there's no hope," she finally whispered.

"Jinny, look at me." Clarissa's voice took on a commanding air like she might have used with her students, and Jinny automatically obeyed, meeting her mentor's eyes. "You have three things going for you as I see them. First, you are an extraordinary reader, far stronger than your professors and supervisors have ever given you credit for. Second, you are not *yet* close to the point of a full breakdown, at least from what I can see right now...."

She trailed off, and Jinny knit her brow. "And the third?"

"The third thing going for you is the one you won't want to hear: your father. He's the foremost genetic scientist of our time. If there is something in your genetic code that is special or unique that may cause this, there is no one more qualified to identify and perhaps even solve the problem. And likely, no one more motivated. You are his only child."

Jinny digested this. The way Clarissa talked about it, she worried her mentor might know more than she was letting on about Jinny's secret, but she quickly dismissed the thought. She was under no illusions that if Clarissa Lowry knew her secret that she would have years since found herself sitting in a prison cell, or worse. The woman might be her mentor, but she was also an established member of the Reader Corps, and her first loyalty would be to the Corps and the Council. Still, if she was willing to keep *this* secret for Jinny... *No, it's too risky. Not just for me but for her if she chooses to hide my secret and it comes out later.*

"Jinny, you may need to talk to your father," Clarissa said quietly, misinterpreting her protégé's hesitation. "Whatever happened between you cannot be worth your sanity."

"You'd be surprised," Jinny said, shaking her head. "I'm afraid that talking to Frank is out of the question."

Clarissa looked disappointed but didn't argue the point further. She sat back, removing her hand from Jinny's and taking a long sip of her largely untouched wine. The waitress chose that moment to bring them their food, forestalling further conversation, though the woman certainly noticed the downcast expressions and damp faces of both readers and beat a hasty retreat as soon as they were served.

For several minutes, they both ate in silence. To Jinny, the normally wonderful dish tasted like ash in her mouth, and she passed the entire meal without a single iota of enjoyment. After mechanically eating only a third of what was on her plate, she stopped and set her utensils down.

"Is there anything I can do besides going to Frank?" she asked Clarissa, who was intently studying the mashed potatoes on her plate as she shoved them around with her fork.

The older woman looked back up and sighed. "I don't know, Jinny. This is relatively uncharted territory, and the past examples we have never ended well. But if anyone can get through this, I believe it's you."

She paused. "Let me do some research on the topic. What I remember is light on details, something I read years ago from a book, not a person. It's possible I missed something in my recollection. How long do you plan to stay on New Brussels?"

"I'm leaving tomorrow. I could only take so many vacation days."

"Then I'll send you whatever I learn via courier ship. Don't worry," she held up her hand to belay Jinny's objection, "I'll encrypt it using a key that I'll share with you before you leave. That way, only you and I will be able to read the contents of any message I send you." She smiled slyly. "Believe it or not, you're not the first young reader to come to me to discuss matters of an intensely personal and explosive nature. I know how to keep confidences."

"Thank you so much." Jinny meant it. Despite giving her little hope today, Clarissa's offer to keep diving into the problem gave her something to at least look forward to. As the woman had said, not all hope was lost.

---

## PRESENT DAY; JUNE 4, 731 P.D.

Fleet Admiral Tamara Chen, supreme commander of the Council Navy, looked at the simulation scores with a sour expression. Just four weeks ago, they'd received the latest batch of conscripts from the Council. Consisting mostly of men and women who had largely never been on a spacecraft as anything other than an occasional passenger,

## THE FOUR WORLDS - SUBVERSION

they were horribly unprepared for life crewing warships, and they simply weren't learning fast enough.

She knew enough about Project Epsilon to know that it was all about creating enacters using food and water additives. That was the extent of her understanding, except for the Keeper's continued assurances that the enacters created through this new process would be just as loyal and obedient to the Council as those that were naturally born with the gene. She was surprised that the project had continued, essentially without pause, even after Kendra Siefred and the reporter Todd Crowley had outed it. But such was the power of the media, she presumed; people would believe just about anything told them with enough authority, especially if it was easier to believe the lie than the truth.

As an enacter herself, perfectly obedient to the Council whom the Keeper represented, she was doing exactly what he asked by taking these new conscripts and training them to crew her naval ships. But it simply wasn't working as planned, and even someone as loyal as she had to admit that the Keeper, and by extension, the Council, had simply been wrong.

Doubting them cost her nothing more than a bad headache; it was disobeying that would be agonizing.

Still, she knew, and felt a low-grade pain building in her head as she thought of it, that at some point, she would have to break the bad news to the Keeper and *suggest* a different course. While not strictly disobedience, it would still cause her a good amount of pain to question her orders that way. But she'd just have to deal with that pain because, without a change in approach, she wouldn't be able to fulfill the larger orders they had given her to subjugate the Sol system and the Four Worlds within one year's time.

Because the simple fact was that these new enacters *weren't* like born enacters at all. Sure, they followed all orders given to them... eventually. But for men and women who had lived the better part of their lives with their own free will, it was amazing how many times they had to test the limits of their new genetic programming before they would simply accept that they *must* follow those orders.

Until they reached that point, they would test and test and test to see if there was a way around it.

One woman, a former accountant from Fertility, had initially refused an order to take her new station at the *CNS Excalibur's* bridge sensor array. She'd stood just two meters from her station for 45 seconds while sweat broke out on her brow and she clenched her teeth in the obvious pain of her disobedience. Finally, the pain had become so intense that she collapsed onto the bridge deck and dragged herself to the sensor station. Only once she had painfully reached up a hand to touch the sensor control panel did the pain dissipate enough for her to pull herself up into the seat assigned to her.

Three more times that same day, the woman had balked at simple orders until the pain became so intense that she had no choice but to obey, just to make it go away. Momentary delays, but potentially catastrophic in combat where fractions of a second counted.

There were dozens of stories like that, coming in from all over the fleet, as the new crewers simply and obstinately refused to accept their new lots in life.

On top of those, there were stories of more passive resistance. Unlike the crewers the Council fleet had started with, all enacters from birth and indoctrinated properly from the age of five, these new crewers didn't *want* to be there and showed it in little ways. Officers on the training details found themselves having to give orders for the simple and mundane, orders they would never have to give willing crew.

For example, there'd been a man out of Mako 7's asteroid mines who had skipped almost every meal before anyone noticed he was too weak to perform his duties. One of the training officers finally detected the man's weight loss and gave him explicit orders to arrive on time for every meal and eat a healthy serving, and only then did the conscript regain his strength.

Another conscript, a former software engineer from Nova Tejas, had stopped bathing to the point where her stench became unbearable for those around her and distracted them from their training. Again, once the training officers noticed and ordered her to shower daily, she complied. But never in their most pessimistic projections had Chen and her training officers thought they'd have to explicitly order their crews to eat and groom themselves and take care of other necessary day-to-day tasks like that.

It was becoming a bigger and bigger problem.

And then there was the trouble with imprinting. Born enacters were separated from their parents at the age of five, a full year ahead of the age when most enacters imprint on an authority figure, forever tying themselves to that figure's commands and orders with the genetic imperative to always obey. The Council took them at such a young age to ensure that they *only* imprinted on the government and so that no one could ever force an enacter to imprint on an individual with less savory intentions.

The men and women coming to Chen now as newly-created enacters had no such early indoctrination outside of that which took place normally in schools. The Keeper had explained that constant subliminal messaging in every media available to the public would ensure that these new enacters imprinted on the Council as well, but Chen was seeing cases where that wasn't true.

In one instance, a man who'd been a first mate on a short-haul freighter out of Calcutta had clearly *not* imprinted on the Council. He ignored all orders issued to him by the training officers, even after multiple reminders that they represented the will of the Council, until one officer noticed he *did* obey any order passed through his former ship's captain, who was part of the same training cadre.

After multiple experiments of orders given both directly and through the former captain, Chen's officers could only conclude that the man had indeed imprinted on his captain rather than on the Council. Needless to say, Chen had ordered both men immediately executed. It was far too dangerous to have enacters not imprinted on the Council *or* to have a non-Council representative, like the captain in question, who could demand that sort of loyalty from *anyone*. So, they had to die, and it was a terrible waste, given that they were both able spacers.

Since that time, they'd found at least 180 more instances where the Council's subliminal messaging had failed to produce the right imprinting, and in each case, Chen found herself signing more execution orders and regretting it every time.

At the end of the day, of the over 15 thousand conscripts in the latest batch, Chen's training officers believed that only about 60 percent would turn out to be suitable to use on her ships, and about two-thirds of those only in non-critical roles that required little independent thought—where orders could be given to conduct specific actions without relying on the willingness of the crewer to think beyond the specific orders for ways to help their ship or the fleet.

It was a disaster, and the report she was putting together for the Keeper was going to lead to undoubtedly the most difficult discussion she'd ever had with the man.

---

Jinny awoke screaming and drenched in sweat. For a moment, she thrashed the covers off her, her brain not registering where she was, and she cried out for help. But then she recognized the small bedroom of the O'Leary's guest house and forced herself to calm down. Still, it took several minutes for her heartbeat to slow its pounding rhythm, not helped by her worry that she'd perhaps screamed loud enough for Corey and Debra or one of their staff to hear from the main house.

Luckily, after five minutes, no one came to check on her, and she was able to regain a semblance of calm. Even then, an underlying stress remained that she knew would not go away anytime soon.

The nightmares had stopped for a while when she'd been stationed on Nova Tejas. But they had started up again just after Ryder Cruz's death, the same time she'd met Alan Daily and brought him into the rebellion. But they hadn't been as frequent as before, so she had largely ignored them. However, about two weeks after arriving on Earth, she'd woken up screaming in the guest room of Professor Tichner's home. This was before she'd even met the O'Leary's. The old man had heard her cries and come in to check on her, but she'd explained it away as just a simple night terror.

She knew that he'd believed her at first but that he'd grown suspicious after it happened every few nights thereafter. The old man was polite enough not to confront her about it, but that didn't matter so much to Jinny, who was terrified that the dreams were now coming again *every* night, and often more than one nightmare per night at that. At least now, with her bed in the guest house removed a hundred meters from the O'Leary's main house, she was less worried about someone hearing her and wondering why she woke up screaming so often.

Of course, the worst part about the nightmares coming back was what they portended: a not-so-gradual and virtually guaranteed descent into insanity.

The most frequent nightmare she had, not surprisingly, was of Alan Daily's death. She experienced it at least twice every week, sometimes playing the role of Tyrus as the killer and other times playing the role of Alan himself. It was terrible either way, as her own formed memory of the event combined with the read memories from both Tyrus and Alan to make the details especially vivid.

She dreamed of other violent crimes as well. At least four times, she had dreamed of breaking her own mother's neck, reliving the memory she'd read of the event from Frank Ambrosa, again made more poignant by her own memory of the event from her childhood. The serial killer Hendrix was another frequent visitor to her nightmares, with Jinny taking his role in murdering all 12 of the black-haired women who reminded him of his ex-wife.

Two nights before, she'd dreamed of Ryder Cruz's death, with Jinny pulling the trigger on the sniper rifle that killed the speaker; it was another of Tyrus' memories.

Tonight's dream had been from the point of view of a man who had murdered a coworker at the Copernicus trade ministry over envy at a promotion and a perceived slight. That one had always been a source of frustration for Jinny. The murder had happened three months before the man had been picked up for an outstanding warrant for traffic violations. The guardsman who booked him into jail for the night thought that his profile matched that of the murder suspect and had called for a reader. This was during one of the rare times on that planet that Jinny wasn't confining herself to only loyalty screenings, and she was the on-call reader for the evening.

The guardsman who had called her in knew it was a long shot, but hoped that the man had perhaps done something in the last 18 or so hours that would point to his guilt. He hadn't. But, of course, Jinny could still see the murder in his memories; she just couldn't admit to that.

She'd considered lying and claiming that the man had bragged about the murder or even muttered to himself about it in the last half day. However, from her reading, she also knew that the suspect had been with his girlfriend for two days straight. With a witness to the entire 15 and 1/2 hours she could officially read, she couldn't risk making anything up that the girlfriend might refute. Even though the courts would have trusted a reader over any alibi, it might have been enough to make her superiors in the Corps suspicious. So, the man had gone free for the murder.

Tonight, she had dreamed of choking the life out of his female coworker in the woman's own hovercar, which Jinny, experiencing things from the perspective of the murderer, then took and burned to a crisp in an industrial part of town with the dead woman inside it, destroying any DNA evidence on both the body and the car.

She turned on the television—she had no idea why everyone on Earth insisted on calling their larger viewscreens that—hoping to distract herself, and navigated to a stream that played 24-hour news. The anchor was talking about some inane debate set to take place in the coming days in Congress about unemployment subsidies. It seemed ridiculous for that to be the top news item when Earth and her sister planets were, at best, mere months away from an all-out invasion by a force they couldn't hope to stop.

*Maybe that's why the nightmares have returned,* Jinny thought sourly. It wasn't just that the United Earth government was dragging its heels on preparing for the coming war—her unsuccessful testimony in front of the Congressional Committee on Foreign Affairs earlier that day certainly attested to that—it was that it almost didn't *matter* if they prepared or not. Tyrus had told her that there was a decent chance that all the warships the Four Worlds could field wouldn't equal the numbers and tonnage that the Council could send. It was simple economics, he explained, a subject they'd unfortunately only glossed over at the Reader Academy. There was no way that only four planets, even if they represented the birthplace of humanity, could equal the industrial might of 47 planets, many of which were more populated than Earth itself.

Still, if the Four Worlds were to have *any* chance, it would only be if Earth and Mars could work together. However, President Pereira and his Blue Party seemed unconcerned about allying with Mars—even outright hostile to the idea—and more concerned about continuing to use them as the bogeyman for what passed as their foreign policy.

Jinny switched off the television, disgusted at the anchor's prattle about issues of no galactic import, and sat in silence for a long time, staring at the moonlight coming through the bedroom's window and the shadows it cast through the leaves of the trees outside the guest house. It was a long time later when she finally drifted back to sleep and back into another nightmare.

---

## TWO YEARS AGO; 729 P.D.

Jinny walked back into her small apartment in the block of buildings close to the Reader Corps planetary headquarters on Copernicus, in the city of Landing. Her luggage followed her through the doorway obediently, and the suitcase headed off toward her bedroom on its own as she stood by the still-open door and surveyed the small space disconsolately.

Just a couple weeks before, when she'd left for her trip to visit Clarissa Lowry on New Brussels, the modest apartment had been Jinny's place of solitude and shelter from the demands of the Reader Corps. Now, it was somehow different. The neutral gray tones that she had found relaxing before now seemed drab and washed out. The simple minimalism of the space—she had always had a light touch in decorating—felt sterile and impersonal, like she was just passing through her own life as a casual observer, not an active participant.

She'd had a lot of time to think about things on the voyage home from New Brussels—a week spent traveling through the void. The passenger liner on which she traveled afforded little physical privacy, but as a reader, she had been given an upgrade to the business class cabin, which at least gave her a private sleeping pod and a lounge area equipped with privacy fields so that she could be free from the noise and conversation of other passengers. In that silence, she had considered the ramifications of what Clarissa Lowry had told her and had come to one firm conclusion.

*If it's only a matter of time until I lose my mind. I need to make that time matter.*

Of course, she had little idea how she *could* make the time matter. She had no choice of vocation; she was a member of the Reader Corps, plain and simple. There were no alternative career options for her. She didn't have a family or any close friends on Copernicus, either. There had been the occasional man in her life, but the latest one, Parker, had left her a message that had pinged her watch as soon as the passenger liner had come into range of Copernicus' planetary Internet. It was over between them; he had found someone new who wasn't a reader. And Jinny found that she really didn't care.

No, the answer wasn't to go find herself a new boyfriend to make her happy. The answer had to be about bringing more meaning to her *own* life, not relying on someone else to bring that meaning for her. She just didn't know how to go about doing that. There was trauma in her past that she had never acknowledged—and could never acknowledge —to anyone else, and she had to admit that it was holding her back. The secret she had to keep from the galaxy meant she could never fully open herself up to anyone, but *maybe* she could bring down some of her walls and find a better way to use her abilities.

She shut the apartment door behind her and moved into the small living room to sit on the even smaller couch. Pulling up her watch's holo, she began composing a message to her friend Sakura on Greater York. Perhaps a visit with the one real friend she'd ever had would be a good place to start bringing down her walls. She couldn't tell Sakura her big secret—that would put the girl in too much danger—but talking about the nightmares and the disturbing revelations from Clarissa with someone else she trusted might help her find the solution on her own… or at least help her figure out the best way to make her last years of sanity more meaningful.

She'd lied to Clarissa Lowry about needing to run back to Copernicus because of limited vacation days; the real reason for keeping her time on New Brussels short had been to decrease the chances of Frank tracking her down. In reality, she'd seldom taken an actual break from her duties, so she had enough vacation time stored up to take the time transiting to Greater York and back with a week or two of time to spend there, even after her trip to the galactic capital.

*Yes,* she thought, *a visit to Sakura is what I need.* She almost believed it.

# CHAPTER 4

PRESENT DAY; JUNE 5, 731 P.D.

Riggs sat across from Jinny in the restaurant at the top of the Space Needle in Seattle. She'd ridden an atmospheric shuttle from San Diego to meet him, and they'd taken advantage of the warm summer weather to walk the six blocks from the shuttle terminal to the thin anachronistic building that rose to a height less than a quarter that of the surrounding skyscrapers, yet somehow seemed to dominate the city's skyline.

He had attempted to draw her into conversation several times during their walk to dinner, but each time, the effort had died quickly. It was clear she had a lot on her mind and was in a shell of her own thoughts and concerns.

This was the fifth time they'd gone to lunch or dinner together in the three months since arriving on Earth, and each time Riggs had left just a little more smitten with the beautiful reader. Thus far, however, he'd gotten no solid signals that she reciprocated his feelings. He'd tried to talk about it a few times with Jynx, but she'd just sneered and asked him why he was wasting his time. After those first few attempts, he'd given up confiding in his co-pilot.

Finally, as the waiter walked away with their order and they'd finished some small talk about the view of the Puget Sound from the restaurant's rotating platform, Jinny had started to loosen up just a bit and engage him in real conversation. But the topic wasn't uplifting.

"I just don't know if the government is taking the threat seriously at all. They have no real concept of nor even seem to care about what is headed toward them. They won't even acknowledge the facts that are right in front of their faces," Jinny said as she carefully spread butter on the warm bread the server had left behind.

Riggs looked around nervously to make sure no one was listening to their conversation, but the table's privacy field was engaged, and he was still getting used to being in a society that allowed and even *embraced* critical talk about the government.

"Well, I'm not sure what you can do about it," he said, trying to soothe her. "You've already told them what you know dozens of times. So has Tyrus. Even Jynx and I have shared what little *we* know, though they haven't asked us any follow-up questions since they stuck us up here to rot on that little island."

Jinny eyed him with a half-smile. "That little island is one of the most beautiful places I've ever seen," she said. "I'd love to stay there too if it didn't mean an even longer commute to Houston three or more times a week."

He shrugged. "Oh, it's beautiful, but it's *so* boring. There's absolutely nothing for me to do, and Jynx misses working on the *Monk* so badly that last week she took apart my house's environmental system and rebuilt it, supposedly to make it better. Now it bounces between arctic cold and desert heat five times a day, and it's driving me nuts."

Jinny giggled, and despite his complaints, he was glad to see her relax a little and stop acting as if the fate of the entire galaxy rested on her shoulders alone. She just looked so exhausted, though she had shrugged off every one of his attempts to talk about her obvious lack of sleep.

"How is Jynx? Any better?" she asked.

He frowned and shook his head. "No. She'd go back to the colonies in a heartbeat if they'd let her, even if it meant taking her chances with the entire Guard *and* the Council Navy. She still blames you and Tyrus for dragging us into this, and she's basically like a tiger in a cage most times I see her."

Jinny reached out and placed her gloved hand on top of his bare one. "And how are *you* doing, Cal?" she asked, her liquid brown eyes fixed on his.

His heart raced a little as he gazed back at her and swallowed the lump that had instantly formed in his throat. "I'm... uh... I'm good."

"No, you're not," she said with a half-smile. "I know you well enough by now to know when you're lying. And it has nothing to do with that island you're on."

He grinned back at her. "Even though you can't read me?"

Jinny scrunched up her nose like she smelled something bad. The first and only time she'd tried to read Riggs had not gone well for her. Instead of getting his memories, she'd gotten the equivalent of a mental shout and quick eviction from his head.

"Are you ever going to tell me how you did that?" she asked him softly.

He sighed and became all-of-a-sudden very interested in the piece of bread in front of him. He had thought through a thousand different ways he could tell her the truth about that day on Rinali Station— about what he was—but he couldn't ever bring himself to do it. "One day I might," he replied. "But I'm just not ready to go there yet. Besides, it's not *my* secret to share."

She gave him a quizzical look but then nodded her understanding. "Well, let me know when you're ready. There's still a lot I haven't shared with you about my past, so I guess we'll just have to both open up a little more as we go."

Catching her wording, he blurted out without thinking: "As we go where? I mean... uh... Where are we going... with this?" He felt the blood rushing to his face and ears in embarrassment, but Jinny pretended not to notice.

Instead, she just shrugged. "I don't know, Cal." Jinny was the only one in the group who regularly used his given name. *He* hadn't even used it all that much over the years and wasn't sure Jynx even remembered it half the time. "You know that it's taken me a while to get over what happened to Alan," she continued.

It was his turn to nod his understanding. But again, without thinking, he spoke. "And Tyrus?"

She looked surprised and shook her head rapidly. "No. Tyrus and I are just friends. We'll never be more than that." It sounded to Riggs like she was trying to convince herself as much as him, but he chose not to prod more.

"But you and I are…" she trailed off. "Well, I'm not sure what we are. If we had time to explore it, I think this could grow into something, but with me in San Diego and Houston, and you here…." She shrugged as if to say that it just wasn't meant to be.

Riggs wasn't ready to give up that easily. He reached out and placed his other hand on top of the gloved one that she still had lightly resting on his. "Jinny, I… Well, I think you're amazing, and I'm willing to take it as slow as you need to. But I do want us to be more than friends."

*I want us to be more than friends?* he thought frantically. *What am I, a twelve-year-old trying to get his first girlfriend?*

Jinny smiled brightly at him, oblivious to his self-castigation. "I'd like that too," she replied, and his heart leapt. "For now, how about we take it one dinner at a time, though?" His heart sank just a little.

Then her eyes widened to match her dazzling smile, and Riggs felt a glimmer of hope. "After dinner tonight, why don't you take me to that little ice cream place on Bainbridge that you mentioned last time? The one with blackberry ice cream. I can catch a late shuttle back to San Diego." Blackberries didn't grow in the colonies for some reason, and the little team—even Jynx—hadn't been able to get enough of the tart fruit since they'd arrived on Earth.

Riggs smiled and didn't remember another thing they said for the rest of the dinner.

---

Jinny was happy that she and Riggs elected to take the longer water ferry ride to Bainbridge Island rather than the local Loop. And not just about avoiding even a brief ride on the dark and claustrophobic Loop. She had never been on a real boat prior to coming to Earth. There had been no need for it and no time either, as she'd spent the better part of her life learning how to be a member of the Reader Corps or working in the same. So, she tried to find an excuse to ride the ferry whenever she visited Riggs. Even though it took a full half-hour longer than the near-instantaneous Loop ride under the Puget Sound.

They stood together on the front of the boat and watched the lights of the island approaching. Though it was a relatively warm summer's evening, the cool breeze off the water lent a slight chill to the air, and Jinny found herself instinctively huddling against Riggs for a little extra warmth. Cal tentatively put his arm around her shoulders as she leaned into him.

*Wow, he must think I'm a schoolgirl. I can't even tell him what I want or how I feel because I don't even know myself. But the first opportunity I find to string him along, I take it without even a thought.*

The problem was that Jinny really *didn't* know how she felt about Riggs. In a way, he reminded her of Alan Daily. Though the two couldn't be more different on the surface—a true blue, straight-arrow guardsman versus a smuggler and habitual rule-breaker—they both had the same earnest desire to do what was right, especially when it came to helping other people. And if she was honest, even more particularly when it came to helping *her*.

But it was more than just reminding her of Alan. Riggs had his own gentle nature and was just so easygoing with their budding relationship. It was clear he liked her and wanted to get closer, but in the three months they'd known each other, he'd never once made her feel pressured into moving any faster than she was willing to.

That was important when less than three *and a half* months ago, she'd seen her now best friend—then mortal enemy—shoot the love of her life in the head.

Thoughts of Alan's death brought back thoughts of the nightmares, a place in her mind that she'd sworn she would keep suppressed so she could enjoy her night off with Riggs. But the worry was still there, like a phantom always in the periphery of her vision, no matter how hard she tried to ignore it.

When the ferry docked in Eagle Harbor on Bainbridge Island, Jinny pushed aside her grim thoughts, intent on forgetting about her descent into insanity at least for the remainder of the evening, and looped her arm through Riggs' and continued leaning into him as they walked the short distance from the ferry terminal to the main drag of Winslow, the island's small central town. They walked slowly down the avenue lined with trees and shops with architecture that made her feel like she was seeing a part of Earth's history, long forgotten, before the massive world war that had decimated the population and ultimately spawned the Council government just over a millennium ago.

They neared the end of the avenue and turned into a small outdoor plaza. Down a short distance sat the quaint ice cream shop Riggs had told her about. But as they got closer to their destination, she felt him stiffen next to her and heard him let out a groan. Broken from her reverie, she followed his gaze to the front door of the ice cream shop and let out a little gasp of her own.

"Tyrus?!" she exclaimed. "What are you doing here?"

"And why now?" she heard Riggs say, almost under his breath. She elbowed him slightly, and he gave an exaggerated grunt.

Tyrus smiled widely at the sight of the one person in the galaxy he considered a friend, and he gave a respectful nod to Riggs as well. "I may be separated from the part of the galaxy I call home," he replied, "but I can still brush off and use my old skills when needed."

His smile lessened, and he looked at them both soberly. "In all seriousness, Congressman O'Leary told me you were having dinner with Riggs tonight when I commed looking for you, and I remembered you mentioning you wanted to visit this shop next time you were up here, Jinny. Plus, we really all need to sit down and talk, so it made sense to meet you here on the island."

Riggs was skeptical and didn't make any effort to hide it in his tone. "So, you've just been standing outside an ice cream shop for hours, hoping we'd arrive?"

Tyrus shrugged. "I may have had other ways to track you both down. That's not the important thing right now. Can we go somewhere private and chat?"

Jinny narrowed her eyes at him and then looked up at Riggs, seeing the disappointment on the pilot's face. She looked back at Tyrus. "We can, but only after Cal and I get the ice cream we came here for. You're welcome to join us, or you can just stay out here on the sidewalk and look like a big, mean government agent for the next half hour."

Tyrus' smile returned. "I guess I'll join you then."

Jinny ignored the small groan from Riggs.

A little over an hour after encountering Tyrus at the ice cream shop, Jinny, Riggs, and Jynx gathered with him in the small kitchen of Riggs' borrowed home. Except for Jynx, they sat at the kitchen table. The sour-faced co-pilot took up a position leaning against the wall where she could glare openly at Tyrus.

Having swept the house for bugs using an app on his watch, Tyrus had found and destroyed six of the listening devices before he indicated it was safe for them to talk. Now, with all of them gathered, he first turned to Jinny.

"OK, tell us your honest impression. How seriously is the government taking the threat from the Council Navy?"

She thought for a moment, then exhaled loudly. "They're not," she admitted. "Corey and his Red Party are taking it seriously enough, but they're the minority right now and don't have the votes to push anything through. I've still never met President Pereira or had the opportunity to sit down with the man and talk about the Council threat directly. Though, from Corey, I get the impression that the president simply doesn't want to believe it's as bad as we say. His political party sure doesn't seem to think it's worth worrying about."

She looked around at everyone at the table and at Jynx against the wall. "I just don't think they're going to take it seriously in time to do enough to prepare for it." She'd known that for quite some time, of course, but saying it out loud seemed to bring a finality to her failed efforts to convince the leaders of Earth to prepare to defend themselves.

Tyrus nodded. "That's my impression too, and I know that a lot of the top military leaders feel likewise, even if they can't say it openly. Those are the people I would tend to trust when the chips are down, and none of them have a great deal of confidence in their commander-in-chief or his party right now."

"But isn't that how a democracy is supposed to work?" Riggs interjected. "Isn't the whole point that the civilian leadership *isn't* supposed

## THE FOUR WORLDS - SUBVERSION

to be as hawkish as the military leadership, to provide a counterbalance? Isn't that why we all think they're better than the Council, or have we changed our minds about that already?" He had obviously not been sitting idle in his time sequestered on the island, and Jinny was impressed that he'd been studying up on the strange form of government the people of United Earth embraced.

She answered before Tyrus could, knowing that Riggs would listen more willingly to her than the big ex-assassin. "The principles are good, as far as I can tell, but it goes beyond that with Pereira and his Blue Party. It's like they're being willfully ignorant of the danger the Four Worlds face because it's inconvenient to their policies and political platform. I don't understand the saying, but I've heard a few Earthers say that Pereira is 'drinking his own cool aid', which I think means that he's a full believer in his own rhetoric about how Earth is ready for anything the Council can throw at them, but that the more important issues are closer to home."

Tyrus gave Jinny a smile of gratitude. "I think you're right. Normally, that wouldn't be so bad. The president only serves a six-year term and can only serve a maximum of two terms. So, he or she wouldn't have time to do any actual damage, even if they *were* delusional. But Pereira is only two years into his first term, and with the imminent attack from the Council, he can do a *lot* of damage in a short time simply by doing nothing."

"So what?" Jynx cut in, not trying to hide the hostility in her voice. "What do we care if these idiots get themselves fragged?" She looked around the room for support, casting a dirty look at Riggs when he shook his head at her. "I mean, come on," she continued, "we've given them the warning; we've taken all the risk so far. If they choose not to listen, that's not on us. We should get the *Monk* back and get out of here before the Council comes and kicks their sorry butts."

"I don't know, Jynx," Jinny said, shaking her head. "I'd feel pretty terrible about this planet and everyone on it dying or getting put into effective slavery to the Twenty just because I didn't do everything I could to stop it. Besides, where would we even go?"

"Haven't we done everything we can to stop it already?" Jynx argued back, ignoring Jinny's question. "It's up to that idiot Pereira and his bunch of fools now. And this Corey guy, maybe. It's not on any of *us* anymore."

Tyrus responded this time, which immediately caused a darker cloud to come over Jynx's features. "You're right, in one respect, Jynx. We can only do what we can do; there has to be an effort from others. We can't force Earth or any of the Four Worlds to build up their militaries or put in place the right defensive measures. But we haven't yet done *everything* we can do to help them get there."

"Oh yeah," said Jynx combatively. "Just what are you suggesting, *Alpha*?" As always, she said Tyrus' old title like a curse. "Are we supposed to flap our arms real hard and fly up to the shipyards and build our own fleet to face the Council when they come?"

"Actually," Tyrus said, "you're not that far off the mark. But we don't fly to Earth's shipyards. We go to Mars."

Stunned silence greeted him. Even Jinny, who could usually tell what Tyrus was thinking, was stunned.

It was Riggs who finally broke the silence. "What do you mean, go to Mars? Listening to the way the Earthies talk about them, they're a bunch of wackos out there, and they're just as likely to throw us in a jail cell and dissect us for study as they are to listen to us."

Tyrus nodded slowly. "That's a definite possibility. Still, I feel like all of us have done everything we can here on Earth to convince the leadership of the threat. Jinny," he turned to look at her, "has done a terrific job convincing a good chunk of Congress *and* the military leaders that they need to prep for this. She even has the sympathy of most of the general public right now, which means something here. But the majority party and the executive branch are still largely ignoring the threat. Even some of the folks in O'Leary's Red Party are no better—too focused on placating their local constituents instead of doing what's right for the system as a whole."

He pulled up a holo of the Sol system on his watch, disabling the privacy field so they all could see. Pointing at the mass of Jupiter, he said, "Europa only has a small Navy and limited shipyards to build a bigger one. They've relied on a mutual defense pact with Earth to protect them against any Martian aggression for centuries."

He pointed next to the fourth planet from Sol. "Only Mars has the military and industrial capacity to rival Earth's. So, if Earth isn't going to prepare for war, we need to convince Mars to do it. And time is running out."

They were all silent for another long moment as they digested what Tyrus had said.

This time, it was Jynx who broke the silence. "So, what? We go and convince a bunch of dictators—or who knows what government they have out there—to help us prepare to defend the Four Worlds? How do we even get there? Last I checked, we didn't have a ship."

"I don't have a way to get us there," Tyrus admitted, putting a smug smile on the woman's face. "But we need to go in person; they've ignored every attempt at communication. So, we need to start thinking about it now, so that *when* the opportunity to go arises, we're ready for it."

"Wait just a second!" Riggs said. "Are we *sure* about going to Mars? Like I said before, there's no guarantee they won't just kill us. There has to be something else we can try *here* first."

Tyrus cocked his head and regarded the man, not with anger but with genuine curiosity. "It's certainly worth talking about," he said. "Jinny, what's your take? *Is* there a way we can convince Pereira and his supporters?"

Jinny thought carefully. "Honestly, probably not. They have two sticking points. First, beyond the *Monk's* sensor recordings and a few pieces of data that Siefred gave us, we really don't have any proof of the Twenty's intentions. Second, and this may be the bigger issue in reality, they can't understand *why* the Keeper and his cronies would want to invade the Four Worlds."

Riggs scoffed. "Really? They dealt with the Council for hundreds of years before the schism, and they don't believe that these guys are greedy and power-hungry enough to come back and try to conquer them again?"

"No, no. Wait, Riggs," Tyrus said. "Jinny has a point. This has been bothering me ever since we met with Siefred. Because she made it sound like it was all about power. But the Twenty has taken a number of major and risky steps to prepare for this invasion. That navy they built has to have cost them hundreds of trillions of credits, and the risk of public backlash they've incurred with their little project to try to turn everyone into enacters is a big deal. I'm afraid I agree with the Earthers to a degree on this. The motives just don't make sense, especially when weighed against the cost."

Jynx threw up her hands. "You *would* agree with them," she said accusingly to Tyrus. "Just because you can't understand why they're doing it, doesn't mean that the motives aren't exactly what Riggs just said."

"He's right, Jynx," Jinny said. "It's been bothering me, too. Every time I have to try to explain it to a new congresswoman or committee panel, I just don't feel like the motives of power and greed make sense on their own. And not just because the democratic rulers of United Earth have a hard time imagining that level of thirst for power. The Council has 47 worlds under their control and at least 20 times the population spread across them as the Four Worlds have. Unless they're insane, it just doesn't make a lot of sense to go to all this trouble for so little reward."

"What if we're looking at this wrong?" said Tyrus. "What if the answer isn't about power or money, but about something else the Four Worlds have that the Twenty feel they need?"

"Like what?" asked Riggs.

"I don't know."

"Australia," Jinny said, surprising even herself with the statement. Everyone turned and looked at her. She had given the topic a lot of thought, but she hadn't felt she was ready to share it with the others yet. Either way, it was out there, so she continued.

"What if," she started, "it's really about the enacters and other enhanced in Australia?"

"How so?" Tyrus asked.

"Well, who says you were the first enacter to disobey an order?"

Tyrus shrugged. "There's no record of it happening before. Still, I suppose that doesn't mean it hasn't happened, and they just suppressed it. I imagine we'll never know."

"Yet, here on Earth, they also have *no* records of enacters being able to beat their programming; and they've *tried* to make it happen. And there's something else. When I was at the Reader Academy, there were rumors that the average reading time was decreasing."

"Reading time?" Jynx asked, her voice softer than usual, genuine interest overshadowing her normally hostile expression.

"The time period a reader can read from a living person or recently deceased corpse," Jinny explained. "Publicly, we tell people it's 18 hours, but the average is closer to 12, officially, at least inside the Reader Corps. But at the Academy, the average for my class was closer to ten hours. There were even rumors that it *used* to be 18 hours on *average*, but it's been steadily getting shorter for the last several generations. I've never even met another reader who can read that long."

"What would that have to do with Australia?" Riggs asked.

"What's the key difference between the readers, enacters, blenders, and speakers in Australia versus those in the colonies?" Jinny asked in return.

Riggs shook his head, but Tyrus jumped forward with the answer. "Purity of bloodlines!"

Jinny nodded. "That's right. In the colonies, the enhanced can and sometimes do marry the unenhanced. I was a reader not because my mother and father were but because two of my grandparents were. It skipped a generation."

"But didn't your father turn you into a reader?" Riggs asked.

"No, Frank couldn't create a reader from nothing; he used to complain all of the time about that knowledge having been lost with the original records of the genetic engineers who created the enhanced. I had the gene already; he just found a way to enhance it. I was a reader first because of my bloodline, but the line was so diluted I probably wouldn't have been all that strong of one.

"At least a quarter of my classmates were born to single-reader families. Even enacters sometimes marry non-enacters, though it rarely works out. I imagine it's the same for blenders and speakers. Perhaps the bloodlines are getting weaker in the colonies, which could allow some enacters, like Tyrus, to disobey even the Council. And maybe that's why the readers aren't able to read as much anymore."

Tyrus nodded his understanding. "Which could mean that the entire invasion isn't about gaining *new* power but about keeping the power the Keeper and the Twenty already have. Because how do they maintain that power? Through the enhanced. Not only are they speakers themselves, but they rely heavily on blenders and readers to be their eyes and ears. And they absolutely depend on the enacters to carry out their orders without question. And not just alphas like me, but *all* the enacters, especially those in the Guard. If those genetic traits are weakening, they would be at risk of losing even the power they currently have."

Jinny was getting excited now, as the idea she'd toyed with only in her head seemed to make sense to the others as well. "Exactly. But here on Earth, the enhanced have never been allowed to mingle with the general population, much less intermarry. So the bloodlines would be purer. The Twenty could be hoping to use the enhanced in Australia to reinvigorate their bloodlines in the colonies."

She stopped, looking at each of them in turn. Tyrus looked excited, Riggs looked terrified, and Jynx just scowled.

"It makes sense," Tyrus said slowly now, his expression turning thoughtful. "Except for one part. If the colonies have had no contact with the Four Worlds in centuries, how would the Twenty even know about Australia and the segregation of the enhanced?"

Jinny shrugged. "Candidly, that's where my theory falls apart. Unless they somehow have spies on Earth…."

She trailed off. All of them knew that if the Twenty had spies on Earth, that meant they also had another way through the Rift. The Solside entrance to the one known path through the Castilian Rift, nicknamed the Front Door, was never left unguarded by the various naval forces of the Four Worlds. The *Blind Monk* had been intercepted almost immediately after surfacing there. But the idea of there being a second path, one known only to the Council government, was almost too scary to be worth contemplating. It would mean the Council Navy could easily spy on or even attack the Four Worlds by surprise.

"Well," Tyrus said. "Where do we go from here?"

"I think O'Leary might help us," Jinny said softly, drawing another round of surprised glances from the group. "It's clear he's worried about Earth's lack of preparation and Pereira's particular reticence. He's also one of the few politicians I've heard speak staunchly in

# THE FOUR WORLDS - SUBVERSION

support of more direct measures to contact Mars and work together with them on this. All the rest of them seem to treat Mars like it's a threat worse than the Council. The Martians are a favorite villain for every political party, but Corey might be the exception to that. I think he might have some deeper connection to Mars, even, but he changes the subject when I bring it up."

Tyrus frowned. "Are you sure we can trust him? Have you read him?"

Jinny shook her head and grimaced. She didn't like the automatic assumption that she was reading *anyone* on Earth. "No, and I don't *plan* to read him. That would betray his trust. Even so, I'm as sure as I otherwise can be."

"How long do we think we have?" Riggs asked, even though he knew none of them had an answer.

Tyrus shrugged. "Could be days. Could be months. Could be a year. But I think we have to assume it will be sooner rather than later. The faster we get Earth and Mars to prepare, the better off we'll be when it does happen."

No one responded to this, each of them lost in their own thoughts.

"OK," Tyrus said, breaking the silence. "We're not going to figure out everything tonight. We all need to be thinking of ways to get to Mars and watching for opportunities. Who knows, getting them to prepare may even prompt Earth to do so just so they don't get left behind in an arms race. Jinny, be careful with O'Leary, but if you see an opening, take it.

"Riggs, hopefully we can get the *Monk* back when the time comes. Just in case, start studying up on Earth spacecraft controls. There should be quite a lot of information publicly available on the Internet. I think there are even some simulator games online. As a pilot, it won't be too suspicious for you to take an interest in those. And we just don't know *what* we'll have to fly in to get to Mars, so you need to be ready."

He stopped and looked at Jynx, who frowned deeply at him and seemed to dare him to assign work to her.

"Jynx can do the same as me," Riggs interjected quickly, for which Jinny was grateful. They didn't need another fight between Tyrus and

129

the woman. "I'll need a co-pilot, and you'll need a backup if something happens to me."

Tyrus nodded, and Jynx didn't argue. None of them mentioned that Tyrus could easily pilot most spacecraft almost as well as Riggs.

"Good," Tyrus continued. "Now that we've settled all that, anyone up for a game of cards?" He smiled lightly, doing his best to break the tension they all felt. "I'm not ready to go back to the officer's barracks in Houston quite yet."

When Jinny finally left Riggs' home late that night, escorted by Tyrus back to the Seattle port to catch a shuttle back to San Diego for her and Houston for him, they hadn't come up with a plan to get to Mars or test Jinny's bloodlines theory in a way that any of them thought would work. Still, it felt good to know that they were at least planning *something*.

However, she knew they really did need to better understand the Twenty's motivation for attacking the Four Worlds. And she was convinced now that the answer lay somewhere in Australia, with Earth's enhanced population. She needed to go there and get the answers; then, perhaps she could convince the rest of the United Earth government to believe the danger they were in.

It felt good to have her mind working on a problem that wasn't related to her nightmares.

# CHAPTER 5

### SEVEN MONTHS AGO; 730 P.D.

"I'm glad you came." The simple statement carried with it an immeasurable volume of import, though that may have just been Jinny's imagination. After all, the man saying the words was a speaker, and they could easily make their words sound just about any way they wanted the listener to take them.

"I'm glad I came here as well," she responded, looking across the crowded bar and not meeting Ryder Cruz's gaze. She was talking about her decision to come to Nova Tejas but not to this bar. It seemed strange to be having her first official meeting with the rebellion in such a public place.

"There won't be any other readers here," he assured her, picking up on her anxiety. "They tend to drink at establishments closer to their headquarters. Plus, this particular bar isn't known as being friendly to the enhanced."

She looked at him dubiously. She'd only met the speaker once before, when he'd approached her after Sakura's suicide on Greater York with a vague promise that she could be part of an organization that kept the Council government and its minions accountable. So, she wasn't ready to fully trust him quite yet. She hadn't even been sure it was a rebellion he was talking about, and she still wasn't entirely sure; she only suspected. Still, she had made the colossal step of transferring herself to the Nova Tejas Reader Corps on the vague promises he'd given. Maybe it was a sign that she was already more insane from the nightmares than she cared to admit.

"You're here," she said, pushing aside that troubling line of thought. "Is it so much to believe that there could be other enhanced here? Any of these people could be a reader... or a blender."

He shrugged. "The first thing you have to learn, amiga, if you're going to be a member of our little group, is that nothing we do can ever be one hundred percent safe. You'll always be at risk. You just manage the risk the best you can and let fate take care of the rest."

It was strange to hear a speaker talk of something as immaterial and semi-religious as fate, and it, unfortunately, reminded Jinny of the message she had received earlier that day.

More than a year and a half had passed since she had visited Clarissa Lowry on New Brussels. They had stayed in contact using the encryption key Clarissa had shared with her, but further conversations had yielded no solutions to Jinny's problem. The nightmares had continued and even gotten worse after she'd read Sakura's body. Jinny had found herself taking fewer high-intensity assignments, asking to be assigned to loyalty screenings instead of murder investigations and the like. It had slowed down her progression in the Reader Corps, and for a while, it seemed to slow down the dreams. But nothing had stopped them altogether.

And this morning, she had received a final message from Clarissa.

***Clarissa Lowry: Jinny. I've exhausted all my own ideas for dealing with this. I know it's complicated, but you really need to reconsider bringing your father into the loop. If anyone can help solve this, it's him. Otherwise, you may be out of options.***

Of course, Jinny had already discarded the idea of going to Frank. Even if her father were willing to help her, she would rather suffer the psychotic break that all of Clarissa's research suggested was inevitable than live a single day beholden to that man. Plus, this was a problem of *his* making; he had been the one to mess with her genetics in utero, and she had zero doubt it was her *special* abilities that also gave her this *special* problem.

Even if she had been able to forgive Frank Ambrosa for doing what he'd done to her *and* for killing her mother, forgiveness did not equal trust. The man had repeatedly shown that he was undeserving of that from her or anyone else. To trust him again would be akin to picking up a poisonous snake and hoping that this time it wouldn't bite.

By Clarissa's calculations, Jinny had at most another year before the dreams caused significant psychological problems for her. That estimate was based on the typical timelines between the first dreams and the eventual and inevitable psychotic breaks suffered by every other reader who had had this issue. But realistically, it was little more than a semi-educated guess; even worse than that, given that Clarissa didn't know just how unusual Jinny's talents were.

Still, it had taken almost a full year and a half, the death of her best friend, and finally reading a crooked Assembly speaker, for Jinny to finally figure out how to make the rest of her life more meaningful. That had taken the form of trusting the man sitting across from her and the mysterious group—probably a rebellion—he claimed to represent. And now she was here, hoping she hadn't misread the situation.

In retrospect, she might have been shocked by how quickly she'd come around to the idea of betraying everything she'd ever known to join Ryder's cause. She supposed she'd always resented not just her father for what he'd done to her, but also the system that had enabled men like him to exercise absolute power over others. The death of Sakura, caused by petty Reader Corps politics, had been the last straw for Jinny, but certainly not the first. She imagined now that her path to treason and rebellion had likely started the day when, as a young child, she had watched her father murder her mother to safeguard the secret of the special abilities he'd given her. The same day she'd seen other representatives of the Council government cover up that murder to not lose one of their top science advisers.

"You're brooding again," Ryder said with a sympathetic smile. "Want to talk about it?"

She shrugged and gave him a wan smile. "Just wondering what I've gotten myself into."

"A world of pain and regret, most likely," he replied, drawing a sharp look from her. He held up his hands in mock surrender. "Sorry, just trying to lighten the mood. But seriously, this could all end as poorly as your worst fears suggest, or we could help liberate the entire galaxy. There's no way to know. All we can do...."

"Manage the risk and trust in fate?" she finished for him.

He grinned. "So, you were listening, amiga."

*OK, so almost definitely a rebellion.* She looked out again over the crowd. "You still haven't explained why we're meeting here instead of in a more private location."

"Well, there are some people I want you to meet." He must have signaled to someone in the bar in a way that she hadn't detected because, at that moment, two individuals slid into the booth, a man next to Ryder and a woman next to Jinny.

"Jinny, meet John and Joan. They're members of our little group, and you'll be working with them while you're here on Nova Tejas."

Each of the newcomers nodded, but neither offered their hand in greeting. She was mildly disappointed. Given the location and clientèle of the bar, Ryder had advised her not to wear her gloves; they were a sure tell she was a reader. Still, she supposed, surreptitiously reading these two strangers was probably not the best way for her to make a good first impression.

She studied John and Joan, certain those weren't their real names, but she was willing to play along. John was short, with sandy blond hair and an olive complexion. He had hazel eyes and an average build. Joan was completely the opposite. She was tall and skinny and had spiked bright red hair and a ring in her nose. Her skin was dark, probably of African descent, though her features looked more Asian to Jinny's eye.

"And what do the two of you do?" she asked with feigned casualness.

"We're the muscle," Joan deadpanned, and Ryder rolled his eyes.

"John and Joan are specialists. They can get in where others can't and find things out for us. Right now, they're working on a job that could use someone with your talents, though."

Jinny raised her eyebrows. But before she could ask what kind of job, Joan jumped back in.

"No way. We're not bringing a newbie into this. We're too late in the game."

Ryder looked at her with a frown and shook his head. "Does that mean you've solved the security code problem?"

Joan frowned, but it was John who answered. "No. It's the last piece of the puzzle. Problem is, it keeps rotating. They change it every hour, on the hour. So even if we hacked in ahead of time, it wouldn't work. Besides that, their security is excellent. They would quickly detect any ongoing hacks and shut them down, not to mention that it could take an hour to hack them or ten with a trial-and-error approach. That means a live hack on the day of the job is out."

"We'll figure it out. We don't need her," Joan cut in sharply. "First rule is not to introduce an unknown element this close to go time."

"Normally, I would agree with you," Ryder responded. "But this job is too important to leave to chance. And Jinny can get us that code."

Joan shook her head, but before she could voice a retort, Jinny jumped in. "Anyone mind telling me what this job is?"

John looked at her appraisingly for a moment and then shrugged. "See that guy at the bar over there?" he motioned with his eyes. "The one in the green jacket."

Jinny tried to glance over at the bar without making it obvious but was pretty sure she failed miserably, given the look Joan shot her. The man was average height and stout, with a few days' worth of unshaven stubble and a perpetual frown. He had a half-empty beer glass in front of him and was studying its contents like they held the answer to a question he wasn't even sure of.

"What about him?" Jinny asked.

"He's a security guard for the local Galactic News Service bureau across the street from here," John replied. "They have something in that office that we need to get our hands on."

"What is it?" she pressed.

"No." Surprisingly, the refusal came not from Joan or even John but from Ryder. "This is your first job, Jinny. You get to take part, but we keep things on a need-to-know basis only. You simply don't need to know what we're trying for in order to help us on this one. Entiende?"

She frowned at him. "And what if I refuse to help unless you tell me?"

He shrugged. "Then we part ways here, amiga. Remember, *you* called *me* after all this time for a reason; even got yourself reassigned to our lovely planet. You want to make your life mean something? This is the price of admission."

She started at his words before she could stop herself. Jinny had mentioned nothing to Ryder about searching for meaning in what time she had left; he didn't know about the dreams or the timer on her sanity, either. But speakers were notorious for picking up on non-verbal cues and using them to weave their words and manipulate their subjects. In that regard, they were a little like readers. Still, what he said made sense. She wasn't ready to trust them without question; it was only natural that they weren't willing to trust her entirely yet, either.

"OK," she relented, "so where do I come in?"

"We have a key card that will get us into the building," John replied. "We know the exact location of the item we're trying to get. We can be in and out in less than ten minutes. What we don't have is the rotating security code for the building's alarm system."

She thought about that for a moment. "When do you plan to go?"

Joan answered before John could. "We could go right now if we had the blasted code. It's," she looked down at her watch, "11:24 PM. The building is right across the street, and he went off duty and left the office just after 11:03, at which point he would have had to enter the code to exit the building without the alarm going off. The code will change again at midnight. His watch contains an app that tells him the rotating code, but it's keyed to his biometrics and won't even show *him* the code if it detects elevated stress levels, so capturing and interrogating him wouldn't do us any good."

"But if you had the code he used to exit the building, you could use that to get in and out before midnight?" Jinny asked.

Joan regarded her skeptically. "Sure, but we'd have to get it in the next few minutes, and I'm willing to bet he isn't just going to share it with us."

"OK. No problem."

John and Joan looked at Jinny sharply. All Ryder did was give a half smile.

"Do you mind?" she asked Joan.

Joan kept her eyes on Jinny, brows knit together in concern, but slid out of the booth and stood up so she could exit. Jinny stood and walked past the woman without a backward glance, making her way directly to the bar.

She bellied up to the bar right next to the security guard but paid the man no mind. Holding up her hand, she signaled the bartender, a young man who eagerly came over to help what he saw as just another pretty young blond girl at his bar.

"Four shots of tequila for me and my friends," she said, purposefully slurring her words. A speaker would have done it better, or a blender, but faking drunkenness wasn't all that hard.

The bartender smiled and nodded and set about filling shot glasses in front of her from a bottle of surely cheap-as-dirt liquor from under the counter. He probably figured she was drunk enough not to catch that he was selling her swill. But Jinny didn't care about the actual drink; it had only given her an excuse to come to the bar.

"That'll be 30 credits," the bartender said, his eyes wandering down to her chest.

She resisted the urge to roll her eyes. She wasn't exactly well-endowed, but some men still couldn't keep their leering gaze off any girl. "Put it on the tab of my boyfriend over there." She gestured toward Ryder, who raised his hand for the bartender to see. The young man nodded and walked away after a frown toward Ryder and a lingering glance at Jinny.

She reached out her hands to take two shot glasses in each and, in doing so, brushed the back of her bare right hand against the exposed forearm of the security guard. He glanced over but said nothing, and Jinny pretended not to notice the momentary contact.

She walked back to the table with feigned clumsiness, spilling a little of the cheap tequila as she went. She set the drinks on the table, and Joan scooted over to let her back in the booth.

"What was that all about?" the other woman asked, disappointment in her voice. "You didn't even talk to the guy long enough to learn anything."

Jinny shrugged and took an exploratory sniff of her shot glass. If it tasted as bad as it smelled, she didn't want any, even if she hadn't sworn off drinking after the debacle with the predatory assemblyman back on Copernicus. Without looking up from the drink, she spoke casually. "The code is seven seven four A B one C eleven G nine."

Joan gaped, and John's eyes widened. The punk-looking woman spoke before her friend. "You're a blasted reader!" she said in a whisper that was loud enough to still draw a warning glare from Ryder. By the way the woman moved away from her and started rubbing her arms, Jinny knew she was trying to remember if she'd had any skin-to-skin contact, even a momentary brush, with Jinny. She hadn't, but it was a little fun to watch her squirm.

Jinny smiled and met the woman's surprised stare. "And you're a blender like your friend over here," she nodded toward John, "but you don't see me getting all worked up about it." She hadn't read them, but she was playing a hunch, and by Joan's reaction, she'd gotten it right.

Ryder laughed quietly, and Jinny's smile widened. She had no idea what she was getting herself into, but for the first time in her life, she felt genuine excitement at the unknown.

---

## PRESENT DAY; JUNE 7, 731 P.D.

Jordan Archer watched the pretty blond reader from across the Capitol Cafeteria. Despite the place's pedestrian name, it was one of the most exclusive restaurants in all of Houston. Only members of Congress, their staff, and their invited friends were allowed to eat there, and it had the reputation of being the place where more deals were made than anywhere else in the capital city and seat of United Earth's government.

Jordan's employer, the enigmatic Iasonas, had gotten him an invitation that allowed him to come and go as he pleased, using a specially hacked ID that changed with his ever-changing appearance. He still had to be careful never to space his visits to the place too closely together. The last thing he or his employer needed was to have one of the service staff or anyone else in the place notice someone who came in multiple days in a row but looked just a little different each day. Most citizens of United Earth had never knowingly met a blender, but that didn't mean they wouldn't get suspicious and recognize the signs of one. Being caught away from Australia would be highly inconvenient for him.

The reader was an interesting case. She wasn't from Australia like the rest of the readers in United Earth. She wasn't even from *Earth*. Archer's employer had asked him to keep a close eye on her, though the man, or woman, had been coy about what the plan was exactly. But for what he was getting paid, Archer could get comfortable being in the dark temporarily.

Now he watched her eat in the company of Congressman Corey O'Leary of the Red Party. She looked solemn, which Archer knew came from another frustrating day of hearings with members of Congress and bureaucrats who had no interest in listening to what she had to say. Archer himself didn't subscribe to any of the UE's major political parties—he worked for all of them with equal enthusiasm if they paid him well enough—but Iasonas had somehow secured him the videos of some of the closed-room sessions Jinny Ambrosa had testified in, urging the UE government to prepare for the impending Council invasion. After watching them, even Archer sympathized with her over the ruling Blue Party. Too bad none of those recordings would ever be made public. They contained little more information than what she'd already shared publicly, but Archer guessed that the average UE citizen wouldn't look kindly on the way the politicians were bullying her in the sessions. Perhaps, if this job allowed for it, he might consider leaking one or two of the videos just for fun.

Right now, he wasn't impersonating anyone in particular, just one more harried-looking congressional aide grabbing a quick, albeit gourmet, lunch before getting back to his 16-hour workday. Even so, he intentionally sat in a place where he could see Jinny Ambrosa, but she was unlikely to see him. The woman was from the colonies and had probably worked with enough blenders to know the telltale signs. There was such a thing as looking *too* average; that tended to happen to blenders when they spent a lot of time in public: they became an average amalgamation of everyone they came into contact with. And given the broad representation of ethnicities and races that lived and worked in Houston representing their constituencies across United Earth, Archer was starting to look a little funny, even though he'd only had a few days since impersonating Dave Watts, and Cecily had accompanied him to Houston so he could still use her to partially reset his appearance each night.

Archer studied and cataloged Ambrosa's mannerisms without even thinking about it. He had learned through practice and experience how to also change his mannerisms, accent, and even twitches and style of movement to match up with his chosen subject. So even though he knew he could never be called upon to mimic the young female reader—gender swaps like that simply weren't part of a blender's bag of tricks—he still studied her closely. At the very least, the knowledge could come in handy later when he made contact with her. People often naturally trusted those who spoke and acted like them.

Ambrosa got up from the table and walked off, probably toward the ladies' room, and Archer surreptitiously followed her with his eyes. She was attractive, he had to admit, and he certainly wouldn't mind spending enough time near her to take on some of her features. But he quickly shoved aside the thought. Not only was he unfailingly loyal to Cecily, but he was also on the job, and such thoughts were a distraction.

His implant buzzed, and he checked the message on his palm.

**Iasonas: *It's time to make contact.***

Archer stood up to go speak directly with O'Leary; they would have to talk quickly before Ambrosa returned. He stumbled halfway there as the congressman looked up from his meal and looked straight at him. Was that recognition that flashed in the man's eyes?

Another day, another sense of unending futility.

After lunch with Corey at the Capitol Cafeteria, Jinny had testified in yet another congressional meeting, this time in front of the Committee on Science and Technology. It had quickly become obvious that the committee members had no interest in talking about the coming invasion, but they did have all sorts of questions about colonial technology. Jinny was no expert by far, but they still hung on her every word, and they were especially anxious to learn about interactive holo displays and colonial star drives. It seemed that the Four Worlds were at least a hundred years behind the colonies in star drive technology, probably because the ships in the Sol system really had nowhere to go. The only thing they used their star drives for were hops to the outer system, particularly the Oort Cloud and beyond, where United Earth had a number of asteroid mining operations.

There was even a large planet beyond the Oort Cloud called Scotus, so far from Sol's light that it was nothing but a pitch-black, rocky wasteland, and so close to the mysterious border of the Castilian Rift that ships attempting to go much farther beyond its orbit were never heard from again—no one knew what it was about the Rift that prevented even sublight ships from traveling through it safely.

That should have made Scotus a place to be avoided, but the planet, it turned out, had an unusual concentration of the rare metals used in the construction of warship hulls. As such, both United Earth and Mars had laid claim to Scotus, fighting several wars and smaller battles over it throughout the centuries before finally settling on an uneasy détente, in which the UE mined Scotus' northern hemisphere while Mars mined the southern.

So even though they had less use for their star drives, the members of the Committee on Science and Technology were practically salivating over colonial star drive tech, which would shorten the already-short ride from Earth to Scotus by an hour or so. Jinny thought it was all a bit silly, but one of the congresswomen raved about how that hour savings would add an 18% increase to mine productivity.

Whatever. At least they weren't calling her a liar like Hastings or most of the other Blue Party committee leaders. So, Jinny was happy to answer their questions, though the discussion was incredibly boring.

Afterward, she and Corey had returned to the O'Leary's house for dinner with Debra, but Jinny had begged off an after-dinner game of chess, insisting she wanted to get a little extra rest. The truth was that she was horribly sleep-deprived from her nightly dreams, and she desperately needed as much rest as she could get. So, she quickly bathed and went to bed, taking an over-the-counter sleep aid in the hope that it would put her in a deep enough slumber to avoid another round of nightmares.

It didn't work. She tossed and turned throughout the entire night and woke up screaming once again.

If anything, tonight's latest nightmare had been among the most disturbing of the last few weeks. She had played the role of a young woman she had read on Copernicus, Ophelia O'Neil, who had been murdered in gruesome fashion during a home invasion and assault. Normally, a reader with Jinny's limited experience should never have been allowed to read the victim of such a violent crime, but a snafu of scheduling had put her as the only on-call reader in the area that could reach Ophelia's corpse in time to get the information the Guard had needed.

That Ophelia's assailant had been caught, jailed, and later executed for his crimes didn't change the trauma Jinny still carried from the reading. She had felt a lingering sense of the violation the young woman had experienced for weeks afterward. Now, dreaming of the event from Ophelia's point of view, those feelings came rushing back and left her gasping for breath and struggling to remind herself that it wasn't *her* memory she was reliving.

She looked at the clock. It was 6:15 AM. In a few hours, she and Corey would board the Loop for another useless trip to Houston to talk to politicians who were more concerned about handing out social entitlements to buy reelection votes than actually saving the people they represented. It almost made Jinny think the Council had gotten a few things right. *Almost.* Even in her most cynical moments, she had to admit that at least on Earth, the government couldn't order anyone killed on a whim; even Tyrus had noted that, as far as he could tell, the UE government had no secret cadre of assassins playing the role the alphas had for the Twenty.

Beyond that, people in the UE generally had freedoms that no one in the 47 Colonies enjoyed. Whereas the Twenty controlled the media in the colonies and suppressed most information that could paint the Council government in a poor light, there were entire news services on Earth that did little *but* criticize the government.

Then there was the religious freedom. Alan Daily's mother had instilled in him a sense of religious belief that he had kept hidden his entire adult life; *being* religious on its own wasn't strictly a crime in the 47 Colonies, but *practicing* religion in any way was. Even having copies of religious texts in your home was grounds for arrest, as Jinny had learned in her first loyalty readings with Clarissa Lowry. So, Alan had been careful not to let his beliefs become known to his fellow guardmembers. But in reading Alan multiple times, Jinny had seen the depth and strength of his trust in what his mother had taught him.

Still, those teachings had been relatively vague, and Alan had struggled to solidify his ambiguous beliefs in the absence of any interchange of ideas with other like-minded individuals. Only a few banned religious books, passed along by his mother, helped him put some limited structure into how he worshipped in solitude. But even those he rarely picked up, ever cautious that a random loyalty reading would expose him.

When Alan died, Jinny had made a vow to further explore that part of his life that had been so important to him. She wasn't convinced that religion was a good or a bad thing, nor did she feel a personal need to learn about any deity, but she made the promise as a way to stay connected to the one man she'd ever loved. Perhaps it would serve to keep a small part of him alive in her.

Coming to Earth had given her the chance to do that. Churches abounded here, and once she'd learned what to look for, she'd been surprised by just how many religions there were. While Tyrus had been in the hospital, she'd used periods of silent vigil next to his bed to search the Internet and study a variety of Earth belief systems. Some felt somewhat aligned with what Alan had believed; others felt incredibly different. But none of them matched up perfectly or made her feel any real desire to keep learning about them.

When Tyrus had been released from the hospital, she'd started visiting churches in person, hoping that it would be different to hear the various beliefs in person. In some ways it was—there was an indescribable but vague feeling of peace she got in some churches more than others. Even so, her frustration continued to grow. For three weeks she visited three or four different churches per week, and all had different teachings, none of which felt particularly close to Alan's beliefs. Worse, the visits quickly began to feel like a chore, and she felt guilty for doing nothing more than going through the motions to keep her promise to Alan.

Just two weeks before, she had decided it was time to give up. Maybe she would revisit her quest after she had somehow saved the Four Worlds from the coming invasion. But until then, it was easy to justify halting her search, telling herself it was only a distraction from her main purpose in coming to the Sol system.

However, this morning, after the horrific nightmare she'd just experienced, she felt a sudden urge to talk to someone, *anyone*, about what she was going through. It was possible, she hoped, that sharing her problems with someone else would grant her some temporary relief from the dreams. Something similar had happened when she'd eventually told Ryder Cruz and her fellow rebels about her special abilities—as if the cathartic release of stress at sharing her biggest secret gave her a reprieve from the nightmares. It had only lasted a few weeks before the deaths of Ryder, John, and Joan brought the nightmares roaring back. But it *had* worked until then, so maybe could work again.

She knew it was a long shot, but she felt she had to try *something*.

Several times now, she had toyed with the idea of telling Tyrus or even Riggs about the nightmares and what they portended. But she had held off for two very important reasons. First, she didn't want to burden either of them when they each already had so many worries. Second, and more critically, she didn't want to change the way either of them saw her. She was conscious of the fact that both men had placed her on a pedestal; Tyrus especially had invested her with every virtuous attribute he could, including several she didn't feel she deserved. However, she had sensed early on that the man *needed* to see her that way, especially since he had betrayed everything he'd held dear for his entire life to follow her on her quest to aid the rebellion. It was as if she had replaced the Council in the big ex-enacter's mind as the ultimate authority that he would follow.

That thought alone was scary, and she sometimes had to try hard in Tyrus' presence not to show him just how uncomfortable his dogged loyalty made her. But she also suspected that telling him about the nightmares and her slow descent into insanity would risk breaking the big man's already-fragile mental state. Because no matter how calm and assured he appeared to the rest of the world, Jinny knew that underneath it all, he was like a starship that had lost its station-keeping thrusters, drifting wantonly and clinging to whatever he could—in this case her—to give his shattered world any sense.

So, telling Tyrus was out of the question. And Riggs... She had no idea where that relationship was going, but telling him she would soon have a psychotic break didn't feel like it would help matters.

Maybe instead, she could find a religious leader to talk to; supposedly, they had to keep anything told them in confidence, so that gave her a measure of protection from the government or her friends finding out. Even then, there would be the risk of exposure, but it felt manageable next to the bigger risk of not doing anything and accepting her fate.

She slipped out of bed and got dressed quickly, then made her way to the guest house's small garage, where Corey and Debra had left a hovercar for her use; the Earthers called them 'aircars' but she couldn't shake the habit of the colonial name. Five minutes later, she was on Interstate Five, heading south into San Diego proper.

She had no idea where she was going, but the simple and familiar act of driving immediately lessened her anxiety to a more manageable level. After several minutes of savoring the experience, she told the car's AI to search for a church that was open this early, not really expecting to find any. But to her surprise, the aircar directed her to one that was only a few miles away, just off the freeway.

The car pulled to a stop outside a relatively plain-looking building that lacked the adornment of many of the churches she'd seen. She could see lights on in the windows but no movement. For several moments, she left the car on, debating whether to drive away and forget her morning's quest or push forward. Now that she was here, the idea of telling anyone, even a religious leader sworn to secrecy, about her nightmares was suddenly much scarier than it had been less than a half hour earlier when she'd left the house.

She put the car back into gear and was about to leave when the building's side door opened, and a man wearing a shirt and tie walked out carrying a bag of garbage toward a dumpster in the small parking lot. The image of the man dressed formally but taking care of such a mundane task almost made her laugh out loud and distracted her from her decision to flee. Too late, she realized that he had spotted her car and was making his way toward it after dropping off the trash.

He neared and waved cheerfully, and Jinny lowered the window in resignation.

"Can I help you, Miss?" Now that he was closer, she could see that he was easily in his sixties or seventies, with a shock of unruly white hair and laugh lines around his eyes. He smiled widely as he greeted her.

"Uh. I... I guess I was hoping to talk to someone," she answered haltingly, feeling that the words sounded ridiculous as they left her mouth. How did she explain that she was a reader from another part of the galaxy who was having nightmares that would eventually drive her into a psychotic break, but probably not before she failed to save this man's planet from an invasion fleet full of fanatically obedient soldiers? Even in her head, it sounded like the plot of a bad holo vid.

He ignored her awkwardness and kept smiling back at her. "Well, this is a pretty good place to talk to someone, in my opinion," he said in a friendly tone. "My wife is inside; we're just cleaning the building, but we're happy to chat with you, and you can tell us whatever you came to say."

Realizing that she couldn't drive away now without looking rude, Jinny reluctantly got out of the car. Standing now outside the vehicle, she could see that the man was about her height, and if he meant her any harm, she was fairly confident she could take him on or run away faster than he could follow. But his manner was so open and friendly that she almost instantly felt safe and secure in his presence.

He led her toward the front door of the church, chatting with her like they were old friends about the weather, the model of her hovercar—apparently, it was a really nice one, though Jinny didn't know much about cars, having always used the Reader Corps motor pool and never owning one for herself—and asking if she was following the local football team that was apparently in a rebuilding year.

She mostly let him do the talking, and they entered the building where warm and cheery lighting revealed a simple foyer with comfortable-looking couches and paintings of various religious scenes on the wall, none of which meant anything to her. But it had a homey feel and settled some of her unease. Every moment in the man's presence, she felt less like bolting back to the car and the safety of the O'Leary's house.

He invited her to sit on one of the couches and excused himself to find his wife. Jinny almost still made for the door as soon as he disappeared, but curiosity and her need to talk to someone won their battle with her fear, and she sat down and decided to play things out. She had come this far, after all.

A moment later, the man returned with a woman of similar age, dressed in a simple blouse and skirt. She sported almost identical whitish hair and laugh lines to her husband but had darker brown skin that hinted at South American ancestry, assuming Jinny wasn't mistaken in her Earth geography.

"I'm Juliana Taylor," the woman introduced herself, smiling and offering her hand. She had a husky, rich voice that reminded Jinny of Clarissa Lowry's, further putting her at ease. She reached up and took the woman's offered hand with her own gloved hand in greeting.

"May I?" Juliana asked, gesturing toward the couch cushion next to Jinny.

"Of course."

She sat down and looked back up at her husband. "Paul, why don't you let me and this young woman chat? The chapel still needs vacuuming. I'll come get you if we need you."

"Yes, dear," the man replied in a long-suffering tone belied by a grin and a quick wink at the two women. When he had departed the room, and the sound of a distant vacuum cleaner could be heard, Juliana Taylor turned to face Jinny on the couch.

"Now tell me, dear, what did you want to talk with someone about?"

Jinny squirmed, unsure of how to broach the sensitive topic.

The other woman gave her a moment to respond, and when she didn't, she reached out and patted Jinny's knee lightly. "Come now, Reader Ambrosa, there's no need to be nervous. You can tell me whatever you'd like."

Jinny looked up at Juliana and met the other woman's eyes, her heart abruptly falling into her stomach. She supposed it had been naïve of her to hope that the woman and her husband wouldn't recognize her, but she was disappointed, nonetheless. With the stigma against readers in the Four Worlds, she was prepared for the woman to show her the door. At least two pastors at churches she'd visited had done just that, one telling her that reading was the 'devil's work', whatever that meant. Even those that had welcomed her had viewed her with a healthy measure of wariness and suspicion. In most cases, it had made her so uncomfortable she had left their sermons and meetings early.

To her surprise, however, Juliana Taylor's facial expression didn't change. She still had the same warm smile that reached her eyes. Finally, Jinny worked up the courage to respond in some way. "Anything I tell you is confidential, right? Just between you and me?"

Taylor nodded. "Of course. Paul and I are missionaries. So, unless you admit a major crime to either of us, we won't tell a soul. There are laws that protect anything confessed to a member of the clergy. I won't even tell my husband anything you tell me unless you give me permission to."

Taking heart at the woman's promise, Jinny thought carefully about how to start, staring down at her gloved hands as she mulled over the right words.

Misinterpreting her silence for reluctance, Juliana reached out one of her hands for Jinny's. "May I?"

Jinny looked back up at her in confusion, unsure of what the woman meant. Slowly, the missionary reached out with her other hand and gently removed Jinny's glove. Then, when she didn't resist, Juliana lightly grasped her bare hand in her own.

Jinny gasped. Many readings were painful affairs for her. When she read someone, she got *every* memory, the good and the bad. For many of the people she'd read in her career with the Council Reader Corps—murder victims, criminals, abuse survivors, and even disgruntled government employees—the negative outweighed the positive in the depth and color of the memories, if not in sheer quantity. Even before the nightmares had begun, Jinny had felt like a small part of *her* died almost every time she read someone.

There had been a few exceptions that were far more positive, like Alan Daily, her friend Sakura, and others. But even those had eventually soured when she'd been witness to their deaths, either via reading the corpse afterward as with Sakura or direct experience as with Alan. But now, she had another positive set of memories: those of Juliana Taylor.

It wasn't that the woman was free of any negative memories or had lived a particularly easy or even pleasant life. She had been born in poverty, struggled in school as a child, suffered multiple miscarriages in her first marriage, and eventually divorced an abusive husband. These memories were sharp in Jinny's reading of the woman, but they were all overcome and overshadowed by the woman's indomitable spirit.

Determined to break out of her family's poverty rather than stay trapped in its cycle, Juliana had cherished her opportunities for education. And when a learning disability had made school difficult for her, she had doubled her efforts and taken help from sympathetic teachers who knew that, in the slums of Venezuela, the young woman's only chance at a life of any kind was to learn everything she could.

By the end of high school, Juliana Encarnación, her maiden name, had the grades necessary to make it to one of the better colleges in South America. There she had reveled in the new opportunities to learn. She had also met her first husband there, an idealistic and charismatic student named Lyle. They had shared a year of marital bliss before her first miscarriage shattered their early hopes of starting a family. Something broke inside Lyle when they lost that first baby, and he had grown distant from his bride. Eager to repair the damage to their marriage, Juliana had gotten pregnant again. But when that pregnancy ended the same way, Lyle had overtly blamed her and turned toward abusing her in retribution for the imagined sins and defects that he was convinced had earned her the tragedy of losing two of their children.

Juliana had suffered under Lyle's hand for five years, leaving him multiple times but always coming back when he promised to change. But the change never lasted, and finally, broken and bleeding from the man's latest beating, she had left him for good with the help of an old college roommate and a sympathetic doctor who had treated her wounds.

It was a horrible story at first as Jinny read the woman; it was so similar to so many stories of tragedy that she had *experienced* in her many readings. However, Juliana hadn't let the tragedies hold her back. She had put her trust in the God she somehow still believed in—Jinny couldn't fathom how the woman could keep faith in *any* higher power after having been treated so poorly by life—and pushed forward. Recovering with the help of good friends from before her marriage and a few religious leaders, Juliana went back to school and finished the degree that she had put on hold to marry Lyle and start a family. With the same work ethic that had boosted her through high school, she studied her way to nearly the top of her graduating class in just two years.

After graduation, Juliana moved to North America, seeking a fresh start. For several years, she worked in her chosen field, counseling young women who, like her, found themselves in abusive relationships. She helped many of them recognize that they deserved better and should finally leave, but she also lost many of them when they could never come to grips with such a weighty decision. For years she toiled, helping some and losing others, but never giving up on any of them.

Then, in her early thirties, she met Paul Taylor. Paul was a few years older than her and had lost his first wife to an aircar accident, leaving him alone to raise their two children, both under the age of ten. In him, Juliana found a kindred spirit in need of healing like herself. Together they faced their grief and challenges, and she grew to love Paul and his children.

Two years after meeting, Paul asked Juliana to marry him. She said no. The pain of her relationship with Lyle had largely faded from her day-to-day thoughts, but not enough that she felt she could trust *any* man that deeply ever again. She'd expected Paul to leave after that, but he had done something that surprised her. He had stayed. And never once had he shown the slightest resentment of her rejection. To her delight, things went right back to normal, as if the proposal had never happened.

A year later, almost to the day, Paul asked her again to marry him. She again said no. This time, however, it wasn't because she didn't trust him. Rather, she was too afraid to tell him she couldn't have children of her own. She didn't feel that she could inflict that upon Paul, who had talked of wanting a large family beyond the two children he already had. But again, he stayed, even when she could not openly explain *why* she continued to reject his proposal.

A year later, he asked her a third time. This time, she broke down and tearfully explained that she couldn't give him the additional children he so desperately wanted. In response, Paul looked her in the eyes and slid the engagement ring onto her finger. "With you, I have everything I could ever want or need." There were tears in his own eyes to match hers, and Juliana finally said yes.

Five years of hard but happy marriage—full of ups and downs but also of growing trust, love, and mutual respect—passed like the blink of an eye. Then a miracle. Juliana had gone to the emergency room one evening for a pain in her lower abdomen, and the doctors had found a tumorous growth. Skilled surgeons had been called in to remove it, and after the successful procedure, one of the doctors sat down with Juliana and Paul and explained that the growth, undetected by previous scans, had been the cause of her miscarriages and that it would be safe now for them to start a family.

Fast forward another 30 years, and Paul and Juliana Taylor had four living children, including Paul's original two whom Juliana had raised as her own, and now seven grandchildren whom they doted on and spoiled, to the chagrin of their parents. Their life had been far from easy; there had been financial struggles, health scares, and even the death of their fifth and youngest child to a rare and incurable disease.

But through it all, Juliana and Paul had leaned on each other and on their shared faith in a God they had never seen but deeply believed in.

Juliana Taylor was the first person whom Jinny had read since arriving on Earth. And as the woman finally withdrew her hand, she knew her cheeks were wet with tears that flowed freely.

"How?" she asked. "How did you stay so happy through all of *that*?" She posed the question without thinking; she was so sleep-deprived and in such a state of mind that it just slipped out before she could stop herself. When she saw the look in the other woman's eyes, she felt her heart drop once again.

"You saw more than most readers, didn't you?" the woman asked in awe, and panic rose inside Jinny. In a single unguarded moment—a single second of stupidity—she had let her most deeply held secret, and not the one she'd come to share, slip to a *stranger*. But then, through her tears and growing fear, she saw something she hadn't expected. Juliana Taylor was smiling broadly.

"Oh, darling," the woman said, reading the confirmation of her question in Jinny's eyes, "you are so special. What a wonderful gift you've been given. But I imagine it is also a terrible burden. Tell me, is that why you're here?"

Jinny nodded, not trusting her own voice at that moment. Her surprise increased when the woman did not shy away but instead reached out and enveloped her in a gentle but strong hug. Skin touched skin again as the woman's cheek brushed hers, and once again, she relived all the moments of Juliana Taylor's life—the bad and the good. To her continued shock, reading the woman a second time was a comfort and gave her a feeling of familiarity and home that she had never experienced with her own family and had read in few others. Tears sprung to her eyes.

"You poor dear," Juliana said, still holding her tight, and it surprised Jinny to hear the matron's voice break as she cried along with her. "I imagined you can't tell *anyone* about this, can you?"

In a raspy voice, Jinny finally spoke. "I'm so scared. I don't know what's happening to me."

And right there, she broke down the remaining walls she'd spent her entire life building. She told Juliana Taylor about what her father had done to her, about her special abilities, and finally, about her nightmares and the horrible prognosis she'd received from Clarissa Lowry. She'd come looking for a place to unload her burdens but had never imagined she could even open up the way she did, sharing things with this woman that she'd never shared with anyone else. But somehow, the fact that Juliana was a relative stranger made it easier than she imagined it would have been to tell any of her friends, especially Tyrus.

At the end of her tearful monologue, Juliana pulled her into another hug, patting her back and soothing her the way her mother had done in the few years before Frank had killed her. In the background, the droning sound of Paul's distant vacuuming lent a comforting, domestic air to the exchange.

"I'm sure no one who hasn't been through what you're going through has any real answers to give you," Juliana said. "But will you allow an old woman to give you two pieces of advice?"

Jinny leaned back as the woman let her out of the hug. Part of her yearned for the embrace again. She had hugged so few people in her life: her mother, Alan, Riggs, and Tyrus when he'd finally woken up in the hospital. It felt *so* good to be held by another human being again that it broke her heart for it to be over.

Still, Juliana Taylor didn't break all contact. She kept one hand on Jinny's shoulder as if sensing that the girl needed a comforting touch.

"First," she began, "your gift has a purpose. Everything in life has a purpose, though we often don't know what it is for a long time. When my first husband abused me the way he did, I thought it was my fault, and it took me a long time to realize that I bore none of the blame. But once I got through that, I was able to build a life around helping other women in the same situation, helping them in ways I would have never been capable of if I didn't understand their pain firsthand. You may not know your purpose now, but I *promise* you have one.

"Second, no matter how hard things get, you *can* get through it. But it's important to recognize that you can't do it alone. Just like when I had to get over those years with Lyle, I couldn't do it without a lot of help. For me, that came from friends, family, and, most importantly,

God. You may take a different path, but you need to let someone else bear the burden with you.

The woman stopped speaking but smiled warmly and beamed at Jinny with a powerful sense of peace and love that she hadn't experienced since the brief time with Alan on the *Lucille*, the only period in their brief relationship when they hadn't been in immediate danger of capture or death.

"How do you know?" she asked.

"About your purpose? Because I've yet to meet someone who didn't have one. Even Lyle, whose purpose may only have been to give me the experience I needed to help others. I also sense that you are a genuinely good person. I've seen the news and read your story. You came here to save all of us, even though you'd never met us or even knew we existed until a few days before you arrived. But you still came, and that level of selflessness is uncommon and special."

The words hit Jinny so hard that she started crying anew, burying her face in her hands. She felt Juliana put an arm around her shoulders, holding her as she sobbed. They stayed that way for several minutes, and Jinny let herself feel the bevy of emotions, good and bad, that she had suppressed for so much of her life in the name of duty, first to the Council, then to the Rebellion, and finally to the people of the Four Worlds.

Finally, her tears spent, she looked back up at the older woman. "And what about God? How do you know He's even there? I was always taught…." She stopped, not wanting to challenge the woman's faith but desperately wanting to understand how such a self-sufficient, strong person could believe in superstition with no proof. She had wondered the same about Alan when she'd first read him and had yet to find an answer in her time on Earth.

Juliana smiled again. "You were taught that God didn't exist; that he *couldn't* exist. But frankly, I wouldn't want to live in a world where that's true. Even in my darkest moments with Lyle, I felt Him near, watching over me. It's so hard to explain to someone who hasn't experienced it for themselves, but trust me that He *will* be there for you as well. He will help you bear your burdens. It's OK if you don't believe

## THE FOUR WORLDS - SUBVERSION

me now, or ever. He still won't abandon you. Even if you don't believe in Him, He will believe in you."

When she finished, the two sat in silence, Jinny absorbing what the woman had told her, unsure of it but trying to memorize each word. None of them gave her any solid ideas on how to solve her problems, either with the politicians of United Earth or with the nightmares and her descent into insanity. And the words alone certainly didn't convince her to believe in any god or religion. But they made her feel a sense of peace and rightness as if they might reveal more answers to her if she studied them later. She recognized in that feeling a parallel in how Alan had thought of his own vague religious beliefs. He'd often been frustrated by how little he understood the few things his mother had tried to teach him, but he'd always held out a hope that someday things would become clearer to him.

That hope was something Jinny now desperately needed for herself. Perhaps the difference between religious faith and simple hope might have been less than she had supposed; that thought felt like she might have cracked some fundamental code of Alan's beliefs. But it still didn't give her any concrete solutions *now*.

After a few long moments, she broke the silence, putting her lingering doubts into words. "I want to believe there is something that can help me out there, but I just haven't been able to find it yet. And time is running out for me. Right now, it just feels like a race to see whether the Council invades before or after I lose my mind."

Juliana smiled sympathetically and patted her knee again. "Have you tried talking to other readers about this?"

Jinny shook her head. She'd asked Corey the day before to organize a visit to Australia for her, mostly so she could satisfy her curiosity about the Twenty's motivation for invading the Four Worlds. But he had gently deflected her request. She had never even considered asking the readers there about her nightmares, but the idea now sounded so obvious that she resolved to press harder on him that very day.

Misreading her hesitation as further doubt, Juliana continued. "There is an entire continent of readers down in Australia. Why not go and ask them your questions? It's possible they can make sense of what's happening to you."

"Thank you. I think I'll do that," Jinny whispered. When she spoke with Corey today, she wouldn't take no for an answer.

Juliana patted her hand again. "That's wonderful. But promise me something, will you?"

Jinny nodded, not caring what the woman might ask, but resolved to give it if within her power.

Juliana Taylor leaned in close and smiled broadly, the crows' feet around her eyes giving her an air of kind wisdom. "Whatever happens, promise me you'll come back and tell me how it went."

Jinny nodded and, before she could stop herself or even think about it too hard, threw her arms around the woman and surrendered herself to another warm embrace, letting the hug and the soft noise of the distant vacuum soothe her frayed nerves.

# CHAPTER 6

## THREE AND A HALF WEEKS LATER; JULY 2, 731 P.D.; FOUR MONTHS AFTER THE REVELATIONS

Admiral Chen looked at the disembodied head of Keeper Ian Petrov, floating in front of her above the ready room desk on *Excelsior*, and steeled herself for the difficult discussion to come.

"I've read your full report, Admiral," the man said, nodding to her. "But do me the favor of summarizing the key points so I can make sure I didn't miss anything."

Chen took a deep breath and then started speaking. "Your Excellency, as we prepare for the invasion of the Four Worlds, ships aren't the problem. We already have a larger Navy than our intelligence suggests the combined Four Worlds have. But our personnel are untested, and most have never seen actual combat. We even lack the same experience as the Guard Space Force. At least they occasionally fight pirates and rebels.

"Furthermore, the enacters from Project Epsilon are not as naturally obedient as we had hoped. I have sent you my reports on them and their minor rebellions. They chafe under their new status and must often learn the hard way that their bodies and minds will not allow them to disobey. But even their merest hesitations may spell doom in actual battle. And then there are those that are not even imprinted on the Council, all of whom we have put to death.

"With the enacters we now have in training, we only have enough personnel to crew half the fleet. However, between their inexperience and minor rebellions, we can only crew a quarter of the fleet reliably. I project this puts us well beyond the year deadline to invade the Four Worlds. If current trends hold, we are looking at up to an additional year's delay."

The Keeper frowned. "That is unacceptable, Admiral Chen. I expect you to do better."

Chen resisted the urge to frown back. Why did politicians insist on such vague statements? *Of course*, he expected more; he demanded it. But he was noticeably short on suggestions on how to get there, and she could only work with the tools she had been given. Her thoughts gave her a light headache, even as the logic of her internal objections warred with the emotional and subconscious imperatives of her enacter gene. It was an unpleasant experience to *know* you were right but to *feel* that you were doing something wrong.

"Respectfully, sir, we cannot meet the deadline with our current resources and the slow progress of Project Epsilon. But I do have some ideas on how to close the gap."

Petrov's frown remained, but he raised an eyebrow. "I am listening." Clearly, he *hadn't* read her full report as he'd claimed to, or he would already know what she was going to suggest. That might not be a bad thing; it meant he wouldn't have objections already prepared.

"First, sir, I suggest we begin drawing enacters from the Guard, especially the Space Force or Paralimitary Force. They are natural enacters, not those created by Epsilon, so they are already conditioned and loyal and have been from childhood. With them, there will be none of the minor rebellions we are getting with the newly created enacters. And we can take advantage of the training they already have. They will assimilate into the fleet far faster."

She saw the Keeper wince at her words and wondered how much of the rumors that had reached her from Panamar were true. Was it possible that the Guard's enacters were somehow breaking their programming as well? She shook off the thought and continued. She wasn't expecting him to agree to that suggestion anyway. It was a purposeful overreach so that he would be more amenable to compromise to the alternative she would offer later.

"Second, we need to battle test our fleet and our crews. The more they fight together, the more they will be prepared for the war that is to come. I believe that even the new enacters will overcome their reticence to follow orders if they see it as the difference between life and death. Only combat can impart that. I propose that the Council Navy immediately take over all anti-piracy actions from the Guard Space Force *and* that we take over the hunt for the rebel fleet that fled Panamar two weeks ago."

The Keeper shook his head. "What you suggest would require making the existence of the Navy public. We are in no position to do that."

"Yes, sir," she continued, trying to keep a level of confidence in her voice. "The original plan was to make them public right after Rinali, to answer the threat of the supposed Four Worlds' fleet that destroyed the station along with its Guard forces, and—"

"Those blasted Revelations made that option untenable," the Keeper spat. "All that planning down the drain because of Siefred and that pet reporter of hers."

There wasn't a question in the man's words, so Chen swallowed and continued. "Yes, sir. But that doesn't mean the plan still can't work. The government has never fully admitted one way or another what happened at Rinali and the Rift, so there is no official explanation for it. What if there was *another* event in which the Guard were to be attacked by enemy forces? Then you would have evidence to further back up the originally planned story."

The Keeper shook his head again, this time more emphatically, and she knew she was losing him quickly. "It has been over three months since the catastrophe at Rinali, Admiral. Where *your* forces failed to stop that ship from getting through the Rift. We've worked too hard to quash the story of what happened there to bring it back up now, even to attempt to spin it to our benefit."

Chen resisted pointing out that it had been the late and unlamented

Admiral Piers Lamont who had commanded the fleet during that engagement, not her, nor did she point out that the escape of a small schooner through the Rift had nothing to do with the internal PR nightmare the colonies and the Council government had faced afterward. Politicians didn't like it when you called out their illogical arguments, and Chen was experiencing enough pain already as it was.

"Sir, what I am saying is that we should stage *another* attack, but this time take advantage of the rumors flying out of Panamar. Instead of blaming this attack on the Four Worlds, let's use the genuine threat of the rebel fleet. Then we can expose via a careful public relations campaign that the Council, in all its wisdom, had ordered the creation of a small navy—an auxiliary to the Guard Space Force even—because of the rising threat from the rebels and the Four Worlds. Basically, we go with *your* original plan, which was sound, just delayed a bit to give the public another reason to believe it."

She saw his mouth quirk up a bit as she indirectly praised him. She pushed forward.

"That will allow us to openly employ our naval ships in anti-rebel and anti-piracy engagements. We can do so with small task forces so that the full size of the fleet never reaches the public view. It will simply seem that the Council was being prudent by preparing a modest, secret force to keep the people of the colonies safe. It will also give our people the vital experience they need before we go up against the more tested militaries in the Four Worlds."

She stopped there, afraid to go further until she saw his reaction. For a while, Petrov said nothing but stared at something out of Chen's field of view. Then he looked back at her and gave a small nod.

"It's an interesting proposition, Admiral, and one that I am willing to take to the Council for discussion. How, exactly, would you propose staging this attack? Using your forces with false markings as we did at Rinali won't work if we're trying to duplicate a ragtag rebel fleet."

Chen smiled. He had asked the exact question she was hoping for. "Sir, I know the Jaguari Pirates were virtually all destroyed at Rinali, but they were hardly the most capable or heavily armed pirate group in the galaxy even before that. I'm sure one of the other groups can be… persuaded to be in the right place at the right time to simulate the rebel fleet."

The Keeper actually smiled at this thought. "Yes, I'm sure we can arrange something. Perhaps the Vultura group would be a good patsy this time around. Some of their activities of late have displeased the Council greatly, and this could be an opportunity to make two problems go away." Then his smile disappeared, and he was all business again. "Admiral, we will consider *this* recommendation, but until we see how it all works out, we will *not* be giving you any of the enacters from the Guard. The Council has already made it clear that we need the Guard where they are, for now, to keep peace in the colonies. Perhaps after successfully taking the Navy public, we can reconsider."

"Yes, sir. Thank you, sir." She was all right with that answer; she had a backup proposal ready. "May I suggest that if we can't draw natural enacters from the Guard, that we perhaps focus Project Epsilon on exclusively converting merchant fleet spacers to enacters? They will at least already have the basic training of crewing spaceships. That, coupled with the crucible of combat, may hopefully be enough to turn them into obedient crewers and perhaps even capable officers." It was a risky proposal; they were having the same disobedience issues with the merchant crewers they were already getting through the Epsilon pipeline, but if *all* their new enacters came in that way, at least they could focus less on the basics of crewing a spaceship and more on loyalty conditioning. Chen's training officers thought it just might work.

Petrov considered this for a full 20 seconds and then nodded. "I can see how that would be helpful, Admiral. I will discuss it with the Project Epsilon leads and see if we can make the adjustment.

"Await my next communication with the Council's decision on all of your proposals. Until then, please draw up a limited engagement plan to hunt down the real rebel fleet, as you have proposed. If the Council approves your plan, we will want to move quickly."

She nodded respectfully. "Of course, sir. There is one more thing, however."

The Keeper glared at her and frowned deeply but stopped from cutting off the line. For a moment, Chen wondered if she should back off and not push the man too far in one meeting. But she shook off the nerves. She and her senior officers agreed strongly on this next point. Even if it hurt her to bring it up, she owed it to the men and women under her command to at least present it.

Chen consciously straightened her spine. "Your Excellency, we know so little of what awaits us in the Four Worlds. We need more intel so we can properly prepare our forces. That intelligence gap, coupled with the need to test more of our forces in combat, leads me to recommend that I be allowed to lead a mission to the Four Worlds *now.*"

The man shook his head in exasperation. "I'm confused, Admiral. Did you not just finish telling me that your forces are not ready and will not be ready for quite some time? How can we possibly move on the Four Worlds now?" There was an angry tone to his voice that warned Chen against continuing to push, but she shoved aside her doubts and pressed forward anyway.

"Yes, sir, but I am not speaking of the invasion. Rather, I am suggesting a reconnaissance in force. We send an over-strength task force that still represents only a fraction of our power. It will allow us to discover exactly what the forces there look like, as well as the political situation. We still don't know if we will be fighting a united Four Worlds military or each planet separately."

The Keeper shook his head again. "Our scouting missions through the Goat Path have already shown that there are three distinct governments in the Sol system and that Mars and Earth are not likely to fight together. What more could we possibly learn by sending through a larger force where they can see it?"

The Goat Path was one of the Council government's most closely guarded secrets. For 800 years, conventional wisdom and knowledge had held that there was only *one* path through the Castilian Rift. But a hundred years ago, the Council had started a campaign to find alternative routes. They sent survey ships along the edges of the Rift, scanning for space-time signatures similar to those found at the Back Door.

It had taken 70 years, but they had finally found a likely candidate on the edge of the Odyssean Waste, a large swatch of star systems with no known planets suitable for terraforming or colonization. It had taken 15 years more and dozens of lost survey ships to map the actual path through the Rift from that point. Part of the challenge had been that the new path continually changed and shifted, and a ship had to be fitted with a special and extremely expensive sensor suite to ride the void through it, surfacing multiple times, taking new readings, and making course adjustments before submerging again.

Finally, one of the survey ships had gotten through, finding that the Goat Path, called that because of a long-forgotten war on Old Earth in a place called Thermopylae, let a ship surface in the Sol system outside the orbit of Neptune and well above the ecliptic plane. That put the path's exit in an ideal position, where it would be incredibly unlikely for Earth or any of the other Four Worlds or their navies to detect a ship surfacing, no matter what kind of sensors they were using.

The Council government had been using the Goat Path ever since to send spy ships to gather intelligence on the Sol system. They had even built the secret military installation at Delta 3, where Chen now sat, within the Waste and close to the entrance to the Goat Path for convenience in invading the Four Worlds. That assumed the Council's scientists could ever figure out how to send a proper *warship* through rather than just small survey or spy ships. So far, any attempt to send anything larger than a schooner had resulted in the ships being lost to the void.

"The surveys through the Goat Path," Chen answered carefully, "have gained most of their intelligence by listening in on unencrypted comm traffic and media signals. We have learned, for instance, that Earth and Luna share a government, but that Mars and Europa are separate polities. But there are two critical items of intel that we have *not* gotten from those missions."

"Go on," the Keeper prompted, his eyebrows raised. They surprisingly had quite a bit of intelligence from other sources within the Four Worlds as well, ones that the Keeper kept secret, even from her. But she firmly believed that there was an enormous difference between what people *said* and what they actually *did*. The best way to figure out how a Mendozan bearcat would react when threatened was to poke it with a stick.

"First," she said carefully. "We have solid intel on the number of enemy warships and roughly where they are in the system, at least for the polity of United Earth. We have similar intelligence on the Europan fleet. But we know little of the Martian Navy other than what we can capture via long-range passive sensors. If we go through the Rift and attack, the Martians may react and show us what they have.

"Second, and even more important, we will see how all the Four Worlds' governments and navies react *together* when they are threatened. I know our intel suggests Mars and Earth will not work together, no matter what. However, if we're wrong on that count, it could catastrophically shift the calculus of the battle out of our favor. We need to give them a threat to react to *now* when we can do so with minimal risk to ourselves and see how they deal with it: separately or in unison.

"Since they already know we're coming, we won't be giving anything away by showing up now. Sending only a small force may even give them a false sense of security that we can exploit later. Not to mention that it will give some of our best officers the chance to see a real battle against an evenly-matched foe, experience that will be vital when we lead the true invasion later. And given what our intelligence says they have stationed at the Front Door, we can send just three task forces and still overwhelm them with relative ease. That represents only a $16^{th}$ of our total eventual strength, so we won't be revealing anything about the size of our forces."

She stopped, holding her breath and awaiting the man's reaction. His face was hard and impassive, and she could not tell if he was about to endorse her idea or remove her from command for even recommending it. Then his eyebrows knit together in concentration, and to her relief and gratification, he started nodding slowly.

"I like it, Admiral. I will, of course, present it to the Council for approval, but I believe they will give their blessing to *this* recommendation. I may also be able to think of some ways we could use such a mission to sow discord amongst the Four Worlds and make it even less likely that they will face us as one. We have been internally debating ways to do this without revealing the existence of the Goat Path, and your proposal gives us an opening we hadn't considered.

"Assuming we approve it, how long will you need to make it happen?"

Chen pretended to think for a beat. The truth was, she'd already had her tactical planners and logistics people prepping for the mission for several weeks now; she had wanted to be sure of its feasibility before she proposed it to the Keeper and the Council. "Four weeks from today should be sufficient, Your Excellency."

"Good. Good. Start preparations now, Admiral Chen. I will take this to the Council and return with the final authorization in a few days. Until then, proceed as if the mission is approved."

Chen couldn't quite hide a smile. "Yes, sir!"

Petrov's holo image vanished, and Tamara Chen slumped back in her chair and sighed loudly. Like all conversations with the Keeper, this one had been exhausting for her. Not only did she have to deal with the man's mercurial nature, but she often had to subtly manipulate him into giving her what she needed by asking for things she knew he would say no to so that her follow-up requests would seem more palatable.

It didn't help, of course, that the very act of manipulating the Council's voice to her had given her what was now turning into a massive migraine. It wasn't direct disobedience—that would have her writhing in agony on her office's floor—but it skirted close to the edge. She dimmed the lights and leaned her head back, rubbing her temples and clearing her mind. The pain would fade in time, but the victories won in a simple meeting today could mean the successful culmination of everything the Council had created her fleet to accomplish.

But before her mind cleared fully, she had one last unsettling thought. *What if the Revelations are right and the Council doesn't exist? What if Petrov himself is the true ruler of the galaxy?* It was a terrifying thought; before, she had always felt better about the man's occasional irrational nature and emotional outbursts because she *knew* the Council and all of its wisdom was behind him, keeping him in check. But now, *what if?*

That thought more than doubled the pain in her head, and she thrust it aside quickly. The Keeper had long since ordered her, with full Council authorization codes, to not believe anything the Revelations said and to clamp down on any spread of them within her fleet. She had done the second with enthusiasm but was finding the first order hard to obey. Belief, after all, was not always a conscious decision.

Reaching over to her desk drawer, she removed a bottle of pain pills and took one without a drink, swallowing it forcibly and hoping it would be enough. She had a lot of work ahead of her. Part of her fleet would leave for the Four Worlds in less than a month, and if all went well, another part would start its first open engagements in colonial space against the rebels. There were also reports of a rebel base somewhere on the border of the Coreward Rim and the Expansion Region that she had to look into.

As she waited for the medication to do its job, she smiled despite the pain.

---

The display on the bridge of the *UENS Monitor* showed relatively empty space all around the moon Titan. No other ships were detected within the ship's active sensor range of a hundred million kilometers or in the much larger range of its passive sensors. Only the bulk of Titan, Saturn itself, and the massive gas giant's other moons cluttered the display. Finding a ship in that vast open area was often like finding a needle in a haystack, but it was the exact purpose for which SWACS (Space Warning and Control System) ships like *Monitor* were built.

"See anything?" Captain Rosita Perez asked the man beside her. Short, even for a spacer, and thin, she was dwarfed by the two-meter giant next to her. The massive black man turned and took her in with green eyes that gave her chills—both good and bad ones.

"Nothing," he replied in his smooth baritone. That voice gave her only the good sort of chills. It reminded her of one of her high school crushes, an R&B singer, of all things.

The large man continued talking, unaware of her internal musings. "Nothing on sensors. Can't even see anything occluding any of the planetary bodies or stars, at least not within visual range."

She nodded back at him. "Neither can the computer, and *Monitor* has the most advanced AI and sensor packages in the fleet right now, even amongst the SWACS platforms. If there was something out there to see, we'd see it."

"So, why are we out here?" He looked at her expectantly, even though she was as in the dark as he was. *Why did my orders specify I bring* Monitor *to these exact coordinates and wait here? And why did they tell me to swing by Charlie Station and pick up a colonial ex-assassin on my way?*

Another man cleared his throat behind them, and they turned to see the medium-height blond man, who had accompanied them into the small bridge, smiling wryly. He had *also* been waiting to board her ship when she'd docked at Charlie Station, a small repair and maintenance depot that serviced Second Fleet's station at Waypoint Charlie, the semi-permanent fleet station that guarded the line between Mars and Earth. Frustratingly for Perez, the blond man *did* know why they were here but had been unwilling to tell her before now. "Mr. Tyne," the man said smugly, "that question will be answered in about ten seconds."

Tyrus Tyne raised an eyebrow at the man that went ignored. Rosita could see the shorter man's left hand moving rapidly and knew he was noiselessly interfacing with its subdermal implant. Tyrus had mentioned that even four months into his time on Earth, he was still getting used to people having their computerized companions *embedded* inside of their bodies versus carried in a watch as they did in the colonies. But the Four Worlds had had almost 600 years of complete disconnect from the rest of humanity, leading to wildly diverging technological development. In some areas, the Four Worlds were more advanced, while in others, the colonies took the cake. Rosita longed to get her hands on the rumored tactile holo tech that the colonials had supposedly developed.

"Ah, there we are," said the blond man, interrupting her thoughts as he nodded back forward toward the bridge view screens.

Tyrus and Captain Perez turned back and saw... nothing. Several moments passed with the same. Then, to their surprise, the empty starscape in front of the *Monitor* shimmered. Suddenly, they were looking at a massive warship that dwarfed Rosita's small corvette and that couldn't have been more than a few thousand kilometers away based on the now screaming sensor pings and proximity alarms.

"Dios mio," Rosita said under her breath, while Tyrus just stared in astonished silence.

"Captain Perez, Mr. Tyne, allow me to introduce you to UENS *Enterprise*, the most advanced ship in the United Earth Navy's arsenal. It is also our most closely guarded secret."

The blond man—Rosita knew him only as Drake, which was certainly just a code name—who was a high-ranking member of UEN Intelligence, didn't wait for them to overcome their awe and continued speaking.

"What you're seeing is a carrier with full stealth technology. You'll notice that we flew directly through the space it was in just hours ago before we started our survey. It obviously wasn't there then; otherwise, we could have hit it. It was on the far side of Titan and moved to the spot it now occupies *while* we were scanning the space through which it traveled."

Perez threw the man a scornful look, feeling her defenses go up as he, by implication, impugned the skills of her crew and ship. "That's impossible. We would have picked up on the heat signatures of their drives."

In response, Drake lifted his hand and spoke into it. "Captain Holm, please turn and show us the back of your ship." Then to Tyrus and Rosita with barely concealed glee: "Watch this."

With surprising grace for a ship so large, *Enterprise* pivoted in space to show its rear to *Monitor*.

"What? There are no drive nozzles!" exclaimed Perez. Tyrus nodded, his eyes uncharacteristically wide.

Drake stepped up beside the two of them now. "None at all, Captain Perez. The *Enterprise* uses a new type of experimental sublight drive. It's so secret that I can't even give you a hint as to how it works, but I *can* tell you it gives off no detectable heat while the ship is in transit. As for the normal heat of the ship's operations, the carrier stores that in specially designed heat sinks and can go a day or so of normal activity without having to shed any heat to surrounding space. After that, it can radiate the heat in any direction its captain pleases to reduce the chances of detection.

"How many fighters does it hold?" Tyrus asked, speaking aloud for the first time since the new ship had appeared.

"Alas, only 26," Drake replied with a shrug. "Ten fewer than our Essex-class fleet carriers. The new drive technology and the heat sinks take up a tremendous amount of the ship's internal space. But, even with that limitation, we have…."

"An undetectable launch platform that can sneak 26 fighters to where the enemy will least expect them." Tyrus finished the thought for him.

"Exactly." Now Drake's smile was even wider, and Perez found herself grinning as well.

Even Tyrus allowed himself a lopsided smile, and she thought she could read the big man's thoughts. With ships like these, Earth *might* stand a chance when the Council Navy came to invade. And Rosita believed they *would* come, as did most other naval officers, regardless of what the government's official position may be.

A ship that could move without detection would be a trump card in any engagement. Even just 26 fighters could pack a wallop and take down just about any capital ship, especially with the element of surprise.

"But wait, there's more," the usually reserved intelligence man said in a fairly good imitation of a salesman. "Captain, please point all your active scanners at this grid." He flicked his hand to transfer a set of coordinates to Perez's palm implant. "And let's do the deepest scan your AI can accommodate."

She frowned but relayed the grid coordinates to her sensor officer, and then they all waited in silence for the results. Five minutes later, the man looked back at her and shook his head. "There's nothing there, Captain." His normally professional tone held a heavy hint of his disappointment.

Drake lifted his palm implant and spoke into it again. "Admiral Bol. Care to show us the rest of your task force?"

As they watched, space shimmered again, and two more massive carriers appeared out of nowhere, directly in the center of the search grid the *Monitor* had just unsuccessfully scanned.

"Now," the intelligence officer continued, "here are the *Yorktown* and *Midway*. They are both built to the same specifications as the *Enterprise*."

"You built three of them." Tyrus' voice held an undertone of awe.

*Of course*, Perez reflected solemnly, *these are still only three ships*. Based on the limited intel that Tyne and his friends had brought from the colonies, the enemy had several dreadnoughts that were still larger than these new carriers and had far more weaponry and even some fighters of their own. But if these three carriers could be used at just the right time, and not a moment too early or too late, they just might make a difference against the invasion.

Looking now at Tyrus Tyne, she could guess that even he was now feeling a measure of hope.

---

The small atmospheric shuttle felt a bit cramped to Jinny, but as one of its only three passengers, the space allotted to her was absolutely palatial compared to what the average passenger on a commercial airliner got on Earth or any of its colonies. Her crowded feeling was less about the space itself and more about the company.

The UE government bureaucracy had finally agreed to Corey O'Leary's requests that she be allowed to go to Australia. At first, even he had been reluctant to have her go but eventually had thrown his weight behind the effort after she'd strongly insisted. It still took a couple of weeks for her travel papers to be approved and, in what she was sure was a slight by the ruling party toward the top member of the opposition, O'Leary's request to accompany her had been denied.

Instead, Jinny had been sent along with two government-appointed minders. She'd nicknamed the two men on the shuttle with her the 'hulk' and the 'snake'. The hulk was, fittingly, an overly tall, brown-skinned man—she guessed he was of Arab ancestry—with muscles that looked like they were more for show than for any actual use. He seemed to perpetually be puffing out his chest and had trouble holding his arms straight at his sides, like the bulbous muscles of his shoulders and arms were always getting in the way. He didn't walk so much as lumber, and despite his titular position as her bodyguard, she hoped they didn't meet any threats that required running or even moderately paced walking. He wasn't a sterling conversationalist and had barely said three words to Jinny or anyone else on the plane.

The snake was almost the hulk's polar opposite. Short, pale, and skinny, he moved in ways that seemed jerky, like he was constantly surprised at how fast his limbs reacted to the signals from his brain. In the course of the four-hour flight, he'd knocked over two drinks in the cabin with his spastic movements. His eyes darted to and fro in a reptilian manner, and he even had the habit of almost constantly licking his lips. The snake was supposedly a member of some United Earth intelligence service and was there to 'brief her on the situation in Australia'. She smiled to herself as she remembered a phrase she'd heard Corey O'Leary repeatedly use when speaking of useless government meetings: 'that meeting could have been a text message'. Well, the pro forma briefing the snake had given her could have certainly been encapsulated in a very *brief* text message.

In fact, a text would have been far more helpful. The man spoke in such low tones she could barely understand him, only spent about 15 minutes briefing her, danced around the answers to the few questions she'd asked, and made it clear he had no genuine interest in providing any intelligence to her. Rather, it was abundantly clear the snake had been sent along more to *watch* her than to actually *brief* her, though he'd honestly spent more time watching the shuttle's one and only flight attendant, an attractive woman in her thirties who did her best to ignore the man's leering gaze. He'd even tried to leer at Jinny for a moment, but the look she'd given him in return was enough to make him devote *all* his attention to the poor flight attendant after that.

So, hulk and snake were less-than-stellar company on the otherwise luxurious private shuttle, and the flight attendant spent as little time in the cabin with them as possible to avoid the snake undressing her with his eyes. That left Jinny with no one to talk to and two men who made her completely uncomfortable and who were sitting way too close to her. Her worst fear was that she might accidentally make contact with one of them in the brush of a hand or some such and have to *read* them. Just the thought of reading either man made her feel like she might need a shower when the flight was over.

When the shuttle's pilot, who had wisely stayed locked and separated in the small forward cockpit for the entire flight, came on the intercom to tell them they'd be landing in Sydney in fifteen minutes, Jinny had to stifle a sigh of relief. That was before the snake decided to speak again.

"Now, Miss Ambrosa, we have a full itinerary while we're here. We'll be meeting with the governor this evening, of course, at a reception in your honor. Prior to that, we have meetings with his secretaries of agriculture, transportation, and commerce. They will be able to give you a picture of life in Australia for the... enhanced."

He said that last word reluctantly as if he would have preferred to use a different word or not sully his tongue with any reference to the readers, blenders, enacters, and speakers who entirely populated the continent of Australia.

"I think I would get a much better picture of life in Australia if I had a chance to walk the streets and talk to the people," Jinny said, purposefully fixing the man with an intense stare and gratified to see him look away first. It confirmed her impression of a bureaucrat who preferred to work in the shadows—a spy. Though if this was what Earth had as spies, then it would only be a few weeks before Tyrus knew *all* their secrets. This thought almost brought a smile to her face, but she was still glaring at the snake and awaiting his response.

After licking his lips several times and studying something out the shuttle's window intently for a moment, he finally replied. "Unfortunately, I believe the schedule is quite too busy to allow for much wandering of the streets, but perhaps we could ask the local government to convene a small focus group of citizens for you to talk to?"

Jinny frowned and mentally checked a box. For some reason, the UE government was nervous about her even being here on the large island continent, and they obviously weren't going to let her deviate from their carefully constructed script.

Which would make the two goals of her trip extremely hard to fulfill. She needed to learn as much as she could about the abilities of the enhanced on Earth to see how they compared with those in the colonies. If her suspicions were correct, finding that the enhanced here had stronger abilities than their colonial counterparts would support her theory of why the Twenty felt such a strong need to invade the Four Worlds now.

Second, and no less pressing, she needed to discover if anyone here could help her with her nightmares. That meant meeting with other readers, preferably in a private setting, and definitely not with anyone who directly worked for the government. If even a hint of her declining mental state made its way to the Blue Party or even Earth's media, they could use it to discredit her in the eyes of all and undermine her and Tyrus' quest to get the UE prepared to meet the coming invasion.

Because really, without Jinny as the public face of their little group, they had no hope of swaying public opinion. She loved Tyrus dearly, but his charisma seemed to only come out when he was playing his role as a spy—pretending to be someone else. When he was just being himself, it was like he had to sometimes stop and think about how to speak or react, and he'd had a hard time generating much sympathy in the few interviews he'd given. It didn't help that everyone on Earth had heard his story and knew he'd been a Council assassin most of his life. On top of that, viewer polls had described him as bouncing between robotic and overly intense. It only took a few interviews before Corey had 'encouraged' the big man to focus his time and efforts on working with the military leadership, letting Jinny handle the public relations for their little band of colonials.

Jinny laughed to herself gently as she thought of the *one* time Riggs and Jynx had been allowed to take part in an interview that had never been broadcast. It had been in their first few weeks on Earth, before Tyrus had even woken up, and their host at the time, Professor Tichner, had somehow convinced the network not to air the footage. That had been made easier because many of the choicest words Jynx had used were not allowed on a public news program. And she had repeatedly threatened the interviewer in some very creative ways, while Riggs just sat and glared at the camera. The two smugglers hadn't been invited to give any more interviews after that.

The snake looked at her funny when she chuckled, and she threw him a frown that made him immediately look away. She thought about poking him with a few more questions about the situation and living conditions in Australia but knew he would evade them all in what he probably thought was a subtle fashion. So she just turned her attention out her window to the sparkling blue waters below the shuttle and the brown of the approaching coastline.

That Earth insisted on completely separating all the enhanced from the general population was offensive enough to Jinny's sensibilities, though she could almost understand it given how the ancestors of the enhanced had, for centuries, been used by the Council to subjugate the peoples of the Four Worlds before the schism. What really disturbed her, however, was how secretive and evasive *everyone* she spoke with was about the Australian continent and how the enhanced there lived. It was clear, even to one who lacked Tyrus' finely honed instincts for espionage, that the United Earth government was hiding something big on the southern continent.

She sighed inwardly. As usual, it looked like she would have to take matters into her own hands. She sensed that getting to the hidden truth in Australia, much less meeting either of her two goals for the trip, might be the hardest challenge she'd yet to tackle on Earth. But glancing again at the snake and the hulk, she resolved once again to get to the bottom of whatever the UE was hiding in Sydney.

---

## FIVE MONTHS AGO; 731 P.D.

Jinny sat across from the man and tried hard not to fall asleep. He had been droning on about his job for the better part of an hour, which was bad on a first date, but it was doubly worse because his job was just so *boring*.

The man was a traffic control officer for the New Dallas Prefecture. What that really meant is that he was a programmer, working on the algorithms that controlled the flow of hovercar traffic in and around the city. What it meant for Jinny was that she got to suffer through an hour of talk about advanced AI learning and the great traffic jam of 728, which, to hear this man talk, had been more intense than being a Guard Space Force officer fighting pirates.

Then again, Jinny supposed nearly *everyone* had an overly inflated sense of the importance of their own job. He must enjoy it, at least, to prattle on about it so.

She just wished he would look at her face when he talked instead of at her body. She wondered, not for the first time, if guys really thought that women didn't notice where their eyes wandered and lingered. This guy was so unsmooth that he didn't even try to hide his ogling, even when the server had taken their dinner order. Poor guy probably thought he had a real chance with Jinny. For someone who supposedly understood algorithms so well, he didn't seem to question the supposed dating app algorithm that had matched the two of them up.

Or maybe he just thought that guys with buck teeth, beer bellies, and receding hairlines normally pulled buxom brunettes with hourglass bodies.

That thought almost made her laugh. And the next thought—imagining what this guy would think if he knew that most of her hourglass shape from a stuffed bra and prosthetics in other places—*did* make her laugh, and she awkwardly passed it off as a reaction to some inane thing he had said.

"You're doing great, Jinny," Ryder's voice said in her ear. "I'm almost in. But I still need him to say the rest of the code words."

Jinny already knew what the code words were. Halfway through dinner, the creep had tried to make a move, putting his hand on her bare knee that was exposed by the slit in her dress. She'd let him linger for exactly how long it took for her to search his memories for what she needed, and then she had giggled and pushed his hand off playfully, even though what she'd wanted to do was punch him square in the face.

*Next time, Ryder, you're the honey trap,* she thought with no small amount of resentment. Unfortunately, Ryder didn't have the skills, the body, or the gender to pull it off in this case. Of course, Jinny didn't have the body either, which was why she was wearing so much padding and prosthetics. Based on their hack of his dating app history, this guy had a type, and she was literally modeled to be the woman of his unrealistic dreams.

It also helped to disguise her in case they ran into anyone she knew, which was a distinct possibility this close to the New Dallas Reader Corps headquarters; the brown wig and cheek prosthetics helped with that as well. Jinny almost hadn't recognized herself in the mirror. Hopefully, no one else would, either.

"Tell me more about the traffic light at third and main," she cooed —at least, she thought she was cooing; she'd never really understood what that meant—and batted her eyes at him. "What kind of sensors does it have?"

He grinned widely. "They're aerial disturbance sensors. They can detect the displacement of air caused by a hovering vehicle. That way, they know the size, speed, and even the approximate mass of every vehicle and can adjust the traffic lights accordingly to minimize traffic jams."

*'Sensors'. Check. 'Detect'. Check.* Mentally, she ticked off the words she needed him to say to the microphone in the small earpiece she wore that let her hear and converse with the rest of the team.

"And what is the maximum altitude you said it can detect hover-cars at?"

He smiled again.

*He must really think I'm into him.*

"Up to three hundred meters, though with atmospheric pressure changes due to weather, sometimes we can detect vehicles as high as four hundred meters."

*'Three'. Check. And he threw in 'four' as well. Bonus check.*

"That's so fascinating," she gushed. "And what kind of AI model did you say it uses to adjust the timing on the light?"

"Well, it's pretty complicated," he bragged. "It's an unsupervised model where the AI uses Janisovian factors to predict the sine waves of traffic movement in a simulated three-dimensional environment."

*Thanks for the detailed explanation, but all I needed you to say was 'model',* she thought.

"Where do you monitor all of this from? Do you get to work from home?"

"No," he said, happily oblivious to the fact that he was answering questions he'd already covered in his long monologue earlier.

*He just didn't say the right words before.*

"I do it only from the main station. Traffic control is *way* too important to trust to an unsecured home connection." He looked serious for a moment and leaned in close to her across the table. "If someone ever hacked us, people could *die*."

She pretended to be suitably impressed. But what she was thinking was: *Or a shipment of weapons meant for the Guard can be rerouted to a place where a rebel cell like mine can more easily intercept it. Oh, and 'station'. Check.*

That should give Ryder everything he needed. Despite this man's conviction of the importance of traffic control, the station he worked in didn't have any live guards or even a night shift staff; most of the day-to-day operation was left to a fairly rudimentary AI, which also was in charge of guarding access to the facility. The most troublesome part of getting past that AI was a voiceprint analysis of a spoken code word sequence, which Jinny's 'date' had just happily and helpfully provided in pieces to her and, via her, to Ryder.

When she'd read him, she had also confirmed the exact time of the weapons shipment, which was taking place the next day. The programmer had been told just this morning so that he could be sure to get in early and ensure the AI kept the route clear. What he couldn't know is that Ryder was now using his physical access to the station to install a worm in the AI that would reroute the shipment to a different flight corridor, all the while showing this guy and his colleagues that it hadn't deviated from the preset path.

Now, the hardest part of the evening for her would be to extricate herself before the guy got any more handsy. Poor slob probably expected her to follow him back to his place, but Jinny had long ago learned how to put off overeager young men who wanted her for her looks.

She jumped as if startled and pulled up the holo on her watch in privacy mode. To the programmer, it would look like she had been surprised by a message alert.

"Oh no," she said, putting her hand to her mouth in mock surprise.

"What is it?" he asked, putting on his best look of concern.

"A pipe in my apartment broke, and it's flooding the unit below me. They can't reach the super, so they need me to give the plumber access so they can fix it before it causes more damage. I need to go right now."

She stood up, but he reached out and grabbed her bare forearm. She winced as she read him once again. He really did have a boring life. At least she was fairly sure she would forget all of it relatively quickly; there was little in his memories that stood out enough to stay with her.

"Wait," he said, "I can come and help you."

*Blast,* she thought. *Didn't think he'd get all chivalrous on me. Of course, he probably just doesn't want to let me get away from him before he can seal the deal.*

"Oh, I can't make you do that," she said in her best try at an appreciative tone. "Besides, you still need to pay the check, and I need to run now. Message me later tonight, OK, and maybe we can pick up where we left off." She winked and turned to make a hasty exit before he could think to say anything else.

Outside, she jumped into a waiting hovercar, which sped away just as the young programmer burst from the door, clearly having decided not to let her get away so easily.

John looked at Jinny from his place behind the wheel as he merged the car into the higher lanes of traffic.

"Good date?" he asked.

"Sure, if you consider playing defense to get his hand off my thigh half the night good. I was worried he'd end up feeling the prosthetics."

John laughed lightly as he swerved the car around a hovertruck that had tapped on its brakes for no apparent reason. "Well, Ryder got in and out quickly, and mission accomplished. We're passing the info along to another cell to make the actual intercept tomorrow."

Jinny frowned. "I thought we would be doing that ourselves."

John regarded her with a smirk in the rear-view mirror. "No way. Joan tapped a cell of regs for that. No use jeopardizing a team of enhanced. There are things we can do that the regs can't, but only if *we*

THE FOUR WORLDS - SUBVERSION

stay alive. And there will be guardmembers with the shipment. Let the regs handle the bullets, I say."

"I just wish we could at least be there to see the results of our efforts."

He shrugged as he changed lanes again and swerved around a garbage hauler; John's driving always made her carsick. "You know the rules, Jinny. Compartmentalization. Only Joan knows the identity of the other cell, and she only knows who their leader is, not even the rest of the members."

When she'd first started working with the rebels, Jinny had thought Ryder was in charge of their small cell. It had surprised her to learn that the taciturn Joan was the cell leader. It made sense, she supposed. Ryder was way too public as a member of the Speaker Corps and an employee of the Nova Tejas Prefecture at that. Joan had the natural anonymity that all blenders had, even within the Blender Corps. So did her boyfriend John, but he was content to be a foot soldier, not a leader.

"Speaking of Joan," she said, "how did it go?"

"We're picking her up next, so you can ask her yourself." John pushed down on the control wheel, and the hovercar shifted to the lowest lane of traffic at street level. Then he pulled over to the side of the road in front of the Reader Corps headquarters for New Dallas.

The rear passenger door opened, and Jinny had the surreal experience of seeing *herself* slide into the backseat of the car next to her.

Whereas Jinny looked little like herself right at that moment with the wig and prosthetics, Joan looked *exactly* like Jinny, right down to the mole on her neck and the small, faint scar under her left ear where she'd been pushed in her first year at the Academy and hit the corner of a coffee table in the girls' dormitory.

"That still freaks me out," she observed, and other-Jinny just smiled at her.

"Well, if it makes you feel any better, your job is pretty boring," other-Jinny/Joan told her. "Mostly just pretending to do paperwork like you said, though they did pull me in for a loyalty screening."

Jinny looked at the blender in horror. The plan had been for Joan to do anything possible to avoid pretending to *read* anyone. She had been sitting at Jinny's desk in the bullpen, in plain view of the other readers who all habitually worked late, for the express purpose of giving Jinny an ironclad alibi. When the Guard weapons shipment turned up missing, there *would* be an investigation, and it wouldn't take long before it zeroed in on the traffic control station and the same programmer she had just been on a fake date with. That meant there would undoubtedly be a search for the mysterious woman he had been out with, especially when she didn't return his calls or messages.

Joan had been convinced that Jinny had nothing to worry about, especially after she and John had put her disguise together, but they had chosen to err on the side of extreme caution. This was the most active role Jinny had taken in an operation to date, and as the rebellion's only reader on Nova Tejas (at least that's what they told her), they wanted to protect her at all costs. So, the plan had been for Joan to be seen working busily at Jinny's desk so that no one would ever suspect her of being the programmer's mystery date, no matter how deeply they dug into the false identity.

But if Joan had actually had to pretend to *read* someone, it might undermine the entire operation.

"Don't worry," Joan soothed, seeing Jinny's worry. "It was a simple case. I used the script we went over, and they didn't suspect a thing. The guy was a lowly bureaucrat who had missed his first appointment for some reason or another. Your boss pulled me from my desk at random but didn't even stick around for the reading. I just held the guy's hand for a few seconds and then checked the box on the desk holo to say he'd passed the screening. No fuss, no muss."

Jinny was still worried but allowed her posture to relax a bit. "So, what now?"

"Now, I get to go home to *my* apartment for a good night's sleep, and you get to go home *alone* to yours."

For the past week, Joan—supposedly on vacation from her own Blender Corps job—had stayed in Jinny's apartment day and night, ensuring that Jinny was the only human with whom she had any contact. That had triggered her blender mutation to alter Joan's physical appearance, and even internal structures like vocal cords, to match Jinny in every way conceivable. The process had been awkward, as every day Joan looked and talked more and more like Jinny. By the end of the week, the only difference between the two women had been at the level of their DNA. Blenders could and would change their DNA to match up with another person, but that required a blood transfusion. However, there had been rare but serious complications when blenders received the blood of other enhanced individuals—something about their different genetic mutations conflicting—so they had avoided it this time.

"Just make sure no one sees you get out of the car in front of your place," Jinny reminded the blender.

Joan threw her a dismissive glance, which looked really weird on Jinny's face. "You know, I've done this before. I can disguise myself pretty handily, even without my mutation. Speaking of which, you need to get out of that getup before we get to *your* place."

John kept his eyes respectfully on the road in front of him while Jinny changed clothes in the backseat, putting on an outfit identical to the one Joan now wore. She sighed with relief when she removed the bulky hip prosthetics and the padded bra and even more when she took the painful cheek prosthetics out of her mouth.

She finished just as John pulled up in front of her apartment building. Bidding goodnight to the two blenders, she started to exit the car.

"Uh, Jinny. Forgetting something?"

She looked down at herself and saw nothing amiss and then looked back up at Joan. Her clothing was an exact copy of what the blender was wearing, and the prosthetics and padding were all removed. Then she saw Joan looking upward and reached up in chagrin to remove the brown-haired wig from her head.

"Oh."

Joan just smiled at her. The woman had been warming to her recently, which had made the last week together not as horrible as Jinny had expected. "No worries. Have a good one, Jinny."

She said another goodbye and slipped from the car, heading across the sidewalk and into the building. Her first stop, she resolved, would be the shower to wash off the programmer's oily touch. After that, she would lie awake in bed as she always did after an operation, reviewing it in her mind to think how she might do better next time. *At least,* she reflected, *I won't have any nightmares tonight.*

---

## PRESENT DAY; JULY 2, 731 P.D.

"And so, Miss Ambrosa, you can see that there is a bustling trade of goods between Australia and the rest of the UE. Even the daily cargo shuttle flights to and from Luna mean that the inhabitants of our humble island have access to all the best that the UE has to offer. We are truly part of the global and interplanetary community."

The portly Secretary of Commerce for the Governor of Australia continued to drone on, telling Jinny all about how the enhanced people kept prisoner on the continent wanted for nothing and had free and open commerce with the rest of the population of Earth and Luna. As if 'free' or 'open' could realistically be applied to people who were rarely allowed to even *interact* with the rest of humanity. When she'd asked about communication between Australia and the other nations of Earth and its sisters, the man had quickly sidestepped her question and gone on to tell her all about how the enhanced supposedly preferred to keep to themselves and avoid too much interaction with the other peoples of the solar system. But had he mentioned that they had access to all the latest entertainment programming from across the UE? He had, she assured him, though she noticed that the flow of programming into Australia was only one-way. Nothing in the way of information about the people here flowed *out* to the rest of the UE, though she'd had to learn that by her own observation and reading between the lines of the man's droning monologue.

While he spoke, she pretended to take copious notes on her tablet. Tyrus had helped her break the tablet's administrative controls prior to her leaving for Australia, and now Jinny was using the tablet to surreptitiously log into multiple social media and communications apps. In every case, she found she wasn't able to get *anything*. The first social media app gave her a message that 'We're sorry, but our service is not available in your present location'. A messaging app simply told

## THE FOUR WORLDS - SUBVERSION

her it was 'unable to connect to the server'. App after app, she got the same basic response. The people of Australia were clearly and intentionally cut off from the rest of the system.

"Now, Miss Ambrosa, I would happily take any questions you might have, but I'm afraid we're out of time, so we will have to leave those questions for a future conversation," the secretary was now saying to her. *Yeah, and I just bet you timed it just perfectly so you wouldn't have to take any more questions from me,* she thought as the man gave a few more meaningless platitudes and took his leave from the conference room that had been Jinny's de facto jail cell since the shuttle had landed on a pad on the top of the government building in Sydney.

From her perch high in the office building's upper floors, she had a majestic view of Sydney Harbor, including a very modern bridge that crossed the waterway that juxtaposed with the ancient ruins of a large building on the water's edge. Jinny had read that the ruins marked the location of an opera house that had been renowned the world over for its architecture and acoustics. Now only the building's foundations remained. Seeing the world outside reminded her that her requests to walk the city had been politely but no-less-firmly refused by every government official she'd spoken with today.

The other so-called secretaries had been just as generally unhelpful as this last one. At least he hadn't spent almost the entire conversation staring at Jinny's hands as if she might leap across the table, remove her gloves, and read him against his will. The severe-looking woman who was Australia's Secretary of Agriculture had done just that, rarely taking her eyes from Jinny's gloves. It was so uncomfortable that it was almost a sure thing the woman had almost no regular interaction with readers, which was unusual for a person who supposedly helped to govern a continent that housed every reader in the UE.

In fact, Jinny didn't need to be a reader to see that everyone she'd encountered so far in the government building was neither reader nor blender. No one was wearing gloves, and no one had the telltale generic features that characterized blenders. If she had to guess, she was fairly certain that everyone she'd met was, in actuality, a speaker. Their words were just too oily and smooth, and the Secretary of Transportation, an attractive but vain middle-aged man who could have passed for a holo actor, had subconsciously mimicked Jinny's colonial accent within two minutes of meeting her. It was a definite speaker move. Even if the latest secretary had been the most boring speaker she'd ever listened to.

"Now, Miss Ambrosa," the snake said, interrupting her thoughts. "We'll be moving to the top floor to attend a reception in your honor with the governor. It is quite gracious of him to make the time."

Jinny shrugged noncommittally and allowed herself to be escorted from the room and through a short hall to the lift. In transit, they passed many empty desks, as if the floor they were on had been cleared of the usual government workers specifically so Jinny wouldn't see them. She had the suspicion if she had seen them, they would also be free of readers or blenders. One couldn't tell an enacter or a speaker just by looking at them, but she was also fairly sure there were none of the former and plenty of the latter inhabiting the government offices.

After a quick ride on the lift, she followed her two minders into a hall that was broader and had higher ceilings than anything she'd seen in the building so far. She instantly pegged it as the floor where the higher-ups worked, especially as they passed art on the walls that was of clearly better quality than the generic photographs and posters that had hung in and outside of the conference room they'd come from.

Following a walk down the thickly carpeted hall, the three of them arrived at a set of wide double doors that were propped open, revealing a lush and spacious reception room full of people. As Jinny entered on the heels of the snake, all in attendance hushed their conversations and turned to face her. There were probably fifty people in the room, but a middle-aged woman with a fake grin stepped forward and symbolically opened her arms as if she might give Jinny a hug from five meters away.

"Miss Ambrosa, welcome to Sydney. We are *so* delighted to have you here with us on our humble little island."

*Yep, she's a speaker too,* Jinny thought wryly. There was no mistaking the smoothness of even her simple little speech. The woman had obviously been listening to recordings of Jinny's voice because she was already mimicking her New Brussels accent.

"Allow me to introduce you to the room," the woman continued. "I

## THE FOUR WORLDS - SUBVERSION

am Deborah Locksley, the governor's chief of staff. Governor Jacobson will be along shortly and is *so* looking forward to meeting you. In the meantime, we've gathered a variety of government leaders here to meet with you and answer any questions you may have about our wonderful home."

*I just bet you have,* Jinny thought uncharitably, taking in the room. Her first impression was that the people in the reception hall were in four distinct groups. The group in the center, from which Ms. Deborah Locksley had emerged, was probably a group of speakers. To their immediate left was a group of people wearing gloves—almost definitely readers. To the right of the speakers was a small group of plain-looking folk that were probably the blenders. The last group—huddled almost defensively near the wall furthest from Jinny—by process of elimination must be the enacters. It was gratifying to finally see people from the other enhanced groups, but by the way they all refused to intermingle, it was also clear that there was no love lost between them.

"This is Mr. Timothé Laurent, Secretary of Education and a fellow reader." A man stepped forward at Locksley's words, emerging from the group of readers to the woman's left. Jinny had the distinct impression that while he'd been standing *with* the group, he'd not truly been *part* of it. The other readers subtly didn't look toward the man and moved as a group to maintain a distance from him, even as he made his way through them.

"Reader Ambrosa, we are so grateful that you've made the trip to visit us, and we look forward to sharing in the exchange the knowledge by readers from two different parts of the galaxy," Laurent said, bowing his head deferentially to her. His voice was smooth and cultured and set off alarm bells in her head.

"Perhaps you would like to join us and speak with your fellow readers while we await the governor's arrival?" he asked, but the way he motioned her toward the group made it clear that it was less a question than a strong suggestion that she would be wise to accept. Jinny decided to go along with the charade for a while and see what she could learn.

"Of course," she replied. "After all, that is one of the main reasons I came to visit." She walked toward the group of readers, several of whom nodded to her with tight but uncomfortable smiles as if they themselves were following a script.

It was obvious after just five minutes of conversation with the group that there would be no actual exchange of knowledge. Laurent did most of the talking, mostly in the form of questions directed at her. When she asked the man anything, he expertly danced around the answers, delivering a message about 'prosperity' and 'open commerce' that was almost identical she'd heard from the parade of secretaries earlier. When Jinny directed a question to any of the other readers, she got short and shallow answers, with most of them throwing glances toward Laurent throughout as if looking to him for approval of their words.

The jig was up. Jinny knew almost immediately that Laurent wasn't a reader. He was just too smooth and didn't talk like any reader she'd ever met. And when she asked about the government positions of the other readers, who she was almost certain really *were* readers, the answers were evasive and vague. It was clear this group of readers had been brought here strictly for her benefit and had no actual place in the government.

Her first conclusion: Australia was entirely ruled by speakers. In that regard, it almost felt like home.

It was the same story with the blenders. One plain-looking woman led the conversation, clearly a speaker chosen because she was nondescript enough to *almost* pass as a blender. It was even more clear with the enacters. None of them would meet her gaze or say more than two words to her *except* for the speaker implanted in their midst and playing at being an enacter himself.

Her second conclusion: the other types, *especially* the enacters, feared the speakers in the room. She wondered if that same fear carried over to the general populace.

When the governor finally arrived, a tall patrician man with silver hair and an erudite nose, he briefly shook Jinny's hand, gripping it limply as if he were afraid she might read him through her glove. He then introduced his wife, welcomed Jinny to their 'humble little island', and left almost immediately, explaining that he had an important issue that demanded his attention.

Jinny wished she *could* have read the man—it would be worth breaking her self-commitment to read no one unwillingly after she'd arrived at Earth—to finally get to the truth of just what was going on in Australia. Because it all stunk.

The breakthrough didn't come from her brief conversation with the governor. Nor did it come from any of the formal conversations in the room, scripted as they were. Jinny had given up all hope of learning anything at the reception until, under the watchful gaze of her minders, she was at the long buffet table against one of the side walls grabbing some food (so that the night wouldn't be a *total* waste). As she browsed and selected some items, one of the male readers casually walked over and began browsing and selecting food from the other end of the table.

Out of the corner of her eye, Jinny saw Laurent, the fake reader, watching the man with a hawkish intensity. But the man either didn't care or pretended not to notice. He didn't even look up at Jinny until they'd made their way to the center of the table and were a mere meter apart. At that point, Laurent was almost bouncing on the balls of his feet, getting ready to come over and intercept the man before he could do anything to spoil the little ruse.

Jinny decided to initiate conversation, if for no other reason than to upset Laurent even further. She had taken an instant dislike to the man and suspected she'd loathe him even if he hadn't been lying to her all evening.

"Is there anything here you would recommend?" she asked the other reader.

He looked up at her quickly as if startled. "Oh... I... um," he stammered as if he'd really been completely unaware she was at the buffet table—which perhaps he had been given the absent-minded way he'd been focusing on the food in front of him. "Sure. The pavlova is a local delicacy." He picked up something that looked like a small fruit tart from a platter on the table with his gloved hand and held it out toward Jinny, nodding toward the plate in her hand.

Jinny took a step forward as Laurent launched off his toes and started closing the distance to the table to intervene. But the man didn't engage Jinny further. He simply placed the pastry on the small dish she carried in one hand. As he did so, Jinny looked for an opening or some sort of signal from the man, but he refused to even meet her gaze, and she couldn't just rip her glove off and touch him—not with Laurent watching and agitated. While the fallout of such a bold move would probably not result in any harm to Jinny, she didn't know enough about the strange dynamic here in Sydney to be sure how the other reader might be punished for her impudence.

She almost instantly resigned herself to the night continuing as a total failure when she felt the tip of one gloved finger lightly brush the exposed wrist of her hand holding the plate as the man withdrew his hand from the pastry. But it *wasn't* a gloved finger; there was a light tear in the fingertip that was invisible on a mere visual inspection, which allowed the man to push his finger forward just enough to expose the skin.

She knew all of this not because she could feel the tear or even the skin of the finger but because, for that brief instant of contact, she *read* the man.

Jinny covered up her reaction by quickly reaching for the pastry with the other hand and taking a bite. The other reader moved away as if nothing had happened, passing by Laurent, who had halted his march toward the table and was glaring at the reader like he'd assaulted Jinny. But the imposter reader with the French name said nothing to the real reader passing him by; he merely nodded respectfully to Jinny and said something about letting him know if she had any more questions about the food before turning and heading back to the huddled knot of readers.

The contact had been incredibly brief, but even had Jinny not been exceptional by the standards of every reader to have ever lived, she would have clearly received the thought at the top of the other reader's mind:

*Trust no one. If you want the truth, a black car will be parked outside the front of this building at 1:00 AM tomorrow morning. If you can get to it, we will do the rest.*

# CHAPTER 7

Dr. Hiroto Takahashi pulled at the collar of his starched dress shirt for the tenth time in the last seven minutes. He was never comfortable outside of his lab. Worse, the man across the desk from him seemed to have designed his spacious office in a way that was most disconcerting to the fussy scientist.

Creighton Horvath, Senior Assembly Speaker, was from Nova Tejas, and took his cultural heritage seriously—much *too* seriously, in Hiroto's opinion. Dark, grainy woods lined the office, floor to ceiling. The desk at which the speaker sat appeared to be carved from a single tree. Everything was far too… earthy. Or perhaps the proper word was organic. Either way, to Hiroto, the space just felt wrong.

In his line of work, he much preferred the white-on-white cleanliness and sharp lines and angles of a good laboratory, with humming ventilation and air purifiers and smooth white floors that were easy to clean in the event of a spill. To him, wood was just one more uneven surface where bacteria and other germs could find purchase and multiply. Never mind the grotesque stuffed animal heads that seemed to be Horvath's preferred method of decorating his walls. Even though Hiroto knew intellectually that they were stuffed and well-preserved, the thought of *dead animals* as wall decoration made his stomach turn.

The germs that could live in that fur... The animal heads were also a sign of Horvath's power; hunting for sport had been outlawed in the 47 Colonies since even before the schism with the Four Worlds. The message was clear: 'The rules of mere mortals don't apply to me'.

He really hated coming here to report to his de facto superior. In reality, Hiroto Takahashi served the Council directly as a member of its Council of Scientific Advisors—its senior member since the downfall of the disgraced and now missing Frank Ambrosa. More importantly, Takahashi had also inherited Ambrosa's role as the administrator of the top-secret Project Epsilon. It was for that reason that Horvath had summoned him from his lab early this morning like a dog summoned from his food bowl on his master's whim.

"These numbers aren't promising, Hee-row-tow," the Nova Tejan drawled in that annoying accent he loved to use. Takahashi had corrected the man's pronunciation of his name a dozen times and had finally given up when it became clear the speaker had no intention of saying it correctly. Which was doubly insulting, given he was a speaker. The man could no doubt learn and speak fluent Japanese in a week if he didn't already know it. He could *certainly* get Hiroto's name right, but he obviously didn't care.

Or maybe it was just part of his strategy to throw people off. He seemed to do a lot of little things aimed at that, like making Takahashi always meet him in his horrible office rather than in one of the comparatively sterile and comfortable conference rooms that were commonplace in the Assembly office building.

"Yes, Horvath-san," Hiroto replied, bowing his head slightly in acknowledgment of the man's criticism. "The trial results were mixed. Besides the unfortunate suicides," the speaker frowned, as he always did when Hiroto used that word, "there have been several unanticipated side effects. However, I am pleased that in 98.4 percent of cases, the genetic mutation was successful with no material negative consequences."

"But they're not listening to us, are they?" demanded the speaker as he lightly slapped a palm onto the desk surface between them. "They're not imprinting on the Council. So, your 98 percent means as much as a cow that won't give milk, doesn't it?"

## THE FOUR WORLDS - SUBVERSION

As far as Hiroto knew, Horvath had grown up in urban New Dallas, so the man's constant farm references were confusing, especially to Takahashi, who had never even been on or seen a farm. Still, he understood the general message.

"Yes, honored speaker. In 4.7 percent of cases, the subliminal conditioning failed, and the test subjects imprinted on an authority other than the Council, usually a manager at work or a loved one, like a parent or spouse."

Horvath hit the desk harder this time. "They're not test subjects, you fool!" In his anger, his accent slipped for the barest of moments. "The test subjects were those people we brought to your precious lab back when you said the treatments and conditioning were nearly one hundred percent effective. *These* people are citizens of the 47 Colonies who live out in the wild, as it were. Some of them on my home planet. And when they imprint on the wrong authority figure, it doesn't just cause your tests to fail; it causes all sorts of chaos in the real world! You realize you promised us that these newly created enacters would be even *more* obedient than the naturally born ones. As far as I can tell, you've failed to deliver on *every one* of the promises you made regarding Project Epsilon. Over 50 years of work at risk of going straight down the drain!"

He leveled a finger at Takahashi and shook it. "We're looking to you to make it right, or else."

Hiroto inclined his head again, mentally shoving aside the unsubtle threat and knowing that arguing with the man when he was like this was a losing proposition. Besides, he needed to save his arguments for later in the conversation. "You are right, Horvath-san. We could not anticipate all the variables of wider distribution of the project, nor did we expect the failure of the subliminal conditioning at these levels. But," he hastened to add before the other man could blow up again, "we do believe we have a solution."

Horvath sat back in his overstuffed real leather office chair and regarded Hiroto with a cool expression that reminded the scientist of a snake inspecting a rat it was going to have for dinner. The speaker inclined his head and waved a hand for his guest to continue.

Hiroto swallowed and then began talking quickly. "We need to effect the transformation in a more controlled environment. Instead of continuing to send the formula out to the populace, we must bring the populace to *us*. That way, we can control what they see and hear and how they imprint. There will be virtually no chance that they fail to imprint on the Council. As a bonus, we can observe them and identify the ones exhibiting unstable or even suicidal tendencies and separate them from the rest of the subjects. It is the perfect plan. I just need the approval to execute it."

Horvath's frown had deepened as he'd listened to the scientist. His face took on a stormy disposition that made Hiroto shrink in his seat when he stopped talking and came up for air.

The assemblyman leaned forward and steepled his fingers in front of him, his eyes boring into Hiroto's. When he spoke, his voice was icy, and he slowly bit off each word as if speaking to a young child. "Let me get this straight. You expect me to go to the Council and tell them that the trillions of credits we've spent on getting your precious formula out to the populace is money wasted? That they can't get the billions of enacters you promised by the end of the decade; that they'll have to settle for what, a few thousand instead? Blast it, man; we need another half million just to crew the fleet!" He slammed his hand down on the desk, harder this time.

Hiroto jumped and then shrunk further into his seat. "No, not at all! The Council *will* have their billions. This is just temporary while we rework the formula and the indoctrination mechanisms. We have some ideas on that—good ones! But they will take time to implement. This way, we do not have to stop altogether while we wait for the new solutions; we can continue, just with smaller groups. I estimate we could create close to two *million* enacters, perfectly loyal to the Council, in the next twelve months."

Horvath did not respond at first but studied Hiroto over steepled fingers as he considered the man's proposal. Then he looked down, pulling up something on his desk holo that Takahashi couldn't see. Hiroto sat there in uncomfortable silence for a long moment until Horvath looked back up and raised his eyebrows as if surprised the scientist was still in the room.

"I will present this to the Keeper and the Council. You're dismissed," he said in a monotone that hid his feelings well.

Hiroto quickly gathered his pad and hurried to the office's entry door. Just as he put his hand on the door control to open it, Horvath spoke behind him in a low voice that he had to strain to hear.

"If the Council says yes to your proposal, you *will* get me those two million enacters in one year. And I need the first million done within six months; no excuses."

It wasn't a question, and for a barely fleeting second, Hiroto considered reminding the Assembly speaker that he'd promised *close to* two million and said nothing about the timing of the first million, but thought better of it and scurried out the door.

---

When the scientist was gone and the door closed behind him, Horvath keyed the comm on his holo desk. "It's Creighton," he said to Keeper Ian Petrov on the other end of the call, his affected Nova Tejas drawl completely gone. "Dr. Takahashi has an idea that will at least get us enough crew for the rest of Chen's Navy ships in the next six months. But we need to move fast."

He listened for a moment as the other man spoke. "Merchant crews, huh? Chen wants Merchant crews?" he mused. "Well, that would fit Takahashi's plan perfectly.

"Still, to be candid, I don't trust our friend Hiroto to deliver; not sure he's motivated enough as it is. I think it might help to have one of the alphas pay his family a visit. Nothing violent, just to send a message."

He listened again to the Keeper's response.

"Yes, sir. I have just the alpha in mind. The one who took out Farnsworth for us. He's a scary bugger, and he'll do an excellent job of conveying our message to even a thick-headed scientist."

He listened again to the Keeper's reaction and final instructions. Then he keyed off the comm.

*If only that fool Ambrosa hadn't run*, he thought idly to himself. *We need to figure out what he did to that daughter of his; he certainly raved about it in that crazy manifesto we found. Bunch of rambling; the guy was losing it even before the truth about him came out in those blasted Revelations. But who knows, maybe we can get that daughter of his back, too, when we take Earth. Then we can lure him out or just get what we need without him.* The Keeper was probably already thinking along those lines but had declined to share his plans with the rest of the Twenty. Petrov was keeping more and more to himself these days, and even thinking about it made Horvath's blood boil.

So Creighton switched to his favorite line of thought. Earth. The ancient homeworld and the last place in the galaxy that stood in need of the peace and order that only the Twenty could bring it. Of course, his more cynical side also knew that the same peace and order couldn't survive if they *didn't* take Earth. Frank Ambrosa had been right about one thing: they were mere decades away from losing the effectiveness of the genetic enhancements in the colonies and, with them, a good portion of the power the Twenty held over the populace.

It would start, as it always did, on the Edge worlds—balls of dirt like Panamar or Phoenix—where the enhanced were already few, and open rebellion was never more than a breath away. But if allowed to fester there, it would eventually spread to the Expansion Regions, the Coreward Rim, and possibly even the Core itself. They could *not* let that happen, which made accessing the enhanced bloodlines on Earth imperative, especially considering Takahashi's failures to create reliable new enacters.

Luckily, Creighton was one of the few, even among the Twenty, who knew exactly how large the Council Navy was in relation to the combined forces of the Four Worlds. Their invasion *would* be successful, assuming they could generate enough new enacters to crew the fleet in time.

*They don't stand a chance*, he thought with a grin to himself. He was still grinning when he placed the call to the alpha Collins to order him to pay Hiroto Takahashi's wife and children a little visit.

Corey O'Leary sat at his desk working on a speech he was to give the next day to the entirety of the United Earth Congress. Well, to half of them, at least. So many of the lawmakers simply didn't attend meetings unless they featured a high-profile vote. It was infuriating to someone like Corey, who took his responsibility to his constituents quite seriously.

The son of wealthy parents who owned a dozen different companies, Corey could have theoretically relied on his trust fund and lived in extreme comfort for his entire life. But his parents had made it clear from his early childhood that they expected him to take over the family business. With that in mind, they had sent him to the absolute best private schools on Earth and even to two semesters studying abroad on Mars when the red planet had briefly opened its borders during a period of relative peace in the Sol system. That had been almost a decade before the Six-Month War.

As a result, he had two different bachelor's degrees, plus a Master of Business and another in Interplanetary Affairs. His parents had insisted on both advanced degrees as prerequisites for him to fill their shoes. But it had backfired on them. Corey had found the business degree dreadfully boring, but the interplanetary affairs lessons had been exhilarating!

Shortly after his graduation with the latter, he had announced to his parents his intention to enter government service and eventually run for public office. They had immediately cut him off financially and stopped talking to him for five full years.

Then, Corey's father had died in an accident while inspecting one of his businesses, a commercial shipyard at Lagrange Point One. Corey, then an aide to an influential congresswoman, had rushed home from a summit on Europa to be with his mother. In the tender days that followed, mother and son reconciled, and Corey's estrangement ended.

Welcomed back into the family with open arms, he'd resumed his place as heir apparent, though with the understanding that he would never directly manage the family's businesses but would instead serve as the chairman of the board for each. Other men and women handled the day-to-day affairs.

His mother had died twenty years later from one of the few remaining incurable forms of cancer, drifting away in a luxurious private hospital room while her only child held her hand and cried silent tears.

That made Corey O'Leary one of the ten richest men in United Earth and easily one of the top 15 across United Earth and Europa—no one knew enough about Mars to say where he would have ranked there.

But all that money had done nothing to help him make a difference in his role as a congressman. His companies were prohibited from donating to any politician's campaign, given his ownership stake, a rule that Corey agreed strongly with. But his fellow members of Congress had at first looked down on him, assuming that he'd somehow bought his position rather than earning it as they did. It had taken two solid decades in Congress to change their opinions and a full 40 years as the representative of Western North America for him to rise to his party's top position. Now there was even talk of him running against Luiz Pereira in the next presidential election, but Corey wasn't entirely sure he wouldn't be retiring before then.

Still, he loved serving in the government, even if, at times like now, it was horribly frustrating.

His failed attempt to concentrate on his speech was interrupted by a vibration in his left hand. He looked down at the screen built into his palm and smiled. Placing his hand flat on his desk, he transferred the call to his office's hardware. On the room's opposite wall, a large viewscreen brightened to reveal the smiling face of a large Russian man.

"Mikael, what a pleasant surprise," Corey said graciously, which would have been a shock to anyone who'd ever seen him interact in public with Mikael Gorsky, UE Secretary of Justice and a staunch supporter of President Luiz Pereira. The stories of the hatred O'Leary and Gorsky had for each other were legendary in Houston circles... and they were completely false.

"Corey Ivanovich," Mikael said with a large grin, using the Russian honorific name he'd long ago assigned to his Irish friend. "How are you this evening?"

Corey shrugged. "Working on a speech no one will listen to. So, the usual, I suppose. To what do I owe the pleasure of this call?"

Gorsky's smile disappeared, and he looked solemnly at his friend. "We may have a problem, Corey Ivanovich. I understand that your reader friend is in Sydney."

O'Leary returned the frown. "Yes, I'm afraid she is. I tried to gently dissuade her from going, but she was very insistent."

The Russian shook his head. "I understand, but the timing could not be worse. Givens is using the trip to convince Pereira that Ms. Ambrosa's true loyalties lie not with the UE but with the enhanced in Australia. She has even gone so far as to recommend that the young woman not be allowed to return to Houston, but that she be required to stay in Australia with the other readers. There was talk of legal action if she defied the order and returned to North America."

Corey's frown deepened. Tabitha Givens, chief of staff to President Luiz Pereira, was a continual thorn in his side. She was an ambitious woman whom many, Corey included, believed was the genuine power of the Pereira administration. "That would be a drastic and dangerous move, Mikael. Even the president has to know that the public has grown quite fond of Jinny. My latest polling suggests that 72 percent of UE citizens believe she is here trying to help us, no matter what the president's pet members of Congress and the media have been saying. Surely, he must—"

Gorsky held up a hand to interrupt his friend. "She *will* be allowed to return. When Pereira asked for my legal opinion, I told him that Ambrosa, who is not even a UE citizen, could be considered to have diplomatic immunity as the representative of the Free Colonies polity."

The congressman raised an eyebrow. "That's a stretch, even for you. Especially since the Free Colonies is more of a movement than an actual nation, at least the way Tyrus and Jinny tell it."

The larger man shrugged. "Yes, but coupled with the poll numbers, it worked to convince Pereira *not* to make a move right now. Besides, I am the durak's Secretary of Justice. He must at least pretend to listen to me occasionally on matters of a legal nature." The man's face darkened, and he started speaking faster. Whenever he used Russian words mixed in with his English, it was a sure sign he was agitated. "But that does not mean he will not do something later. The man is increasingly under the sway of that ved'ma Givens. If our plan is to work, Corey Ivanovich, we may have to consider more extreme measures. Pereira *must* be removed from office."

Corey shook his head. "We don't have the support yet for a vote of no confidence. The Blue Party still has far too much control over the moderates. You know that better than I do."

"And you know, Corey Ivanovich, that I am speaking of *other* measures."

Corey gave a frustrated sigh. "We've talked about this, Mikael! I can't even *consider* what you're proposing," he shot back. "We have to trust the system. What you're talking about flies in the face of the Constitution itself!" Mikael had never shared the full details of what he wanted to do to force Pereira out of office, but the broad outline had been enough for Corey to know he wanted no part of it.

The big man was silent for a moment. "And if we fail? There will *be* no more Constitution. My friend, we are both trying to save our nation and its people."

Corey's jaw tightened, though he said nothing in response. Gorsky watched him silently from the viewscreen and then shrugged in surrender. "Are you convinced still that Pereira can be made to see reason?" the Russian asked.

O'Leary considered his answer for a moment. Then he shook his head. "Honestly, no. And I'm not even as close to him as you are by a large degree. But I *do* believe we can use public opinion to convince him it would be politically expedient for him to at least *pretend* to take the threat of the Council invasion seriously."

"Nyet," Gorsky shook his head. "He does not stand for reelection for another four years. We have discussed this."

"You're correct. But a third of his supporters in Congress *will* be up for reelection later this year. He could lose his majority, and that would make him a lame duck, unable to pass any of his policies without Red Party support; he would have to compromise with us on the military buildup. Or better yet, we could even flip enough of the seats to get our vote of no confidence."

The big Russian grimaced. "That may be true. But by the time that happens, it will almost certainly be too late for us. The Council could come *tomorrow*, my friend, and we would be almost completely unprepared. Can I ask you to at least think on my proposals some more? They may be our only hope."

Corey sat back in his chair and stared at the ceiling, his mind racing along the lines that Gorsky was suggesting. Finally, he sat up straight and looked back at his friend's visage. "OK, Mikael. I promise I will *consider* more active measures. However, know that my answer is unlikely to change, for now, at least. There are still things we need to try before I can condone working *outside* the system."

Gorsky smiled tightly. The admission that such measures might eventually be necessary was a much larger concession than he had ever gotten out of his friend before. "I will take what I can get, Corey Ivanovich. Let us talk again next week."

When the connection ended, Corey sat back in his office chair again, staring into space, all thoughts of his coming speech driven from his mind. He and Mikael Gorsky lived just three kilometers apart, but they'd had few in-person conversations for the better part of a decade, and they were rarely seen together in public. They were members of different country clubs, rarely attended the same parties, and had hidden their friendship from the world since their very public —and very *staged*—falling out in a congressional committee meeting.

The reasons for their fake animosity had been political. Gorsky was an up-and-comer in the Blue Party, whereas Corey was the minority leader of the Red Party. In a town where everyone was watching you and expected you to toe the party line, a friendship between leaders of such divergent parties would have cast enough suspicion and dispersion on both of them to undermine any hope either had at higher office.

The staged falling out had also served another, deeper purpose. Not only did it cement their party loyalty in the minds of their peers and supporters, but it also allowed them to work together on things in subtle back channels, building policies and legislation that were more palatable to members of both parties, as well as to the near-dozen smaller parties they often had to ally with.

Corey always smiled as he imagined the reaction Pereira, Givens, and windbags like Hastings might have if they knew just how many lines of Blue Party legislation over the last decade had been written by Corey himself, feeding the words to Gorsky much as the big Russian did for Corey when authoring Red Party bills.

However, now they were doing something much riskier than merely helping each other write more moderate legislation. Both of them agreed the Council threat was real. And even though they differed in their opinions on the best way to meet that threat, they were completely aligned that Pereira was failing their nation. But while Corey had held out for working via democratic channels—shaping public opinion to sway the president and his party—Gorsky had been advocating for more direct action, both in the political arena and in the darker fringes of Houston. He hadn't shared all of those plans with Corey, likely understanding how his friend would react, but the little he had shared offended Corey's sensibilities even though he knew it came from a good place in the big Russian's desire to save the people of United Earth.

Corey only hoped that it wouldn't come to that. For now, Gorsky's report that Pereira and Tabitha Givens were considering legal avenues to silence Jinny was enough for him to send a message to one of his family attorneys. Then, he sent one more message to the fixer and blender, Jordan Archer. Better to be ready for every eventuality.

---

Jinny's elation at receiving the message from the reader in the reception hall quickly faded when she contemplated the challenge now in front of her. She was under no illusions that *anyone* in the Australian government building would let her casually stroll out to a waiting car. Even if the Sydney government officials would somehow allow it, her two minders, the hulk and the snake, certainly wouldn't. In the reception hall, they'd never strayed more than a few meters from her, and it had been a minor miracle that the snake hadn't somehow interposed himself between the other reader and Jinny at the buffet table.

After the momentary feeling of hopelessness passed, she set her mind to work on the problem. She consciously thought about the times she'd read Tyrus, looking in his memories for inspiration, and found some. She also thought of how Riggs and Jynx might handle the situation but deduced with an inner smile that there was no way she could get her hands on a flame thrower or grenade launcher, so their way was out.

After the reception, she'd been escorted to a new floor in the same building that was residential in nature. The snake explained with false courtesy that the floor was for visiting dignitaries and that the governor had graciously offered it to Jinny to stay in before arising early for more meetings and the trip back to North America the following day.

Jinny pretended to be suitably impressed at the governor's generosity and gave all the appropriate 'oohs' and 'awes' as they arrived at her assigned room and showed her the amenities. The room was nice, if a little small. But she had no interest in the entertainment console, the drink dispensers, or the finely tiled shower and tub. She was looking for exits.

Ironically, the earthbound reader she'd encountered couldn't have known just how powerful Jinny's talent was. She'd not only gotten the message from him that he'd intended but also enough of his memories to know exactly where the black car was going to take her and whom she would meet there. The momentary contact hadn't been enough for her to read more than a few months of his most recent memories, but she still *almost* had enough information to skip the meeting altogether. However, she was intrigued by what else she might learn and especially by the woman she was to meet. She, therefore, considered it imperative that she be in that car at one in the morning, as the man had told her to be.

She still didn't have any promising ideas on how to get there. She checked the clock in the room and saw it was 9:08 PM, leaving her almost four hours to figure it out. So, she sat back and set her mind again to working on the problem.

*First problem, the room I'm in is almost definitely bugged for sound and possibly video. Or at least Tyrus would tell me to assume it is. So, I will.*

*Second problem, the snake told me he or the hulk will be outside my room* at all times 'for my safety and convenience'. They're acting as my jailers for the entire night and will stop me if I try to leave.

Third problem, the lift uses a key card, and I don't have one. So even if I can get out of the room and down the hall, I can't get the lift to take me anywhere.

Fourth problem, even if I can get the lift to take me to the first floor, there will undoubtedly be security there, and they will just as undoubtedly be warned to watch for any attempt on my part to leave the building.

Fifth problem, even if I can get out without being caught, I will have to do it all again in reverse to get back in before the hulk and the snake wake me up for the morning meetings.

She thought through the five problems repeatedly, forming and discarding several plans. She even briefly considered a false seduction of the hulk or the snake but immediately rejected that plan as not worth it, even to find out what was happening in Australia. She also doubted her ability to pull it off, not from a lack of looks—the snake, in particular, seemed amenable to anything with feminine features—but from a lack of experience in such things. She may have played the honey trap in a few missions with her old rebel cell, but in all those cases, she had merely been trying to get information, not subdue or sneak past anyone.

The numbers on the clock marched on, and it was now 11:56 pm. Gone were three of her four hours with *nothing* to show for them except a list of problems and discarded plans. She simply wasn't a spy like Tyrus and wished there was a way for her to call and ask his advice, but he was off planet on some secret assignment with the Navy. Her mind was turning to despair again when a light knock came at the door.

She hadn't changed her clothes yet for sleeping, convinced she was going to find a way out, but was worried the snake or hulk would be suspicious if she answered the door fully clothed. So, she called out, "Coming!" and quickly kicked off her shoes and threw on a robe that had been hanging in the closet. Halfway to the door, she realized it looked ridiculous, as anyone could easily see the top of her blouse and the legs of her pants sticking out, but she had no other options.

She opened the door a crack, expecting to see either of her minders checking up on her. But to her surprise, the person at the door was a woman wearing a maid uniform, her face shadowed beneath the brim of an official-looking hat, pushing a cart on wheels and covered with a white tablecloth that went down to the floor.

"Excuse me, Miss Ambrosa, the governor sent me to check on you and offer you a tea service to help you sleep. I apologize if I woke you."

Jinny looked past her to the hulk, who was alone on guard duty and showed no outward sign he knew or cared that the woman was there. She shrugged and opened the door wider so the maid could push the cart into the room.

After placing the cart in the middle of the bedroom, the woman made a show of wordlessly preparing the tea. Then she looked over at Jinny, who had taken a seat on the edge of the bed, and smiled. It was at that moment that Jinny first really took in the woman's appearance, and she had to fight to control her reaction. The maid looked much like *her*. She was Jinny's height, with a similar build and complexion. Her hair was the same blond color under the hat as well, and she also had brown eyes like Jinny. Her facial features, while generally similar, were different enough to spoil the comparison, but the woman still could have passed for her in a crowd.

"Ma'am, have you been shown the functionality of the shower yet? It's different from what you might be used to." As the maid spoke, her eyes met Jinny's and flicked back and forth between her and the bathroom repeatedly.

"No, I was wondering about that. Do you mind showing me?" Jinny asked, taking the hint.

The maid nodded and motioned for Jinny to follow her. Once they were both in the bathroom, the woman made a big show of turning the shower on and showing her how all the dials and controls worked. Only once the water was running did she lean in close and talk directly into Jinny's ear.

"The running water will interfere with the microphones, and there are no cameras in the suite. We have a plan to get you out. You and I will switch clothes, and I'll stay here until you get back. Now, I'm going to turn off the water before they get suspicious. You'll need to ask me questions about the shower or other fixtures long enough for us to make the switch."

Jinny nodded, and the woman started chatting inanely about the shower controls as she turned them off. Jinny asked a few questions but largely let the maid do most of the talking as she played the role of the chatty help to perfection. While they spoke, each undressed quickly and changed into the other's clothes. After just a couple of minutes, they were each dressed as the other had been when Jinny first opened the door, even down to the awkward combination of full clothing and a robe on the maid, just in case the hulk had indeed been paying attention. Jinny also wore the maid's hat, pulled low over her face to hide her features.

"Well, Miss Ambrosa," the maid said cheerily, "I should let you get back to your tea." Then she led the way out of the bathroom and to the front door, where she opened it a crack so the hulk could hear their conversation but not see either of their faces.

"Are you sure you want me to leave the tea cart here? I can collect it in the morning." the maid asked while subtly nodding her head.

"Yes, I may want to refresh the tea later if I have trouble sleeping," Jinny replied, taking the queue.

"Very well," said the maid in the same cheerful tone. "I'll be back around seven in the morning to collect the cart and take your breakfast order. Does that work?" Another subtle nod.

"Yes, that will be perfect. Thank you so much," Jinny replied. She let the maid, dressed as her, open the door fully and usher her outside the room. With the hat pulled low, Jinny walked right past the hulk without a glance and made her way to the lift, fingering the access card the other woman had slipped into the pocket of the maid uniform.

Though Jinny had not read the maid, the woman had imparted just enough information by word, gesture, and facial expression for Jinny to know what she needed to do. She arrived at the lift a moment later and pressed the call button. Once it arrived, thankfully empty, she stepped inside, scanned the card on the reader, and selected the ground floor.

Now the problem was that she was leaving the building *too early*. The conversation and clothes switch with the maid had taken less than five minutes, and it would be nearly an hour before the time appointed for the black car to arrive.

But the maid had thought of that. There was a small scrap of paper affixed to the back of the access card. On it was a simple set of instructions.

Three minutes later, Jinny was on the ground floor and safely ensconced in a small office with a door plate that read 'hospitality services'. There were four desks in the room, all deserted, and by the pictures on each desk, she quickly deduced that one belonged to her savior maid. There she waited in terrified boredom until five minutes to one am, at which point she simply couldn't wait any longer. Quietly, as if the building itself were listening for her to mess up her escape, she eased out of the office door and made her way through a service hallway to the main lobby. There she kept her hat low but waved at a bored-looking security guard who called out, "See you tomorrow, Ursula," without more than glancing up from his tablet.

Twenty seconds later, she was outside the building, at the edge of a large circular drive, but the black car wasn't there!

Even though she was still a few minutes early, panic nearly seized her. *What if the car doesn't come?* A dozen scenarios flew through her head, all of them ending in interrogation rooms where the snake leered at her and asked her questions she couldn't answer. Just as the clock struck one, and she was ready to turn tail and try to make her way back to the relative safety of the maid's office, she glanced across the circular drive and the main road in time to see a small black car pull up and park on the opposite side of the road from the government building.

Breathing a sigh of relief, Jinny walked slowly across the main boulevard, grateful it was free of other traffic at this hour. As she neared the car and saw the tinted windows, she had another thought. *What if this is all a trick? What if this isn't even the right car?* But it was too late for second thoughts, and she took a deep breath as she opened the rear door facing the street and ducked her head down to peer into the car.

She released the breath when she saw that the back seat opposite her was occupied by the same reader who had passed her the information in the reception hall. Except gone was the deferential and skittish manner he'd adopted there. In its place was a straight back, a gaze of cool confidence, and a handsome face wearing a small smile.

She nodded to him and entered the car, seated herself, and pulled the door closed behind her.

"Are you ready, Reader Ambrosa, to learn what Australia is *really* like?" he asked in a firm voice, so at odds with his earlier stutter.

"I am."

"Then let's take a ride. I promise all your questions will be answered shortly."

---

## FOUR MONTHS AGO; 721 P.D.

"Hey, honey, I'm home," Ryder called out as he walked into Jinny's apartment.

"Funny," she said drily from her place on the couch. "You know that gets old after the 20$^{th}$ time you do it, right?"

He smiled widely and put his shoulder bag down on the small kitchen table before he walked over and started rummaging through her fridge. He had been coming to her apartment every night for the last three weeks, posing as her boyfriend. Since they were both members of the enhanced community, no one would bat an eye, even though they had different genetic mutations. Speaker-reader pairings were common enough that it wouldn't raise any suspicions. And it allowed them to more closely coordinate efforts as they tracked what was becoming an odd spate of suicides reported by some of the other cells across the colonies. Ryder was doing his best to use his position in the Department of Health and Welfare to find additional information, but it had been slow going.

To help, Jinny had gotten herself temporarily assigned to nothing but loyalty readings. It served the purposes of her rebel cell just fine; the information they often needed was better known by government employees than by murder suspects. It also served Jinny's purpose of continuing to reduce the number of traumatic memories she read that might add to her nightmares, though she hadn't shared that reasoning with the team.

However, Ryder was becoming suspicious, especially after she'd woken up screaming multiple nights, loud enough for him to hear from the living room couch. He had asked her about it, and she had played it off as a normal part of being a reader, but she could tell he wasn't buying the explanation.

"Ryder, sit down. We need to talk." In the three months she had been with Joan's rebel cell, she had quickly grown to trust them. Still, that trust wouldn't have been enough for what she was about to do, except that she had also realized one important fact: the team was putting themselves in unnecessary danger by not using her talents to the fullest. They had been operating under the assumption that she could only read the last 15 and 1/2 hours of her subjects' memories. So, they had employed other means on multiple occasions to learn things from outside that period, all the while not knowing that Jinny could have done it for them with much less risk.

She felt like she had enough blood on her hands over the years from the people she hadn't been able to save, or from the killers she hadn't been able to put in prison, all in order to keep her secret. She couldn't bear the thought of adding Ryder's, John's, and Joan's lives to the toll.

"What's up?" Ryder asked, plopping down into the lone chair in the small living room that sat at a right angle to the couch and balancing a plate of cold pizza on his knee and a bottle of beer in one hand.

"I…" she trailed off, not sure of how to continue. But speakers were nothing if not patient; careers as bureaucrats and politicians usually required being comfortable with silence as a way to learn about your opponents. Being a rebel on top of that, Ryder had turned patience into an art form, so he waited while she sorted through her feelings. Finally, Jinny found her voice.

"I'm not what you think I am."

"Hmm. You're not a reader?" he asked, grinning and taking a bite of the pizza slice. "Or you're not a natural blond?"

She frowned. "This is serious, Ryder. Can you stop the joking for just one night?"

Immediately, the speaker's face went deadly serious, and he leaned forward and set the pizza and the beer down on the small coffee table between them. "Sorry, you have my full attention."

Jinny opened her mouth and just started talking. Before she knew it, Ryder knew almost *everything*: her special abilities, her father's experimentations on her, and the death of her mother.

In the end, she told him far more than she had intended to, but the words came out in a rush, and the feeling of catharsis at *finally* telling someone the things that only she had lived with for so long was heady and intoxicating. She chased the feeling like a drug, telling him more and more. The only things she kept back were the nightmares and her inevitable psychotic break; she convinced herself that was far enough in the future that she wasn't a danger to the team quite yet, but really, she just wasn't ready to share that with anyone yet.

It took almost an hour, with Ryder staying largely silent except for a few pointed questions he asked for clarification. At the end of her monologue, he broke out into a wide smile.

"Jinny, you just made my year!" he exclaimed. "To think, all this time, I've been hanging out with the most valuable member of the entire rebellion, and I'm just now realizing it. This is terrific!"

Jinny's jaw dropped in surprise. "You mean, you're not mad?"

He gave her an incredulous look. "How could I possibly be mad? I mean, this is the greatest thing I've ever heard, amiga! We are going to do *so much* good with your abilities; we may finally stand a chance against the Council. The possibilities are endless."

"But I withheld critical information from you."

Ryder's smile didn't falter, but he looked her straight in the eyes. "In your position, I would have done the same thing. To be honest, we've kept a lot of information from you as well in the name of compartmentalization. And given what the Council would do if they ever found out about you...." He shrugged. "There's no way you could have trusted us at the beginning enough to tell us something this big."

Then his grin widened. "All I can say is that it's a good thing you've never read *me*, amiga. My level of awesomeness would have filled you with insane jealousy."

Jinny threw a couch cushion at him and laughed. "Sure! You've told me enough stories. I don't need to read you to know that it was *you* who set loose the greased pig in the Speaker Academy dorm hall your final year!"

He dodged the pillow and sniffed theatrically. "I still maintain that it was Charlie Kim and that I had no idea that the pig would defecate in the headmaster's office. That was just a bonus."

She laughed again, the feeling of catharsis of not only sharing her gift but *joking* about it with another person almost too much for her to bear.

They talked through the night, her sharing more and more of what her gifts meant and Ryder scheming about how they could turn the Council's operations on Nova Tejas and beyond on their heads. They even came up with specific plans on how to use her abilities to track down information on the rash of suicides they were investigating.

Ryder also helped her game plan how she would tell John and Joan at their next meeting of the full cell. Surprisingly, when she did tell the two blenders a few days later, it was far easier than even when she'd told him. And the two blenders had received the information with almost equal excitement.

Jinny felt freer than she had since she had told off Frank in the hovertaxi after her Academy graduation, threatening him with the exposure of his and her secrets if he ever contacted her again. Except this time, the catharsis was even greater because it wasn't based on her hatred of her father but on genuine friendship and open honesty, such as Jinny had never experienced before.

Then a funny thing happened. For the first time in months, Jinny had no nightmares. The next several nights were the same. It was as if the release of finally telling someone her secret had opened up a floodgate of suppressed trauma that had taken away whatever was causing the nightmares to plague her.

Now Jinny realized something: she finally had meaning in her life. And blast it all; she was going to *live* that life!

The next week, she told her boss she was open to doing more crime scene readings but specifically asked if she could work suicides, given her experience with reading Sakura after hers. He enthusiastically agreed. The suicide detail was one of the hardest slots for the Corps to fill; most readers aggressively avoided it as the despair in the readings added up. It was even riskier for Jinny, given her abilities and her dreams. Still, with the nightmares stopped for the moment, and in the name of a higher purpose, she felt it important that she take it on.

A few weeks later, she also read the New Dallas Guard Commissioner and learned not just about the greater extent of the suicides across the colonies but also about his plans to terminate two earnest guardsmen who had asked a few too many questions about the same. That very night, Jinny, Ryder, Joan, and John met to come up with a plan that, unbeknownst to them, would shake the very foundations of human space and result in three of the four of them not living past the end of the week.

## PRESENT DAY; JULY 3, 731 P.D.

After following a circuitous route, the black car deposited Jinny and Charles Mattingly—the reader from the reception hall, who had needlessly introduced himself given that Jinny had plucked his name from her reading—in front of a single-family home on the outskirts of Sydney. The home was nondescript in every way and looked just like every cookie-cutter house in the neighborhood. No lights shone through the front windows, but a dim porch light illuminated the front door.

Charles got out of the car and led Jinny up to the door. A dog at a neighboring home started barking loudly as soon as it heard the car door closing, startling Jinny and making her glance around in near panic. But Mattingly ignored it and walked right up to the home's front door, where he knocked in a peculiar rhythm while throwing a small grin her way. She knew from the reading that he enjoyed this cloak-and-dagger spy stuff more than he should—certainly more than a true professional like Tyrus—but that he was also fairly good at it.

The door opened, and a man peered out. He studied the two of them and then held out his bare hand. Charles took off his glove and grasped the hand, and the two men waited a few seconds, reading each other. It was smart, Jinny thought, to ensure that neither of them was operating under duress.

"Good, all according to plan then," the man inside the door finally said in a gruff voice, opening it wider and motioning for them to enter. They found themselves in a small hallway that was only dimly lit, but Jinny could see a brighter light emanating from the far end toward the back of the house. Without prompting, she walked in that direction with Charles and the new guy on her heels making no move to stop her.

The light at the end of the hallway proved to be the doorway to a well-lit kitchen with a small breakfast table. Two large-stature men leaned against the counter in the kitchen, and a lone woman who looked old enough to be Jinny's grandmother sat at the table, peering at something on a pad in front of her. She didn't look up when Jinny entered the room, but the two men studied her intently. They were clearly the muscle. And everyone, including the older woman, was wearing gloves.

Jinny stopped just inside the doorway, and Charles entered and stood at her side.

"Majko," he said, the single word carrying obvious respect and reverence. "This is the reader from the colonies: Jinny Ambrosa."

The woman didn't react immediately but finished reading whatever was on the pad first. When she looked up, Jinny was struck by her startlingly bright blue eyes that seemed out of sorts with her weather-worn and tanned features. The woman said nothing but nodded once, and Charles gestured to Jinny to take a seat at the table.

The Majko—Jinny knew it was more of a title than a name, again from reading Charles—watched her as she approached. When she'd finally seated herself across from the old woman, the Majko gave a small smile and opened her mouth to speak. Her voice was stronger than Jinny would have expected of a woman her age, and it seemed to resonate in the small room. It was the voice of a woman used to others listening when she spoke.

"Charles tells me that your intentions are sincere. He's quite talented, you know," she inclined her head toward Mattingly, who had taken up station leaning against the counter with the other two men. The man who had opened the front door had not followed them into the kitchen. "Charles can read faster than most any other reader," the woman continued. "He was able, through the brief contact with you, to read not just the last several hours of the boring government meetings you sat through, but also that you came to Australia to truly learn how the enhanced are being treated."

She paused, staring intently at Jinny. "But more so, that you came looking for something that you don't believe you can get anywhere else."

"Impressive," Jinny responded, sensing that the time for her to ask her questions had not yet come.

"Yes, it is," the Majko agreed, nodding slowly. "But I believe your talents far exceed even those of our dear Charles. Am I right?"

The question shocked Jinny. Having never met this woman, there was no way she could know her secret. Outside of Tyrus, Riggs, and Jynx, only Juliana Taylor knew even the basics of Jinny's full abilities. And she had told no one, not even Tyrus, about Juliana. She was also certain that Tyrus, Riggs, and Jynx would not betray her—Tyrus and Riggs would keep her secret out of loyalty to her; Jynx would keep it out of loyalty to Riggs and because she simply didn't enjoy talking to *anyone*.

"What makes you say that?" she asked the woman, cocking her head in a look of feigned confusion and playing for time to think.

"Don't worry," the woman said perceptively. "No one has betrayed your secret. Nor will anyone in this room. I learned it not from anyone's lips but from careful observation backed up by years of experience. You could say that as a reader, I have worked to develop *all* my skills of perception, not just those granted to me by simple genetics."

The Majko paused again, staring intently at her. When Jinny didn't respond, the woman's smile grew broader.

"I have watched every clip of video we can get on you since you arrived on Earth. You are clearly close to the man Tyrus Tyne and the man Riggs. Both of them know your secret. It is obvious by the way they act around you."

She leaned forward, continuing to make intense eye contact with Jinny, making the younger woman feel like she couldn't possibly look away. "They trust you; that much is clear. But they still keep their distance and are wary of your inadvertent touch. Especially Tyne. It is also obvious that he trusts you and you *alone* in this galaxy. Still, he avoids your touch, as does Riggs. Their wariness of you in the face of so much trust and even love suggests to me that there is something far beyond the capabilities of a normal reader that gives them anxiety. Tyne especially would not react the way he does around you if all you could see were the last day or so of his memories.

"So that leads me to the conclusion that you can see much *more* than the average reader. Am I right?"

Jinny was astounded at the woman's perceptiveness and had to try hard to tamp down any visible reaction. By the look on the Majko's face, she wasn't entirely successful.

The woman sat back, and her smile grew sly as she regarded Jinny. "Yes, I thought so. How far back can you read?"

Jinny's mind raced for a moment—a dozen different lies and half-truths that she considered and discarded. Ultimately, she took the straight and honest road. "All of it," she replied. "I can read *everything* a person remembers."

Now it was the Majko's turn to look astounded, which gave Jinny a fleeting sense of gratification. But quickly, the woman's features resolved into a broad enough smile to show her teeth. "Even more than I suspected. Amazing. Your online bio makes little mention of your parents, except that your father was a science adviser to the Council government. I'm assuming that he had something to do with this. Unless *all* readers in the colonies now have this astounding talent?"

Jinny shook her head. "As far as I'm aware, just me. And I may share a lot of things with you, but my father is not a topic that I will discuss."

The Majko's smile didn't fade, but she nodded her head at the tacit acknowledgment of her suspicions. "Very well. You have already told me much about yourself, though, to be fair, most of it I'd already surmised. I imagine you know much already about what I will tell you, given that you read Charles. Nonetheless, let us speak openly of it so that nothing is lost or confused.

"As you've probably guessed or read from Charles, the government you're meeting with in their fancy downtown building is nothing more than an occupational puppet government appointed by the UE to keep the enhanced in line. They rarely leave their building and the surrounding residential area. I think they know that if they did, the people would tear them apart." Her smile turned grim at the thought.

"I'm sure you've also guessed that they have no intention of letting *you* roam the city outside the building. That's because you would quickly notice that *everyone* in Sydney is a speaker. There are three major metropolitan areas left on the Australian continent that survived the pre-diaspora wars and were in good enough condition for our ancestors to rebuild when they were exiled here. Sydney, the present capital, is populated entirely by speakers. Perth is where the readers like myself and Charles live. And the blenders live in Brisbane."

"What about the enacters?" Jinny asked, though she already knew part of the answer.

The Majko's smile disappeared. "The enacters don't have a true city. They live in a series of small settlements spread throughout the interior of the continent—an area long known as the Outback. You see, the darkest truth of our society is that we, as the enhanced, do not even trust each other. The speakers don't trust the readers to learn all of their secrets. The readers believe all the blenders are potential spies. The blenders have nothing but disdain for the manipulative words of the speakers.

"And no one trusts the enacters. How could we? Any enacter you meet could be loyal to the government, to their parents, or to any unknowable third party. You can never guess what they will do in the name of genetic obedience. Even worse, we all fear what they could do if any of the other groups harnessed their power. Imagine an army of enacters loyal only to the speakers, sent to subjugate the readers and the blenders."

"Sounds familiar," Jinny observed drily.

The other woman's eyebrows raised. "Yes, I suppose it might, to you. But the truth here is that we fear both what the enacters are and what they could be made to be. So, by mutual agreement and through mutual fear, we shun them and banish them outside of civilization to eke out a sustenance living in the wilderness, much the same way the regulars have banished all of us here to Australia. Doing the same to the enacters is far from our finest accomplishment and gives us great shame, but we see no other way."

The woman bowed her head and closed her eyes for a moment. Jinny didn't need to read her to see the pain behind her expression.

"Who is 'we'?" she asked the woman. This part had been murky in her all-too-brief reading of Charles.

The Majko opened her eyes and peered back up at Jinny with a serious expression. "We are the real rulers of Australia, my dear. An oligarchy, if you will. I rule the readers as their Majko, the traditional title of the perpetually female leaders we've had since the beginning of our exile to this island. I rule by hereditary right to some degree because my bloodline has always represented the strongest of the readers by ability." She nodded toward Mattingly. "Charles is my nephew, which is why he is so capable. I believe you knew that already. However, I am also confirmed by a vote of the people in Perth as my eventual replacement also will be.

"The speakers have a legislature and make a big show of being more democratic than we are, but ultimately, their aptly named 'Speaker of the House' makes all the actual decisions and represents them in our oligarchic council. The blenders? Well, no one is sure what their actual form of government is. Their representative to the council is always called 'John Doe' or 'Jane Doe', both as a name and as a title. I'm not even sure that they send the same representative each time we meet, as there's no telling them apart, and the person looks different every time and often switches genders.

"But the enacters, by our design and to our everlasting shame, have no central government of their own. We work to keep their settlements isolated from one another so that no single leader can gain enough of an obedient following to be a threat to us. Therefore, they also have no seat on the council."

She stopped talking and took a deep breath. Jinny used the break to ask her next question. "Why keep all of this from me? Why did the government not just let me go to Perth and meet with you and the other readers?"

The Majko took on another grim expression. "Two reasons, my dear. First, the UE has been lying to themselves for so long about the true nature of government here that I'm not sure even President Pereira or most of the members of Congress understand how little influence the so-called governor and his speaker cronies have outside of their building, even with their own kind in Sydney.

"But second, it's clear that they fear *you*. You are an unknown factor, representing an unknown and hidden force—the rebellion against the Council. And a politician fears nothing more than that which he cannot understand, and by understanding, control. If you were to learn the truth about how the enhanced are treated—cut off and isolated by the rest of the UE, shunned as second-class citizens, and forced to live in relative poverty—then you might use what influence you have with the colonial rebels to turn them against Earth.

"Or worse yet, you might find a way to make an alliance with Mars. If there's anything, my dear, that the UE government fears more than the enhanced, it's the Martians."

"But, I—" Jinny began, but the Majko raised her hand to cut her off.

"I'm sorry, Reader Ambrosa, but time is of the essence. I am expected to be in an early morning meeting back in Perth, and my absence would be noticed and suspect in its timing with your trip. So, I must be leaving shortly.

"So let me get to the real reason that I set up this clandestine meeting; the real reason I traveled in secret into a city I'm forbidden to enter without a formal invitation from the Speaker of the House.

"As I said, I've watched you closely and listened to every word you've spoken in public, and in some situations, not so public, since you arrived on Earth. One thing has stood out to me. You may be an immensely powerful reader—indeed more powerful than even myself or my ancestors—but you have an incredibly narrow view of your capabilities. There are things we could teach you… things *I* could teach you that would magnify your capabilities beyond anything you can imagine.

"Now, I am going to ask you a question, and I need you to answer me truthfully. I promise in advance it will betray no confidences you may hold with your colonial companions. But before I ask, you must promise to give me a truthful answer, regardless of the question. Can you do that?"

Jinny's mind raced. She had just met this woman, and the only proof of her identity and sincerity was a brief conversation with her and a briefer reading of Charles Mattingly. And judging by how much this Majko knew of her abilities, it may have even been possible to somehow manipulate her all-too-brief reading of Mattingly to only show what the Majko wanted her to know.

Despite these doubts and every shred of logic telling her to refuse the request, Jinny listened to another voice deep inside and simply said, "Yes."

The Majko smiled again, in a grandmotherly sort of way. But when she spoke, her voice had a far more serious tone. "Tell me, Jinny, have you ever found yourself doing something that you can't recall ever having learned for yourself? Yet you do it like it's second nature—almost muscle memory?"

Jinny considered the question, her mind racing to the time she'd flown the fighter after reading Tyrus. *But I was so bad at that? Wasn't I?*

"I don't think so," was her response. The Majko frowned immediately, so Jinny continued. "I'm not trying to hide the truth. I can think of one or two occasions that *might* fit with what you're asking, but I can't be sure."

The Majko's frown softened, and the old woman nodded solemnly. "Then I see we have much to teach you about the nature of the reader gene. Even before the Council left the Sol system, they worked hard to repress this knowledge, and apparently, they continue to do so. But in our centuries of isolation here on this continent, we've rediscovered what we are capable of. And it is so, so much more than what they taught you."

The woman leaned forward again, speaking faster, her excitement obvious. "Jinny, when you read someone, you don't just get their memories, or even their thoughts and intentions, as some of the strongest readers have been known to perceive. You also get their *knowledge*. Anything they've learned to do in the period you're reading, you get the same learning as if you were right there with them. This has always been a limited ability, as most readers cannot read back further than 24 hours, but we've used it to impressive effect. A reader in Perth can get through schooling in a fraction of the time of normal humans. Imagine four students going to four different classes during the day and then reading each other that evening. It's as if they had *all* gone to all four classes. It compresses days of teaching into a single day for them.

"Now, multiply that by a dozen students. There are limits, of course, to how much knowledge even a strong reader can absorb in a single day's worth of readings, but...." She sat back again now, a glint in her eye.

"...but now imagine yourself. You don't *just* read a single day. You read *everything*. A lifetime of schooling in a single reading, or a lifetime of specialized training. Imagine having the piloting skills of your friend Riggs, the spy craft of your friend Tyrus, and whatever skills rattle around in the head of the woman Jynx. Imagine having all of that and being able to *use* it.

"That's why I came all this way, under threat of imprisonment or even death, to meet you. Because *you*, Jinny Ambrosa, are the penultimate reader. With your abilities combined with my knowledge, we can finally break the readers free of the UE government's discriminatory rule. You are the one who can be the savior of us all!"

She stopped, a little spittle on her lip from her frantic exclamations, and the Majko looked a little sheepish at her excitement, so at odds with her earlier confident and aloof behavior. Jinny sat stunned and tried to process everything the woman had just told her. Slowly, she shook her head.

"What you're saying sounds impossible. I mean, why would I have never noticed this before? Is it possible it's unique to readers on Earth? And what about the 15-day rule?"

"Bah!" the old woman replied dismissively with a wave of one hand. "It's all part of the original gene mutation. Our records go back far enough to verify that. We will open those records to you so that you, too, can realize your potential. For centuries, the Council has told readers in their so-called academies what they are and are not capable of doing. Tell someone that often enough, and they naturally believe it. As for the so-called 15-day rule, that is where actual practice comes in. Like anything you learn, the things learned from reading must be practiced to retain the knowledge. Because by applying the knowledge you have read, you make it *yours*, and then the 15-day rule no longer applies.

"You only have never noticed any of this is possible because they taught you it was impossible. And I'm telling you that's wrong. It *is* possible, and I can teach you how. I want you to come back with me *today* to Perth. We'll hide you there. The UE will search for you, but your power is worth hiding, and I have contacts in the government who will help. I will train you personally, and in six months, perhaps a year, you'll be so powerful that you will be able to help the Four Worlds win the war against the Council *and* help us get our freedom from this island and reenter human society. We *need* you, Jinny. All of humanity needs you. Will you come with me?"

Jinny sat silent, stunned at the woman's words and the sheer audacity of her request. Still, she only considered it for a few seconds, then shook her head. "No. I can't. My friends need me. And I won't put your people at such risk to hide me. But it's possible I can come back later, and you can teach me then." She added the last part hastily, not knowing if it would ever happen but feeling the need to give the old woman *something*.

The Majko abruptly stood up, glaring down at her. "No, it has to be *now*!" She smacked the table with her fist. "If you leave now, you will never come back to us. *You* know it, and *I* know it. Even if you choose to, the government won't let you. It has to be now!"

"Then it will be never," Jinny said sadly. "I can't abandon my friends, not even for what you promise. I'm... sorry. I also thank you for all you've told me today. But there are things I've also come to ask of you before I go."

The Majko sat back down in her seat, deflated, making no sign that she'd even heard Jinny. She forged ahead with her first request anyway.

"I've been having dreams, terrible ones. Memories of those I've read, long past the 15-day period, but so vivid that it feels like they're my own. And they won't stop. Have you encountered anything like this before? Can you tell me how to make them stop?" She realized with chagrin that her voice had taken on a desperate, pleading tone.

The Majko regarded her coldly, but then something softened in the old woman's gaze, and she nodded sadly. "Yes, I have encountered it before. It is the dark side of the same abilities I've just discussed with you. Sometimes the memories of those we read become so muddled with our own that our brains lose their grasp on the reality of who we are. I have, thankfully, never experienced it myself. More thankfully, it is quite rare. It usually happens with readers who have read too many people, or young children who have read something terrible in their early years, before they were ready for it.

"I imagine that with your abilities—with the sheer quantity of memories you absorb every time you read even a single person—that such a thing may have been inevitable."

"And does it...?" Jinny started to ask but couldn't finish the question.

The other woman shook her head and grimaced. "Sometimes they get over it. Unfortunately, it more often drives them insane. Some kill themselves to make it stop—especially the younger ones who don't tell their parents or some other adult what they're going through because they're ashamed. Even many of the adults break down completely and are never right again. Only a few, very few, seem to ever get better."

"Is there anything you can tell me that might help?" Jinny asked, now overtly pleading without shame.

The woman frowned. "I wish there was, Reader Ambrosa. Your case is... unique. Never before have I encountered a reader with your abilities. So, I am unsure what advice I can give you. But," she stopped and gave Jinny a small smile, "if you return with us to learn what I have offered you, then perhaps we can work together to find the solution to your problem as well. We have many doctors and psychologists who work exclusively with readers. If anyone can find a solution, it will be them."

"Thank you. As I said, I will do my best to return once my mission here on Earth is done." Jinny said this reluctantly, eager to grasp even the thin straw of hope the Majko offered her. Then she guiltily remembered the other question she'd come to ask—the more important one that she owed to her friends and all the people of the Four Worlds.

"I have one more question," she told the Majko sheepishly. "You mentioned readers here can't see further back than 24 hours. What's the average?"

The older woman frowned. "Twenty hours is the average, though some readers can only read 16 or 17. Why do you ask?"

Jinny shook her head. "It's better that you don't know; that way, no one can learn it from you."

The woman's frown remained, but she nodded this time. "That is wise. What would be wiser is for you to come with me now and learn what I have to teach you. And so that we can perhaps figure out the solution to your nightmares as well."

That final carrot, presented again, was almost enough to convince Jinny. But to betray and abandon her friends, she would need a lot more than 'perhaps', and she could see from the Majko's expression that the old woman knew that as well. She was making the request one last time as a duty to her people, just as Jinny was turning it down out of duty to hers.

"I thank you, and I promise to try to return," she said simply and softly. Then she turned and looked at Charles Mattingly. "I'm ready to go back to the government building now."

It was the first time she had looked at him since she and the Majko had begun speaking, and she was sad to see the clear distress on his features, though she wasn't sure if it was aimed at her or his aunt. He said nothing but nodded at her request.

They left the Majko sitting at the kitchen table and looking after Jinny with equal parts pleading and sympathy. Twice on the way to the front door, Jinny almost turned around to tell the woman she *would* come with her. But she and Charles exited the house into the warm night to the sound of the same dog barking. She saw the black car immediately pull up as if it had been waiting just down the road for them, which it probably had been.

Only once did she look back at the house as they drove away, wondering if she'd just made a noble decision or the most foolish one of her life.

---

Jordan Archer watched Jinny Ambrosa and the man she had traveled with depart the small home only 27 minutes after they had entered it. He swore softly to himself. It had taken him too long to maneuver himself to a place where he might pick up on their conversation using a directional laser microphone he carried for just that purpose.

Whoever had chosen this house and neighborhood for their clandestine meeting had chosen well. It was the Sydney equivalent of a lower-middle-class neighborhood, which meant that most of the speakers who lived here worked normal daylight hours. So, anyone seen out on the street in the middle of the night would raise suspicions. But it wasn't wealthy enough to breed paranoia, so few houses had security cameras of any type installed.

That latter part should have served Archer as much as it did Ambrosa and those she was meeting. Unfortunately, the houses on both sides of the one she'd entered also had dogs in the backyards. One had whimpered as Archer had approached the house, forcing him to stop dead in his tracks and hunker down behind a bush until the animal lost interest and wandered away from the fence. He'd been unable to get any closer and hadn't picked up anything when pointing his microphone at the home's front windows. That made him suspect the meeting was taking place in the rear part of the house. He'd been slowly working his way around the side yard, moving carefully and pausing frequently to ensure he didn't alert the neighboring canine, when he'd heard the front door open again.

The dog had barked as soon as it heard the door opening, and Archer had used the disturbance to mask his own quicker movement back toward the front of the house, where he arrived in time to see Jinny and the man get into the same car they'd arrived in and speed off.

As he got back into his own aircar, he reluctantly sent an update to his employer.

## THE FOUR WORLDS - SUBVERSION

*Castor: Reader met with unknown individuals in Sydney suburb. Unable to get audio or eyes on whomever she met with. Following again now.*

He knew that the response from Iasonas would not be enthusiastic.

---

Jinny and Charles arrived back in downtown Sydney a full two hours before the seven AM deadline the maid had given her. Charles instructed the driver to go to a different part of the city, and they pulled up outside a small diner.

"I know the owner. He's a speaker, but he's sympathetic to the reader cause. And the UE government has no cameras or spies in this place. They wouldn't last long," he explained as he escorted her out of the car and into the eatery. The driver stayed behind in the car, waiting for them.

At five AM, the diner was empty except for the patrons at a single table, an older couple who ignored them completely. Charles led Jinny to a table, and a waitress magically appeared a moment later and took their orders. Jinny, who hadn't eaten after Charles' surreptitious communication at the reception, found that she was ravenously hungry. She downed several cups of coffee and two large slices of apple pie. Only after she finished did Charles say anything.

"Look," he said almost too quietly for her to hear, "my aunt is a passionate woman, and she probably came on a little strong. You just have to understand that we've waited centuries for an opportunity like this one to come along. Centuries of living as literal prisoners on this continent, cut off from the wonders of the world and the rest of human space, feeling like we have no chance of progression or purpose beyond a meager day-to-day existence. They keep the parts near Sydney nice for when government dignitaries visit, but most of Australia is in poverty, including Perth. Even most of the speakers can't afford to live in Sydney itself and live in the poorer suburbs on the outskirts. Only the ones who are willing to sell out their own get to be part of the UE's puppet government."

He fiddled with his fork, moving what was left of his pie around the plate in front of him as if debating how to continue.

"You have the potential to change all of that. Someone with your capabilities could finally make the government listen, or even overthrow them. My aunt has long spoken about a revolution, though she shares her plans with no one, so I don't know the details. Still, I do see the incredible potential of someone like you.

"So, my aunt got a little too excited about it. But I understand your decision, even if I don't like it. And it *has* to be your decision because there's one thing my aunt didn't say...."

He trailed off, and Jinny said nothing, waiting for him to finish his thought and sensing that any coaxing on her part would convince him not to. As she waited, the bell on the diner's door clanged as another patron entered: a plain-looking man walking in the slouch and tired gait of a manual laborer. Something about the man tickled Jinny's senses, but before she could think about it, Charles continued his thought. He spoke low so that she had to strain to hear him.

"She told you that you could be our savior and the savior of the Sol system, that you could liberate the readers. There's another side to that. If you learn what she can teach you, and you decide to use it for your own purposes, you could also be the destroyer. It's not an exaggeration to say that a human with the knowledge and learning of dozens, even hundreds, of lifetimes could be the most powerful person in the known galaxy.

"I know, I know," he waved both hands, palms down. His hands, like hers, were bare; they could not risk being outed as readers in the middle of a speaker stronghold. "It sounds like hyperbole or a fairytale. But truthfully, knowledge *is* the path to power. Imagine a single person who could hack any system, counter and overcome any battle plan, infiltrate any group, and speak with such knowledge and authority that people would fall all over themselves to follow her—like a speaker but with the understanding to back up her words. And with skill sets even beyond those of your friend Tyne. Imagine it. That kind of power would allow this person to do more good throughout the galaxy than any other person before her, or to do more damage.

There's no middle ground with that kind of knowledge. It *has* to be used."

He looked up and met her eye. "You need to know that *before* you decide. No matter what my aunt thinks."

Jinny almost reached across the table and laid her bare hand on his, then stopped herself. She also didn't smile. The gravity of the information he'd just given her would not allow her to show any happiness right now. She met his eyes, and it seemed to give him a modicum of strength.

"Thank you, Charles." Anymore, she couldn't say. There was far too much to take in, and she needed time to reflect on his words.

He nodded and gave her a small and fleeting smile. "I'll take you back soon. Consider what we've told you tonight. And consider what you told my aunt; maybe we *can* help you with your other problem. You're always welcome back."

He withdrew a small piece of paper from his shirt pocket and slid it across the table for her to pick up, careful not to let his bare fingers brush hers. "I could let you read me again, but I imagine *you* don't want me reading you right now. So, commit this to memory between here and the government building. It's a comm number and an address in Perth. You can reach me there and, through me, the Majko. Use it whenever you decide to come back. And I *do* hope you come back, Jinny."

He looked at her, his piercing blue eyes captivating her attention. For the briefest instant, Jinny imagined what it would be like to turn away from her mission to the Four Worlds and instead go with this man and his mysterious aunt. But almost immediately, she felt another twinge of guilt at the merest consideration of abandoning her friends, even if refusing to go to Perth now meant that she might go insane.

---

Archer watched from behind his menu as Jinny Ambrosa and the unknown man left the diner together. When he was sure she'd gone, he lowered the menu and frowned. The way Ambrosa's eyes had locked on him as he'd entered and the flash of suspicion on her face had terrified him. He'd known that, as a colonial experienced with blenders, she would be likely to pick out the signs of one, but the sheer speed with which she'd seemed to key onto him had shocked him. Luckily, her companion had distracted her long enough to let him get to a table out of her line of sight. From there, he'd surreptitiously photographed the man she was meeting. He'd also made a recording of everything they had said after he'd entered using his directional microphone.

He sent those pictures and the recording now to his employer.

The waitress came over to take his order, and he smiled and ordered a cup of coffee and a slice of pie; he thought that what Jinny and the mystery man had ordered looked good. But he would eat and drink quickly and be on his way. He hated being back in Australia. Visiting here always made him feel like he would never escape it again.

His palm vibrated.

*Iasonas: Disappointing that you did not get a recording of her first meeting, but this other recording is helpful. No need to follow further; she returns to Houston this afternoon. Need you back here sooner. There is a message waiting for you from Corey O'Leary. You are to take the job he offers you.*

Archer sat back in the diner booth and considered his employer's message. He'd only met Congressman Corey O'Leary for the first time that day in the Capitol Cafeteria almost a month prior. O'Leary had a reputation for being one of the few completely honest men in Houston and had never used Archer's services or, as far as he could tell, the services of other fixers like himself. So, when Iasonas had ordered him to make contact with the man that day, he'd been skeptical. But O'Leary had clearly been expecting him to do so, and since then, Archer had wondered if perhaps O'Leary *was* Iasonas.

It would make sense, he supposed. The man was known for his ability to work across party lines but also as a staunch and unyielding critic of the Pereira administration. It would be entirely possible that he was the mysterious political player working to fund candidates across all parties that would oppose the sitting president. Even the most outwardly honest individuals often had dark secrets. Archer would know.

His thoughts were interrupted by the server bringing his food, and he settled in to enjoy a surprisingly good slice of pie.

---

The anonymous driver of the black car took Jinny and Charles back to the government building. When they arrived, Jinny only nodded at Charles and got a small smile in return.

She was still wearing the maid's uniform and passed the guard in the lobby with no incident, used the card to take the lift back to her floor, and walked down the hallway. There was a moment of near panic when she saw the snake outside her room. She thought he would surely see through her disguise. However, the man couldn't take his eyes off her backside as she walked past and knocked on the door. She doubted the leach ever saw her face.

A few moments later, she was back in the small room. The real maid was already dressed in a copy of the uniform Jinny wore and said nothing as Jinny went to the bathroom and changed into a set of pajamas from her luggage. Then the other woman pushed the tea cart out of the door, Jinny's discarded uniform hidden under the tablecloth, and called back to her, "I'll have your breakfast order up in about half an hour," before letting the door close on the leering visage of the snake. Jinny wondered idly if the man would notice that the rear end he now watched leaving the room differed slightly from the one he'd seen arrive, but the creep made no cry of alarm, and Jinny flopped into the bed and stared at the darkened ceiling as a million thoughts flew through her mind.

But the one that kept coming to the surface concerned her the most. The readers here could read 20 hours or more! In the colonies, the average was so much lower. It *had* to be part of the reason, if not *the* reason, the Twenty were so intent on conquering the Four Worlds. Doing so would give them access to pure bloodlines that they could use to strengthen the enhancements back in the colonies. It still left the open question of *how* the Twenty knew about conditions on Earth; they had to know that the enhanced had been segregated from the rest of the population, or why assume the bloodlines here would be stronger?

Which brought up the question of how they were getting such intel when they hadn't even sent a survey ship through the Rift for over a hundred years. It was becoming increasingly likely to her way of thinking that the Twenty must have discovered another path through the Rift. That scared her greatly.

She thought of all of this for several minutes, consciously willing herself not to dwell on the darker issue, that the readers of Australia had had no sure answers for her personal situation. Because unless she found a way to stop the nightmares on her own, she was doomed. That thought would hang over her like a death sentence during all of her meetings in the government offices that morning and throughout her flight back to North America that afternoon.

# ACT II

The most jarring thing about the original genetic enhancements is that we still do not understand how they actually work. What causes an enacter to imprint on one, and only one, source of authority in their lifetime? How does a blender's body change its DNA to match that of its intended subject without losing the genetic mutation that makes him a blender? How does a reader see the memories of a corpse she touches, even after the brain is dead and all neurons have stopped firing? How does a speaker learn a new language fluently within days with no formal training other than being exposed to those who speak it, even knowing the meaning of words he has never heard spoken aloud?

We cannot answer any of these questions even after a thousand years. And why? Because the Council still insists on hamstringing our study of genetics in general and the enhanced mutations specifically. Not only did the 5th Council destroy all records of the original genetic engineering projects that created the enhanced, but their laws forbidding research into the enhancements still stand, an archaic absurdity after so many centuries, especially now that we face the waning of these capabilities because of the Council's equally foolish decision to allow the enhanced to intermarry with the regs.

It was all done with good intentions, or so the Council says. And in some ways, they may be right. Even I can imagine the catastrophe that could have arisen had someone outside the Council government gotten their hands on the secret method for creating their own enacters. Imagine one of the pirate lords building an army of enacters. Worse yet, imagine enacters more loyal to their parents than the government; it would be impossible to teach them anything!

The restrictions are also why it took 32 years of crash research to even come up with the baseline formula for Project Epsilon, and we're still likely ten years or more from being able to implement it. And the Council still insists on foolishly prohibiting our research into the same for readers, blenders, and speakers. For those, the Keeper has hinted there is a plan to reintroduce purity into the bloodlines. Still, unless there's some long-forgotten colony full of pure enhanced bloodlines, I can't see a way for him to be so sure of any plan he and his dullard friends in the Assembly come up with.

Sometimes I think the Keeper oversteps his bounds and may be hiding things even from the Council itself. It would be so easy for him; the Council members never communicate directly with any of us. It all runs through him.

That is why I have taken matters into my own hands. I knew that my wife and I both carry the dormant reader mutation, which meant that our child was likely to be a reader, albeit a weak one. But I found a way to enhance the baby's abilities! I won't go into details here; no one would believe me even if I shared the entire formula. But if it works, she may become the strongest reader to have ever lived. If not, she will most likely die before she reaches the age of manifesting her abilities, and I will have to start over with a new fetus.

Virginia doesn't know, of course. The poor woman is nothing but a simpering beauty queen. She was such a disappointment to her family when she wasn't born a reader herself, and she's actually convinced herself that it was a good thing! Someday she will see that I am right when our daughter is the model for all future enhanced. Someday the Council will see as well, and they will hail me as a hero. Until then, I must keep it a secret.

Now that the baby is born, I am running tests and collecting samples. Soon I will know if...

-Excerpt from the *Manifesto on Genetic Enhancements,* from the personal files of Dr. Frank Ambrosa

# CHAPTER 8

### TWENTY-SEVEN YEARS AGO; 704 P.D.

"Jynx, stop pulling your sister's hair!" The exasperated voice of Luanne Koppel chided the younger of her two twin daughters as she took the girl's sister into her arms to comfort the crying child.

"B-but Momma," whined seven-year-old Jynx, "she pulled my hair first."

Luanne regarded the girl with a raised eyebrow as the older twin, Dax, continued to sob into her shoulder, wetting her worn t-shirt. "Now, Jynx. What have I told you about lying to me?!" she snapped.

The little girl, wearing her favorite faded gingham dress, started to tear up, her lower lip quivering. "B-but Momma," she wailed, "I'm not lying. D-Dax is mean!"

Absently patting the still-crying Dax on her shoulder, Luanne shook her head emphatically at her other daughter. "Jynx, you apologize to your sister right *now*, or I'll have your father spank you when he gets home. Is that what you want? Is it?"

The floodgates opened, and Jynx cried in concert with her twin. "N-no," she forced out between great gasping sobs. "D-don't sp-spank me!"

"Then say you're sorry, Jynx."

"I'm s-sorry, Momma!"

Luanne shook her head again. "Don't tell *me*. Tell your sister."

Jynx was about to argue but saw the anger building in her mother's eyes and gave up the fight. "I'm s-sorry, Dax."

"For what?" Luanne prompted.

"For p-pulling your hair."

Dax turned and gave her sister a look and then turned back to bury her face anew in her mother's shoulder.

"OK, Jynx, now go to your room until your father gets home."

Jynx didn't argue but turned and ran, still crying, to the upstairs room she and Dax shared in the family's small house on Drake's World.

"What am I going to do with that child?" Luanne said to herself, but loud enough for Dax to hear. The little girl gave no sign she'd understood but continued to cry into her mother's shoulder for a full minute before her sobs subsided. Then she turned her head to look up at Luanne, eyes pleading.

"Mommy, can I have ice cream?"

Twenty minutes later, fully satiated on three whole scoops of ice cream—a rare delicacy in the Koppel home, where money was always scarce—Dax skipped through the door of the twins' shared bedroom. There, she found her sister lying face down on her tiny twin bed, occasionally still gasping with a sobbing spasm.

"I got three scoops," Dax said triumphantly. "Chocolate."

Jynx ignored her older twin, turning her face to look directly away from her, not wanting her sister to see her tears.

Dax smiled. "Jynx, maybe next time I'll get you some ice cream, too. Would you like that?"

Jynx just shook her head, not trusting her voice. Dax was always asking questions like that, hinting that 'next time' there might be something good for her sister. But next time was always the same: Dax started trouble, and when Jynx finally got pushed to the brink and fought back, she went running to their mother and blamed the whole thing on her younger twin. And for some reason, Momma always believed Dax.

Perhaps it was because Dax was the pretty one. Even though the twins were identical, no one would ever mistake them for each other. Dax always wore her hair in pigtails or braids, had a clean face and hands, and smiled a lot. She played with dolls and other girly toys her parents bought for her. Dax wasn't afraid to talk to adults and was the darling of the second-grade class they attended. She always had the nicest clothes the Koppel family could afford: pretty dresses with lace and bows in bright red, yellow, and green colors. The other girls at school would copy Dax's hairstyles and beg their parents to buy dresses to match the ones she wore.

Jynx, on the other hand, never kept her hair done. It was too hard to keep a braid in when she was always running around outside. She liked to explore the small desert chaparral behind the Koppel home on the outskirts of Harkness City and would often come home covered in dirt and with twigs and leaves in her hair. Most of the time, her brown locks were so tangled that her mother had largely given up brushing them each evening, as she did with Dax. Nor was the older Koppel woman willing to dress her younger daughter in new clothes that she would ruin out in the dusty desert, so Jynx usually wore hand-me-downs from other children in their neighborhood and was found just as often wearing boy clothes as anything else.

The simple truth was that Luanne Koppel, a former cheerleader and debutante herself before life dragged her into suburban stagnation, related much better to her older daughter and didn't know what to do with the younger twin. Or maybe it was more that she and her husband had only planned for one child, and the second twin had come along as an inconvenient and costly surprise. Either way, she doted on Dax and largely ignored Jynx except when scolding her.

All this might have still been fine if Dax had been a good sister. But the little girl had a mean streak, of which Jynx was the most common target. Other children in their class at school and in their neighborhood also suffered at the hands of the oldest Koppel twin, but so many of them craved the attention of the popular Dax that they kept coming back for more.

Jynx was no exception. She simultaneously hated and worshiped her twin sister. At school, Dax would occasionally let Jynx sit with her at lunch or recess, and despite her older twin using these as opportunities to poke fun at her, she hoped every day that she would be allowed to join Dax and just be around her.

Everyone, including Jynx, favored Dax. Except for their father.

Perhaps it was an awareness of how Luanne placed Dax on a pedestal. Maybe it was that Jynx acted more like the son the elder Koppel had always wished for but had no hope of having; Luanne had declared her baby-making days ended. Or possibly, it was a deeper understanding of how Dax showed two different faces to the world, most often at her sister's expense. In any case, Ned Koppel seemed to find a kindred spirit in his withdrawn and quiet youngest daughter. Whenever he would return home from work before the twins were in bed, he would pull Jynx onto his lap while he ate dinner and told Luanne about his day. He would read books to her while Luanne brushed Dax's hair before bed. And he would often lie down on Jynx's little twin bed next to her and lightly rub her back as she fell asleep. These were the most treasured moments of Jynx's childhood.

It wasn't that Ned treated Dax poorly. As a father, he doted on both of his girls as much as his meager salary as a high school history teacher would allow. He just spent just a little extra time with Jynx. Dax resented him for it.

The night after the hair-pulling incident, Ned Koppel returned home from work earlier than usual. When he walked in the door, he hugged his wife and then picked up Jynx and whirled her around as he often did. Dax ignored her father's homecoming; she was too busy playing with a new doll that Luanne had purchased for her at the store that day while shopping for groceries.

Ned must have somehow known that Dax had gotten a new toy and Jynx hadn't, because when he set the little girl down, he motioned for her to stay close while he crouched down and opened his satchel. Jynx watched with amazement as he pulled out a little stuffed tiger.

Two months before, on a weekend, Ned had taken the twins to the Harkness Zoo while Luanne had been home with a minor cold. Father and daughters had roamed the entire zoo, which wasn't exceptionally large, intent on seeing every animal. Dax had oohed and aahed at every exhibit, running ahead and pointing and calling out to the animals and to her father in her perpetually exuberant tone. Jynx had been more sedate, as usual, grasping her father's hand and refusing to leave his side.

But when they'd come to the tiger exhibit, Jynx had dropped her daddy's hand for the first time and scurried up to the glass enclosure in amazement. She had seen pictures of tigers in books about Old Earth, but the animals had never been brought to Drake's World; large predators that could pose a threat to humans were rarely seeded on any of the terraformed colony planets. But Harkness had just recently received a breeding pair from a sister zoo on Greater York as part of a cultural outreach program for the Expansion Region, and Jynx was awestruck to see the big cats with their orange and black stripes. Pressing her hands and face against the enclosure's glass, she watched them pace back and forth with such beauty and grace that it transfixed her and made her forget where she was for a moment.

The spell had been broken when Dax started shouting that she wanted to move on to see the flamingos. Still, Jynx had not forgotten how she'd felt watching the massive felines that day.

So, when her father took out the stuffed tiger, she gasped in joy and grabbed it to her chest, hugging it tightly and smiling as she felt its soft fur tickling her chin. "Thank you, Papa," she whispered, too afraid to speak loudly lest her sister notice her new gift and throw a fit that their father had brought her nothing. Ned smiled warmly and patted her on the head.

Luanne called the family to dinner and told the girls to go wash up. Jynx bounded up the stairs and put her tiger in her bed, under the covers and out of sight, before joining Dax in the small upstairs bathroom to wash their hands and faces. While Jynx splashed water onto her face, Dax watched her silently in the mirror.

After dinner, Luanne took Dax upstairs to brush her hair while Ned sat and read a book to Jynx. It was the story of Tom Sawyer, one of her favorites, and she envisioned herself romping through the woods with the main character and his crew of semi-wild children in a long-forgotten time. She would later learn that it was an illegal book, censored by the Council government for its anti-establishment leanings, and that her father kept a small stash of such books passed down through his family. At that age, she wouldn't have cared. She simply loved it when her father read to her.

When it was time for bed, Jynx rushed to her room and pulled back the covers, excited to see her new tiger again. But the stuffed animal was gone!

Through her youngest daughter's sobs, Luanne tried to understand what had happened—Ned had retired to his small study to plan his next day's lessons—and finally, with as much love as she ever showed her little girl, convinced Jynx that they would find the small tiger in the morning before school. After her mother had left, Jynx lay awake, crying silently for a full hour before finally succumbing to restless sleep.

The next morning, the family woke up to a scream from the girls' room. Their mother dashed into the room to find an inconsolable Jynx holding something tight to her chest. It took several minutes to calm down the distraught little girl and pry open her arms to see what she held. It was her stuffed tiger's decapitated head, which she'd woken up to find on the pillow next to her.

To any other mother, it might have been obvious what had happened: that one twin, in a fit of jealous pique over what her sister had gotten, had made sure that neither of them could be happy. However, it was as if Luanne Koppel utterly refused even to consider that Dax, her perfect little bright princess, could be guilty of such a heinous crime. It was never even suggested that it might be the case, and thus continued one of the hardest trials of Jynx's life: seeing Dax praised and exalted by all those around her while also seeing her secretly doing all she could to make everyone but herself miserable.

---

## PRESENT DAY; JULY 30, 731 P.D.; FIVE MONTHS AFTER THE REVELATIONS

Just beyond the orbit of Jupiter lay the small patch of space known as the Front Door. It was the entrance to the only known path through the Castilian Rift, which emptied out at the Back Door on the colonial side.

A good ship could make the transit in eight hours, but no one from the Sol system had even attempted it for over two hundred years; every attempt before that had never returned, interdicted and destroyed by the Guard quarantine fleet perpetually waiting at the Back Door.

Humanity could travel farther out in the Sol system itself, of course, but no one who had ventured more than a few light weeks beyond the Oort Cloud had ever returned. Something about the Rift made sure of that. As a rule, few ships ventured out further than the orbit of Scotus, and even that was too close to the Rift for comfort.

This meant that for any invasion that the Council sent to the Four Worlds, the governments of the Sol system *knew* that the enemy ships would have to surface from the void within the Front Door's small area of less than 1.5 million cubic kilometers, an astoundingly small patch of space in astrological terms. Added to this was a little-understood feature of the void, which was that it was inherently unpredictable, at least to the level of precision that would allow a traveling ship to exactly pinpoint its exit coordinates for any extended travel through the nothingness. This 'void drift' was fractionally small compared to the distance traveled, and the relationship was nonlinear. A ship traveling ten light years through the void could usually expect to surface within 314 kilometers of its planned exit point. A ship traveling one hundred light years could expect to surface within 504 kilometers.

The distances involved in void drift were infinitesimal compared to the vastness of space. However, that still hadn't prevented the occasional accident, especially in the early days of void travel. In one case, two ships traveling together to Eridani b2 had each drifted just enough that when they surfaced, they both attempted to do so in the same volume of space. In another case, a ship on approach to Terra Nova had surfaced in a spot already occupied by another ship outbound from the planet and preparing to submerge. This especially was an incident of such staggering low probability to defy imagination, but it happened, nonetheless. In both cases, the results were immediate and disastrous. Suddenly forcing two objects to occupy the same space caused the component atoms of both to violently repel each other in a massive release of energy. In other words, each event resulted in a

# THE FOUR WORLDS - SUBVERSION

spectacular explosion and the instant annihilation of all ships and people involved.

Despite the low probabilities of such incidents ever occurring again, the Council government did as governments do best. Sensing an opportunity to exert more control over human space travel, the Council decreed new ironclad rules for ships entering and exiting the void in groups. To facilitate this, they adopted Hopper's Law, the equation discovered by Lawrence Hopper of the Centauri II Institute early in the post-diaspora days, that calculated the relationship between distance traveled through the void and probable drift upon exiting. They used this equation to dictate how far two or more ships traveling together had to space out their planned exit points to avoid potential collisions upon surfacing from the void, logarithmically proportional to the distance they would be traveling through the void. Two ships traveling five light years had to space out their exit points by a minimum of 280 kilometers, for example.

Alternatively, ships could choose to space out their exit *times*. So instead, the two ships could enter and then exit the void a minimum of five seconds apart, which was overkill, but ensured the first ship would have traveled enough distance after resurfacing to leave space in which the second ship could safely surface.

Even putting aside the Council's artificial rules, Hopper's Law had a very *real* effect on travel through the Castilian Rift. The Front Door was an area of only 1.5 million cubic kilometers, roughly in the shape of a cone, with the apex of the cone representing the true exit from the Rift and fanning out from there toward Sol, with a base of roughly 150 km diameter and a length of a bit less than 250 km. Travel through the only known path in the Rift was a distance of 4.3 light years, meaning a potential drift of up to 274 kilometers. This meant that a ship could literally surface *anywhere* inside the cone that represented the Front Door.

As such, pre-schism space travel rules had dictated that only one ship surface at the Front Door at a time, with a separation of at least five seconds. Military strategists in the Four Worlds, planning for the eventuality that one day a hostile fleet might appear at the Front Door from the Council side of space, had calculated that no more than three ships could safely surface at once within the cone before the probability of a collision became too great for even an aggressive military force to stomach. They also estimated that the minimum time between groups surfacing would be at least 1.2 seconds.

That meant, in practical terms, a defensive force stationed at the Front Door would have 1.2 seconds to take on three or fewer invading ships before the enemy could surface the next set of reinforcements. This also meant that a relatively small defensive force could hypothetically hold against a much larger invading force, like the 300 Spartans of old against the Persian hordes at Thermopylae.

When the *Blind Monk* had surfaced in the cone of the Front Door just five months before, they had been intercepted by a cruiser assigned to the Coalition Security Force. The CSF was the product of the Coalition Space Treaty, signed by Earth, Mars, and Europa over three hundred years before, meant to protect the Four Worlds from outside threats. The treaty had been signed during a period of unusually good relations between Earth and Mars and mandated the creation of the CSF as a peacekeeping and maritime security force, like the Coast Guard of old. Their roles included defending the Four Worlds and patrolling the interplanetary trade routes in the Sol system against pirates and smugglers. They also served as a search and rescue force for ships in distress.

The CSF started as a large enough force to fulfill its mandate, with ten capital ships and accompanying escorts, roughly equivalent to three full task forces in the United Earth or Martian navies. Unfortunately, but predictably, Mars had changed governments just 48 years later, and the planet's new rulers had declared their part in the treaty null and void. This left Earth and Europa to stand alone, with Mars also declaring that the CSF was no longer welcome in Martian space and that it no longer had authority to stop and board Martian-flagged vessels.

This battle of wills, coupled with politicians on Earth and Europa who saw the CSF as a convenient place to pull funding to pay for domestic initiatives, meant that by the time the *Blind Monk* surfaced in the Sol system, the CSF was down to just eight ships. None were capital ships; instead, they had only three older generation light cruisers, four destroyers, and a single aged battlecruiser that spent more time in shipyards than patrolling the system. Essentially, the CSF became nothing more than a token force. However, since neither Earth nor Europa was willing to dissolve the Coalition Treaty unilaterally, and keeping it in place was seen as spitting in the Martians' faces (something both Earth and Europa derived satisfaction from), the token force remained, perpetually understaffed and underfunded.

Still, there were automatic escalations built into the Coalition Treaty. Despite the United Earth government's unwillingness to take the Council threat seriously, the mere arrival of the *Monk* through the Rift automatically activated the treaty's mutual defense clause for a period of no less than twelve months. Within weeks, Earth and Europa had each dispatched the required task forces (36 ships for Earth and 18 for Europa) to the Front Door. A pro forma announcement of intent and obligation under the treaty had also been sent to Mars, asking that they assign a task force of 36 as well, as dictated by the treaty. Predictably, the Reds did not even send a response. Their only show of acknowledging the *Monk's* arrival was to shift two task forces from their Fleet of the Eagle slightly closer to the Front Door but still 15 light minutes away.

Therefore, the result was that for the last four months, after allowing a one-month delay for the slow wheels of government bureaucracies to turn, a fleet of 36 Earth ships, 18 Europan ships, and three lonely CSF ships (the rest were still needed to meet their space-lane patrol duties) had sat at the Front Door just waiting for something else to come through.

Today, that wait would end catastrophically.

---

Captain Dietrich Wagner sat in utter boredom in the command chair of the *CSFS Numenor*, one of the Coalition Security Force's light cruisers assigned to guard the exit from the Rift. He and the *Numenor* had been on station at the Front Door for two months straight, as the CSF's small size didn't allow for frequent rotations of duty stations. For that entire period, Wagner had experienced the double frustrations of absolute boredom and crippling envy.

His aged cruiser was crewed at less than two-thirds of its nominal complement of spacers. Moreover, even the crew he had was not the cream of the crop. The Coalition Space Treaty required Earth and Europa to staff the CSF in proportion to their funding of the Coalition itself, but it hadn't defined *who* they had to staff it with. As such, for at least the last hundred years, both navies had used the CSF as a dumping ground for their dregs; spacers with discipline or performance issues regularly found themselves transferred to the dead-end assignment of crewing Coalition Security Force ships.

Wagner, therefore, had nothing but disdain for most of the officers and spacers under his command. They made constant mistakes and were often borderline insubordinate, with few exceptions. Of course, Wagner never stopped to consider that he had been assigned to the CSF because of *his* mediocre performance ratings in the United Earth Navy. As with most narcissists, a club in which he was a member in good standing, he couldn't even conceive that many of the discipline issues on his ship were due as much to his poor leadership as to the actual quality of the men and women under his command.

So, spending the last two months on station with 54 regular navy ships, each staffed and run in accordance with the highest standards of thousands of years of water and space naval forces, was enough to make him rage silently (and sometimes out loud to his executive officer in the privacy of his small office ready room) about the stark contrast between *his* CSF forces and the UEN and EN forces surrounding them.

The Coalition Treaty had never specified who would command a joint defense force at the Rift. Since no one could agree on that, even now, the CSF, UEN, and EN forces operated as three distinct bodies. As the senior officer for the CSF, this technically put Wagner on equal footing with Rear Admiral Peter Zelinski of the UEN and Commodore Amanda Lee of the EN. But given his objectively lower rank of Captain and the far inferior size and effectiveness of his force, neither treated him like an equal. Again, he never stopped to think that perhaps the way he acted in their weekly meetings may have also had something to do with their obvious disdain toward him.

What was worse, in the bi-weekly drills the three naval forces had agreed to hold, the CSF always showed up poorly, its reaction times and simulated effectiveness far lower than the two regular navies. Though both Zelinksi and Lee were politic enough not to make a big deal of this directly with Wagner, he could see in their after-action reports just how little they thought of his force's capabilities.

Seeing how smoothly the UEN and EN operated during the drills, Wagner naturally blamed the men and women under his command rather than himself and held a disdain bordering on hatred in his heart for the officers and crews of his tiny 'fleet'. This hatred fed his envy, and he became convinced that if he had the same resources and quality of personnel that Zelinski and Lee had access to, he would match them and even beat them in the simulation scores.

He sat now in his command chair, brooding over all of this and idly thinking of the glass of wine awaiting him in his cabin after his shift was over, when everything went to hell.

The harsh sound of the ship's klaxon jerked him to full awareness and caused him to knit his brow in confusion. Wagner hadn't been on station when the *Blind Monk* had come through, so he'd never heard that alarm outside of a drill. And he hadn't scheduled any drills for today nor been made aware of any joint drills with the other two fleets.

His first thought was that his XO, Lt. Commander Slattery—the man seemed to be perpetually overeager since his assignment to the CSF six months before, as if he thought performing well in the small force would allow him to get back to his previous station in the UEN—had gotten ahead of himself again and scheduled a drill without remembering to tell his captain. The young man seemed to think that more drills on their own would somehow allow the crew of the *Numenor* to improve their performance in the larger joint drills, as if this group of misfits could ever do *anything* right, even with practice.

But all thoughts of drills and strangling his XO went out the door when Wagner glanced toward the sensor display.

*Who in the—?*

The massive ship that had just appeared off *Numenor's* port bow, just within the cone of the Front Door, opened fire, pouring its lasers into the small CSF light cruiser. As bad luck or fate would have it, its second shot speared through the ship in the exact location of the bridge, opening it to space and ending the life of Captain Dietrich Wagner and his bridge crew. The rest of *Numenor's* crew was only seconds behind them.

---

Rear Admiral Peter Zelinski quickly set down the coffee mug he'd been drinking from, and the cup's regulation lid did its job and prevented any from sloshing out onto his ship suit. But the potential for coffee stains was the furthest thing from his mind as he watched the sensor screen on the flag bridge of the *UENS Egypt*, his Missouri-class battleship that, until recently, was one of the largest warships by size and tonnage to ever ply the spacelanes of the Sol system.

The three ships that had suddenly appeared out of the void within the cone of the Front Door had just changed that math considerably.

Zelinski had been in the room just under two months ago when Tyrus Tyne had given a briefing to the command staffs of the United Earth Navy and had seen the comparisons of size and firepower between Earth's battleships and the Council's dreadnoughts. But that briefing had not prepared him for the monsters that now bore down on his task force and started firing the instant they had surfaced from the void.

Around Zelinski was controlled chaos. The sensor AIs of each ship in his fleet had been programmed to sound the alert if *anything* was detected surfacing nearby. Spacers and their officers were already rushing to battle stations, and Zelinski's staff on his flag bridge were already barking out updates and information to him.

He tuned it all out and issued the one command only he could give. "Full attack! Pattern beta six."

By now, the three massive enemy dreadnoughts had flown beyond the Front Door, and behind them had already appeared *five* battlecruisers. The Council Navy's commander seemed to be recklessly throwing their ships through the Rift without regard to the risk that they might collide upon surfacing, openly defying the UEN's best strategists with their blatant disregard for Hopper's Law.

Another 1.2 seconds passed as Zelinski's ships began returning fire on the Council ships. Another wave of enemy surfaced from the Rift, this time two more battlecruisers and four light cruisers. The invasion force, if that's what it indeed was, had fired first, removing any responsibility on Zelinski's part to decide if firing on them was warranted. But the battle so far had been short and one-sided. The Council Navy had destroyed all three of the CSF ships, a light cruiser and two destroyers, in their first volley and had since disabled a Europan Navy battlecruiser and destroyed a United Earth Navy destroyer.

Now Zelinski's ships, as well as Commodore Lee's, were getting their own punches in. One of the Council battlecruisers, part of the second wave, exploded in a brilliant flash of light as the *Egypt* and one of Zelinski's other three Missouri classes, the *Gujarat*, converged their fire upon it. The combined fire of three Europan light cruisers and destroyers also destroyed a Council light cruiser and were already working on a second. But then another Europan ship, a heavy cruiser, succumbed to fire from one of the Council battlecruisers and cracked in two as her spine broke under the barrage of lasers.

Worse, nothing seemed to phase the three Council dreadnoughts that had burned hard to slow their initial velocity and were now bearing down on Zelinski's force from behind the main defensive line. Laser fire from the UEN ships did nothing more than put pockmarks on the behemoth's hulls, and Peter Zelinski realized too late the terrible mistake his fleet and the others guarding the Front Door had made.

In an effort to take advantage of the limited number of ships that could surface at once through the Rift, the CSF, UEN, and EN had positioned their fleets on the edges of the cone-shaped space that constituted the Front Door, well within laser range of anything within that cone. The intent was to instantly engage ships as they came through, taking advantage of the 1.2-second delay between enemy waves.

What they had failed to account for was that the enemy might start by sending through more ships than even the most pessimistic of military planners would expect. That they would send not one but *three* dreadnoughts in the first wave had been unthinkable. Now those massive ships were covering the rest of the Council fleet as it came through and were shrugging off any volume of laser fire the Four World navies could throw back at them.

*We should have stayed further out; used our missiles,* Zelinski thought in a moment of epiphany. *Instead, we've played right into their hands.*

Because the Council fleet had one major advantage in this engagement: they had known when they were coming. The Four Worlds' ships, on the other hand, had lost critical seconds reacting to the enemy fleet appearing from the Rift, and those seconds had been long enough for the aggressive enemy commander to roll the dice on sending far more ships through the Rift than anyone had thought possible in so short a time.

"*Egypt* is taking fire from Dreadnought Beta!" the flag tactical officer called across the bridge.

"Order the *Tacoma* and the *Amsterdam* to flank the enemy ship," replied Zelinski, checking his plot and identifying the two closest ships, both battlecruisers. His voice was much calmer than his mind as he saw his task force was down to only three battleships. *Argentina*, on the opposite side of the UEN formation, had been destroyed by the combined fire of several enemy ships, but had at least taken a Council battlecruiser and two heavy cruisers with her before she died.

He made no commands related to the direct defense of his flagship; that was Captain Yellin's job on the command bridge, and the woman certainly didn't need her admiral looking over her shoulder or countermanding any of her orders in an engagement likely to be over in minutes at most and seconds at worst.

Zelinski watched on his sensor screen as the two UEN battlecruisers, *Tacoma* and *Amsterdam*, took station on either side of the gigantic enemy ship and began hitting it with their broadsides while dancing their ships in random patterns to avoid the dreadnought's return broadside fire. But the big ship ignored the two smaller attack ships completely and instead turned its own broadside toward *Egypt*, pouring a surprising amount of laser fire into the smaller battleship.

"Hull breaches on decks four, six, and nine!" cried one of Zelinski's staff.

"The Europan task force is down to half strength!" a female voice cried out in a tone that should have been panicked, but to the sensor officer's credit, was urgent but professional.

"Enemy strength up to 40 ships," the same woman continued. "Three dreadnoughts, six battleship analogs, and 12 battlecruisers. The rest are heavy cruiser and below, but they keep coming through!" Then she switched to a tone of exultation. "Explosion at the Front Door! Two or more enemy ships collided due to drift!"

Zelinski knew it would make no difference. "Signal the *Gujarat* to join the attack on Dreadnought Beta," he commanded.

"I can't raise *Gujarat*!" the comm officer replied, and his voice *did* carry a genuine tone of panic. "It appears they've been disabled, sir!"

Zelinski's heart fell into his stomach. Less than two minutes into the invasion, he had already lost two of his only four capital ships. His sensors showed the two smaller Europan battleships were likewise out of action, one destroyed entirely and the other disabled and venting atmosphere into space.

He opened his mouth to call out a new set of orders, but the words never left his throat. The *UENS Egypt* and its crew of over two thousand spacers and officers, including Rear Admiral Peter Zelinski, disappeared in a massive explosion as a laser breached their reactor's containment field.

Had Zelinski lived only a few minutes longer, he would have seen the shrapnel from his ship's destruction damage the attacking Council dreadnought almost as much as his force's returned fire had. However, the same explosion also critically damaged the battlecruiser *Tacoma*. She and her sister, *Amsterdam*, lasted only another 15 seconds against the dreadnought's now concentrated fire.

After that, Zelinski would have witnessed the destruction of his fourth and final battleship and the last surviving capital ship in the combined Four Worlds' fleet. The *Norway* had drawn the attention of one of the other Council dreadnoughts and had lasted only seconds longer than the *Egypt*.

Nine minutes and 34 seconds after the first Council ships had surfaced through the Front Door, the entire force of combined CSF, UEN, and EN ships stationed to stop them had been destroyed, disabled, or, in the case of two lucky UEN light cruisers and one EN heavy cruiser, had retreated far enough away to escape the same fate after seeing the battle was lost.

The Council had taken its damages as well. Of the 75 ships that Tamara Chen had sent against the Four Worlds, 22 had been destroyed or critically damaged—those were already limping their way back to the Front Door to escape into the void. But in trade, fully 54 ships of the Four Worlds combined navies had been taken out. And all three incredibly dangerous and hard-to-kill Council Navy dreadnoughts were still combat effective.

Ironically, the battle could have gone far differently had either Earth or Europa sent along a single carrier. Fighters packed a disproportionate punch for their size and were incredibly hard to target and kill, given their small size and maneuverability. On top of that, the Council fleet could not immediately launch its own fighters, given how quickly and closely together its ships surfaced from the Rift. Even a few dozen UEN or EN fighters could have potentially turned the tide. But carriers and fighters were expensive to maintain and operate—and even more costly to replace—so neither of the Coalition powers had seen fit to send any of the high-priced ships along. In the end, politicians and accountants, along with a few tactical mistakes, had sent almost 24,000 military personnel to their deaths, with trillions of dollars of lost ships and equipment, all for the sake of saving a few hundred million in operational expenses.

But that thought wouldn't occur to anyone until days later, as for now, almost the entire remaining Council fleet set a course directly for Earth, leaving just five combat-effective ships back to guard the Front Door.

---

Another day, another ride via the Loop from La Costa to Houston. It was past the point of being monotonous, especially with no hope of any genuine progress in the endless congressional committee meetings.

But today was different.

Jinny and Corey had barely gotten five steps from the capsule when Corey stopped walking and raised his left hand to study it intently. When Jinny had first arrived on Earth, it had been strange to see so many people pay such close attention to their hands, especially before she knew about the subdermal implants most citizens of the Four Worlds had. She imagined it was equally strange for them to watch her poke the air above her watch, reacting to a holo only she could see. But even had she wanted one of the ubiquitous palm implants, the requirement that she always wear gloves would have rendered it essentially useless.

Next to her, she heard the congressman suck in a sharp breath, and she was distressed to see that he'd turned several shades whiter, a nontrivial feat for a red-haired man of Irish descent.

"Corey, what is it?" she asked anxiously.

After a few moments' hesitation, as Jinny began to doubt he'd heard her and was about to ask again, Corey raised his eyes to look at her, his face slack and his mouth stuck agape.

"We've run out of time. They're here."

Jinny didn't have to ask who 'they' were. She instinctively looked up toward the sky, though she would have seen nothing, even *if* the station's roof weren't in the way.

The Council Navy had arrived. The invasion of the Four Worlds had begun. And they weren't even close to ready.

# CHAPTER 9

"That's only a fraction of their fleet," Tyrus said to Vice Admiral Mary Bol on the bridge of the *UENS Enterprise*. "It's roughly the same size force they sent to Rinali and the Back Door to destroy the Guard fleet stationed there. We know they had more beyond that. So, this has to be a mission to test our defenses."

"I would tend to agree," Bol replied evenly. "But that doesn't mean it's not a vanguard force for a larger fleet still to come through the Rift. There's even," she admitted, "a slight chance they know of another way through the Rift that we don't."

Bol turned to the sensor officer on her flag bridge. "Anita, anything on the TS?"

"Tachyon sensors show no other ships surfacing at the Front Door or anywhere else in range," the trim lieutenant replied, and Bol nodded in acknowledgment.

Tyrus had been on Mary Bol's flagship for four weeks, and he was unsure why he'd been there so long. At first, he had worried that the politicians on Earth had sent him out on a shakedown cruise with the UEN's three most secret ships as a sort of exile; it had to rub them the wrong way that the naval leadership back in Houston was more inclined to listen to his warnings than the false assurances of civilian politicians with their own agendas. Sending him out for a month with three ships under strict comms silence had probably struck them as an excellent way to get him out of their hair.

But Mary Bol had let it slip early on that the orders to keep Tyrus aboard the *Enterprise* as an observer and adviser had come indirectly from Fleet Admiral Lopez himself. That put them in a new light, and Tyrus started paying careful attention to Bol and how she ran her small task force. If the old fleet admiral wanted him here, there had to be a reason.

What he had seen had encouraged him greatly. The calm and steady Bol maintained a tight ship, and the crew both liked and respected her. Seeing the level of professionalism firsthand that the UEN was capable of on their warships gave him further encouragement that their training and naval traditions would be a real advantage against the relatively newborn Council Navy. It had also given him the opportunity to strategize how best to use her three stealth carriers against the larger enemy forces once the invasion began.

Of course, he had to admit there was also a personal reason he was not disappointed to have spent so much time on *Enterprise*: Mary Bol herself. Tall, just a few centimeters short of Tyrus' two-meter height, and lithe of build, with ebony skin almost as dark as his own, Bol was not what anyone would call a classically beautiful woman. Her features were too sharp, and her build lacked much in the way of traditional feminine curves. However, that didn't stop her from having one of the most commanding presences of any man or woman he had ever encountered, and to be around her was to naturally trust and defer to her. For Tyrus, that had translated into no small amount of attraction, despite her being eight years his senior.

In his more cynical moments, he supposed it probably had to do with his subconscious mind trying to find an authority to replace the Council. Whatever the cause, he couldn't deny his attraction to the older woman, and he studied her closely now as she issued commands to her staff in efficient manner. Of course, dwelling on her right now was probably also his brain's shocked response to the start of the invasion he'd feared for months.

"Mr. Tyne," she asked him, breaking into his thoughts; the admiralty had dropped the 'commander' from his title shortly after that first briefing, "do you think the Council Navy may have a way to jam our Tachyon sensors?"

Tyrus thought for only a moment. "Doubtful. As far as I know, Council scientists have done little with Tachyons thus far. We—the colonies rather—use gravitic sensors to track ships surfacing from the void; anything surfacing sends out a gravitic wave burst equivalent to a large comet suddenly appearing out of nowhere. There were experiments in faster-than-light communication but centered on quantum entanglement, not Tachyons. It wouldn't surprise me if the Council Navy already has *that* technology integrated into some of their ships, though I recall hearing that early prototypes required a space fully the size of a destroyer as well as a planetary power grid. However, to my knowledge, almost nothing had been done regarding Tachyons." Still, he shrugged to convey that anything was possible.

Bol nodded and said nothing in return. Tyrus knew that, until recently, all the Four Worlds navies had also used the type of gravitic sensors he was describing, which had a relatively limited range. Tachyon technology was in its relative infancy—only two decades old—on Earth and hadn't even been formally shared with Europa yet, though they had mysteriously developed their own version just five years after the UE. Naval leadership assumed Mars had likewise stolen the tech, but no one could know for sure.

Tyrus watched with an impressed eye as the Enterprise's flag bridge crew quickly recovered from the severe shock of watching an entire UEN task force destroyed. They didn't even seem flustered seeing the remainder of the Council Navy fleet set course directly toward Earth. Much of their calm demeanor had to do with Bol, who had ignored some of her officers' and enlisted spacers' shocked gasps and had calmly issued orders in the same quiet but authoritative tones she used to order coffee from her steward. She seemed to know what her crew needed to see and hear from her, and he briefly wondered if her question to him about Tachyon sensor jamming had been simply to calm *his* nerves.

"Anita," Bol again addressed her sensor officer, "work up a plan to do a full active scan of this sector but hold on executing pending my order. No sense in showing them we exist unless we absolutely have to."

"How long until we get orders from Houston?" Tyrus asked.

Bol did the math in her head. "The light of the battle would have reached them five minutes ago. So, we should hear something anytime now, assuming they're not waiting to see what Mars will do first."

"What do *you* think Mars will do?"

The admiral shrugged. "I've learned the hard way not to try to second guess the Reds. They don't always act rationally, though I'm sure they think the same about us. I'm more worried about what *we'll* do." She said this last part in a lower voice that wouldn't carry across the bridge.

Left unsaid was how disappointed Bol and most of the senior military leadership were in just how slow President Pereira and his administration had moved—or rather hadn't—in the face of the warnings brought to them by Tyrus and his companions. He had to agree with Bol that he was equally worried about what Earth herself would do. Pereira had been elected on an Earth-first platform, focusing on economic reforms and the buildup of social entitlements. The way he talked, Tyrus felt he would have fit in well with the Twenty. The Council, aka the Twenty, used social entitlements, like universal income for the unemployed, for a variety of reasons, but one of them was to make the majority of the colonies' populace as dependent on the government as possible.

Tyrus didn't know what Pereira's true motivations were. On the outside, the man seemed genuinely desirous to help the relatively small but still concerning poor populations of Earth and Luna. But one of his first actions on taking office had been to further cut Earth's already meager funding to the Coalition Security Force, endangering an organization already operating on a shoestring budget and forcing many of the fleet's aging ships into mothballs; it also made it harder for them to guard the Front Door with any true defensive force.

In fact, in an unusually candid moment, Bol had let it slip to Tyrus that the president had come close to shutting down the top-secret program that had developed and launched the *Enterprise, Yorktown,* and *Midway* but had held off only because a strong voting bloc in

Congress made it clear that cutting funding to the project would make it harder for him to get his other programs through the legislative body that co-governed Earth with him. That Bol herself hailed from Nigeria, one of the Blue Party's electoral strongholds, hadn't hurt. Despite being at odds with most of her countrymen politically, the first Nigerian woman to reach the lofty flag rank of vice admiral had quickly become a national hero.

"All we can do is wait for orders," the admiral said softly now. "Wait and watch." Yet, despite her words, she continued to issue calm commands to her crew, preparing them for whatever those orders might be.

---

Corey had led Jinny away from the Loop station and straight to Government House, which contained the offices and residency of President Luiz Pereira. After gaining entrance to the building, no quick process given the tight security, they boarded an elevator that took them straight *down* to the presidential command bunker, also known as the Situation Room.

Jinny had rarely felt more out of place than she did at that moment. When she and O'Leary had been admitted into the top-secret bunker, they'd been quickly shown to a modest-sized conference room where President Pereira was in deep conversation with the entire Joint Chiefs of Staff and his civilian advisers. This being her first time physically in the president's presence, Jinny was immediately flustered. She'd gone to take a seat on one of the chairs in the outer ring against the conference room wall, hoping to stay small and out of sight, but O'Leary had gently but firmly grabbed her by the arm and instead guided her to the seat next to his, *at the table!*

Now, she felt every twitch of her face and worried endlessly that everyone in the room was focused on how nervous she was. That was ridiculous, of course, as only General Cruz, Chairman of the Joint Chiefs of Staff and an acquaintance via Corey, had briefly nodded to her and O'Leary when they'd entered. The rest of Earth's power brokers had studiously ignored them.

Suddenly, that changed. Cruz's voice broke through Jinny's wall of nerves and heightened her anxiety by bringing every gaze at the table to rest on her.

"Mr. President. We are all shocked at what's happening, but we must think carefully before reacting. Without Tyrus Tyne in the room, our best expert on the Council Navy and its capabilities is Ms. Ambrosa. I suggest we hear what she has to say before we proceed any further." Cruz turned to Jinny, his green eyes under his graying black hair softer than she would have expected from Earth's top military commander, as he nodded respectfully to her. For a moment, she sat in shock. Corey had explained en route what had happened at the Front Door—he had received a briefing via his palm implant. But she hadn't expected to be asked for *her* thoughts on the matter in front of the president and his advisers!

"Ms. Ambrosa, what would you suspect the Council is up to by sending what we believe is only a fraction of their available force?" Cruz continued, gently but helpfully prompting her.

Jinny gulped and glanced at her hands on the table but then steeled her nerves and forced herself to meet first the gaze of Cruz and then of the president himself. Pereira had the calm look of a wise patrician, his hair barely graying at his temples and contrasting handsomely with his tan brown skin and bright hazel eyes. He reminded her of a few Assembly speakers back in the colonies, which wasn't a good thing.

She opened her mouth to reply to Cruz's question but had to clear her throat when the words first wouldn't come. Underneath the table, she felt Corey give her a quick pat on the knee, nothing flirtatious, just a small and welcome reminder that she wasn't alone. She finally found her voice.

"I'm not a military expert, but I know how the Twenty thinks. I... I read one of them before I left the colonies, and I've read Tyrus—Mr. Tyne—on multiple occasions, so I have much of his knowledge as well. I also spoke extensively with another member of the Twenty, Kendra Siefred, as you know."

She could see the obvious discomfort on the faces of everyone but Corey O'Leary as she referenced her status as a reader but pressed onward with her answer.

"If I understand correctly, this fleet seems smaller than what I believe the Twenty would reasonably send against us. Certainly smaller than what Tyrus has said to expect. That suggests the Twenty are probing you—us—to see how we respond. I assume they are also trying to see what we will respond *with*. You yourselves have acknowledged that it's been a century and a half since you've had contact with anyone from the colonies. That means the Twenty know less about your defensive capabilities at this point than you know—from Tyrus and me—about their offensive capabilities. They're almost certainly trying to learn more. I believe, most importantly, that they'll be looking to see if each planet responds independently or if we coordinate our actions."

She took a deep breath and looked over at Corey, who nodded his support. She had surprised herself by how well she'd gotten through that; she certainly had practice from the endless committee meetings and discussions of probable Council tactics with Tyrus, but this was an entirely different kind of audience.

General Cruz nodded and lightly pounded the table with his fist. "I concur. It's just as I told you, Mr. President. This is a reconnaissance in force. They are trying to see how we react to it and cause as much damage as they can in the meantime."

Pereira pursed his lips and regarded Jinny with a skeptical glance. When he spoke, his voice had a nasal quality that was more pronounced in person than on the vids, which instantly reduced the impact of his handsome looks. "I disagree, and so does my national security team."

He turned and regarded Cruz as if Jinny were no longer in the room. "While I'm sure that Mr. Tyne, Ms. Ambrosa, and their companions believe in the bogeyman they've told us about, by their own admission, they and their Ms. Siefred left behind a rather tumultuous situation in the colonies when they broadcast the truth about the Council to all the member worlds."

Jinny sat up straighter. Siefred hadn't yet broadcast *anything* by the time she and Tyrus had escaped to the Four Worlds through the Rift. They knew she had been *planning* to reveal the truth about the Council and its lies to the colonies, but they had no way to verify that she actually had. But here the president was, talking about it as if he *knew* it had happened. It could have been a simple slip of the man's tongue, but it nagged at her.

She saw Pereira glance to his right at a sour-faced woman in a severely conservative business suit. He paused, and Jinny noticed the woman give an almost imperceptible nod. At this subtle signal, the president sat up straighter and puffed out his chest slightly as if taking all his confidence from the dour woman's approval or consent. That troubled Jinny immensely, and the nagging feeling increased.

"Surely they've had to re-task much of their invasion fleet," the president continued, his tone even more confident than before, "to maintain the peace domestically, leaving them less to send against us. This is likely all they *could* send, and if we win this battle decisively, they'll have no choice but to leave us alone." The man smiled in a way that felt oily to Jinny. "Besides, they are heading directly toward Earth, so the best thing we can do is send our fleet to stop and destroy them. That way, the threat will be over, and we will have defended our home. There's no downside." He quickly glanced again toward the woman on his right.

"I don't think that's true at all." The words shocked Jinny, but not as much as the fact that they came from *her*. They also surprised Pereira, who looked back at her for the first time since starting his monologue and openly gaped with astonishment. The woman at his right threw Jinny a look that could melt titanium alloy. Before either of them could object openly, Jinny squared her shoulders and forged onward.

"With all due respect, Mr. President, that isn't how the Twenty thinks. They're arrogant beyond anything you can understand in a democratic government." She doubted that was true from the little she'd seen of Pereira's and several congress members' own lack of humility, but she felt that a little indirect praise might help her case. "There have been no legitimate challenges to their rule since they left the Four Worlds behind and then destroyed the Council. And the Guard itself is quite capable of putting down isolated rebellions. Add to that the fact that the Council Navy has been kept secret from their own populace. Remember that when the Twenty sent them to destroy

Rinali Station, they went out of their way to make it look like it was a naval invasion from the Four Worlds, not from the Council government itself. For all we know, the people bought that story and have given this invasion their full support.

"Even if that is not the case, I suspect they are in full propaganda mode and are relying primarily on misinformation campaigns backed by the might of the Guard to keep the populace in line, despite the disclosures from Ms. Siefred, which, candidly, we're not even *sure* went out after we left."

"Are you suggesting that your mission to get the information to Siefred so she could release it was a failure?" the woman seated to the president's right asked with the beginnings of a sneer. "Or are you suggesting we leave Earth undefended and just let them come?"

Jinny shook her head, tamping down a rising anger. She decided to focus on the woman's first question and ignore the second for now. "No, but we didn't stick around to see if and how the information went out. We just trusted that she would take care of it. A *lot* could have happened. Even assuming Speaker Siefred was successful, I don't think it would change the Twenty's goals in relation to the Four Worlds. The way they think, it might even make retaking the Four Worlds all the more urgent."

She was about to share her theory on the real reason for the Council's invasion—the need for the purer enhanced bloodlines from Australia—but a little voice inside told her to keep that to herself for now.

Instead, she continued: "If they can use their propaganda machine to turn the populace of the colonies against the Four Worlds, which we *know* was part of their plan, then they could easily rally the people around a common enemy and distract them from Siefred's message."

The table was quiet for a moment as everyone absorbed her words, but the grimace on the woman next to the president only became more pronounced. Jinny was debating what she might say next.

Cruz broke the silence, addressing the president directly. "Mr. President, I urge you to listen to Ms. Ambrosa. Even with no intel on us, it would be entirely unreasonable for the Council to think that only 75 ships could take on the entire military and civilian infrastructure of the

Sol system. Everything suggests that this is just a recon mission, and I believe the move toward Earth is a feint to see what we'll throw at them and whether we will respond as Earth and Luna alone or united with Europa and Mars.

"We need to accomplish two goals today." Cruz held up two fingers and ticked them off as he spoke. "First, make them think we're all united against them. Let's reach out to Mars and see if they'll coordinate with us. They haven't responded before, but this could be the opening we need now that the threat has proven to be real.

"Second," he kept speaking quickly before Pereira or any of his advisers could argue with the first recommendation, "we *cannot* reveal all of our ships. The remainder of Second Fleet should be enough to defeat what the Council sent, even if Mars and Europa don't send their ships. We should continue to hold First Fleet back in Earth orbit with its engines cold so that they don't see our full order of battle."

Jinny knew from speaking with Corey and Tyrus that United Earth had two numbered fleet units aside from a few task forces for system patrol and customs interdiction. Second Fleet was habitually stationed between Earth and Mars, just outside a sphere of space surrounding the red planet that included both Martian-owned territory and a narrow demilitarized zone. Second fleet moved with the orbits of the two planets to maintain that station. Their shifting location in space was referred to as Waypoint Charlie and included a small repair and maintenance station supporting Second Fleet's semi-permanent posting there.

First Fleet, sometimes called Home Fleet, was in orbit around Earth itself. It largely kept its main engines cold, using maneuvering thrusters to shift each ship's orbit around the planet in intricate random patterns designed to make it difficult for the Martians to keep track of the exact number of ships. The Reds did the same with portions of their fleet, going back hundreds of years in the ongoing arms race between the two planets.

What Cruz was suggesting made sense to her. The enemy had surely already seen Second Fleet by the thermal signatures of its fully powered ships, so using it to intercept the Council Navy didn't tell them much more than what they could already see on their sensors.

But lighting up First Fleet's main drives and moving them away from the sheltering bulk of Earth and Luna would give the Twenty a full count of essentially all the UEN's warships. And it would do so for no real gain, given the relatively small size of the attacking force.

Cruz stopped speaking but kept his eyes on President Pereira, holding the man's gaze. For a moment, it looked like the president might relent and listen to his top military officer in the room. Then the woman next to him engaged a privacy field and cupped her hand to speak directly in the president's ear so that no one could read her lips. Pereira's face hardened as she spoke, and Jinny's heart sank further.

A moment later, the privacy field disengaged, and the president spoke. "Order all of Second Fleet to move immediately to engage the enemy. Have First Fleet go to full battle readiness and prepare to repel a possible Martian attack while the Council has Second Fleet distracted. They are to move half their force away from Earth and take up station at Waypoint Gamma, where they should be able to move to either help Second Fleet repel the Council invasion or defend against an incursion from Martian forces."

Jinny wasn't familiar with Waypoint Gamma, but that didn't matter. The president had just gone entirely against the recommendations of his Joint Chiefs in what could be a disastrous move for United Earth.

Cruz's jaw dropped, showing his own shock in an obvious fashion, but the president ignored it and continued. "And in terms of working with the Martians," he shook his head vigorously, "I don't think there's time, nor do I think they would be receptive. They are much more likely to turn this situation to their advantage. Contacting them and telling them our plans in the vain hope that they might reciprocate would only shift the balance of power in their favor should they decide to use this as an opportunity to attack."

His eyes bored into Cruz's from across the conference table. "General, you may know tactics," he turned to stare at Jinny, "and you, Ms. Ambrosa, may understand the motivations of the *few* Council government leaders you met or read." He said the last word like a curse. "But *I* understand politics, and war is a political decision."

Pereira nodded curtly as if to show agreement with his own words and then stood up to signal the end of the meeting. "Dismissed."

Before anyone else could stand, General Cruz quickly interjected. "But sir, you have to reconsider—"

"No, he doesn't!" snapped the woman to the president's right. "And you, General," she pointed a bony finger at Cruz, "need to understand that your commander-in-chief has given you an order. Now go and do your job!" Jinny had the abrupt mental image of an enacter receiving orders from a Council representative. The tone the woman used with Cruz was the same that many bureaucrats had used with Tyrus in the memories she recalled from reading him. To find it used here in a place where free will was so valued was disconcerting in the extreme.

Luiz Pereira said nothing to defend his top general from the woman's attack but gave another curt nod, then turned and left the conference room with the sour-faced woman and his other civilian advisers in tow.

When they were gone, and the soundproof door had shut behind them, General Cruz shook his head slowly and muttered something under his breath that Jinny didn't catch. Then he looked up at her, and his eyes softened.

"I'm sorry, Ms. Ambrosa, for putting you on the spot like that. I'd hoped you could convince... Never mind what I hoped. I just think it was important to bring out all the information, directly from the source, in this meeting."

He turned to the other three military leaders in the room. "Kurt," he said to the man in the white Navy uniform festooned with ribbons, "you heard the president. Send orders to Admiral Lafayette and Second Fleet to set an intercept course for the lead elements of the Council fleet. They've seen what happened to Admiral Zelinski's force going toe-to-toe with those dreadnoughts, so suggest to Lafayette that a missile and fighter engagement at range may be more effective.

He paused, the conflict clear on his face. Then he seemed to lose some internal battle with himself and sighed. "And send a message to First Fleet. Tell Admiral Showalker to prepare his forces for battle. He is to light up all his drives, launch his combat space patrol, and set course with half his force for Waypoint Gamma, just as the president ordered."

Then Cruz stood, squaring his shoulders, clearly upset but also turning from the mode of arguing strategy with politicians to putting his whole mind to implementing the directed plan.

Before he could leave the room, Corey O'Leary spoke for the first time since he and Jinny had entered. "Admiral, may I suggest a small tactical adjustment to how you carry out your orders?"

Cruz stopped, and the eyes of every military leader in the room turned and fixed on O'Leary with an intensity and obvious hope that the chairman of the Committee on Military Affairs could somehow turn what they all viewed as an inevitable intelligence disaster into something a little less so. After all, Corey held that position, even as a member of the minority coalition, precisely because the smaller members of Pereira's Blue Party majority coalition had been nervous about the president's lackadaisical approach to military matters.

Corey continued, his voice casual but pitched low. "The president ordered you to have Second Fleet intercept the enemy but did not specify how quickly or where they should do so. Based on the intelligence Ms. Ambrosa and Mr. Tyne brought us, we believe the top speed of our carriers and battleships to be approximately ten percent higher than that of the Council's dreadnoughts. May I suggest not revealing that fact to the Council fleet at this time?"

He stopped, looking calmly at Cruz. The general regarded him thoughtfully for a moment, and then the corner of his mouth twitched ever so slightly upward. He turned back to the man in the white uniform.

"Kurt," he said, "make it clear to Admirals Lafayette and Showalker that they are to keep their speed to only 85 percent of full military power unless doing so will risk too many lives. Their discretion on that, but we should have enough of a numbers advantage that the speed differential won't be a primary factor in the engagement… assuming they actually let us engage them."

The admiral smiled and nodded to acknowledge the order. Cruz continued, looking back at Corey and Jinny, both still seated at the table. "Let's hope your interpretation of the president's orders is correct, Congressman, but I'm afraid my career will be the least of our worries if we're wrong about all of this."

With that, he turned and left the room, the rest of the military officers following hastily.

When they were alone at the table, Jinny looked over at Corey and saw his previously calm face had taken on a red countenance. "That man!" he said aloud to her and then cursed under his breath. "He probably doesn't see the irony in how his overconfidence is playing right into the Council government's arrogance. No matter what happens today, we're revealing nearly every card we have. We're showing just how fragmented we are. To not even consider *calling* the Martians...."

He looked over at Jinny and gave her a wan smile. "I'm sorry, my dear. You did great, better than I hoped when Cruz and I agreed to set up this little ambush. And I'm sorry for that as well. If anyone could make the president see reason, it was probably you. You are more persuasive for your earnest and open nature than you probably realize. But now we have to play with the hand we've been dealt and hope for the best."

Jinny nodded slowly. She knew she should be angry at O'Leary's and Cruz's ambush—for putting her on the spot with the president—but she wasn't. Though she did have the terrible feeling that the most crucial battle of the coming war had already been lost in this very room.

---

On the bridge of *CNS Invictus,* Admiral Tyler Prudhoe couldn't stop smiling. The first engagement against the Four Worlds had been a rousing success. They had caught the defenders off guard with their daring in sending large numbers of ships through the Path all at once, risking the possible destruction of a few from void drift in order to get as many ships through as quickly as possible. That they'd lost only two ships, both light cruisers, to collisions was the icing on the cake.

Now, he was also pleased to see that Earth had taken the bait. The fools were sending an entire fleet to intercept him *and* moving a portion of another fleet away from Earth orbit. His sensor officer had also reported a smaller fleet from Europa breaking in half, sending one part toward Earth for its defense and keeping the other on a line between his fleet and their own planet. He was now confident that he had an accurate count of virtually all of Earth's, Luna's, and Europa's naval forces, and it matched up with the pre-mission intel rather nicely. Wherever the Keeper and Admiral Chen were getting their information from, it was highly accurate.

Only Mars had done nothing, so they hadn't yet gotten a good reading on the Martian naval forces. But Mars' lack of action had given him another gift, the sure knowledge that the Four Worlds, unlike the 47 Colonies, were *not* united in government or purpose. Even the actions of Europa, whose fleet seemed to be slow playing the transit to defend Earth, told him that the actual invasion was likely to face a disjointed and uncoordinated force, with each planet effectively fighting on its own. It seemed that not even a direct threat could unite the three separate polities in the Sol system, and that would make it far easier to defeat them in detail.

Despite all the early intelligence wins of the mission, however, Tyler Prudhoe's greatest sense of satisfaction came from being in *command* of the entire endeavor. He knew that Fleet Admiral Chen had recommended to the Council that *she* directly lead the first armed incursion into the Sol system in almost six hundred years. But she had lost that battle; the Keeper had reportedly told her she was too *valuable* to risk. Of course, the implication was that her chosen replacement to command the mission, Prudhoe, wasn't as valuable, but he was fine with that assessment. Because after his victory here today, no one would ever question his value or capabilities again.

His smile grew wider. He had lost 22 ships to get this information and cement his legacy, but victory on this mission was a price well worth even double those losses.

Now, he and his remaining ships were en route to Earth, minus five that he had left to guard the Front Door and ensure his fleet had an escape path when the time came. Five ships might feel like a pittance versus the multitude of warships that the Four Worlders could send to take back the entrance to the Rift, but one of those five was the *CNS*

*Indomitable*, the most damaged of his three dreadnoughts. Rear Admiral Atkins had destroyed one of the four largest battleships that had faced them at the Front Door but had gotten too close in his zeal to engage it, and the enemy ship's explosive destruction had damaged the *Indomitable* moderately enough that it made sense to detach her and leave her on rearguard duty.

Besides that, none of the Four Worlds' fleets were making any move toward the Front Door. Not even the Martian task force sitting just 15 light minutes away had started toward it. It appeared the Martians were entirely content to watch rather than engage his forces. And Prudhoe had specific orders on how to deal with that. The red planet had no way of knowing that they were playing directly into the Council's hands.

"Time to Earth?" he asked his sensor officer.

The young man, whose name he had forgotten, looked up. "At current speed, we will intersect Earth's orbit in 20 hours and 17 minutes, sir."

The admiral nodded. Of course, it would take much longer than that if they wanted to attack Earth, as they would need to decelerate down from their current and still increasing speed of 0.005c to have any meaningful time to engage the planet's defenses, but Prudhoe had no intention of getting that close. Attacking Earth itself was not part of his mission orders.

"How long until the closest enemy fleet reaches weapons range?"

"Twelve hours and 46 minutes, sir."

"Very well. Captain Norwood, wake me if anything changes. I will be in my cabin resting after the battle we just had."

Captain Henrietta Norwood acknowledged his order and took over the command chair for the long wait for the next phase of their plan.

---

"Ma'am," called the bridge officer at *Enterprise's* comm station. "Tachyon telegraph from Houston. Our orders are to slip in behind the invading force and shadow them. Full stealth protocols and only engage if threatened or on further orders."

Bol nodded and gave Tyrus a look that included a tight-lipped smile. "Thank you, Scott. Send no acknowledgment."

To Tyrus, she explained, "Even though we assume the colonials don't have Tachyon sensors, let's not take any chances at revealing our location or our existence yet. Even a directional sublight comm at this distance could diffuse enough for that fleet to catch its edge and track it back to its source."

"That's wise," Tyrus admitted.

Bol began giving orders to her staff, leaving him alone with his thoughts. Inevitably, they drifted to Jinny Ambrosa, and he wondered if the beautiful reader was aware of what was happening right this moment in the outer Sol system or if she was oblivious to all of it on Earth.

Thoughts of Jinny brought with them a set of warm and confusing feelings. Tyrus was reasonably sure he had no romantic delusions about his relationship with her. He certainly didn't feel about her the way he was starting to feel about Mary Bol; those feelings terrified him in a way he couldn't explain. But Jinny had been his first, and still *only*, real friend since being ripped from his parents at the tender age of five for his enacter indoctrination and alpha training. Their friendship was surprising in so many ways. He'd killed most of her rebel cell on Nova Tejas *and* the man she loved in that alleyway on Centauri II, and he and Jinny had spent only a week together on the run from the Twenty's agents before arriving here in the Sol system.

Still, she had been there for him when he'd first woken up on one of Earth's orbital stations. One of the nurses there had told him that Jinny had waited by his bed almost day and night for those first couple weeks. Even after he'd regained consciousness and been moved down to a unit in the Houston Naval Hospital, she had visited him nearly every day. It had given the two of them time to talk and get to know each other better now that no one was shooting at them. And it had only strengthened the fledgling friendship they'd almost accidentally begun in colonial space.

And he had needed that friendship desperately. As he had recovered physically, he'd also been forced to come to grips with the emotional fallout of his actions in the colonies. He had killed *so many* people at the Council's direction; at the time, he had been led to believe that each and every one of them was a threat to the peace and order of the 47 Colonies. He had also believed, as any enacter did, that he had no choice but to follow the Council's orders. But Kendra Siefred's revelations about the true nature of the government and his own eventual break with his genetic programming—due to Jinny's revelation that he hadn't actually killed his mother during his training—had brought both of those previously incontrovertible facts crashing down around him. And while he was happy to now be free of his slavery to the Twenty's insidious agenda, that freedom came with a heavy price: a lifetime's worth of guilt.

He saw the faces of the people he'd killed in both his dreams and his waking hours. Logically, he knew that it was counterproductive for him to feel guilty for things he did while under the control of his genetic programming. But that didn't stop him from thinking through each Council mission, replaying them in his head and looking for ways that he might have broken his programming earlier or even just found loopholes in his orders to leave more of his targets alive.

These thoughts had led him to some very dark places in his first several weeks after waking up in the Sol system, and he had found himself wishing on several occasions that he had just died saving the *Monk*. Anything, he thought, would be easier than living with the crushing guilt of all his crimes committed in the name of the Council.

The only thing that had kept him from completely spinning out and self-destructing in the face of that overwhelming guilt was Jinny's steady companionship. They spent hours in the hospital talking through his missions and memories, which she had read from him on multiple occasions. She held his hand while he broke down, crying for the first time since he had woken up next to his mother's corpse—falsely believing he had killed her—in the Enacter Academy's secret Alpha indoctrination chamber.

Jinny didn't call attention to his grief or try and talk him out of it; somehow, she seemed to understand that would have only made it worse. Instead, she was simply there for him, ready to listen or to sit in companionable silence so that he didn't have to be alone. He had talked through so many things with her, confessing crimes that she already knew from her readings but that he still felt he needed to say aloud to someone. And slowly, it had brought him back from the brink.

He wondered if she knew she'd saved him. A man with his training knew a thousand ways to take a life, and he could have easily ended his own at any moment in that hospital had he chosen to do so. He didn't think he would have actually gone through with it, but deep down, he shuddered to ponder what might have happened without Jinny's present and deep friendship.

So Tyrus wondered now in the quiet of his mind, notwithstanding the controlled chaos surrounding him on *Enterprise's* clean white bridge, where Jinny was and what she was doing. And whether she was going about her day ignorant of the battle fought and the one yet to come, or was watching tensely from the sidelines as he was.

# CHAPTER 10

The mood in the Situation Room was beyond tense. Jinny had been there for the better part of six hours now, enough time to witness the aftermath of the disastrous engagement at the Front Door... which was basically nothing. In essence, the only thing that had happened since Pereira had issued his questionable orders was that several blue and red dots on the room's giant viewscreen had moved slowly toward one another, while a clock underneath counted down the hours and minutes until the Council and United Earth fleets closed to within weapons range of each other.

Of course, even she knew that their assumptions of the Council fleet's weapons range could be entirely inaccurate, but Tyrus had worked with the UEN to make their best estimate based on what he knew of the Guard Space Force.

"Why are you still here?" a voice snapped from surprisingly close, causing Jinny to jump in the seat she occupied on the back edge of the room, spilling thankfully lukewarm coffee in her lap as she did so.

She looked up to see the scrunched, sour face of Tabitha Givens, the president's chief of staff. Givens—Jinny had since learned the woman's name from Corey—had been the one speaking into Pereira's ear in the meeting when she'd first arrived in the Situation Room, who had given

Jinny a bad feeling by how the president seemed to look to her to confirm every decision.

"I... uh... Congressman O'Leary asked me to stay here with him as his adviser," she replied unsteadily, using the words Corey had told her to say if anyone challenged her presence in the room. Obviously, he'd had the foresight that this little confrontation might happen.

"He has *no* authority to do so," the sour woman snapped back. "I demand you leave at once!"

Jinny felt her hackles rise, and she recognized in Givens the same power-happy bureaucrat that seemed to inhabit virtually every senior reader and mid-level bureaucrat she'd encountered back in the colonies. She looked around to see if Corey was nearby, but he had gone to the restroom a few minutes earlier and had still not returned.

Luckily, she had lots of experience dealing with petty bureaucrats. And even as a mid-level reader, few outranked her in the colonies, so she was used to speaking with authority herself. "I'm sorry," she said respectfully but firmly, "but the congressman asked me to remain here. You're welcome to take it up with him when he returns."

The woman's face turned a deep shade of red, just as Jinny knew it would. What most people never understood about readers was that a good reader didn't *need* to read a person to understand how they would act or react in certain situations. Reading others gave them a good baseline on human behavior, and they learned to recognize verbal and nonverbal cues in others that revealed quite a lot about the person they were observing. Blenders and speakers often developed similar talents to augment their enhancements and make them more effective. And Jinny knew she had pegged Givens correctly, as not just a power-drunk government lackey but also as a woman who was not used to having her authority questioned and didn't quite know how to react when it happened.

"I don't care what O'Leary said," the woman retorted, purposefully stripping the congressman of his title, which came as no surprise. "I demand you leave this instant!"

Jinny smiled again, knowing it would further infuriate the woman but not caring after watching tens of thousands of Earther and Europan spacers die just a few hours before, largely because of the incompetence and petty politics of this woman's boss. "I'm sorry, but no. I'll stay here until Congressman O'Leary returns and you can discuss it with him."

Now Givens was *furious*, and it oddly gratified Jinny to see the woman's claw-like hands curl into fists. "You there!" she shouted across the room, drawing quite a few stares. She pointed at one of the Marine guards that flanked the entrance to the bunker. "Come here!"

The Marine dutifully walked across the large command center, slipping between rows of duty stations crewed by civilians and military personnel alike. Jinny noticed with satisfaction that the man didn't hurry, and every second it took him to arrive fueled Givens' rage. When the Marine finally came to parade rest next to the two women, the chief of staff turned her ire on him.

"I demand you remove this woman from this bunker immediately!"

The Marine looked confused and looked first at Jinny and then at Givens. "Ma'am," he said respectfully to Givens, "I'm afraid you will need to speak with my commanding officer. I am not authorized to take orders from civilians outside of the president himself."

Jinny had to put her hand to her mouth to stifle a smile and laugh and hoped Givens didn't see. The poor Marine might as well have removed all the stops on an already melting-down reactor. The chief of staff looked like she was going to have a stroke right then and there, the vein in her temple pulsing as she tried to process the man's refusal on top of the one she'd already gotten from Jinny.

"Is there a problem here?" a calm but authoritative voice asked, rescuing the lonely Marine. Jinny hadn't even seen General Cruz approach but was glad he was there now.

"Sir!" the Marine snapped to attention.

Givens whirled on Cruz, but then seemed to hesitate. *Didn't count on having to order around anyone with* real *authority, did you?* Jinny thought wryly.

Unfortunately, the chief of staff was game. "This man," she pointed accusingly at the Marine guard, "refused an order to remove this woman," she pointed at Jinny now, "from the bunker. She has no right to be here, and having her in this room, especially as a *reader*, is a security risk. I demand she be removed at once!"

Cruz waited patiently through Givens' rant and betrayed little emotion, though Jinny saw a fire in his eyes that the other woman no doubt missed. He turned calmly and looked at Jinny. "Ms. Ambrosa," he said, his tone respectful, "have you read or attempted to read anyone since you arrived on the premises?"

"I have not, General," Jinny replied, matching his respectful tone.

Cruz nodded once and looked at the Marine guard. "Corporal, has anyone in your chain of command ordered you to remove Ms. Ambrosa from this facility?"

The Marine, still at attention, answered back quickly. "No, sir."

Cruz raised his eyebrows and looked back at Givens. "I'm sorry, Ms. Givens, but this Marine has done nothing wrong, and your request to have the military remove Ms. Ambrosa from this bunker is denied. She has done nothing inappropriate since her arrival and is a vital source of insight and intelligence for the other Joint Chiefs and myself while she is here. Of course, if the president himself were to order me to have her removed in his capacity as commander-in-chief, then I'm sure the young corporal here would obediently fulfill the order. Until then, will there be anything else?"

Jinny watched Givens with interest. The woman had tightened her jaw and turned an even deeper shade of red during Cruz's respectful yet unmistakable rebuke, and Jinny knew that the chief of staff could choose to play this one of two ways. She could decide to go over Cruz's head to the president himself or to back down and try to save face. Either way would undermine her future authority in the eyes of everyone in the room, as they were all now surreptitiously watching the exchange.

Going to the president would mean disturbing Earth's leader for a trivial matter. He had gone to the surface a few hours before for some meetings with congressional leaders to brief them on the situation, leaving his military commanders and advisers in the Situation Room to monitor things and call him if needed. And Jinny was betting that the irascible Givens would avoid pulling the man out of his meetings. That meant the most likely scenario would be for the woman to make some

## THE FOUR WORLDS - SUBVERSION

sort of excuse and back out of the confrontation, trying to salvage what dignity she could.

But what Givens ultimately did surprised her.

The woman looked daggers at General Cruz. "Well done, General. You may have won this round, but remember that you serve at the pleasure of President Pereira, and I am his top adviser. So, in the future, I would ask yourself if this *reader*," she spat the word, "is worth destroying your career over." She threw one last hateful look at Jinny and then walked away.

Jinny had to admit she honestly hadn't expected the woman to take the direct approach like that. She sensed that perhaps another battle had been lost and not in the direction she was expecting. Cruz dismissed the Marine, who moved gratefully and hastily back to his post, and then sat down in the chair next to her.

"Never you mind that woman," the general said softly so that others couldn't hear but so he also didn't have to engage an obvious privacy field. "She's like a pet snake I had as a kid: always looking for a way to bite."

The man's candor surprised Jinny, and she decided to be equally direct with him. "I hope that my being here is not going to lose you your job, General. I can leave if it's a problem."

The older man smiled at her warmly, though it didn't reach his eyes, which were filled with a deep sadness that Jinny had seen briefly from him in the conference earlier with the president. "Now don't you go worrying about me, Ms. Ambrosa," he said casually. "I've dealt with snakes like Tabitha Givens my entire career. *Nothing* you could do today would make her any more or less inclined to get me fired from my job. Worst case, my wife finally gets her wish and I'm home more to help her spoil the grandkids."

His joking tone at that last statement failed to cover his obvious worry, but Jinny wisely decided not to call him on the lie. Instead, she returned his smile. "You're a good man, General Cruz, exactly the type of leader I was hoping to find when I came to warn Earth about the Twenty's plans. I hope you keep your job for a long time."

Warm gratitude momentarily replaced the worry in his eyes, and he reached over and patted her gloved hand. It was the first physical contact anyone in the room had dared have with her besides Corey, who had grown used to being around a reader. Even through the glove, the man's brief touch conveyed far more than words the trust he felt toward her. Jinny had to resist the urge to choke up and instead turned her gaze to the mission clock.

"Do you think they'll really attack Earth?" she asked, her whisper so quiet that Cruz had to lean closer to hear it.

He shook his head. "They'd be crazy to with so few ships, but that's what worries me. When the enemy does something that *looks* crazy to us, it usually means we don't fully understand their reasons or their plan. And charging the entirety of our Navy with an oversized task force doesn't make any sense with the information we have now. So, they're up to *something*. We just don't know what it is yet."

Jinny suppressed a shudder. After watching a portion of this same enemy fleet ruthlessly destroy their supposed allies, the Guard, at Rinali and the Back Door, she was certain that any surprise they had for the Four Worlds would be equally nasty. Either way, she didn't need the coffee she'd spilled on her pants to keep her awake while that mission clock ticked down.

In that moment, she made a decision.

"General, I think there's something you need to know."

He looked at her with a raised eyebrow.

"Can we talk in private? Where no one can overhear?"

---

"How stupid can they be?" Tyrus muttered under his breath, eyes riveted on the small pad Bol had handed him. "They've revealed *everything* United Earth has, just to what, intimidate a couple of Council task forces?"

Bol nodded solemnly. They were alone in her ready room, him sitting across from her at her desk, so he knew she could be more open where those under her command couldn't hear her express doubt over the orders from the civilian government.

"You're not wrong," she said in a flat voice. "But that's how democracy works, for better or worse. The civilians run the show, and we follow their orders." To Tyrus, it sounded as if she were trying to convince herself as much as him.

"You know, just following orders has been the greatest source of pain in my life," he said, raising an eyebrow and looking at her skeptically across the small desk; even on a massive carrier and in the Admiral's own domain, space was at a premium.

She returned his look with a sympathetic one. "I understand where you're coming from, Tyrus. And while the law gives Admiral Showalker the right to refuse unlawful orders or those that would constitute crimes against humanity—like sending kinetic rounds toward an inhabited planet—these particular orders fall into neither of those scenarios. So, he *must* follow his orders and move half of First Fleet away from Earth, even if the rest of us think those orders are… less intelligent ones. None of us are enacters, but we are duly sworn officers in the United Earth Navy."

Tyrus grunted in response. His skepticism of civilian government leaders had grown from a seed of doubt during his days as a Council assassin to almost full-blown distrust and paranoia since finding out about the Keeper's and the Twenty's lies. The reticence of the United Earth government to do *anything* to prepare for the Council invasion only heightened that distrust.

"On the bright side, if Second Fleet catches them before they can return to the Front Door," continued Bol, "there won't be anything left to return to the colonies and provide them any intel."

Tyrus shook his head. "Destroying all of them is overly optimistic, Admiral. You know as well as I do that the first thing every one of those Council ships did after destroying your forces at the Front Door was to recharge its star drive. They can reverse course anytime in the next ten hours and make it back to the Front Door and into the void before Second Fleet gets into missile range. And the damaged ships they already sent back would have taken sensor logs of the initial engagement with them." He shrugged. " Plus, even if you got these three wonderful ships there ahead of them, you'd be obliterated as soon as you dropped your stealth measures to engage them."

Bol frowned and nodded. "You're probably right, Tyrus. And in private, please call me Mary. It's only out there," she gestured to the door leading the bridge, "that I have to play the indomitable and unapproachable admiral."

He smiled despite the situation. Love had never been in the cards for him since the first day the instructors at the Enacter Academy had selected him for the special Alpha program. One of the standing orders all alphas had was to avoid romantic or emotional entanglements. That meant no wives, lovers, or even close friends. Tyrus had gone along with it—not that he had a choice—knowing that his life was not his own anyway and, he thought, having come to grips with that fact.

Now that he was free of all that, he was in uncharted territory as he tried to come to grips with his feelings toward Mary Bol. Tyrus had wondered if it were even possible for him to feel these emotions toward *anyone*; he'd thought that it was likely his long stint as an enacter and alpha, and all the terrible things he'd done, had killed that part of him. So, having these feelings now for the admiral was disconcerting at best. And his lifelong training as a Council servant and assassin had included nothing helpful for this type of situation. When it came to human relationships, especially those of the romantic variety, he felt like he was five years old again, desperately trying to figure out the answer that was expected of him.

"Tyrus, you still with me?"

He looked up in surprise to see Mary Bol regarding him with a half-smile. "Sorry... I was thinking about some things."

She raised an eyebrow. "You know, a lady prefers a man's attention be on her when she's talking. And an admiral *demands* it."

Tyrus felt a moment of panic rise in his chest. Her words hinted at flirtation, and he even hoped that they were a signal that she felt about him the way he was beginning to feel about her. Except he had no idea *what* he should do. He didn't even know what to say in response!

Bol seemed to sense his confusion and even be amused by it. She smiled wider. "Look, let's talk business if it makes you feel better. Because I know we're both still worried about what Mars might do."

Tyrus gratefully took the lifeline offered. "Uh, of course. Mars is the real wildcard, but they've already shown the Council fleet that they don't play nice with others. I imagine by now that the admiral of that fleet knows well that the Four Worlds aren't all one happy family. He or she can monitor the comms traffic, or the lack thereof, between Earth and Mars as well as we can. Plus, no one can miss that the Martian Navy hasn't made a single move to engage the Council Fleet or defend Earth from them. Even the Europan fleet is dragging their feet—only moving at 70 percent maximum thrust and not even on a direct intercept course; they seem to be more worried about that fleet changing course toward Europa."

Mary nodded. "I agree. But just because the Martians haven't made a move yet doesn't mean they won't. My concern now is whether or not the Martian task force that has been sitting and watching the Front Door will try to engage either the five ships the Council Navy left behind or even the larger enemy force when it inevitably returns to flee through the Rift. I'm almost rooting for them to do so, but it would introduce another unknown variable into an already-complex situation. As for the Europans... Well, they're only doing the smart thing. We don't *need* them to defend Earth against such a small force, and they can't risk leaving their worlds uncovered. Yet it does make our lack of coordination even more obvious to those Council ships' intel folks."

"I agree," Tyrus replied, his confidence back now that he was focused on matters of war and tactics. "My money is on Mars continuing to watch as they've done up until now. My big question is what *you* and your ships will do if the president orders you to reveal your presence and engage the enemy."

Bol frowned deeply. "Well, so far, no one has ordered me to do anything but shadow the Council fleet. Still, if I am given a direct order to reveal these ships and join the battle, you must know I *will* obey it. If I don't follow my orders, the whole system breaks down. The civilian leadership may not always be right, but the long-term cost of disobeying them is far higher than the short-term cost of following even orders I disagree with. If you don't believe me, study up on the history of the Roman Empire when you get a chance. When the military stops listening to civilian leaders, bad things happen to civilization."

"I hope that's true," he responded. "Because the cost of following those orders may be quite high and may not be short term at all. Especially with all they've already learned about us, we need to keep what secrets we have if we're to have any hope when the *real* invasion force arrives."

Bol nodded. She and he were of one mind: the relatively small force the Council had sent was *not* the promised invasion but a reconnaissance in force. She arched an eyebrow. "You seem to have a nasty habit of saying things I know are true but don't want to think about too hard. I'm not sure I like that quality in a man."

It may have been Tyrus' imagination, but he thought he saw her smile a little right before he looked away in confused embarrassment.

"Now, if you don't mind," she continued nonchalantly, "it's been a long morning. Even at maximum acceleration, we won't reach the rear of the Council fleet for another six and a half hours, and that will still be a full five hours before we expect the rest of Earth's fleet to intercept their forward elements, assuming they don't turn around before then. An hour at battle stations can drain the body like three hours in normal time. So I'd like to get some rest and rotate my command crew to do the same, even if none of us will likely get any sleep. I suggest even you try to relax a bit. Things are going to get... exciting this evening."

With that, she graced him with a warm smile and stood up from her desk. Tyrus did likewise, and they shook hands, both lingering for the barest moment before she left him to go and give her crew orders from the flag bridge. Tyrus left via another door that took him out into the corridor and headed toward the small cabin set aside for visitors in the ship's officer country, still feeling the warmth of her hand on his.

---

"That's incredible. How sure are you of this?" General Cruz's green eyes bored into Jinny's as they sat in his small temporary office in the Situation Room bunker. They were alone save for Corey O'Leary, who had joined them slightly after Givens' blowup.

"Honestly, it's just a theory. But it's the only thing that makes sense," Jinny replied evenly. She had just finished sharing with the two men her hypothesis that the Twenty was invading the Four Worlds expressly to gain access to the pure enhanced bloodlines in Australia.

"But that would suggest they have spies already on Earth," Corey argued. "And we would have seen something come through the Rift; there's no stealth technology good enough to get past our pickets there."

Cruz frowned momentarily in a way that Jinny noticed, but O'Leary didn't. Something about Corey's comments on stealth technology had made him flinch, but she didn't press on it. "It would suggest that," she agreed with Corey. "Like I said, it's just a theory. But if they're not coming for the enhanced, the only other motive we've been able to come up with is simple greed and thirst for power. And if that's the motive, then why now? Why not hundreds of years before this? The Twenty have been secretly ruling the colonies for centuries; do we think they're just *now* getting around to expanding their power back into the Sol system? Or why not wait until later since we exposed their plans; even a few years would be long enough for most citizens of the 47 Colonies to forget all about the rumors of a secret navy. Their moving so quickly implies a level of desperation, as does their quest to artificially create so many new enacters to crew their warships."

Corey shook his head in frustration. "I agree that the timing supports your theory, even if I don't want to believe it's that simple. From what you say, it sounds like the degradation in reader abilities has been accelerating, which could mean that they're looking at a complete breakdown in enhanced bloodlines in the colonies sooner rather than later. The real question is, how does this change things for us?"

Jinny stayed silent, watching the wheels spin in Cruz's head as the man stared at a spot on the wall behind her. When he finally spoke, his voice was subdued. "It changes things quite a lot. *If* the Twenty are just after the enhanced, they don't need to fully conquer Earth. All they need to do is scare us bad enough that we'll *give* them what they need."

"You mean...?" Jinny couldn't finish the question as the horror of what he was suggesting sunk in.

He nodded with a grimace. "You've been around our leadership enough in the past few months, Ms. Ambrosa. You've seen that many of them will do just about anything to get reelected and hold on to their power. In that regard, they're little different from the Twenty." He turned and fixed his gaze on O'Leary. "Tell me, Congressman, could you see your peers in Congress voting to surrender the enhanced to the Council Navy to save United Earth and their own skins?"

Corey was silent for a long count of ten, but by his reddening face, Jinny knew he was *not* convinced of the integrity of his fellow world leaders. Finally, he sighed. "I suppose they would do it if it looked like the Council Navy had the upper hand. It also changes things in another significant way that we haven't discussed yet. Our Navy is pretty evenly matched with the Martians right now. If Europa takes our side in a conflict, we have the upper hand, but there's no guarantee the Europans would choose either side the next time Earth and Mars go to war. The Coalition Treaty only unites us in the face of threats from *outside* the system.

"So, with the losses sustained today, it's already going to throw the balance of power off. Imagine if the full Council Navy were to arrive and focus their attack only on United Earth. It wouldn't take many losses before we'd start to feel disadvantaged against future Martian attacks, which means…"

Cruz finished the thought for him, his frown pronounced. "…it means that there is a low threshold of losses we could sustain before Congress and the president decide giving up the enhanced is better than opening ourselves up to Martian conquest. We might even raise the white flag the second a larger fleet comes out of the Rift and starts burning towards Earth."

"I'm afraid so," Corey agreed with a matching frown. "This is pretty explosive if it's true." He turned back to Jinny. "You were right to share this with the two of us, but don't share it with *anyone* else. We need to play this close to the vest, or there may be talk of even preemptively offering the enhanced to the Twenty to make a deal before the actual invasion comes. Especially since Pereira and the Blue Party will likely be clutching at straws after today's little fiasco."

Cruz sat back and blew out a long breath. "And especially because the alternative is for them to admit they were wrong and start the military buildup in earnest. That fool Hastings is already trying to drum up support to send an emissary through the Rift to negotiate peace

# THE FOUR WORLDS - SUBVERSION

with the Council. After today, a negotiated peace would be one of the *few* ways the Blue Party comes out looking good after they refused to make any real military preparations based on your warnings, Ms. Ambrosa—Jinny."

She shook her head. "The Twenty wouldn't honor any agreement they make with the Four Worlds; they would just use it to lull you into a false sense of security so that you'd be easier to invade."

"Everything you've told us about them supports that," Corey said. "I believe you, and I even believe that *giving* the enhanced to them would only delay an inevitable conquest. But I'm afraid not even my Red Party colleagues are likely to balk at giving up the enhanced to save Earth." He looked at Cruz and Jinny in turn. "So, we tell no one, correct?"

"Agreed," Cruz replied. "In truth, it's only a theory. So, keeping it from the other Joint Chiefs and Government House isn't technically withholding vital intelligence. Though it comes close. I also don't like the implications that the Council has some way of spying on us here. We might need to order some additional pickets in the outer system to look for the Tachyon signatures of any spy ships surfacing from the void along a different path through the Rift, but that's a *lot* of space to cover and will leave those ships out of position to defend Earth when the full invasion force arrives."

"Agreed," Jinny said, responding to Corey's question, though she also understood Cruz's dilemma. "That's why I only told the two of you. It's just a theory, as you said."

The three of them adjourned and left the room, and Jinny noticed Givens throwing them a dark look as they emerged back into the main floor of the Situation Room. *She doesn't know what we were talking about,* she thought, *but she knows we're keeping something to ourselves.* It would only add to the woman's ire. Still, that didn't seem all that important right then.

---

Admiral Terrence Lafayette, commander of the United Earth Navy's

Second Fleet, swore as he watched the viewscreen in front of him on the flag bridge of the *UENS Texas*.

"Sir," reported his sensor officer, "the enemy fleet has begun turnover deceleration and is burning on an intercept vector with the Front Door."

Lafayette had seen the same thing on his own sensor screen before the young man had even informed him, but he acknowledged the information with gratitude and then set to thinking about what it meant. He had expected this, of course, as had Admiral Clancy, General Cruz, and the rest of the Joint Chiefs. None of them had thought that the Council Navy was insane enough to attack Earth with only 48 ships, even if two of them were those magnificent and infuriating dreadnoughts. They *had* to turn back around at some point and make their escape.

However, knowing something was likely to happen and watching it happen were two different things. He knew from the mission clock on his screen that, even were his fleet to go to full military power, which they'd been expressly ordered *not* to do, they would never catch the Council fleet in time to engage them before they submerged back through the Rift. And it didn't look like the Martians, who potentially *could* intercept them ahead of their escape, were even going to twitch their fleet in that direction.

That meant the peoples of the Four Worlds and their navies would miss the chance to avenge their fallen comrades. It especially rankled Lafayette, who was the commanding officer for *all* of Second Fleet, including Task Force 23, Rear Admiral Peter Zelinski's fallen command. Those had been Terrence's men and women, as much as Zelinski's, who had died in the fiery sucker punch from the enemy fleet that was now showing him its rear.

"We could do an in-system hop, sir," the voice of Captain Lakshmi Dasgupta said softly from his right.

He looked over to see *Texas'* captain, who had come to the flag bridge from her normal station on the battleship's command bridge specifically to talk tactics with him in person. Even a real-time internal comm couldn't replace the flow of ideas and information that came from two people sitting in the same room and watching the same screen.

He shook his head reluctantly. "We could, but we'd lose part of the fleet."

Star drives required a massive amount of power to both submerge and surface a ship. When done properly, a star drive the size of the one on *Texas* needed a good thirty minutes to charge its capacitors in preparation for either. That effectively gave the drives a minimum distance that they could travel a ship through the void because it would take at least half an hour for the drive to store up enough power after submerging to surface the ship again to normal space. Smaller ships could do shorter hops, as their drives required much less power, but a battleship simply couldn't manage it.

Military ships *had* a workaround to that: to temporarily tie the star drives into the main reactor, removing the safeties and bypassing the capacitors while the reactor ran on overdrive. Unfortunately, it was extremely dangerous, and the latest specs Lafayette had seen—all theoretical, of course; no one was crazy enough to test it—suggested that a 'crash emergence' using that method would cause an energy feedback loop that would destroy the ship approximately five percent of the time. That meant that doing it now would lose him roughly a $20^{th}$ of his fleet, but there were no guarantees it wouldn't be far more.

Even worse, the impact would be outsized on the larger capital ships, as the energy surge required to power a star drive was exponentially larger the more a ship massed. Therefore, the risk was more significant for larger vessels, close to ten percent. So not only would he probably resurface without part of his fleet, but it might also very well be the part he needed most to engage the Council's force.

"I agree, but I just thought I'd raise the possibility," Captain Dasgupta said. Her job as flag captain was to raise options with him, even if they weren't ones he would agree to. *Especially* the ones he wouldn't usually agree to.

He looked over at her and smiled. "And keep doing that, Lakshmi. I have a feeling we're going to need to explore *every* option before this war is done." There, he had said it. War. Even if the president and his advisers refused to acknowledge it after today, the Four Worlds were unquestionably at war with the 47 Colonies. And 47 vs. four were odds that Terrence Lafayette didn't like.

"Besides," he said. "Even if we could catch and destroy that main element, it would be a Pyrrhic victory. We'd have to destroy or capture every one of them to keep the intel they've gathered from getting back to the Council. Which is probably exactly why they left those five ships back at the Front Door, to submerge back to colonial space if anything happens to the main fleet."

Dasgupta nodded solemnly. "Still hurts not to be able to show them what happens when they *don't* catch us by surprise."

"That it does, Lakshmi. That it does."

"Sir!" called the comm officer. "TT from Houston. We are to continue pursuit at current course and speed until the enemy has left the system."

"Thank you, Adams," Lafayette said, reading the short message and then looking over at Dasgupta. "Well, it seems the decision has been taken from us anyway. Makes sense. Still, would have been nice to see how those dreadnoughts stand up to a missile fight."

His flag captain frowned, and he watched her patiently as she clearly worked through something in her head. "What if there were still a way?" she said slowly.

He raised an eyebrow. "What are you getting at?"

Dasgupta reached out to the display that hung from the flag bridge ceiling in front of them. Using a reverse pinching motion, she zoomed in on a portion of space roughly between the enemy fleet and the Front Door but a little to the solar west of both. Two small green blips and one blue one showed in the expanded image.

"The survivors of TF 23?" Terrence asked in confusion. In all the excitement, he'd largely forgotten about the three small ships that had fled the engagement at the Front Door once all hope was lost and their commanders' duties turned to keeping their ships and crews intact. Only two had been part of TF 23, both light cruisers. The slightly larger blue blip, a heavy cruiser, was a Europan ship. None of them could do much to hurt the Council fleet, even if they weren't fleeing with all of their remaining acceleration.

"None of those ships can fire capital ship missiles, and their broadsides only house a few of the smaller anti-ship missiles," he said to Dasgupta. "Most of their tubes are configured only to fire defensive and anti-fighter armament. So what good would they do against one of those dreadnoughts or even a Council destroyer at that range?"

His flag captain smiled, which he'd always reflected on the woman looked like a shark who had spotted a school of fat and slow fish. She zoomed out and gestured to another part of the screen, where there were no blips, but there *was* a thin, dotted, gray line representing the estimated course for a group of ships that couldn't be seen even by the sophisticated and powerful sensors on a Missouri-class battleship. As his flag captain, she was one of only a handful of people in Second Fleet, along with Lafayette himself, who knew what that gray line represented.

Terrence Lafayette smiled for the first time that day.

---

"Incoming TT from Admiral Lafayette on *Texas*, Admiral. Your eyes only." The internal comm message instantly brought Mary Bol out of an unexpected but fitful sleep, and she was off her bunk almost before she consciously registered the words.

"Send it to my day cabin," she replied to the empty air of her cabin, knowing the ship's AI would relay her response to the flag bridge.

Less than five seconds later, she was sitting at her desk and reading the brief message. Tachyon telegraphs were new tech for the Four Worlds, less than 20 years old. They were based on the same principles as the Tachyon sensors that could detect ships surfacing from the void and required enormous amounts of power, usually limiting communications to terse and abbreviated messages with simple encryptions. Still, they allowed for instantaneous comms across the Sol system. The one she was reading now was short but infinitely sweet in its import.

"Captain Holm." The AI relayed the message, and the man answered immediately, looking like he had been awaiting her call. As her flag captain and lord and master of the carrier itself, it was his job to know *everything* that went on in his ship, even when his admiral got a secret communique from another flag officer.

"George," she told her flag captain. "I want your CIC to run some numbers for me. Can you join me in my ready room and bring Commander Davies?"

Technically, Mary could have called the *Enterprise's* combat information center herself, but whenever possible, she liked to keep the line between admiral and captain clear. She may be the master of all three of the top-secret carriers in her armada, but nothing degraded a crew's confidence more than having their admiral play captain and micromanage her flagship. So, whenever she could, she tried to work through Holm instead of around him. He made it easy, doing his job so competently that it never felt forced to keep him in the loop.

Two minutes later, having fixed her uniform and short hair, she walked through the door from her small day cabin into her ready room. She found Holm and Davies already there, waiting for her. With a wave and a voice command to the ship's AI, the room's main viewscreen changed to show a tactical map of the space surrounding the Council Navy fleet.

She laid out Lafayette's request, and both Holm's and Davies' eyes widened. This was her other reason for not calling directly to the CIC; she wanted her senior officers to absorb the audacious plan before it hit the ship's rumor mill, which often seemed to move faster than even the Tachyon telegraph.

She hadn't invited Tyrus Tyne into the discussion, also on purpose. After a month in his company, she trusted the man completely. Still, even with Fleet Admiral Lopez's recommendation, he wasn't cleared for the full capabilities of the *Enterprise* and her sisters.

"It just might work, Admiral," Commander Tiffany Davies, the *Enterprise's* tactical officer, said. She ran some quick calculations on her palm implant. "But we would have to go to full military power to get there in time to do anything meaningful, and those three ships would have to cut their acceleration now and burn back toward an intercept, which will also put them in range of the Council fleet's missiles."

Bol nodded her acknowledgment but said nothing, looking to her flag captain for his thoughts.

Holm rubbed his chin thoughtfully. "We're still supposed to be on our shakedown cruise, so we've never run the drive at full power for that long. One minor hiccup in the compensators and…."

He didn't have to finish that sentence. Technically, the *Enterprise* and her sisters could accelerate tens of times faster than any other ship in human space. But doing so would tear the ships apart, not to mention turning every human on board into so much jelly spattered on the walls. So, the real check on how fast the three ships could accelerate was in the operational limits of each ship's reinforced frame, its artificial gravity generators, and, most importantly, its inertial compensators. The three massive carriers had next-generation tech. Their compensators should allow them to go to an acceleration of 71 g's, almost twice that of the fastest human ships previously in existence and *more* than twice that of a Missouri-class battleship or Essex-class fleet carrier.

"Once we get there, does the rest work? Or will we be revealing ourselves?" she asked the two officers, trying not to sound too anxious. She had run the numbers herself the instant she'd gotten the TT from Admiral Lafayette, but she had to be *sure*.

"That part, I believe, is easier," Davies replied, flicking her left hand toward the screen to show something she'd been working out on her palm implant. A three-dimensional model with vectors and formulas popped up. "It's all a matter of perspective. If we keep those three ships directly between us and the Council fleet, the chances of them seeing us are less than four percent. Even if they do, they'll likely misinterpret it as sensor ghosts caused by launch flares."

"I concur," Holm chimed in. "And for what it's worth, I recommend we do it. Not to sound too eager, Admiral, but this is *exactly* the type of thing these ships were designed for."

"That may be," Bol replied, appreciating the man's enthusiasm but also running it through her own cautious filters. "Still, just because we *can* do something doesn't mean we should. The existence of these carriers is about the only thing the Council Navy *hasn't* learned in their little foray here. If we're detected, we risk letting them get away with everything they need to know to come back and invade us for real next time."

"But if we pull it off," argued Davies, "then we will make them stop and think before they come back again. We might even buy ourselves some much-needed time while they try to figure out what happened and how to counteract it, and all the while, they'll be trying to solve the wrong problem, giving us an edge when they do return."

Left unspoken was the effect it would have on the UEN, whose officers and crews would already be demoralized by the tragedy at the Front Door earlier that morning. If they pulled this off, it could change the entire perception of the battle amongst the troops. Not to mention what it might do in the political arena if they showed there was indeed hope of defeating the enemy.

Having said their piece, Holm and Davies now waited patiently for Bol to work things out and make a decision. She turned back to the viewscreen and studied the vectors and time codes again. After about two minutes, Mary looked back at her subordinates.

"Let's do it. Send the orders via tight beam laser to Captains Forrester and Kopolov. Don't send any messages back to Second Fleet. Admiral Lafayette is ordering those cruisers to do their part regardless and left it up to me to decide if we do ours. But our ships will not broadcast *anything* that could reveal our position and existence. Those cruiser captains may not know what's coming any more than the enemy will, and they're taking a massive risk, but we *will* be there to back their play."

Holm and Davies nodded, each throwing her a quick salute as they practically ran from the room to fulfill her orders. When they were gone, Bol turned back to the viewscreen and studied the vectors again. Davies was right: pulling this off would give the enemy something heavy to think about. But failing at it would show the last trump cards Earth had. Supposedly there was one more experimental craft in Earth's arsenal, but… Either way, it would be a test of the three ships they now commanded and their crews, and Mary Bol would ensure they did their jobs to perfection.

# CHAPTER 11

### EIGHTEEN YEARS AGO; 713 P.D.

Jynx sat in her third-period 11$^{th}$-grade English class in her customary place at the back of the room. Though her stutter had finally faded several years before, she still clung to the habit of avoiding speech whenever possible. Sitting at the rear of all her classes allowed her to listen and learn without the exposure that might require her to answer more questions or speak frequently.

The class started like any other. Old Mrs. Finch, the elderly English teacher, began by asking for volunteers to recap what they'd read in the homework. Jynx had done the reading; the book was *Stories of the Colonization* and a favorite of hers, and she had read it several times before Mrs. Finch had ever assigned it. She loved the stories of first landings on a dozen different colony worlds, tales of terraforming, and descriptions of encounters with new species on the few colony planets that had already supported multicellular organisms. She especially enjoyed the stories of the pioneers who had branched out from the main landing settlements and conquered the frontier wildernesses of planets like Utsukushi-sa, Daimantas, Unidad, Dixie, Ceti III, and

Diego Nuevo. Even if she knew that many of them were stylized and embellished to teach the principles the Council felt young students should learn. And even if all the characters were unflinchingly loyal to the Council—very unlike Tom Sawyer.

Despite her passion for the topic, she declined to raise her hand or answer any questions Mrs. Finch posed to the class. Even though Dax, who hadn't even done the reading, provided several of the answers—Jynx knew that she had looked up a summary on the Internet and that Billy Lee, one of her older twin's adoring hangers-on had also given her his notes—Jynx still stayed quiet. She knew later she would even purposefully answer some of the reading quiz questions incorrectly. Ever since Dax had switched her test and Jynx's in the seventh grade, giving her younger twin her failing grade, Jynx had purposefully not done as well as she could have in school. Somehow it felt better to do poorly on her own than do well but let her sister take the credit.

Then something happened that turned that class period from the usual fight *not* to be noticed into a one-of-a-kind day for Jynx. Kurt Stevens passed her a note.

It popped up on her watch holo via a messaging app that the school's network firewalls had failed to stop students from using—there was an eternal arms race between teenagers who wanted to talk secretly during class and the school administrators and techies who tried to stop them. As she read the message, she blushed. He was asking her to a dance! And not just any dance, the fall formal! Dax had gone every year, even though ninth or tenth graders could attend only if a junior or senior asked them—Dax had never had problems finding older boys who wanted to take her out. But Jynx had never been asked to *anything* by any boy.

After reading the note, she turned and regarded Kurt, a shy boy who also rarely spoke but had rakish good looks and hair that she had imagined running her fingers through during more than a few slow days in class. With a smile, she nodded, and he smiled back. Jynx kept her watch holo open, privacy field engaged, and read his message several more times throughout the class. She was so distracted that she even forgot to answer some quiz questions incorrectly. She didn't even notice Dax casting her and Kurt curious glances from the front of the room.

It was Friday, and the dance was three weeks away. Still, that same night, Jynx used her old, half-broken pad to go online and look at dresses for the formal. She found a few she thought her parents could afford and rehearsed how she would ask for one. Her plan was to approach her father first and enlist his help to convince her mother. She dreamed about it all weekend.

The following Monday at school, Jynx was over the moon. Finally, *she* was the center of attention, even if only from one person. She repeatedly cast glances at Kurt in third period, but he avoided her gaze. She started to worry but convinced herself it was only the boy's normal withdrawn habits returning.

At lunch, Jynx looked everywhere for Kurt. She had practiced what she would say to him as well. She would ask him what color he planned to wear so they could coordinate, but she mostly just wanted an excuse to talk to him. However, the boy was nowhere to be seen in the places he usually hung out.

Finally, she spotted him but stopped short. Kurt was sitting at the popular table, a place he would have never been allowed to get close to before. The reason he was there now was apparent. Sitting right next to him, leaning into him, and batting her eyes at the boy, was Dax!

Jynx stood there, rooted in place ten meters away, staring. Her mouth worked in silent despair as she watched her twin sister hang all over the boy who, just a few days before, had asked *her* out. Then Dax looked up and met Jynx's eye. She smiled, a cruel smile belied by an evil glint in her eyes, and then turned and pulled Kurt's face to her own and kissed him! It had all the appearances of a passionate kiss, and Jynx felt a gasp escape her lips as her sister stuck her tongue down Kurt's throat. But Dax's eyes stayed open the entire time, fixed on her younger twin sister. Jynx turned and ran as the tears started to flow and spent the rest of the lunch period crying silently in a bathroom stall.

By the end of the day, it was known all over the school that Kurt was Dax's new boyfriend. They dated for two and a half weeks until

Dax publicly dumped the boy in the middle of the hall between classes. Kurt ran off, fighting to keep from crying, pushing past a stunned Jynx without even noticing her.

Still, Jynx held out a sliver of hope that Kurt would remember that he had asked *her* to the dance, which was just three days away. But the boy avoided her and refused to even meet her gaze in class. At lunch, she searched everywhere for him, but to no avail. He wouldn't even respond to her messages.

On the night of the dance, Dax was dressed in a low-cut black gown with a slit high up the side that showed her legs and cleavage to devastating effect. She wore a thin sweater over it so that Ned wouldn't see and demand she put something more substantial on; Luanne helped distract her husband as part of the plan.

Jynx stayed in sweatpants and an old ratty t-shirt, crying her eyes out as she watched Ian Forster, the school quarterback and Dax's boyfriend before—and apparently after—Kurt, pick up her sister and take her to a waiting hovercar.

Luanne was caught up in her favorite daughter's night of glory and utterly oblivious to Jynx's suffering, but Ned came up and knocked timidly on the closed door to the room the twins still shared. He asked through the thin door if his younger daughter wanted to join him for a movie with popcorn. Jynx didn't even answer him.

She withdrew even further into herself for the last year and a half of high school, refusing to talk to any of the boys in her classes, including the few that expressed some interest. But even in her despair, she watched her sister with envy and *knew* that someday they would put aside their differences and love each other as only sisters could. Because surely Dax would grow out of her ways, and they could finally be close. Jynx would trade a dozen Kurts for that chance.

---

## PRESENT DAY; JULY 30, 731 P.D.

Corey had been the one to admonish General Cruz and Jinny Ambrosa *not* to share Jinny's theory about the Twenty's real reason for invading the Four Worlds with anyone else. It was simply too explosive, and it was only a theory still. But deep down, he knew it made too much sense not to be true, though the implications were staggering.

So, breaking his pact with the others, he had almost immediately sent a message to one other person outlining the theory and what he believed it meant for the coming Council invasion.

Fleet Admiral Horatio Krishna Lopez, who, in the Six-Month War with Mars 49 years ago, had earned the nickname 'Hunter Killer' in a play on his initials, was also a good friend of the O'Leary family. He was only 11 years older than Corey, so the two had careers that overlapped for most of their adult lives. During that long period, they had learned to trust each other completely.

Lopez was the only active UEN officer with the title of Fleet Admiral, the highest possible rank that the Navy could bestow, making him senior even to Admiral Clancy, the naval representative on the Joint Chiefs of Staff. Despite that, he had been removed from the formal chain of command two years prior, shortly after Luiz Pereira's election to the presidency. Lopez, who in his old age had stopped caring about being politically sensitive, had broken naval tradition and openly expressed his support for Pereira's Red Party opponent in the months leading up to the election. He had been concerned by the Blue Party's talk of decreasing military funding, even before they knew about the impending Council invasion. The Martians had literally just launched their failed missile attack at Luna, and Lopez wasn't convinced that it was a one-time affair. He saw Pereira as a dangerous option for the UE, and did his best to keep the man out of office.

Unfortunately, his voice wasn't enough to sway public opinion, especially when Pereira unveiled his pork-laden plan for increased social entitlements and higher taxation of the 'evil corporations' that ironically employed most of his voter base but made an easy target for his populist rants. But Lopez had turned the new president into a solid enemy. The lucky thing was that he was too famous and well-respected, inside and outside the military, for Pereira to order him to resign or to forcibly retire him. So instead, the president had removed him as Chairman of the Joint Chiefs, installing the apolitical General Cruz of the United Earth Army instead, and then forced Lopez into a teaching role at the Naval Academy on Luna. Publicly, he stated it was so the old admiral could impart his wisdom to the rising generations of naval officers. But, privately, everyone in the Navy knew it was simply a way to tuck old Hunter Killer out of the way where he couldn't bother the president anymore.

However, Horatio Krishna Lopez had survived the administrations of seven different presidents before Pereira, and nothing the Brazilian politician could do could remove the man entirely from the naval hierarchy. Even his staunchest rivals in the admiralty, such as Admiral Clancy, had to begrudgingly admit that the man was far too much of a strategic and tactical genius to leave on the sidelines. Furthermore, he was one of the few UE military officers the Martians respected, having won several key battles against them in the Six-Month War. So, if they were ever to hope to get the Reds to join forces with the rest of the Sol system to defend against the Council, Lopez would be essential to that plan.

With all that, the old admiral's influence in the military waned very little, even with the formal reduction in his role. If anything, by removing him from the direct chain of command, Pereira inadvertently expanded the man's intrinsic authority, as even the new Joint Chiefs sought him out frequently for his counsel, and he was able to give it in a less filtered fashion.

Knowing this, Corey forgave himself for quickly sharing Jinny's theory with the man via an encrypted text message. As was his way, the old admiral responded quickly.

**Horatio Lopez: Not surprising. Have suspected the same. Wise to keep it quiet.**

**Corey O'Leary: How did you suspect? Was news to me.**

**Horatio Lopez: Reading between the lines. Hints from interviews with Ambrosa and Tyne on reader and enacter capabilities in colonies didn't match up with what we see in Australia. And the Twenty's plan to create enacters from the populace felt like a brash move. Too risky if it doesn't work. They would only do it if they had no other choice.**

Corey considered this. If he hadn't already believed Jinny was right, Lopez's confidence and independent arrival at the same conclusion would have swayed him completely. The man hadn't survived over 65 years of naval service, including winning the Navy Cross three times during the Six-Month War alone, without being incredibly thoughtful and intelligent.

*Corey O'Leary: What do we do?*

*Horatio Lopez: Keep the secret. I have contacts down south. Ambrosa met one of them when she was there. Can't say more over text. But I may float the idea with them to see if they have thoughts.*

*Corey O'Leary: I trust your judgment. What happens if the Twenty sends a formal demand?*

*Horatio Lopez: Will deal with it when it comes. Keep building support in Congress to do the right thing. May need to find help elsewhere as well. You know where. We can't do this alone.*

Corey sat back in shock in his seat along the back wall of the Situation Room's command center. If he was reading Lopez's intent, the man had just essentially told him they might have to solicit support from Mars directly. What he was talking about, given the current state of relations—or lack thereof—and the formal policies of the UE government, amounted to high treason. Of course, Corey also couldn't argue with it. He had known for quite some time that someone, possibly even him, would *have* to talk to the Martians. He had history there and would be a natural choice in saner times to head any talks with the Reds. But it sounded now like it might have to happen sooner than he'd expected and outside of formal channels altogether.

He chose not to respond to Lopez's last text. Instead, he turned his mind to a bigger problem: how to get to Mars. He had a way, but it would require leaning on an old friend who might not still be a friend at all. And that scared him almost as much as the Council fleet that still lingered in the Sol system.

---

"Ma'am, at your command."

Mary looked up from the small systems display on her command chair and fixed her gaze on her comm officer. "Send the order, Scott. Flank speed ahead."

Five seconds later, all three of Bol's massive stealth carriers surged forward at an acceleration that boggled the mind.

Mary's father had enjoyed restoring antique automobiles. Some of it had been out of necessity. By Earth's standards, most of Nigeria was still extremely poor, and aircars were expensive. So, Jonathan Bol had made a decent living fixing up old, wheeled vehicles and selling them at bargain prices to other families in their modest community. Of course, most were electric, but he'd even found two that had desperately old internal combustion engines to fix up—they were all collector reproductions, of course; nothing outside of a museum had survived from the period when gasoline-burning engines had been the norm. But those reproductions had eventually sold at an obscene price to a collector in Europe. The money from that sale alone had allowed the elder Bol to send his only daughter to college in North America, which became Mary's gateway into a career with the UEN.

Even at an early age, Mary had enjoyed watching her father work, and she had loved riding in the old cars after he was done fixing them. There was something raw and visceral about being pressed back into your seat as an old automobile without inertial compensators rapidly accelerated at ground level, where you could see the trees and the signposts fly by and feel the bumps in the road underneath the tires. It was something you just didn't get in a modern aircar. Somehow those old cars felt faster, even though the aircars could easily outpace any wheeled vehicle.

Now, as the *Enterprise* leapt forward with a tremendous surge of power, Mary got to experience part of that feeling again as the rapid acceleration of the ship pressed her into her command chair with a force equivalent to four gravities. Of course, it was a far cry from the 71 g's of actual acceleration that the ship was pushing, but the inertial compensators were canceling the vast majority of that out, which was the only thing that allowed Mary and her crew to live through it. Even then, if the compensators had so much as a momentary failure, they would all be dead before they even knew what had happened.

"This is surreal," Tyrus Tyne grunted under the four g's of pressure from his seat in the bridge chair to her right. "It's so quiet."

"Yes, it is quite a novel experience, isn't it?" Over the years, Mary had served on and commanded everything from a four-person patrol boat to one of the enormous Essex-class fleet carriers that out massed everything else Earth had, including the Missouri-class battleships. In every case, she had learned to read her ships' acceleration and the health of her engines via the vibrations in the deck. *Enterprise* lacked those vibrations entirely, which had taken some getting used to. It was a strange juxtaposition against the feeling of being four times her weight with the ship's acceleration.

"Still not going to tell me how the drive works?" Tyrus asked, pitching his voice low so that only Mary would hear.

She looked over at him and smiled. "No. It's so classified that telling you would get me court-martialed in an instant. Of course, I'm happy to hear any theories you have, though not here. Perhaps after the battle, over dinner, in my quarters?"

Tyrus nodded, seemingly interpreting her invitation as a working dinner, robbing her of the comical picture of the big ex-assassin blushing. Not for the first time, Mary wondered just how blunt she had to be with the man. She could tell he was attracted to her despite their age difference, and the feeling was mutual. Still, he wasn't picking up on any of her hints, even the ones she dropped as heavy as a hammer. It had been more than a decade since Mary herself had had a proper relationship with a man, so she knew she was out of practice. But Tyrus made her look like a worldly savant; it was almost like the man didn't know *anything* about women or relationships.

Still, she wouldn't be able to tell him about the sublight drive that powered *Enterprise* and her sisters. It was possibly the most significant military secret that Earth had held since the invention of the atomic bomb more than a millennium ago. And it was what allowed the large carriers to be genuinely stealthy.

Over the centuries, humanity had experimented with a multitude of different ways to make a spaceship undetectable. Everything from photo-adaptive outer hulls to active jammers that clouded sensors had been tried, and they had almost all worked to an extent. Most had even made their way into *Enterprise's* design. But none of them had ever solved the biggest problem: heat. Put simply, the main drive on any starship generated a tremendous amount of heat as it burned reaction matter to propel the ship forward. Even ion drives generated significant heat in their operation. Therefore, against the cold vacuum of space, no amount of active jamming could hide a thrusting warship from the simple thermal cameras and sensors that all warships mounted for that very reason.

What that all meant was that, until recently, the only way for a ship to be undetectable was to have it cold coast with only small maneuvers and corrections or to have it come from the direction of a more prominent source of heat, like a star or gas giant, which was a difficult thing to manage unless the enemy was extremely accommodating.

Then researchers on a secret UEN base way out in the Oort Cloud had invented the singularity drive. As she had shown Tyrus and the crew of the *UENS Monitor* weeks ago, *Enterprise* had no main drive nozzles. Indeed, it had no reaction drive at all that pushed it forward. Instead, its drive *pulled* it forward. The carrier could create an artificial singularity, a miniaturized black hole, and project it out in front of the ship's bow in a specially crafted containment field. This caused the massive ship to effectively *fall forward* toward that singularity as if it were spiraling down the gravity well of a large star. But because the black hole moved with the ship, the carrier never reached the bottom of the gravity well—if it ever did, the results would be catastrophic as the singularity ripped the ship apart. The containment field around it even made it invisible to gravitic sensors, though the scientific explanation for how that worked was beyond even Mary's working knowledge of physics.

As a child, Mary had seen a cartoon where a rabbit had ridden on top of a tortoise, propelling the animal forward by hanging a carrot from a fishing pole in front of its face. The tortoise chased the carrot but never caught it as the carrot moved with it. The singularity drive was not so different in principle, as the carrier chased the black hole but never reached it.

The size of the singularity controlled the rate of acceleration for the Enterprise. Technically, the drive could produce a black hole large enough to reach several hundred gravities, but safeguards were in place against that, as the ship and its crew would never survive such acceleration. Instead, the drive was capped at 71 gravities at full military power, which was still almost twice as much as the fastest conventional ship known to man.

However, it was quiet and brought none of the deck vibrations a reaction drive would, making it feel *slower* than a typical warship except for the four g's bleeding through the compensators. Just staring out the viewscreen, one would never even know that the three carriers were quickly ramping up to a fraction of the speed of light, as the stars themselves were too far away for the movement to translate. Only the ship's plot showed them moving across the Sol system.

It was eerie and unnatural, but it was the future. Unless, of course, Mary managed to tear her three carriers apart on this little trip.

---

Admiral Tyler Prudhoe was still a cheerful man, especially after his nap in his day cabin. So far, everything had gone *better* than planned. Not only had he successfully destroyed a non-trivial portion of the Four Worlds' defensive fleets, but he had also gathered enough intel to keep Admiral Chen's intelligence weenies fat and happy for the next several months. That intelligence would be critical to the *real* invasion when it started. He even allowed himself to imagine that if Chen herself fell out of favor with the Council, his success here would make him the next natural choice to command the invasion. The thought warmed him; he liked Chen, but that didn't mean he wouldn't happily take her job.

His ships had long ago killed their forward momentum toward Earth and were burning at full acceleration back toward the Front Door, where all was quiet, as reported by the ships he had left there. It looked like they were going to escape the Sol system without further losses and with their complete intelligence boon, while the Earth and Europan navies chased them impotently from behind, and the Martians watched impassively from the sidelines. It had to be frustrating, he thought with a smile, for the admiral in charge of the Earth fleet to have come so close to weapons range, at least in astronomical terms, only to have Prudhoe's ships execute a perfectly timed maneuver to decelerate and head back the way they'd come, keeping them just a few hours outside the Earth fleet's missile range.

Yes, everything had gone almost perfectly, and one of the best parts of the mission was yet to come. It was time to sow a little chaos, courtesy of the Keeper himself.

"Comms, are the Project Firebrand messages ready to send?"

"Yes, sir, queued and ready at your command," came the reply, and Prudhoe sat back in his command chair and smiled again. No one in the fleet except him knew the contents of the two encrypted messages waiting to be sent. But soon, everyone in the Four Worlds would know, and his only regret was that he would be long gone and back to the colonies by then and unable to watch the explosive results.

The Four Worlders, of course, had been hailing his fleet nearly continuously since they'd arrived in the system. Nevertheless, he'd steadfastly ignored them, refusing to respond either to the commanders of the opposing naval fleets or to the world leaders. He'd been especially amused by several messages from a President Luiz Pereira, ruler of Earth and Luna. The man's first comms had asked for an open dialog and peace talks. His later messages had been impotent promises of reprisals if the Council fleet did not respond. They hadn't

So, the messages Prudhoe was about to send, while not direct responses to any of those entreaties, would be the first and only transmissions from the Council fleet that the people of the Four Worlds would receive, at least until the full invasion fleet was bearing down on them and demanding their unconditional surrender. He smiled at that mental image.

"Send them," he said to the comm officer, unable to keep the smile out of his voice. And with one press of a button on the woman's console, arguably the most critical part of Prudhoe's mission had been completed successfully. Now all he had to do was settle back and wait for the eight hours it would take his fleet to reach the Front Door and return to Council-controlled space.

"Sir, *Texas* reports intercepting two light-speed transmissions from the enemy fleet: one directed at Mars and one directed here."

General Cruz looked up from the monitoring station he had commandeered in the Situation Room for his personal use. "Contents?"

The comm officer shook his head. "Encrypted, sir, and too large to send via TT. Texas is forwarding them via light-speed comms, and we'll have the AIs get to work on them as soon as they arrive. Based on what *Texas* could tell us, we're estimating a few hours at least to break the encryption."

Cruz frowned. While good news on the surface, a few hours made no sense. United Earth had encryptions strong enough that even the most advanced AIs in the Sol system would need *days* to crack them. And by all accounts from Jinny Ambrosa and Tyrus Tyne, encryption technology was even further advanced in the 47 Colonies, where the government had made an art of controlling the information available to the public. That meant one of two things: either the Council Navy was sending the messages to someone with limited decryption capabilities, or they *wanted* the Four World governments to decrypt and see the contents of each message.

Either option stunk to his way of thinking, but there was nothing he could do about it until the contents were decrypted and revealed. In the meantime…

"Sanderson, what's the status on Attack Plan Nemo?" he asked the tactical officer who had been in the Situation Room for every one of the 13 hours since the Council fleet had first arrived, popping stim pills and mainlining coffee to stay awake and alert despite the stress.

The commander looked up at Cruz. "Sir. Element A is on its way to the intercept point. Still no word on Element B, but that's expected."

Cruz nodded. Element A comprised the three cruisers that had initially fled the massacre at the Front Door. Only two of the ships formally answered to him. The third and largest, still only a heavy cruiser, was part of the Europan Navy. Cruz had been on the light-speed comm with its commander and with Admiral Jason Namora of the Europan Poseidon Fleet—the *only* fleet Europa technically had—to get their cooperation with the plan, thought it had meant he had to let them in on at least part of the secret of the *Enterprise* and the other two stealth carriers. He could do so by stretching his own authority, keeping the explanations purposefully vague, though he knew that if the plan failed, it would be his head on the chopping block for that and everything else that had gone wrong today.

At least the lack of response from Element B wasn't cause for concern. Element B was the *Enterprise* task group, and they had been ordered not to respond, even via TT, so there would be no chance of giving up their existence or position to the enemy. But Cruz and Admiral Clancy both had faith in Admiral Mary Bol. She had been hand-selected for the command by Fleet Admiral Lopez himself. Despite what Cruz's boss might feel for Lopez, and even though the man's removal had paved the way for his own ascension to the chairman post, he trusted the old admiral to be an excellent judge of the officers in the UEN. Barring an equipment malfunction, Mary Bol would be there on time.

---

"Admiral, those three escort ships are still on a vector to intercept," the sensor officer on *Invictus* called out. The three ships had turned hours before, but no one on the bridge of the Council Navy dreadnought had believed they actually wanted to *catch* the invading fleet. It was suicide.

"Show me," replied Prudhoe, and the holo display in the center of the spacious bridge changed perspective to zero in on the three laughably small cruisers that were now supposedly trying to make an attack run on his fleet.

"Risk assessment?" he asked his tactical officer.

The man stepped up next to his admiral at the holo display. "Extremely low, sir. They won't ever close to laser range, and given their size, we do not believe their missiles will be large enough to carry the fuel to catch us. Even if they do, we anticipate minimal damage from warheads that small."

Prudhoe nodded and studied the vectors and timestamps on the holo display carefully. He couldn't find anything wrong with the tactical officer's assessment, but something was still nagging at him. Because surely, the captains of those three cruisers knew the same thing he did, but they were *still* accelerating toward a missile engagement envelope with his forces.

Maybe they were trying to get him to launch some of his missiles so they could capture and study them. Or maybe they were suicidal or overcome by the fog of war and blood lust. He really had no idea, but either way, according to the timestamps on the holo, they would know in two hours.

# CHAPTER 12

Commander Karina Maze of the *ENS Voyager* looked around the bridge of her heavy cruiser. She had held the command for only a month before being sent to guard the Front Door along with Task Force 12 of the Europan Navy's Poseidon Fleet. So she vividly remembered the first time she'd seen *Voyager* sitting in its dock at Ganymede Naval Station. It had looked like pictures of a Kraken, the massive and deadly ocean predator that had lived deep below the ice on Europa before the moon had undergone terraforming and destroyed the alien animal's natural habitat.

As with most existing multi-cellular life on terraformed worlds, scientists had attempted to keep the Kraken alive in captivity after the terraforming was complete, harvesting several mating trios before the climate and chemistry of the moon were changed enough to kill them all. But the large predators hadn't lasted even a single generation in the enormous tanks built especially for them. It was too late when the scientists realized a Kraken needed more than frigid salt water and regular feedings to survive; it needed to hunt. Robbed of the opportunity to hunt and kill their food, the captive Krakens quickly became listless and sedentary, refusing to mate, eat, or even swim. One by one, they had settled to the bottom of their tanks and simply allowed themselves to die.

The scientists *had* figured it out, but by that time, only one male remained alive, and it took three different genders to produce Kraken offspring. And all cloning attempts failed; the large predators had little in common with DNA-based lifeforms on Earth, so conventional methods were useless. The last remaining specimen had lived several years more with live fish and whales in its tank to hunt, even though it couldn't fully metabolize the Earth-based organisms. Ultimately, it had still gotten bored with the ease with which it caught its prey in the enclosed space, and had settled down to wait for death like its mates before it.

That's how the *Voyager* had looked and felt to Karina. It was a predator, and it needed to hunt to stay alive. She had secretly been excited at the prospect of being sent to guard the only known invasion path for the Council Navy and had hungered for the chance to prove her ship and crew in what she was certain would be a victory at the Front Door whenever the enemy was foolish enough to come through.

All such thoughts were gone. *Every* other EN ship sent to the Front Door with her was gone, along with over 11 thousand of her friends and colleagues—that didn't even count the UEN and CSF losses. And her ship had been able to only assist in destroying a single Council Navy destroyer and lightly damaging another before the battle was over, and she chose the better part of valor and ordered the retreat.

That decision had been the right one; staying would have only added her ship and crew to the list of casualties, but in the 14 hours since the battle, survivor's guilt had set in. Karina recognized it for what it was, but no amount of detached, clinical analysis of her mental state made it any better. She somehow *knew* that she had let down her fellow officers and spacers in some intangible and mysterious way by not staying and meeting the same fate they had. And she could tell her crew felt the same way, as illogical as it may be.

At least now they were being given a chance to fight back. Karina had no idea how the Earthers had cracked the code of stealth space travel, but apparently, they not only had, but they had built multiple stealth ships that could do real damage to the Council fleet before it left the system behind. They just needed Karina and her ship to make it happen without revealing their existence to the enemy, and she was more than happy to oblige. Even though deep down, she knew what the likeliest outcome for her and her ship would be.

Now, like the Krakens of old, it was time for *Voyager* to go hunting.

---

Tyler Prudhoe watched the plot carefully, so he was not surprised when the sensor officer called out: "Missile range in thirty seconds, Admiral."

Captain Henrietta Norwood, *Invictus'* commanding officer, stepped up next to him. "Should we prepare our own missile barrage?" she asked in her typical efficient manner.

"Not yet," he replied, still disbelieving the sheer foolishness of the three small cruisers that thought to take on the might of his task force. "That may be what they're hoping we'll do. We've gotten a tremendous amount of intel on this trip. But destroying those ships would allow the enemy to study our missiles. Why give them that small benefit just so we can swat at three harmless gnats?"

"Yes, sir," Norwood replied simply.

"In range now!" called the sensor officer... and nothing happened. A few more seconds passed, long enough for the light of any missile launches to reach Prudhoe's fleet.

"Perhaps it *was* a feint only to get us to expend some of our missiles," the captain observed.

Prudhoe was opening his mouth to reply when the holo display flashed red.

"Missiles inbound, sir!" cried the tactical officer, the excitement and dismay clear in the young enacter's voice. "There's... 33 of them. Ship killer size! Wait, there's 33 more. And another 33. Ninety-nine ship-killers inbound, admiral!"

"That's impossible!" Norwood snapped back, her usual unflappable manner abandoned. "No ship as small as those could carry so many missiles that large."

The man at the tactical station looked back at her in confusion, unsure how to respond to his captain's statement, which conflicted with the reality he was seeing.

Norwood's face turned red. "Check again! It must be a sensor issue. Could they be jamming us to make it look like there are more missiles than they could have launched?"

The man didn't argue, not that he really could have, and set to work checking the sensors. A moment later, he looked back up. "No, ma'am. It's not the sensors or jamming. The missiles appear to be real."

"I concur," the sensor officer called from the other side of the bridge. Prudhoe frowned deeply and looked back at the holo plot.

"Full defensive measures across the fleet," he barked. "Bring the escorts back to us. Let's make sure nothing gets through."

---

Karina Maze had seen the same thing that the tactical officer on *Invictus* had, but from a different angle and far more up close. She had waited in stressful anticipation as she turned her ship to present its meager broadside to the enemy at the edge of missile range, doing just as she'd been instructed and at precisely the ordered timestamp and coordinates. She hadn't seen any sign of the supposed stealth ships, but her orders had been clear.

"Fire!" she had called out, and her small ship, along with the two UEN light cruisers—temporarily also under her command—belched out their small broadsides of close-range anti-ship and anti-fighter missiles, all set to launch but only burn their engines for a short distance before going dead and cold coasting. They would never reach their targets.

But directly behind *Voyager* relative to the enemy fleet, an enormous ship suddenly showed on Karina's sensor plot. The behemoth, smaller than the Council dreadnoughts but larger than even one of the United Earth or Martian battleships, belched fire from its broadside as 11 giant ship-killer missiles left their tubes and sped toward her relatively small heavy cruiser.

Karina saw death coming for the barest of instants and was certain the carrier's captain had miscalculated. But to her relief, all 11 missiles passed by *Voyager* harmlessly, though within just a few hundred meters—spitting distance in terms of space battles—of her dorsal and ventral hulls. Twice more it happened in rapid succession until 33 missiles had flown past *Voyager* toward the enemy.

From the enemy's perspective, she knew it would look like her heavy cruiser had launched those missiles; they would be unable to see even the much larger stealth ship as the bulk of her ship and the sensor scatter from *Voyager's* own meager launches would have interfered with their view of it. To the enemy, it would seem like her small ship had cycled its missile tubes at insanely fast speeds, launching three broadsides of missiles that would have barely even fit in her ship's magazines. It would give the Council Navy folks quite a confused picture, especially as the two *light* cruisers next to her appeared to do the same thing simultaneously, aided by two more of the large stealth ships, sending a total spread of 99 missiles in three fast waves.

Before the last missiles had swept by *Voyager*, all three stealth ships disappeared again. Then, try as she might, Karina couldn't find them anywhere on the sensor plot. Not even a ghost.

---

"Fire back!" yelled Tyler Prudhoe after only a brief hesitation to make sure his ships were moving into their ordered defensive formations. "Full broadsides. I want all three of those ships dead before their missiles can reach us!"

It was a massive overreaction spurred by his own lack of battle experience coupled with the surprise of the unexpected shipkillers heading his way. But it was an order, and his tactical officer was an enacter. So the officer didn't argue but immediately relayed the command and designated targets for each Council Navy ship so that missiles would fly toward all three of the enemy escorts. Less than two minutes later, just over a thousand missiles left their tubes and zeroed in on the three helpless Four World ships.

Ninety-nine missiles total from *Enterprise*, *Midway*, and *Yorktown*, no matter how large or sophisticated, versus so many Council ships should have been easy odds. Every ship in the Council fleet was equipped with defensive laser clusters and Gatling guns designed to take out anything that got past the lasers.

However, in their complacency and certainty of victory, the CN ships had allowed themselves to break tight formation. They had moved naturally into a loose convoy, with the larger and slower dreadnoughts at the rear and the rest of the smaller, faster escort ships up ahead. This eliminated the overlapping defensive shields that would typically be the best way to ensure nothing got through to damage any of the Council ships.

Even then, at an average of just about two missiles per ship, the Council Navy should have had no problem swatting the enemy missiles from space before they got close enough to do any damage. Except that the enemy had known that too, and they had concentrated *all* of their fire on the two CN dreadnoughts.

Without organic crew or heavy reinforced hulls and armor, the missiles were able to accelerate much faster than any ship, including even the *Enterprise* and her sisters. Each UEN missile had ramped up to over 150 g's of acceleration almost the moment they'd left their launch tubes, adding to the speed already imparted by the ships that launched them.

In Council-controlled space, missile warfare was rare. For generations, the Guard had been the only legitimate space force in the 47 Colonies. They had primarily relied on their disabling weaponry and fast interceptor fighters to take care of the pirates and smugglers who were their occasional foes. Because the Guard's doctrine was to board, search, and seize rather than standoff at a distance and destroy, they focused their true offensive weaponry more on short-range lasers. The Council Navy, of course, had better tech than the Guard Space Force, but it was still *based* on what the Guard had, just a generation or two ahead.

As a result, Admiral Prudhoe and his staff were about to learn just how outmatched they were in a standoff missile battle.

"Admiral," his tactical officer called, "the enemy missiles are accelerating at 175 gravities, sir!"

Prudhoe started, sure that he'd heard the man wrong. "How fast did you say?"

"One hundred and seventy-five gravities, confirmed. At this rate, their intercept time will be less than 23 minutes."

Prudhoe swore. Their own missiles only accelerated at a rate of 105 gravities, making their total flight time almost 30 minutes long. That would be a significant disadvantage in future engagements. On the other hand, it was also vital intelligence that he could take back to the colonies.

He waited in silence with the rest of the bridge crew. His original order to move to defensive formations meant his fleet's escorts had already cut acceleration in hopes that they could make it back to the two dreadnoughts in time to help shield them from the relatively small number of incoming missiles aimed at them. Unfortunately, with the distances involved, only a few would arrive in time.

A few minutes later, his tactical officer cried out again, this time in exultation. "Enemy missiles have cut acceleration! They're gone from our scopes!"

"What? Are you sure?" Prudhoe asked though he knew the question was stupid. Still, it defied logic and belief that the enemy missiles would have such a short range. If they were going to make the rest of the trip ballistic, then avoiding them would be almost laughably easy.

He shrugged, the movement hiding his relief at the news. "Captain Norwood. Cut thrust for sixty seconds, change your vector to mark 45, and engage full acceleration for five minutes. Comms, signal *Invincible* to do the same."

With that command, both his dreadnoughts cut their thrust and fired maneuvering rockets to yaw up at a 45-degree angle relative to the system plane. After waiting sixty seconds, which would throw off the attacking missiles in one direction, both ships went to full power on their new vector, ensuring that any ballistic missile launched at their previous course would fly safely underneath and ahead of the two ships. And if they reset their course reasonably soon, the move would only slightly delay their arrival at the Front Door. The change would, however, now make it impossible for any of their screening cruisers and destroyers to catch them in time to mount a missile defense, but the tradeoff seemed clear in Prudhoe's mind.

*Let's see them hit us now,* he thought and settled back in his command chair to wait, gratified to see on his personal holo that *his* fleet's missiles were still accelerating on course for the three small Four Worlder ships that had somehow launched broadsides the size of which should have only been possible for capital ships. He shook off that worry; there would be plenty of time to analyze the mission recordings later and try to piece together how three small cruisers could throw that many ship-killer missiles his way. For now, he would be content that their missiles would miss while he would kill them no matter how they ran.

After five minutes of thrust on their new vector, his two dreadnoughts reset their courses back to the Front Door and continued burning home.

---

"Come on, come on." Mary Bol thought she was saying the words only in her head, but Tyrus threw a look at her from his place on the bridge to her right.

"I suppose they're thinking they've won," he said.

"You're confident they won't be able to see the missiles while they're ballistic?"

He shrugged, which did not fill her with confidence. "The Guard, at least, only used thermals to track incoming missiles. It's possible, I suppose, that the Council Navy has improved upon that and actively uses magnetometers like your ships do, but I believe not. Missile battles are rare in colonial space, a product of us not having any wars to fight against evenly matched foes for six centuries."

"I hope you're right," Bol replied. "Because we're definitely going to lose those three ships to that overkill barrage the Council fleet sent their way."

None of them had been able to believe that the Council fleet had launched full broadsides from *every* ship against the three small cruisers. It was massive overkill, but it was the sad reality they now dealt with. The one EN and two UEN cruisers and their brave crews had no hope of escape.

Tyrus hesitated for a long moment. "You could," he started, "use your anti-missile defenses to come to their aid. Maybe even launch your fighters?"

Bol shook her head sadly. "Against so many missiles, it would do little good. And my orders were to go dark and get out of dodge." She could see from Tyrus' confused expression that he didn't understand her analogy. "I mean, get out of the path of any counterattack. Defending those three ships would be a momentary win but would reveal the existence of these carriers without a doubt to the Council. We took a big enough risk as it is; they'd have to be idiots to think a light cruiser can launch the broadside we did. Even with the way we spaced them out."

Tyrus nodded his agreement. "True, they will suspect something. But they won't *know*, and that's an enormous difference. Suspecting there's a bogeyman, but not knowing where he's hiding or what he looks like, is far scarier than actually seeing him. With luck, this stunt buys us time; the Council Navy will have to plan for multiple contingencies and probably consider upgrading their missiles and defensive measures before they come here again."

Bol smiled tightly, though she didn't tell the man that his words mirrored the conversation she'd had earlier with Holm and Davies. Tyrus was smart when it came to tactics, and she idly wondered if she could keep him on board as a consultant for the duration of the conflict. There would be other… benefits to that arrangement as well. That thought softened her smile for the merest second before it disappeared entirely as she turned her thoughts to the crews of the three doomed cruisers.

---

"Status?" Admiral Prudhoe called out.

"Still no sign of the incoming missiles. We project they are behind and below us, sir," the tactical officer replied. "Our missiles are two minutes from impact, tracking true. The enemy has started firing counter missiles."

All that had happened five seconds ago, given the time it took light to travel between the two forces. But it was as close to real-time as things usually got in space, so Prudhoe was satisfied that all was well.

He wriggled a bit in his command chair. He'd been sitting for so many hours with only occasional walks around the bridge that he was getting sore. He wondered idly if he might return to his day cabin and…

"Missiles inbound!" the panicked voice of the tactical officer practically screamed. "Read 99 ship-killers accelerating at 175 g's."

"They fired another round at us?" Prudhoe demanded.

"No, sir! These are the same missiles we tracked them firing earlier. They're two-stage! They've adjusted course and vector to intercept; two minutes out."

Prudhoe felt the blood drain from his face. A two-stage missile was on the development roadmap for the Council fleet, but more as a concept than an actual project. Now it looked like the Four Worlders had beaten them to it. He listened as Captain Norwood took command of fighting her ship, giving crisp, clear orders to her crew. He imagined that the *Invincible* was doing the same thing at the moment and found himself in the unenviable position all flag officers find themselves in occasionally, of literally having nothing to do other than to trust the people under him. The *good* flag officers, at least, who didn't micromanage their subordinates or relegate their ships' captains to the role of passive observers. He had learned that much by watching how differently Tamara Chen ran her fleet versus the late Piers Lamont.

So, he sat and listened to the controlled chaos around him, watching the holo plot closely as 50 of the 99 missiles maneuvered straight toward *Invictus*.

---

Karen Crosby was a *housewife*, not a naval gunner! So how she had come to be stationed in the starboard number three defensive laser cluster on the *CNS Invictus* was a tragedy of epic proportions. One day she had been taking her kids to and from soccer practice on the planet Ivanov, lamenting her life's monotony; the next day, she had gotten a comm call from the Planetary Prefecture. She didn't even *know* anyone at the Prefect's office, but the voice that had come on the phone had spoken with authority and commanded her, in the name of the Council, to leave her home immediately and come to the government port for 'processing'.

Her first inclination had been to laugh nervously and refuse. But the instant she'd done so, a debilitating pain had struck her in the head, like a thousand headaches all at once. It had driven her to her knees and taken her breath away. The only sound she was aware of beyond her own cries of agony was the voice of the man on the other end of the comm call, calmly telling her that the only way to make the pain go away was to do *exactly* as he had ordered.

Apparently, Karen was an enacter now; she wasn't even sure how that was possible. She also had no idea what her husband had thought when he'd returned home with their two small children—he had taken them out to ice cream on his day off work while she got some things done around the house—but every day since she had been filled with a sense of despair as she thought of how betrayed Carl must have felt to come home and find her gone with no explanation. She could have no way of knowing that her husband had also been enlisted as a new enacter in the Council Navy. Both of them had been victims of Project Epsilon, leaving their children to become wards of the state, as their respective extended families were told they'd died together in a hovercar accident. It was hoped that the children would also exhibit the enacter mutation from Epsilon and be able to join the Academy at the appropriate age.

Five months of forced training later, she was Gunners Mate Third Class Karen Crosby, assigned to the starboard number three defensive laser cluster on Admiral Tyler Prudhoe's flagship, invading *Earth* of all places!

"Crosby!" barked her commanding officer. "Be ready; those missiles are less than a minute out. Let the AI do most of the work, but be ready to take command manually if you see anything going wrong. Got it?"

"Yes, sir," she replied. Not acknowledging orders promptly always brought the pain with it. But nothing could hide the resentment in her tone. She wasn't alone in that; on *Invictus* she had encountered hundreds of other new enacters who had also been ripped from their families and lives. All of them resented it, but none of them could do anything about it. Even though they so desperately wanted to.

On her holo display, Karen saw that the ship's gunnery AI had assigned eight of the incoming ship-killer missiles to her defensive cluster. The computer had calculated targeting solutions on all eight and was waiting for them to enter maximum defensive range in just a few seconds before it engaged.

*Be ready to take command manually if you see anything going wrong.* The orders of her commander echoed in her head. *Anything wrong… anything wrong… anything wrong… taking me away from my family was wrong!* With that thought, Karen found an almost microscopic loophole in her orders. And even though it still hurt her head in excruciating fashion to do so, she slammed her hand down on the manual override button on her console, removing the AI from the firing loop and letting all eight of the incoming missiles proceed unmolested straight at *Invictus*, while she slumped in her seat, twitching from the pain of her triumphant disobedience.

---

The space around the two Council dreadnoughts looked like an old-style fireworks show. Defensive lasers speared the darkness, seeking the heat signatures of incoming missiles and doing relatively well at it, despite a few that inexplicably failed to fire. Of the total 99 missiles coming at the massive ships, 74 were destroyed before they reached each dreadnought's fifty-thousand-kilometer close defense bubble. For those that penetrated that bubble, the Gatling guns affixed all over the hulls of the two dreadnoughts fired a near-constant stream of deadly metal chaff into space, making it look like an old Earth movie of flak used in World War II. Of course, no one on any of the ships involved would have made that connection, but it was apt.

The Gatling-gun-fired shield of chaff caused 21 of the remaining missiles to detonate prematurely. This left only four missiles still alive, and three of those had been targeted at *Invictus*. One missed, detonating after its onboard AI detected it had passed under its target, the explosion doing nothing more than pepper the dreadnought's tough outer skin with shrapnel and some light radiation that didn't even make it through the hull. But the other two hit, one amidship and the other at the stern.

The effects were near instantaneous, and there was nothing Tyler Prudhoe, Henrietta Norwood, or anyone else on *Invictus* could do about it. The missile that hit the middle of the gigantic ship detonated with a nuclear fire that opened four decks to space and instantly killed 483 of the ship's total complement of 3200, including Gunners Mate Third Class Karen Crosby. That destruction would have been a crippling blow on its own, but the rest of the crew could have contained the damage if given the chance and possibly even gotten the ship through the Front Door and back to friendly space.

But by sheer happenstance, the second missile—one of the eight that Karen Crosby had let through the defensive laser shield with her mutinous action—hit near the main reactor. The reactor itself shrugged off the blow; it was the most heavily shielded part of the ship, but the nuclear blast severed multiple power conduits that came off the reactor to critical ship systems. Two of those were the redundant lines that powered the artificial gravity generator, which also provided the ship's oh-so-critical inertial dampening.

Tyler Prudhoe's mind had little time to process what happened as he and everyone else on the *Invictus* were suddenly subjected to the full 30.7 gravities representing the dreadnought's maximum acceleration. In an instant, too quickly even for the built-in safeguards to shut off the main drives, the admiral went from 95 kilos of weight to a crushing 3,100 kilos. His last brief sense was of terrible pressure and pain, then he and everyone else on the dreadnought were dead. Had Karen Crosby lived for just another few seconds, she might have smiled.

*Invincible* had it somewhat better. The single missile that got through the ship's defenses impacted just behind its bow and ripped much of the forward portion of the ship open to space. This left the warship unusually susceptible to the inevitable micrometeor and space dust strikes against which the bow was typically heavily armored. But worse, it damaged both of the vessel's redundant star drives.

Even so, the dreadnought would be able to limp back to the Front Door, though it could never enter the void without extensive repairs. Council Navy standing orders now demanded only one thing of its commander and crew.

On the bridge of *Invincible,* Rear Admiral Cindy Zhou swore as the pain in her head built to unfathomable levels. She knew her orders, but her conscious mind desperately argued that there *must* be another way. However, in the end, as always happened with enacters in her experience, genetic programming and her subconscious mind won out, and she haltingly typed in the code on her command chair arm. She then slowly reached forward and pressed the large flashing red button that appeared in her holo field.

---

"The second dreadnought just exploded, Captain!" cried *Voyager's* sensor officer. "I think it may have self-destructed?" The question in his voice was unmistakable.

*What an odd concept,* Karina Maze thought, studying the viewscreen plot. *We would never ask one of our ships to sacrifice itself and its crew like that.* Europan ships didn't even *have* self-destruct capability.

She pushed that horrific thought aside and consciously forced herself to bask in the satisfaction that her small ship had played even a tiny part in taking out both Council dreadnoughts. That sweet emotion was the last thing she felt as the first wave of the Council's launched missiles got through her ship's mostly automated defenses and left nothing behind but the unconstituted atoms that had once belonged to Captain Karina Maze, the skeleton crew that had refused to evacuate when she'd ordered them all to escape pods, and the *ENS Voyager.*

It would have saddened her to know that both of the UEN light cruisers on her flanks succumbed to the enemy fire at almost the same instant, though only one retained its command crew; the third commander had decided *not* to go down with his ship in a vain attempt to defend it from the missile strikes. As it was, the nuclear fire still took him out, along with a third of the escape pods that had launched from all three vessels.

---

Despite knowing what was coming, Mary Bol watched in horror as the *ENS Voyager, UENS Socrates, and UENS Shen* all disappeared from her viewscreen plot under the hail of over eight hundred missiles that had penetrated their defenses. The Council ships had launched so many missiles that the outcome was never in doubt, and it was the first hundred or so missiles to arrive and penetrate the defensive shields that had done the job before the others even caught up. That first wave had exploded almost as one and destroyed the three small ships and a good portion of their launched escape pods.

Even the satisfaction of seeing both of the targeted Council dreadnoughts destroyed first—their light reached her only moments before that of the cruisers' demise, didn't soften the blow of losing more brave comrades in arms who had willingly sacrificed themselves for a chance to strike back at the invaders. Still, none of them had thought the Council fleet would fire *every* missile it had in the tubes just to take out three small ships, even if those ships had seemingly launched an impossible barrage their way.

That, coupled with the apparent self-destruction of the second dreadnought, chilled Mary to the bone. *This is what pure evil looks like,* she thought grimly. *No quarter given, for foe or friend, as long as it serves the Council's purpose.* Despite not being a religious person, she felt compelled to say a silent prayer for the crews of the three lost Four World ships and even for the crew of Council Navy enacters who had been compelled to take their own lives on the orders of a group of power-hungry men and woman who would never see the front lines of this war.

Well, they would if Admiral Mary Bol had anything to say about it.

"There was nothing you could have done," Tyrus said softly, parroting her earlier argument back to her. "Even if you'd stayed, no ship can survive that many missiles. Even all those escape pods could never have gotten clear in time. If you'd stayed to pick them up, your ships would have been destroyed as well."

She knew he was right—he was echoing what she'd told him earlier—but it didn't take the edge off the pain. Especially because she couldn't risk exposing herself to Council sensors to even pick up the surviving escape pods, and no doubt more brave men and women would die from radiation exposure and other injuries before Second Fleet could reach them.

The pain still had faded little four hours later when the light reached *Enterprise* from the Front Door, showing the remaining Council fleet, including the small number of ships they'd left behind to guard the entrance to the Rift, flicker out of real space and submerge into the void.

# CHAPTER 13

**FIFTEEN YEARS AGO; 716 P.D.**

Jynx was so tired. She had worked a 12-hour shift at the small factory that built wooden furniture for the citizens of Harkness City and the rest of Drake's World. The job paid poorly, but after her father had been forcibly retired—for reasons still unclear to her—from his teaching job, their little family needed every credit they could earn. Especially when they were paying for college tuition.

The tuition wasn't for Jynx. When she and Dax had graduated high school, their parents had made it clear that they could only afford to send *one* twin to even the government-subsidized Council University in faraway Landing City, on the opposite side of the planet. And there was never a question in Jynx's mind whom they would send.

Jynx may have had the better grades, but for Luanne, Dax was the one with the future. She was the bright and effervescent one. Her younger twin was still the quiet little shadow who could never equal or surpass her sister. For Ned, it wasn't nearly as cut and dried. But he had learned to pick his battles with his wife, and Jynx's purposeful underperformance in school meant that her grades weren't all that great either. So Dax would be the one to go to college.

Resigned to her lot, Jynx had taken a job instead at the Peterson Furniture Factory, bringing in a few hundred credits a week, roughly two-thirds of which went to pay for her sister's education. Drake's World didn't have the free college system that served the Core, nor could the Koppel family afford the passenger fare to send Dax to a Core world even for the free schooling. The rest of Jynx's meager earnings supplemented her father's small pension and the money Luanne made by cleaning houses for other families in the city.

Jynx tried hard not to resent her parents and Dax for the situation; she even blamed herself at times, lamenting her choice to hold back in school and not earn grades that matched her potential. She also still harbored hope that one day Dax would come home and apologize for all that had passed between them, so they could finally be *sisters*. Even after all her older twin had done, Jynx was still under her spell.

On this day, as she entered the small apartment her parents and she had been forced to move into when her father lost his job, she could feel in the air that something had happened that would change everything.

Luanne was sitting at the small kitchen table, reading something on her pad, her eyes puffy but her countenance oddly cheerful. Ned sat next to her, a hand on her shoulder, a sad frown on his face.

"What happened?" Jynx asked.

"Oh, it's so wonderful!" Luanne cried. "Your sister got a job!"

"What?" Jynx cocked her head to the side. Dax had only been in school for a year and a half and, by all accounts, had *not* been doing well at all. Jynx had stayed in touch with a couple of classmates, girls like her who had never had many friends but had gone to the same college as Dax in the planet's eastern hemisphere. By their report, Dax spent more time partying than going to class and had even gotten involved with a crowd of petty criminals operating out of the dorms. They mostly stole people's identities online and used their account information to purchase small items the Guard wouldn't care to track down. Now there were rumors they'd been getting into bigger thefts. Dax had found her calling, not as an academic, but as a hacker.

Dax had always been smart. She had just used Jynx and others to avoid having to put the work in at school. But one thing she'd always been invested in had been programming, which eventually turned to hacking, starting with infiltrating the high school servers to subtly change her grades. Her skills had only increased in college, where she supplemented formal coding classes at the university with illegal online courses that delved into the darker side of programming. From there, she had learned quickly that her skills and her natural leadership capabilities meant others would come and work *for* her, allowing her to live well beyond her family's meager means. She still, of course, accepted her parent's tuition money every month without complaint.

Jynx knew all of this but had never had the heart to tell her parents what their hard-earned money was funding. Now she couldn't help but prod. "What job?"

"Your sister was offered a position with a transstellar software company operating out of Cannes in the Parisian system," her father replied with a wan smile. He might attempt to be happy for his oldest daughter, but he was far less blind to the story's logical gaps than Luanne.

"She's taking a break from school," her mother bragged, oblivious to her husband's reservations, "so she can learn on the job for a year or two; then she'll come back and finish at the university."

"No!" Her parents looked at her in shock as Jynx cried out the single word. For the first time, she felt a courage rising inside of her. For years she had held her tongue, but her parents *needed* to know!

"Don't you see?" she forged ahead, speaking quickly to get it all out in a flood of more words than she usually spoke in an entire afternoon. "It's all a lie. She doesn't even go to class. Why would some big company want to hire *her?* She's lying. She has to be! Don't you see? It just doesn't make sense."

"How dare you!" Luanne Koppel stood up from the table, dropping her pad on the chipped plastic surface. "After all your sister has done for you and this family, how dare you say such awful things about her!"

"But Mom, you *have* to see." Jynx put her hands together in supplication. "I hear it from Bree and Helena all the time. Dax isn't studying anything at that school other than how to steal money online. She's failing most of her classes, and she's started hanging out with some bad people. She—"

"Shut! Up!"

Jynx stopped as if struck as her mother screamed the words at her. She opened her mouth again to continue, but she couldn't force anything out; her instant of courage failed her. She looked to her father for support, but Ned Koppel wouldn't meet his daughter's gaze. Then an awful realization hit her.

*They know. All this time, they've known. They just can't bring themselves to admit it; they can't admit that their perfect little girl is a monster because it would mean that they've been wrong all these years—especially mother.*

"You've always been jealous of your sister," Luanne accused, pointing a finger up at her taller daughter—both girls had gotten their height from their father. "You've never been able to cope with her success or your failures. Get. Out."

"But—" Jynx took a step forward, eyes wide and pleading.

"Get. Out." Her mother bit off each word in anger, a look of hatred in her eyes.

Jynx looked to her father again for support. "Daddy?"

Ned's head hung low, and he still wouldn't meet her gaze. Despite all that he had tried to do for his younger daughter over the years, he had never been able to stand up to Luanne. But the worst part now was that he showed no sign that he even *wanted* to. Jynx's last vestiges of hope for her family disappeared in that moment.

"Get out!" Her mother pointed toward the back bedroom that Jynx used. "Get your things and get out. Don't come back until you're ready to apologize for the terrible things you said. In fact, don't *ever* come back!"

Quietly, head hung low, Jynx moved to the bedroom, packed her few things, and then left the small apartment.

She slept on the street for a few nights, using the bathrooms at the factory to wash and dress herself each day before work. Then she found a co-worker willing to let her crash on his couch for a few weeks, though she moved on quickly when it became clear he wanted more than her friendship in return. Slowly, she saved up just enough money for a ticket to Landing City.

She never saw her parents again. They died in a car accident a couple of years later. Jynx heard about it while doing a year's sentence in a prison in Landing City. Desperate for money, she'd been the getaway driver for a crew that robbed a jewelry store but got caught, luckily before anyone was hurt, or anything was stolen, or the sentence would have been much worse.

Part of her died the day she heard of her parents' accident, but part of her was glad—glad they had died without ever finding out the truth about Dax. The 'job' she had taken in Cannes was with a forgery and hacking ring. She would quickly rise to the top of the ring and take it over, convincing a poor fool named Jetter to marry her in return for his services as the forger while she worked as the hacker. So she'd learned *something* from college, at least.

Three years after her parents' deaths—while she was apprenticing in the engine room of a tramp freighter doing local runs in the Expansion Region—Jynx heard of her sister's demise. Somehow that news hit her even harder than the deaths of Luanne and Ned Koppel had. Because in that moment, all her hopes of reconciliation with Dax, of finally getting to be sisters, also died. They were taken from her, and Jynx vowed to find out the truth about what had happened to her twin.

It would be years later, around the same time she met up with Cal Riggs and signed on as his engineer and co-pilot, that she would learn about a man named Jake, who wasn't what he appeared to be. Even later, she would come to know his real name: Tyrus Tyne, the man who took her sister and their future away from her.

---

## PRESENT DAY; JULY 31, 731 P.D.

Corey O'Leary had read the third paragraph of the Admiralty's report on the Council incursion at least six times and still hadn't retained a word of it. He was distracted instead by the information he had recently received from the CEO of Celtic Securities, a cybersecurity company in which he, as the sole heir of the O'Leary family, owned a majority stake.

The government hadn't been the only party to intercept the messages broadcast by the Council Navy, and Celtic Securities had the best codebreakers in the Sol system. It was no contest when they could pay so much better than the UE government for their code geeks.

As far as Corey knew, Naval Intelligence was still trying to decode the two messages, but Corey had known what they both said for the last two hours, and it wasn't good. He had immediately forwarded the contents to Mikael Gorsky and had only received a two-word response.

*Mikael Gorsky: Just wait.*

He had been checking his palm screen almost every two minutes since, waiting for the big Russian to say more. Finally, he couldn't be patient any longer and sent another message.

*Corey O'Leary: Will they be arrested?*

The wait for Gorsky's response felt interminable, but after only three minutes, he messaged back.

*Mikael Gorsky: When P sees, likely. But do not worry. We can use this.*

*Corey O'Leary: How?*

*Mikael Gorsky: G likely to convince P to go too far. We expose it, P has to backpedal. Loses face. Maybe enough for vote of no confidence.*

Corey considered what the Secretary of Justice was suggesting: that they could use Pereira's inevitable overreaction to the messages—spurred on by Givens—to discredit the man. He forced himself to stop and think about it from multiple angles before answering.

*Corey O'Leary: Too risky. Must warn them.*

When the response came, his heart rate jumped.

*Mikael Gorsky: Too late for that. P will move fast. Warning your reader friend will start internal investigation. And they run; they look guilty. Must play hand that is dealt. Especially if more active measures are off the table.*

Corey didn't like it but struggled to argue with the man's logic. Not warning Jinny, Tyrus, and their friends that the UE government would be coming for them felt like a colossal betrayal. But if they *did* warn them and they ran, they would look far more guilty; Mikael was right about that. Then the public opinion that Corey had been counting on to work in their favor would instead be used *against* them. And without the public behind Jinny and Tyrus' message, they had no chance to save the entire *system* from the Council's wrath. Besides, he only had his suspicions of the active measures Gorsky was proposing, but he knew he wasn't ready to go that far. Which left the only option to do what his friend was suggesting, and *let* Jinny and her companions be arrested, no matter how much it rubbed him the wrong way.

Finally, slowly, he typed in his response.

**Corey O'Leary: OK. We don't warn them.**

However, his agreement to follow his friend's plan didn't mean he couldn't take his own measures. A month ago, he had convinced one of his family attorneys, Clark Jeffries, a single man with no family, to take an extended vacation to one of Corey's fishing cabins in the American Rockies. Paying the man's salary to sit around and do nothing but fish was expensive, but not nearly as expensive as hiring a blender named Archer to *also* stay at the cabin so he would be ready to impersonate Jeffries on a moment's notice if the need should arise. There were things a good fixer could do that an honest attorney like Jeffries would never consider nor agree to. It had all been a costly precaution against potential legal action from the Pereira administration aimed toward Jinny.

A month in with no additional talk of such from Pereira or Givens, and Corey had been about to pull the plug on the whole affair. It seemed they weren't going to try to banish Jinny to Australia with the other readers as Gorsky had indicated they might. But now he sent a message to the blender. He would need the man's services after all.

---

While Corey fretted about the inevitable arrest of Jinny and her friends, Mohammed Qureshi was busy with his team in the Octagon's depths, doing their best to decipher the two messages that *Texas* and several listening posts had intercepted from the Council fleet. He had no way of knowing that he and his team were already behind O'Leary and Celtic Securities.

The Octagon was the United Earth Military headquarters building in Houston, named not for its actual shape, but because someone had once claimed it was even harder to navigate than the ancient United States Pentagon. It was in the building's fourth sub-level that Mohammed and his team worked feverishly to decode the Council's messages.

Mohammed was a hands-on leader and had started his career as a cryptoanalyst before being promoted to lead his current team. So, as usual, he was busy at his workstation when one of his people called him over.

"Boss, you're gonna want to see this," Makena Maina called across the room.

Mohammed got up from his desk and stretched, feeling his spine pop as he stood erect for the first time in several hours. They had initially projected that the encryption on the Council messages would only take four-to-six hours to crack, but thus far, it had taken closer to 12 hours with no success. He had been fielding calls from the Situation Room every thirty minutes since the original deadline asking for status updates. It was incredibly annoying. Couldn't they just let him work?

He sauntered over to Makena's seat. The young African girl was a legitimate prodigy in the cryptoanalysis field, one of the few that hadn't been seduced away from government service by the promises of big corporate money, and also had an uncanny talent for working with artificial intelligences, which were often heavy on the 'artificial' and light on the 'intelligence'. One had to know how to phrase questions just so to an AI to get the most out of it, and Makena seemed to speak their language even better than English or her native Kikuyu.

"Whatcha got?" he asked, stifling a yawn and thinking it was about time for another energy drink. Then all sleepiness fled as he moved his eyes down to Makena's flatscreen display and saw what she had pulled up there.

"You decrypted them?" he asked incredulously.

"Of course," she answered in confusion. "I decrypted them 20 minutes ago."

Mohammed resisted the urge to shout in frustration. Makena was a genius, but she was an absentminded one who often forgot to share valuable information when she got distracted by another bright and shiny problem. "So, what are you working on now?" he asked, trying hard to sound patient.

"This." She pointed at a line of code on her screen below the decrypted text of the two messages. "It's a data packet attached to the message sent to Earth."

"I can see that," he replied, "but why is it so interesting to you?"

She looked up at him again in confusion as if the answer should be obvious to him. "Because it only appeared after I cracked the message's encryption, like an attachment on an encrypted email. But it has its own encryption that is *much* more sophisticated than the one on its parent message. It's weird, that's all."

Makena also had a gift for understatement.

"Send me the decrypted messages right away and keep working on the data packet," he said. "And good work, Makena."

"Oh, thanks," she replied, but he could tell she was already back inside her head, trying to work with the AI to tackle the new challenge she'd found.

Mohammed practically ran to his desk to see the text of the messages Makena had finally decrypted. When he read the two short lines of the first message, the one sent to Earth, he immediately engaged his palm implant and placed an urgent call to the Situation Room.

---

Jinny was dreaming again, but this time it was her *own* memory. She was back in the small safehouse apartment in the Little Tijuana district of New Dallas, where she'd first had Alan Daily meet her. She was reliving watching two of her friends and fellow rebels die.

Ryder's death had been the most dramatic. Ryder Cruz had always seemed larger than life. He was smooth talking and gregarious, as most speakers naturally were. But he was better than most Jinny had encountered because he didn't take himself too seriously, which gave him a genuine sense of humor that instantly endeared him to people. He was also one of the bravest men she'd ever met.

Jinny had always imagined that *if* Ryder died in the fight against the Council, he would go out as spectacularly as he had lived. She envisioned something like a hail of bullets or an explosion in which the speaker sacrificed himself to save a bus full of school children.

Instead, Ryder had been simply sitting on a couch and talking when Tyrus Tyne had pulled the trigger on the long-range laser rifle and blew up the speaker's head. It had been shocking in the abruptness with which Jinny's friend had ceased to exist and left behind only a headless corpse and brain matter cooked into the wall behind his body.

So far, she had seen it happen at least a dozen times in her dream, each time rushing to warn Ryder but getting caught or slowed down in various ways so that she was always an instant too late. But at least this time, she wasn't dreaming from Tyrus' perspective and acting as the one who pulled the trigger.

In the current version of the dream, she heard the Guard Special Tactics team banging on the door to the small apartment and was in the process of leading Alan into the room off the kitchen that had an escape hatch built in. Except that the knocking was much louder than she remembered it, and there was also a lot of yelling…

Jinny slammed awake as the door to her bedroom flung open, and two black-clad figures rushed in, shining unreasonably bright lights in her face and screaming at her to put her hands behind her head. She was vaguely aware that she was also screaming at them in terror.

Regaining more of her consciousness and faculties, she was horrified to see that the lights shining in her face were attached to the barrels of nasty-looking assault rifles.

"Get down on the ground, face first, with your hands interlocked behind your head!" one of the men was shouting at her.

Confused and scared, Jinny did as he asked, not seeing any choice but to comply. There was a sudden weight on her back that ground her chest painfully into the room's carpet through the thin fabric of her nightshirt, and she felt gloved hands harshly wrench her arms down and attach them together with what felt like thin but unyielding plastic straps that dug into her wrists.

"What's going on?" she cried.

"Jinny Ambrosa, you are under arrest for violating the Espionage Act of 2481. You have the right to remain silent...." The voice continued droning on with more words that didn't register for her. *Espionage Act?* she kept thinking. *But I'm not a spy.*

She grunted as the man got off her back and yanked her unceremoniously to her feet, which were still bare. She was wearing only her pajamas and felt suddenly self-conscious and even violated in the thin clothing as the lights of more flashlights turned on her in the dark room. Then she was unceremoniously herded out into the brightly lit hallway, where she was surprised to see that the men and women who had come to take her were wearing the uniforms of the United Earth Federal Police. About half of them, including all those holding the assault rifles, were also wearing body armor. It seemed like overkill for a single young woman's arrest.

The man roughly pushed her down the hall and out the front door of the small guest house, where finally, she heard a voice she recognized. Looking forward, she saw Corey and Debra, him in nothing but shorts and a t-shirt and her wearing a long nightgown. A pair of federal police officers were holding them back from getting close to her.

"Jinny, don't worry!" Corey called out to her. "This is all some horrible misunderstanding, and we'll get it sorted out and get you back here as soon as we can." Then she saw him turn and start berating a man wearing a suit with a physical badge hanging from his neck. He was still yelling at the man when she was thrust into the backseat of a black hovercar and driven away from the O'Leary home.

---

General Cruz held his head in his hands inside the conference space of the Situation Room. He was alone in the room now, but moments before, it had been filled with the rest of the Joint Chiefs, the president, his staff, and the secretary of justice, a big Russian named Mikael Gorsky had always rubbed Cruz the wrong way.

The meeting had not gone well. The contents of the two messages intercepted from the Council fleet and later decrypted were short but damning in the extreme. So much so that, along with the relatively unsophisticated encryption used, Cruz was utterly convinced that the messages were *meant* to be read by them to trick the United Earth government into reacting a certain way.

Unfortunately, President Pereira and his advisers had not agreed with Cruz's assessment and had reacted in *exactly* the way he suspected the Council wanted them to.

The messages had been simple. The one addressed to Earth had read:

**Execute Phase Two. Use resources acquired at Rinali.**

No one knew, of course, what Phase Two was, and Cruz suspected it probably didn't exist. But while the message hadn't called out Jinny Ambrosa or Tyrus Tyne by name, the reference to Rinali Station, their last stop before coming through the Rift, was a heavy-handed hint. It also neatly implicated their companions, Riggs and Jynx, who, by their own admission, they had met, or 'acquired', on the station.

It was far too neat in Cruz's mind. The first rule of spycraft was never to assume that the enemy couldn't read your mail, and in this case, not only had the encryption protocols been almost laughably simple, but the message had been far too direct. A genuine message to an implanted spy would not openly reference a location like Rinali that would immediately implicate its recipients. That alone should have been a red flag for anyone who read it. Unfortunately, though not surprising in retrospect, Pereira had refused to listen to reason and had ordered the immediate arrest of Tyne, Ambrosa, Riggs, and Jynx. 'Until we can be sure', had been his explanation, but Cruz could see that both he and Tabitha Givens were practically giddy over the prospect of arresting the group of political thorns in their sides.

The second message, the one directed at Mars, had been more disturbing in some ways. It simply read:

**Your terms are acceptable. Stand by for instructions.**

Again, the message reeked of being fake, but Pereira was so intent on using the Martians as bogeymen that the man had needed no excuse to believe they were double-dealing against Earth with the Council government. And just like that, Cruz had seen any dwindling hope of working together with the Martians abruptly end. The president hadn't even been amenable to *calling* the Martian government with a fleet breathing down his neck; now, with this message, he was intent on exploring a preemptive attack against them and had ordered Cruz and the Joint Chiefs to draw up options. If only he'd shown that same fire in preparing earlier for the Council's inevitable attack.

All of this was even worse in light of Jinny Ambrosa's theory about the true motives behind the Council's attack. Because further isolating Earth from Mars and heightening the fear of a Martian attack played right into the scenario she, O'Leary, and Cruz had discussed. He could almost hear Pereira surrendering the enhanced on Australia to an invading Council fleet in the vain hope that it would save enough of the UE Navy to fight off a follow-up Martian attack.

The only silver lining of the small but disastrous attack and the two intercepted messages had been that the president at least finally acknowledged the need to ramp up military spending and production to prepare for the actual invasion that would inevitably come. The Council had done them a small favor, Cruz supposed, in sending the smaller recon force first. It showed that Tyne and Ambrosa had been right about the invasion, but it might be too little too late. The Council had also just demonstrated that they could practically swat the UEN like flies; even the destruction of two of their three dreadnoughts was symbolic, at best, though Pereira was sure to play it up as an inspiring victory in the press. It was a sobering and depressing thought.

Cruz's palm implant pinged, and he looked down. The caller's name was no surprise, and he sighed as he answered.

"What is going on!?" demanded an angry Congressman Corey O'Leary. "Armed federal police just battered down the door of my guest house and took Jinny into custody on charges of espionage. Do you know what's happening?"

Cruz took a deep breath and started to explain. Had he been less sleep deprived or stressed beyond reason, he might have noticed that O'Leary did not seem overly surprised by any of his answers.

## CHAPTER 14

As they often did at night when she was alone, thoughts of Dax marched through Jynx's head as she walked through the darkness along the secluded forest path. At the center of Bainbridge Island was a large, forested area crisscrossed with trails and aptly, though perhaps ambitiously, named the 'Grand Forest'. Some trails were wide and well-worn and often busy with joggers, bikers, and even horseback riders—that had been a surprise the first time Jynx had rounded a blind corner and come face-to-face with a real-life horse! Others were barely visible game trails where few humans ever ventured. It was to these that Jynx gravitated, almost always at night when she could be assured of meeting no other human in her wanderings.

Unlike Riggs, Jynx had grown up on the surface of a planet, although Drake's World often barely qualified as such. But growing up there on the arid desert world had made her appreciate and even come to love the greenery of the Pacific Northwest, though she would never openly admit it to Riggs or anyone else. Even all these years after parting company with Dax, Jynx still guarded her feelings closely, even with her partner.

She knew that the carefully constructed shell of cynicism and sarcasm she wore like body armor kept Riggs and everyone else in her life at a distance. Yet, even with that self-awareness, she was wary of sharing her authentic emotions or self with anyone, even the man she'd grown to trust and, in less guarded moments, would admit was her best friend.

No, the only times she could genuinely be herself were on these midnight walks through the forest when Riggs and her United Earth government handlers all thought she was safe and sound in the bed in her temporary house.

She'd found a way out of the house and into the forest at the edge of the backyard that avoided all the so-called security cameras placed around the property. She, like Riggs, knew those cameras were more to watch than to protect the two of them, but they played along with the fiction. Still, Jynx enjoyed fooling those that were watching them.

Tonight, as she made her way silently through the woods, nearing the back of her home, she abruptly halted. Something felt *wrong* about the night the closer she got to the house. She stood there, not moving, simply thinking and searching the darkness around her for what had triggered her sense of wariness. Then she realized what it was: there were no sounds.

Late at night and even this close to the line of homes on the border of the Grand Forest, there was usually a small cacophony of nighttime wildlife sounds, from the buzzing of insects and the chirping of crickets to the occasional howling of the local packs of coyotes. Somehow the forest had embraced Jynx, its music barely quieting as she moved through the dense trees most evenings, even when it rained.

But tonight, all was silent near the houses, as if something else was intruding on the forest and lending it a preternatural calm. Jynx stood without moving and listened intently, pulling tighter the sweater she had worn for this evening's walk. Even in the summer, when the sun set in the Pacific Northwest, the temperature dropped well below what she considered comfortable—she'd grown spoiled by the constant climate she enjoyed in a spaceship's controlled environment—and she'd been looking forward to getting back to her bed inside the warm house.

She stood that way for several minutes until she started wondering if the unnatural quiet was her imagination or conceivably because of a passing predator she couldn't detect. Then, just as she was about to take another step along the narrow trail to the house, she saw movement.

A man stepped into view around the side of the house. From his vantage point, he might not be able to see Jynx standing several meters inside the dense forest at the far end of the yard, and besides, his attention was fully fixed on the back door to the house itself. He was dressed all in black and, to Jynx's surprise, was carrying an assault rifle, its shape obvious to her even at this distance in the dim moonlight. She saw more movement, and an identically dressed and equipped figure stepped around the other side of the house. From the way this one moved and the build, Jynx guessed it was a woman.

The two figures stayed at the corners of the house, their rifles trained on the back door, a large sliding glass opening that led onto a small wooden patio from the kitchen, from which steps led down to the grassy backyard.

Jynx's adrenaline spiked, and she was worried that the pounding of her heart would give her away, but she stayed perfectly still. It was likely that the two intruders had thermal vision, so if they looked her way, they would probably see her, especially from the woman's vantage point. Luckily, they seemed to assume she was inside. If this was a smash and grab, then there were probably a couple more of them in the front, who would enter the home to take her while these two made sure she didn't escape out the back. If they were the local version of the Guard...

Slowly, Jynx took a step backward along the path and then another. She was on a timer. Once the team in front of the house breached and found her missing, she would only have moments until they started searching the surroundings. If she were still within sight of the house, her heat signature would stick out against the cool forest like a tramp freighter at a high-end shipyard.

Luckily, a small hill rose in the forest behind the house and then dropped away into a shallow gully. If she could reach the top of that hill and get over and into the depression before they looked her way, she could make her way along the low ground, shielded by the gully wall, until she was a safe distance from the house.

She heard no loud sounds as she moved but saw both the figures in the backyard stand up straighter and stiffen. She took that to mean the team in front had entered the house, and the lack of sound meant they were true experts. Or they had the code to the door.

The first thing Jynx had done when the government had assigned her to the house was to change all the door codes to sequences only she knew. Even so, she wasn't a hacker like her deceased sister and was sure there was a master code she hadn't known how to change. It was likely that this team had that code, which made them government.

*Riggs!* she thought suddenly and almost stumbled as she fought the urge to bolt in the direction of her friend's house and warn him. If it was the government coming for her, they were undoubtedly coming for him as well. Still, it was just as likely that they either had already taken him or had come for them simultaneously, so one couldn't warn the other. She forcefully shoved aside all thoughts of helping him; she could do more if she stayed free and had to prioritize that for now.

Jynx breathed a quiet sigh of relief as she reached the trail at the top of the small hill, turned, and fled silently into the gully on the other side, still choosing with care where she stepped to avoid making noise. As her head disappeared behind the crest of the hill, she finally heard a crash from the direction of the house, which sounded like someone had flung open the sliding back door. Her captors knew she wasn't there and would likely search the forest soon.

---

Riggs had gone to sleep in his house around 10 PM like he usually did and woken up just over an hour later to bright lights in his face and voices yelling at him to surrender himself. Then he'd been whisked away into a dark hovercar with his hands in cuffs behind him.

There'd been no explanation. And no sign of Jynx.

In fact, while his captors had never spoken directly to him after putting him in the car, he'd heard them talking to each other enough to guess that Jynx had somehow evaded them. *Go Jynx!* he thought to himself. *Whatever's going on here, we need you on the outside.*

He thought in terms of 'we' because he supposed that any reason the UE government would find to arrest him and Jynx would undoubtedly drive them to capture Jinny and Tyrus as well. It was probably something to do with the battle out by the Front Door that the news had reported just hours ago. The government hadn't yet acknowledged that it had been the Council fleet, at least not by the time Riggs went to bed. Still, enough amateur astronomers and in-system freight haulers had seen the light from the battle that the president's office had issued a brief statement promising the threat had passed, and more details would be shared later.

Riggs had been tempted to stay up late and wait for those further details; he'd even messaged Jinny to see if she could tell him more but never got a response. Finally, he went to bed. He figured Houston was only two hours ahead of Bainbridge Island, and the president was unlikely to give a press conference in the middle of the night. And he knew well that sitting around and waiting for ships to spend hours moving across a star system, even in a battle, wasn't the best use of anyone's time. That made him resigned if not content to learn what he could along with the rest of Earth's population in the morning.

But whatever had happened, it had resulted in Mama Riggs' little boy sitting in the back of a black government hovercar. Not that it was the first time, but Cal Riggs had largely kept out of the hands of the Guard for the last five years since he'd acquired the *Blind Monk*, aside from a few 'drunk and disorderly' nights in the brigs on various stations.

The longer he was in the back of the government car, the happier he was that Jynx was out there. He knew that his co-pilot and friend was cranky, challenging to get to know, and downright mean sometimes. But if he had to choose one person to be on the outside, thinking of ways to get him out, it would be her. *Or Tyrus Tyne*, he reflected, but he'd grown to know and trust Jynx over the years, and he knew she wouldn't rest until she'd gotten him free.

Jinny and Tyrus? She'd probably happily leave them to rot in jail, but she wouldn't do that to Riggs. Then once she got him out, he'd convince her to spring them too. Of course, they were on a strange planet, with the entire planetary government arrayed against them. He tried not to think too hard about that. All he had was hope, and he wasn't going to lose that if he could help it.

---

"Admiral, urgent TT from Houston. Your eyes only!"

"Send it to my private display," Bol commanded. Tyrus couldn't see what she was looking at because of the privacy field she engaged, but he saw her facial expression go from curiosity to surprise to anger in the course of less than a few seconds. Whatever the message was, it wasn't good.

When she finished reading the telegraph, she disengaged the privacy field and looked over at Tyrus, a speculative look in her eyes that sent a minor chill down his spine.

"Boats," she said calmly to the chief petty officer who stood at the back of the bridge. "Orders from Earth. Place Mr. Tyne under arrest and put him in the brig."

Tyrus stared at Mary Bol in shock but recovered quickly. "What's going on here, Admiral?" he asked as sedately as he could, his mind racing for ways out of the situation.

"By order of the president and under the Uniform Military Justice Code section four, paragraph 16, Mr. Tyne, you are under arrest," Bol recited calmly, almost robotically, throwing him a look that said he wouldn't get any more information than that. Briefly, he considered incapacitating the chief petty officer as the man grabbed him by the arm, but immediately discarded that path. Escape would be an option later when he wasn't on a ship surrounded by loyal United Earth Navy spacers. Not only was there nowhere to escape to, but he loathed the thought of hurting Bol or any of her crew. For now, he'd go quietly and see what information he could gather on the reason for his arrest.

But immediately, another thought struck him: if they were arresting him, they were probably capturing his friends as well! As the anger rose inside him, he swore to himself that, whatever game Pereira was playing, if Jinny Ambrosa were hurt, the man and anyone associated with him would learn what an alpha was capable of.

---

Jynx moved swiftly down the bottom of the gully, thankful it was summer and that the small stream that had no doubt been here during the rainy season had dried up. She didn't stop to rest or even think about Riggs or her next move until she was a full kilometer from the house and nearing the parking lot of one of the Grand Forest's main entrances. She only paused twice in her flight, both times thinking she'd heard subtle sounds of pursuit but neither time hearing anything more.

She thought briefly about stealing a hovercar from a nearby house but didn't know enough about Earth technology to trust that she'd be able to find and disable the tracking mechanisms. Nor did she think it would be easy to get off the island via the only bridge to the Kitsap peninsula or the ferry to Seattle. When the government goons realized she wasn't in or near the house, they were sure to put in place roadblocks, depending on how badly they wanted her. The assault rifles made her think they wanted her enough to do whatever it took to apprehend her.

Instead of walking through the empty parking lot, she skirted its edges, staying in the tree cover, making her way along the side of the road, and heading south. On an optimistic day in late spring, Riggs had tried to get Jynx out of her self-imposed funk—or maybe it was an attempt to get *himself* out of the funk he was in—and take her to the beach. There, Jynx had seen the one sure way she could get off the island without worrying about roadblocks.

She made her way along the sides of various roads for several kilometers, thankful for the half-moon that gave her just enough light to see but still allowed her to hide in the shadows. Where she couldn't find enough tree cover at the road's edge, she made her way deeper into the woods or jogged quickly along the edge of the road, ready to lie down and hide in the short grass if a car happened by.

There was a close call a couple of hours later—she didn't know how many; she'd left her watch in the house when she'd gone to take her late-night stroll—when a car almost caught her in its headlights as she was crossing a quiet intersection. She'd hastily dived into a small drainage ditch, just in time to see an old-style pickup truck—it even had rubber wheels instead of the more ubiquitous hover matrix—pass through the intersection without even slowing for the stop sign. The driver probably figured it was late enough that no one would notice or care.

She had another close call when she was about to step out into the road but heard a car coming. She crouched down behind a large tree stump as a black hovercar came around the corner without its lights and drove by her slowly, less than a meter off the ground. In the dim moonlight, she spied the extinguished light bar on top of the car and knew it must be looking for her. By pure chance, she'd found the one tree stump in the area large enough and thick enough to hide her thermal signature from its scanners.

Another hour or two later, she finally neared her destination, a small rocky public beach with a deserted parking lot. She was on the southern tip of the island and could see the lights of Bremerton in the distance, her ultimate target.

Jynx had lived a good portion of her life running. After her sister had abandoned her and gone off to her short stint at college, and after her parents had kicked her out, Jynx fell in with the wrong crowd herself and even landed in prison. Drake's World was known throughout the colonies as a hotbed for crime. The local syndicates controlled the planet more than the Council government's representatives, and even the Guard wouldn't enter certain neighborhoods without armored paramilitary mechs. Drakes World was also the center of the 47 Colonies' drug trade, and the most common vocation for those who left public school without the benefit of college was to turn to a life of crime. Jynx was no exception, though she found it ironic that Dax had *still* ended up in a similar place despite going to college and being handed the perfect opportunity to get out.

But despite her life on the gray side of the law, Jynx had decided that a single stint in prison was enough for one lifetime. So, she had learned a thing or two about avoiding the authorities and had helped

Riggs get out of plenty of trouble in their years together. She'd chosen her destination for the evening's journey with careful deliberation. Bremerton was a good 50 kilometers away from Bainbridge Island's center by hovercar—they couldn't fly directly over the water; it didn't provide enough resistance for their hover matrices, and they would plummet from the sky and sink unless they had backup vertical turbines for lift—so the authorities would be unlikely to expect her to get that far on foot or otherwise. Bremerton was also home to a modest-sized training base for the United Earth Navy. Those that fled government authorities rarely fled *toward* government strongholds, so it would not be the first place they looked for her.

Now, all Jynx had to do was get there. And while it may be 50 kilometers on *land* to get there, she judged it was only about two kilometers by *water*. She had hope that she could make it, because the main thing she had noticed on that beach trip with Riggs had been all the boats. Bainbridge Island was a place where crime was practically nonexistent. So, the beach she had reached had a plethora of small boats pulled up and left on the shore for their owners to use when they visited; they weren't even locked up!

Searching carefully through these craft, Jynx found what she was looking for. She always carried a small utility knife with her, even on her midnight strolls, and most of the boats here were tied to rocks or old pier posts along the shore just in case the tide came in far enough in a storm to pull them out to sea. Working quickly, she cut several of these lines and tied them together until she had about 50 meters of rope.

She picked a small one-person kayak, one with an attached waterproof bag. The owners had also helpfully left a lifejacket and paddle inside. She carried the boat to the water's edge, then stripped down to her undergarments and put her clothes inside the bag. Then she quickly searched the waterline for one more thing she needed before calmly pushing the boat into the water, bracing herself against the cold.

About 45 minutes after Jynx entered the waters of the Puget Sound, one of the police boats patrolling the shores of Bainbridge Island—its crew roused out of bed to assist in the search for a woman in her mid-thirties who had escaped from federal authorities—spotted a small blue kayak floating in the water and moving slowly toward Bremerton.

The police boat put on speed and turned its flood lights onto the kayak while also aiming its thermal scanners at the craft and the surrounding water. But the police lieutenant in charge was puzzled to see no thermal image inside the kayak or anywhere near it. When he and his team reached the small boat, he looked down at an empty vessel with a paddle jammed inside along with a life jacket.

"What do you think?" he asked the police sergeant standing on the deck next to him.

The other man shrugged, stroking his bushy mustache thoughtfully. "Don't know, sir. Could be one of those boats folks leave over there on Lytle Beach that just got loose and drifted out this way. No indications that anyone's been in it, not that they'd leave much evidence. The life jacket looks pretty dry, and so is the inside of the kayak. If someone was in here and jumped out, they wouldn't have left everything so neatly arranged."

He turned to his superior, eying the younger man and arching an eyebrow, hoping for the correct response to his next question. "Should we report it, sir?"

The officer considered this for a moment and then sighed and slowly shook his head. "With those federal guys involved, can you imagine the paperwork we'd have to fill out just for a drifting kayak? No, let's keep patrolling. No sense in ruining all of our evenings just because some idiot didn't tie up their boat."

The sergeant smiled and let out his own held breath. He was pleased that his example was finally rubbing off on this normally by-the-book young officer. That boded well for their working relationship. He *hated* unnecessary paperwork.

Under his direction, the other two cops on the boat pushed the kayak back out into the Puget Sound, and the lieutenant gunned the boat to make up for lost time in their patrol pattern.

## THE FOUR WORLDS - SUBVERSION

Jynx tried hard not to gasp loudly for air as she broke the water's surface and watched the police boat continue on its way. She had been worried they might choose to bring the kayak on board, in which case they would have wondered at the 50-meter rope connected to it. Until she'd spotted the patrol boat coming toward her, the other end of that rope had been tied to her waist.

She'd never been in the kayak; it had always been nothing more than a diversion, designed to do precisely what it had done in drawing the police craft's attention so it wouldn't notice the woman swimming 50 meters in front of it, using a small piece of driftwood to stay afloat. Jynx now swam back to that piece of wood; it had floated away from her with the current after she'd let go of it to dive under the water and hide. That same current had pulled her farther and farther away from the decoy kayak while she'd been submerged, helping her avoid the boat's scanners.

She got back to the driftwood and held onto it to keep her muscles from getting overly tired as she swam. Jynx hadn't exactly learned how to be the strongest swimmer on her desert home planet but had spent enough time at public pools on hot summer days that she wasn't a slouch either. Still, she hadn't counted on the cold temperature of the water, even in the Pacific Northwest summer, and was suffering from numbing pain in her extremities. She was also chafing where the waterproof bag with her clothing rubbed against her bare back.

Regardless, there was nothing to do but keep swimming, though the lights of Bremerton didn't seem to get any closer. It was about two hours later when she finally felt painfully sharp pebbles against her frigid feet, and she practically crawled out of the water and lay on her back gasping for several minutes on a small patch of sand on the beach.

Once she finally caught her breath, she looked up at the darkened home that loomed above the beach—the home she'd picked as her destination from a few hundred meters out *because* it had no lights on inside or out. Not bothering to struggle back into her clothes yet, she made her way up the beach, wincing at the rough rocks and dirt underneath her soles, and crept up slowly to the home's back window.

Peering inside, she saw no sign of movement or habitation. Making her way around the side of the house, she found the window to the garage and was relieved to see no cars there or in the narrow but long driveway. Even better, the house had high wooden fences that shielded it from view from the houses on either side and was set back far enough from the road with enough trees in between to have a good amount of privacy in that direction as well.

After looking through several more windows and confirming her suspicion that no one was home, she dug into the waterproof bag and pulled out her utility knife. It took her just a few minutes to break open the home's back door. When she was inside, she stopped dead still and listened carefully, hearing nothing that would hint at a security system or anyone inside the house besides herself. Still, it was only after a careful and quiet survey of every darkened room, including the garage, that she felt comfortable enough to go into a bathroom with no windows and turn on a light.

There, she slipped back into her clothing, not bothering to dry off her wet undergarments. She didn't trust the noise of the clothes dryer she'd spied in the laundry room and wanted to be ready to flee at a moment's notice. Her only concession to comfort was to quickly wash the sand off herself in the bathroom's small shower. Then, when she was dressed and had her shoes back on her feet, she crept into one of the smaller bedrooms and lay down on top of the sheets of a twin-size bed that was clearly for a child, though the relative lack of decorations in the room and anywhere else in the house made her think it was a short-term rental or a family's vacation home.

Knowing that she'd need sleep for what was ahead and reasonably confident in her survey of the home that she'd tripped no alarm systems and seen no obvious cameras, she ignored her wet clothing and fell into a fitful sleep from the exhaustion of her hours of swimming across the frigid sound.

Her last thought as she drifted off was an imagined mental image of Riggs in comically large chains being led from the front door of his house and pushed roughly into the back seat of a black hovercar.

# ACT III

Jinny threatened me again to tell our secret if I didn't stop contacting her. Foolish girl. She's so much like her mother. If only she knew that she holds the key to saving humanity from chaos. If the Council falls, so do the rest of us. Surely, she must see that, or what did they teach her in that blasted Academy?

Still, stupid girl that she is, at least she understands what would happen to us both if her secret got out. It's the same reason I don't even write all the details here and why I won't ever put in writing the full extent of her abilities, which I gave her. They're more mine than they are hers, but the secret must be kept.

All I need is a little of her blood. I've used all the samples I took before she left for the Reader Academy. Unfortunately, she hasn't let me close enough to take any since, but I'm so *close* to replicating what I did with her. I just need more.

Just a little blood. A few vials; that's all. Then I can unlock the code. I have to make Jinny see, somehow, that she needs to do this for me. For the galaxy. Perhaps I can...

- Excerpt from the *Manifesto on Genetic Enhancements*, from the personal files of Dr. Frank Ambrosa

# CHAPTER 15

### EIGHTEEN YEARS AGO; 713 P.D.

The woman led the small boy, just five years old, by the hand through the stark white hallway of the New Brussels Enacter Academy. He clutched her hand tightly; he was wary of his new surroundings, but his discomfort was leavened with an excitement that quickened his steps.

When they reached the door at the end of the corridor, the woman keyed it open with a wave of her watch and motioned the boy to enter, releasing his hand as she did so. He looked up at her with wide eyes and then looked forward and took a tremulous step into the room. She put her hand on his back and pushed him forward a bit more before she waved the door shut behind him. She stayed out in the hall.

The boy looked around the room with his arms at his side. All he saw was a single chair and desk, both sized for his small frame. The rest of the tiny square room was white—walls, ceiling, and floor.

He stood at the threshold of the door, not daring to move, waiting for instructions, wanting to get things perfectly right. A chime sounded, and a portion of the floor in front of him lit up with a green arrow that moved from where he stood, across the floor and toward

# THE FOUR WORLDS - SUBVERSION

the desk and chair, just a meter and a half away. When the arrow reached the chair, it disappeared and then reappeared in front of the boy, once again moving from him toward the chair.

The boy took the hint and hastened to the chair, looking around as he moved to make sure there was nothing else in the room that required his attention. When he reached the chair, he sat and stared at the blank surface of the desk before him. He stayed that way for five minutes in nervous anticipation until he noticed the room's lighting dim. He looked around with a smile but saw nothing and no one.

Then, another chime sounded, and the wall in the front of the room began to glow, resolving itself into a screen with the 3D image of a small blue ball at its center. The ball grew in size for a few seconds and then faded to be replaced by an image of a rotating galaxy with words around its border.

Even though the boy was only five, he could already read at the level of a much older youth. So, he clearly understood the words surrounding the small galaxy: 'The Council of the 47 Colonies'. He'd seen this image and its wording before, emblazoned like a logo on the jumpsuits of the few adults who'd interacted with him today, including the woman who had dropped him off in this small room just moments before. More importantly, his father had the symbol hung in every room of their small apartment.

A male voice spoke, seeming to emanate from every corner of the room. "Welcome, D5746J14L1. And happy birthday."

"It's my birthday," the boy responded, not a question but a simple agreement of the fact.

"Why yes," the voice responded. "You're five years old today. That's why you're here."

"I know; Father told me." The boy sat up straighter and higher in his seat.

"Yes. You're very special, and it's time for you to learn just how special you are. That is what you will be taught in this room."

"Yes, sir," the small boy replied in a voice of confidence that he'd rehearsed with his parents in the weeks leading up to this special day. He listened to his own words, wondering if he'd gotten the tone right;

the proper show of emotion wasn't something that came naturally to him.

"Now," the voice continued, "there's no need to be afraid. I'm going to teach you today about the Council and all the wonderful things that it does for humanity. Would you like to learn about the Council, D5746J14L1?"

The boy didn't even have to consider. He nodded emphatically. "Yes, sir. I want to learn all about the Council."

The screen in front of him changed, and the boy watched in silence. It was like his mommy and daddy had said. He was finally home.

---

## PRESENT DAY; AUGUST 1, 731 P.D.; FIVE MONTHS AFTER THE REVELATIONS

Jynx stayed just an hour or two in the abandoned house. She had little idea of how law enforcement worked on Earth, but she'd had enough run-ins with the Guard in the colonies to know generally what to expect. By now, they would have extended their roadblocks to a radius of several dozen kilometers, but they probably assumed she was still in relatively close proximity to Bainbridge Island.

They also probably suspected she was off the island but not on the Seattle side. The only way to get there was by ferry or by a much longer swim than she would have been capable of doing. A big city like that would also have a strong... whatever the Earth equivalent was of the colonies' street network—a system of cameras and other sensors that would make it nearly impossible for her to move about freely there. The Earthies she'd met staunchly claimed that no such network existed on their perfect little planet, but she knew better.

Such systems had a lot more ground to cover and tended to be less dense in their coverage of suburban and rural areas like those on the Kitsap Peninsula side of the Puget Sound, so that was where they'd really concentrate the human search for her, probably starting in Poulsbo and Silverdale, the two closest towns to the island, which she had bypassed by swimming directly across to Bremerton. They probably wouldn't assume she'd go north to Kingston or anywhere in that direction, as the only ways to escape from there were a few highways or ferries that could be easily blocked.

No, they'd know she was heading south, toward Tacoma and the surrounding environs, where she could lose herself more easily in the networks of rural roads and escape south to Oregon, east to a place called Idaho, or circle back around Seattle and head north into British Columbia. Always wary of being trapped *anywhere* without multiple escape routes, she had carefully studied the maps of the surrounding areas almost as soon as she and Riggs had been placed on Bainbridge Island. South gave her more options.

So, while she was fairly confident she was currently outside of their search cordon, it wouldn't be long before they would think about Bremerton and before they might even start door-to-door searches. And she couldn't know if the crew of the police boat had reported the empty kayak; she suspected they hadn't, given how they'd raced away from it, but they might change their minds later.

With that in mind, she allowed herself just a short stretch of restless sleep and then a quick meal from the little nonperishable food the owners had left in the vacation home. Then she started walking, carefully ducking behind a tree or laying down in a drainage ditch every time a car passed. After about an hour, she found herself in what was clearly a seedier part of Bremerton, the low-income housing and less-than-savory businesses that, in her experience, always sprung up around major government installations.

It was almost as if the strong positive charge of a Guard facility, or in this case, a naval base, always required the offsetting negative charge of a borderline slum. Or perhaps it was just that underpaid and over-disciplined young men and women who usually crewed such installations needed a place to find a release. Either way, it warmed Jynx's heart to see the beginnings of the poorer neighborhoods—they could have been facsimiles of the area she'd grown up in on Drake's World—and it wasn't long before she found exactly what she was looking for.

As the sun rose, she found herself in a street of tiny, rundown homes on smaller plots of land, and she spotted the car. From the outside, the hovercar—aircar—looked nondescript. Black in color and conservative in appearance, it was the heavily tinted windows and damaged license plate that gave it away. As she got closer, she knew what she'd find inside. Sure enough, the driver's side door was unlocked. No one in their right mind would steal *this* car… not unless they had a genuine death wish.

Jynx didn't have a death wish, but she was out of options. Besides, while it was possible the owners of this car could track it, it would be almost certain that those same owners had disabled any tracking mechanisms the *government* could use to find her. If either found her, they were likely to kill her—she had no faith in the United Earth government being any less shady than the Council, despite what they may say publicly about human rights and freedom. But she would take her chances with the criminals of Earth before their monolithic government.

She briefly searched the car's cabin and further verified her suspicions, even finding a physical starter key hidden just under the front passenger seat. She also found the trunk release and opened it. Inside, just as she'd known there would be, were a number of small bricks of a white powdery substance wrapped in thick, clear plastic. For a moment, she marveled at how similarly criminals operated on all worlds. Apparently, even those cut off from the rest of humanity for hundreds of years.

Carefully removing the drugs from the trunk of the car, she put them on the bare dirt around the base of a nearby tree, watching the growing light around her nervously. The owners of the car would pursue her either way, but they'd be much more motivated if she left with a fortune's worth of their product. They could replace the car far more easily.

And Jynx absolutely needed *this* car. Not only was it unlikely to have any functional tracking beacons, but it would also likely be equipped to go faster and higher than the typical hovercar. Possibly high enough for her to altogether avoid many of the roads that the police might block searching for her.

Just as she finished removing the last of the drugs, she heard a noise across the street, like a rock falling or hitting a fence, and ducked down low behind the side of the car. There was enough light now that being seen was a real possibility, and she was surprised no one leaving their home for work, or other activities, hadn't stumbled on her yet. But after several moments of tensely watching for the source of the sound, she was satisfied that no one was about.

Quickly, she stood up and reached over to the back of the car to push the trunk closed, her eyes still fixed on the spot across the street but seeing nothing there. Then she returned to the car's cabin and turned the key in the old-style ignition—no biometrics for this hovercar—and was relieved to hear it hum smoothly to life. Slowly, she pulled away from the curb and, obeying every traffic law to a fault, drove south out of Bremerton. She didn't know where she was going yet but knew she had to get as far away from where she was expected to be, as quickly as possible.

And as much as she hated to admit it, she had to find the one and only person who could help her free Riggs. She had to find Tyrus Tyne.

---

Tyrus sat in an outwardly calm fashion in his cell in the *Enterprise's* brig. Inside, he was anything but. He still didn't know why he'd been arrested; none of the guards would even talk to him. By the timing, it had to have something to do with the Council Navy's recent attack, and he had a few suspicions along those lines, but that's all they were.

It was five hours later that he looked up and found Admiral Mary Bol looking at him through the small window in the cell's hatch. He saw her lips move and heard her voice coming through a set of speakers in his cell.

"So, Mr. Tyne. It seems your ruse is over."

He looked at her with confusion but held his tongue, waiting for her to say more.

"That Council fleet tried to contact you, but we cracked the message. To imagine, this entire time, you've been working for them. Not the reformed enacter you would have us all believe, are you?"

"Admiral, I have no idea—" he began to respond, but Bol kept talking as if she hadn't heard him.

"We're sending you back to Earth to stand trial. I'm sure it will be fair, given the complete faith and trust I have in our civilian leadership. We'll be putting you in one of our stealth shuttles within the hour, and if you behave on the way to the lunar naval station, I'll be sure to have the three guards put in a good word for you with whomever from the civilian side is picking you up there. I imagine you'll eventually be joined by the rest of your friends."

Tyrus fought the urge to scrunch his brows together in puzzlement as she turned heel and walked away without a backward glance. Her words made sense… but they also didn't. To anyone who hadn't gotten to know her on a personal level, Bol's words could have been taken at face value. But to Tyrus, who had become a confidant, it was almost instantly obvious that the admiral was telling him *everything* he needed to know.

Someone from the invading fleet had broadcast something that made the UE government believe he was operating as a Council spy here in the Four Worlds.

He was being arrested, supposedly to stand trial, but Bol didn't really think that would happen. The line about her complete faith and trust in civilian leadership gave that away. She respected the civilian leadership and obeyed their commands, but 'faith' and 'trust' did not define the way she felt about them, especially in the way they micro-managed naval tactics.

She was sending him in a *stealth* shuttle with only three guards. She was literally telling him he should try to subdue the guards and escape. And the part about behaving was her subtle plea not to hurt those guards as he did so.

The admiral had also told him he was meant to be taken to the lunar naval station—that would be the military side of Lunar Base One—where he would be turned over to someone *outside* the military; she wouldn't have made a point of telling him he was being picked up there by civilians unless it was important. It was possible she didn't truly know who was picking him up or what their intentions were and was warning him to be careful. Or she knew and didn't like the answer.

Either way, it probably meant he should avoid Luna at all costs and make his way directly to Earth after his escape. As he thought about it, arresting him and sending him to Earth's moon made sense. It would put him largely out of the public view; some of United Earth's most secure military—and non-military—installations were on Luna for that very reason.

Still, he tried to think about her message from a few different angles as he continued to sit in his cell in silence. It was a habit he'd developed over the years: to not simply go with his first impression or conclusion in situations of ambiguity. He thought about a dozen different interpretations of Bol's words, including the literal one—that she really was convinced of his guilt and was simply gloating at him.

However, everything he'd learned about Mary Bol told him she wasn't the type to gloat to a prisoner, especially one with whom she'd formed a professional—bordering on personal—relationship. The message was so out of character for her that he was sure there *was* a hidden meaning to her words. She was telling him to subdue the guards, escape in the shuttle (that's why she had made special mention it was a stealth shuttle; it would be easier to avoid detection after his escape), and make his way to Earth. She also wanted him to know that Jinny and the others had been arrested, which meant he would have to figure out a way to rescue them.

Fighting a rising anger at the thought of Jinny in prison, Tyrus laid back on the bench in the cell, figuring he could catch 30 minutes of sleep before Bol's promised deadline to move him to the shuttle for transport. It would be a long trip to Luna in a shuttle, but he didn't know exactly when the opportune time for his escape attempt would present itself. So better to get what little rest he could now.

His own escape would be the easy part. The hard part would be finding and freeing Jinny, Riggs, and even Jynx.

---

Jynx drove through the morning, sometimes skimming along rural roads and sometimes floating along just above the treetops where she hoped the dense forest would mask her radar signature; she couldn't do that too often, as the varying heights of the trees and density of their branches made it hard to maintain the hovercar at a constant altitude. Twice she set the car down in forest clearings to avoid the searchlights of passing airships, and once, she sped right by a well-hidden country cop who must have been napping and didn't even turn on his lights to follow. She would have preferred to wait to travel only at night but knew that it was imperative to quickly put as much distance as possible between herself and Bainbridge Island.

By the time the sun had risen high in the sky, she was well into Oregon, taking the long way around something called the Portland Impact Crater and steering clear of Portlandia, the largest city in the region. She had to figure out her next move, and traveling in a straight line away from the Seattle area wasn't it. It was too predictable. Even so, she had to maximize the distance before she could get cute with the route.

First, she was hungry. She had searched the car unsuccessfully for a stash of food left by the previous drivers, but her swim across the Sound had burned a lot of calories, and the meager supplies she'd eaten at the vacation home hadn't been nearly enough.

Her stomach was rumbling, but she couldn't just stop and buy food. She had to assume that sometime in the last 14 hours since her escape, the authorities had released her picture to the public. Which meant she needed to find a place to go where the people were unlikely to have seen the news yet.

In that same vein, she had another problem. Jynx had no money. Her government babysitters had supplied everything she'd needed since arriving on Earth; they'd even allowed her to go shopping in the little town near the Bainbridge Island Ferry dock and paid for pretty much anything she wanted. But they had never given her any money of her own.

However, she had watched to see how the economy of the UE worked in those various transactions. She knew that most people used their subdermal palm computers to transmit financial information to receiving units set up in stores to make purchases—much the same way people used their watches to pay in the colonies. But, on a few rare occasions, she'd also seen people pay with physical cards made of plastic. These people appeared to be exclusively from the lower working classes; some of them didn't even have the near-ubiquitous palm implants. She'd heard them call the plastic pieces 'cash cards', or 'prepaid cards'.

A month ago, she'd evaded her handlers for a short period inside one store and bumped up against one of the people she'd seen use a plastic card. It had been an older man dressed in work clothes, with heavily calloused hands and a world-weary look. In the momentary tussle, she'd picked the card from his jacket pocket, where she'd seen him slip it after he'd paid for his small bag of groceries. Instead of stealing the card, she'd flung it onto the floor. Then, pretending to notice that the man had dropped it, she knelt to grab it and quickly examined both sides as she straightened up to hand it back to him.

She only had it in her hands for a couple of seconds, but that was enough time to see that there was no name or other identifying information on it, just a number. And in small print on the back side were the words 'funds on card fungible for the bearer'.

She'd had to look up the meaning of 'fungible' when she'd returned to her home that evening; her high school education was well behind her. She still wasn't ready to use the word in a sentence, but she learned enough to know that the cards were not tied to any single individual. Anyone holding the card could spend whatever money was on it.

So now, she had to find someone with one of those cards, and this time she had to steal it.

She found *him* at a roadside fast-food joint with a pickup window at the back that served a group of weary men and women who were obviously getting off the morning shift of some sort of manual labor job. They were dirty and tired, and most of them kept their eyes on the ground in front of them except for a few small groups that engaged in quiet conversation. None of them looked as sad or desperate as some of the poor she'd witnessed in the colonies, but they were beaten down by comparison with the higher-income folks she'd largely been around on Bainbridge.

Humans were humans everywhere, and that meant there were Haves and Have Nots. It was the same on every planet and station she'd ever been on, and even some of the larger ships. Put more than a few dozen humans together, and they just naturally separated into social classes. Jynx's family had been relatively poor by galactic standards but almost middle-class by the standards of the hole that was Drake's World. And she had learned to move amongst all sorts in her relatively brief career, so she carefully studied the men and the women around her as she loitered at the edge of the small gravel parking lot. She hoped that their working the morning and possibly even part of the previous night away had left them little time to watch the news and see her mugshot. She'd also parked the drug mule car half a block away so she wouldn't draw too much attention to herself.

*There!* After several minutes, she mentally picked one of the men. He was younger, the stubble on his face thinner and somewhat scraggly, as if he was desperately trying to adopt the unshaven, rough look of his peers but wasn't quite able to hack it. He stood alone, wearing a tattered t-shirt, not interacting with any of the others. And she'd seen him pay with one of the cash cards. He was also casting quick glances over at her every few moments but in an interested rather than suspicious fashion. She knew she couldn't look that good in yesterday's clothing, but she also knew some men wouldn't really care.

Jynx slowly and casually worked her way over to him. When she was about five meters away, he noticed her coming and looked at her with a mix of interest and wariness. By the way he scanned the surrounding crowd, she could tell he was a man with a past that hadn't been good to him. A small part of her felt just a sliver of guilt for what she was about to do, but she quashed it quickly. She hadn't survived this long by being sentimental.

His eyes stayed fixed on her until she was standing right in front of him, and she casually leaned one hip against the dirty pickup truck he was standing next to; she thought it probably wasn't his. She threw him a small smile and tried her best to make it look a little shy.

"Haven't seen you here before," she said, her voice soft and pitched higher to make her sound younger. She blinked and looked at the ground before looking back up and meeting his eyes. "You new?"

He shrugged, a look on his face that Jynx associated with no small amount of terror. This was not a man used to the attention of good-looking women. "I just started at the shipyard last week," he said, his voice cracking just a little on one syllable.

Up close, he was cute in the same way a mangy dog adopted off the street is cute, but he'd never be called handsome. But Jynx wasn't looking for a date, though she needed him to think that was on the table.

"That's nice," she said, still playing the part of the timid girl. "I'm looking for a new job myself. How is it there?"

"At the shipyard?" he asked dumbly, as if she might be asking about anything other than the place he'd just mentioned. She nodded, letting some of her hair fall in her face, and then reaching up slowly and tucking it behind her ear and kicking at the gravel of the parking lot. She was laying it on *thick*.

"Well," he said. "It's a job. Building ships for people with lots of money." He shrugged again and looked away from her gaze.

"Does it pay OK?" she asked, thinking she was going to have to prod every word out of him.

He shrugged again. That seemed to be his go-to move. Jynx fought the urge to roll her eyes. "I guess so," he replied. "A little more than minimum wage, but the benefits are OK: health; no dental unless you pay for it, but you get a discount at least."

She smiled, and he gave a shy smile back before breaking her gaze again.

"Sure sounds nice. I've been out of work for a couple of months now. Times are hard."

He nodded, taking on a sympathetic look.

"Foster family kicked me out a few years ago," she said, playing a hunch. She might be in her thirties but knew that men often thought she looked a lot younger when she wasn't glaring daggers at them. She had used that in several cons she and Riggs had played.

His eyes came up, meeting hers with sudden interest. "Orphan?"

She nodded, her hair falling across her face again.

"Me too," he said, his voice taking on a little more life.

"Really?" She looked at him with mock surprise. Her hunch had paid off. "But you seem so... put together," she lied.

He smiled at this and subtly puffed out his chest a little. The quickest way to manipulate a man, Jynx knew, was to make him feel good.

"Well, I got lucky. Found this job and the one before it," he said, then followed up quickly, "but it wasn't always this way. There's been hard times—a lot of 'em. But you just get through 'em and keep going."

"Wow," she said, brushing her hair out of her face again. *Could he be any more formulaic?* "I wish I had your optimism. Nothing ever seems to work out for me."

The instant the sympathy showed in his features again, Jynx knew she had him and tried not to smile.

"Well, you hang in there, and good things will happen to you, too," he said, a measure of newfound confidence in his voice.

Then, as if he'd just had the greatest thought of his life, he brightened further and said, "Say, why don't I get you an application from the shipyard? I'll even put in a good word for you."

Jynx made her eyes go wide and her mouth open in a bigger smile than she'd shown before. "You would do that? But we just met. You don't even know my name."

He held out his hand, some of the shyness returning. "I'm Toby. What's your name?"

She reached up and grabbed his hand. "I'm Victoria, but you can call me Vicky." Make him feel like he was in an exclusive club to get her nickname.

"There," he said with satisfaction. "Now we know each other, and I can recommend you for the job."

"You're so great, Toby. No one's ever this nice to me." She was laying it on *really* thick.

"Well," he said, breaking eye contact and kicking his shoe at the rocks this time, his embarrassment evident. "I'm just watching out for a fellow orphan. We've gotta stick together in this world, or it eats us up."

Jynx felt another twinge of guilt but hid it behind another smile. "Yeah, we really do."

Now came the harder part. Well, the harder *parts*. First, she was hungry.

"Say, Toby, I'm... never mind." She looked down at the ground and refused to meet his eye.

"What is it, Vicky?" He asked, the timbre of his voice going lower—the strong man there to save the damsel in distress. "You can tell me."

"I haven't eaten since breakfast yesterday. I ran out of money last week and got kicked out of the shelter I was staying in. Too many people. You wouldn't..." she looked hopefully at the window serving food, not having to feign the facial expression this time. It smelled great to a stomach as empty as hers.

"Oh, of course. Yeah. I can get you some food."

Fifteen minutes later, they sat at an outdoor picnic table on the edge of the parking lot while she ravenously downed a hamburger and a healthy serving of fried potatoes—it was amazing how fast-food staples were so similar in the Four Worlds and the colonies despite more than half a millennium of separation.

While she ate, Toby picked at his own food and opened up, telling her a good chunk of his life's story. Parents dead at the age of five—car accident. Some time in a state-run orphanage and then from one foster family to another. Some physical abuse here and there and a lot of emotional abuse at pretty much every stop.

Jynx made the occasional comment or asked a question to keep him talking. The more he told her, the more he convinced himself that he trusted her and the guiltier she felt. *I must be going soft,* she thought to herself more than once. Six months ago, bouncing around the galaxy with Riggs, she would have robbed this kid blind without so much as a second thought. Riggs was the conscience of their operation, not Jynx.

Perhaps it was the time alone that softened her, or maybe it was her worry over the fate of her one and only friend. Whatever the reason, she was kind of starting to like this Toby kid. But that didn't change what had to come next.

When they were both done eating, she put the shy and scared look back on her face. "Toby, do you think you could walk me to my car? I can give you my comm code there so you can call me about the job application, but I'm really kinda scared to walk there by myself."

"Sure, I guess." He looked around the parking lot in confusion.

"It's parked around the corner," she quickly added. "I, uh, I slept in it last night and was trying to figure out what to do all morning before I walked over here for food. Before I remembered I didn't have any money left."

"OK, let's go then." He stood up and reached out, grasping her hand to help her to her feet. It was *so* awkward, but it broke a little piece of the heart that Jynx had forgotten she had. *Poor boy. He's just a baby.* He was at least ten years younger than her.

She debated with herself all the way to the car. Her plan from the start had been to lure him here, away from the other men and women at the fast-food joint, so she could steal his cash card and anything else of value he had on him. She'd knock him out and leave him to sleep off the headache that would follow in the bushes by the side of the road while she made her escape.

However, by the time they got to the car, she was reasonably convinced that she couldn't go through with it and was preparing to wish him goodbye and keep driving until she found another mark. She should have just enough charge left in the car to make it to the next town and get herself in the right frame of mind to do what she needed to do to survive.

She was so troubled by this and so deep in thought that she completely missed noticing the other car parked about 20 meters behind her stolen one. But she did notice the two hulking men who stepped out from around her car when she was just a few meters away. One held a wooden bat, and the other proudly displayed a pistol in the waistband of his pants.

Toby gasped, and Jynx's heart fell.

"Thought you'd get away with stealing the boss' car, did you?" the man with the bat addressed Toby, ignoring Jynx. The other man wasn't ignoring her, but the look on his face wasn't one of accusation. He wanted something else from her than a car.

"What?" Toby asked in confusion, his voice heavy with fear. "I don't know..." he trailed off and looked at Jynx. "Vicky?"

Jynx cowered behind Toby, putting him between her and the two men and silently wishing to whatever power there may be in the universe that this wouldn't go the way she was certain it would. But momentarily freed from the distraction of her guilt, she was all Jynx again, and she was working all the angles.

"This isn't my car. I don't know whose it is," Toby said lamely as the two men approached. Even faced with a beating and possible death, he wasn't throwing 'Vicky' to the wolves.

"Oh, yeah?" said the man with the bat smugly. He stepped forward toward Toby, raising the bat to strike. Toby reached back to keep Jynx behind him and lifted the other arm to try to deflect the swing of the weapon. But his hand behind him found only air.

Jynx ducked around Toby, all pretense of the shy, scared young woman gone. She lashed out with her foot, right into bat man's knee, hearing and feeling the satisfying crunch as the thug screamed in pain. He involuntarily dropped to the ground, and Jynx grabbed the bat out of his hands and leapt toward the other man, who was about a meter behind his buddy.

The second man hadn't thought to draw his gun before, figuring that the wimpy-looking guy and scared girl were easy pickings, but now he fumbled for his weapon. Just as he finally got a grip on it and drew it from his waistband, the bat connected with his head, and he, too, crumpled to the ground.

Jynx reached down and grabbed the gun out of the second man's limp hand and then whirled to face the first thug, who was rocking on the ground and holding his shattered knee. Jynx stepped over to him, staying just outside the range of any stupid move he might make, and pointed the pistol at his head.

"Vicky?" Toby asked in confused awe, his mouth hanging open and his expression flitting between relief and terror.

"Sorry, Toby. I'm not who you think," she said, throwing him an apologetic grimace.

The man on the ground swore, saying all sorts of nasty things about her parentage and even calling her a few names she didn't recognize. His creativity almost impressed her. When he was done with his tirade, he looked her in the eyes. "Do you have any idea *who* you stole from?"

"No, and I really don't care. But you *are* going to tell me how you found me."

"Go to—" he spit out but stopped when she waved the gun in his face.

"Now that's not nice, especially since I'm being so generous that I haven't even shot you yet," Jynx said, putting cold steel into her voice. "Now, you're going to tell me how you tracked the car, or I'm going to put a bullet in your other knee and then work my way up from there. Understand?"

He glowered at her but said nothing. She didn't really want to fire the pistol. It was her first time holding, much less using, an Earth gun, and she genuinely wasn't sure if she had the safety off or if the gun had an integrated silencer or not. The last thing she needed was someone calling the cops and reporting gunfire. But she still held the bat in her left hand. A moment later, the man was screaming again as it shattered his other kneecap.

The string of new curses and epitaphs he let loose would have made even the hardest colonial criminals blush, and now Jynx was *definitely* impressed.

"Next one aims just a little higher than your knees, if you know what I mean," she told him coldly.

"Tracker," he gritted out through clenched teeth and a look of pure hatred.

"Where?"

"Under the left rear hover matrix. Painted to look like part of the metal."

"Watch him," Jynx said to Toby, who still stood with his mouth gaping open. It amazed her he hadn't turned and run away yet. "Make sure he doesn't make any calls." Toby just nodded dumbly at her.

She walked over to the car and lay down next to where the man had said the tracker would be. Feeling around, she found a bump with a slightly different texture than the rest of the car. With a little tug, it came loose, and she examined it and then dropped it to the rocky ground and crushed it beneath the heel of her shoe.

Walking back to the suffering thug, she examined the gun and found that, similar to colonial weapons, there was a stun setting. She keyed it on and shot the man. The blue bolt connected, and he went still and quiet, though she could see the rise and fall of his chest. She then checked on the other thug. This one had a head wound from where the bat had hit him, and his pulse was thready.

Now it was her turn to swear. She didn't want to add murder, even in self-defense, to the reasons that the Earthies wanted to lock her up. She looked up at Toby.

"You need to get out of here," she told him. "And forget that you ever saw me. Can you do that?"

He looked at her in confusion mixed with horror. She sighed. "After I'm gone, please call an ambulance. This guy needs medical attention."

Toby shook his head and walked over to where she knelt next to the man while she watched him with a look of confusion now on *her* face. He knelt down opposite her and grabbed the passed-out man's left hand, pressing in a certain spot and holding it for several seconds. The subdermal screen in the hand started flashing red.

"That just called an ambulance and gave them his exact location," he explained in a low voice. "But if you were from here, you'd know that."

*Blast*, thought Jynx. *He recognizes me now.*

"Listen," she told him. "Thanks for the meal, but you really will be better off if you forgot you ever saw me."

He just shrugged.

She stood without another word and walked back to the car, getting in the driver's seat and switching on the engine, ready to drive away. It surprised her when the passenger door opened, and Toby got in.

"What are you—?" she started to ask, but he just shrugged again.

"In for a penny..." he said. She hadn't heard that phrase since leaving the colonies, and it gave her a little brief sense of home to hear it used here, even in this situation. She really didn't want him to come, she told herself. She also didn't have time to argue with the boy. The sound of distant but fast-approaching sirens filled the air.

She gunned the engine and sped down the road, passing the ambulance as it came from that same direction. When she reached a fork in the road, she took the more rural looking of the two options. She needed some distance from the town, and then she could stop and think about what to do next. Hopefully, that included convincing this idiot in the passenger seat that staying with her was a bad idea.

---

Jinny stewed in the small waiting room, dressed in a drab orange jumpsuit complete with sewn-in gloves and a hood—everything but her face and the front of her neck was covered; someone had thought about her being a reader—and chains around her wrists that were fastened to a ring in the center of the room's small metal table.

From outside, she heard a buzzer sound, and the far door opened, admitting a man she'd never seen before. He was of medium height and handsome in a soft and out-of-shape kind of way, with brown hair and brown eyes to match. He regarded her with a solemn and sympathetic smile and sat down wordlessly at the table across from her.

He took a moment to open his left hand, where most Earthers had their subdermal implants, and peck away at it with the fingers of his right. Then, as if satisfied with what he saw on the integrated screen, he looked up at her and nodded.

"Ms. Ambrosa, my name is Clark Jeffries. The O'Leary's have hired me to be your attorney in the matter of United Earth versus Ambrosa. You've been charged with espionage, and it's my job to defend you against those charges."

Jinny eyed him suspiciously and said nothing in reply. She'd seen enough government subterfuge in her years as a reader that she wasn't ready to trust anything or *anyone* at face value. Even if the man did say Corey and Debra had sent him.

The attorney's mouth quirked upward in a knowing smile. "Congressman O'Leary said you'd be skeptical and cautious. They will kick me out if I make any contact that would allow you to read me. But O'Leary said I should mention Tyrus' mother."

Jinny said nothing but felt a sense of immediate relief. She and Tyrus had been careful not to tell the Four Worlds media about the reason she'd been able to turn him from killing her in the alleyway after he'd shot Alan Daily—that she had revealed to him that he *hadn't* actually killed his mother as part of his alpha training. Tyrus had told no one, and she had related the fact to only two people: Professor Tichner and Corey O'Leary. That this man knew to mention Tyrus' mother was enough to show that he was likely from O'Leary, as he claimed.

"OK, so let's say I believe you. What's my situation?" she asked.

"You're in federal custody in Houston, awaiting transport to a secure holding facility on Luna. The government says that's for your own protection—to avoid potential vigilante attacks here on Earth. I don't believe them. I think they're trying to get you out of the public eye, and so does Congressman O'Leary."

Jinny looked around the room frantically, worried that he'd just spoken so blatantly against the government in view of all the cameras and microphones she was sure were spread across the room.

Jeffries shook his head. "Don't worry. It's illegal for them to listen to a conversation between an attorney and his client, and they can't record video either, just watch through the two-way glass. So, unless they've got a really expert lip reader on the other side of that glass, they can't listen in or reconstruct our conversation later.

"Plus, we do things a lot differently here on Earth than you're used to in the colonies. I can say whatever I want against the government, and so can you, though I wouldn't advise saying *anything* to anyone without me present. They will use everything you say against you.

"Besides," he smiled. "I have an app on my palm implant that is scrambling the signal of the one camera and microphone they *do* have illegally hidden in this room."

She nodded slowly.

"So, right now, before they come up with a pretense to kick me out," he continued, "I need you to talk to me so we can plan your defense. Tell me exactly what they told you about why you're here."

"Well," she said slowly, "They mentioned some message, supposedly from the Council fleet, that suggested that Tyrus and I are spies here, and the agents who arrested me talked about espionage. It's all a lie," she hastened to add. "I'm not a spy, nor are my friends, and we've done nothing but *help* Earth since we got here." Her tone at the end let her resentment show through.

Jeffries nodded dismissively. "I know that, and so does Corey. It's the judge we'll have to convince, though I may push for a jury trial if we can find one that hasn't been unduly influenced by the government's propaganda. The message from the Council fleet hasn't been released to the public yet, but I'm expecting a convenient leak out of Houston anytime now. It is likely to turn a good amount of public opinion against you."

"So, what do we do?" she asked, frowning at the pessimistic picture he was painting. "You're my attorney. Do you expect me to just plead guilty and rot in here? I don't know how the legal system here works, but I know enough to understand that would be a bad idea."

She was immediately sorry for the harsh tone of her voice, but she had to admit she was a little on edge and upset after being betrayed by the same government she'd spent so much time trying to help over the last five months. Luckily, Jeffries took it all in stride and didn't look offended in the least.

"Of course not, but we *will* have to be thoughtful about your defense. For now, I can give you some potentially good news. They've arrested Cal Riggs and Tyrus Tyne, but somehow, they missed your friend Jynx. For what it's worth, that may keep them occupied looking for her for a while and give us the time we need to build the case to keep you out of prison.

"I've already filed a motion with a federal judge to dismiss your case based on the scarce evidence, but I don't expect it to go through. It's all pro forma at this stage," he continued.

Jinny had little concept of what that meant; even as a member of the Reader Corps, she'd had little interaction with the court systems in the colonies, and she imagined things worked much differently here. "So, again, what do I do?" she asked, trying to bring the conversation back to her original question.

He shrugged and smiled at her. "For now, trust your friends, the O'Leary's. And know that I am *very* good at my job."

He leaned forward, cupping his hands around his mouth so that only she could see his lips. Then he mouthed a few words before removing his hands and sitting back. Jinny suddenly understood that Corey O'Leary was sneakier than she'd ever given him credit for. She was also scared. Because if Corey had felt that the legal system would be on her side in this fight, he would have indeed sent an attorney like Clark Jeffries. But this man wasn't Clark Jeffries, and the only reason she could think of for Corey to send a blender instead was if he thought things wouldn't go her way and more active measures might be required to get her out of jail.

---

Jordan Archer mouthed just three words to Jinny Ambrosa: 'I'm a blender'. By the way her eyes widened afterward, she not only understood what he'd said but also the import of it. That was good. Because Iasonas had told him enough for Archer to know that, guilty or innocent, elements connected to someone high up in the UE government would make sure that the pretty young reader *never* left custody alive. O'Leary had been likewise frank when he'd messaged Archer just 24 hours before: if legal options failed, the blender would be called upon to get Ambrosa out by any means necessary.

Their conversation done and a few more platitudes exchanged, he left the meeting room where Jinny remained chained to the table. Once outside the government facility that held her, he sent Iasonas a message with the details of their conversation. He then sent a separate message to O'Leary—just in case he and Iasonas were *not* the same person. After that, he set about preparing for his next meeting as Clark Jeffries.

Before he got too deep into that, he sent yet another message to Cecily. She hadn't been responding to him for the past several days. It wasn't that unusual for them to go weeks without speaking to each other—it was often the norm when he was on extended assignments—but usually, when he did find an opportunity to reach out, she was quick to respond. The only thing he could think of was that she'd had to leave for Europa as she sometimes did to manage the businesses her father had left behind when he'd fled.

*She's probably in all-day meetings on Ganymede or Europa itself, or it's possible the messages aren't getting through because of a solar flare or something like that,* he reassured himself. But deep down, he knew something was very wrong.

# CHAPTER 16

As the three guards had walked Tyrus to the shuttle bay and led him aboard one of *Enterprise's* two stealth shuttles, he had watched them carefully, looking for any weaknesses he could exploit later to escape. It turned out that he was wasting his time; Mary Bol had one more surprise in store for him.

The launch from the *Enterprise* was uneventful. They were in orbit around a large moon—Tyrus guessed it was likely Titan; he could see the rings of Saturn out the viewport—probably to shadow the shuttle launch from prying eyes. He knew from Bol that anytime the *Enterprise* launched a fighter, a shuttle, or even a missile, it was momentarily visible to sensors, so she and her captains were careful where they did so.

The guards had put Tyrus in the shuttle's troop bay, which usually housed a boarding force and was fairly spacious for just one person, while they and the pilot stayed in the forward crew compartment. This represented both an opportunity and a wrinkle. While he was sure the guards were watching him via cameras, he was also reasonably sure he could get out of his shackles without making it obvious what he was doing. But then the problem was what to do next. With none of the guards in the compartment with him, all they had to do was leave him locked in there or even evacuate the air for just long enough to knock him out. Then he'd be right back where he started.

But all of his musings and planning became a moot point when, two hours after launch, all three guards made their way into the troop compartment and sat facing Tyrus from the opposite row of inward-facing seats.

One of them, whom Tyrus recognized as Chief Petty Officer Straczynski, *Enterprise's* chief of the boat (the carrier's senior enlisted man), was the one who had originally arrested him on the bridge. The other two he'd never seen before.

"Mr. Tyne," Straczynski said, nodding to him with an impassive expression.

"Chief," Tyrus replied, keeping his tone calm and civil.

"I want you to know, Mr. Tyne, that I don't trust you," the man said next and then sat and stared blankly at Tyrus as if waiting for him to respond.

When Tyrus didn't, he continued: "But Admiral Bol trusts you, and I trust her."

He nodded at the two spacers next to him. "And Roberts and Chang trust me."

When he said nothing more for a few moments, Tyrus broke his silence. "Where is this going, Chief?"

The man regarded him coolly for another moment, then shrugged and responded. "The Admiral thinks that the only thing waiting for you at Luna is a quick and *accidental* death before you can stand trial. Don't ask me why, but she's convinced. So, here's how this is going to work.

"In about 14 hours, we're going to reach the midpoint of our journey to Luna. We're taking a roundabout route to avoid the normal shipping lanes, so we can be sure to stay undetected and come into Luna from a different vector. Don't want anyone tracing our origin back to empty space and wondering just what might be out there."

He paused again, and Tyrus nodded as though to agree with him. The man was obviously going to mete out information at his own pace.

"So," continued the chief, "at that point in our journey, you're going to escape and subdue me and the boys here. You'll get your hands on Chang's gun and force the pilot to turn over the control codes to you using that."

Tyrus was genuinely surprised at the matter-of-fact way the man discussed betraying his duty as a sworn UEN spacer, and once again marveled at the loyalty Mary Bol inspired in her crews. Straczynski kept talking.

"After you've taken control of this shuttle, you're going to jam the three of us, plus the pilot, into that small escape pod down there." He inclined his head toward a hatch that led to the belly of the shuttle. "Then you'll launch us into the cold of space and take this shuttle and go do whatever it is you need to in order to stop this craziness. Understood?"

Tyrus considered for a moment. "Understood, Chief. And I'm guessing the reason you're telling me now instead of 14 hours from now is so that just in *case* the government breaks its long-standing bias and uses a reader to reconstruct events after you're rescued, they won't be able to go far enough back to see this conversation. Which also means that I need to act from here on out as if we haven't spoken, and when the three of you come back here in 14 hours, I need to make it look real."

For the first time, Straczynski smiled slightly. Then he turned and looked at Roberts and Chang. "See, boys, I told you this one is quick on the uptake."

He stood to leave, and so did the other two spacers, who preceded him out of the hatch. Just before leaving himself, Straczynski stopped and turned back to regard Tyrus, all evidence of the smile gone from his grizzled features.

"Understand one thing," he said in a low voice laced with menace. "You'll need to truly subdue us to make it look good for the medicos and any readers that come along. That means leaving a few bruises, maybe even a black eye or two. But break any bones or do any permanent damage to those two lads or the pilot, and you'd better *kill* me. Because if you don't, no amount of being quick on the uptake or as physically fast as I hear you are will protect you when I come after you. Not even God or Mary Bol will be able to shield you from me."

He paused, and Tyrus simply nodded to show he understood.

"And one more thing. You betray Admiral Bol; me and every man or woman who has ever served under her will hunt you down and then dance on your grave. Got it?"

Tyrus nodded again, keeping his face solemn.

After Straczynski left the bay and closed the hatch behind him, Tyrus leaned back in the uncomfortable jump seat. He didn't know the chief petty officer all that well, even after a few weeks on the *Enterprise*, but those last comments made him genuinely like the man and understand why Bol had chosen him for this mission.

What he couldn't understand was why Bol, Straczynski, or any of the others were taking such an enormous risk to free him before he reached Luna. The chief had said Bol believed he'd meet an untimely demise there, made to look like an accident. That, plus her willingness to commit treason on his behalf, meant there was *a lot* more going on here than he was aware of. He tried to think back to someone on Earth he might have upset enough since leaving the hospital that they would want him dead, but he couldn't think of anyone. There were plenty of people from his past life, but none were here in the Four Worlds aside from Jynx, and she wouldn't resort to subterfuges; she would stick the knife in his gut herself.

The only reasonable explanation was that someone wanted to silence him and his friends and stop them from agitating for United Earth to properly prepare for the Council invasion. And it had to be someone here in the Sol system. Because even if the Council fleet had sent a message implicating him as a spy, there would be no reason for anyone in the United Earth leadership to believe it unless they *wanted* to. On top of that, whomever it was had obviously decided to work outside the legal system and make sure he never got a chance to testify on his own behalf.

An officer like Mary Bol, loyal enough to not only make admiral but also to be given command of the most secret force Earth had at its disposal, did not betray her own government without an overwhelming reason. Though Tyrus knew there was a mutual attraction between them, it certainly hadn't progressed to where she would even consider betraying her oath for him. He also doubted she would let him go on her own initiative alone. Something was going on, and someone unseen was pulling the strings, both against him and in his favor.

He was still reflecting on that as he allowed himself to drift off to sleep, now knowing that he had a little less than 14 hours to wait before making his move.

---

## THIRTEEN YEARS AGO; 718 P.D.

The young boy called D5746J14L1 sat at the table, eating alone as he always did. Every day, he'd come to the small mess hall and ignore the other children there. They weren't special like he was. They knew it, and he knew it. In fact, he wasn't like them at all. So, they didn't mingle or mix. They just co-existed. And D5746J14L1 existed above them all.

He wasn't lonely; he didn't *need* anyone else. He had all he needed and all he wanted. He had the Council. The Council that had formed after a horrible war back on old Earth. That had stripped the despots and ineffectual world rulers of that day—the ones responsible for the war, either by causing it directly or being too inept to stop it—of all their power and privilege. The Council that had become the government—a benevolent government with no thirst for power, no predilection toward corruption, and no other desire than to bring peace and prosperity to mankind through reason, logic, and science. But even more importantly, he had the *purpose* that the Council had given him.

Because that same Council had chosen *him*. He was one of trillions of people, billions of ten-year-old boys, and they had chosen *him*. The thought made him... satisfied. Not happy—he could feign that emotion well enough but didn't really understand it. No, satisfaction was the right word for how he felt, and it was more than enough to know that in a galaxy in which everyone was equal, he was *better*.

He was better in every way: more intelligent, more talented, more physically perfect, and, most vitally, more loyal, which was interesting when he reflected on it. After all, he differed from every other child in the mess hall in one important way, one that they would never guess.

It made his loyalty to the Council all the more impressive. They told him that every day, the woman in the hall and the man's voice in the little white room. While he sparred with the fighting instructor, the silent older woman who never said an unnecessary word to him, he could hear another voice broadcast throughout the room telling him he was *special*.

And he believed it. He exacted every order with perfection, never having to miss a meal because he answered a question wrong or failed to put the Council first. He also didn't have the silly ties to his past life that plagued some of the other students. His parents had told him from the time he could remember that he was *not* theirs. He belonged to the Council. His father had talked about it as 'going home'. 'When you turn five, we'll take you home.' It had always been clear that his home wasn't with the man and woman who had birthed him and briefly raised him but with the Council that had made it all possible. Even his mother had almost looked relieved on the day they had dropped him off here.

He was content and satisfied here. The learning satisfied him. So did the fighting. A year before, they'd stopped simple hand-to-hand sparring and had begun training him on weapons. Not just the knives and guns and even telescoping batons he had been expecting, but weapons drawn from everyday life. He had learned how to maim with a bag of rocks, permanently injure with a kitchen spatula, and kill with a simple metal screwdriver. He'd appreciated the challenge of it, knowing that it was preparing him for remarkable things.

Then this morning, the voice in the room had told him it was almost time—almost time to *finally* use his training. It was almost time to exercise the will of the Council that had raised him to be their ultimate servant. The next phase of his training was to begin.

A bell chimed softly in the mess hall, and all the children, including D5746J14L1, stopped eating and obediently took their trays to the disposal area. Then they moved out of the room single-file through one of the three main entry doors at the front of the room. All except for him. He followed the instructions the voice had given him earlier and walked toward the lone door at the back of the room.

He heard some of the other children whisper as he did so, for none of them had ever seen that door used. But the voice of one of the women of the hall called out, "Quiet children," and the whispering immediately silenced. One would expect nothing less from a room full of the Council's enacters—its servants in training. *Useless genetic mutation,* the boy thought with disdain. *They should be loyal to the Council because of what it gives them, not just because some genetic code compels them.*

When he reached the never-opened door, he waved his watch in front of the control pad, and the door slid aside with barely a hiss. It was dark beyond, but he stepped through without hesitation and sensed the door sliding shut behind him, taking with it the light of the mess hall. The boy stood there in the dark, at rigid attention, waiting and listening.

Then the lights started. They *screamed* at him, so bright that they overrode his senses from multiple angles and almost drove him to the floor. But ever loyal and obedient, he did not allow them to move him, and within seconds he'd forced his eyes to remain open and not even squint, though the lights blinded him to the point of physical pain.

Then the multiple lights seemed to converge into just one, and a voice echoed in the room. It was a new voice, one that he had never heard before. It did not yell, but it was laced with authority. He had to strain to catch it as the light tried to deaden all of his senses.

"Who are you?" it asked a second time before he understood it.

"D5746J14L1, reporting as ordered," he answered.

"Why are you here, D5746J14L1?"

"I was ordered to report for a special exam."

"So, you were. Tell me, D5746J14L1, who is your father?"

His back straightened further as he understood the exam had already begun. "The Council," he answered with all the conviction he could muster in his voice.

"Good. And who is your mother?"

"The Council."

"To whom are you loyal, D5746J14L1?"

"To the Council," he answered, now with a sense of supreme satisfaction. This test was even easier than he'd expected.

"What does the Council provide?"

"Everything. The air we breathe and the water we drink come from the Council's terraforming. The food we eat comes from the Council's agricultural programs. The school we live in was built by the Council for its enacters and people like me to be safe and to learn how to serve the Council. The Council gives us *everything*."

"All correct, young D5746J14L1. But does everyone feel the way you do?" The question didn't surprise him because not everyone could be trusted, but *he* could be.

"No. Some people are bad and don't follow the Council," he answered firmly.

"That is correct," the voice answered simply.

Then the light abruptly silenced, and for an instant, he was mildly concerned that he'd somehow failed the exam. That would be… inconvenient. Then the room lit up again, though not as bright. This time, the light came from a holo hovering in front of him. It showed a view of the world outside the walls of the Academy, where men, women, and children walked happily along a street where hovercars moved sedately.

Then, suddenly, one of the hovercars veered off the road and into a number of the pedestrians, throwing bodies into the air while others fell beneath it. Men and women screamed or gaped in astonishment. Children cried. The car impacted the side of a building, crushing a woman in a business suit against it, and then came to a stop. The sunroof of the car opened up, and a man stood up from inside dressed all in black, including a black head covering and mask. In his hands, he held an assault rifle, which he brandished menacingly as he yelled something the boy couldn't make out.

Then the man started firing randomly into the crowd. After a minute or so, he stopped firing and yelled again. "Death to the Council!" D5746J14L1 could now plainly hear it. Then the man started firing again and again and again…

The boy smiled at the scene, which surprised him. Displays of emotion usually took intentional thought on his part, but this smile happened naturally. Watching the bloody massacre, he felt something he'd rarely felt this intensely before. He was *excited*!

Every day from then on, the boy visited the small room at the back of the mess hall after lunch. Every day the voice asked him the same questions. But every day, the holo it showed him was different. One day it was of a woman drowning her own children because she hated the Council and wanted to make a statement. Another day it was of a child blowing himself up in a rural school to protest the Council's educational curriculum. And another day, it was of a man blowing up an entire shopping center because he hated the peace the Council brought to humanity. Every time, the boy smiled and savored the excitement the images and videos produced in him.

Day after day, the holos continued, and day after day, he learned what it meant for men to be evil. And he learned that the evil resonated with him like a harmonic frequency. It was delicious.

---

### PRESENT DAY; AUGUST 2, 731 P.D.

Tyrus freed himself from his bonds minutes before Straczynski, Roberts, and Chang came into the compartment to 'check on him' at the set time. Less than 60 seconds later, all three lay incapacitated on the ground, Chang's gun covering them from Tyrus' large hand. He put them into the escape pod and used the pistol to stun all three of them and prevent them from trying to escape. Then he went to the cockpit to confront the pilot.

The man behind the controls was quick; he reacted instantly upon seeing his prisoner loose and almost cleared his pistol from its holster before Tyrus was able to subdue and disarm him. Luckily, he didn't need to resort to torture or even press too hard to get the man to surrender the shuttle's command codes, making him wonder if the pilot was also in on it but had made a show of drawing his weapon strictly for the cockpit recording devices. Either way, a stun blast from Chang's confiscated pistol sent him into oblivion, and Tyrus had to carry the man down the ladder and manhandle him into the escape pod with the other three.

In the end, Straczynski had a mildly broken nose, while Roberts and Chang were each bruised and banged up in various ways that would leave them sore for the duration of their stay in the escape pod but would otherwise heal quickly. The pilot would suffer nothing but a hangover from the stun blast and a bruised wrist from Tyrus' disarming blow.

Still, he was glad he wouldn't be anywhere near the four men when they awoke. They'd have nasty headaches and even worse dispositions, given that the escape pod had clearly *not* been designed with the comfort of four full-grown men in mind.

Comfortable or not, the pod would have more than enough life support for them to be rescued, even if the rescue vehicle had to come all the way from Earth's orbit. Tyrus was tempted to send a message to the UEN now to ensure a quick save but knew that he needed every minute he could get to burn clear from the scene, even in a *stealth* shuttle with full silent running protocols in effect. For all its accouterments, this shuttle had a normal reaction main drive and not the secret heatless drive that allowed its mother ship to be truly stealthy.

The question remained of where exactly he needed to go: Earth or Luna. Bol had hinted he should stay away from Luna, but if Jinny and the others had already been captured and transferred to the moon, then he would need to ignore the admiral's counsel. He got his answer an hour later when he was checking routine broadcast traffic from Earth and caught President Pereira's press conference. The man started with a fantastical and severely embellished account of the battle with the Council Navy, mischaracterizing them as a full-blown invasion force that the UEN and EN, under the president's fearless and steady leadership, had defeated and turned back. It was fantasy, but the man was careful not to say anything patently untrue that might come back to bite him later—political double-speak at its finest.

Tyrus wondered if the average citizen could do the math that the battle happened too far away for Pereira to have played any real-time role at all. Even with the Tachyon telegraph, the faster-than-light communication method only allowed small bits of information to be passed at a time, making it near impossible to micromanage a battle from afar. Based on some of the questions from the reporters, Tyrus didn't think they were fooled, either. But the president ignored them and pushed on.

For the first time, he also got to see the message that the Council fleet had sent to Earth, albeit surely an edited version, which was played halfway through the press conference. Then the president preened before the cameras as he not-so-subtly boasted of his quick thinking in having Tyne arrested without violence at an 'undisclosed location'. He heavily implied, but was careful not to state explicitly, that he thought Tyrus and Jinny were guilty of the acts of espionage the Council fleet's message had pointed at.

The man spoke more solemnly about taking Jinny and Riggs into custody than he did about Tyrus. For Jinny, he showed a poorly staged mugshot from the hours following her arrest. It was obviously calculated to downplay her attractiveness and reduce the public's sympathy for her. In Tyrus' opinion, it backfired. Jinny looked sleep-deprived and upset and had a wicked bruise forming on her cheek, but nothing could hide her natural beauty. If anything, it made her look more vulnerable and, therefore, more deserving of sympathy.

Riggs was scowling into the camera, and in the video that showed him being led to a government car in his underwear, he even threw a rude gesture with his bound hands, though it didn't translate well on Earth. It would have made Tyrus chuckle if not for the gravity of the situation.

Then came the interesting part of the press conference. The president shared a picture of Jynx and identified her as having escaped the Federal Police sent to arrest her and Riggs. He called for a worldwide manhunt and noted that she'd last been seen at her home on Bainbridge Island but was suspected to be far away from there by now.

Tyrus sat back and considered the implications of what he'd learned. Jynx on the loose meant he had an ally, assuming she didn't shoot him on sight. But he'd have to find her first. He wondered idly if doing so would even be worth it; perhaps it would be better just to rescue Jinny and Riggs on his own. But he quickly discarded that option. Despite the woman's antagonistic feelings toward him, Jynx was still part of their little team and deserved saving as much as the other two. She was also a capable operator and might be a significant asset in rescuing the others.

He was still thinking through the angles, using cold logic to tamp down his growing anger at Pereira's betrayal, when another press conference came on, this one from Congressman Corey O'Leary, presenting the view of the opposition. Tyrus already respected the man, mostly because Jinny trusted him, but he listened carefully to his statement for any clues as to the man's genuine sympathies. O'Leary didn't play to the cameras nearly as much as Pereira had and didn't have the other man's natural charisma and showmanship. Instead, he talked plainly to his audience and answered the reporters' questions with a direct earnestness that, in Tyrus' opinion, made him come across as far more trustworthy.

His message was simple. The battle had been a disaster, and the president and his party's lack of planning and unwillingness to take the warnings from Jinny, Tyrus, and their friends seriously were to blame. He hovered just on the edge of calling Pereira a liar about the events of the battle, probably to avoid anything that the president could condemn as revealing classified information. But he did go on to call the man out directly for his 'unfounded' arrest of Jinny and her compatriots based on a 'message clearly sent specifically to fool the administration into making such a heinous move'. He even presented analysis from an expert who claimed that the encryption of the Council messages was so laughably simple that it obviously pointed to the messages being *meant* for quick decryption.

Whereas the president had put most of the focus on arresting Tyrus, playing to his audience's fears of shadowy government assassins, O'Leary played to their sympathy for an innocent young woman. He downplayed Jinny's status as a reader—there was still so much fear of the enhanced on Earth—and played up her selfless and tireless dedication to helping the UE government prepare for the inevitable Council invasion. He shared a video of her working at a local food bank in San Diego, and another of her visiting a church—all imagery that would play well to a broad audience. He called her 'like a daughter to myself and my wife, Debra', his eyes misting up as he did so. He was good because he was genuine, and Tyrus was relieved to find himself honestly believing the man was still an ally.

Whether anyone listening would believe O'Leary's message was left to be seen. Tyrus had ever been amazed by how easily the public of any world would believe convenient and comfortable lies, especially when the lies were more palatable than the truth. It would be easy for most Earthers to accept that the Council threat had passed and that the government had wisely arrested spies in their midst, acting quickly to keep the populace safe.

Regardless, O'Leary had done his best, and Tyrus was grateful to him for it. Furthermore, he suspected the man was someone he might call upon for help in rescuing Jinny. But despite his conviction that O'Leary was an ally, he also didn't know how the man would react if asked to break the laws of the government and the people he served. So, he resolved to file away any use of the congressman as a plan C. Plans A and B he was still working on.

After the two press conferences, Tyrus set course for Earth—it sounded like that's where Jinny was still being held—and listened for a while to the meaningless debate by the news pundits, each adding their own speculations but no additional facts. Around the hour and 15-minute mark, he turned off the broadcast and forced himself to focus on building a plan of attack.

If the government of United Earth wasn't ready to take the fight to the Council, then perhaps it was time for Tyrus Tyne to take the fight to them.

---

Riggs had not expected to miss the modest house on Bainbridge Island. It had felt like such a prison to him; he never before having been tied to a planet-bound home for so long. But compared with actual prison, it had been a paradise.

For a day and a half now, he had sat in a solitary cell, his only human interactions the occasional guard walking by or bringing him one of his three daily meals. The first morning after his arrest, he'd been purposefully rude to them, hoping to spark some kind of reaction; angry people tended to talk too much or even brag about their actions to put the aggressor down. That could have given Riggs some kind of information about his predicament. However, the three guards placed over him had stoically ignored him.

By the end of that same day, he'd switched his strategy to polite but insistent questions. He thought that they'd at least be willing to tell him *why* he was being incarcerated. All he'd been told at the Bainbridge house was that he was being held on suspicion of something or another related to being a spy. What they could be referring to, he had no idea. He'd always been biased toward the criminal side of the law in the colonies, but *spy*? Never. They must have mixed him up with Tyrus.

Unfortunately, the guards stayed silent despite what Riggs felt was an earnest effort on his part to be... well, to be *earnest* with them.

So, since they'd brought him his breakfast on this, the second day, he'd largely stayed silent. Though occasionally, just to break the monotony, he broke out in song. Riggs liked to sing, though almost never to an audience. He'd walk around the *Blind Monk* singing at the top of his lungs sometimes, enjoying the sound of his own voice echoing off the mostly metal corridors. Jynx hated it. She said it reminded her of two cats fighting while they simultaneously drowned. Riggs had to admit he didn't have the best natural singing voice. Some of the high notes caused his voice to crack, and he often went monotone when he got to a bass part. But he still enjoyed it immensely.

So now, every few minutes, he'd open his mouth and cut loose with a loud rendition of *Home on Fertility*, *Ride the Void*, or *Rum on Rinali*. Each song was from a different genre, and Riggs only knew about half the words, so he filled the gaps by repeating the ones he knew or sometimes ad-libbing about the physical characteristics of one or all three of the guards. He sang especially loud when they brought him his lunch, extolling in song the virtues of smashed peas and rice.

He could tell by the guards' facial expressions that they didn't particularly enjoy his singing or the lyrical genius he displayed in singing about their halitosis, thinning hair, or pimples. But he shrugged it off. *Everyone* was a critic, and it helped break the boredom of being stuck in a cell on a planet where he'd never even committed a major crime (possibly one of the few in the galaxy with that distinction) and waited interminably for *someone* to tell him why he was there.

That afternoon, that someone finally appeared. The guards brought

Riggs into a small room with a metal table and left him there, hands chained to the table. Even though the design of the handcuffs differed slightly from what the Guard used in the colonies, they were similar enough. Riggs figured he could be out of them in about 60 seconds, 20 if he could get his hands on a safety pin, which would also save him from dislocating a thumb. But he decided it was in his best interest to keep that a secret until he was more assured of being in a position to escape. He was thinking about options when the visitor entered the room.

He was dressed quite unlike the guards, wearing a business suit and carrying an expensive-looking leather satchel that reminded Riggs of one he'd 'borrowed' off a business associate on Berlin Station in orbit of Neues München. The visitor was of medium height and reminded him of one of the holo vid stars from back in the colonies—handsome but in a soft and nonthreatening way—like you could trust your girlfriend around him while you were off pulling a score, as long as you weren't gone for more than a week or two.

The man sat across from him and smiled, showing perfect teeth below brown eyes and an almost identically colored mop of hair. "My name is Clark Jeffries," he began without preamble. "I'm an attorney, and I've been retained by the O'Leary's to represent you and Ms. Ambrosa."

"They have Jinny?" The words escaped Riggs' mouth before he'd really had a chance to think or absorb the identity and mission of the man.

Jeffries gave him a sympathetic look. "They took her from Corey O'Leary's house about the same time they arrested you. Just after they decrypted the transmission from the Council fleet."

"Transmission? From the Council fleet? What transmission?" Riggs felt like he was sitting down to watch a dramatic holo vid halfway through and had missed all the story setup.

The man, Jeffries, adopted an expression of sharp interest. "You mean they haven't told you why you're here?"

"They haven't told me anything!" Riggs practically yelled at the man, suddenly finding that this anger and frustration at the silence of the guards the past 36-plus hours was pouring out unbidden at the one and only man who had talked back to him in all that time. A day and a half didn't seem like all that long when you were on a spaceship you controlled and that could take you anywhere; in a jail cell, it had felt like weeks. This Jeffries wasn't necessarily a guilty participant in the crimes against Cal Riggs, but he was a convenient target for him at that moment.

"Not only that," he continued, "but they ambushed me in my house at night. Barged in the door, yelling at me to get on the ground. I was in bed! Asleep! Got the feeling they really enjoyed marching me outside in my underwear."

Jeffries looked upset now and shook his head with his mouth pressed into a thin line. "Did they at least read you your rights?"

Riggs scrunched up his face. He really didn't know what that meant. "They started to say something about a right to be quiet or some such nonsense—but then they all got distracted by something and just jammed me in the back of a car. Someone said something about me being a suspected spy, and then they haven't said so much as a *word to me since*!" He yelled these last words, turning his head back to the door through which he'd come, hoping the guards on the other side could hear him.

When he looked back at Jeffries, the man had a small smile again. "Listen to me carefully," the man said in a grave voice. "Did they ever mention the Espionage Act of 2481? Or did they ever tell you that you had the right to an attorney?"

Riggs thought for a second, then shook his head. "Not a word of either."

"Interesting," Jeffries said with a satisfied grin. "If they forgot to read you your rights and haven't even told you what you're being charged with...." He seemed to think a long time about such a simple thing, which made Riggs wonder if the guy was even a good lawyer. Of course, his bar for comparison was pretty low; most defense attorneys in the 47 Colonies were employed by the Council as so-called public defenders but really had little interest in helping people like Riggs.

Finally, Jeffries slapped a hand on the table, causing Riggs to jump slightly. "Well," the man said, "we might be able to get you out of here pretty quickly. I just probably need to call a judge."

Riggs sat back, crossed his arms, and let loose a grunt. What did he mean *'probably'*? "Yeah. Sure. It'll be my word against theirs. I know how this works."

Now Jeffries was smiling even wider. "No, Mr. Riggs. With all due respect, you know how it works back in the colonies. But here on Earth, we still have the rule of law and a constitution. And if they can't prove they read you your rights, with body cam footage or something like that, then they can't hold or even charge you. Keeping you for even a day without telling you the charges is against that constitution, which still means something on Earth. You give me two hours to make a few calls, and I'll be back here with a judge's order to let you go free."

Riggs felt his mouth open a bit in unabashed astonishment. "Seriously? Just like that."

The lawyer nodded. "Indeed. Just like that."

Riggs nodded, feeling the corner of his mouth involuntarily quirk up in a smile of his own as a wave of relief washed over him. He even felt some burning in his eyes but quickly convinced himself he must be allergic to something in the jail; they couldn't be tears. Then he stopped and stared hard at the man.

"Wait, you said you're representing me and Jinny. But what about..." he trailed off, his fine-tuned criminal instincts not allowing him to say the names of other accomplices, even though he knew that was ridiculous and *everyone* on Earth knew exactly who his traveling companions were.

Jeffries nodded solemnly in reply. "Well, I'm fairly certain that commotion that distracted the federal police from reading you your rights was them discovering that your friend Jynx wasn't in her house like they'd thought. I suspect you guessed the same. Her face has been all over the news for the last day and a half, and they haven't found a trace of her outside of a possible sighting in Oregon yesterday."

Now it was Riggs' turn to grin. Jeffries continued. "And Tyrus Tyne. Well, he was taken into custody by the Navy and put on a shuttle to the lunar naval station. However, he overpowered the guards on the shuttle, stuffed them in an escape pod, and stole the ship." He paused and, as if it was an afterthought, added the word: "Allegedly."

"Where is he now?" Riggs asked, his voice falling to a whisper.

Jeffries shook his head and shrugged. "No one knows. Just like Jynx."

Riggs sat back as far as the chains would allow and looked up at the ceiling, grinning even wider, causing the lawyer to cock his head to the side and give him a look of confusion. "I'm surprised, Mr. Riggs," he said. "I would have expected you to be much happier about your co-pilot being free than Mr. Tyne, who, by your own narrative in the news, you'd only known about a day before arriving in the Sol system."

Riggs shrugged. "I'm pretty happy about Jynx getting away," he said, looking back at the man. "But your government has absolutely no idea the *hell* they've released upon themselves with Tyrus Tyne on the loose."

Jeffries looked confused again. "Well, I had heard he was some kind of government assassin, but that supposedly he's turned over a new leaf and broken his enacter programming. So, why should our government be that afraid of him?"

Riggs scoffed in response and shook his head, then smiled still wider and showed his teeth like a predator, leaning forward to look Jeffries square in the eye. "Because 'assassin' doesn't describe a tenth of what that man can do. He wasn't just a government agent. He was *the* government agent. I have it on good authority that he single-handedly put down a rebellion on Phoenix and later ended a civil war on Yukon solidly in the Council's favor. There isn't much that man *can't* do.

"And he is obsessed with the safety of one person—Jinny Ambrosa. You see, they're friends, and he doesn't have all that many of those. So, if she's in government custody…" he paused, savoring his next words, "he will burn this planet to a cinder if that's what it takes to get her free."

Jeffries sat back in his seat, wearing a look of deep thought tinged with just a bit of a mirror image of Riggs' wicked glee. "Well then, Mr. Riggs. We'll just have to hope that I'm a good enough attorney to get

Ms. Ambrosa out of the government's custody *before* Mr. Tyne feels he needs to do it himself."

Riggs nodded. "Now, you keep talking, mister, about some message from the Council Navy that supposedly got me and my friends in the government's crosshairs. How about you tell me all the things I've missed being stuck in here the last couple of days?"

Jeffries did just that. Then, true to the man's word, ten minutes short of his estimated two-hour deadline, a visibly upset guard escorted Riggs out the front door of the jail, where he saw sunlight for the first time since his arrest and found Jeffries waiting in a large hovercar that took them to the nearest Loop station. From there, they boarded a capsule for La Costa, near San Diego. There, in Corey O'Leary's home office, 'Jeffries' dropped the act, and Riggs officially met Jordan Archer.

---

For the first few hundred kilometers, Jynx and Toby had ridden in relative silence, stopping only to charge the car at a power station once, which Toby had wordlessly paid for with his cash card. Now, just over 24 hours after they'd first met, they were sitting in a copse of trees somewhere in rural Idaho, having just awoken from a brief nap and waiting for darkness so they could resume their travels.

It was then that Jynx finally decided that she wasn't going to beat the boy at a contest of who could stay sullenly introspective the longest, and she started talking.

"You don't have to do this—come with me—you know. It'll just get you in trouble."

He seemed to consider this thoughtfully for a moment but then gave one of his patented shrugs and smiled. "Yeah, because this is so much worse than heading home to my dirty apartment I share with five other guys and trying to get some sleep before I work the *next* early morning shift. At least this car is quiet. *You* try finding some peace with five dudes who all work different hours and are coming and going constantly."

"What..." she didn't know what to say after a statement that was so incongruous with the gravity of their situation, so she asked the first question that came to her mind. "What's a dude?"

He looked at her funny and then shrugged again. It had been somewhat cute the first time he'd done it when she was flirting and trying to get him to buy her food and then follow her to her car so she could rob him blind. But *now,* the constant shrugging was just getting annoying.

"I don't know. I guess a dude is just a guy. Unless it's a girl, which it can be. It's slang, you know."

Jynx just nodded. "OK, but at least in your dirty, noisy apartment full of dudes, no one is hunting you down to *kill* you."

He smiled oddly at that as if she'd just told him he'd won a contest for a free vacation. "Well, you haven't smelled the apartment, so you really have no idea."

Despite herself, Jynx guffawed and then laughed out loud. The sheer ridiculousness of his casual manner contrasted with the desperation she'd been feeling for so many hours that she couldn't help herself. Before she knew it, she was still laughing, but tears were falling down her cheeks. And then she wasn't laughing anymore.

Jynx couldn't remember the last time she'd cried. It might have been when Dax had stolen her high school dance date, Kurt. She hadn't even cried when she'd learned her mother had died, though perhaps she had shed a few tears for her father.

But she cried now, and it felt like she would never stop. It was as if all the frustration of the last two days since her escape, plus all the caged nervous energy from her five-month involuntary 'vacation' on Earth, came out in a single moment and mixed with the suppressed emotions of her years of loneliness. Or at least, that's what Jynx would have thought if she were a self-reflective type of person. But she wasn't, so she quickly tamped down all thoughts of *why* she was crying and just let herself cry.

"Was it something I said?" she heard Toby ask in a faint voice from the passenger seat. He sounded genuinely confused, and she couldn't help but laugh a little again through the sobs and the tears.

Fifteen minutes later, when Jynx had cried out every tear she had and reverted to silent contemplation of the car's steering wheel in front of her, Toby chose to break the stillness.

"Look, what I had back there wasn't all that bad, really, but... Well, I guess you could say that I've never had an adventure in my entire life. I've bounced from orphanage to foster home and back again, but my life has been just living one day at a time and trying to survive to see the next one. So, when I saw you take out those guys and realized who you were...." He shrugged again and went silent, and Jynx felt a burning desire to break his shoulders to prevent him from ever shrugging again, warring with an equal desire to ask him to finish his thought. For his own safety, she just stayed silent.

Finally, he opened his mouth to speak again. "Well, I guess I thought to myself, 'Toby, you've been looking for some kind of adventure and never thought it would come. Maybe it's time to get in the car with the pretty and dangerous girl and take a risk'." He shrugged again. "So, I did."

Jynx considered it. It was so cheesy it could have come from a B movie holo vid. It even reminded her of one she'd seen back in the colonies, though Toby would have no way of knowing that. Then she frowned. "You know, I was planning to *rob* you back there," she said. "I brought you back to my car so I could get you away from the crowd and steal your cash card. Those thugs showing up saved you from *me*."

At her unexpected—even to her—admission, he surprised her as he harrumphed and shook his head. "No, you *were* going to rob me. I knew that from the moment you walked up to me."

She looked over at him with a suspicious glare. "How? How did you know?"

He shrugged—she was *really* going to break his shoulders at some point on this trip—and smiled awkwardly. "You don't spend your life in foster care without learning to read people's hidden intentions. I knew, but I played along. I thought it might be nice to have lunch with someone who, well, you know, looks like you, even if it was all a farce."

Jynx shook her head. "So then, *why* did you follow me to my car?"

He shrugged—again!—and looked over at her with a smirk. "I thought maybe I could rob *you*."

"Wait," she said in exasperation. "You bought me lunch because you thought I was pretty, even though you knew I was going to rob you? And you followed me into my trap because you thought you could turn the tables on me? Oh boy, are you lucky those drug dealers showed up and saved your butt!"

Then she threw him another look. "You said I *was* going to rob you. What did you mean by that, exactly?"

He didn't shrug this time, but he smiled. "Well, about halfway to your car, I could tell you'd changed your mind."

Jynx couldn't help smiling back now. "Well, aren't you something? And here I thought *I* was conning *you*. When all you wanted was some time with a pretty girl, and what? A ride out of town?"

Toby's smile grew wider, and he shrugged again. "I mentioned adventure, too, didn't I? And getting away from that smelly apartment!"

Jynx laughed again, and this time it didn't turn into a bout of sobbing.

---

## THE NEXT DAY; AUGUST 3, 731 P.D.

"I need you to read one of the guards," the blender impersonating Clark Jeffries said calmly to Jinny from across the small metal table.

This time when he'd visited her, just two days after his first visit, he'd said nothing upon entering the small room but first waved a device from his pocket in the air. When it had beeped, he'd momentarily left the room. As the door was closing behind him, she'd heard him yelling at the Guards about a listening device. When he'd finally returned and waved the device again—this time with no beeping from it—he'd told her it was safe to speak openly. Apparently, he trusted whatever the little device was more than the app he'd used to scramble the listening devices on his first visit.

"Are you insane?" she asked in a sharp whisper. It had been three days since she'd seen more than the paltry bit of sunlight the small square window in her cell admitted, and she was irritable and terrified.

"They watch me like a hawk and never let me get close enough to touch any of them." She held up her hands, covered with the gloves sown to the sleeves of the prison jumpsuit. "It's not exactly like I can just reach out and touch them with my hands, either." The gloves also made her personal hygiene somewhat challenging, but she chose not to share that with the blender.

The man nodded. "You're right, of course, but I have a way to guarantee that *they* touch *you*."

She eyed him skeptically, refusing to ask him to elaborate. This was just his third visit to her in as many days, and each time he'd asked a lot of questions of her but gave up almost nothing in return. It was already growing frustrating and making her doubt he really had any plan to help her. Though she had been gratified yesterday to learn he'd gotten Cal out on a technicality, he'd given no hint of how he planned to get *her* out.

Finally, he seemed to give up the mental game of chicken and chose not to wait for her to ask him what he meant. He reached inside his coat pocket and withdrew a pen and a piece of paper. He slid them across to her side of the table.

"The guards aren't listening anymore, but they *are* watching. So, I want you to take that pen and write a few random numbers on that paper. They'll think you're giving me information to help with your defense. After you're done writing, I want you to put your finger on the tip of the pen and click the button on top."

"And why would I do that?" she asked skeptically.

"Because it encases a small needle that will pierce through your glove and deliver a poison directly into your bloodstream," he said, so matter-of-factly that she looked back at him in confusion instead of the outrage she should have felt. He smiled as if knowing he'd won their little war of words.

"Don't worry," he continued. "It won't *kill* you. It will make you sick. It will also, unfortunately, be extremely unpleasant, but it will help you display symptoms you could never fake. You'll start to sweat profusely, then you'll have a convulsion—you should really try to keep your tongue away from your teeth—and then you'll collapse and look to any reasonable person like you're dead."

She raised an eyebrow at him. "You've got to be kidding me."

His smile disappeared, and he took on a serious tone. "No, because if you do that, then the guards will come into your cell, and the first thing one of them will do is check your pulse. It will be a reflexive part of their training, and they're likely to do it *before* they think twice about you being a reader. And while you will *look* like you're completely unconscious, even dead, this particular drug only affects the body, not the mind. You'll be in hell, paralyzed for an hour or more, unable to even open your eyes. But your mind will be fully alert. That will make the paralysis an absolutely horrific experience for you, but it will have the positive effect of allowing you to read the guards when they touch you to take your pulse and later to move and treat you."

She looked at him with horror. "And you're sure it will work? Have any other readers tried this?"

He shrugged. "You know where I'm from. Is it so hard to believe that this might have already been tested on folks just like you?"

She frowned, recognizing that he hadn't actually answered her question. Then she recalled where she was and wiped all expression off her face. "Just how is this going to help me get out of here?" she asked, whispering again, not fully trusting his assurances that the guards couldn't listen in.

He replied in a normal tone. "We know they were planning to kill Tyne when he got to Luna. Don't ask me how, and don't worry; he's escaped." *That* was new information for Jinny, and she fought the urge to smile.

"Now," he continued, "they're transporting you there, as we knew they would. But we don't know what their full plan is. If the plan is to kill you when you arrive on the moon, then we need to get you out *before* you're moved up there. That, unfortunately, involves some fairly serious risk on the part of myself and everyone else involved, including your friend, Corey." He shrugged as if accepting the risk was second nature to him.

"But, if they're *not* planning to kill you when you arrive there, we can get you out on Luna, especially if they take you to any of the government-run prisons there. We have contacts in nearly all of them. So, if our legal options fail, it would be easier to rescue you up there when the government is feeling all warm and secure than it would be here. And that's only assuming we can't get you out the legal way, which I'm working on."

He stopped and looked down at the pen and back up at her expectantly. Jinny wasn't quite convinced.

"Two questions," she said in a no-nonsense tone. "First, Cory obviously brought a *blender* in," she mouthed the word, not quite ready to say it out loud even with the guards only watching, "so why couldn't they bring a reader in who could secretly read the guards with a simple handshake? They wouldn't be avoiding a reader they've never seen and whom they don't know was one. And second, why would the guards have any knowledge of what's going to happen to me on Luna? What makes you think they're looped in like that?"

He sighed, an unexpected reaction from the normally collected man, and cocked his head with a strangely sympathetic look on his face. "To answer your first question, let's just say we don't have any other readers available to help us right now. I'm a bit of an anomaly myself; there aren't all that many blenders who risk doing what I do, and even fewer readers. Being caught operating outside Australia carries a pretty stiff penalty. As to your second question, whoever is planning this whole thing, and we suspect but don't know for sure it's Pereira or any of his people, will want to keep the circle small so that nothing gets out. But they also will want to manage the risk. That means keeping at least one guard in the loop so that they're close to you and can make sure everything happens according to plan.

"Still," he shrugged, "there's no guarantee that the guard who checks your pulse will be one who knows anything. So, there's risk in all of this. But either way, we'll have more than we have right now."

Jinny sighed, knowing that, with no other options, she was going to agree to go along. "So, what happens *after* I read them?"

"Well," he sat back and looked a bit more comfortable, sensing her surrender. "Protocol says they have to call your attorney immediately if anything happens to you. A seizure and near-death experience certainly qualify. Of course, if they *don't* call me, that tells us something as well. Either way, I'll be back here within a few hours, and you can tell me then what you learned. So..." he looked down meaningfully at the pen and paper in front of her again.

She pursed her lips and gazed at him intently, her eyes boring into his. Of course, they really *weren't* his eyes; they were counterfeits of the real Clark Jeffries' eyes. She had no idea if she could really trust him. He'd told her that Corey O'Leary had been denied his petition to visit in person, but she only had his word and that one little tidbit about Tyrus' mother, to know that Corey had sent him. What if someone had somehow gotten that information out of the congressman? If that was the case, this could all be an elaborate ploy by the government to kill her before she even got to Luna.

But if it was, it was way too complex and convoluted to make sense. There were better ways for her to inconveniently but accidentally die while in custody. Besides, if they wanted to administer a drug like the blender was talking about, they could just slip it into her food.

So, Jinny took a leap of faith, a word she'd only learned the meaning of since arriving on Earth, and picked up the pen. Twenty seconds later, after writing down two words and some numbers, she slipped the pen down so that she pressed the tip against the palm of the same hand that held it and clicked the top. She felt a small pinch through the glove and handed the pen back to Archer. It had been her minor rebellion to inject the poison into her palm instead of her finger as he'd instructed, but his facial expression didn't betray that he'd even noticed.

About half an hour later, after Archer had left and she'd been put back in her cell, she felt the first wave of heat and then chills. She broke out in a cold sweat and stumbled as she made her way to her cell's small sink to splash water on her face. She intended to walk back to her bunk before the convulsions and eventual paralysis hit, but she never made it. Halfway across the tiny room, her body spasmed, and pain coursed through her.

She fell in a heap to the floor, her head bouncing painfully on the hard tile of the cell, and her body jerked and shook there, bruising her elbows, heels, and the back of her head even more as she flopped around.

After what seemed like an eternity, her body finally stopped convulsing, and her eyes involuntarily closed. She went to open them and felt a trickle of worry when her eyelids didn't respond to her command. That trickle turned to panic when she tried to move her hand up to her face, and it didn't respond, either. She could feel her entire body, but she couldn't make it do *anything*!

Through the cloud of panic, she remembered what the blender had told her about the paralysis and the horror she'd feel. But now that she was in it, her clinical understanding of what was coming had not prepared her in the least for the absolute terror of being trapped in her own body, unable to move or react in any way. Her one and only solace was that she was still breathing, but she had no control over that, as her body's auto-responses took over, and it filled her with a dread that even that might stop after every breath.

As the man had said, she was in hell. She tried to scream, to call out, to do *anything*, as an intense feeling of claustrophobia came over her. It was like she was buried alive, unable to move to help herself. Had she known what this would truly feel like, she never would have agreed to do it.

Such was her state of hysteria that she almost didn't hear the footsteps approaching rapidly down the hall. She did hear the cell door clank open and felt what had to be two fingers press against the artery in her neck, checking for a pulse.

The fingers lingered for only a few moments, but it was enough. Memories, thoughts, and intentions of the guard flooded into her mind. She saw nearly his entire life in an instant, in the typical overwhelming way she'd grown accustomed to. She even had enough time to go deep into his memories, clinging to them like a life raft as she desperately sought *anything* to distract her from her horrible predicament.

Had Jinny been physically capable of gasping at that moment, she would have done that and more when she came to the part of what the guards and their shadowy leaders had planned for her when she arrived on Luna. It wasn't the accidental death that Archer had expected at all. It was so much worse!

# CHAPTER 17

"How could you have let this happen?!" demanded Corey O'Leary, the shout sounding louder than it was in the confines of his home office. The only other occupant of the room watched the outburst placidly, betraying no emotion whatsoever in response to O'Leary's accusing tone.

"I brought you into this to get her out, not to get her deeper in! Assuming she's even still alive!" the tirade continued, and Corey slammed his hands down on the mahogany desk and stared daggers at his guest.

Jordan Archer pressed his own lips into a thin line. The worst part of the congressman's tirade was that he was right to be so upset. Faking Jinny Ambrosa's collapse and near-death to get her a chance to read her captors had been Archer's idea. He'd sold O'Leary on it as the best plan to gather intelligence on the president's intentions for the reader and her friends. He'd come up with the plan in the moment, during a brainstorming session with the congressman, who had reluctantly given his blessing. Jordan had texted the plan to Iasonas afterward, and his unknown employer had neither endorsed nor condemned the move, so he'd chosen to proceed.

He'd fully expected the guards to either shrug off the incident as just a fainting spell or to brush the entire thing under the rug to avoid it appearing that they'd been neglecting or abusing their prisoner. But in the end, they'd done the one thing Archer had failed entirely to anticipate. Which is why, hours later, he was here in O'Leary's office instead of back with Ambrosa, learning what she'd read from the guard.

"We knew it was a risk," he said simply. "But we... *I* miscalculated." Jordan had learned early in his career that accepting personal responsibility for his mistakes was the best way to not only diffuse the anger of his accusers but also to learn from his errors and avoid similar ones in the future.

"Miscalculated? Hmph," replied O'Leary, his voice only slightly calmer as he got up and paced the room. "I'll say. They're telling us she's *dead*." The man's eyes turned soft, and for a moment, Archer thought the elder statesman might cry. When he spoke again, his voice was low and caught a bit. "Do you... Do you think she really could be?"

Archer had been considering that question since he'd been turned away at the prison by a guard who had solemnly told him that Jinny Ambrosa had collapsed in her cell, hit her head, and died from brain trauma shortly thereafter. He'd considered it all the way in the aircar to the Loop station, on the Loop ride to San Diego, and on the quick trip from the station to the O'Leary home.

In all, he'd been considering that question nonstop for the last two hours. In that time, he'd arrived at his answer, mulled it over, attacked it from various angles, and settled on it with a firm conviction. He still paused and appeared to consider O'Leary's question once again, for no other reason than to show the congressman just how seriously he took it.

He finally spoke slowly and deliberately. "She's alive. I've requested to see the body, which normally an attorney can do immediately; at least, that's what Jeffries told me. I got nothing but evasion. Even when Jeffries called one of our friendly judges, she refused to consider a court order until tomorrow. Someone obviously got to her first."

"But what does it possibly buy them to claim that Jinny's dead if she isn't? The truth has to come out eventually when there *is* no body, doesn't it?" asked O'Leary, his expression showing his dissatisfaction with Archer's answer, but his eyes betraying his sincere hope that the fixer was right.

The blender nodded slowly again and rubbed his nose. "Listen, sir. Bodies get lost in the system. It happens. Or they could claim a biological hazard and that they had to cremate her. She *is* in jail for suspected espionage against Earth, so it wouldn't be a stretch for the public to believe she was trying to somehow infect the prison staff with a biological or chemical agent, and it backfired on her. There are a number of creative ways they can explain a missing body."

He shrugged. "In retrospect, I should have guessed they might use her near-death experience to fake her actual death. We knew they'd suspect me of slipping her something; there was no way to do it without the timing being pretty obvious. Since they didn't know the rest of our plan, they may be throwing us a curve ball to see how *we* react, especially since there's really no way for us to *know* that they're lying. They probably hope that we'll assume our plan went awry and walk away."

O'Leary nodded thoughtfully and reached up his hand to rub his own nose. It was an affectation of his when he was thinking deeply, and Archer hadn't been able to help but mimic it throughout the course of this meeting. The curse of being a blender.

"So, we can't know for sure, but if we want any hope of pulling this thing off, we *have* to assume she's still alive," the congressman mused.

"Are we sure they're really Pereira's people? The ones pulling the strings against Jinny? It would really help to know for sure who we're up against."

Corey rubbed his nose harder and shook his head again. "I don't know. That's the most infuriating part of all of this. We *suspect* Tabitha Givens is up to her eyeballs in it. But either Pereira really is clean and just too dumb to know what his chief of staff is doing right under his nose, or they've done a terrific job at keeping his involvement a secret."

"And your best guess?"

The nose rubbing stopped, and the congressman took on a sober look. "Luiz Pereira may be many things—stubborn, misguided, politically hungry, even downright underhanded at times—but I don't honestly believe he's that dumb. He *has* to at least know Givens and her cronies are up to something."

Archer nodded thoughtfully. "That complicates things. We thought we were fighting against a political appointee, but now we think it's the actual leader of the world that's against us, at least by proxy. The *elected* leader, no less."

"Don't you think I know that?!" O'Leary snapped, then looked chagrined. "Apologies, I'm a bit on edge. All this," he waved his hand vaguely in the air, "is driving me to drink, and I promised Debra years ago I'd given that up for good." Archer almost snorted. He'd met several times with the congressman over the last month and rarely seen the man in his private office without a drink in his hand. Still, the fact that O'Leary had apologized to him spoke volumes. Few of Archer's previous employers cared about his feelings at all; he was an employee, practically a piece of furniture, and not worthy of their consideration. O'Leary was different. It was the one major thing about the man that made Archer doubt his theory that O'Leary and Iasonas were one and the same.

"But I agree," the congressman continued, "that we have to assume you're right and that Jinny is still alive. We also have to cope with the fact that we very well may be fighting *directly* against United Earth's elected leader. That removes all ambiguity in what we're doing. It's high treason. There's no technicality we can use to get off if we're caught. On top of that, there's only one outcome that gets us to success, and it *doesn't* necessarily also lead to us getting out of this alive."

"You're absolutely right," Archer said matter-of-factly. As a spy—and worse, as a blender operating illegally outside of Australia—he was used to being on the edge of treason and death, but it was an unfamiliar experience for the congressman. Nonetheless, Jordan wasn't about to coddle the man. He'd made his bed and all that. "However, if she's still alive, sir, all we have to do is alter the plan a bit. First off, we should assume that they'll move her to Luna faster. We also have to assume that they won't send her to any of the government-run prisons; too much paperwork and no way to hide someone who is *supposed* to be dead. That leaves only one option on the moon, and she's probably already on her way there. So, we'll have to go with Plan C and get her from the Luna black site instead of while she's in transit."

Corey's eyes widened. "Plan C? Wasn't that the one you said had less than a 20 percent chance of success?"

"No. I said less than 15 percent. But that's still more than zero, and those are the chances of our first two plans succeeding with this new wrinkle."

Corey sat down hard in the overstuffed leather swivel chair behind his desk and regarded Jordan with a concerned frown. "So that's what it comes down to, does it?" He sighed and sat up straighter, his eyes never leaving his guest. "What do you need from me to maximize our chances of this working?"

Jordan Archer allowed himself a small, tight-lipped smile. He'd brought a list. But first… "Is Cal Riggs still in your guest house?"

Corey nodded, narrowing his eyes. "Hasn't stepped foot off the property since you brought him here."

"Good. Because we'll need his piloting. What about Tyne? Do we have a way to contact him yet?"

O'Leary frowned. "I might. He disappeared the moment he stole that shuttle. And the admiralty has closed ranks against anyone who asks about it. But I'm talking with an old friend over there and think I've convinced him that I'm on their side."

Archer nodded. Had O'Leary not said something to that effect, Iasonas had ordered him to push harder on the man to find a way to contact the ex-alpha. It cast further doubt on his theory that Iasonas and O'Leary were the same person, though the congressman could be playing a subtle game to keep Archer off balance.

"Good," he said. "Because the only plans I can come up with involve a man with Tyne's special talents. We need him on this." That was true, and not just because Iasonas *insisted*, for reasons he'd chosen not to share with Archer, that Tyne be part of any attempt to rescue Ambrosa.

"I know that!" snapped O'Leary. "I'll get that part done. You just start laying the rest of the groundwork. And try and figure out something more concrete than the vague plan you outlined earlier. This *has* to work!"

A few minutes later, after going through the rest of Archer's list of things needed to even start planning the escape, the meeting was over, and the blender left. On the aircar ride back to the Loop station, he sent a summary of the discussion to Iasonas, mildly amusing himself with a mental image of O'Leary reading a synopsis of the meeting he'd just been a part of.

# CHAPTER 18

Tyrus sat quietly in the large building that felt like a portal to a world from the past. The desk at which he sat had a touchscreen display built into it and was as modern as anything outside the establishment. But surrounding the small cluster of desks were row upon row of shelves that held something Tyrus had rarely ever seen in the 47 Colonies: paper books.

He'd come into the building because it was largely deserted and boasted of a direct feed into the global Internet at every seat. However, on his way in, he'd been overwhelmed by the sight of so many physical books and had stopped for several minutes just to pick a few off the shelves and read the first few pages, carefully and reverently rubbing the paper between his fingers as he did so.

He had no idea why he felt such awe in doing so. The first book had been a dry historical text about a long-forgotten war. The second had been a cookbook about something called an artichoke. And the third had been a romance that started with such a scandalous first scene that he'd quickly returned it to the shelf, his ears burning as if his dead mother had walked into the massive building and caught him reading it.

No, his reverence had nothing to do with the contents of the books he saw here. Still, he couldn't deny that reverence just the same. Even had there not been signs urging silence throughout the building, he would have walked these rows of shelves in quiet solitude, fearing that his voice would break the spell they held over him.

Even the smell was overwhelming, and he caught the building's lone other occupant, an old woman behind a huge wooden desk, eying him strangely when he lifted one book to his nose and inhaled deeply.

He thought it must be what these books represented that moved him so—the free and unfettered access to information and truth. In the colonies, truth had been a fluid thing. He recognized it now that he was free of his enacter chains. The Council, or really the Twenty, had held an iron grip over what information was shared and how it was disseminated to the public. Every history book, biography, school lesson, and news report was carefully crafted to support the fiction of the Council and its benevolence, and they were all strictly digital. The government had outlawed physical books less than a century after they'd fled the Four Worlds, citing environmental concerns in both manufacturing and disposing of the books. But Tyrus suspected it was really so that they could ensure that only their edited digital versions of the books were read in every household.

The Council had even controlled popular entertainment, though in a slightly less obvious way. No holo movie Tyrus had ever seen had even hinted at government conspiracies, the Guard abusing its authority, or enacters being asked to do anything wrong by the Council or its bureaucrats. Except for a few B movies that showed dystopian alternative realities in which the Council wasn't shepherding humankind in peace, the enhanced were nearly always the heroes of every vid.

However, on Earth, Tyrus had seen all sorts of media, of both informational and entertainment varieties, that portrayed the government in a negative light. It was almost like the people of Earth reveled in their ability to poke fun at and even expect the worst of their own leaders. There were whole 24-hour news channels that did nothing but criticize whatever part of the government wasn't in agreement with their chosen views. It was surreal to someone raised under a monolithic authority that brooked no dissent.

He'd spoken to Jinny about her strange obsession with various

Earth religions since they'd arrived in the Four Worlds. She'd even told him some about her meeting with Juliana Taylor, though he knew she was holding something big back from him in the telling of that story. What stuck out in those conversations with Jinny, however, was that she *still* hadn't found anything she really believed in. But the mere fact that those different beliefs *existed* for her to choose from seemed to excite and dismay her at the same time.

He hadn't really understood why that was at the time. Now, standing amongst so many different viewpoints and uncensored ideas, he thought perhaps he finally got it.

Tyrus only took a few more minutes to indulge his awe at this building and what it represented. There were no libraries like this in the colonies, and judging by the lack of clientèle, they weren't exactly popular here on Earth either. Despite that, their very existence felt wonderful to him.

But now, he was back to the reality of his situation as he deftly used the touchscreen at the small table to look up the latest news on the manhunt for himself and Jynx, who, it appeared, was still at large. As he did so, he was surprised and happy to see the news report that Riggs had been released from custody on technicalities related to his arrest and was last seen entering the gated community where Congressman O'Leary lived with his wife—where Jinny had stayed for several months before her arrest.

For the briefest of moments, Tyrus considered again contacting O'Leary but quickly decided it wasn't yet the time. Then another alert popped up on the news site he was browsing, and his heart dropped into his stomach.

***Suspected Council Spy Jinny Ambrosa Found Dead in Custody; Cause of Death: Suicide by Unknown Biological Agent***

Tyrus fought to control his breathing. He suddenly found himself combating the unbearable urge to tear the entire building he was in—the library he was just recently admiring for all its virtue—to the ground. He wanted to destroy *everything* dear to these Earthers that had taken Jinny from him.

It took him several minutes to get himself under control, and he was gripping the table in front of him so tight during that time that it surprised him he didn't leave indentations in the wood surface.

*She can't be dead!* he thought in despair. Then anger rose inside him. *I'll kill them all!*

And he would. There was no question. It was what he'd been born and bred to do. He would track down every single person on Earth, in the 47 Colonies, or anywhere else that had had a hand in Jinny's death, including the president if necessary, and he would kill every single one of them without mercy and without...

*Suicide?* The word bubbled up to the top of his mind. Suddenly he recalled a conversation that he'd had with Jinny while she had sat next to his hospital bed during his long recovery after they'd first arrived on Earth.

She had spoken to him about the suicide of one of her friends, Sakura, and how it had affected her and eventually led her to the rebellion. The way she had talked about her friend taking her own life... No, there was no way Jinny Ambrosa would *ever* kill herself. It was unthinkable; she had been through too much and weathered too much pain without losing her optimistic streak to give up like that now, especially when she *had* to know that Tyrus would never let her rot in prison.

So, the government was lying about how she'd died. Which meant they could be lying about her death as well.

Frantically, Tyrus opened the article and read through it. It was light on information, so he checked a news aggregation site and opened another article on her death. Then another. Finally, he found a single piece of data that gave him hope.

**Ms. Ambrosa's attorney, Clark Jeffries of the O'Leary Family Foundation, has expressed his dismay that the government has refused his requests to examine Ms. Ambrosa's remains. The Department of Justice has cited a possible biological agent used in her death as the reason the remains are being kept in isolation. Officials suggested that cremation may be necessary to safeguard the health of the public.**

And with those words, Tyrus felt a tremendous weight come off his heart. Suddenly, he could breathe again. For someone who had been part of so many government cover-ups himself, he knew one when he saw it. *Jinny's not dead!*

A small voice in the back of his mind questioned whether he really believed that or was just grasping at any straw of hope, but he quashed it quickly. Until he knew for sure, he would operate under the assumption that she was alive.

Now he had to keep her that way. He *had* to rescue her. And that meant first finding someone to help him; he had to find Jynx.

A day ago, when he'd landed the stealth shuttle in the dead of night in a forested area near a town called Park City, Utah, he'd been crestfallen at how he and his companions had gone from saviors who brought news of the impending Council invasion, to hunted fugitives who could find no help with any of the people they'd come to save.

But in the last 24 hours, he'd realized with mixed emotions just how *good* it felt to be back doing what he was best at: hiding, evading, hunting, and ultimately striking. It wasn't that he wished any of the people of Earth any harm—oh, he'd kill a *lot* of them if Jinny were really dead, but for now, they were safe—but it felt oddly satisfying to have a mission again, after months playing adviser and observer but not really *doing* anything.

Of course, that feeling was fading quickly as he made literally no progress in finding Jynx. He'd been using the shuttle to connect to the Internet and consume information but had been careful not to send any message or transmit any data himself. The shuttle's stealth systems made that easy. Still, despite years of experience hunting people by the small but steady data trails they left, he could find absolutely *nothing* anywhere online that led him to Jynx after a news report that showed she'd been in Oregon and had possibly abducted a local man there after assaulting two others severely—he wondered what they'd done to upset the mercurial woman. *It could be they just looked at her wrong. Or worse, maybe they reminded her of* me!

All that told him was that she *might* be moving south. But he guessed she wasn't, given that she would also know that direction would be obvious now to anyone hunting her. And south in California was heavily populated, and she would be wary of urban areas.

He'd chosen to land in the mountains of Utah consciously because it was less populated than the surrounding areas and had good mountain and forest cover to hide the shuttle from scanners and visual searches. Now a part of him wondered if his subconscious had prodded him to choose this area as well because it was in the rough direction that he now believed Jynx was probably heading.

Of course, that still left him with the giant problem of *finding* the woman. He had no idea how she was traveling; he assumed hovercar, or aircar as they called them on Earth, but couldn't know the type or color. He also didn't know if she was alone or if the man she'd supposedly abducted was still with her.

So, this morning, on the second day of his time back on Earth, he'd disguised himself and made his way via a circuitous route to the edge of Park City, where he had found this public library building. From the anonymous touchscreens spread throughout the building, he would now risk *sending* a message.

It was a simple one and not one he thought the authorities would catch. In fact, there was a better-than-average chance that not even Jynx would catch it. But by his reckoning, it was his best hope of finding her in a short enough time to make a difference. He would need her help to rescue Jinny from wherever she was, but if he couldn't find the woman, or if she refused to help him, he'd just have to do it himself. Either way, time was running out.

---

"Hold the capsule, please!" a familiar accented voice shouted within the echoing confines of the La Costa Loop station. With a sigh of exasperation, Corey O'Leary pressed the button that paused the capsule's closure and launch and waited until the red and puffing face of Mikael Gorsky peered at him from under the extended capsule door and raised his eyebrows to ask if he could board.

Corey shrugged and jerked his head unhappily toward the capsule's small interior. To anyone watching, it would look like two political rivals who stumbled into having to share a Loop ride but were both too politic to refuse each other's company.

However, when the capsule door closed and left the light of the station, the two men clasped hands warmly. Their respective bodyguards sat silently in the other two seats, among the only people in all of United Earth who knew the genuine relationship between the men, but both loyal enough—and well enough paid—to never share it with even their own spouses.

"Is it clean?" Gorsky asked in his heavy Russian accent.

Corey nodded and held out a small bug-scanning device that usually rode in his hip pocket. "Do you mind?" he asked the senior bureaucrat.

Gorsky feigned a look of hurt but nodded, and Corey ran the scanner over the man and then his bodyguard, nodding with satisfaction when it turned up no listening or recording devices. He then submitted as Gorsky ran his own scanner across him and his bodyguard to verify the same and then double-checked the rest of the capsule's interior just to be safe.

One could never be too careful, and even old friends turned political rivals turned secret compatriots could only afford to trust each other so far.

"What's the word?" Corey asked, getting down to business.

"All bad, Corey Ivanovich," Gorsky said with a shake of his head. "Givens suspects Admiral Bol had a hand in Tyne escaping, but even she's not tupoy enough to openly accuse a senior admiral of being complicit in such a thing. Besides, the Nigerian congressman is a member of the Blue Party, and Givens will not risk offending the party's base in that country."

Corey nodded but said nothing. Gorsky only reverted to using Russian words when he was genuinely upset.

The big man continued. "All it means for us right now is that Tyne is, as you Americans would say, in the wind. It makes him look guilty. As I told you the other day, we know that Givens or someone close to her had arranged for him to have an accident once he reached Luna—he is too dangerous for her to leave alive—but his escaping means I cannot protect him. I could have countered Tabitha's plans on Luna, but now there is nothing to stop her pet agents from shooting him on sight as an escaped prisoner. It will be even easier for her to explain away; no one questions when an escaped fugitive dies in a gunfight with the politsiya. If we do not find him first, I can do nothing for him."

Corey frowned. Like Givens and Gorsky, he suspected—more accurately knew—the admiralty had played a direct hand in helping Tyrus escape. Lopez had all but admitted it in their last call. But he decided to keep that tidbit to himself. He trusted the big Russian, but that didn't mean he would tell him everything when compartmentalization may be the only thing that saved them all from going to prison together.

"There are too many players in this game," he growled in frustration instead. He wasn't kidding. He'd even yelled at old Hunter Killer Lopez when he'd found out about Tyrus' escape. Had the man consulted him beforehand, he would have warned him off of helping the ex-assassin for all the same reasons Gorsky had just enumerated.

Gorsky nodded. "And all of their motives are suspect, and no one can speak openly about any of it, so even those of us on the same side cannot coordinate efforts."

The Russian had stated exactly what Corey was thinking. Lopez and Bol could have had no idea that they'd interrupted a carefully laid, albeit last-minute, plan to discredit the president and his staff. Corey and Mikael had planned to foil Givens' assassination attempt and release the details to the public. Now, all they could do was play defense and try to salvage something from the mess.

"And Jinny?" he asked, afraid of the answer.

Gorsky took on a sympathetic look. "Nyet. I have been digging, Corey Ivanovich, but Pereira seems to genuinely believe the reader is dead. He either hides the truth well or is not part of whatever plan Givens and her druz'ya have hatched. And the men watching her were loyal to Givens, even if they technically do work for my agency.

"I suspect she still lives, my friend. But I have not been able to confirm it or find where they may have transferred her to. Which almost certainly means the Crater, as I am sure you have already surmised. Beyond that, I am afraid you may be on your own to find her.

"I read the summary of your attorney's visit to her. He did well. I suspect he used a poison pen, am I right? An attempt to read one of the guards, perhaps?"

Corey said nothing, doing his best to keep his expression impassive.

Gorsky leaned forward. "Tell me, Corey Ivanovich. The attorney: who is he, really?"

Corey looked up in feigned surprise. "What do you mean?"

Mikael laughed. "Come now, my friend. Do you take me for a fool? The man is obviously a blender posing as that lawyer of yours. But I do not pry if you are not ready to tell."

O'Leary grunted and shook his head. *One day, Mikael's astuteness will get him in real trouble,* he thought to himself. Out loud, he said: "How about the search for Jynx?"

Gorsky gracefully accepted the change in topic. "Nothing new. Almost four days now since she gave us the slip, as you would say, on that little island up north, and three days since the report of her leaving those two drug runners beaten and bleeding in Oregon. My kind of woman. Since then, nothing. Wherever she has gone, she is extremely good at running."

"And the young man they said was with her?"

The Russian frowned. "As near as we can tell, he does not exist. We canvassed the area where they were seen with the boy's picture; no one recognized him. He is not in any of our databases. Of course, that means little. He could have joined up with her anywhere between Bainbridge and Oregon, and perhaps if he has never been arrested or worked for the government, it is plausible we would have no picture of him for the facial recognition AIs to find. Still…"

He didn't have to finish. Even in the relatively lax democracy of the UE, where the government openly touted the citizenry's right to privacy, that they couldn't find the boy's face in *any* database stretched the imagination. Either way, he was a wild card in an already complex and fluid situation.

Gorsky continued, "Pereira wanted to keep the arrests quiet at first. So, I only sent a few federal police to get her and her friend, Riggs. When she escaped, we had to use the local island politsiya, and by the time we were allowed to expand the search and go public, she was already gone. Now everyone on Earth and Luna assumes she is truly guilty because she ran. Just as we feared."

Corey sighed in frustration. "Nothing is going according to plan."

The Russian shrugged his broad shoulders again. "Few things ever do, Corey Ivanovich. But we cannot lament what might have been. We can only push forward in the new reality."

Corey rolled his eyes. Gorsky was always saying things like that. They sounded profound but were entirely unhelpful. "It was supposed to be relatively easy all things considered. They all get arrested, we make a stink in public, and then we watch closely and leak any overreaches of authority to the newsies—get them on Jinny's side as the victim of a government plot to discredit her and her friends. It would be a bonus if we could stop any attempts to kill them in custody and leak those as well. Now, Jinny might be dead, Tyrus and Jynx look guilty because they ran, and the only one left is Riggs, who is pacing a rut into the carpet of my home office. And I am for sure not putting *him* in front of any cameras again."

Gorsky looked sympathetic again. "Assuming the reader is still alive, and you find her, exposing the lie about her death would be sufficient to get us back on track. But that means a more direct action than you have been willing to take before now."

Corey checked his watch, mostly as a way to avoid meeting Gorsky's gaze. It was just after 4:00 am in San Diego now, and Houston was two hours ahead. Pereira had been giving daily morning press conferences, supposedly updating the public on the hunt for the colonial fugitives but saying little of substance.

"You have your daily counter-speech prepared?" Gorsky asked, guessing his thoughts.

He nodded in reply. "Another condemnation of Jinny's supposed death and another demand that Pereira give us immediate access to the remains. Calling the arrests a travesty of justice, etcetera, etcetera. I made sure to put in a few choice remarks about you and the Department of Justice being Pereira's stooges and all that, just for good measure."

"Corey Ivanovich, you wound me so," Gorsky replied in mock severity. "What do you plan to do about Tyne? It is too dangerous for me to step in there now that he is loose. Givens does not know I am directly working against her, but she knows I am her chief rival within the party, so she is always watching me closely. Just as I am watching her."

"I'll take care of it," Corey answered shortly.

Gorsky raised his thick eyebrows. "How?"

Corey shook his head. "I said I'll care of it. The less you know, the better."

The Russian shrugged and looked upward at the blank ceiling of the capsule, which was now well on its way to the capital. When he continued speaking, his voice had grown thoughtful. "Tell me, my friend, do you know why there are so few people of Chinese or Indian ancestry in the Four Worlds and probably the colonies as well? They used to comprise a third of Earth's population before the diaspora, but now they are less than ten percent."

Corey was startled at the abrupt change of subject and merely nodded for his friend to go on.

"In the nuclear holocaust of World War III, China and India were no harder hit than anywhere else. Missiles took out all of their major cities, but the same was true of the United States, Europe, and Russia. It took three hundred years to rebuild Houston itself if you remember. Our precious San Diego looks nothing like it did before the war. The whole coastline is different; the Sea of Angels used to be a city even larger than Houston! Though we have used many of the same city names to pretend some sort of continuity, my own Moscow is not even in the same place as its namesake, as with your New York.

"However, it was not the attack itself, despite its brutality, that destroyed China and India. It was infrastructure."

Corey was mildly surprised by the statement. It was an argument he vaguely recalled hearing in his college history courses, but he couldn't remember the details, so he raised an eyebrow at the Russian. It always amused him when Gorsky spoke of academic topics. His accent and propensity to mix Russian words in his English seemed to fade away when he did so.

Gorsky smiled solemnly. "You see, my friend, the infrastructure, especially *medical* infrastructure, of the former United States and

Russia were fairly spread out by the time World War III hit. Our rural areas had just as much medicine and medical manufacturing and distribution facilities as our urban areas, at least on a per capita basis. And our supply chains were already set up to feed those rural areas.

"But China and India? For nearly a century leading up to the war, they had focused virtually all of their economic development on a handful of major cities. *Everything* flowed into or through those cities as hubs. When those large urban areas were the first to be destroyed by nuclear fire—much of it admittedly launched by my own country—the entire infrastructure of both states crumbled to dust with them. The rural regions could grow food, but all the means to process, package, and preserve it were in the cities. So many people starved when they were mere kilometers from surpluses of spoiling crops.

"Even those that survived starvation in the immediate aftermath did not avoid the fallout. Especially when the stocks of anti-radiation treatments were manufactured *and* stored in the same major cities that were most likely to be destroyed first. Those that did have the medicine could not get it to the rural populations in time because their roads and highways outside of those metropolitan areas had been neglected for years.

"That same lack of medical infrastructure meant that even those who survived the fallout became more susceptible to minor diseases. In one province of China, a simple coronavirus, one that had been cured decades before, killed a fifth of the population before someone from what was left of the government got the right vaccines and medicines there. It was a human tragedy of epic proportions."

The big Russian paused, his lips pressed tight into a thin line that belied his powerful emotions on the topic.

Corey broke the silence, speaking gently. "Where is this going, Mikael?" He was genuinely curious but also tried to keep the impatience out of his voice. Given the opportunity, the big Russian would pontificate for hours, but they only had 20 minutes left until they arrived in San Diego, and Corey had much to think about already from their conversation.

Gorsky feigned a look of hurt but resumed talking. "Quite simply this, Corey Ivanovich. In the years immediately following the war, the

United States and Russia ended up with populations larger than both India and China, a huge reversal from the pre-war period. Add in a few countries that managed to largely stay out of the war, like Brazil, and the balance of population *and* power shifted drastically in the post-war era.

"The same thing will happen if we go to war with Mars. Earth and Luna have their manufacturing and military infrastructure spread out across the surfaces and orbits of two worlds. You could even destroy Houston, and the impact would be fairly minimal. Mars, on the other hand, even since finishing their terraforming so long ago, has tended to keep its infrastructure concentrated in its original settlements, its rural settlements largely depending on them for everything; this we can observe through telescopes even if they refuse to talk to us. They use a classic hub and spoke model, similar to what India and China used before World War III.

"So, when war comes again, and you and I both know it inevitably will, Mars cannot win against the industrial might of United Earth. Unless…"

He paused, looking pointedly into Corey's eyes.

Corey nodded slowly. "Unless we're stupid," he finished for his friend.

Gorsky gave a sad smile. "Da. As you say. Unless we are stupid. The same is true when the Council finally sends a real invasion. They may win the first battles. They may even decimate our industry. But they'll never subdue us completely without a much larger force than we believe they are capable of building…."

"Unless we're stupid," Corey finished again, his voice almost a whisper this time.

"Da. Good luck to you, my friend. And give my regards to Aphrodite."

Corey let his surprise at that last statement pass. He wasn't ready to discuss that phase of the plan openly yet with *anyone*. Though, as always, Gorsky seemed to have guessed more than he should know. The two friends rode the rest of the way in silence; each man lost in his own thoughts of the terrible but necessary chain of events they'd almost unwillingly put into motion.

It wasn't until the end of the ride that Corey had a terrifying thought. Mikael had been wrong on one count: being stupid wasn't the only way United Earth could lose to the Council. If the enemy was somehow able to infiltrate the UE from within...

---

Jynx and Toby had now been on the run for four full days. During that time, she had learned much about Toby Haight, and he knew almost as much about her as Riggs did... maybe even more. Despite his incredibly annoying habit of shrugging every five seconds and despite being a full decade younger than her, something about Toby made Jynx feel comfortable telling him things she'd never willingly told anyone. Possibly it was that he represented someone she would almost certainly part ways with soon and never see again, but she'd already told him all about Dax and even about her plans to one day kill Tyrus for murdering her sister.

He'd seemed confused about why she would want revenge on a man who'd killed a sister who had abused and tormented her and so many others, but he was wise enough not to ask a murderous and capable woman too much about her motives.

From him, she'd learned that he'd been orphaned when he was too young to remember his parents well. He'd broken into the office of the orphanage late one night when he'd been 12 years old and found in his file that he had a brother somewhere, but there had been no details beyond a single mention—not even a name. He'd spent a good portion of his rare free time since researching to see if he could discover his sibling's identity, but the files were sealed, and he'd been turned away at every attempt.

He was now 24 years old and was bouncing around between a series of dead-end jobs. He'd had exactly one relationship with a woman in his life, and it had ended after just a month when she had figured out he had no proper education or skills and wasn't keen on getting any.

Toby wasn't what Jynx would characterize as the motivated type. He bounced around in life because he was content to do so, and his only real ambition was to find his long-lost brother, though he couldn't articulate why. Still, she probably understood better than he did, given her experience with Dax.

She also got the sense that, despite his admission that he would have robbed her if given the chance, he was a fairly decent person. In fact, the *only* reason he'd considered robbing her was because he knew she was planning on robbing *him*. According to his moral code, that made her fair game. Had she truly been the innocent and downtrodden fellow orphan she had pretended to be, she would have been perfectly safe in his company.

That realization gave Jynx a certain warmth that she couldn't explain and that she quickly tamped down under her natural layer of cynicism every time it bubbled up to her conscious mind. Still, she had to admit that she had quickly grown to trust Toby and was oddly delighted to find that he seemed to trust her as well.

Now they drove along in the darkness over a deserted country road in a place called Utah, which Toby said he'd never visited. They were moving far slower than Jynx would have liked, traveling only at night, avoiding major roadways, and finding places to park the car out of sight in the daylight hours. Toby was too poor to have ever afforded a palm implant, so they couldn't use it to look up directions. On the plus side, that also meant the government couldn't use it to track them, so it was a fair tradeoff, especially since a radio news report had told them that the authorities had questioned people at the roadside diner and had figured out that Jynx had 'abducted' poor Toby.

Now, all Jynx could do was keep the car pointed roughly southwest and follow the occasional sign on the road. She knew they were headed toward a place called Salt Lake City but planned to give it a wide berth to avoid any official entanglements. Her rough strategy was to take the hovercar off-road and above the trees to circumnavigate any population centers they came across, which had so far been blessedly few since leaving Oregon.

After the second day, she'd let Toby drive a few hours here and there so she could grab sleep. But right now, it was nearing daylight, and she should have already found a place to pull off into the forest, park, and allow both of them to get some much-needed rest. For the last hour or so, Toby had been dozing, and Jynx had turned on the radio to listen to what passed for music on Earth in an almost vain effort to keep her eyes open.

She had just spotted a promising overgrown turnoff from the road that led deeper into the forest when the music paused, and the voice of the radio station's host came on.

"Thanks for listening to 97.1, The Slopes, bringing you Utah's favorite Earth oldies mixed with Lunan and Europan favorites. Now, folks, I have a special message from one of our listeners to their old flame. Sounds like they really miss 'em; this is the second day they've asked us to play this tribute. It says, 'Dax, I miss you. We were better together. If you're lonely on the road, come to Park City, and we can relive old times and see old friends. Love, Jet'."

Jynx slammed her foot on the car's brake pedal, killing their forward velocity and jamming her and the sleeping Toby against the shoulder restraints. He woke up with a confused grunt and threw up his hands as if to ward off an attack. For the briefest instant, his quick movements reminded her of a cat, but the impression quickly fled as he looked around in confusion.

She ignored him and listened intently to the radio. "Whoever this Dax is," the announcer was saying, "I suggest you get to Park City and give this Jet guy, or girl, another chance."

"What's going on?" Toby asked, his eyes wide and looking around inside and outside the car like he was scanning for threats.

"Shhh," Jynx admonished and fixed her attention back on the radio. But the host had moved on and was playing a very pitchy love song to match the message he'd just read.

She turned to Toby and briefly explained exactly what she'd heard. The thought of keeping it from him didn't even enter her head, she would reflect later. If he was all in on her little adventure, it seemed she was also now all in on him joining it as a full participant.

"So, wait. Let me get this straight," he said, blinking the sleep out of his eyes while Jynx pulled the car off the road and along the overgrown path she'd spotted before she'd heard the message. "You're saying that this Tyrus guy, *the guy who killed your sister*, is sending you secret messages through the radio using her name, and you're considering *doing what he says?!*"

"Well," she paused and thought for a moment. "Basically, yeah. And this doesn't mean I forgive him," she hastened to add, "but with your entire scudding planet looking to kill me or throw me in prison, he's just about the only person I can count on for help."

Toby looked abruptly hurt, which confused her for a second until her own fatigued brain caught up with her. "Oh… I uh… I didn't mean…" she started lamely. "I mean, I can count on you, too. Obviously."

"Sure, whatever," he said in a voice that promised he wasn't truly OK with her lame semi-apology. "So, he's in Park City. I vaguely remember that being somewhere in the mountains past Salt Lake. They had the winter Olympics there when I was a kid, but I've never been."

"Olympics?" Jynx asked, but Toby kept right on talking.

"If it really is him, then it's probably as good of a place to meet him as any other; not so big that the cops will target it in their search for you—us—but not so small that the locals will notice strangers."

He nodded as if getting used to the idea. "So, the real question is, do you think it's really him? Or is it a trap?"

She shook her head emphatically. "No one else who didn't come here with me would know about my sister and her husband. It's not like I'm big on sharing," she felt a little blush as she suddenly realized just how much she *had* shared with this relative stranger, "and Tyrus himself is a locked box. He's outgoing enough to suit his purposes, but he only tells people what *he* wants them to know. Riggs doesn't talk to *anybody* about anything of substance. He just tells them whatever they need to hear so he can steal their cargo and make a few credits."

It was her turn to shrug.

"And the other one? The reader?" Toby asked, skepticism clear in his youthful voice.

Jynx frowned. "She's a bit more talkative, I suppose. But what possible reason would she have had to share details of *my* personal life with anyone outside of our group? She seems to pretty much pretend I don't exist." She grinned. "Jinny thinks I'm… inconvenient."

Now Toby shrugged. "Maybe she mentioned it in passing, you

know, when someone asked why you hated Tyrus. Or maybe she was drugged or interrogated while in custody. I mean, even your friend Riggs was on the inside for a few days. Who knows what they got out of him."

Now Jynx was frowning. Internally, she was kicking herself, first, for jumping so quickly to believe it actually *was* Tyrus sending the message because she wanted so badly to believe someone out there really could help her. And second, because she realized that she'd been momentarily *happy* at the thought of seeing the man who had, in cold blood, taken away her chance to ever reconcile with Dax.

She shook her head. "You're right; it probably is a trap." She meant to say it with a calm, steady voice, but she almost whispered it and even heard her voice break a bit at the end.

"I'm not saying it is or it isn't," corrected Toby. "I just don't want us to rush into anything without considering all the angles. It could be him, and even I admit it sounds like it probably is. Though I'm a little suspicious that it's this convenient. I mean, we're in Utah planning to head further east, and he just *happens* to be in Utah to our east?"

He frowned. "Look, I can't decide whether to talk myself into believing it's this Tyne or thinking it's a trap set by the government or the police or whoever is after you now. I *do* know that both of us are way too tired to be making any big decisions right at this moment. This is a fairly good place to stop. Let's conceal the car better and then get some rest. We can talk about this more when we wake up and decide the best way to go forward when we're not both nearly hysterical with fatigue."

She nodded silently, not trusting her voice. He nodded back once and then got out of the car and gathered downed branches and leaves to throw on top of it, providing a little more camouflage in case someone happened to see the small clearing they'd parked in through the trees.

When he got back in the car, he opened his mouth as if to say something more but stopped himself when he saw the look on Jynx's face, switching back and forth between hope and despair as her thoughts argued and raged. So instead of talking, he leaned his seat back and settled in to go back to sleep.

Jynx stayed sitting upright for several minutes, unable to stop playing the radio host's message over and over again in her head. The thought that Tyrus might be waiting for her just hours away filled her with a bevy of confusing emotions.

On the surface, she still hated the man for what he'd done—not just for killing Dax, but for everything he'd done to support and prop up a corrupt government that preyed on the downtrodden like Jynx. She also hated him for sucking her and Riggs into this mess by bringing them, or making them bring him and Jinny, to Earth.

Nevertheless, deep down, in her fatigued vulnerability, she had the fleeting thought that it was possible she didn't really hate Tyrus for what he'd done. Maybe he was simply an easy target for the years of hate and aggression she'd stored up against her twin. He'd not only taken away her opportunity to repair things with her sister, but he'd taken away her chance to get *even* with Dax.

Jynx had role-played in her head a million times what her first meeting with her sister after years of separation would be like. She would be a successful captain by then, with her own ship and a thriving trade business. She'd swoop in to save Dax from a deal gone bad, and then she'd rub her sister's face in her success, sneering at her faux marriage to Jet and the petty criminal she'd become.

In her fantasies, it was *Dax* who begged *Jynx* to be reconciled. It was Dax who made the first move and sought her sister's approval. Jynx would eventually give it, but only after making her sister wait and then apologize for every bad thing she'd ever done to her twin.

Only after Jynx had extracted her full psychological revenge would she extend the hand of forgiveness and friendship to her sister, and they would reconcile and become the partners they were always meant to be. Except Dax would be Jynx's co-pilot, following *her* lead for once.

But Tyrus had gotten to Dax first and ended the chance for all of that. Not because he hated Jynx but because he had no choice but to obey his orders from the Council. Dax *had* been a criminal. Of course, so was Jynx.

She shook her head violently, clearing her brain of the terrible thoughts that could exonerate her hated enemy if she took them too far. She leaned her seat back in a huff and closed her eyes, trying to think about anything *but* her sister and Tyrus Tyne in a vain effort to fall asleep.

What she found her thoughts turning to was Toby. She opened her eyes a crack and peered over at him, seeing his chest rising and falling in a slow rhythm that *probably* meant he was asleep. She'd learned not to assume she could read him as well as she thought. He could be feigning sleep, giving her the space to process the emotions he knew she was struggling with.

He was oddly compassionate that way. Besides her father, Jynx couldn't remember the last person who had shown her any genuine compassion. Her mother had never really given her what she so desperately craved, choosing to heap her praise and love upon Dax and treating Jynx as an afterthought. Even Ned had failed her there at the end when he'd chosen Luanne Koppel and Dax over his youngest daughter.

Riggs, as close as they had become, had never thrown much compassion her way either. He'd treated her as a business partner and almost, but not quite, a friend. That had never bothered Jynx consciously before, and in retrospect, she knew it had likely been a simple response to her prickly nature that broadcast to the world that she didn't *want* those things from anyone.

Despite all that, Toby had seen through her shell, listened to her, said nothing while she cried, and given her space when she needed it while still managing to *be* here if she needed that instead. She wasn't sure exactly what this emotion she was feeling for him was leading to, but it was new and foreign to her, and… she liked it just a little.

Nowhere close to sleep now, she continued watching him. Then, slowly, deliberately, she slid across the cabin of the hover car, moving her legs to straddle the drive selector on the floor between the front seats, and leaned her body into the crook of Toby's arm.

She heard his breath catch, but his eyes didn't open. Whether he was asleep or just pretending, he wasn't doing anything to stop her, so she lay there stiffly, leaning against him, her head resting on his shoulder.

After a few moments, she allowed her body to relax. She couldn't remember the last time she'd had human contact quite like this. Unlike so many of the women who circulated in the smugglers' community, Jynx had fended off every advance made her way, never seeking even the momentary companionship of a drunken tryst. So, she wasn't quite sure how any of this worked.

But she let her body relax a little more, sinking deeper into Toby's side, finding comfort even in his bony and oddly muscular frame, and finding that she felt somewhat safe for the first time in the days since fleeing Bainbridge Island. Or was it longer than that since she'd felt like this?

She was just starting to contemplate going to sleep when she felt Toby's arm wrap around her shoulders and pull her closer to him. She looked up and saw his eyes were now open, and there was a strange look in them she hadn't seen before on him.

Before she knew what was happening, he was kissing her, and she was kissing him back. And then she really stopped worrying about how she felt about Tyrus, Dax, or anyone else in the galaxy.

---

For students of Earth and particularly North American history, it had always seemed ironic that the world's capital had ended up in Houston, since that city was inside the historical borders of the state of Texas. Before the third world war had destroyed most of the world's governments, Texas was well known for its often utter refusal to go along with the rest of its own country's political norms, much less those of the larger world. It had been a quality that had drawn many people to move to that state in the century preceding the war, a war which many now attributed to the very political trends that Texas had long eschewed.

So, at first, after the Council had been driven off the planet, it had been strange but oddly natural that the state that had so long embraced political independence should now be the seat of a new democratic government to rule *all* of Earth according to the same principles. But over the centuries, as the political norms of the world shifted in patterns that would have been all too familiar to the people of pre-WWIII Earth, the irony was that those norms now had an iron grip on Houston and the surrounding environs. It was inevitable that they would where there was such a high concentration of politicians and bureaucrats. So, the very place known for fierce freedom-loving independence and the rejection of federal authority was now the place where those same ideals figuratively went to die.

Rising up to take Texas' place was an unlikely location that had once been populated entirely by government employees: Luna. Over the centuries, Earth's moon had gone from a simple research station to a collection of government and military installations to a thriving world in its own right. In fact, it took only a few decades after the conclusion of WWIII and the creation of the Council—historians often argued over the exact timeline—for Luna's population to grow large enough to be a full-fledged colony world rather than simply an extension of Earth.

At the time, the Council was in its early years and still held to many semi-democratic principles, including a policy of self-determination for any extra-Earth populations. So, when the people of Luna had voted to become an independent nation apart from Earth, the Council had initially wished them well.

Less than a century later, but a few decades before the Silent War that had resulted in the Council's annexation of Mars, that all changed. Another vote was held on Luna, but this time it was one that would forever be tainted by rumors of inappropriate Council influence at best and downright manipulation at worst. That the vote had still passed with only a 53 percent majority in favor of joining the Council's rule was a testament to the fierce streak of independence that permeated Lunar culture. The people of Luna would forever resent that vote and their newfound subjugation to Earth's government.

Therefore, it was no surprise that when the Council was driven from the Sol system, Luna created its own independent government. But alas, its independence was ended again, though this time by economic concerns. The Council, in a ploy to keep Luna from ever considering independence under their rule, had shifted much of the moon's industry to orbital platforms—in orbit of *Earth*, not its moon—or to the surface of the homeworld itself. And unlike the terraformed colony worlds, Luna had always had trouble growing enough food to feed its own populace. So less than three generations after declaring independence, the people of Luna resentfully, but legitimately this time, voted to join Earth and created the United Earth nation.

Even now, hundreds of years later, the resentment and fierce independent streak that had once characterized Texans stayed with the Lunans. That included a strong desire for privacy and a tough criminal justice system. Both of which made Luna the perfect place to hide a secret private prison.

Unlike Mars and Europa, Earth's moon had never undergone any sort of terraforming. It remained the airless and lifeless ball of gray dust that had first greeted Neil Armstrong and Buzz Aldrin over a millennium prior. But beneath the surface, initially for protection against radiation and asteroid strikes, but later out of stubborn habit, civilization flourished.

Now, over four billion people lived underneath the rock and dust of Luna in tunnels that ranged kilometers deep, rarely seeing the surface of their world except through the thick glass of the rare domed observation habitat. Those that gazed upon that surface typically did so quickly, eager to return to their underground paradise and put behind them the reminder of the cold space outside. Far from the warren of narrow tunnels and small caverns that had supported the first permanent research stations on Luna, the current population now thrived in massive hollowed-out spaces that supported lush parkland, shining city squares, and all manner of entertainment and attractions.

Unlike early travelers to the moon, who had only stayed short periods to minimize the inevitable loss of bone density from the lower gravity, citizens of Luna had now thrived for many hundreds of years with artificial gravity sown throughout their habitats, typically set for 0.9 g, or 90 percent the gravitational pull of Earth. Of course, several low-gravity sporting events had developed over the years where the arenas were kept to the normal 0.17 g native to the moon. A particularly fun-to-watch but violent form of American football, played almost in three dimensions with reduced gravity, even drew a large following among spectators from Earth and Europa.

If a maze of underground living spaces, no matter how grand, lent itself to anything, it was to hiding things from public view. The

Council had commissioned secret prisons for political dissenters on Luna early in the colony's history. Those had been buried during the revolution, but over the centuries, new government facilities had been built. Most of these supported United Earth's growing naval forces, particularly as the Martian threat waxed, waned, and then waxed again over the years. It was far easier to launch new ships and supplies from Luna than from the gravity well of Earth, and the moon's facilities quickly supplemented and then overtook the orbital shipyards of the larger homeworld.

There were also a handful of facilities that had nothing to do with the military. Instead, these belonged to other shadowy organizations within the United Earth government or, sometimes, to private concerns. One such was the space officially called Area 17b, ostensibly a secret but simple research station managed by civilian contractors on behalf of the government. But those who worked there, as well as those unfortunate souls that the government sent to be more permanent residents, collectively referred to this little slice of hell as the 'Crater'.

There was no research done in the Crater. But it *was* run by civilian contractors, all of them from Blackmont Industries, which was well known for being a private military that sold its services to the highest bidder. Even under the single government of United Earth, history had deep roots, and enough national pride and resentment existed around the world for minor wars to pop up over the years. Blackmont seemed to always find itself in a position to profit greatly from those. There were even rumors of the company being used by Earth's government to conduct deniable raids on Martian interests. There were just as many rumors of them conducting similar raids on United Earth interests under Martian employ. They were an equal opportunity mercenary outfit known for their lack of scruples in achieving the goals of those who had the money to pay them, and half of their employees had even served hard prison time themselves.

The Crater had a population of 514 Blackmont employees overseeing 2,851 residents, less politely called prisoners. It was the last stop for serial killers, Martian spies, prisoners of war, and all other manner of humans who were best tucked out of sight and out of mind.

Their population had just risen to 2,852 with the addition of one new and extremely special prisoner, transported from Earth and kept in solitary confinement in a part of the prison that wasn't even shown on the blueprints. In fact, of the 514 Blackmont staff in the Crater, only seven, including the facility director, knew of the presence of the new prisoner, and only five had actually seen her. The chances of anyone else ever seeing her from that day forward were extremely low. After all, the rest of the Sol system thought her dead.

When the Crater had been built, it had relied on two things for its security: first, absolute secrecy; and second, the lack of any tunnel connections to any other part of Lunar society. The Crater was a facility on its own, hidden near one of the moon's poles, an area that ordinary citizens avoided out of the same ancient primal programming that had kept most humans away from Earth's poles even after the planet had warmed enough to make them slightly more habitable.

As a result, the Crater was a completely self-contained facility. It had its own landing pads in a deep lunar crater—hence the name— that allowed shuttles to come and go unobserved. The only way for anyone to escape the facility, beyond somehow stealing one of the heavily guarded shuttles that delivered supplies and personnel once every week, would be to walk across the airless surface of the moon. In fact, in the history of the Crater, 39 inmates had escaped the facility only to all run out of oxygen in their stolen spacesuits hundreds of kilometers from the nearest source of breathable air.

In 34 of those cases, the Blackmont guards had watched the escapees via live drone feeds and placed bets on everything from the direction the escapees would walk to the exact timing and order of their suffocation and death.

Under the leadership of one less scrupulous Blackmont director, inmates had been shown an airlock that stayed perpetually unlocked (but with no attendant spacesuits) and were openly dared to attempt an escape through it. Even the desperate men and women who reluctantly called the Crater home refused to take that offer.

So now the Crater's 2,852$^{nd}$ prisoner was effectively lost to society and her friends forever. But certain people in the government and at Blackmont had more in store for her than simple incarceration. And because she'd read the guard who had checked her pulse in the small cell on Earth, Jinny Ambrosa had the horror of knowing, in broad terms, just what her captors intended to do with her.

Had the unlocked airlock been an option at that point in time, she almost might have taken them up on it rather than face the fate that awaited her. And if she'd known how bad it was truly going to be, she might have done all she could to dig through the rock around her and burrow to the airless surface.

---

Tyrus waited patiently at the small café. Luckily, it was still summer in the northern hemisphere on Earth, so the normally snow-covered streets of Park City were warm, clear, and sun-drenched. This allowed him to sit at a small table outside of the café itself, separated from the sidewalk by a short metal railing, giving him the perfect vantage point from which to inspect every aircar and pedestrian that came up the small downtown's main road.

He didn't know if Jynx had changed her appearance. He certainly had, using makeup to lighten his normally dark complexion and dye to change his black hair to a light brown.

In a moment of unexpected melancholy, thoughts of the disguise took him back to Skyhook Station in the Alpha Centauri system over five months before, where he and Jinny had used electronic means to change their skin and hair colors. That had been less than a day after she'd watched him gun down Sr. Guardsman Alan Daily, the man she'd loved. And the same amount of time since he'd disobeyed an order from the Council for the first time and chosen *not* to give Jinny the same fate.

At that point, Jinny was with him only out of necessity, and any hope of forming a friendship was the furthest thing from Tyrus' mind or expectations. But to both of their surprise, they'd gone on to form an attachment to each other that was deeper than Tyrus had had with anyone since his own parents. Now he was discovering new depths to that attachment as he struggled to keep his anger in check at her imprisonment and potential death.

Now he sat at the café table, hopefully waiting for someone who could help him rescue her. But if Jinny had overcome her hatred and fear of him—and even forgiven him unconditionally for murdering Alan Daily, Ryder Cruz, and her other fellow rebels—to build a relationship of friendship and trust, Jynx was further away from that outcome than anyone could be. In the few times he'd seen her since arriving on Earth, always in the company of Riggs and Jinny, she'd made no attempt to hide her loathing. On two occasions, she'd even bluntly reminded him of her intention to kill him for what he'd done to her twin sister.

Tyrus regretted every life he'd taken as part of his involuntary service to the Council government. He'd regretted them at the time, even though he'd tricked himself into believing the Twenty's lies that they all deserved the death he brought them. Still, he had to admit, with some consternation, that he regretted Dax's death *not* so much because of Dax but really because of Jet.

Though he suspected, and now even knew, that many of the people he'd been sent to kill were innocent of any crime other than disagreeing with the government, Dax had truly been a criminal with ill intent and no scruples. During the short time he'd spent undercover as an enforcer with her crew, he'd watched her brutally beat a man who owed her a pittance of money and ruthlessly turn in a former member of her crew to the Guard only to eliminate the *possibility* that the woman might be competition for Dax's operation.

Tyrus regretted killing Dax because he never *wanted* to kill anyone. However, he also knew that Dax was headed down that road with or without his intervention. But her husband Jet was another matter entirely.

Jet was a socially awkward genius who had the rare mix of artistic and programming talent required of forgers. He wasn't as good a hacker as Dax, but he was the best in his one area of specialization. Give the man a watch connected to the Net and a few photos, and he could make you a false ID and history that would fool even the Guard. He'd been doing just that as part of Dax's crew, but Jet never did it for his own greed; he did it for her.

Jet had been madly in love with Dax from the day he'd met her, following her around like a puppy dog when she'd brought him into her crew to handle the forgery side of the operation. Still, he'd shied away from some of the crimes she asked him to commit, his own moral compass intact enough for him to draw the line at hurting people in certain ways.

Until, of course, Dax found the right ways to motivate him. That had led to a sham marriage, at least for Dax. Jet was fully committed to her and faithful to her in thought, word, and deed, every second of every day from even before they'd said their marriage vows.

Unfortunately, Dax felt no love for Jet in return. That had been clear to Tyrus the first time he'd met the two. She simply knew she needed the man for his skills and manipulated him the same way she did everyone else on her crew. One of her enforcers loved getting drunk, so Dax plied him with cheap booze in expensive bottles every chance she got. One of her smash-and-grab girls had a thing for gambling, so Dax comped her rooms in station casinos, negotiating a share of her losses with the casino managers in return for sending them an easy mark. And Jet... Well, Jet loved her, so she gave *herself* to him, or at least pretended to.

In front of Jet, Dax was the loving wife. But Tyrus had witnessed her cheat on her husband no less than half a dozen times and knew he hadn't seen most of what she did behind the man's back. She'd even made a pass at him on two occasions, both of which he'd successfully deflected.

So, when Tyrus had finally shot Dax in a way that made it look like she'd been downed in a firefight with a disgruntled customer, he'd actually told himself he was doing Jet a favor. And because his orders didn't specify he had to kill Jet as well, he'd been able to let the man—whom he'd taken a strong liking to—walk away alive.

Alive but broken. Jet had never recovered from losing his wife. Over the years, Tyrus had made a point of keeping in touch with the forger, using his skills for official and not-so-official reasons but really keeping contact to make sure he was OK.

He wasn't. Sure, he got slightly better with time, but Tyrus doubted Jet would ever love anyone again. He became a hermit, taking jobs from people he knew like Tyrus—the man he knew as Jake

—but otherwise keeping to himself and mourning his dead wife in solitude.

After learning he could somehow defeat his genetic programming and disobey the Council, Tyrus had told Jinny he one day intended to tell Jet the truth about Dax's death and accept any punishment, including death, that Jet saw fit to dole out.

He was resolved to keep that promise. But first, he had to survive, and that meant trusting the sister of the amoral woman he'd killed, and her trusting the man who had killed her twin. If it was a holo movie, it would have made for high drama. As the one and only genuine hope of saving the Four Worlds and every human living on them, it 'sucked'. He'd picked up that bit of slang from some of his United Earth Navy acquaintances, and it fit the situation well.

Several hours into his sojourn at the café table, during which he'd quietly put off the subtle and then not-so-subtle hints from the waiter that he give up the table for new customers—he'd ordered something small each time the man approached to keep him off his back—he spied a black car with heavily tinted windows hovering slowly up the incline of the main street toward him.

He couldn't see the driver of the car, nor could he tell if they were alone inside, but his instincts screamed at him to pay close attention. Perhaps it was because it was exactly the type of vehicle he might have chosen as a getaway car, or maybe it was some of that divine inspiration Jinny had told him about after one of her trips to visit Earth's churches.

Either way, he locked his attention on the car as it passed and then got up to follow it on foot, waving a cash card at the table's terminal to pay his bill. The cash card hadn't come from Bol; there was no way she could leave any of *those* lying around the shuttle and then claim she hadn't meant to help him escape. Luckily, one of Tyrus' talents developed as an alpha had included picking pockets, and he'd turned that to good use in his short time back on Earth. He regretted stealing from anyone, but he also needed to survive. Nothing could or would impede his mission to rescue Jinny. Of course, he had no idea how he was going to secure fuel for the stealth shuttle when it eventually ran out, but he had to tackle one problem at a time.

Now he followed the black car as it made its way up the street, glad that the speed limit was a mere 15 kilometers per hour to protect the heavy pedestrian traffic drawn by the shops, cafés, and bars of Park City. Finally, the car parked at an open meter, and Tyrus' heart sank as a man—a boy, really—got out of the passenger seat and waved a cash card at the meter to pay for the space.

He stopped his walk toward the car and was about to turn around when the driver's side door opened, and a woman stepped out. Her hair was platinum blond, and she wore too much makeup, shadowing her eyes in black and her lips a dark burgundy. The makeup was applied in a way that subtly changed her facial features, but Tyrus recognized Jynx instantly.

As the perpetual criminal on the run, Jynx habitually scanned the street and sidewalk around the car the second she got out, and within seconds, her eyes locked on Tyrus. He felt a pang of disappointment that she'd seen through his own disguise so easily, but he was distracted from the thought when an unexpected look of relief flashed across her face, only to be replaced by a thin-lipped frown an instant later.

She jerked her head, indicating he should get in the back seat of the car before she spoke to the man across from her at the meter, and they both climbed back in their respective doors.

Tyrus approached cautiously. Jynx didn't trust him, and he didn't trust her, but they needed each other at the moment. And the guy with her didn't *look* like a government agent or a cop, but Tyrus himself had made a career out of looking like something he wasn't whenever it was necessary. Either way, he was wary.

Nonetheless, he squared his shoulders and drummed up some of that faith Jinny talked about and walked to the passenger side rear door of the sedan, opening it and climbing in. Faith or no, he intentionally put himself behind the unknown man, where the guy would have to turn awkwardly to point any kind of weapon. And Tyrus still had the gun he'd taken off his guards on the shuttle.

"Jynx," he said nonchalantly as he settled into the car and closed the door. "Who's your friend?"

She eyed him with her customary fiery hatred but then abruptly softened in a way he'd never seen before as she looked over at the skinny guy in the passenger seat. "This is Toby. He's been helping me. We can trust him."

Tyrus was surprised by the look she'd given this Toby, and by the look the man returned to her, but he wasn't ready to take Jynx's word that the boy could be trusted. Still, he held his tongue and simply nodded once. "You got my message?"

Jynx almost smiled and nodded back. "Clever using those particular names, though not the way to get me to like you any more than I already do."

Tyrus shrugged and was surprised to see a flash of annoyance cross Jynx's face at the simple gesture. Toby squirmed uncomfortably but kept his hands where Tyrus could see them. She had probably instructed him on that. If she liked this boy as much as her gaze toward him suggested, she probably didn't want Tyrus hurting or killing him over a misunderstanding.

"Nice to meet you, Mr. Tyne," the interloper said in a nervous and youthful voice. "I've heard a lot about you."

Tyrus nodded at him through the car's rear-view mirror and turned back to Jynx. "They have Jinny, but Riggs got out."

She nodded but said nothing.

"I'm fairly sure they were planning to kill me when they got me to Luna. She's probably there already, so we have to get her out before they kill her too."

Jynx frowned, then looked away and out at the street beyond the parked car. When she looked back, her face was hard. "That's your problem, the way I figure it. And from what the news has been saying, she's probably already dead. I just need you to help me and Toby disappear. Preferably with Riggs and the *Blind Monk*."

The answer wasn't surprising; Jynx had always looked out for herself first. What was surprising was her inclusion of the boy in the statement *and* the tone of her voice—she'd sounded almost embarrassed or regretful. Tyrus raised an eyebrow at her. By the look on her face, she knew he'd caught the tone.

"Look," she said, her voice softening only slightly. "The way I see things, it's your fault, and Jinny's, that Riggs and I are here in the first place. So, I just want to collect my partner, find our ship, and get off this rock and back to the colonies where, if I get arrested, I *know* what it's for. So, give me one reason I should help you rescue your pretty little reader friend, assuming she's even still alive."

Tyrus said nothing. By the wording of the question, he knew Jynx was either trying to convince herself that she didn't *need* to help or that she didn't *want* to help. In that frame of mind, she'd latch onto anything he said and turn it toward her argument, so silence was the better path for him at this juncture.

They sat there staring at each other for several moments. The boy, Toby, squirmed more in the passenger seat, turning awkwardly to look at Tyrus and then back at Jynx. Finally, he couldn't take the staring contest anymore and broke the silence himself.

"Jynx," he mumbled. "Come on. She's your friend too."

The simple, imploring statement shocked Tyrus, though he didn't let it show. The familiar way the boy talked to the woman and his words implied that she'd somehow opened up to him, and Tyrus didn't think Jynx was capable of opening up to *anyone*. But when she broke her stare with Tyrus and looked back at the boy, her face took on an expression Tyrus hadn't believed Jynx could form with her perpetually sour features.

*Oh no, she's infatuated with this kid,* he thought. Any other time he might have been happy to see Jynx show a measure of joy—or any emotion not associated with her hatred for him—but right now, he needed the sharp and pragmatic Jynx who had escaped from federal agents, not this love-sick, distracted woman in front of him.

But Jynx surprised him once again, nodding curtly and turning back to Tyrus, her features sharpening again but not showing the measure of anger she usually flashed at him. "OK, fine. We'll help Jinny *if* she's alive. It's not her fault she's your friend."

At this, Toby snickered, causing both Jynx and Tyrus to throw him a sharp look. The boy sunk lower in his seat and shrugged, but a weight seemed to leave the car. "All right," Jynx continued. "Do you have a plan? Because Toby and I have been brainstorming a few things on the drive here." Clearly, at least some of her reticence to help had been purely for show.

Thus began the most civil and by-far-strangest conversation Tyrus had ever had with Jynx. As they drove toward the edge of town an hour later, preparing to ditch the car and make their way on foot to Tyrus' hidden shuttle, they had the barest beginnings of a plan. But to his chagrin, they couldn't seem to get any further until they knew for sure *where* on Luna Jinny was being held.

That problem was unexpectedly solved when Tyrus entered the shuttle anew and saw the comm light blinking. Hesitantly, and only after urging Jynx and Toby to leave the shuttle and take up an overwatch on a ridge a hundred meters away, Tyrus accepted the message.

The text was short and terse. Corey O'Leary had decided to contact *him* instead of waiting for the ex-alpha to reach out on his own. Which meant someone in the United Earth Navy had obviously given the man the means to get in touch with the lost stealth shuttle. The congressman also claimed to have some ideas on how to rescue Jinny. It was a start.

# CHAPTER 19

### ELEVEN YEARS AGO; 720 P.D.

It had been exactly two years since the first time D5746J14L1 had entered the small room off the back of the mess hall. Since then, he'd entered that same room at the same time every day. And every day, he'd seen holos of enemies of the Council doing horrible things, each time building his level of excitement, which he kept carefully hidden from the adults who were no doubt watching him.

But today, the 730th time he entered the room, happened differently. Today, after asking him the standard set of questions about the Council's place in society and whether everyone felt loyal to it—he had those answers down so well that he had to make a real effort to show any feigned emotion when answering them—the holos did *not* start. Instead, the voice asked a new question that the boy hadn't heard before.

"D5746J14L1." The voice had continued to use his number for the duration; the sound of the boy's given name was now foreign, even inside his own head. "Does knowing about the enemies of the Council frustrate you?"

"Yes. I hate them," was his emphatic response. He knew it was expected, and it was true to an extent. Yes, he *disliked* them, as he disliked just about every human being he'd ever encountered or heard of, but more so, the men and women who committed the crimes he watched in this room every day *fascinated* him.

"That's good, D5746J14L1. These things frustrate all of us. Would you like to do something about it?"

Without hesitation, he replied, "Yes. That's why I'm here. Someone needs to stop them." He left unsaid his true desire. *I want to hunt them. So, I can learn how to become like them.*

"That's wonderful, D5746J14L1. Because the Council needs your help."

Suddenly, the lights in the room, which were still blinding and had never turned off for the expected vids, went out except for a small circle of light in the center of the room, right in the space usually occupied by the holos.

But today, instead of holo videos, the space was filled by the kneeling form of a woman. She was dressed in an orange jumpsuit and was bound by plastic cuffs around her wrists and ankles. Straps around her legs held her to the floor, and other straps kept her in a kneeling position and prevented her from removing her bound hands from her lap. She wore a blindfold and a gag and moved her head around as if trying to determine her surroundings by sound alone.

"This," the room's voice continued, "is a very bad woman. She killed a family last week—a mother, a father, and their three children. And she did it because they were loyal to the Council, and she isn't. She was so jealous of the wonderful life they lived as a reward for their loyalty that she plotted and executed their gruesome murder. The Guard arrived too late to stop her but was fortunate to catch her leaving the scene with the murder weapon. There is *no* question of her guilt."

The boy could feel his excitement growing to levels that teased him and promised greater things. He fought the urge to leap forward and attack the bound woman, not for what the voice said she'd done, but because he *could*. Still, he carefully kept his face impassive and awaited what came next.

The voice continued, unaware of his eagerness, as if it felt the need to further convince him of what had to be done: "She confessed fully to the crimes. In fact, she was *proud* of them. She detailed how she took her time torturing the little family before finally ending their lives. She even wrote 'Death to the Council!' with the husband's blood on a wall after she'd finished slitting his throat. It turns out this wasn't her first crime, either. She's killed *dozens* of other good, loyal families just like this one. Only now, she's been caught.

"The Assembly convened a special session of the Guard court and tried the woman. The court recommended death, and the Council agreed. Don't you agree, D5746J14L1?"

The boy tried hard not to smile and considered carefully the proper response. "Any decision the Council makes must be right. I agree."

"That's a good answer, D5746J14L1."

Another circle of light appeared in the room, and the boy saw a narrow pedestal had risen from the floor. On top of it was a large tactical knife. His excitement rose even higher, and his entire body tingled with anticipation. He barely stopped himself from rushing forward to grab the blade. "This is the murder weapon," the room's voice told him. "This is the knife this woman used to kill that family and so many others. The Council decreed she is to be killed with the same weapon so that she can feel what those poor people felt in their last seconds of life."

The boy said nothing, for the voice had asked him no questions. He glared at the knife and then back to the woman in the center of the room, willing the voice to continue and set him loose for what he desperately hoped was coming.

"D5746J14L1, I speak for the Council. You know this. Pick up the knife."

He walked briskly to the pedestal and, without even the barest hesitation, reached out and grabbed the wicked-looking knife. The shine of the blade in the room's light was the loveliest thing the boy had ever seen. His body shook in pent-up anticipatory delight.

"D5746J14L1, the Council is pleased with your progress in your training. They have decided to give you a grand reward. You have the honor of carrying out the sentence—the Council's will—on this woman."

A long pause followed as if to let the boy contemplate this.

"D5746J14L1, slit the woman's carotid artery with the knife."

Finally set free, the boy leapt forward, placed the knife's serrated edge against the woman's throat from behind, and sliced upward and across quickly and powerfully. The blood began spurting from the woman's neck in waves, splattering the boy's hands, and he watched it run down her body to pool on the ground. The doomed prisoner struggled jerkily against her bonds, but the boy held her tight, savoring the feeling of her life ebbing out of her as her struggles calmed, and she quickly went still.

D5746J14L1 stood there for a full minute, staring down at the woman's corpse and savoring the beauty of what he had just done. But strangely, he was left with a sense of... disappointment. It had happened too fast. Had the voice not explicitly decreed the form of death, the boy thought he could have found more creative and slower ways to drain the woman's life from her. Perhaps then it would have given him the release he craved, the feeling of supreme satisfaction he knew was just out of reach.

"D5746J14L1, what you just did was very good. The galaxy is much safer because of your actions, and the Council is proud of you. I know it wasn't easy, but it was *necessary*. Do you believe me?"

"Oh yes," the boy replied, smiling and showing his teeth.

"Good D5746J14L1. I'll see you again tomorrow."

From then on, the boy would kill a Council prisoner every day in the small room. Soon, the voice stopped even telling him about their crimes. He didn't care; he didn't need to know. It was enough that the Council let him dispense justice by his own hand. Eventually, the voice also stopped telling him exactly how to kill them, and he let it play out more slowly, savoring every moment, sometimes torturing his prisoners for 15 minutes or more before finally granting them death. Nevertheless, each time left him strangely disappointed and hungry for more. None of the killings gave him the satisfaction he craved. Instead, the hunger grew with each life he felt fade under his hands until the voice couldn't have stopped him if it tried.

Because he was different from the other boys and girls in the building.

He was part of the new generation of alphas, or so they had told him: men and women trained to be fiercely loyal to the Council and carry out the most dangerous and necessary of missions. Except, unlike previous generations of the Council's assassins, D5746J14L1 and his contemporaries were *not* enacters. They didn't need to be. Their very desire to bring death and order to the chaos of the galaxy ensured they would stay forever loyal to the Council government... as long as the government kept letting them kill.

---

## PRESENT DAY; AUGUST 10, 731 P.D.

"Now that she's in the prison on Luna, there will be no getting her back," Tyrus said, his voice hard with an edge of frustrated but controlled anger... controlled at least for now. It had been five days since Corey had first contacted the man and arranged to meet him, Jynx, and the boy Toby. And despite several false starts, they *still* didn't have a solid plan to save Jinny.

"How can you say that?" snapped Riggs from across the small table, his voice carrying his own anger in greater measure. "Aren't you an alpha? What good are you if you can't figure out a way to break her out?!"

Corey O'Leary interjected, doing his best to diffuse the tension. "Come now, gentlemen, arguing won't get us—"

"Riggs, I want her out of there as much as you do. Maybe even more," Tyrus said, ignoring Corey's attempt and cutting him off. "But we can't just—"

"Just what? I thought alphas could do *anything*! Sure seemed that way when you and your buddies were doing the Council's bidding back in the colonies. What, now that you're on the right side, you suddenly *can't* do your job? I'll ask again, what good are you?"

"Gentlemen!" Corey tried again to draw their attention. They went on as if he hadn't spoken.

"Riggs, I'm sorry." Tyrus' voice didn't sound apologetic. "But no one can just walk into a maximum-security prison and break out their highest priority prisoner. Not anywhere! Much less on an airless moon, where the prison is buried under ten meters of solid rock, with only one way in or out. It's suicide!" By the tremble in his voice, it was clear the man was on the edge of a breakdown as he spiraled further and further into defeatism.

Corey turned red in the face, shaking his head at the obstinance of the two other men who insisted on taking their frustrations out on each other rather than calming themselves to find a proper solution. His exasperation with their behavior rode on top of his own already-high anxiety; they were staying at and meeting in his family's fishing cabin, the same one recently inhabited by the real Clark Jeffries. It was better than his San Diego home for the purpose of avoiding the eyes of federal agents. But that didn't mean they were in the clear, and the risk of discovery carried with it a penalty of high treason if he was caught.

Now, his frustrations were bubbling to the surface, and he was opening his mouth to yell at the two men to pipe down and listen. Someone else beat him to it.

"Riggs! Shut it!" Jynx surprised them all with her outburst as she slammed both palms down on the table in front of her, causing the normally unflappable Tyrus to show a brief startle. Riggs just turned and stared at her, mouth agape. Even the boy Toby, who seemed to be Jynx's new boyfriend if Corey wasn't misreading things, looked taken aback by her outburst.

"And you!" Jynx said, ignoring her partner and whirling to face Tyrus. "You know as well as I do that there is *always* a way. So instead of telling us what can't be done, put that galaxy-class sneakiness to work and figure it out!" She bit off the last three words, making it clear that no one was to argue with her. Now it was Tyrus' turn to go slack-jawed in surprise, though Corey couldn't tell if it was with shock that she would speak to him like that—he doubted that given what he'd heard about the woman's feelings for Tyne from Jinny—or more likely at the fact that she'd buried a backhanded compliment in the rebuke.

"Well," Tyrus started slowly but quickly regained his composure, "there's possibly a way. But we would need a hacker far better than myself."

Jynx frowned. "How good?"

Tyrus answered in a low voice. "Dax quality; probably even better."

The woman's frown deepened as she regarded the ex-assassin, and something passed between them that Corey didn't understand. Then she turned to him, catching him off guard with a question. "Well, how about it, Mr. Government? Know anyone like that?"

Corey shook his head. He knew that many of his colleagues in Congress made use of semi-legal and even blatantly illegal hacks to collect dirt on their opponents, but he had never agreed with nor condoned the practice. Though, if he was perfectly honest, he couldn't say for sure that the opposition research firms he occasionally hired didn't skirt the edge of legality, but he certainly didn't know any of the hackers himself.

"Ahem." The sound of a throat clearing behind Corey reminded him of the silent presence of one more person at their little clandestine conference.

Everyone at the small table turned to regard Jordan Archer. The blender leaned back against one of the small dining room's walls and had worn an expression of barely interested boredom during most of the discussion. Aside from responding to a few minor questions here and there, mostly with one-word answers, he had been entirely silent. Now, he levered himself off the wall to stand up straight.

"I might know of one," the man said. "I don't even know his real name. He just goes by the handle of Neon Mouse, but—"

He was interrupted by Jynx guffawing at the hacker's chosen name. He ignored her and pressed forward. "We don't exactly run in the same circles, but he's supposed to be one of the best, or rather worst, depending on your point of view. He hacked the Octagon's network a few months ago, by all accounts, just for fun. I'm sure he wouldn't come cheap, but he'd be the one to use.

Corey sat back, contemplating the possibility and trying to ignore Jynx's eyes boring into him and Archer in turns. "Money wouldn't be a problem. Even without tapping into my foundation's accounts, my personal accounts are more than sufficient; I have a few of them that even the Department of Revenue doesn't know about." He was reluctant to admit that. He liked to play above the board in both his personal and professional life. But his father, domineering tyrant that he was, had taught Corey the importance of having a nest egg that the government didn't know about. Just in case.

"Well?" Jynx asked impatiently, her eyes still on Archer. "Can you get in touch with this Purple Rat or not?"

"I can get us in touch with a woman who knows the Neon Mouse," Archer replied, ignoring Jynx's purposeful distortion of the hacker's handle. "I'll reach out after we're done here and see if we can get an offer to him via her."

"How long would it take?" asked Tyrus before Jynx could interrogate the blender again.

Archer shrugged. "It's difficult to say. If Neon Mouse is even on Earth right now, it could take a couple of days. Maybe less. Maybe more. The woman I know who can likely get in touch with him wouldn't have his direct contact info. She uses a series of cutouts and digital dead drops. If Neon Mouse even checks them, it could take days or even weeks."

"Is he good enough to hack the secure servers at Area 17b?"

Archer's only response was a quick nod.

"Is there anyone *else* you can think of who could hack them and would be easier to get in contact with?" Tyrus pressed further.

---

Archer pretended to think about Tyne's question for a bit, then shook his head. "There's a man on Luna and another here on Earth. Unfortunately, I wouldn't have the faintest idea of how to even start contacting either of them." That was a blatant lie; he had them both on loose retainer. Every fixer needed a few good hackers.

"I know someone on Ganymede who's easier to reach, but *if* she decided to help us, it could take weeks for her to make her way to Earth or Luna, and it's a long shot that she would even be willing to come. And she would *have* to come; there's no way to conduct a hack that complex from half a light hour away. It has to be real-time, likely even *inside* the facility. Besides, none of the others are as good as Neon Mouse." That part was certainly true.

"Well then," Tyne said, turning back to look at the others. "If we can find this Neon Mouse and get him to help us, and if he can hack into the Blackmont servers, then I might have the beginnings of a plan." He turned back to look at Archer, an eyebrow raised. "But it also requires the help of a blender."

Archer frowned but nodded. He had expected that part, even counted on it. But it wouldn't help if he looked *too* eager. Iasonas had been adamant that Archer himself needed to be *with* Tyne and the others when they went to rescue Ambrosa, just as he had made it clear that the Neon Mouse had to be involved in any rescue plan. But Tyne made Jordan nervous, and he would likely pick up on him trying too hard to be included.

From there, the big ex-assassin started to lay out his rough plan for the rest of them. Riggs interjected several times, poking and prodding, and Archer himself gave several pieces of constructive feedback, both to make the plan better and to subtly—he hoped—ensure that his part in it stayed necessary. Even Jynx had a few surprisingly calm suggestions. After about an hour, they had something that they all thought just might work.

---

The time in the small cell had quickly started to blur.

Jinny wasn't sure exactly how many days it had been since she'd been transferred via shuttle to the underground prison on Luna. There was no clock in her cell, and there were no windows—not that the strange day/night cycle of Earth's moon would in any way match up with a standard planetary day. Even her meals seemed to be brought to her at random intervals as if the guards didn't want her to know how much time was passing.

No one had spoken to her in all the time since they had put her in the cell. The two guards who brought her meals opened a single slot in the transparent door to hand the food trays through to her. They collected the tray from each previous meal when they brought the next one. One of them was the man she'd read back on Earth.

She'd tried to force them to talk to her at first, ignoring them when the tray slot opened, assuming they would call out to her to have her come and get the food. Instead, they'd simply waited about five seconds and then withdrawn the proffered tray of food without a word. Then she could have sworn they didn't even bring her food for the next meal, skipping it altogether. When they'd finally come again, she moved quickly to grab the food tray as soon as they shoved it through the slot.

She knew what they were doing to her. It was psychological conditioning. They were trying to disorient her and make her pliable so that, when they finally did come to talk to her, she would be so desperate for human contact that she would answer all of their questions without even thinking. She'd seen the Guard use similar tactics when softening a suspect who was arrested too long after their alleged crime for a reader to be of any use.

But these prison guards didn't know who they were dealing with. They thought she was all alone.

She wasn't.

Jinny had memories to keep her company, not just *her* memories but the most poignant memories of everyone she had ever read. Of course, the memories of people she read faded over time from her mind much faster than her own experienced memories did. However, like her own memories, the most colorful—both good and bad—stuck around far longer. That was the reason for her nightmares, but also now the reason for her salvation.

While awake, Jinny lived a myriad of lives in the time she sat alone in her cell. She was the happy recipient of five different childhood birthday parties, full of love and laughter. She relived the taste of over a dozen first kisses. She experienced the pain and joy of childbirth six separate times. She felt the warmth of three particularly enjoyable Thanksgiving dinners with family and friends whom she'd never met but intimately knew nonetheless. She was married, divorced, and married again a dozen times over.

But when she slept, the nightmares also came. She shot Dax, Jet's wife and Jynx's sister, in the back, as Tyrus had. She lived through the beatings at the hands of her friend Sakura's father, and she relived

Sakura's later suicide on Greater York. She shot Ryder in the head from Tyrus' place behind the sniper rifle on Nova Tejas. She snapped her mother's neck while a younger version of herself watched and cried. And she relived half a dozen other horrific crimes perpetrated by degenerate men and women she'd read through the years.

At least every fourth dream was of Alan's death. Sometimes, she was herself, watching him crumple dead to the ground; sometimes, she was Alan, seeing the borehole of Tyrus' pistol right before the shot that killed him; and sometimes, she was Tyrus, pulling the trigger that ended the life of the only man Jinny had ever loved.

She'd forgiven Tyrus long ago for what he'd done in that alley, and she really felt no anger at him for it even now as she relived it. But that didn't stop the pain of seeing it over and over again when she closed her eyes. The memory had even started to intrude on her conscious daydreaming, always in the back of her mind, taunting and threatening her with its very existence.

Still, at least she wasn't alone. Because she also relived the way Alan had tenderly held her when she'd woken up sobbing from a nightmare on the *Lucille*. And she got to experience anew, from her perspective and his, the first kiss they'd shared in the same small crew cabin—she felt his love for her in that moment in a way that still brought her indescribable joy.

She also relived the experience and joy of seeing Tyrus wake up for the first time in the orbital station hospital above Earth, still relatively fresh from his ordeal saving her, Riggs, and Jynx from the explosion of the Council Navy dreadnought.

Her friend, Tyrus. She didn't feel about him the way she'd felt about Alan. But they'd had more time together than the mere days she'd had with the senior guardsman, and their friendship had grown a depth that even her fledgling relationship with Alan had lacked. Now, in the never-ending twilight of her small cell, she relived every moment in the formation of that friendship, mostly from her perspective but some from his, though she hadn't read him again since fleeing the colonies.

Thoughts of Tyrus made her smile. Not only because of their

friendship but because she, more than anyone in the galaxy, knew *exactly* what the man was capable of. And the evil men and women who held her captive would learn it as well. Because even in her darkest moments alone in the small cell, she never once doubted. *Tyrus will come for me.*

# CHAPTER 20

"She might be interested, but it will cost." Archer's informant, a plump middle-aged woman with dark hair and a ready frown, looked up from her coffee concoction at the outdoor seat in the small café in Bern, Switzerland, and regarded the blender skeptically. "Last I checked, you don't have that kind of scratch. Not for Neon Mouse's services."

Archer showed no surprise or any other emotion in response. He hadn't even shown his reaction when the woman had corrected the Neon Mouse's gender. He simply shrugged and replied evenly. "Money won't be an issue in this instance. But she'll have to do the job in person and in real time. No cutouts, no dead drops, and no remote connection. She'll have to be *with* us, physically, though I won't say where, except that it won't be outside of United Earth space."

The woman opposite him laughed as she shook her head. "No way. Neon Mouse does *nothing* in person. *I've* never even met her. I haven't even heard her real voice. She's incredibly private."

Archer raised an eyebrow. "I find everyone is willing to step outside their comfort zone for the right price."

The woman licked her lips and regarded him with hunger in her eyes. "And just what is the right price?" With that question, Archer knew he had her.

"Double her usual fee." He didn't even know what Neon Mouse's usual fee was, though he could guess, but Corey O'Leary had vast amounts of family money and had given him a blank check to get the reclusive hacker on board. And Iasonas had been quite insistent on this *specific* hacker being part of the team. "That and the opportunity to hack something most people would say is unhackable."

The woman regarded him skeptically, though she'd had a tough time suppressing her gleeful excitement when he'd mentioned the large fee. Her customary cut as the broker would probably be enough for her to skip any kind of genuine work for a year if not two. "You'd better not be talking government," she said. "They're too *easy* to hack; Neon Mouse doesn't even get out of bed for most government servers. You have something more challenging in mind?"

Archer smiled for the first time. "Ask her if she's ever hacked Blackmont Industries."

Now it was the plump woman's turn to smile. She waved her left palm at the payment reader on the table and stood to leave. "Give me a day. I'll reach out via the normal channels tomorrow with Neon Mouse's answer."

After she left, Archer sent a message to his employer.

*Castor: Neon Mouse is in play. And she's on Earth.*

The response came quickly.

*Iasonas: Are you sure she will take the job?*

*Castor: Fairly certain. O'Leary has deep pockets, so money not an issue. Will know for sure tomorrow.*

*Iasonas: Good. Her involvement is critical to the plan. Make sure she says yes. Do whatever it takes.*

---

Two days after his meeting with his contact in Bern, Archer maneuvered the hover van over the broad road leading to the McCarran Shuttle Port in Las Vegas, Nevada. Despite being home to multiple military bases, mostly research-oriented ones, at the time of Earth's third world war, the area surrounding Las Vegas had held little strategic value. So, it had escaped any direct hits by nuclear weapons, though a chemical attack had been directed at one of the nearby bases.

As such, Las Vegas itself had gone on relatively unmolested in the days immediately following the massive war. However, when the Council had strictly outlawed gambling (a decision he'd heard from Riggs they had reversed after the schism), it had, for a time, destroyed the desert city's economy. Without the casinos, the place really was little more than an overly hot and isolated wasteland. For the duration of the Council's rule in the Sol system, the shrinking town had been little more than a shell of its former self, almost uninhabited except by those too poor to build a life anywhere else.

Later, when the Council had left the Four Worlds and democracy had returned to Earth, the change had brought with it both the virtues and the vices of a free society. And Las Vegas had always thrived on the darker side of freedom; six hundred years later was no different. Today it was once again the thriving center of gambling and other forms of entertainment for the North American continent.

There had, as of yet, been no direct communication with the hacker called Neon Mouse. But Archer's contact had come through, and the blender now wordlessly drove the van to the passenger pickup area of the shuttle port. There, he pulled over and waited at the designated spot, setting a green baseball cap on the van's dashboard in the agreed-upon sign.

He saw no one take any interest in the van or the baseball cap over several minutes' time. Normally unflappable, the excitement of being part of a conspiracy that spanned not just United Earth but the entire galaxy—not to mention pretending to be employed by Corey O'Leary while really serving the mysterious Iasonas, who possibly *was* O'Leary—had him on edge. On top of all that, he *still* hadn't been able to reach Cecily, and over two weeks had passed since their last conversation. A dozen times, he had composed messages to Iasonas, telling his anonymous employer that he needed to renege on this job to instead go and find his girlfriend. But he hadn't been able to press send on any of them, held back by a strong intuition that the conversation wouldn't end well for him. Iasonas seemed to have some personal stake in the outcome of this mission.

Now, with every minute that passed beyond the agreed-upon time, his stomach sank as he became increasingly convinced the mysterious hacker wasn't coming, further adding to his problems.

So, he was relieved beyond measure when a short feminine figure wearing a sweatshirt with the hood pulled low and carrying nothing but a backpack, made a beeline for the van and entered quickly through the front passenger door. The woman closed the door without ever showing her face to Archer, and sat looking straight forward, the hood masking her features.

"Neon Mouse?" he asked, his voice low, even though the van had enough countermeasures artfully hidden to thwart anyone trying to listen in on their conversation.

The figure nodded, and the woman hesitantly turned and faced him. Once again, Archer's customary nonchalance failed him. The hacker, who had over the last few years become the scourge of the United Earth government and private institutions across the Sol system, was little more than a young *girl*. At most, he guessed her to be 18 or 19 years of age, with olive skin, bright green eyes, and a small tuft of black bangs visible from under the hood.

"Drive," she said, in a voice that sounded like it belonged in the soprano section of a children's choir, but in a tone that made it clear she expected to be in charge.

Archer thrust down the urge to laugh, put the van in gear, and headed out of the shuttle port and back to the small motel where Tyrus Tyne waited. He would be interested to see how long the girl thought she was in charge with *that* man in the room.

# CHAPTER 21

His name was Pedro De Vasquez, and he was an auditor for the United Earth Department of Prisons, a lesser unit of the Department of Justice. It was a job he'd held for the last 24 years, and he had long since reached the highest rank he ever would, even if he didn't want to admit it.

The simple fact was that Pedro was an unpleasant man. He knew it and even took a sort of smug satisfaction in how much he put other people off with his cold, haughty attitude and sour expressions of disdain. It was an attitude that made him the perfect auditor, feared by government contractors all over Earth and Luna. It also guaranteed he'd never be promoted to anything *above* an auditor. In his more sober and rare self-reflective moments, he acknowledged this fact to himself. But in the far more frequent moments of bitter hatred for even his own agency, he used the perception of unfairness at his plight to feed back into his poor attitude.

It was a cycle he would never escape from, but that was largely OK with Pedro De Vasquez. Because even as he lamented his inability to be promoted above the role of auditor, he also openly and fiercely enjoyed the job. He enjoyed making people squirm as he dug up the dirt they were trying to hide from him. He reveled in it when they subtly—and sometimes not-so-subtly—offered him bribes to look the other way. He exulted in telling them no to those offers... most of the time, that is.

De Vasquez had taken a few bribes here and there—what government employee hadn't? After all, he often reflected, even members of Congress who were supposedly above such graft took pricey lobbyist jobs after their terms of service were over. And wasn't that the ultimate form of bribery? *Make a few problems go away for us while you're in office, and we'll give you a cushy job playing golf and tennis for millions of dollars a year after you're done with government service.* The irony was thick in De Vasquez's mind. *Everyone* was for sale, even the men and woman who would act most shocked to find that a lowly auditor in the Department of Prisons was taking a cut on the side.

Pedro had amassed a healthy nest egg in a Europan bank that was notorious for refusing to cooperate with UE government investigations. They would *never* catch him. He was too careful. He didn't own a flashy car or live in an expensive townhouse. Instead, he lived purely within his means, or what his means were supposed to be as a government employee. Meanwhile, the money just kept adding up.

Sometimes, though, it was the non-monetary compensation that truly delighted him. Like today. She was a lower-level functionary with Tartinwell Consolidated, one of the second-tier government contractors the Department of Prisons used to provide food to inmates held in North American installations. She had no actual power within her company, but her boss did. And when she had caught Pedro's eye at the last audit, right around the time he'd uncovered that same boss' complicity in double-charging the government for some of the company's foodstuffs, an arrangement had been made.

Now, in order to keep her job and her own name out of any indictments for her boss' wrongdoing—it was so easy to frame underlings for such activities—she met Pedro once a month at a nice hotel on a white sand beach in Miami. She had just left his hotel room after one of those visits, and Pedro was genuinely looking forward to sleeping in the next day. Some sort of computer glitch at the office had the system insisting that he was overdue on taking his vacation days, triggering a mandatory three weeks off starting immediately. Even Pedro's boss, who should have known better, wasn't going to argue with the department's all-knowing AI. Nor was Pedro going to correct the error.

So here he was, with three weeks off and just enough money transferred from his secret Europan account to enjoy it. Life was good.

He was just drifting off to sleep when there was a knock at the door to his room. Grumbling, he levered his large, flabby body out of the bed and stumbled to the closet, where he grabbed one of the hotel robes. All the while, the knock at the door became more insistent.

"I'm coming," he growled irritably at whoever had the gall to disrupt his sleep. Still, he was smart enough not to just open the door, and stopped and looked through the peephole instead.

The young woman who had so recently left his room stood on the other side of the door, wearing a broader smile than he'd ever seen from her before. Grunting, he unlocked the door and pulled it open, a lascivious grin on his own face.

"Back for more?" he asked.

But before the woman answered, and before Pedro's foggy brain registered anything amiss, she stepped aside, and a much larger figure stepped from the side of the doorway and pushed Pedro into the small room, slamming the door behind him.

The man before him was a giant—at least two meters tall and covered in lean muscle. Something about him rang a bell in De Vasquez's mind, but he never completed the thought before a blue flash thrust him into darkness.

---

"You want me to blend into *that*?" Archer asked sourly as he looked at the still robed but otherwise nude form of the short, balding, chubby, and sweaty Pedro De Vasquez.

Tyrus gave him a sympathetic look. "Is the body type a problem?"

Archer shook his head, still frowning. "No, but the weight gain means it will take at least eight or nine days for me to pass for him. And I'll need *a lot* of food. I'm just really getting sick of blending into people with overactive sweat glands."

The blender had found the young woman from Tartinwell Consolidated at the hotel bar, where their intel suggested she always stopped for a stiff drink after a forced night with the despicable De Vasquez. She had been all too happy to accept the large wad of cash—enough to buy her time to find a new job—and the memory chip with enough information to blackmail her boss into letting her go without a fight, courtesy of the Neon Mouse. But she'd seemed most excited at the promise of teaching De Vasquez a lesson he wouldn't soon forget, and she probably would have taken far less in exchange for helping them get into the man's room.

Tyrus supposed he should have been surprised it had worked so well. The average person would probably wonder why De Vasquez would accept, without question, the woman coming back to his room. Surely, she was done with him and wanted to get as far away as she could. However, men like Pedro De Vasquez, in Tyrus' experience, lied to everyone, *especially* to themselves. The man probably thought the young woman *enjoyed* her forced liaisons with him.

Tyrus had already decided, whether or not the rest of their plan worked, that this would be the *last* time De Vasquez used his position to take advantage of any woman. After the operation was over, he'd make sure the Neon Mouse arranged for a note outlining the man's many crimes and bribes to be delivered to his supervisors and the Federal Police.

Now, he felt almost as bad for Archer as he had for the unfortunate young woman. He'd worked with enough blenders in his time under the Council to know that they didn't just take on the appearance of other people; they quite literally *became* them, all the way down to their DNA changing enough to fool most DNA sequencers. That meant that in just a single extended week of being in proximity to De Vasquez and a few blood transfusions, Archer would be just as out of shape and sweaty as the man himself.

"Are you sure you can risk staying here with him?" he asked the blender, looking around the nice hotel room.

Archer nodded. "He paid for the hotel for three weeks; planned to spend his whole vacation here. Idiot used his supposedly hidden account on Europa to pay for it, too. Our Mouse found that in about 15 minutes of light digging after she hacked the AI that gave him his surprise vacation. But I doubt anyone cares about the man enough to follow that trail, so we should be safe here. Just to be certain, I've also rented the room adjoining this one in case I need to move him or for when I have room service deliver meals.

"Besides," he nodded toward the suitcase he'd brought with him into the room, "this isn't my first rodeo. I'll hook him up to an IV drip that will keep him pretty placid. I'll let him be just conscious enough to talk to me so I can adopt his tone of voice and some of his speech patterns and mannerisms, but on enough happy juice that he won't even think to call for help or try to escape. The worst part will be how bad he starts to smell after a week without a shower."

Tyrus had never seen a rodeo—he heard they still had them on Nova Tejas—but he got the gist of the blender's comment and shuddered a bit at the thought of the odor to come. "Well then, I'll let you get to it. I suppose if I stay here too long, you'll start to look like some weird amalgamation of this guy and me. So, I'd better get going."

Archer gave a wan smile. His skin was already several shades darker just from the few days in Tyrus' company. The ex-alpha was wearing enough makeup that he almost looked white, but somehow that never seemed to matter to Jordan's blender gene. It was as if his genetics changed him based more on what he *knew* the person looked like rather than what they tried to look like around him. He'd also gained three centimeters in height and several kilograms of muscle from being around Tyne, which would give him that much more to lose and convert to fat as he took on the form of the short, obese man passed out in front of them.

"Help me get him into that chair over there before you go. And put the 'do not disturb' sign on the door on your way out, please. The last thing I need is for a maid to come in and see this guy passed out and hooked up to a bunch of tubes."

They worked together to get De Vasquez into a chair, and Archer was already starting the IV drip when Tyrus left the room, a hat pulled low over his face, walking in a slouching gait that made him appear several centimeters shorter than he really was. Not for the first time, he marveled at how easy it was, even for a wanted fugitive, to move around a world that—unlike every planet of the 47 Colonies—didn't have cameras at every corner.

---

When Tyrus had left, Archer looked down forlornly at the unconscious figure of Pedro De Vasquez. As a blender, he'd gotten extremely good at hiding the way he felt from those around him. But Tyne scared him. Not only was the man clearly dangerous, but he was almost preternaturally observant, even more so than most readers Archer had met. He had to watch himself closely to not let his genuine emotions show through in the man's presence.

Chief among those was a level of anxiety that went beyond normal mission jitters. Because he finally knew what had prevented Cecily from answering any of his messages for the last two and a half weeks.

With shaking hands, he pecked at his palm implant to pull up the text he had received the night before.

*Iasonas: Failure on this mission is not an option. Watch Tyne closely. He will be vital to the mission's success. I have plans for him on Luna. But if he suspects you, then there will be consequences. Cecily says hello.*

The implication was obvious and horrifying. Whomever Iasonas really was, whether Corey O'Leary or someone else, he had Cecily and was holding her to ensure Archer's cooperation and success in the increasingly convoluted and risky mission to rescue Jinny Ambrosa. For the first time in a long time, Jordan Archer was genuinely and unashamedly terrified.

---

Jynx watched in silence over the girl's shoulder as the hacker, Neon Mouse, worked for her third straight day on breaking into the main servers of Blackmont Industries. Several empty cans of energy drinks littered the desk around the young woman, but the girl ignored the mess as she fixated on the code on the screen in front of her.

And it was an actual *screen*—two of them, in fact. Real physical screens that had been folded up in the girl's backpack. The technology was so archaic as to be ridiculous, at least by the standards of the interactive holos that had been ubiquitous in the 47 Colonies for the last two hundred years. Even so, it didn't seem to slow the hacker down in the least. The girl moved so fast through the lines of code that, even though she hadn't bothered engaging a privacy screen, Jynx wouldn't have been able to follow anything of what she was doing. It didn't help that the programming languages used here in the Sol system were so wildly different from those used in the colonies, though she assumed some of the basic principles of computer logic were at least universal. But she'd never been much of a hacker anyway; that had always been Dax's domain.

"I'm in," the girl said in her overly high-pitched voice, surprising Jynx. The hacker sat back and motioned toward the screen with one hand. As if the lines of unintelligible, foreign code would make any sense to Jynx.

"You're sure they didn't detect you?"

In response, Mousey—Jynx refused to think of the girl by her stupid, full moniker, though it certainly fit her squeaky voice—looked back at her with a frown. "Of course. It wasn't easy to get in; Blackmont has much better security and encryption than anything those government idiots use. But at the end of the day, it's all just qubits."

Jynx nodded as if she could empathize. "Great. I'll tell the others."

She walked over to the window of the small motel room. Through the thin tinted glass, she could feel the stifling Las Vegas heat. Originally, she had balked at the idea of hiding in such a densely populated area. It only took one person recognizing her, Riggs, or Tyrus from their faces being plastered all over the media for them to be found. But Tyrus had argued that if Blackmont or the government *did* detect their hack, they would have a much easier time disappearing in the crowd of Las Vegas' millions of residents than they would in a secluded forest cabin where their heat signatures would stand out for kilometers to any searchers.

Mousey had looked offended at Tyrus' implication that she *could* be detected but had nodded to back him up anyway. Besides, the motel was relatively uncrowded, being one of the cheaper, more rundown lodgings on the outskirts of the large city, far away from any of the gleaming casinos. Toby had been the only one they'd allowed to leave or interact with any of the motel staff, and even he wore a disguise while doing so. He had done all of their grocery shopping and other errands, including running to a dozen different electronic stores spread around the city to buy the various things Mousey had needed to set up her hack.

Now it had paid off. The diminutive hacker, who without her hoodie was an adolescent girl with a boyish figure and way too many piercings and tattoos for even Jynx's criminal taste, had been an easy roommate for Jynx. She'd almost never left her computer except for the occasional bathroom break and a few hours of sleep at random times of day and night. Now she had completed the second part of the job they, or rather, O'Leary as the money man, had hired her for. The first had been the hack that had delivered them Pedro De Vasquez and the means to access him.

"They were using a 14-petabyte quantum encryption scheme; it was downright organic and would have taken me years to break even with a fleet of co-opted AIs churning," the hacker was saying. "But I found a vulnerability that one of their lazier people left open in an API that gave me a tunnel right into the system after I attached my worm to a data packet coming in from one of their satellite servers. Once I was in, I just had to convince the software I belonged there before any of their watchdog security AIs found me. When they eventually did, I already had a password and encryption key that made me look legit.

"From there, I still had to force my way up through the higher levels of security, but I was able to do a little social engineering with one of their VPs. Idiot isn't too careful of what he posts on social media; likes to impress the ladies with his nice office and fast cars. He thinks he's been texting a twenty-year-old model named Gigi for the last two days. But it's really been one of my chat bots farming him for information. It's amazing how many imbeciles use the name of their first childhood pet as a password key yet think nothing of posting all about that same dog in their throwback social posts.

"Then a pretty face, or what they think is a pretty face, asks them a few deep questions to get to know them on a dating app, and they fall

all over themselves, revealing just about everything a decent hacker would need to steal their entire identity."

Jynx nodded along with the girl's monologue. It was the most Mousey had spoken in the week they'd been in the motel together. The things the hacker was saying made some sense to her now, at least the parts about social engineering. Jynx had been known to chat up drunk businessmen at bars to gather information for one of hers and Riggs' scores more than once.

"Anyway," the girl continued to babble; Jynx was surprised and annoyed at how talkative she was now that the initial work was done. "That guy's access got me to 90 percent of what we needed, but I was able to use it to spoof the AI controller into a logic loop that ended with it giving me root access."

The girl smiled widely. "Now I *own* Blackmont—at least their Earthside systems. The stuff on Luna is a different matter; as far as I can tell, it's all air-gaped for maximum security. But once I get a connection, I should be able to use what I've built here as a strong starting point. It's highly likely they even use the same encryption schema."

"Good," Jynx said, only half listening now. Instead, she was wondering how the other parts of the plan were coming together.

---

Tyrus frowned. He'd been watching the building through the long-range scope for almost three full days, only pausing to catch short naps, drink from his water supply, eat some of the nutrition bars he'd packed, and occasionally use a nearby tree for the call of nature. He hadn't even changed once out of the camouflage ghillie suit he wore, courtesy of Corey O'Leary. It had a built-in refresher setting, but that had only worked with any effectiveness for the first two days without a shower.

Unfortunately, in the three days he'd been here, he'd found few vulnerabilities he could exploit.

This had always been the riskiest part of the already incredibly risky plan he'd cooked up with Riggs, Jynx, Archer, and O'Leary.

However, the part with Archer and the government auditor had worked out so far, and an encrypted message from Jynx an hour before told him that Neon Mouse had done the second part of her job, gaining them full access to Blackmont's Earthside servers. But Tyrus' part, this last part before they could embark on the next phase, was not looking good at all.

The building he watched was a supply and personnel transfer depot for Blackmont Industries. It was a small warehouse with an equally small shuttle pad behind it. Inside the building, Tyrus knew—Neon Mouse had found the information they needed early on, without having to do much real hacking at all—was the processing center for Blackmont employees who were sent to Area 17b on Luna, aka the Crater.

Of course, they still didn't have confirmation that that was where Jinny was being held, but they had early on eliminated all the official government prisons on the moon, leaving only the privately run Crater as a possibility. And the Neon Mouse's recently completed hack had revealed a faint money trail originating from an account tied to Tabitha Givens, President Pereira's chief of staff, to another account tied to the CEO of Blackmont Industries on the same day that they suspected Jinny had been transferred to Luna. A little voice in the back of Tyrus' head continued to nag him that Jinny might *actually* be dead, as the news reports said, but he quickly pushed it down. The evidence, at least to his way of thinking, all pointed to her still being alive and imprisoned in the Crater.

Assuming he was right, this building he watched now was the key. Blackmont employees who were set to do rotations at the Crater first came to this depot in the mountains of Colorado, where they went through multiple layers of security to get a uniform keyed to the prison's facilities. Without one of those, no one could get into the Crater or move around inside of it, at least not until they'd had a chance to hack its systems. And according to the Neon Mouse, the *only* way to hack the Crater's systems was to get someone on the inside first. It was the classic chicken before the egg situation.

Tyrus had, from a distance, shot a small spy device onto the collar of one employee's coat as he'd entered the facility. The few minutes of video it had beamed back hadn't given him anything to be optimistic about. Employees entered the facility once a week in the morning before the regular shuttle flights. They used their Blackmont corporate identification cards, which were encoded with their credentials and biometrics, to enter. Those cards were scanned at the outer door, but that only got them into the lobby. There, armed Blackmont guards compared the photo on the card to the appearance of the employee in front of them *and* to the photo of that same employee stored in the Blackmont server records.

After the employee passed that checkpoint, they entered a room where they went through *four* different biometric tests. First, the fingerprints and palm prints of both hands were scanned and compared with the server records. Then, they inserted a finger into another device that took a drop of blood to make a DNA comparison to the central Blackmont records. He suspected that the DNA test was well beyond normal specs and could probably even catch a blender. After that, they did the same with a retinal scan. Finally, they gave a urine sample that was tested for both illicit substances and as a backup DNA comparison.

Only after they'd passed all those checks were they allowed to proceed into the main part of the facility. There, they watched a short briefing video on what to expect at Area 17b; this was actually quite helpful for Tyrus, as the small camera picked up the video and audio and sent it back to him.

But that briefing described in only light detail—enough to be concerning but not enough to reverse engineer anything—the uniforms that the Blackmont employees would wear on their way to and while in the Crater. The uniforms were special issue and had integrated electronics that were biometrically paired to the wearer. They alone allowed each employee to go into the sections of the Crater that they were cleared for, and no one could use the uniform of another employee; the biometrics saw to that.

Tyrus didn't get to see where the uniforms were handed out. While his tracked employee was ostensibly on his way to get his, he passed through an antechamber where a mini-EMP blast fried Tyrus' small bug. He surmised by measuring the time from that point to the shuttle launch that getting the uniform was the last step before the employees were loaded into the shuttle for the flight to Luna and Area 17b.

All in all, nothing Tyrus saw gave him much hope that they could sneak one of their own into the facility under disguise as a Blackmont employee. Even with Neon Mouse's full access to their servers, they had no idea of how far in advance the uniforms were manufactured and programmed with employee biometrics. It could happen a month ahead of time, or it could happen mere hours before. He surmised that the facility itself handled the manufacturing of the uniforms in-house, so it wasn't even workable for them to capture a uniform en route. And except for a weekly download of employee biometrics the Mouse had found, the depot had *no* live connections to the main Blackmont servers for her to hack. It was a simple but highly effective firewall against exactly what Tyrus and his team were trying to do.

Someone had been very smart and extremely paranoid in setting up the security measures. They wanted to be sure that no one who didn't belong in Area 17b ever got close to it. Not surprising for a secret prison used primarily for spies, foreign combatants, and the odd psychopath. Even democracies, it seemed, had their dirty secrets they preferred to tuck away out of sight.

Tyrus sighed and settled in to watch the facility as darkness fell. It would be another long, chilly night in the mountains for him and his silent vigil. Hopefully, day four would yield something he could use.

---

"You know, that holo tech you've got sounds pretty slick. Don't suppose you'd let me take a look at your ship when this is all over?"

Jynx sighed openly. The young hacker in front of her hadn't spoken more than a few words during her day and night hacking of Blackmont Industries. But now that her initial part in the plan was done, she hadn't *stopped* talking for two whole days. Even the few times that Jynx had gone next door to spend some alone time with Toby in the other rented room, she assumed that Mousey just kept on talking while she was gone.

It was getting seriously annoying.

A knock came at the door. Mousey didn't even take a breath but kept right on chattering while Jynx got up and looked through the tinted front window to make sure it was Toby. Satisfied, she opened the door and let the young man in.

That led to the second thing that annoyed her about Mousey: the way Toby looked at her. Oh sure, Jynx supposed the hacker was attractive enough, even if she was too young and undeveloped. But she was far closer to Toby's age than Jynx was. And she overcame her otherwise plain appearance by wearing cutoff shorts with long black stockings and shirts that showed off her multiple naval piercings and the bevy of tattoos that encircled her abdomen and continued up under her shirt and out the top of the low-cut garment. The tattoos, piercings, and clothing drew attention to her body in ways that made Jynx always think she would have to clean up Toby's drool from his chin.

She was most upset with herself for even caring. She and Toby had made no promises. They'd never even talked about the possibility of such. Jynx was a decade older than the young man, and his clumsy innocence, albeit levied with the cold dose of reality he'd gained growing up in the foster system, was so far from anything she had ever thought would attract her in a man. On top of that, he was only a half-decent kisser; even in her own relative lack of experience in that area, she could tell he hadn't done it all that much before her.

Yet no matter how many times, usually lying awake in the uncomfortable motel bed at night when Mousey had finally stopped talking and gone to sleep, Jynx convinced herself that she didn't—*couldn't*—want Toby, all it took was one look at him drooling over the girl to get her hackles up.

At least Toby seemed to have finally clued into her reaction, because this time when he entered the room, he made a purposeful show of not even looking over at the Mouse, who right that minute was wearing a shirt that left little to the imagination. There was no way for him to ignore her naturally; the girl was continuing to talk nonstop. But Toby kept his eyes riveted on Jynx's and sat down on one of the beds with his back awkwardly turned away from the table where the girl sat. Jynx sat down next to him, facing the hacker.

"Archer sent the all-clear again," he said to Jynx. "And Riggs reports that he and O'Leary are ready on their end with the shuttle all fueled up and in position. Nothing yet from Tyrus."

The flash of anger that had normally come to Jynx with any mention of the ex-assassin's name was still there, but it had faded to little more than background noise at this point. "Don't worry about him," she replied begrudgingly. "If anyone can take care of himself and get his part done, it's the alpha."

Toby studied her for a moment, not responding. When he opened his mouth again, she could feel his hesitation, like a thick cloud in the room. "Jynx," he started in an uncertain tone. "Why do you hate Tyrus so much? I mean, I know he killed your sister, but didn't he not have a choice in the matter? He's an enacter, right?"

She let the question linger for a long moment, and even Mousey seemed to sense the tension and was waiting in perfect silence for her response. For a time, Jynx told herself she wasn't going to answer, especially not with the hacker girl in the room. But the earnest and hopeful look on Toby's face eventually overcame her defensive walls.

"He *did* have a choice," she said softly. "He didn't kill Jinny, did he? Even though he had orders to. That means he had a choice with Dax, too."

"Enacters don't have a choice. They have to do whatever they're told."

Jynx threw a look at Mousey to show that the girl's input wasn't appreciated, but the hacker didn't take the hint and kept talking.

"So, you shouldn't be mad at him. He had to do what he was told."

"You know nothing," Jynx said, a menacing tone in her voice that was meant to make it clear that she would brook no arguments on the topic.

Mousey ignored the hint again. "He seems pretty set on helping this reader friend of yours. He doesn't act like an assassin."

"He. Killed. My. Sister." Jynx bit off each word, struggling to keep her voice under control.

"Was he under orders from that Council thing?" the girl pressed.

Jynx frowned. She could see from the look on Toby's face that he was interested in how she would choose to answer the question. She relented. "Yes, it was on a mission for the Council. And yes, from what

I've gathered, it was a direct order. But that doesn't make it right!" She said the last part to Mousey directly, her expression daring the other woman to argue with her.

The hacker cocked her head in confusion. "So, why are you mad at him? He couldn't disobey a direct order. So, it's not his fault your sister is dead."

Jynx felt her face grow hot with anger. "Well, he obviously *did* disobey a direct order when he didn't kill the reader, didn't he?!" It was a repeat of her prior argument, but this time she said it loud enough that she saw Toby throw a quick glance around him as if to remind her of the motel's thin walls. Jynx kept her challenging gaze riveted on Mousey, doing her best to ignore him.

The hacker still looked confused. Despite her clear propensity to live more in the code of computers than in the world with the rest of humanity, she, like everyone else on Earth, had heard the basics of Tyrus' and Jinny's story. It had been plastered all over the media for a full month after they'd first arrived on Earth. "But he didn't know at that point he even could disobey. Right? So even if he was able to do it later, it doesn't change the fact that he didn't know then, at the time he killed your sister. So why are you mad at him for doing something he had no choice but to do?"

"You wouldn't understand!" Jynx snapped back.

The hacker shook her head and kept pressing. "No, you're wrong. I know a lot of enacters. Everyone shuns them. They're not even allowed to leave their enclaves in Australia. But I visit them sometimes, especially when I need to hide from… well, anyone. They're good friends, and they don't betray their friends without a direct order, and almost none of them have imprinted on the government, so I don't have to worry too much.

"I know that even *they* were surprised when they heard the story on the news—when you all first came to Earth—about your enacter friend disobeying the Council. They thought it was a lie; it sounds like it wasn't the way you're talking about him. But if some of them, even after hearing the story, can't believe it, how could your friend have believed it before he ever saw himself do it?"

The circuitous nature of the question aside, Jynx didn't know how to answer.

"She has a point," Toby practically whispered from next to her at the foot of the bed, speaking for the first time since he'd asked the original question.

Jynx shot him a look, but the disdain she tried to put into it just wasn't there.

"No. He could have stopped himself," she said. Instead of the words coming out with their usual sharp anger, she knew her voice sounded almost pleading. She felt her face growing hot again, but from tears forming in her eyes, not from the anger she'd felt before. "He *should* have stopped himself," she mumbled to herself huskily, barely loud enough for Toby to hear just a dozen centimeters away.

"You told me about your sister," Toby said quickly as if he was trying to cover up her obvious vulnerability. "How she tortured you and took your things; how your parents always favored her, but she was nasty to you all the time. It sounds like it was horrible. So, I get she was your sister, but I just don't understand why her death has affected you so much. Why are you so upset that Tyrus killed her, especially when he was just following orders?"

Jynx leapt to her feet and glared down hard at Toby, surprising him so that he leaned back as if to put more distance between them. "Because he got to her before I could!" she practically screamed in the small confines of the motel room.

She stood there for a long moment, glaring first at Toby and then at the hacker girl, daring either of them to speak first. Her hands were balled up in fists, and her shoulders were hunched tight in rage. Someone in the room below them banged on the floor beneath her feet to tell them to keep the noise down, but she ignored it.

Then, slowly, the rage drained out of her. Her shoulders slumped, and she put her hands on her knees as she struggled to stay upright. Tears flowed freely from her eyes, and she gasped for breath.

By some unspoken agreement, both Toby and the Neon Mouse stayed silent, waiting for her to catch her breath, collect herself, and continue. When she finally did, she spoke in a low, almost whisper that they both had to strain to hear. "I never got the chance to see if things could be different between us. I even thought…" her voice caught, but she steeled herself to get the words out. "I even thought that I would find Dax and kill her myself—to stop her from hurting other people like she'd always hurt our parents and me. But I never got the chance. Tyrus took that from me!"

Toby got up from the bed and stepped cautiously to stand in front of her. Slowly, gently, he reached out and grasped her shoulders with both of his hands and pulled her forward into him. It was awkward; he was several centimeters shorter than her, but she leaned into him and cried into his shoulder.

They were still standing like that when the hacker quietly left the room and went to Toby's room next door, leaving them alone with Jynx's demons, which had finally been released.

# CHAPTER 22

It was on another nameless day that they finally came for Jinny. They led her out of her cell and into a small room. It was empty except for a metal table, two chairs, and a mirror on the far wall across from where they sat her down. She knew instinctively that others were watching her from behind the mirror's glass.

They were obviously ready to start executing their plan, the one she had read from the prison guard on Earth. He'd been the one to lead her into the room. She knew his name, of course, but she'd chosen to think of him as 'Lurch', for the way he walked hunched over, with his hands usually in his pockets. He stayed after he chained her to the table, leaning up against the far wall and smirking at her, saying nothing.

Then another man entered, wearing a white lab coat. Wordlessly, the newcomer and Lurch held Jinny down and painfully drew several vials of blood from her arm by jabbing a large needle through the thick fabric of her jumpsuit; it took them several tries to find a vein through the thick material, making her feel like a pincushion. But her comfort was of far less priority to the men than ensuring she couldn't read either of them.

She declined to cry out in pain but glared at the men on either side of her in the mirror's reflection without blinking and without letting any facial expression shine through. She could tell it made the man in the lab coat uncomfortable, and she reveled in that minor victory.

*Kill him!* The voice that hissed in her mind was not her own, and for a moment, it surprised her. She saw Lurch look at her curiously in the mirror as she let her confusion color her face, but she ignored him.

*Kill him!* It came again. It was a raspy male voice… one she faintly recognized.

Suddenly, Jinny was no longer in the room! She no longer *saw* Jinny Ambrosa in the room's lone mirror. She saw Hendrix, the serial killer from Copernicus whom Jinny had once read and sent to prison. The man who had killed a dozen black-haired women on an insane spree to destroy anything that reminded him of his unfaithful ex-wife, and whose memories had been a featured part of her dreams since then. Now, Hendrix smiled back at himself in the mirror and laughed.

The prison guard and the man in the lab coat looked at Hendrix in shocked silence. He sneered at them, showing his teeth, wordlessly promising the terrible things he would do to them if they ever let him free. *Kill them now!* his internal voice raved, and he stretched at the chains holding him, fighting to get to the two doomed men in the room as they took a step back from him and…

Jinny shook her head and gasped. She was back in the room, seeing herself in the mirror where, before, Hendrix had looked out at her and laughed. Lurch and the lab-coated man were looking at her with confused and frightened expressions, and she knew they had only seen her, not the horrible serial killer that had briefly taken her place. *Kill them!* Hendrix's voice said again, but it sounded more distant now as if coming from a fog in the back of her mind that muddled her thoughts and made it hard to concentrate on herself.

Done drawing the blood they had come for, the two men beat a hasty retreat. *Kill them!* Hendrix's voice said again, now a distant whisper. Then they were gone, and so was Hendrix.

But the fog remained. Coming out of it, Jinny heard the urgent whispers of others, far enough away that she couldn't understand their words but could feel the fear and hatred in their voices, and it terrified her. For a while, her hazy mind tried to make sense of what had happened just a few moments before. It had been just like her nightmares—she had *become* Hendrix, seeing herself as him and the world through his eyes—but it had happened while she was *awake!* And that put a deep fear in the pit of her stomach that she fought hard not to show to the faceless men and possibly women who doubtlessly studied her through the glass.

After what seemed like an interminable wait, the room's door opened, and another man entered, accompanied again by Lurch. Like the man in the lab coat, she had never seen this newcomer before. He was a stern-looking man with gray hair who sat wordlessly across the table from her and stared at her for a long time, obviously trying to make her uncomfortable.

She waited him out, purposefully fighting the fog and going to a happy place in her head where she rested in Alan's embrace on the *Lucille* and listened to him talk of his feelings for her. She was kissing him again when the man finally broke the silence. That upset her because the kiss ended too early, and the fog came rushing back.

"We know you read your guard back on Earth. So, you know what we want." His expression was smug as if he held some sort of power over her with that knowledge.

Jinny said nothing in reply. With a concerted effort, she pushed back at the fog, trying to get back her sense of self and steel herself for what she knew was coming. But now Alan was back and stroking her hair. Had that really happened, or was she just wishing it had? Either way, she surrendered to the moment, letting Alan lead her deeper into the fog's embrace.

"Not giving us what we want will only make this more painful for you, Reader Ambrosa. It will be far easier to surrender now. No one can hold out forever, but those who try always regret it."

Jinny ignored him. Now she was holding a little girl. She looked down in awe at the blond baby in her arms, cooing and reaching up for her face. But who? *Virginia!* called a familiar voice in her head. *I'm home early. I came to see you and little Jinny.* That voice. Usually, it brought so much hate with it, but now all she felt was love and admiration. Why was that? *Oh, Virginia, you look so wonderful with our daughter.* Daughter? Virginia? Frank! She wasn't Jinny Ambrosa anymore. She was Virginia Ambrosa, mother to Jinny and wife to Frank. Frank was a good man; he was. He was just a little...

Now she was staring down at a different figure in her arms. This scene was familiar. The willowy woman with flaxen blond hair in her arms was silent, with her eyes open and her neck twisted at an unnatural angle. She was broken. *Virginia!* the same familiar voice cried out again. Frank! She was Frank on the day he'd killed her mother. She looked up, seeing a small girl standing a few meters away, and she reached out her hand toward little Jinny, begging the special girl to read her for the first and only time...

A palm slapping on the table brought Jinny back to reality. "I said, how do you want to do this?!" the man sitting across from her in the small room yelled at her, spittle flying from his mouth and onto her face.

Jinny retreated into the fog, and Frank cocked his head and looked at the man impassively. "Jinny won't tell you *anything*," Frank told the man. "I taught her better than that."

Now it was the gray-haired man's turn to cock his head and look confused. "What are you talking about, Reader Ambrosa? We have questions for you, and you *will* answer them. Let's start with how far back you can read."

Frank just laughed at the man. *Kill him!* Hendrix cackled from inside the fog. Frank ignored the serial killer, though he marked him for later study. Perhaps if they could take some of his genes and splice them with an enacter... No, he was getting distracted.

"Reader Ambrosa, you're choosing the hard way," the man across the table warned.

"Jinny isn't here right now," Frank answered. "Come back later."

He grinned widely at the frustrated man.

Then Frank was gone, and Jinny was back. Well, sort of back. The fog was thicker than before, and the voices that emanated from it now shouted over each other, far louder than the yelling and raving from the man across the table. Jinny ran away from the fog and found herself in Alan's arms again on the *Lucille*. Ryder was there, and John and Joan. Tyrus stopped by to chat for a few minutes, and he and Alan shared a few stories and some laughs about their adventures with Jinny. All was forgiven between them, and they were friends now. Her mother stopped by as well but wasn't able to stay longer than just to say hi. Frank tried to come by, but she turned him away at the door. Hendrix was outside in the hall, ranting about killing some guy in a lab coat.

Then someone *slapped* her! She looked up in shock. Alan, Ryder, John, Joan, Tyrus—all her friends—disappeared, and now it was just the man across the table. The man across the table and her. His gray eyes were unfriendly, and his face was pulled down in a frown. 'Angry Man', she decided to call him—had that been her thought or someone else's?

"Answer my question, or I'll do a lot worse than that to you," Angry Man growled at her, raising his open palm again to threaten her. "This can be so easy for you if you just tell us what we want to know. There's something different about you, and we need it. And we *will* get it."

"And what do you think will happen when you do?" Tyrus asked. He had offered to sit in for Jinny. It was so very kind of him. He was her best friend in the whole galaxy.

Angry Man started as if he hadn't understood what Tyrus said. So, the alpha asked the question again, speaking slower now so the man could better understand him. "What do you think will happen when you get what you want out of Jinny? I'll tell you what. I will hunt you down and kill you and everyone else involved in keeping her a prisoner. But if you let Jinny go now, *maybe* I'll let you live. This is your last chance to survive."

The gray-haired man's mouth opened in shock. Tyrus smiled his billion-dollar smile. "Now, where were we? Oh yes, you were just thinking of what a good idea it might be to let Jinny and all the rest of us go."

Then he laughed, and Hendrix laughed, and Frank laughed, and Jet laughed, and Alan laughed, and Ryder laughed, and Juliana Taylor laughed, and Sakura laughed, and even Virginia joined in. And Jinny was so happy to have such good friends there watching out for her, even if she kept losing them in the fog.

It was on the sixth day, almost as darkness was falling, that Tyrus finally got his break. An unmarked hovertruck pulled up to the security gate at the entrance to the Blackmont depot's fenced parking lot. Out of habit and discipline, he turned his scope and directional microphone toward the truck, though he had heard nothing of genuine interest from any of the previous deliveries over the last several days.

"You're late," he heard the guard say to the truck driver.

"Sorry," the driver replied in a tone that, even from Tyrus' distance and through the digital enhancement, made it clear the man didn't really care. "Had a grav coil give out and had to stop for repairs. Took a day to get the part to me; I was out in the middle of nowhere. Had to sleep in the kiffing truck."

"How terrible for you," the guard said in a voice thick with sarcasm. "Meanwhile, we've got another batch of guards coming through in two days, and the printers are out of thread, waitin' for you. We'll have to run 'em all day and all night until they get here just to have the uniforms ready. We usually have three days for that, not two."

"Hey, I don't service the truck. I just drive it. You wanna be mad at someone, call the motor pool."

"Yeah, yeah. Just get in there so we can get those printers running, will ya?"

Tyrus fought to keep from smiling. He pulled out his comm and switched it on from low-power standby mode. "Base," he said, waiting for Jynx to acknowledge. When she did, he said, "We've got our window. Nine days."

He didn't say the rest on the off chance that Blackmont was monitoring comms in the mountains surrounding their facility. He would be in their place, and he didn't want to take the risk that they could crack his encrypted transmission. Jynx signaled her understanding with a single click of her transmitter.

He had just learned that the Blackmont facility made the specially encoded uniforms only three days before each batch of personnel arrived for shipment to the Crater. So, all they had to do was have the

Neon Mouse hack the server now to change the personnel list for not this next round but the one after that in a week and a half. Then their man could make it through the secure facility and onto the transport, with his own encoded uniform waiting for him, courtesy of Blackmont Industries.

Quietly, Tyrus packed up his things and began to slowly hike back to the rally point, where Riggs and the stealth shuttle would, alerted by a signal from Jynx, rendezvous in three hours to pick him up. As he walked, he smiled to himself for the first time in weeks.

*I'm coming, Jinny.*

# CHAPTER 23

**NINE DAYS LATER; SEPTEMBER 2, 731 P.D.; SIX MONTHS AFTER THE REVELATIONS**

"We're ready." The two simple words, spoken in a calm voice, belied the tension Riggs felt.

Tyrus didn't move or respond at first. He stared at the snowcapped mountains that ringed the small forest valley where the stealth shuttle waited to take him and his team to Area 17b, the Crater. Riggs felt a chill go up and down his spine as he watched the tall black man take in the surroundings quietly.

A month had passed since the Council's attack and Jinny's imprisonment. And weeks had passed since they had first met in secret in Corey O'Leary's small cabin to plan her rescue. In that time, everything had miraculously fallen into place, though not without a few necessary adjustments along the way. Now they were ready to go, and the closer they'd gotten to this moment, the icier and more distant Tyrus had become.

This man was dangerous. Riggs had known it from the moment he'd met him and Jinny on Rinali Station, as they'd approached him posing as minor ne'er-do-wells looking for a smuggler. He'd known it when the man had dismantled by hand a team of pirates who tried to stop them from getting to the *Blind Monk* to escape the dying station. And he'd known it when the ex-alpha had calmly destroyed the Council Navy fighter that had trailed them from Rinali and later when he'd nonchalantly prepared to repel boarders. That was just before the timely intervention of a Guard shuttle allowed them to escape from the massive Council Navy dreadnought that had caught the *Monk* with a shock cable.

Even with all that, he'd never seen the man as cold and as dangerous as he was now.

Riggs knew how deeply Tyrus felt for Jinny. It wasn't romantic; sure, he had sensed some jealousy from the man at the times he had tried pursuing his own romantic relationship with the pretty reader, but it had never seemed to come from a rival for her affection. Rather, Riggs had always had the impression that the ex-alpha simply wanted Jinny's *time*, which made sense, given that the man literally had no other friends.

Of course, always present in those same moments was a clear sense from Tyrus that to hurt Jinny was to incur his wrath, no matter what he and Riggs had otherwise been through together. Cal hadn't needed the reminder to treat the woman well—he may be a smuggler, but his mother had raised him right—but it had been an ever-present weight on his shoulders that reminded him anyway. Even the big ex-alpha's work to help the Four Worlds prepare for the Council invasion seemed to sometimes be more from doing what Jinny wanted him to do rather than from a deep wellspring of personal motivation to save the Earthies.

Riggs cared deeply for Jinny as well; he could even see himself settling down with a girl like her. But in a universe that had continuously betrayed Tyrus Tyne, the big man cared even more deeply for the reader. Because she was, quite possibly, the *only* person or thing he truly cared about.

Now, someone had taken this man's best friend from him. And Riggs felt a surprising measure of sympathy for those responsible for her incarceration and for those that would stand in Tyne's way to gaining her freedom.

*They're going to die. All of them. They don't even have an inkling of what's coming, and it wouldn't matter if they did. They're already dead.*

Tyrus turned, oblivious to Riggs' terrified inner monologue. He smiled thinly at the pilot in a way that didn't reach his hard eyes. "Let's go, Riggs. Let's get Jinny." Without waiting for a response, he walked past the pilot and up the stealth shuttle's ramp. Riggs shivered again from a feeling that had nothing to do with the crisp mountain air.

---

Jinny huddled, shivering, on the small bunk in her cell. She was terrified. The fog was so thick, and she knew that was bad, but she couldn't remember why. And the voices that came from the fog were so urgent—they demanded her attention day and night at every moment, awake and in her dreams. Sometimes they came out of the fog and spoke more to her and even to the guards, and in those times, Jinny could feel herself slipping away, little by little until she started to lose track of herself in the fog altogether.

Tyrus had been by to visit today and had detailed to Lurch exactly how he was going to kill the guard when he came to rescue Jinny. That was OK, though Jinny was a little shocked at her friend's graphic description of dismemberment. But it was the thought that counted.

Then Hendrix had come out of the fog and started shrieking at the guards and the cameras in the room, and he was much more graphic than even Tyrus, so much so that it scared her to even be in the same room as the man... but she hadn't really been there at all with him, had she?

Then her parents had visited, but Jinny had ignored them. To her mind, Frank was worse than Hendrix, and Virginia was just chatting inanely about the drapes she wanted to put in the baby's room. It annoyed Frank, and it annoyed Jinny. Her parents finally left but promised to visit again soon before they disappeared back into the fog.

She had been so scared, but then Alan had come for a while and just lay down on the bunk next to her and held her wordlessly. She had fallen asleep in his arms but woken up from another nightmare to find him gone. Instead, Ryder had been there, telling her all about the team's next mission. It sounded like a fun one; something about a prison break. She hadn't really been paying attention. The fog made it hard to focus on *anything*.

She'd gone back to sleep, but she'd dreamed about Sakura's suicide and had woken up in a cold sweat, recognizing she was in a prison cell and that something was *very* wrong with her. She hadn't been able to decide what it was before Hendrix started yelling at the guards again.

Later, she had been talking to Juliana Taylor—how nice of the kind older woman to come and visit her—when all of a sudden, the matron had disappeared before her eyes, and Jinny had shuddered in panic. *It's here,* she had thought. *The break! I'm losing my mind!*

But then Tammy Johnson stopped by her cell, and Jinny forgot all about whatever it was that was scaring her. It had been so long since she'd seen Tammy or even thought about her, but she was polite enough not to say anything about the woman's missing left hand. That would be so rude to the girl whose crime scene had brought her and Alan together, even if Tammy had already been dead when that had happened.

Now she sat, shivering, on her bunk, terrified but not sure why. After all, she wasn't alone in the cell anymore; all her friends were there with her. She could hear them all the time now, and that was good, wasn't it?

*This place isn't so bad, so long as my friends are all here,* Jinny convinced herself as she drifted off to sleep, doing her best to ignore the roiling fog just out of sight. *And they won't leave me. They'll be here when I wake up.*

---

Reuben Linchfield hated Pedro De Vasquez more than he hated any of the dangerous criminals he was responsible for looking after on a daily basis. Reuben knew that if you took the worst sociopath and removed from him all hope of escape in a way that was impossible by comparison in Earthbound prisons, that same sociopath would eventually become resigned to his or her fate and become, in turn, surprisingly docile.

Of course, keeping every prisoner in Area 17b drugged at all times probably had something to do with that, but Reuben liked to think it was more the knowledge that there was nowhere to go for anyone who escaped his facility. Even though the few true sociopaths they had in residency were given enough of the prescribed drugs to reduce them to drooling invalids.

Still, for every incapacitated sociopath, murderer, spy, or other prisoner the Crater hosted, Blackmont got money, and Reuben Linchfield got an extra few percentage points in his annual bonus. But Pedro De Vasquez, aka the 'Lizard' to the men and women who ran Area 17b, consistently found ways to *cost* Reuben money. The last time he'd visited the Crater, the man had found that one of the senior guards had been padding his expense reports. While the stolen amount had totaled only a few thousand dollars, Reuben had learned that hell hath no fury like a bureaucrat scorned. In the end, Blackmont's corporate headquarters had needed to pay several *hundred* thousand in fines to prove to the government how sorry they were—cutting into corporate profits and Reuben's bonus.

The time before that, the Lizard had mandated the firing of Reuben's administrative assistant, citing the woman's lack of proper qualifications for her post. That the charge had been true had made Linchfield no less livid. He hadn't hired the woman for her *typing* skills. Who was De Vasquez to deny a man of his stature a few comforts in this lonely and isolated post? Of course, the gnome-like little man had suggested that a few thousand dollars could make the problem go away, but Reuben knew that opening that door once with a pig like De Vasquez would mean the man would keep coming back to the trough for more. So, he had feigned righteous anger and instead showed both the government auditor and his own administrative assistant the door. He knew there were other women in the prison's population of guards and administrators who were anxious, or at least willing, to cozy up to the facility's director for a better chance at a promotion.

Now, with the hated Pedro De Vasquez sitting across from him in

## THE FOUR WORLDS - SUBVERSION

Reuben's relatively spacious office, the Blackmont director was all smiles. He had to keep up appearances, regardless of his inner feelings.

"I trust you've found everything so far to your liking and approval?" he asked the Lizard with false amiability as the man blew on the steaming mug of coffee Reuben's new assistant had brought for him. The audit itself had been going on for two full days, with De Vasquez staying in one of the administrative area's guest quarters. This morning was to be the auditor's final report.

The Lizard said nothing but watched Reuben with a cool gaze over the rim of the mug. He did that. A lot. He just stared at Reuben and his people like they were insects; never mind that even the most junior Blackmont guard in the Crater made more than twice the Lizard's annual government salary. He was a petty man who took satisfaction in the power he wielded over the corporate types he considered his inferiors. Reuben had learned the hard way just to let the man have his power trips.

"Your quarterly energy usage is up three percent," the Lizard finally spoke in the annoying nasal voice that sometimes haunted Reuben's nightmares. "Yet I can find no legitimate reason for the increase, so I doubt the government will cover the expense," he ended with a smug, self-satisfied smile.

Reuben stifled an exasperated sigh and looked back at the man blankly. "I will have to check our records, but I'm sure that such a small increase is within normal fluctuations and nothing that the government need be worried about."

The Lizard only shrugged and went back to blowing on his coffee. He'd still yet to take a sip, and Reuben was almost sure that once he finally did, he'd complain about it being too cold.

"There is another discrepancy," the auditor said with mock casualness. "Your records currently show 2,581 prisoners, but I have it on good authority that you really have 2,582 in residence."

Reuben felt his spine go stiff, and he quickly hid the grimace that fleetingly formed on his face. "Are you sure you read the records correctly?" He needed to stall and give himself time to think. There shouldn't have *been* any paper trail showing the new prisoner coming in. Someone on his staff was getting fired after this meeting!

De Vasquez frowned and lowered the mug of coffee. "Of course, Director Linchfield. My sources are never wrong about something like this. I'd hate to think you're trying to hide something from me."

Reuben cursed in his head, but he was proud of how calm his voice sounded when he responded. "As you know, we often take in special prisoners by order of the government. Unfortunately, I am unable to comment on such cases, as even you lack the security clearance for them."

It was the truth and really the only response that *might* work with the bureaucrat, but Reuben tensed for the man's riposte. He knew he was playing with fire. The Lizard would either accept that bureaucrats above himself had made a decision, or he would insist on squeezing Reuben and Blackmont between himself and the other shadowy government officials who had delivered the new prisoner. And Linchfield desperately needed the man to take the first option, because if word got out that the highest-value prisoner in the Crater had devolved into a raging lunatic, it was all over for Blackmont's plans, and by extension, for Reuben Linchfield.

Unfortunately, by the man's deepening frown, Reuben guessed he was choosing the latter path.

"I have full authority over this facility's efficiency ratings and am privy to *all* information required to do my job," the Lizard said.

Reuben tried his best to project a look of calm confidence as he shook his head. "I'm sorry, Mr. De Vasquez, but in this case, I lack the authority to disclose the information you seek. Perhaps if you reach out to your superiors and ask them about it, they will inform you of the same."

He almost returned the inspector's earlier smug smile as he played the card he knew no bureaucrat would attempt to trump. By encouraging the Lizard to call his own superiors, he was showing the man that he already knew what the response would be. Now, the Lizard had to choose between either backing down or losing face by being shot down by his own superiors in front of the same people he was sent to audit, something no government lackey with his overgrown sense of importance would ever do without first being sure of the outcome.

But to Reuben's surprise, De Vasquez didn't shrink or even frown. The man smiled! And when he spoke, it was with an audible sneer.

"Now, now, Reuben," his nasal voice bit off Linchfield's first name. "I'd be happy to call my superiors about this. And when I do, I'll be sure to tell them about the secret account you keep with the Second Bank of Europa. You know, the account where you store the money from your… extracurricular activities?"

Reuben felt the blood drain completely from his face, and a pit formed in his stomach. *How does he…?* "I'm not sure what you're talking about," he said lamely, even to his own ears.

The Lizard shook his head and smiled wider. "Come now; surely you didn't think it escaped my notice that some of the more potent psychedelic drugs you use to keep your prisoners in line have shown up on the streets of Tranquility City? Or that some of the prisoners I saw on my tour yesterday looked much more awake and alert than would be possible at the dosages you *claim* to be administering to them?"

The man let his questions hang in the air as he grinned at Reuben as if to say, 'your move, Director'.

Reuben swallowed audibly. When he spoke, his voice quavered, and he hated himself for the weakness. "What do you want?"

"Simple," De Vasquez said, a glint in his eye at Reuben's obvious surrender. "I want you to transfer half of the funds in your little off-Earth account to an account number I will provide you."

Reuben shook his head in desperation but then breathed out loudly and nodded slowly. If his superiors learned about his skimming of the facility's drug supplies for his own profit, no one would ever find his body. That's how things worked in Blackmont Industries. But he still felt rage building inside him as he considered this worm taking a portion of his hard-earned gains. His hand slowly slid across his lap toward the desk drawer that held his loaded pistol, but then he stopped himself.

*If I give in, that makes De Vasquez complicit. I can use his own greed against him and possibly even make these inspections go easier. Besides,* he thought with an inner smile, *he only mentioned the account at the Second Bank, which means he probably doesn't know about the account at the Citi-*

zen's Bank or the one at the Io Valley Credit Cooperative. So, he's really only getting about an eighth of what I've socked away so far. If that buys me relief from his constant meddling, that might just be worth it.

"Fine," he responded out loud. "But I'll need assurances from you that the matter rests after that."

The man shrugged in response, and despite Reuben's internal decision, the smug grin on the Lizard's face made him still want to pull out his gun and shoot the bureaucratic troll.

"I can make sure that no one else discovers your... indiscretions for a modest ongoing fee," the man said, and Reuben almost did grab the gun. Still, he held back. He just needed to buy some time so he could figure out how to make the man go away. Accidents happened all the time in a maximum-security prison. Letting a prisoner take care of the Lizard would be poetic justice and probably even worth the fines the government would no doubt levy.

"I'm sure we can arrange that," he answered, moving his hand away from the drawer.

The Lizard nodded and then smiled a little wider, portending more pain for Reuben Linchfield. "One more thing," he said, "tell me about this new prisoner. I think you just realized that I *do* have clearance after all."

It was the final humiliation. The Lizard probably didn't care at all for the identity of the new prisoner, but he'd painted Reuben into a corner and wanted him to realize just how little power he had to deny the auditor *anything*. And he was taking his revenge for Linchfield daring to tell him no just a few minutes before.

So Reuben told him all about the 2,582$^{nd}$ prisoner to take up residence at the Crater, except the part about her losing her grasp on reality.

# CHAPTER 24

"We'll be landing at Lunar Base One in two hours, Congressman." The calm and professional voice of Landon Hartman, Corey O'Leary's pilot, was a sharp contrast to the turmoil inside the legislator at this moment.

It wasn't that Corey didn't believe in what they were doing. He'd better, given that he was literally committing treason with the aim of breaking Jinny out of prison. Getting caught would mean the end of both his political career and his life as a free man.

Even success would likely mean the same, but at least it would give them a chance to save the entire system. He was still convinced that Jinny was the key to doing that. She was the only one the public might believe about the threat; additionally, Horatio Lopez had told Corey that Jinny had some sort of special abilities that could also be invaluable in the fight against the Council. Corey didn't know what he meant by that, and the old man refused to share more detail except to say that it was absolutely vital that she be freed before Pereira's and Givens' cronies actually *did* kill her.

And even if none of that was the case, what the government was doing to her was just plain *wrong*, and he couldn't, in good conscience, be a part of it even just by allowing it to happen.

He had spoken at length with his wife, Debra, about it. He'd learned long ago never to make a major decision without her input. They both would have been jailed for violating the State Secrets Act multiple times over had anyone else in the government suspected just how much he confided in her, even on classified topics she lacked the clearance for. But he had found her to always be a voice of reason and calm logic, even when he couldn't count on his closest official advisers for the same.

Debra stood to lose as much as Corey if this plan went sideways. In some ways, she stood to lose even more. If the plan went well from start to finish, Corey would be fleeing to the only place in the Sol system that *might* be willing to listen to the warnings that Jinny and her friends had brought. It wasn't Earth; he had to go to Mars. And the only way he could get there was to call in a favor from an old relationship, one he'd sworn to Debra he would never revisit.

He'd expected her to be upset with him for even suggesting the course of action he was now solidly embarked upon. She'd surprised him by not only accepting the necessity of his plan but by fully endorsing it. Like him, she'd grown to love Jinny as a daughter in the brief time she had lived with them and would do anything to save the girl, even if it meant staying on Earth to face the inevitable fallout from his actions in doing so.

They had discussed the possibility of her accompanying him, of course. In this, Debra had put her foot down and adamantly refused to leave her planet. One of them had to remain for their children and grandchildren, not just to be with them, but to help them understand the *why* behind Corey's actions. Especially when the media began its inevitable assault on his character. It might be *months* or even *years* before Gorsky could arrange to get Corey back to Earth and the charges dropped, and the damage to his public image might never recover.

Worse, Corey had his doubts that what they were attempting would work. But the time for such worries had passed. Even had he wanted to recall the others and scrub the mission, he knew they wouldn't listen. He had seen the look on Tyne's face as they discussed each step of the plan. Like the others, he knew that anyone—friend or foe, it didn't matter—who stood between that man and rescuing Jinny Ambrosa would be as good as dead.

The cold fire that burned inside Tyne had troubled him from the day he'd first met the tall ex-assassin. The man was damaged in a deep and fundamental way, and Corey doubted that any of Tyrus' friends, including Jinny, realized just how unstable the big man really was.

He had been around others who were likewise damaged in ways that weren't always apparent. Politics attracted all kinds of people with all sorts of issues, including more than its fair share of sociopaths. Tyrus wasn't a sociopath; the man had, if anything, an overdeveloped sense of morality, probably stemming from his newfound freedom to choose his own path. In some ways, it was that sense of morality—of strict right and wrong—that made the man so dangerous. For Tyne, there was no gray area; the very concept would probably have confused him. That meant that decisions, actions, and even people could only fit into one of two categories in the big ex-enacter's mind: good or evil. And heaven help anyone who landed in the second category.

Corey knew that many of the guards staffing the Crater, where Jinny was almost certainly being held, were, in fact, evil. He'd read enough reports on Blackmont Industries over the years to know that, even among the gray world of mercenaries, they were one of the worst outfits. He'd tried repeatedly to have them removed from the list of approved UE government contractors, but he'd lost every time. Blackmont had a healthy share of owned politicians in every party, including and especially Corey's.

He had no doubt that some or even most of the men and women staffing the hidden Luna prison had committed enough atrocities to earn the death penalty if the truth ever came to light. But he also knew that others hadn't. Some of them were just men or women doing their jobs and trying to support their families using the perhaps-limited skill sets God or nature had bestowed upon them. None of them would have completely clean hands, but not all of them would have particularly dirty ones, either.

He had tried to explain this to Tyrus before they'd parted ways; he'd tried to tell the big man that some of the guards and administrators at the prison would be innocents and that a light touch may be in order. The big man had simply stared back at him with a nearly vacant expression. His response had chilled Corey to the bone. "If they're innocent, they won't get in my way." Which, of course, left the logical extension of that statement unspoken: 'If they get in my way, then they're not innocent'.

The betrayal—as Tyrus rightly saw it—of the UE government in having him and his friends arrested was enough to make nearly *everyone* associated guilty of gross evil. Even then, Corey or someone else may have reasoned with the man. However, the fact that they'd taken his *best* friend, Jinny, to a secret prison and told the world she was dead, left no room for argument.

Tyrus Tyne was the avenging angel who would descend below the lunar surface and smite all those that impeded his righteous quest. And there was nothing Corey, Archer, Jynx, Riggs, or possibly even Jinny herself could do to stop him. A lot of people were going to die.

The buzzing of his implant interrupted his grim thoughts. He looked down at his palm and saw the caller's name. Even though he was alone in his shuttle's passenger compartment, he still engaged the privacy field when he answered.

"Mikael. What's going on?"

The big Russian answered hurriedly. "My friend, I do not know how you intend to get your reader friend out of the Crater, but I have heard through back channels that someone paid an obscene sum to hire a hacker called the Neon Mouse. Tell me, please, that it was you."

Corey thought about denying it; the less Gorsky knew about the plan, the less chance he could be made to reveal it. But the man *had* been helping Corey with information from inside the Pereira administration. So, he decided to answer what he could.

"Yes, I've hired the Neon Mouse."

"Good. That is quite good," the man responded. "I must ask you a favor, then."

Corey frowned, glad that Gorsky couldn't see his expression on the audio-only connection. "What, exactly, do you need?"

"It is simple, really. When the hacker is done with helping your reader escape, I need you to have her access a certain document in Pereira's personal files and send it to me."

Corey thought for a long moment before responding. When he did, he spoke slowly. "Mikael, I don't like where this is going."

He could almost see the Russian's exasperated expression in the tone of his response. "Corey Ivanovich. I ask you to trust me on this. It is vitally important to our cause but too sensitive to talk about even on this secure line. If we were together in person, I would gladly share the details. But as it is, you must give me your trust as I have given you mine. This may be the only way I can ultimately help you return to Earth."

Corey let out a long sigh. He and Gorsky each now had enough on the other to see them both put in prison for an awfully long time. Even playing a distant support role and feeding Corey the information he needed to break Jinny out of the Crater was enough to have the Russian executed for treason if his role in the plan ever came out. He was *right*, to Corey's chagrin; they had to trust each other.

"OK. Send me the details. I'll pass along the instructions to the hacker *after* we get Jinny out."

"Spasibo, my friend. I knew I could count on you. I am sending the information now."

The call ended, and Corey sat back in his seat and looked out the viewport at the expanse of space between Earth and Luna, heavy with the lights of the daily traffic that moved between the two planets. In the distance, he could see the larger lights of the naval shipyard standing out against the expanse of stars.

He frowned. No matter how things shook out over the next few days, his career, and possibly Gorsky's along with it, was over. So, it was no time to hold back, he supposed. Though a small nagging feeling at the back of his mind refused to go away, he shoved it aside and went over the plan again in his head.

---

"Badge?" It was the seventh time, by Toby's count, that someone had asked to see or scan his badge since he'd entered the small supply depot in the mountains of Colorado. The first check had worried him, even though he'd been expecting it; it was the first test of the false identity the Neon Mouse had uploaded for him to Blackmont's servers. But as he got deeper and deeper into the facility with no alarms sounding, he had to admit the cute little hacker did good work.

One week before, there had been no record of Toby Lazenby—they'd used the same first name to keep things simple, and so he would respond naturally when it was called out—in any of the records of Blackmont Industries. But the Neon Mouse did good work. Three days ago, when the next shipment of supplies for the uniform printer arrived, Toby Lazenby had such a deep record within the Blackmont personnel files that it would fool even his own mother into thinking he'd worked there for the last six months.

That no one would recognize him came from the fact that he'd supposedly been deployed to a Blackmont contingent on Io, a small corporate security team, before being transferred to Earth and now again to Luna. It was a strange path for someone with so little time at the company, but not an *overly* unusual one based on the personnel records the Mouse had hacked.

So, he showed his badge without flinching to the burly guard who had asked for it. The man examined it, scanned it with his pad, and then grunted. "Your uniform is over there in locker B9," he said gruffly, then diverted his attention to the next transferee in the line.

*Almost there*, Toby thought, pushing aside any lingering doubts or worries about the mission. He was in too deep now to turn back, even if he'd wanted to. Of course, his motivations were complex, even to him. But they all boiled down to one thing: get Jynx and her friends into that facility alive. If he could do that, everything else would fall into place.

Jynx had argued *against* him going on this part of the mission. She had volunteered, claiming she could disguise herself enough to pass through Blackmont's security without being recognized. However, for all her bravado, it never would have worked. The depth of the biometric scans meant they also couldn't send Archer to impersonate a real Blackmont employee, and they needed him to play De Vasquez anyway. So, Toby, knowing what he needed to do, insisted on going.

That the others agreed was a small surprise. Jynx had argued more, but they'd impressed upon her that the chances of the guards at the Blackmont facility recognizing the face of one of Earth's most wanted fugitives—even with a disguise—was simply too great. Besides, Tyne himself had argued, Toby's time in the foster system made him not only smart and sneaky but a decent enough actor. Toby hadn't even known the big man had been watching him that closely, and it gave him shudders to think about it.

So now Toby was here, doing his best to break *into* a maximum-security prison. *Well,* he thought wryly, *at least maybe I'll get the girl when this is all over.*

---

"Signal from Archer!" Jynx called out from the stealth shuttle's cockpit, and Tyrus leapt to his feet faster than Riggs could react and rushed forward to see what the blender had sent.

When Riggs arrived in the cockpit, Tyrus was already sitting in the pilot's chair and reading the message on one of the cockpit display screens. Riggs leaned in to see it over the larger man's shoulder.

There were a few paragraphs of words, but more importantly, there was a map of where in the prison they were keeping Jinny—it was the first hard confirmation they'd had of her imprisonment there, and it sent a wave of relief through Riggs.

Then he looked closer. They had all studied the prison map that Neon Mouse had hacked from the Blackmont servers on Earth to the point that they'd essentially memorized it. But the part of the prison where Jinny was supposedly being held wasn't even *on* that map. Instead, the blueprints showed that area as nothing but solid rock on the other side of the prison's administrative areas, far from the normal prisoner cell blocks. It meant they would have to adjust their plans somewhat, but it might actually make it easier for them to get to her in the end.

He glanced back behind him into the passenger/troop compartment. The young hacker who had gotten them the original map was sitting in one of the jump seats along the shuttle's starboard bulkhead, fiddling with a pad. Before they'd left Earth, she had somehow found the time and supplies to dye her hair purple, and she'd added two chains to her facial piercings: one leading from a ring in each nostril to a matching ring in each earlobe. That was in addition to the chain she already had encircling her bare stomach.

Riggs had to admit the look definitely set her apart, though it wasn't exactly attractive by his book, especially with the myriad of colorful but clashing tattoos that covered almost every exposed square inch of the girl's body.

No, despite being an underworld scoundrel himself, Riggs had a surprisingly wholesome taste in women. Jinny, with her girl-next-door looks and vibes, had attracted him from the start. Back on Earth, he had caught Toby sneaking a look now and again at the eccentric hacker whenever he thought Jynx wasn't looking. He wondered if the boy knew just how much fire he was playing with when he did that. His co-pilot was clearly smitten with the young man for reasons Riggs couldn't fathom. He'd walked in on them making out when he'd visited the motel in Las Vegas—he hadn't even known Jynx was *capable* of that sort of behavior. But that wouldn't stop her from cutting the boy apart if she thought he was even considering cheating on her with the Neon Mouse. And Toby seemed to make his co-pilot happy, which wasn't something Riggs wanted to see end.

"Temperance, get up here!" Tyrus' voice boomed practically in Riggs' ear, making him wince. At the sound, the young hacker jumped to her feet and obediently moved forward through the open hatch into the now-cramped cockpit. They'd all thought it silly when they'd learned her real first name. It had come out when she'd first been introduced to Tyrus. He'd thrown her a look of disapproval when he'd asked her name and she'd given her hacker handle. Without raising his voice or showing any overt anger, he'd once again asked her name. She must have seen the hardness of his eyes or heard it in the tone of his voice because she'd immediately shared it.

*How did a girl named Temperance end up as a hacker calling herself the Neon Mouse?* Riggs wondered. Of course, she utterly refused to let anyone else on the crew call her by her real name—only Tyrus. She would ignore the rest of them if they tried to use it. They all had to call her Neon Mouse, though Jynx often simply called her 'Mousy', to the girl's obvious frustration.

"What's up?" Temperance/Neon Mouse asked when she arrived in the small cockpit.

"The supply and personnel shuttle should be arriving this afternoon," Tyrus answered. "Any last-minute checks we can do to make sure nothing goes wrong?"

The girl shook her head. "Nope. It's just like I thought. The whole prison is air gaped. It's not a software firewall; they literally don't even have a live data connection with the outside world. If you want me to hack them, you're going to have to get me inside."

"But to do that, we have to first hack them so we *can* get inside," Tyrus said with forced patience.

The girl either didn't pick up on his tone or chose to ignore it. She just nodded. "Yep. The little spike I gave your friend Toby should do the trick. All he has to do is put it where I told him, and I'll have a remote connection to the surface systems. Should be enough for me to get us in if we move quickly. But it won't take them long to find it, so the timing has to be precise."

That had been another reason they hadn't had Archer take on Toby's part of the plan. They needed his meeting with Linchfield to take place at least several hours ahead of their raid on the facility so that he could confirm both Jinny's presence in the prison and her exact location. But having him plant the spike that far ahead would have drastically increased the chances of Blackmont's security experts finding it and locking down the entire place in response. That part had necessitated Toby's role.

"It better be enough," Jynx growled. She might not be worried about the girl stealing Toby away, but that didn't mean she liked her at all. Of course, that wasn't surprising for Jynx.

"It'll work," the hacker said defensively. "There isn't a system created I can't hack and make dance." Then she looked at Tyrus. "I mean… I'm pretty sure it'll work."

Riggs shook his head in consternation. With most of the crew, the girl spewed the bravado and certainty that was so typical of hackers in any part of the galaxy. But with Tyrus, she hedged. He suspected she knew what he was capable of doing to her if she failed to live up to her promises. Riggs didn't think he would kill or even hurt the little hacker, but he wasn't sure he *wouldn't* either.

He was scaring all of them. The man was a tightly wound spring that was ready to snap. The sooner they rescued Jinny and restored some calm to the big man, the better off they all would be. And the way he kept looking toward the special container O'Leary had sent to be loaded on the shuttle before their departure, the end game couldn't come soon enough.

---

"*Irish Setter*, you are cleared for landing on government pad 4C," the voice of Lunar Base One Control said through the speakers of Corey's personal shuttle. Landon Hartman acknowledged the landing assignment and guided the small shuttle in.

Landon had worked for the O'Learys for nearly fifteen years after he'd been drummed out of the United Earth Navy with an honorable medical discharge when a piece of shrapnel from an overloaded gravity generator had lodged near his spine. The doctors had removed the piece of metal, but a spinal injury of any kind was deemed too risky for continued naval service. So, at the young age of 24, nearly fresh out of naval pilot training, Landon Hartman found himself with no job, no prospects, and a disability pension that wouldn't even pay for a $16^{th}$-level underground slum apartment on Luna, much less anything on Earth.

Then Corey had come across the man's file in his role as the chairman of the Congressional Committee on Military Affairs. Long frustrated by the rest of Congress's refusal to properly fund veteran disability and pension benefits, Corey had seen the file and jumped on an opportunity to make a difference for at least *one* of the many veterans he was continuously striving to help. It just so happened at the time that the O'Leary family's personal pilot was retiring, and he saw something in Landon's file that convinced him to give the kid a shot.

A few weeks later, after a couple of audition flights, the O'Leary Foundation hired Landon Hartman as a staff pilot, assigned specifically to the private shuttle of Congressman and foundation trustee Corey O'Leary. The man had worked in that capacity ever since, despite numerous offers of promotion within the organization. He was completely loyal to the congressman and refused to even consider letting anyone else fly the man anywhere.

It was this same stubborn loyalty that would now probably doom the pilot. Corey hadn't wanted to take him on this mission; he saw no reason for his treason to taint any of his staff. But Debra had quietly let the young man know what was going on, and Landon had insisted on being the one to fly Corey to Luna personally. Because, he had reasoned with his employer, having a wealthy heir and congressman show up on a commercial flight would raise suspicion all by itself.

Corey had still tried to keep the man out of the next part of the plan, even trying to find a way to smuggle Riggs to Luna with him instead. But once again, he'd lost to the combined force of Debra O'Leary and Landon Hartman. He only prayed that it wouldn't destroy the young man.

---

Toby gripped the armrest of the shuttle so hard he thought he might break his own fingers. The excitement of the upcoming mission was overwhelming, and he grinned as the g-forces of the shuttle launch leaked past the craft's inertial compensators.

"We're through the exosphere," the pilot called calmly through the cabin. "Five hours to Luna and Area 17b, folks. Enjoy your flight."

---

"I'm pretty sure your friend made it onto the shuttle," Temperance/Neon Mouse said calmly from her place back in the troop compartment of the stealth shuttle. "I put a watch on the Earthside

Blackmont servers, and I haven't picked up any alerts about an alarm from the supply depot. So, either he's on the shuttle, or they're keeping his capture quiet for some reason."

Jynx glared at the girl, but Tyrus only nodded. Riggs was taking his shift up in the cockpit now, and they sat with the hacker in the back of the shuttle, ostensibly resting for what was to come. In reality, neither was ready to relax or even pretend to. Zero hour was approaching.

# CHAPTER 25

"Congressman, what an unexpected but welcome surprise." The facial expression of Science Director Belyaev, who headed up the team of researchers on the military side of Lunar Base One, showed that the surprise was anything *but* welcome. The man had always hated it when the government meddled in what he saw as *his* personal domain. Unfortunately for him, Corey O'Leary's position as chairman of the Committee on Military Affairs meant he was one of the few men Belyaev simply could *not* turn away, even when he showed up without prior warning.

"Thank you for the warm welcome, Director," Corey said, pretending not to notice the other man's prickly manner. "I've come for a surprise inspection of the work you're doing on Object AA24. This is my personal pilot," he gestured to Landon standing next to him, "and member of my congressional staff, Landon Hartman. As a member of my staff, he is also cleared for the project, and I wanted to get his professional opinion on the object while we're here on Luna."

"Of course, that makes sense." Once again, Belyaev's tone made it clear that it absolutely did *not* make sense, and Corey was sure that the man was dying inside at the thought of letting a lesser life form, like a pilot, or even a congressman, touch his most prized possession.

But it wasn't really *his* possession. It was the property of the United Earth government, sort of. And Corey controlled the committee that controlled Belyaev's budget. So, the man was at least outwardly deferential as he led them to the secret underground hangar buried deep below Lunar Base One.

They arrived at the viewing window into the hangar, and for the first time, Corey saw, in person, what the UE government had deemed Object AA24. He was surprised at the ugliness of the ship. It looked a little like a pregnant whale, in his opinion. But the government's pet scientists had been drooling over it for the past six months, repairing it and then taking it apart and putting it back together to learn all its secrets. It wasn't surprising that they were studying it so closely; it was the only piece of technology from the 47 Colonies that Earth had been this close to in almost 600 years.

Corey wondered idly how Riggs and Jynx would feel to know just how possessive Belyaev and his staff had become over Object AA24, aka the *Blind Monk*.

---

Commander Kevin Fischer was doing his best to appear much more alert than he really was. His command chair wasn't the most comfortable seat he'd ever sat in, but it was often the hardest one to stay awake in. Especially when literally nothing of note had happened for his entire shift on the bridge of his small patrol frigate, *UENS Lunar Dawn*.

The *Dawn* was currently providing close patrol of the space around Luna's southern hemisphere, charged with scanning for any smugglers or other unauthorized ships that dared to get too close to the moon. Even as boring as the post sounded, Kevin often thought wryly, it was actually much *less* exciting than that.

Oh sure, United Earth saw its fair share of smugglers, even the ones they usually pretended not to notice taking harmless goods to the enhanced in Australia now and again—as long as they never tried to smuggle any *people* on or off the island continent, no one really cared if the enhanced got a few extra recreational drugs and game consoles. But the space around Luna was so much smaller, and the viable entry points to the airless world so relatively scarce, that few smugglers ever got close to the heavily patrolled space around the Earth's moon. Earth itself was a much more inviting, and hard to patrol, target, with much larger markets for whatever illicit product the smugglers wanted to sell. It simply wasn't profitable to do the same on the moon.

With that reality, close Lunar patrol was one of the most boring and uneventful assignments for any UEN ship. And *Lunar Dawn* was nearing its third week on station, just long enough for everyone to be struggling to stay awake at their posts. It was especially infuriating after the explosive events of the Council Navy's attack only a month prior, which made any routine duty seem even duller by comparison.

*Only one more week to go,* thought Fischer, for probably the hundredth time just that day. *Then maybe they'll send us to the Front Door or even to patrol the edge of the Martian neutral zone. I'd even take a courier run to Europa.* Anything was more interesting than their current assignment.

"Captain," the voice of the sensor officer on the *Dawn's* small bridge interrupted his wishful thinking. "The computer flagged a transient return in sector 12."

A transient sensor return was about the only excitement this patrol ever seemed to generate. Usually, it boiled down to a piece of debris or an errant small asteroid that Lunar Control hadn't picked up on for destruction by the moon's collision avoidance defense network.

"Analysis?" he asked the young lieutenant, trying to keep the boredom out of his voice.

"I'm not sure, sir," Lt. Hashemi replied, his own voice barely rising above a casual tone. "Could be an asteroid, but when I do a tight scan of the area, I turn up nothing."

"Sensor ghost?" Kevin asked, referring to the not-too-uncommon occurrence of UEN sensor AIs seeing things where nothing was to be seen. The techs on Lunar Base One, the largest UEN naval facility outside of the Lagrange Point One shipyards, had been chasing gremlins in the sensor AIs for Kevin's entire naval career and before, trying to keep them from seeing phantom returns and misinterpreting them as actual objects. It was a never-ending battle. He was personally convinced sometimes that the AIs were just screwing with them.

"Could be, sir. But the pattern was different from the usual; it wasn't stationary but appeared to be moving in a tight Lunar orbit near the south pole. If I had to guess, it could be a ship with cold engines or even some sort of stealth, but it's admittedly a long shot."

"Well," Kevin said, standing and stretching. While the larger Navy ships tended to be all spit, polish, and protocol, the patrol ships—with their smaller, tight-knit crews—were commonly far more relaxed, even on the bridge. "We're not doing anything else at the moment. Let's go check out our long shot, shall we?"

---

Riggs swore loudly from the stealth shuttle's cockpit, causing Tyrus to jump to his feet and join the pilot in the forward compartment.

"What's going on, Riggs?"

"There's a UEN frigate headed our way. Their broad-spectrum sensors painted us a few minutes ago; wasn't the first time, but this pass, they must have gotten some sort of return. They painted us again for just an instant with a narrow-spectrum targeting radar, and it looks like they're coming to investigate now."

Tyrus pursed his lips in thought. Riggs knew what he was thinking. Hypothetically, the stealth shuttle's tech was secret even within the UEN, like its top-secret mother ship, the *UEN Enterprise*, which Tyrus had told him a little about. The shuttle *should* be capable of hiding from even a close-targeted search by the two-generation-old frigate headed their way. At least, it would be as long as it kept its engines cold like they were now.

But that the frigate was even coming toward them was a good sign that the tech wasn't perfect. Despite that, there wasn't much they could do. If they fired up the main drive, they'd be spotted for sure and would have to scrub the mission altogether. And they might never get another shot at getting Jinny out. Their only real option was to stay perfectly still and hope the bigger fish coming to investigate didn't see their little minnow.

"Any rogue emissions?" Tyrus asked him.

Riggs shook his head. "We've been under full stealth protocol since we got here. It wasn't anything we did. My guess, by the lack of urgency they're showing in coming this way, they caught what they think might be a sensor ghost, but they're either just motivated enough, or just bored enough, to come and investigate."

Tyrus put a hand on his shoulder. "Well, then let's continue to play dead. Just to be safe, go through the cold start checklist one more time. If we need to fire up the engines and run, let's make sure we can do it quickly because they'll see us clear as day if we do."

Riggs nodded. There had been exactly zero discussion of the command hierarchy for their mission, but no one, even Jynx, seemed willing to argue or doubt that Tyrus was in charge. So, he calmly set out fulfilling the other man's orders, preparing for the worst-case scenario.

---

"Welcome to the Crater, folks," the voice of the Blackmont shuttle's captain announced as Toby watched the gray surface of the moon quickly rise to meet the descending craft. "Local time is 1600, and the weather is calm and sunny. Be sure not to go outside without your sunscreen and a respirator."

From the groans that sounded through the passenger compartment, the pilot's attempt at humor wasn't well received by anyone on the small ship. Toby sat surrounded by nine other men and two women who were transferring up to the Lunar prison. Seven of the men, including Toby, were arriving for guard postings, while the remaining men and both the women were arriving for administrative roles, clearly denoted by their red uniforms in contrast to the guards' blue ones.

The postings ranged from three months to a year, depending on the person; apparently, no one at Blackmont liked working in the Crater, but they limited the frequency of staff rotations to better keep the place a secret. Or so he'd gathered from the chatter on the flight. He had pretended to be asleep for most of the ride to avoid having to answer any questions that might clue in his companions that he wasn't exactly whom his badge said he was. Even now, he looked out the window through slitted eyelids to keep up the pretense. Still, he couldn't resist the thrill of watching the shuttle land on the Earth's moon, a place he had never thought he'd see this close in person.

Of course, he wasn't there to visit any of Luna's resorts, casinos, or even shopping areas. He had to come to see the one place visitors would avoid most if they even knew it existed. And that excited him even more.

---

"Anything?" Kevin Fischer asked his sensor officer.

"Besides that Blackmont shuttle that we just saw land on schedule, nothing, sir," Lt. Hashemi replied in a dejected tone. "Maybe it was just a sensor ghost or even scatter from the Blackmont shuttle itself."

Kevin smiled, remembering how eager he'd been as a junior officer to impress his first captain and feeling a measure of sympathy for the young man.

"Well," he replied, "maybe so. This is good training anyway. Let's run a search grid on your projected trajectory for the object and see if we get lucky."

The sensor officer perked up. "Yes, sir!"

---

"Why aren't they going away? They obviously haven't seen us," Riggs lamented. He was whispering as if the UEN frigate that was now only four thousand kilometers off their port stern could somehow hear him through the vacuum if he spoke too loudly.

"They're settling into a grid search," Jynx observed from the co-pilot's chair.

Tyrus sat behind both of them, not because he could do any good right then, but because he felt disconnected sitting in the passenger compartment with Temperance the hacker, waiting to see if the patrol would detect them or not.

"Well, all we can do is keep playing dead and silent," observed Riggs. But Tyrus saw the man pull up the operating manual on his display, opening to the crash startup page yet again.

---

Reuben Linchfield sat at his desk, still stewing over the hundreds of thousands of dollars he'd watched transfer out of his account to Pedro De Vasquez's pocket only hours before. Since then, he'd imagined all sorts of creative ways to make the Lizard suffer. Unfortunately, all of them also ended with Reuben himself having to go on the run or potentially becoming a citizen of the same prison population he now watched over.

Still, it didn't stop him from fantasizing for the seventh time about breaking the annoying auditor's kneecaps with a baseball bat. His daydreams were interrupted by his latest administrative assistant, a plain-looking brunette named Yasmine, who didn't fit the bill of what he typically looked for in his admins, poking her head into his office.

"Director Linchfield, the shuttle has arrived and is unloading passengers and supplies now. Head Guard O'Malley wants to know if you'd like to come down to the receiving area and talk to the new personnel.

About half the time, Reuben would have said yes. But he was too upset from the ordeal with De Vasquez to talk to a bunch of greenies this afternoon. "No. Tell him to handle it himself. I have a few things I'm working on here that demand my attention."

With a quick nod, the woman left to relay his message. *At least she's efficient at her job*, he thought to himself. *Even if she doesn't have anything else going for her.*

---

Jinny was back in the small gray room with its single door, metal table, and large mirror. Lurch had brought her here, though he clearly hadn't enjoyed his conversation with Hendrix on the way over. The serial killer had that effect on people—always talking about strangling them or putting a knife in their throat. Jinny would have been disturbed, too, if she were Lurch. But Hendrix's bark was worse than his bite, especially since Lurch wasn't a skinny black-haired woman like the serial killer's ex-wife and chosen murder victims. Still, it was almost fun to watch the guard squirm at the man's threats.

Angry Man now sat alone in the room with her after Lurch and the guy with the lab coat—she called *him* the Pharmacist—had taken her blood once again. They did that *every* time she came to the room. They got plenty of blood today, but she tricked them and gave them Hendrix's instead. Wouldn't they be surprised?

Hendrix was gone now, back into the fog, and Tyrus was there, watching Angry Man calmly as he ticked off his usual list of questions. What had Jinny learned in Australia? How far back could she read? What were the capabilities of readers in the colonies? Tyrus found the questions boring; *he* wasn't the reader. But he had agreed to take his turn in today's interrogation so that Jinny could rest. She was *so* tired.

"Come now, Reader Ambrosa, do we have to resort to violence again today?" Angry Man asked in a tone of false sympathy. For some reason, he couldn't figure out that he was talking to Tyrus instead of Jinny. He never seemed to figure it out, even when they all tried to tell him so.

"Do whatever you have to do," Tyrus answered, letting his boredom show through. What Angry Man thought passed for torture wasn't even half of what he had gone through in his alpha training and indoctrination. Nor was it even comparable to the pain he'd felt when he first disobeyed his orders to kill Jinny.

Angry Man shook his head in frustration. "Just answer the questions, and I promise this can all be over."

"Your plan won't work," Tyrus told him instead. "You seem to think that Jinny has some sort of special ability that you can bottle and use for your little company to exploit the people of this system. Has it ever occurred to you that she's just a normal reader, like the millions you already have access to in Australia?"

Angry Man pursed his lips and frowned. "We *know* you're not a normal reader. So cut the act. There's something special about you, something your father did to you. And you're going to tell us exactly what it is."

Tyrus almost frowned. How had they learned about Frank Ambrosa and what he'd done to Jinny? They hadn't shared that with anyone since they'd arrived on Earth. But he decided it was best to ignore the man's comment and keep playing dumb. "Well, of course *I'm* not a normal reader," he replied with a laugh. Jinny liked his laugh. "I'm not even a reader. I'm an enacter, or I was. But we're talking about Jinny, and she *is* a normal reader."

Then he played a hunch. "Besides, even if you did somehow figure out a way to create your own readers, they won't be able to see enough to do you much good." He could see the man briefly wince at the comment and knew he'd guessed at least partially right.

"*You* are Jinny Ambrosa," Angry Man said, his voice rising as it often did when Tyrus or anyone else tried to get him to understand the truth. "Pretending to be someone else doesn't fool any of us, but it does make these sessions much more painful than they need to be."

He flipped a switch on a device in his hand, and Tyrus felt a surge of electricity course through him, causing muscles throughout his body to painfully spasm and clench. It lasted for five full seconds before the man released the switch and looked at him grimly.

*Let me talk to him,* Hendrix said in Tyrus' head. *I want to tell him how we're going to kill him again.* Tyrus ignored the man. Still, perhaps he could—

Jinny gasped, finding herself in the gray room and sitting across from Angry Man. For the briefest of moments, the fog cleared, and in a stark instant of clarity, she begged Angry Man for the help she knew he wouldn't give. "Please. I don't know what's happening to me. You *have* to help me!"

The gray-haired man knit his brows together in consternation and regarded her quizzically. "Reader Ambrosa, I tire of your games. Are you going to tell me what I need to know or not?"

She wanted to; oh, how she desperately wanted to, just to make this hell stop. But they wouldn't *let* her. Couldn't the man see that?!

*If you tell, you doom us all, you stupid girl!* Frank's voice snapped from inside the returning fog. *Tell him nothing!*

Jinny shook her head, frantically trying to fight back the fog that now billowed in and obscured everything again. She could hear Frank laughing at her attempts. But she still had part of her mind working, and she flashed back to the conversation long ago with Clarissa Lowry about her dreams: '...the cases I've read about... manifests as multiple personalities... a complete psychotic break'.

Was that what was happening to her now? Had she finally broken? She was so afraid. She worried she *had* broken, but she couldn't be sure. Everything was so... jumbled and confusing right now, and the fog was making it worse. If only she could—

*Shh, shh, shh. Everything is going to be OK, Jinny.* Alan's warm embrace enfolded her, and she felt the comfort that he always brought to her. *Just stay here with me and let someone else deal with that man. You just stay right here with me where it's safe.*

It sounded so good, and his embrace was so warm and secure. Jinny surrendered herself to his words and to the fog and let one of the others sit down in her place and talk to Angry Man. This time it was Ryder, and he kept answering the man's questions in Mandarin Trade Pidgin, then Italio-Portugues, which annoyed the interrogator to no end. She giggled along with Alan at Angry Man's red face as he screamed about all the terrible things he would do to them if they didn't answer his questions. Then Angry Man started hitting Ryder, who bore the punishment stoically until Tyrus came back to take the beating in his place.

*He's dead, and he doesn't even know it,* Hendrix whispered. *When I get my hands on him, Angry Man will wish he'd never been born.*

Hendrix's words usually bothered Jinny. She knew the murderer was unbalanced at best and psychotic at worst. Still, the more time she spent with him, the less he worried her. After all, he was her friend now too, and her friends were there for her.

---

After a brief welcome by someone named O'Malley, supposedly the head guard for the prison, Toby was shown to his new quarters to drop off his duffel. The bunk room, which he was told he would share with five other men, was currently empty. Four of the men worked the day shift, and the fifth was probably eating a meal before he started working the night shift, explained a young guard named Mitch, who had been assigned to get Toby settled. Toby himself, as a newbie and junior guard, would also work the night shift, and he had to report to the mess hall in just 25 minutes for training before the inmates arrived for dinner.

"There's your room's computer terminal," Mitch motioned to a small screen that folded up from the room's only desk. "There's no connection to the outside, but you can write messages and store them for review and disbursement. Messages go out every Thursday back to Earth, but you have to have them in the system by end-of-shift Tuesday to give the AI and human reviewers a chance to redact anything that might be confidential. No one outside the company, a few government officials, and the Navy patrols are even supposed to know this place exists, so we're careful with our comms."

The man kept droning on, and Toby just nodded along as he surreptitiously studied the computer terminal more closely. There were no external ports of any kind on the thing that he could see, so he hoped the small device the Neon Mouse had given him would do its job.

He didn't even know if it was still in working order. The hacker had assured him that it was heavily shielded and that it would stay safely deactivated in the supply depot, therefore evading detection *and* surviving the EMP blast. He had no way of verifying that she'd been right, but when Mitch finally left him alone to get settled before his shift started, Toby sprang into action.

Without making it too obvious—he'd been told to assume that Blackmont monitored even its own people closely in the prison—he pretended to scratch at an itch on the back of his neck. Hoping it looked natural to anyone watching, he used his fingernail to find and peel back the slight bump on his skin and pull it up and into his palm. Then he made an exaggerated yawn and stretch, reaching out and grabbing the small computer screen, even though it was far too flimsy to give his stretch any leverage.

It took him only a single attempt, and he took the small device that had been hidden underneath the fake skin on his neck and attached it to the back of the computer screen. Supposedly, it would allow the Neon Mouse to get a signal into the Crater's systems and hack them remotely from the stealth shuttle orbiting above, but Toby could only trust that all would work as advertised.

Now he had to get himself ready to be trained for a job he hoped to hold for less than a few hours. It would all be worth it if Jynx and her friends made it into the facility alive. His mission was *everything*.

---

"I need to see if your guy has installed the spike yet," the Neon Mouse whined from the passenger compartment.

"No!" cried Riggs, answering her plea the same way for the fourth time and losing his patience with the hacker. "That frigate is *way* too close. They might detect any signal you send. Assuming they don't see us and the search pattern continues, we have probably another hour before we can chance it."

"But that will put us behind schedule, and they might detect the spike before I can use it. Either way, I better still be getting my full pay," the girl complained.

"Temperance," Tyrus' voice broke into the argument in a tone that brooked no resistance, "you'll wait for Riggs to give you the all-clear before you even fire up that pad of yours. Understood?"

"Fine," the girl pouted but then blessedly stopped talking so that Riggs could sit there alone with his own troubled thoughts while the UEN patrol boat searched for them, hopefully in vain.

---

"Thank you for the tour and the… comprehensive overview of the work you and your people are doing, Director Belyaev," Corey said, trying to keep the exasperation out of his voice. "But as I said at the beginning, we're here to take the ship on a test flight so I can report back to the committee on its handling characteristics. And we really are in a hurry."

The scientist frowned for the 50$^{th}$ time since Corey had first sprung the surprise inspection on him. "I really must protest again, Congressman. We've already sent numerous reports from our own test flights to your committee. There is really no reason to question our data or take your own unnecessary flight."

Corey sighed. "You may protest all you like, Director, but I'm perfectly within my rights to insist on independent verification by my staff pilot of your findings."

The man mulled this over, obviously dissatisfied that Corey had once again refused to give a deeper explanation of why he insisted on Landon Hartman taking the *Blind Monk* for a short flight. Nonetheless, he had to acknowledge Corey's right to do so.

"Fine, but I'm coming with you," the man huffed.

Corey frowned. He had anticipated this wrinkle, even planned for it, but was still frustrated that they couldn't avoid it. "Of course, Director. Let's leave immediately."

It would take another hour before they finally lifted the ship from the underground hanger's floor and made their way gingerly through the launch tunnel to the airless surface of Luna. It would be several hours after that before maintenance personnel found the tied, gagged, and stunned Belyaev in a storage closet next to the launch bay.

---

"Nothing, sir." The dejected voice of Lt. Hashemi reminded Kevin once again of his own days as a junior officer. Since the last war with Mars 49 years ago, there really had been little excitement for the UEN. Sure, there was the odd skirmish with pirates in the asteroid belt or the Oort cloud, but the UEN typically had pirates and smugglers so outmatched that it wasn't even an exciting fight. Even the few small dustups when Martian forces probed outside the neutral zone were over in minutes and almost always with nothing but warning shots fired.

Despite the near disastrous outcome of the Council Navy's first foray into the Sol system, there were some days Commander Fischer caught himself almost hoping that they would invade in earnest like those crazy fools from the colonies had insisted they would. Of course, any hope or fear of that happening seemed in question now that those same fools had been outed as spies for the Council. But a man could dream.

"Very well. Helm, take us back to our patrol pattern, 30 percent power."

---

"They're leaving," Riggs said, and the tension in the cockpit dissipated in an almost physical release of pressure.

"OK," Tyrus said calmly, "let's give it another few minutes for them to get further out of range, then we'll set Temperance loose on the Crater's servers."

---

"Have you served in a detention facility before, Lazenby?"

Toby almost missed the question. He was intensely studying the stun baton at his belt. Luckily, he caught it with only a small hesitation, one he hoped no one would notice.

"No, sir." The man was more senior to him, even if Toby didn't quite understand the hierarchy around the prison yet. "Just a brief assignment in corporate protection. This is my first guard stint."

The man frowned. "No offense, but I'm really sick of them sending all the noobs to our station." His station was, for lack of a better description, the prison cafeteria. According to the man, it was one of the most dangerous assignments in the Crater. Apparently, mealtime was a common period for the prisoners to start a fight or even a riot, though the few prisoners Toby had seen looked way too high on something to start any real trouble. Dinner was an hour away, but Toby hoped that his 'job' would be done before then.

"Sorry, sir," he responded. "I just go where they tell me."

The man's frown turned into a lopsided smirk. "You and me both, kid. Now let me explain how the riot suppression system works."

"Wow, their security is a joke!" Temperance/Neon Mouse exclaimed with obvious glee. "It's like they're not even trying. They didn't even bother with a different encryption scheme for the Luna servers."

Tyrus didn't respond. He was distracted by his own efforts to get himself into the proper headspace for the upcoming mission. It had been a full six months since he'd seen any real action—the farce with the guards Bol had sent with him in the stealth shuttle didn't count—and it surprised him at how quickly he'd grown comfortable with *not* being shot at. But he was about to enter an environment where it would be kill or be killed, and he had to bring his full skill set. Otherwise, he'd be letting down his friends and the entire population of the Four Worlds. He was much more concerned about the former than the latter; he was having a hard time drumming up much sympathy for the Four Worlders after what they'd done to Jinny and the rest of his friends.

"It's probably that they just trust the isolation of their network to keep it safe from people like you," Riggs noted to the hacker.

The punk girl smiled and shrugged. "*No one* is safe from people like me. But it's not even fun when they don't at least *try* to keep me out."

"That's the dumbest thing I've ever heard," Jynx muttered sourly. Like Tyrus, she'd been largely quiet for the last hour, and he could feel her tension as keenly as his own.

He was thinking about Jinny, all of his crew, and—somewhat less so—the fate of the Four Worlds if they failed their mission. He imagined that their dying in the Crater would end the Sol system's preparations for war with the Council pretty quickly. Jynx felt the stress just as much, even if she was entirely focused on the fate of just *one* member of their little team. Tyrus had to admit that Toby was deserving of their concern, given what a risk the young man was taking for a group of people he barely knew—he'd never even met Jinny and was quite literally risking his life to save her. He still wasn't entirely sure about the boy, but he had to admire his bravery.

Temperance ignored Jynx's jab and kept pecking away at the touchscreen of her pad. "There's still a block around the executive functions that I won't be able to get through until we get inside the facility. Not enough bandwidth from here. But I got everything else: updated maps, guard rotation schedules, even the office gossip on what poor female administrator the prison director is trying to sleep with right now, which seems to include pretty much all of them.

"I don't have the financials, but given what that blender guy you all sent in before us said, they're probably not even on the main server—at least not the *real* records. What with the director skimming the drug supply and selling it for profit and all that. But I hacked everything I needed from his own personal records, so no value there anyway.

"But that part of the prison that they're supposedly keeping your friend in—it still doesn't show up on the maps I can see. Are we *sure* it's there?"

Now Tyrus perked up and focused on the young woman. Temperance shrunk a bit as he did so; she had a habit of doing that whenever he turned his attention on her. Part of him accepted it in stride; it was the same way people had reacted to him in the colonies, assuming they had even an inkling of what he was. But the other part of him felt bad for scaring the girl. She was doing her best to help them, even if she was being paid *extremely* well for it.

"Until we get information to the contrary," he told her, "we trust Archer's intel. It makes sense that there would be a part of the facility that isn't shown on the official records, even those only accessible by Blackmont employees. They would want to have a place where they can keep less convenient prisoners or even handle illegal renditions for the government."

"Speaking of which," Riggs said, clearing his throat, "I know it's too late for this, but our little stunt here is going to make us even more hated by the Earthies. If they're trying to find us and kill us now, think of what they'll do after it comes out that we broke Jinny out of prison. I hope we have a plan for that."

Tyrus nodded. "I trust O'Leary. He said he has that part taken care of, and he's been straight with us so far. But I also believe that once we reveal they lied about Jinny being dead and moved her to a secret prison, the public and even most of the government won't care that we broke her out. Even Pereira will be too busy doing damage control to spend much energy coming after us."

Riggs frowned. "I hope you're right."

"Enough jabbering, you two!" Jynx snapped at them. "We're 15 minutes from doing this thing, and someone needs to get *her* suited up." She nodded toward the Neon Mouse, her distaste for the girl clear on the surface.

"It's time, Temperance," Tyrus said, trying but failing to put a note of gentleness in his tone. "Let's get you into something that will stop bullets."

"You'd better get ready too," Riggs said from behind him, and Tyrus looked again at the container that O'Leary had put aboard the shuttle back on Earth.

"We'd all better be ready," the big man said, too softly for any of the others to hear.

---

Something was wrong. The others should have made their entrance into the base an hour ago by the mission clock, and Toby was getting legitimately worried. The prisoners were only minutes away from arriving at the cafeteria for what passed for dinner, and he'd already had a few close calls where his trainer, Jablonski, had clued into his apparent lack of even the most basic knowledge of prisons and guard duty. And his excuse about not having had any direct experience with either before was wearing thin; he had to assume that *everyone* Blackmont sent to the Crater got at least some basic training.

He hoped the guy was just chalking it up to him being incompetent. It was possible he was even writing the scathing performance review in his head already. It was far better than the alternative, which ended with Toby dead or on the other side of the prison bars before he could complete his mission.

The mess was one of the few parts of the prison that was above the surface of the gigantic crater from which the facility had earned its nickname. It even had an airlock at one end that opened to the outside. Jablonski had said it was so that they could use the mess hall as a gathering point for evacuations. He also snidely remarked that having it open to the surface let them use the threat of a forced depressurization to dissuade any riots in the large room. Toby wasn't sure which he believed.

The mess had another feature that set it aside from the rest of the Crater: windows. They weren't large, just portholes along one edge of the room, too small for more than one man to look through at a time. But they provided a view of the shuttle pads outside that Toby kept trying to sneak a look at to see if the rest of his compatriots were landing yet. But every time he tried to look outside, Jablonski snapped at him to pay attention as he prattled on about proper riot suppression procedures and what to do if a convict spilled his applesauce.

Toby was getting more worried and excited as every moment ticked by on the mission clock. His palms were damp, and he could feel his body tensing. *Great,* he thought, *I'm reacting like a novice.*

"Hey, boss!" the only other guard in the mess with them called out. The man, Hurst, was staring at something outside through one of the portholes, and Toby felt his blood run from hot to ice cold. "We expecting a second shuttle today?"

Jablonski stopped the lecture he'd been delivering on dealing with a choking inmate and looked puzzled. "No. Why?"

Hurst shrugged. "There's a shuttle landing on the pad outside. Looks way different than the normal ones, too."

"What? Lemme see!" Jablonski crossed the room quickly and pushed the younger man out of the way.

Toby hesitated, torn between bolting for the door and following the man to see if it was his crew, though it was almost silly to think it might be anyone else. Ultimately, he followed the older man, stopping and peering out the best he could over Jablonski's shoulder.

"That's strange," the guard said gruffly. "Never seen a shuttle like that before. And usually, they announce all arrivals just in case any of the prisoners get loose. But the boarding tube is extending normally, so they must be expected." The man was talking mostly to himself, and Toby could almost physically see the wheels turning in his brain.

Jablonski shook his head. "Still, maybe I better call it in just to be safe. He reached for the comm at his belt—every guard's integrated hand comm was disabled before they were allowed to enter the shuttle at the supply and personnel depot in Colorado.

Almost without thinking, Toby's hand flew to the stun baton at his belt. He drew the weapon, the sound of it unclipping enough for Jablonski and Hurst to turn and look at him in confusion. The expression on Jablonski's face quickly changed to one of surprise, and then a spasm of shock as the end of the stun weapon contacted the front of his uniform's chest, and Toby flipped the switch to activate it and send twelve hundred volts coursing through the older man's body.

"Hey! Wha—?" the other guard, Hurst, started to ask as he reached down and grabbed his own stun baton from his belt. Toby didn't have time for his weapon to recharge, so he dropped it and threw a punch at the man's jaw. It would have landed solidly enough to lay Hurst out, but the guard tripped over his own foot trying to free his baton, and it unexpectedly caused Toby's fist to hit the crown of his head instead of his temple. He felt one of the bones in his right hand crunch.

"Big mistake!" Hurst yelled and stepped forward again toward the now weaponless Toby, who was forced to leap back to avoid a swipe from the guard's stun baton.

"I, uh," he started to say but couldn't think of any good excuse, so instead, he just lunged forward and hit the man again, this time connecting solidly with his left hand and knocking Hurst out cold. But not, to his chagrin, before the man had hit the alarm button on his comm, and a klaxon sounded throughout the underground facility.

## CHAPTER 26

"Intruder at shuttle tube B2! Intruder at shuttle tube B2!" a mechanical voice wailed, snapping Kit Potter to full wakefulness from the nap he'd been sneaking in the Crater's shuttle control center. As far as he was concerned, his post was only necessary for the 30 minutes every week that the regular supply and personnel shuttle arrived to restock the base and rotate guards and administrators. Otherwise, there were one or two shuttles each month that brought new prisoners or, far more rarely, took away the few that ever got to leave the Crater. Still, policy said that the station always had to be manned, and it was easier than guarding prisoners. So, Kit enjoyed his time napping, reading, and playing a few games that someone long gone had managed to sneak onto the prison's servers.

However, now the alarm was blaring, and displays everywhere in the small room were flashing red. Before he could do more than stand up and look around in panic, the door to the space flung open, and another guard glared in at him. The man was dressed in riot gear and carried an assault rifle, and the look he gave Kit was pure poison.

"Get off your butt and get armed, you idiot!" the man yelled at him. Kit could see three other guards similarly dressed and armed in the hall outside—a quick reaction force assigned to deal with attempted prison breaks, riots, or altercations between prisoners.

Kit nodded dumbly at the man and then reached over and keyed in a sequence on one of the terminals that opened a small locker to the left of the door. Inside was a helmet and set of body armor, along with an assault rifle like the other men carried.

The other four guards didn't wait while Kit got himself suited up but went back out into the corridor and moved rapidly toward shuttle tube B2.

It only took Kit a minute; he didn't take the time to properly cinch on the body armor chest and back plates, nor did he take the time to secure the helmet properly. His entire body was shaking from the adrenaline and fear that he knew he shouldn't be feeling. *I was trained for this!* he kept repeating in his mind, but it did nothing to calm his nerves.

When he emerged in the hall, he turned and headed in the direction the other guards had gone, holding the assault rifle ready.

---

Temperance Jimenez, aka the Neon Mouse, tried to keep the look of fear off her features. She had a visceral reaction every time she looked at Tyrus Tyne in the best of circumstances: something between fear and excitement. She was simultaneously attracted to and terrified by the man.

But now…

She snuck a glance at him again, dressed for battle in the contents of the strange trunk that had sat code locked in one corner of the shuttle's passenger compartment since they'd left Earth. She had hacked the lock when no one else was looking, and what she'd seen inside had been beyond even the tech she was used to dealing with. It was something that shouldn't have existed.

"Temperance," Tyne's voice sounded odd coming from the apparatus he wore on his head and face. "Hit the lights."

She immediately complied, though her hand trembled as it hit the command on her pad.

Kit shook with fear and anticipation as he stood at the rear of the quick reaction force's formation. The men had taken up position on either side of the narrow hall that led to the door of shuttle tube B2, the two men in the front kneeling so the men in the rear had a clear line of sight. Kit didn't know where to stand, so he tucked in behind the standing man on the left and cast furtive glances around the other guard toward the still-closed door. He had to pee and wished there had been time before…

"Has central sealed the door?" asked one of the other men gruffly.

"Negative, sir," answered another. "They're reporting loss of local control. It's like—"

The corridor was plunged into darkness as every light went out.

One guard swore loudly, and a tactical light came on, illuminating the door into the shuttle tube. Then another light, then a third, and a fourth…

In the light, Kit could see the door was open!

"What the—?"

He would never know which guard had asked the question.

One moment there was no one in the glare of the tactical lights; the next moment, there was a flash of movement, like mist rippling through the air. The kneeling guard on the right cried out in pain, a choking gurgle that was cut off in a wet squelch and a thud of something hitting the ground.

"Fire! Full spread!" screamed another guard and pulled the trigger on his assault rifle, holding it down and sweeping the empty hallway back and forth. Kit looked around desperately, trying to figure out what the man was shooting at. He couldn't see anything! The other two remaining guards started firing as well, so Kit also squeezed off a few shots in the rough direction of the open shuttle tube door.

Another flash of movement caught his attention, this time from above, and the figure of a large man materialized as if in a mid-air fall from the ceiling. A flash of reflected light extended from each of the man's hands as he fell, and he rotated in the air, landing on his knees with both arms outstretched and holding what Kit could now see were... *swords?* The two standing guards stopped firing and crumpled to the ground without a sound.

Something bumped against Kit's foot, and he looked down in a panic to see the back of a loose helmet. It bounced off his foot and rolled to expose its front, revealing in the dim flashing lights the ashen disembodied face of one of the other guards. He screamed and felt his bladder release, a warm wetness running down the front of his uniform trousers.

But the humiliation of soiling himself was the furthest thing from his mind. The fourth and final guard, other than Kit himself, had stopped firing, and his light had extinguished simultaneously with his cry of pain, thrusting the corridor into pitch-black darkness again, except for a small circle of illumination from a tactical light trapped under one of the dead men.

Kit kept screaming, barely pausing for a breath, tears streaming now from his face in such volume that he wouldn't have been able to see even with a light. He stumbled back against the corridor wall and slumped to the ground, sobbing uncontrollably, cradling his rifle in his arms.

He felt a presence in front of him, sensed by some prehistoric awareness of the movement of the air, not by sight or even sound. He dropped his gun, flinging it away and holding up his arms in a warding gesture in front of his face.

"Don't kill me! Don't kill me! Don't kill me!" he screamed, begging the unseen foe.

"Where is she?" The words weren't shouted, but they cut through Kit's awareness like a knife, even above his own pleading and sobbing. The voice was cold and mechanical, inhuman, with a hiss of static underlying the words that made them sound reptilian. "Where is she?" the voice repeated.

"Who?" Kit managed to ground out between racking sobs. "Who?" he pleaded again.

"The reader," came the inhuman reply, and he imagined he could somehow feel the enemy's breath on his face.

Kit shook his head in the darkness. "I d-don't know who that is."

There was no response, and Kit whimpered as he pictured the blade that would fall to end his life.

The blow never came. Instead, he looked up to find a new group of people looking down at him in the dim light: a man and two women, one of them only a teenager. The man in front shook his head and muttered something, then pointed a rifle at Kit's face, and a blue flash was followed by darkness of another kind.

---

Toby had fled from the mess hall shortly after the first klaxon had sounded. He needed to get himself to the prearranged position so his own special role in the mission, the one not even the others knew about, could go off correctly.

But in his haste, he had left the mess hall at the wrong end, and now he was lost. He had resisted using the tactical light at his belt, worried that it would be a beacon to anyone who might be looking for him. Now, as more and more guards rushed past in both directions, lights bouncing, speaking in panicked tones to each other and ignoring him altogether, he risked turning on the light to get his bearings.

It didn't help. He was hopelessly lost somewhere far from where he'd started. Even having memorized the map of the facility didn't help him in the confused darkness.

He caught snippets of conversation from other guards as they passed, combined with a myriad of overlapping voices that came through the comm on his belt. The consensus seemed to be that an army was attacking the prison.

*But there's no army, just three colonials and a punk hacker*, he thought with a grin. Still, if he hadn't known what Tyrus Tyne truly *was*, the screaming cries that echoed from the comm would have made him doubt that an army wasn't indeed there.

---

"You decoded it?" Mohammed Qureshi asked anxiously as he moved to answer Makena Maina's waved summons to her desk. The woman had been working for the better part of a month on decrypting the mysterious data packet that had been attached to the Council Fleet's transmissions. Half a dozen other analysts had been tasked to help, along with every ounce of computing power the Octagon could spare, all with no effect.

The encryption scheme that had been used on the mysterious packet was so far ahead of the laughably basic encryption of the first two messages they'd decoded. It was also more advanced than anything they'd ever seen in the Sol system. It was enough to have General Cruz arguing to anyone who would listen that the first two messages—those incriminating the four refugees from the 47 Colonies and the Martians—*had* to be part of a Council disinformation campaign. If the Council government and its navy had access to *this* type of unbreakable encryption, why make those other two messages so easy to decode?

Unfortunately, no one was listening to Cruz nor to the multiple memos Mohammed had sent supporting the general's claims. So, their only hope rested with the decryption of the data packet embedded in the message aimed toward Earth.

And for over four frustrating weeks, they had come no closer to breaking it. Until now…

"It was quite ingenious, really," Makena explained. "The AI thought that the rotating key had to be random, but that made no sense; why build a key that your recipient couldn't ever guess or use because it kept changing in unanticipated ways?"

"What does it say?" Mohammed asked impatiently. He knew it was in vain. Once Makena started explaining an interesting problem and her solution, there was no stopping her until she got it all out.

Ignoring his question, she continued. "Then I decided to pull in some of the astrogeeks." He knew she was using the semi-derisive term for the Octagon's Office of Astrological Survey. It was an oft-ridiculed department in the vast military bureaucracy, particularly since it was seen by many as futile to map the distant stars that Earth could never visit outside the Rift. It was also a department that rarely played well with others, but at least three of the guys working there had a major crush on the oblivious Makena.

"They ran it through their own AI but found nothing," she continued. "So, I had them run it again with some new parameters. It took a full week—their stuff is painfully outdated compared to ours—but finally, it spit out the answer."

She paused, looking at him. Mohammed sighed. "And? What was the answer?"

She smiled. "The key is a combination of the radio signals from six different pulsar stars on the colonial side of space. That's why it took so long; it wasn't just one star, but all six in harmony. Super easy to use and decrypt the message once we figured it out. But took a while to get there."

"And what did it say?"

Makena looked surprised. "Oh, here." She pressed a sequence on her keyboard, and Mohammed's pad dinged to announce a data file received.

Anxiously, he pulled up what she sent him and read it. Then he read it again. Then he read it a third time as he dashed back to his own desk, almost tripping over another analyst's chair as he tried to read and run at the same time.

"Get me a meeting with General Cruz, now!" he called out to his assistant. "Tell him it's urgent! We have a Council spy somewhere on Earth, and it's *not* who we thought it was!"

Without waiting for the stunned young man to acknowledge, he gathered his blazer, the one he wore to make his typically rumpled appearance a little more palatable for the higher-ups, and raced out the door toward the office of the chairman of the Joint Chiefs.

---

Riggs moved in shock through the corridor that led toward the prison's administrative offices. He held an assault rifle at the ready, a bright tactical light affixed under the barrel to cast its harsh glow wherever he swept his aim. Behind him, he was barely conscious of the quiet, timid footsteps of the Neon Mouse as she silently followed, and he was only slightly more conscious of the louder footfalls and occasional curses from Jynx, who brought up the rear.

For Riggs, all of this barely registered when faced with the abattoir he moved through.

Dead bodies littered the halls. At first, they were all guards, some dressed in tactical body armor and some in simple Blackmont uniforms of blue and gray. Then they passed more and more people in the red uniforms of facility administrators. Only a few of the latter were dead, their dropped weapons nearby. The rest sat huddled, sobbing against the walls, and Riggs used the stun setting on his rifle to put them temporarily out of their misery and ensure they wouldn't present a problem on the way out.

He had almost scoffed when Tyrus had withdrawn the two long mono-molecular-edged blades from the trunk in the shuttle; they had come with the special stealth infiltration suit O'Leary had procured from who-knew-where. *No way*, Riggs had thought to himself. *Give me a simple gun instead of some archaic swords!*

He was so wrong. Even seeing the carnage those blades had wrought now in front of and on all sides of him, he still couldn't believe it. He also realized how very wrong he'd been about another matter. He had worried that the Blackmont guards and administrators, along with Pereira and his cronies, weren't prepared for the hell they'd unleashed upon themselves by angering Tyrus Tyne and taking away the one person the *ex*-alpha held so dear.

But *no one* could have prepared for Tyrus Tyne because the man wasn't an *ex*-alpha. He may no longer be an enacter, but he was still an alpha in every other sense of the word: the galaxy's most deadly killing machine. Except now, he didn't reluctantly kill for genetic obedience to the orders of a faceless Council; now, he killed for love and loyalty. It made anything that Riggs could have imagined look tame by comparison. The fact that the man was even exercising enough self-control to leave some of the guards and administrators alive—those that didn't wield weapons or try to fight back—was a miracle that spoke to the man's cold mastery of his anger, which somehow made him even *more* terrifying.

Down the hallway, another voice screamed in terror and was cut off in an abrupt gurgle, and Riggs felt his knees go weak so that he had to pause and lean against one of the corridor walls.

"Riggs, why are we stopping?" Jynx asked from behind, her voice trying and failing to mask her own terror with her usual angry bravado.

"Nothing," he gasped in return and levered himself off the wall, and continued walking.

*We're terrified of the man, and he's on our side. What demon have we unleashed upon the people who are standing in his way?*

Suddenly, the empty corridor in front of him shimmered, and a large figure appeared out of thin air. Cal felt his finger tighten on the trigger before he recognized the massive black-clad form of Tyne. He almost fired anyway, and he heard both the Neon Mouse and Jynx gasp behind him.

"Temperance," the large alpha hissed, the full facemask of the stealth suit distorting his voice and giving it a cold, machine-like quality. "It's time. Open everything."

"Y-yes, sir," the hacker stammered, all her normal bluster gone. Riggs heard her tapping on her pad behind him in the darkness and saw the glow from the device's screen playing off the corridor walls.

Tyrus stood there silently, obscured head-to-toe in the strange suit. The man didn't move as he waited; Riggs couldn't even perceive him breathing hard.

*I should say something,* he thought. *I need to stop this madness.* But he found his throat constricted and his vocal cords paralyzed as if asking the assassin before him to stop would break the spell that kept them on the same side and turn the man's cold and brutal rage on *him* rather than the Blackmont employees. It was irrational, he knew, but it was hard to think rationally when he was bearing witness to what the man was capable of.

"It's done," the hacker almost whimpered back to the tall assassin.

Without another word, Tyrus turned and headed forward down the corridor. A moment later, in a shimmer of mist-like luminescence, he disappeared from their sight.

## ONE YEAR AGO; 730 P.D.

The gray of the void through the forward viewscreen of the *CNS Ephialtes* would have bothered most men. But Commander Jarvis Horn was not most men. He relished the void. For a fast infiltrator like the *Ephialtes*, the void meant safety, security, and even home.

However, the other man who stood next to him on the ship's small bridge *did* bother Horn. He wasn't physically imposing; indeed, the man—boy really, but only by age—was average height and lithe of build, with nothing in his features that belied the deadly potential he contained. It was the eyes that bothered Jarvis. They were, simply put, dead.

Whenever the man's eyes met Horn's, the *Ephialtes'* captain felt like someone had stepped on his grave. The eyes held no emotion, not even hatred. They were totally and completely devoid of feeling, like a snake that Jarvis had once encountered as a child in his backyard on Daegu. And just like that snake, he always got the impression that the young man was only biding his time before he would strike.

"Surfacing in two minutes, Captain," the voice of his navigation officer called out, the tension heavy in the woman's tone. It wasn't surprising; navigating the Goat Path, the second path humanity had discovered through the Castilian Rift, required a full team of astrogators, ever-present and ever-ready to make the minute corrections in the ship's course that were necessary as the path shifted and flexed from the constantly changing influence of gravity and dark matter around it.

"Thank you, Gershon," he responded to the tense woman. The scout crew was fairly lax in their military protocol; when you were stuck together in a small ship in the void for extended periods, it broke down walls of professional detachment. So did traveling repeatedly through the Rift. Mankind still had no idea how or why the Castilian Rift existed; indeed, they had found nothing even remotely like it anywhere else in the relatively small portion of the galaxy they had surveyed. It seemed to be unique to Sol, as if some intelligent and malevolent force had attempted to keep humanity bottled up in its own system. And that same malevolence seemed to translate into the

Rift itself; the Goat Path was so difficult to navigate that it always felt to Horn like the Rift was actively trying to kill him and his crew.

He turned his thoughts away from that dark topic and reluctantly regarded the cold young man next to him, suppressing a shudder as he did so. "Sir, may I suggest you take position in your pod?"

The man turned his dead eyes toward Jarvis, and now the captain was unable to contain the shiver that passed through his entire body, even reaching out to steady himself on the arm of the command chair that sat empty next to him—he'd always preferred to stand during pivotal moments on his bridge, but now he regretted the choice.

The other man said nothing but merely nodded and left the bridge at a brisk walk. When the doors closed behind him, a palpable sigh rippled through the small bridge crew. Even given their familiarity, Jarvis would have usually gently reprimanded them for their lack of decorum, but today, he joined them in the feeling of intense relief that the alpha would finally be off their ship.

They surfaced from the void without incident, far enough away from the yellow sun that it was merely a pinprick of light in the distance. Somewhere, a watery blue planet of legends orbited that sun, but the inhabitants of that planet would never see the *Ephialtes*, nor would the crew of the infiltrator likely ever step foot on the planet.

But the boy with the dead eyes would.

The *Ephialtes* only stayed in normal space long enough to recharge its star drive and plot its course back through the twisting, turning path in the void. Thirty-four minutes later, it disappeared again as it submerged for the journey home. But it left something behind. A small pod, barely four meters long and a meter wide, basically a long coffin with small engines, shot out from a specially designed missile tube in the *Ephialtes* within minutes of the ship surfacing. The pod contained only one occupant, who would be kept in stasis during the long, slow journey to the watery blue world. It would take roughly six months for him to get there, with the pod only firing its engines again at the final stage for deceleration, and it would only awaken him during the insertion through the planet's atmosphere.

All of that subterfuge was necessary, for it simply wouldn't do for the Four Worlders to find the pod and trace it back to its source. The Council's plans demanded that the Goat Path stay secret.

The crew's sense of relief might have been greater if they had understood what their ship had truly unleashed on Earth. For the boy was certainly an alpha, but he was *no* enacter. That much had been shared in the briefing Jarvis had received. This wasn't a man who simply operated under orders; he *enjoyed* what the Council sent him to do. And that made him far more dangerous, and far more unpredictable, than *any* enacter.

# CHAPTER 27

PRESENT DAY; SEPTEMBER 2, 731 P.D.

Reuben Linchfield stood behind his desk in the dim light of a single emergency lamp, trying desperately to give orders and receive updates through garbled comm transmissions from across the prison. At first, it had sounded like there was an army attacking the Crater, though they had all somehow come from a single undetected shuttle.

Then it had seemed like it might all be the work of one man or a small group. Either way, the panicked cries and then silence from the guards appeared to be moving steadily down a single corridor *toward* Reuben's office.

And no one could get a look at what was killing them! The reports were distorted and fragmentary but spoke of a wraith, a ghost, or some kind of demon spawn.

*Surely this can't be the work of only one man!* he thought to himself. Now there were panicked shouts on the comm about the prisoners getting out of their cells and making their way into secure areas as if the doors had no locks!

He had tried to call outside the prison for help but had found his computer terminal had locked him out completely. He had shouted into the internal comm at the guards to converge on his office, to defend him, but if anyone heard him over the screams of the dying, they had ignored his pleas.

"The escape tunnel!" He said the words aloud even though there was no one in his office with him. Somehow speaking out loud made him feel slightly less alone.

He turned to the back wall behind his desk. On all the facility maps, behind this wall was solid lunar rock buried ten meters below the moon's surface. But he grabbed a book on his bookshelf and pulled it down with all his might. Then another. With a rasping, grating noise, a section of the wall split and revealed a corridor of raw lunar rock. Far at the other end was a small hanger cut into the side of another nearby crater, housing a single short-range shuttle large enough to carry one person comfortably and two in a pinch.

It was one of the many secrets of the Crater—that every director since the facility's establishment had a way out if the worst should happen. Reuben had used it only once, sneaking out to see one of his mistresses at Dark Side Base Three. Even then, he had done so more out of the novelty than any genuine need to sneak around. Now he would use it for the purpose it had always been intended for.

The corridor was dark, and Reuben didn't have a flashlight in his office, just the dim emergency lantern, so he ripped it off the wall and turned back to the corridor to make his escape.

To his surprise, in the dim lantern light, a figure stepped out of the rocky escape hallway.

"De Vasquez?!" he gasped, blinking to clear his eyes, unable to believe what he was seeing. "What are you doing here?" Then his eyes moved down, and he saw the pistol in the fat auditor's hand, barrel pointed squarely at his stomach. He tried to cry out, but the words choked off in his suddenly dry throat.

"Now, now, Reuben, you're not leaving so soon, are you?" the corpulent man asked, a grotesque smile forming on his lips. "My friends have some questions for you before you go."

"Your friends?" Reuben asked dumbly, his mind moving slowly as he struggled to decipher the import of the man's statement. *"You're doing this?"*

De Vasquez's smile widened. "There you go. I knew you could do it. Even a slug as stupid as you can piece things together when they're right in front of his face."

"B-b-b..." the director struggled to say something, *anything*, in response, but his words and his legs failed him as he stumbled backward and stopped only when his desk blocked his path and his fall. "But I paid you!" he finally exclaimed through his dry throat.

The other man's smile disappeared, and he waved the gun toward the front door of Reuben's office. "He'll be here any minute, you know," the Lizard said as if he hadn't even heard Reuben's words. "And things will go much better for you if you tell me everything I need to know before he gets here. Because if *he* has to ask, you won't like the way he does it."

"Who?!"

De Vasquez smiled again. "Let's call him the angel of death. It's funny, in a way, because where he's from, he wouldn't even get that reference. But it's fitting today, don't you think?" He didn't wait for Reuben to answer. "I'm hoping that the location you gave me for your 'special' prisoner was accurate. Because if it's not, then he's going to carve the answer from you."

Rueben whimpered, but the auditor kept on talking.

"He's not a bad guy, really, when you get to know him. But you and your friends made a big mistake, Reuben. You took his best friend and locked her up here to die. You brought this on yourselves, and there is no way any of you survive what comes next. Unless you tell me everything."

The man grinned again, and Reuben felt his throat close up completely. He couldn't have answered the fat auditor even if he'd known what to say.

"Of course," continued De Vasquez, "given that the way to that secret cell block of yours goes right through the administrative offices here...." He shrugged. "Well, that pretty much sealed your fate. You probably did it that way because it made it easier to keep your special prisoners a secret from the rest of the facility. But now it's backfiring. So, tell me, Reuben, is she where you told me she would be?"

Reuben found that his entire body was shaking now, and he

reached back with both hands to steady himself against the desk, not even thinking to try and grab the pistol he kept in the drawer there.

"Y-yes," he stammered finally. "She's right where I said she'd be. But I *paid* you!"

De Vasquez shook his head, the smile still on his puffy face. "Even now, Reuben, you just don't understand." He pulled the trigger once and then again. But Linchfield was dead after the first shot.

---

Jordan Archer looked down at the body of Reuben Linchfield in the dim light of the lantern the man had dropped to the floor. He nudged the former prison director's corpse with his foot, satisfied the man was gone.

He quickly pulled up his palm implant and pecked out a message.

*Castor: Linchfield dead. Tyne on the way. All going according to plan.*

He waited only a few seconds before the reply came.

*Iasonas: Team in place and ready. After Ambrosa is rescued, Tyne cannot leave alive. Bring the reader to Earth, alive or dead. Corpse is enough. See to it.*

---

## ONE MONTH AGO

The young man with the dead eyes had been watching his quarry when the arrest order had come through. He hadn't been expecting it but had already been observing her for several weeks, learning her habits and coming up with different ways to insert himself into her life when the time came. He had even followed her on several of her late-night walks through the forest, though she would never know he was there or how tightly he'd had to clamp down on his natural impulses not to kill her in the woods where no one would see.

She should be grateful he had let her live so long.

He was less than 20 meters behind her when she fled from her house and the federal police that had been sent to take her in. He had intercepted the message sent to Earth by the Council fleet and quickly decrypted it, so he knew why the police *thought* they were arresting his little Raven. A special little extra had been attached to that same message, meant just for him. It would take the Earthers much longer to decrypt that part, if they ever did, and it had given him enough instruction that he knew what he was to do. And his Raven factored heavily into it.

He knew the woman's real name, of course. He had been watching her long enough that he knew *everything* about her. But he'd chosen to think of her as his Raven; she reminded him of one of the dark birds in the way she brooded and glared at everyone around her. Breaking her would be a challenge but a fun one.

He watched her flee from the house, leaving her companion behind to be arrested. *No loyalty for criminals and traitors,* the young man thought, confirming his estimation of the woman.

She fled for several hours, with him following close behind. Twice she paused in the forest as if she'd heard him. Once, she almost saw him in the headlights of a passing truck, and another time, the Federal Police almost detected his heat signature when one of their cars drove by looking for her. But he managed to stay one step ahead of all of them. It was child's play, really. He'd trained all his life for this.

It surprised him when she went to the beach and began swimming, a kayak in tow, south toward the lights of Bremerton. His little Raven was smarter than he'd given her credit for. He felt himself growing even more excited at the prospect of doing what he intended to do to her. It was always the spirited ones that were the most fun to destroy.

He was a strong swimmer, so he easily followed her across the Sound, diving below the water two hundred meters behind her to avoid the same police boat that almost caught her. When she reached the shore, he surfaced a few dozen meters up the beach and then idly watched her explore and then break into the dark house.

Unlike her, he didn't sleep. He was content to wait and watch, knowing that she would be moving soon. When she did, he was ready. He followed her, again at a distance, keeping to low spots and behind trees wherever possible and making use of the remaining dark of night as well.

The sun was rising by the time his little Raven found a car to steal. She had unknowingly passed two other perfectly good candidates on her long walk, and it was getting to the point where he was thinking of ways to subtly shift her attention to the next car that came up—it wouldn't do to let the police capture her—when she finally chose the one she did. He moved up closer to her while she was rummaging through the aircar, keeping out of sight but ready to move quickly when the time came.

It came when she finished emptying the trunk of the drugs it had contained. The young man threw a rock he had picked up for the express purpose, hitting a fence across the street. He watched as the Raven tensed, hunkered down behind the side of the car, searching warily for the source of the noise. He smiled at the fear in her posture. While her attention was fixed on the opposite side of the road, he swiftly moved up behind the car and slid silently into the trunk.

Now came the moment of maximum risk. If she looked in the trunk before closing it, he would have to incapacitate her and employ more direct measures. It would throw the entire plan into disarray. Still, part of him *wanted* that; part of him hungered to kill her *now*. But that would be an unsatisfying end to over two months of stalking her. The best part of every hunt was the anticipation—that moment when your prey looked into your eyes and realized who you were and that there was no escape. He would be so upset if he missed out on that with his little Raven. She was his favorite prey so far, and he yearned to reach that moment when he took away the hope he would first give her.

Luckily, as he'd expected, given her haste, she quickly pushed shut the lid of the trunk without so much as a glance inside. Moments later, he felt the whir of the car's turbines and hover matrices starting up and then felt it lift into the air and start moving forward. He smiled, practicing that and a dozen other facial expressions as he often did when he was alone where no one could see. They simply didn't come naturally to him at all.

## PRESENT DAY; SEPTEMBER 2, 731 P.D.

Jordan Archer nudged the body of Reuben Linchfield with his foot. It was the first time he had ever killed anyone as part of his job, but he knew he was actually doing the slick facility director a favor. Because if Tyne had gotten to him first, the man's death would have been far less pleasant. Add to that the fact that he was the only one in the Crater who could possibly hope to piece together what had happened here today and the role that someone posing as De Vasquez played in it, and it was simply too dangerous to leave him alive. Iasonas had been clear on that point, and he'd also made it clear what would happen to Cecily if he refused to carry out the order.

A moment later, the door leading out into the administrative offices slammed open to reveal... no one.

"Mr. Tyne," Jordan said as calmly as he could, but he could hear a slight tremor in his own voice.

The air in the doorway shimmered, and the black-clad giant of a man materialized, head cocked to one side questioningly. He looked at the body on the ground and then back up at Jordan, sending a chill down the blender's spine.

"She's right where Linchfield said she'd be," he told the man quickly. "But I can't guarantee she's in a state to be moved."

"We'll deal with that," the giant's mechanical voice rasped. "She's getting out of here no matter what happens."

Archer nodded understandingly. From around the big man, he spied the three others peeking in through the office doorway.

"Ah, the hacker," he said with a wan smile as he saw the smallish girl wearing a body armor vest that was two sizes too big for her shaking frame. He had seen little of her since he'd picked her up at the Las Vegas port but was unsurprised to see her now watching Tyne with wide-eyed terror. "I think you'll find that this office has full access to *everything* in this facility. If you will?" He got her attention and nodded toward the computer terminal on the former director's desk.

The purple-haired girl timidly stepped through the doorway, almost leaning into the wall to stay as far away from Tyne as she could, watching the big man as if he were a wild animal that might lash out at any moment. Archer felt bad for the girl. No one should have to witness the things she had today. For all the fortune she was being paid for this job, it would never be enough.

Of course, he might feel even worse for the guards. With the experimental military stealth suit that he had procured for O'Leary—with Iasonas' help—and its integrated zero-G belt, most of the guards and administrators here in the Crater would never see what killed them, and death could have come from any direction. Archer reflected on how few people, even with all of mankind's experience in space, ever thought to look *up*.

The Neon Mouse skirted the dead body of Reuben Linchfield much as she'd avoided Tyne but gingerly leaned over the desk and pecked at the terminal. It came to life quickly under her touch, as she'd assured them all it would after she'd locked Linchfield and everyone else in the Crater out of their own systems.

"Any idea where Toby is?" another voice broke in, and Archer looked up to see the woman Jynx shoulder her way past Tyne into the room.

*How interesting,* he thought. *Of all of them, she looks the least surprised and horrified by what Tyrus has done here.*

Even the pilot, Riggs, looked like he was going to throw up, and he kept casting furtive glances behind them at the bodies of the few guards that had made a last-ditch attempt to keep the crew out of the administrative offices and protect their boss' office. Archer peered around Riggs outside the door and was surprised to see in the flashing emergency lights a couple of other guards and a handful of administrators strewn around the office space that *didn't* appear to be dead. One he even saw breathing!

*Interesting,* he thought. *I expected him to kill all of them. An assassin with a moral code. What a novel concept.* Had the big man *stunned* them instead of killing them indiscriminately? If he had, it certainly raised him in Jordan Archer's estimation. An assassin who liked to kill was predictable, but one who could *control* his impulses and only kill when necessary was far more dangerous. It also cast his own orders, those to ensure the man's death, into a new light. Any hope of justifying his actions based on Tyne's wanton killing of the Blackmont employees was gone. So much for that.

"I'm going to get Jinny now," Tyrus hissed, and without even waiting for an acknowledgment, he turned heel and walked out of the door, Riggs practically leaping out of the way to let him through.

"Wait!" Archer cried out. Tyne turned and regarded him impassively behind the mask he wore. Images of Cecily flashed through Jordan's head as he considered what to say to the big man. Warning him meant she would most likely die. But *failing* to warn him meant that Jordan himself could never be the man she had fallen in love with. That had been Iasonas' big mistake; he had thought that the threat of violence against his almost-wife would make Jordan do *anything* he asked. But his mysterious employer had failed to consider that not all men were as amoral as he was, and for all of his criminal activity, Jordan Archer had a moral code. More importantly, Cecily had a moral code, and Jordan cared desperately about what she would think of him if and when this was all over.

The big alpha watched and waited. But Archer had already made his choice, and he pushed forward. "Linchfield mentioned something about a special kill squad. They suspected you might come to rescue Ambrosa. Watch out for them."

Tyne said nothing in response but nodded once and then turned back in the direction of the reader's hidden cell.

When he was gone, the Neon Mouse stopped pecking at the terminal and looked up at Archer with red-rimmed eyes.

"He killed them. So many of them. So much blood. Everywhere," she practically whispered. Then she set back to working on the computer.

Archer laid a fat hand on her shoulder—he would be so glad when he no longer looked and felt like Pedro De Vasquez—and squeezed lightly, feeling her shudder beneath his touch.

"My dear," he said gently, "they brought it on themselves. And it could be far worse, trust me."

It was clear she didn't take comfort in his words. *Oh, little one*, he thought sadly. *He did exactly what we needed him to do. We wanted him to do it. And he'll never be the same for it, but it just might be what saves us all.*

*Too bad he probably won't survive it; that's a man I wouldn't mind knowing better. Maybe he could even help me rescue Cecily.*

---

Hendrix sat alone in the cell, listening gleefully to the alarms that bleated around him. The darkness, loud klaxons, and flashing red lights had frightened Jinny, but she was *weak*, so that didn't surprise him. It was why she was now hiding in the fog, and he was in the cell. The chaos *thrilled* him.

He heard a door clang open somewhere down the hall and then the voices of two men screaming. He vaguely recognized them as Angry Man and the Pharmacist. They were begging for mercy from *someone*—he didn't know who—and the sounds of their frantic pleas made him smile broadly and laugh out loud in the darkness that was interspersed only by an occasional flash of bloody crimson.

Just outside the transparent cell door, the Lurch huddled in a corner in that same flickering light, and he threw a frightened look at Hendrix in response to the laughter. Hendrix smiled back at the man and licked his lips. It gratified him to see the guard look away quickly.

"They're coming for you, Lurch," he growled through his teeth. "And I'm going to *kill* you."

The guard whimpered, and the front of his uniform trousers grew dark. Hendrix laughed again.

The screams of Angry Man and the Pharmacist had stopped, and Hendrix was suddenly aware of someone else in the cell with him. It was that annoying speaker, the one called Ryder. "Thần chết đang đến. Không ai sẽ sống sót," the man said, and Hendrix just sneered. The stupid speaker was always talking in some other language as though he expected Hendrix to understand a word of it.

"What's going on?" another voice asked. "Who's out there?" It was Jinny. She had gotten curious and was trying to come back out of the fog. But Hendrix wasn't ready to let her take control again. It was still *his* turn! It was still—

Jinny gasped as she fought her way out of the fog for an instant. The room was alternating between pitch black and a dim red glow. She saw Lurch backed against the far wall opposite her cell, huddled in the corner where the corridor outside ended. He looked terrified and—

*Stupid reader,* Hendrix thought as he pushed Jinny back down. *She should know when to stay put and let* me *handle things. Better for her to just—*

Jinny screamed, the ferocity of the sound momentarily forcing back the fog again.

"Jinny!" she heard a rough, mechanical voice yell. There was a familiar quality to it, one that she—

"He's coming to kill you!" Hendrix taunted in a sing-song voice at Lurch as he pushed Jinny back down into the fog. The guard was now shaking uncontrollably. Hendrix laughed with glee and anticipation.

Suddenly, the air shimmered in front of the cell between him and Lurch, and an enormous figure appeared clad in black from head to toe and facing toward the guard. Hendrix sneered at the newcomer's back. He knew the man was here for Jinny, but he couldn't have her! *No! She's mine! You can't have her! You can't—*

Jinny blinked her eyes rapidly as if doing so might help clear the fog, though it never did. Her brain was moving too slowly to make out what was going on, but she exhaled in shock when she saw the black-clad giant in front of her. He was terrifying in the flashing darkness, yet there was something familiar—

"No! Get back in the fog where you belong, you stupid tramp!" Hendrix screamed. The sound distracted the tall figure, who whirled to focus on Hendrix in the cell.

"Kill the guard!" Hendrix growled. "He liked to hurt poor little Jinny." The big man cocked his head at him, and Hendrix knew he wouldn't be able to resist playing savior to the stupid little—

Jinny felt hot tears pour from her eyes. She was back in the flashing darkness, and panic seized her as she momentarily forgot where she was. The braying of the sirens hurt her head, and she sobbed in terror.

She lifted her eyes from the bunk where she sat and looked out through the door. She recognized the black-clad figure now. "Tyrus," she tried to yell, but it came out as a whisper.

He didn't hear her. He had already turned back toward Lurch and quickly closed the distance with the whimpering guard. In one swift motion, Tyrus grabbed him by the shirt collar and lifted him up in the air.

"What did you do to her?! What's wrong with her?!" he yelled at the man, his voice oddly mechanical. Jinny opened her mouth to—

"Kill him. He hurt us!" screamed Hendrix, exerting his control again and shoving Jinny away. "He and the others did *terrible* things to us. They beat us and threatened us. Kill him! Do it now!"

For a moment, the big man seemed to hesitate as if Hendrix's words confused him. Then he reached out his other hand, grabbed Lurch around the neck, and shook the man as he choked the life out of him. "Tell me what you did to her! How do I fix her?!" he yelled at Lurch, and Hendrix laughed hysterically and—

Jinny watched Tyrus choke the guard through the fog. She desperately tried to call out to him, but Hendrix wasn't letting her; he would only let her watch. He refused to give her their voice back. The fog billowed around her, making it hard to think, and she felt herself slipping away again.

*Tyrus*, she thought, *don't... don't do it. You don't need to. I'm here, Tyrus. I'm here!* She couldn't form the words to make him hear. Even trying was *so* exhausting. It would be so much easier just to let the fog take her again, to curl up and go to sleep in Alan's arms and let Hendrix handle the situation.

The fog closed in again, and Jinny's view of Tyrus and Lurch blurred, and she was only vaguely aware of the large man yelling more things at the terrified guard. Then, suddenly, she heard a new voice.

*Jinny*, it said. *You have to stop him. You have to wake up and stop him!*

*Alan?* It was Alan! He was holding her again, and it felt so good; she just wanted to surrender herself to his safe embrace. But when she tried to burrow into him and let the fog have her, he pushed her back... back toward Hendrix and the narrow, closing gap in the fog and—

"Tyrus, stop!" Jinny heard her own voice ring out through the flashing darkness, and she saw Tyrus hesitate, his fist drawn back to deliver a killing blow to Lurch, whom he still held in the air by his collar. "Stop!" she pleaded with him, fighting to keep Hendrix from reasserting control as he ranted and raved at her from just inside the fog.

"Jinny?" Tyrus' mechanical voice asked, full of hope and pleading.

"Tyrus, don't kill him! He's not worth it," she gasped, and then she felt her body fall forward and saw the hard floor of the cell rushing up to meet her.

---

Tyrus stared in shock as Jinny toppled over from the bunk where she'd been sitting. Her head smacked the concrete floor of her cell with a sickening crunch, and even in the dim, flashing lighting, he could tell it had knocked her out cold.

The shock of it was almost as bad as the sight of her when he'd first entered the hidden cell block off the administrative corridor. She'd been sitting with unnatural rigidity and a slack look on her face, drool glistening on her bruised chin, and a wild look in her one unswollen eye as she goaded him into attacking the killing the one remaining guard in that part of the Crater. She'd spoken of herself in the third person, and even the hatred in her voice was so unlike Jinny that it was almost like another was speaking through her.

Still, he'd almost listened to her demands and killed the guard, though the man clearly was no longer a threat. Before he'd even entered the facility, a piece of him had *wanted* to kill every single person in the hidden prison, simply for the crime of being complicit—consciously or not—in taking Jinny away from him. But in the moments before he'd left the stealth shuttle and begun storming the Crater, he had asked himself one simple question:

*What will I tell Jinny?*

He knew she would ask him what he'd done to rescue her. And he knew that if he killed anyone and everyone who got in his way, it would *hurt* her and possibly even turn her away from him. He had no idea that his thoughts paralleled Jordan Archer's regarding Ceciliy, but he knew he wouldn't be able to look his best friend in the eye if he indiscriminately killed everyone in the prison to satiate his rage.

So, he'd committed in that instant that he would *only* kill those that tried to kill or stop him. To do anything less was to jeopardize the lives of Jinny, Riggs, Jynx, Temperance, and himself. If someone was aiming a weapon at him or any of his companions, he couldn't rely on even a stun blast to possibly make their finger twitch and pull a trigger; he couldn't do anything less than take them out of the equation completely to protect his crew.

However, for those that *didn't* try to take their lives, he would do what he could to keep them alive in turn. So, he'd used the stun cuffs built into the stealth suit or let Riggs and Jynx stun those he left cowering unarmed in his wake. All so he could face Jinny later and tell her what he'd done to save her without losing her forever.

But all his commitments had gone out the airlock when he'd seen the wild look in Jinny's eyes and her bruised and battered face and heard her yelling about how the guard had *hurt* her. He'd picked up the man by the neck and had every intention of killing him, seeing in him the cause of all the terrible things that had been done to his friend and that had somehow *broken* her. He'd been *so* close to choking the life out of the terrified man, with other-worldly Jinny cheering him on in a voice that sounded nothing like her own. It was too late to stop...

...until he'd heard *her* for the first time and turned to see her no longer with the vacant expression and the wild eyes and the drool, but with his *best friend's* pleading countenance, begging him not to kill her tormentor. Somehow, he'd known that her plea wasn't to save the guard so much as to save *him* from doing something that he and she would regret for the rest of their lives.

Then, as if that simple plea to him had robbed her of her energy and strength, she had toppled over and hit the floor hard.

Tyrus spun back around and grabbed the guard, pulling him to his feet from where he'd crumpled onto the prison floor.

"Open her cell, now!" he commanded.

At first, the man did nothing, but then he scurried unsteadily to the cell door and used his uniform's integrated circuitry to key it open. Then the man collapsed to the floor again as Tyrus touched the back of his neck with one of his stun cuffs and rushed past him into the cell.

Inside, he picked Jinny up gently off the floor, ripping off one of the stealth suit's gloves and checking her pulse, not caring if she were possibly conscious enough to read him in the process. He surprisingly wasn't ashamed of what he had done—of the choices he had made today. The guilt might come later, but for now, he gave it little thought next to his desperate need for his friend to be OK. But she didn't stir, though he detected a strong pulse, so at least she wasn't likely in immediate danger.

Then Tyrus gently slung Jinny over his shoulder and moved out of the cell, past the prone body of the guard, and back toward the administrative offices where the others waited.

---

Toby hid under the small desk as men, and even some women, whooped and hollered and ran past in the hallway outside. He'd gotten sloppy. In his haste to escape and in the confusion of the dark prison corridors, he'd moved in the opposite direction from where he'd needed to go. Instead of heading toward the administrative section of the prison to meet up with the others—to fulfill *his* mission—he had inadvertently moved toward the cell blocks, which were now open and hemorrhaging the prisoners who weren't too drugged to function.

He'd already heard them kill several of the guards, ripping them apart with their bare hands or with whatever makeshift weapons they could lay their hands on, and then grabbing their stun batons or guns to kill even more. And Toby himself was stuck. He looked like a guard—was wearing their uniform—and the prisoners would treat him like any other guard if they saw him. There would be far too many of them for him to take on alone, especially with only the simple stun baton he carried as part of his guard kit.

So, he huddled under the small desk in an empty office off one of the hallways, listening in frustrated silence as the worst of humanity rampaged just a few meters away, knowing it was only a matter of time until they found him. Almost as bad, their shouts of bloodlust were contagious. He felt the excitement rise inside him and knew... he needed to kill.

Tyrus turned the corner with Jinny over his shoulder, moving as quickly as he could to get her back to the prison director's office where Archer and Riggs waited and could help him try to revive her and then get her to the waiting stealth shuttle for their escape.

Perhaps it was a change in air pressure from movement down the darkened hall. Maybe it was a faint sound picked up only by his subconscious. Or maybe it was some sixth sense or even the subtle voice of the God that Jinny had mentioned to him. Whatever it was, it made Tyrus stop dead in his tracks and lunge sideways into an open doorway.

It saved his life and Jinny's. The bullets whined down the hall, ricocheting and careening all over the place as at least three assault rifles opened up on full auto. He knew he'd just found the kill squad Archer had warned him about.

The thermal vision of his stealth suit couldn't penetrate far through the thick lunar rock that composed the walls of the Crater's underground warrens, but the inner walls were still made of conventional materials, so it showed him enough. There were four men waiting for him at the only exit from the secret cell block. By the static in his helmet comms, they were jamming him; he couldn't even call for help. And he had no gun other than a pistol at his belt. That and two swords against four assault rifles and a special operations team that already knew he was there did not give him good odds.

And it wasn't just his life that hung in the balance. He gently set down Jinny's slack body on the small room's sole tabletop. Then he turned back to the doorway and prepared to fight or die. For her.

## CHAPTER 28

"It's time to go back to the shuttle," Archer called to Riggs.

The pilot hadn't spoken since Tyrus had left, but Jynx, who had been pacing the office nervously for several minutes, whirled around and glared at him. "No way! Not until we find Toby. We don't leave without him! And *you're* supposed to wait here for Tyrus and Jinny!"

The big alpha and the reader should have been back by now, and Archer knew that meant they were both likely dead, despite his warning to Tyne. That also meant he needed to find a way to recover the reader's body. Iasonas needed it for whatever plan the cruel man had concocted, and if Archer failed to comply, Cecily was as good as dead. She was probably dead anyway, he admitted to himself with a tremble; Iasonas *should* have no way of knowing that Jordan had warned Tyrus of the kill squad, but his shadowy employer seemed to know many things he shouldn't.

"Oh no," a small voice said from Archer's side, distracting all of them. He looked down to see the Neon Mouse, face white in horror.

"What?!" Jynx demanded of the girl, taking a step toward her in a way that had Archer subconsciously reaching toward the pistol at his belt.

"I found them, but…" the girl turned the terminal's screen so that

Jynx could see it. Archer moved around the desk to stand next to the woman and get his own view. Just inside an area that the schematics said should be solid rock—Archer recognized it as the entry hall into the secret cell block—two blue dots on the screen were blocked by four red ones. The kill team had found Tyne and Jinny. They weren't dead yet, but they were about to be.

Another flashing blue dot on the prison map showed the location of Toby Haight. He was in a small room on the other side of the prison, possibly an office or a supply closet, right off of one of the main corridors... squarely in the area now overrun by escaped convicts: the murderers, rapists, spies, traitors, and other dregs of humanity who called the maximum security, top-secret prison home.

"Send that to my comm!" Jynx snapped, her voice hot and angry. Without waiting for the hacker to respond, she whirled and rushed out of the room, grabbing Riggs by the arm and pulling him after her.

"You help Jinny and Tyrus!" Riggs shouted to Archer before he was bodily dragged out of the room. "We'll meet you at the shuttle."

Archer looked down at the Neon Mouse, who was literally shaking in fear, the pungent odor of the girl's nervous sweat filling his nostrils.

She looked at him with wide eyes and a quivering lower lip, and he could see tears born of terror in her eyes. Then he looked back at the display that showed Tyrus Tyne and Jinny Ambrosa about to die.

"Cecily, forgive me," he whispered to the universe. Then he rushed out the door, leaving the petrified hacker alone in the light of a single dim lamp.

---

## ONE MONTH AGO

The young man waited for the sound of the Raven leaving the aircar and then waited for several minutes after the noise of her footsteps had faded. Slowly, carefully, he opened the trunk. He felt his moment arriving. It was time to make contact.

He slid out of the car and hid behind it, watching as the woman walked toward the small fast-food dive just down the road. Following at a safe distance, sticking to the tree line in case she looked back, he was amused that she didn't even check her six. She had a singular focus right now, one that he could work with.

He knew she had no money. Why would she? The Earthers had given her everything she could want or need, not that she appreciated it. She was so spoiled and deserved what he would eventually give her. After all, she was a traitor to the Council. And traitors had to die, but he could have some fun first *and* achieve the other objectives of his mission. It was so wonderful when work and passion intersected.

The roadside joint's parking lot was crowded, and it was easy for him to slip into the crowd on the other side from where she scanned the diners. As he walked past the dirty men and few women, he watched them carefully and started to adopt their poses and mannerisms. He stopped and rubbed some dirt on his unshaven face. At one parked car, he reached into the window and retrieved a tattered t-shirt that someone had left on the seat.

Then he changed out of his own shirt, which was crusty from his swim across the Sound, and slipped the new t-shirt on. A few men watched him curiously, but he paid them no mind, and they went back to talking about their early morning shift at the shipyards. He listened unobtrusively for a few moments, learning what he needed.

Finally, he reached the front of the crowd of laborers and stood nonchalantly next to a dirty pickup truck that looked like it could have been one of the first hover vehicles ever constructed. Then he started his act in earnest. Every time someone walked close to him, he jumped just a little, putting a startled look on his face to complement the effect. For inspiration, he thought of a dog he had once snuck into the Enacter Academy. It had followed him for a few days there, the instructors tolerating it because of his 'special' case. Then he had grown bored with the animal and started beating it, reveling in how it jumped and shied away every time he came near from then onward. Eventually, he had grown bored and killed it, but the two weeks had been interesting ones.

He saw the Raven casting glances at him now, but she was also scoping out a few others in the crowd. So, he decided he needed to be a little more obvious. He walked to the window and ordered some food, paying with a cash card he had stolen a few weeks before. He made sure that the Raven saw him use the card. Then he walked back to the pickup truck with his order ticket. Now, he pretended to notice *her* for the first time, throwing furtive looks her way every few moments like he was examining her beauty.

She *was* beautiful, he supposed, in some subjective way that would matter to most men. He had different criteria, and what she looked like didn't factor at all into the equation. For him, it was about the challenge, the hope, and the eventual crushing despair—she would experience all of it. And the excitement and anticipation of what was coming hit him like a drug.

Out of his peripheral vision, he saw her walk toward him. When she was five meters away, he met her gaze, watching her the rest of the way as she approached, carefully trying to project an expression of both interest and wariness. He'd learned that mixed expression by watching a criminal he'd stalked and killed as part of his first formal assignment. The Raven was likewise playing a role, her normal confident brashness turned down in favor of a sort of timid shyness that couldn't have come naturally to her.

She stopped in front of him and attempted to casually lean one hip against the dirty pickup truck. The woman threw him a small smile and tried to look shy again. She was fairly good at faking the emotions. As a practitioner of the craft, he could appreciate her skill, but he was better. He didn't have *other* emotions to cover up with his fake ones.

"Haven't seen you here before," she said. He shrugged. Shrugging was a great general-purpose reaction to most things, he had long since learned, and it bought him a second to decide what emotional reactions to display. Here, he followed up the shrug with a look of mild terror. It was exactly what he thought a shy orphan—he'd already decided that she would respond best to that persona—would exhibit when faced with a pretty girl who was out of his league.

"I just started at the shipyard last week," he said, purposefully cracking his voice on one of the syllables.

"That's nice," she replied. "I'm looking for a new job myself. How is it there?"

And the game began.

## PRESENT DAY; SEPTEMBER 2, 731 P.D.

With Jinny safe—or as close as was possible to safe—on the table behind him, Tyrus reactivated his stealth suit and, with a shimmer of air, disappeared into the darkness.

Still, he was cautious when he stuck his head out and peered down toward the four men of the kill squad. He twitched his face in the right pattern to change from thermal vision to low-light optics, and the images of the men resolved. They were wearing a different body armor than the rest of the guards he'd come across, further confirming that they must be the special kill squad Archer had warned him about.

*But why let me get so far into the facility before coming after me?* he wondered. He thrust aside the thought for now. It was time to kill again.

Tyrus ducked back into the room as two of the men started to move toward him down the hall. By the way their eyes had fixed on the doorway when he'd peered out, it was almost like they could see him. Maybe there was something in their helmet optics that could defeat the stealth suit?

Carefully but quietly setting both his swords down, Tyrus reached to his belt and pulled two of the specially designed knives at his waist, one in each hand. Moving quickly, he stepped back out into the darkened corridor and flicked both of his wrists in an underhand throwing motion.

The two approaching soldiers—because that's what they undoubtedly were—dropped their weapons and clung at their throats before collapsing almost simultaneously. The knives had flown true into the windpipe of each man.

Unfortunately, the other two attackers had been waiting for just such a move, and they opened fire before their comrades had even fallen out of the way. After throwing the knives, Tyrus immediately pinched his fingers to activate the controls for the suit's integrated grav belt and then jumped hard upward toward the ceiling.

He was too slow. A bullet hit his left thigh, missing the bone but taking a chunk out of his leg. Worse, it caused the stealth suit to glitch and deactivate its active camouflage as the matrix was broken. Now, whether or not they could defeat the stealth suit with their optics was a moot point.

Tyrus pulled his pistol from its holster as his back hit the ceiling and shot one of the remaining two men in the face—his simple pistol rounds would never have penetrated the man's body armor or helmet. Then he turned his aim toward the fourth and final man, but again wasn't fast enough, and he watched in horror as the soldier's assault rifle tracked up at his head in the dim flashing lights.

The gun spoke even as Tyrus reversed the grav belt's controls in a last-ditch effort to evade, falling hard to the floor at an equivalent weight of 3 g's and knocking the wind out of himself as he inadvertently landed on his wounded leg. He felt the bullets passing over him as the man tracked his downward fall, and he braced himself for what he knew was coming, even as he desperately tried to beat the man to the shot.

A final report of gunfire rang out before Tyrus could draw a bead on the man.

But he was surprised to find that he wasn't dead, and he watched in surprise as the final soldier crumpled and fell to the corridor's stone floor.

Revealed now behind the man, Jordan Archer stood in the flabby form of Pedro De Vasquez, his pistol held high where he had shot the last soldier in the back of the neck. Tyrus pushed himself unsteadily to his feet, favoring his injured hip. Then he nodded to the blender and hobbled back into the room where he'd left Jinny, who was still oblivious to the world around her.

---

Toby tried to make himself smaller as he heard someone enter the small office.

"I smell guard," a voice sneered. "Come out and play, little guard."

Toby shook his head in frustration. *No, you're in the way! You're not the one I came here to kill.* Despite that, he felt the excitement rise inside him.

He readied himself to leap out from under the desk and quickly kill the prisoner, waiting to hear the man step close enough for him to make his move.

But the next sound wasn't what he expected at all. It wasn't the slow sound of the man walking toward him and death but a boom that reverberated through the hall outside.

The unseen convict swore, and Toby heard his footsteps running away, and he smiled.

Another massive boom, this time closer, shook the hall. Then the sound of footsteps reentered the room, and Toby knew the end game had come.

"Toby?" a feminine voice called out.

"J-Jynx?" he asked, putting fear into his voice.

Then she was there, crouching next to the desk and pulling him into her arms, squeezing him so tight he thought he might never breathe again. His body shivered in barely contained anticipation, though he knew she would take it as a sign of his terror.

"Jynx!" Riggs interrupted from outside the door. "I hate to break up your reunion, but I can hear a lot more of those convicts coming down the hall, and there are still guards we have to fight through to get back to the ship. We need to leave *now!*"

"Let's go," Jynx said with unusual gentleness in her tone as she helped Toby to his feet. She put something in his hand, and he looked down to see a pistol. He looked back up at her and saw she carried the shotgun that had made such a racket in the hall and scared away the sneering inmate. Riggs held an assault rifle, and they both wore body armor as well.

"Let's go," she said again to him, more forcefully this time, and grabbed his arm to quickly guide him out into the hall behind Riggs.

"Jynx, take Toby and go. Archer just called to say they have Jinny, and they'll meet us at the shuttle. I'll hold them off long enough for the two of you to get a head start!" cried Riggs.

"Riggs, just come with us!" Jynx called back, pleading with the man.

"They're too close! Go!" he shouted, and Jynx obediently pulled Toby down the hall back in the direction she and Riggs had come from.

Behind them, Toby heard Riggs yelling and triggering the assault rifle in full auto mode.

Jynx ran with Toby right behind, the shotgun held in front of her, moving quickly through the darkened hall, still only lit by flashes of red emergency lamps.

"Jynx," he called out to her. "We need to go find Tyrus and Jinny! They probably need our help." It was *vital* to his mission that he find the big alpha before he left the prison.

"Can't!" she answered without looking back. "They'll be at the shuttle before us. Archer says they're fine, but it sounds like they may both be injured. We have to get back to the shuttle and meet them there!"

Toby shook his head in frustration. He'd come so *far*! To fail now was infuriating. And all because he'd taken some wrong turns in the dark!

He was opening his mouth to argue again, but as they went around a bend in the hall, a prisoner leapt out from a darkened open doorway just as Jynx passed.

It must have been his frustration at a mission gone sideways, or perhaps it was the excitement of all the killing taking place around him, but Toby lashed out without conscious thought. The heel of his hand smashed up and into the man's nose, breaking it instantly and pushing bone and cartilage up into the prisoner's brain, killing him in gruesome fashion. Blood sprayed onto Toby's hand, and he relished the warmth of the liquid. The feel of someone's life leaving their body and leaving its mark on him was intoxicating. It had been more than a *year* since he'd killed anyone, and the release was cathartic in the extreme.

But he didn't have time to revel in the feeling. He looked up and saw Jynx had turned around and was regarding him in horrified shock. And he knew that she'd seen him destroy the man in a way that only a trained killer could.

"Toby, how did you...?" she started to ask, but then her eyes narrowed in suspicion and then shocked realization as the pieces fell into place for her. "Who are you, really?"

He sighed internally. His little Raven had figured him out. It was too bad, really. She'd been a fun plaything, a bonus in his mission to kill Tyne, the mission he'd received in those encrypted orders from the Council fleet.

He'd had a dozen chances to kill the big ex-alpha as they'd worked together to plan Jinny's escape, but his orders from the Council had been clear. Tyne needed to die, but the reader needed to escape and *survive*. So, he'd gone along with and even helped execute the plan to rescue her, assuming he would have an opportunity in the confusion of the prison break to find and kill the big traitorous ex-alpha *after* Jinny Ambrosa was safely back with her other friends.

If only he hadn't gotten lost in the confusion and excitement of a prison in chaos. Oh well, there would be other opportunities to kill Tyne. For now, staying with him and his little group for a bit longer would give him useful information he could pass back to the Council when they finally came to invade this horrible little system. But now that Jynx suspected him...

"Don't worry, Jynx," he said soothingly. "It'll all be over soon."

Before she could react, and even as she swung the shotgun toward him, he stepped toward her and grabbed her roughly, pulling her face down into his forehead, breaking her nose, and causing his little Raven to scream in agony. Taking advantage of her physical and mental shock, he knocked the shotgun out of her hands and then spun her around and locked his arm around her neck, cutting off the blood flow to her brain.

She struggled against him, but he knew she had no chance of breaking his iron grip, trained and honed for years for just such a moment as this.

"Shhh," he whispered in her ear, a shudder running through him at the prospect of feeling her life fade in his arms. "Don't fight it, Jynx. This is just how it has to be. I'm doing you a favor, really. Now you can finally stop thinking about Dax."

She tried to say something back, no doubt some pithy insult about his parentage or personal hygiene or maybe a plea for her life. But she couldn't force the words out as the blood flow stopped to her brain. It only took about 15 seconds, and his Raven went limp in his arms, her last struggles exhausted. D5746J14L1 waited for one more instant to ensure she wasn't faking. Then he repositioned both his hands and twisted violently, breaking her neck.

Jynx's body crumpled to the floor of the corridor. He stood there looking down at her, feeling a warm satisfaction well up inside of him. And he smiled. *That was perfect.* It had been better than he'd even expected, far more satisfying than any previous kill of the hundreds he had executed, first in the Enacter Academy and later on missions for the Council. *Maybe the trick is building a more personal relationship before the kill?* That was an interesting thought for another time.

Then he picked up the shotgun where she'd dropped it and held it by the barrel. Calmly, he swung it up at himself and felt the stock of the gun impact against his face, splitting his cheek and causing blood to pour from his own nose. Then he pointed the gun at the head of the already-dead prisoner on the ground and pulled the trigger, the shotgun's boom reverberating through the corridor.

A moment later, Riggs rounded the bend a few meters away and stopped dead. D5746J14L1 had his back to the man but heard him approaching and identified him by the sound of his gait. And by the stunned gasp that carried a world of pain.

"Jynx, no!" Riggs cried and rushed to where Toby stood, looking down at the woman's corpse. The pilot fell to his knees beside her and picked up her head, cradling it in his lap. "What happened?" he choked out, looking up at D5746J14L1.

For a fleeting moment, D5746J14L1 was grateful that his own broken nose had caused tears to flow down his face, a physiological reaction to the injury that saved him the trouble of trying to fake the tears himself—he'd become proficient at faking most emotions, but crying had always been a challenge for him.

"Sh-she saved me," he gasped out, putting just the right amount of shock and dismay into his voice. "That man," he pointed down at the dead prisoner. "He jumped out and hit me, and Jynx fought him off. But she dropped her gun." He was babbling now, doing his best to emulate a man in shock. "He did something to her... I don't know! But she just fell down, and I... I picked up the gun and shot him. But Jynx wouldn't move. I couldn't get her to move!" He thought he had put the perfect level of panicked despair and grief into that last part.

Riggs stared at him, his mouth agape, tears falling from his eyes, and D5746J14L1 wanted to sneer at how easily the man was fooled.

"We can't leave her here," the pilot pleaded. "Help me carry her back to the shuttle. Please, Toby. We just can't leave her here."

---

Archer watched as Tyrus hobbled along down the corridor, the still body of Jinny Ambrosa in his arms. From meeting her before, Jordan was well aware of the reader's beauty, but now...

Even in the tepid illumination of the red emergency lights, Archer could see that her face was bruised and broken, one eye completely swollen shut, and the other closed to the world. Her nose was off-center on her face and twice its normal size, and her lips were a cracked and bloody pulp.

They had walked along for a few minutes when he finally found the voice to ask: "Is she..." he couldn't finish the question, but Tyrus shook his head.

"She's alive. But not by much." The pain in the big man's voice was equaled only by the anger, but it was a far cry from the cold rage the man had displayed before. It was as if, now that he had his friend back, he was no longer the ruthless assassin that had cut his way through everyone and everything that stood in his way.

"She was alive enough to stop me from..." the big man continued but broke off, swallowing his next words and shaking his head.

"I understand," was Archer's reply. He didn't understand, not fully, but he suspected. And for the first time, he thought he could see exactly why this man had been able to defy the Council and a millennium of genetic programming. It was *her*. She'd found a way to reach Tyrus Tyne in a manner that no one else could. She was his kryptonite, to use an obscure reference from the vintage comics Archer had collected as a boy in Australia. But whereas kryptonite had made the hero weak, Jinny Ambrosa made Tyrus Tyne stronger, but only after breaking him down.

This epiphany for Jordan Archer was interrupted by the small voice of the Neon Mouse, who met them outside Reuben Linchfield's office.

"C-can we go now?"

It was Tyrus who answered, gracing the girl with a slight but surprising smile, though it disappeared as soon as he glanced back down at his broken and beaten friend. "Yes, let's get out of here. I may need help carrying Jinny. I took a bullet through the leg." He said it so casually that Archer did a double take once the import of the words sunk in and saw the blood pooling at the big alpha's foot.

"Is O'Leary in position with the *Monk*?" Tyrus asked, ignoring his scrutiny.

"I got confirmation five minutes ago," Archer replied.

"Then let's go. We need to get Jinny help."

With that, the four individuals—the hacker, the blender, the assassin, and the reader—made their way back to the waiting stealth shuttle.

# CHAPTER 29

"Will she be OK?" Corey O'Leary asked softly, breaking Tyrus out of his thoughts as the congressman crossed the threshold of the *Blind Monk's* small medical bay. Tyrus himself hadn't moved from his silent vigil by her side even once in the three hours since the stealth shuttle had docked with the *Monk*, transferring a few members of the team before both ships started their hard burn toward the safety of the outer system. The Neon Mouse had assured them it would take at least a few hours before the Crater's surviving guards and administrators could regain enough system control to send any outgoing distress messages; so, for now, the two ships looked just like any other commercial shuttles leaving Luna in the rough direction of Europa.

"The auto-doc says she likely has no permanent damage," Tyrus replied, shaking his head. "But she was beaten pretty badly and repeatedly. She just won't wake up." His voice caught. "The capsule has no explanation for why. It's like her mind is refusing to return to consciousness, even though there's nothing really preventing it from doing so. She needs a *real* doctor, preferably one who knows something about readers."

Jinny lay in an enclosed, transparent, coffin-like apparatus that jutted out from the med bay's bulkhead. Most ships didn't have their own auto-docs, but Riggs and Jynx had lived a life that largely avoided official entanglements, and that meant avoiding hospitals for all but the worst injuries. Though, how the two smugglers had afforded their own high-end med capsule was a mystery to Tyrus.

He looked at Jinny, focusing on her face. He'd had to gently remove her clothing so the auto-doc could examine and stabilize her, but he purposefully kept his eyes averted out of respect for the woman. He was pleased to see O'Leary do the same.

Not that there was anything attractive right now about the young reader. Her entire body was a mess of bruises, broken bones, and swollen lumps. Someone had beaten her to within a centimeter of her life and done so multiple times. Just thinking about it made Tyrus want to return to the prison and finish off any of the Blackmont employees he hadn't already killed.

His despair was made even worse by what awaited them back on the shuttle. Shortly after Archer had helped Tyrus hobble in with Jinny on his shoulder—the blender had offered to carry her for him, but Tyrus had found himself unable to let go of his friend—Riggs and Toby had arrived, with Riggs likewise carrying the still body of Jynx. But unlike Jinny, Jynx was dead, and no amount of time in the auto-doc could have saved her.

Intellectually, Tyrus had known that one or more of them might, and even likely would, die on the mission. It would have been a miracle if just the six of them, not counting Jinny, had been able to storm a facility of thousands of dangerous prisoners and hundreds of guards *without* taking their own casualties. Even the decision to let the prisoners loose, knowing that it would distract the rest of the guards from the incursion, was a calculated one that Tyrus knew would add almost as much danger as it helped avoid.

But now that one of them actually *had* died, it was far more painful than he had expected. Tyrus had been around death all his life, but only rarely had it happened to someone he cared about—not since his mother. And he was surprised to find that he truly *did* care about the mercurial co-pilot who had so often threatened to kill him. Perhaps it was because of the uneasy but subtle thawing of her feelings toward him in recent weeks, or maybe it was simply that he'd held out some hope he could reconcile with her, only to have it now crushed. Or maybe it was the guilt that she would never see him brought to justice for killing her sister. Regardless of the cause, he found himself mourning the fiery smuggler with a depth of emotion that shocked him.

Of course, his pain at her death was nothing compared to that of Riggs. The pilot hadn't even shown a sliver of happiness at seeing his beloved ship again when the stealth shuttle had docked with it just outside of Luna's orbit. Nor had he said much as he had gently carried the body of his dead co-pilot off the shuttle and onto the *Blind Monk*, where he gently lay her in her own room and on her own bunk, arranging her body as if she were merely sleeping, before making his way wordlessly to the cockpit and taking control of his ship from O'Leary's pilot.

Toby Haight had been just as disconsolate at the tall woman's death. Tyrus didn't know quite what had been forming between the angry woman and the naïve young man, but it had been *something*, and now the boy seemed to be in complete and utter shock that she was gone, showing no emotion and saying nothing.

Despite the success of their mission, it was a broken and distraught group that now made their way rapidly away from Luna. And it seemed that they really would reach the safety of the asteroid belt before the UEN or the CSF even knew about the prison break. It had all gone according to plan...

...except for the broken and battered reader clinging to life in the medical pod and the dead co-pilot in her bunk.

Misreading the cause of Tyrus' silent reflection, Corey O'Leary looked up at him. "You only did what you had to in order to save her."

Tyrus nodded. "I know." And he did know, surprising even himself with that fact.

Corey shook his head emphatically. "You can't blame yourself for what you had to do, or," his voice softened, "for what came of it. She," he gestured toward Jinny inside the medical capsule, "is our only hope. And not even in the way you think. Her abilities, they're vital. But more importantly, *she* is the key herself."

The man looked up at Tyrus and reached up to put a hand on the larger man's shoulder. "You and me, Tyrus. We do what needs to be done. You may have killed those men in that prison, but I have killed just as many, if not so many more, by my politics. Every decision I've made helps some and hurts others. Every law I've voted for helped some get ahead while others starved and even died. Some of my decisions have sent men and women directly to their deaths in battle. Like your friend, Jynx.

"Like you, I've done it for what I believe are the *right* reasons. But that logic gives me cold comfort when I consider those dead at my hands."

Tyrus nodded. He didn't need the man's words, but saying them seemed to be helping O'Leary himself come to grips with all that had happened, so he let the congressman continue.

"But Jinny," Corey paused, looking again toward the broken girl in the capsule, "she is pure. She is unsullied by such cold and rational decisions. Even when you were going to justifiably kill that last guard, she stopped you. She saved her own abuser." Tyrus had told them all the story of what had happened by Jinny's cell, repeating it robotically as if he'd merely been an observer.

"Only *she* could have done that," Corey continued. "You couldn't afford to let him live, but *she* could. Don't ask me why. It's clear the man had been cruel to her. Maybe she had mercy on him. Or, possibly, she was simply giving you permission not to add one more death to your ledger. I don't know, and we may never know.

"The mere fact that she could overcome all of *that*," he gestured to encompass her injuries, "and tell you to spare him... It shows why she *has* to survive. Because she is everything we're trying to save. If she dies, I'm afraid that all hope would die with her."

Now Tyrus shuddered. What he hadn't told the others was that Jinny had first told him to *kill* the guard before she had begged him to stop and spare the man. He wasn't sure what to make of her strange behavior in the cell, like she was two different people talking to him, first egging him on in his murderous rage and then pleading with him to stop. He didn't intend to tell any of them anything, not until he'd had a chance to talk to her and find out what was going on.

"Pereira and his minions understood that," O'Leary continued, still oblivious to Tyrus' inner thoughts. "They knew she was becoming a symbol to the people, so they had to take that symbol away, first by trying to besmirch her reputation and then by trying to fake her death. When that didn't work, they would have killed her for real. But *you* saved her. And in doing so, you may have saved us all.

"Now, let's take the recordings of her and send them to Earth. There is a man there that will use them to force Pereira to rethink his approach to this war. Then perhaps, finally, we can start to prepare to meet the invasion you all came to warn us about."

The congressman didn't wait for a response but squeezed Tyrus' shoulder once and then departed from the small room.

Tyrus stepped forward and put a hand on the top of the auto-doc, and stared down into Jinny's battered face. He stood that way for a long moment, watching her sleep the untroubled sleep of anesthesia and innocence. Then he dropped his hand back to his side and walked out of the room.

There was still work to be done.

# CHAPTER 30

ONE DAY LATER; SEPTEMBER 3, 731 P.D.

The most common thing that surprises first-time space travelers is the sheer *size* of space, even within a single star system. Those who do not regularly ply the spacelanes simply cannot grasp the volume of emptiness that surrounds a solitary starship in every direction. And those that do try hard not to think about it, lest the lonely isolation drive them insane.

A thousand years after the first human colony was established, the most advanced warships with next-generation sensor suites still couldn't reasonably scan a fraction of the space surrounding them. Even an ultra-modern SWACS ship like the *UENS Monitor* could only detect a cold ship with its active sensors if it was closer than two light minutes away, and then only if she already knew roughly where to look. A warship with its main drive lit was much easier to find, and *Monitor* could see the heat signature of one of those from two light *hours* away. The massive sensor arrays and telescopes on orbital stations and on the surfaces of planets could see further, but even they had to have a rough idea of where to scan. In the vastness of the night sky, there was no way to keep watch on it all.

Captain Rosita Perez stood on the bridge of her ship, staring solemnly at the empty space seen through the forward viewscreen. She had a choice to make; two distinct sets of conflicting orders. And she wasn't sure yet what to do.

"Captain," her sensor officer called. "We've detected a ship that meets the profile of the *Blind Monk*! It's cold coasting on a vector from the outer system into the Martian neutral zone. The *Franklin* is close enough to intercept but hasn't seen her yet. Shall I relay the coordinates to her?"

Anita didn't answer the question at first, and part of her wished the man hadn't even asked it. It would be so much *easier* if he'd just relayed the information to the UEN destroyer on his own initiative; it would be so much cleaner for her if the decision were taken away from her.

She thought about the orders she'd received from Houston, and then she thought about the personal message that had arrived just hours later from her mentor. The man had no *real* authority to countermand her orders from naval headquarters. Those orders came from the *president* himself, albeit filtered through General Cruz and Admiral Clancy.

But she *owed* her mentor her entire career. That meant something to her. Even if he was advising, no *pleading*, with her to commit treason.

Her decision finally made, she looked up and met the expectant eyes of the lieutenant at the sensor station. "Negative, James. That's not the *Blind Monk*. It's a classified research vessel, and we are to let it through unmolested."

With those words, the once-promising career of Captain Anita Perez would surely come to an end. She could only hope that Admiral Hunter Killer Lopez, the man who had recognized her promise as a young lieutenant herself on the carrier *UENS Constitution* so many years ago, knew what he was doing.

---

"Entering the demilitarized zone in ten, nine, eight, seven...." Riggs called out. The space in front of them looked clear, though the sensors could see Martian pickets at oblique angles that were sure to intercept them before they reached the red planet itself. Still, even the lack of an immediate threat did not lessen the tension in the cockpit, and when Riggs' countdown reached zero, everyone held a collective breath, just as they had done when they had cold-coasted within light seconds of a UEN destroyer on their journey in.

Nothing happened.

None of them had really expected anything to happen the *second* they entered the neutral zone, but the fact that nothing did was almost a letdown. The stress they all felt had been building for hours, and they would have welcomed almost *any* reaction to their intrusion, even a negative one, if for no other reason than to break the tension and give them some kind of resolution to the long wait.

"How long to Mars territory itself?" Tyrus asked. Riggs knew the alpha already knew the answer, but someone needed to say *something* to break the nervous anticipation. He was grateful to him for that, even if he'd refused to meet the big man's eyes since they'd left Luna. It would take him some time to come to grips with all that had happened there, especially to Jynx. Right now, Riggs was just... numb. But he knew the crash of emotions would inevitably come, and he dreaded it.

"At this speed, only half an hour," he replied, not taking his eyes off the scanners. "If anyone is having any second thoughts, this is the last chance to get off and hitchhike back to Earth."

Tyrus and O'Leary didn't laugh at his lame attempt at humor—his heart just wasn't in it—but the tension did ratchet down a bit. Toby even let out what sounded like a momentary gagged giggle, as if he wasn't sure whether a laugh was appropriate. It was the most emotion the boy had shown since Jynx's death less than 24 hours before. He'd been avoiding Riggs just as Riggs had been avoiding Tyrus. The only time they'd all come together in any meaningful way had been for an impromptu, but no less poignant, funeral service in which Riggs had said a few words and then launched the body of his former friend and co-pilot out of the starboard airlock on a long spiral course that would eventually intersect with Sol itself. It was the way she would have wanted to go out, he told himself: in a literal blaze of glory. But the rushed service had felt like they were cheating themselves and her of a proper goodbye.

"Any sign they've detected us?" Corey O'Leary asked from the other back seat next to Toby. He was the only one on board who wasn't avoiding anyone or being avoided. He'd still had the wise sense to stay largely quiet during the long cold coast in from the asteroid belt toward the red planet.

"No, though it would take some time for the light of any reaction to reach us," Tyrus replied with forced calm. Everyone in the cockpit knew just how upset the man was about Jinny not being there with them. But he was trying hard to hide it anyway.

Intellectually, Riggs knew he and the others had been right when they'd convinced the big alpha to let O'Leary's pilot take Jinny and the stealth shuttle to Australia. They had no idea what awaited them at Mars, nor did they know how the current Martian government—whatever it may be—felt about the enhanced. They may have killed Jinny as soon as they learned what she was. Even Tyrus was taking a tremendous risk as an ex-enacter, if there really was such a thing. But even so, they still would have followed the original plan and taken her if it wasn't for her desperate need for medical attention. Sending her back to Earth, and to Australia in particular, where other readers could examine her and hopefully help her wake from her coma, made the most sense.

Despite all that, Riggs hadn't been *happy* with the decision either. It felt wrong to send her away when they'd just spent so much to get her back!

Archer had gone with the stealth shuttle and Jinny, insisting that he could smooth the way on the southern continent. The Neon Mouse had also accompanied them. Her part of the job was done, and she had wordlessly shown a frantic desire to get far away from Tyrus as quickly as she could.

Surprisingly, Toby had asked to stay with the *Monk*. He argued that he had nowhere else to go and would be a fugitive on Earth when they discovered his role in helping them rescue Jinny. So now he, Riggs, Tyrus, and O'Leary were in the process of implementing the second part of their audacious plan. They were aiming to be the first non-

Martian ship to breach Martian space in almost five decades. At least the first to survive the attempt.

The worst part was that they had no way of knowing if Jinny and the others would make it to Australia safely and without being captured. For obvious reasons, Landon Hartman, Corey's pilot, could not send them any message to verify Jinny's safe arrival in Perth, so they simply had to accept on faith that the pilot and the blender would get their friend there without incident. It could be *months* before they knew for sure. That, more than anything else, bothered Riggs.

Something in the cockpit dinged at him, and one of his holo displays started flashing red. "New ship on the scanner!" he almost yelled. His sudden sense of relief at having the quiet tension broken was fleeting as he took a closer look. "Scud. It's a *big* one too." He enlarged the sensor holo view so they could all see the new ship that had appeared ahead of them, seemingly out of nowhere, hanging almost exactly at the point where the *Monk* would be leaving the neutral zone and entering Mars' space on their current vector.

It was indeed a large ship—bigger than a Missouri-class UEN battleship by about fifteen percent in both length and tonnage. That put it almost as large as one of Earth's Essex-class fleet carriers but still quite a bit smaller than a Council Navy dreadnought.

"How did we not see that earlier?!" Tyrus demanded, his voice tense.

"I don't know," Riggs replied. "The chances that it just happened to be sitting there cold along our exact vector are low-to-none. They must have had a way to mask their main drive's heat bloom."

Tyrus had told them all a little about his time on *Enterprise* and the mysterious drive technology she and her sister ships used to move in perfect stealth. Riggs wondered if Mars had the same tech, but the heat bloom he now saw from the big Martian battleship's drive made that unlikely. They must have developed some other kind of stealth that Earth didn't know about.

"Uh, what's that blinking red light?" Toby asked, pointing toward another flashing light on the console in front of Tyrus.

"It means they have a weapons lock on us," Tyrus replied calmly, emotion drained from his voice now that there was a threat to respond to. Riggs was wary of the man after his killing spree on Luna but had to admit he was a good man to have in the co-pilot chair. But thoughts of that chair immediately brought back with them the pain of losing Jynx, so he quickly tamped down that line of musing and focused himself intently on watching the scanner for any sign of the big Martian ship firing at them.

"Isn't that a bad thing? Should we be turning around and running?" Toby asked, the anxiety thick in his voice.

"No." The answer came not from Tyrus but from Corey O'Leary. "Hail them, please," he said to Riggs, and the pilot dutifully opened a comm channel. Tyrus may have been the unquestioned leader of their mission to rescue Jinny, but since rendezvousing with them aboard the *Monk*, the congressman had subtly yet no-less-effectively taken over as the group's head. After all, this next part of the mission had been entirely his idea.

O'Leary wasted no time but spoke into the open comm channel. "Martian Navy battleship, this is United Earth Congressman Corey O'Leary on board the merchant vessel *Blind Monk*. With me are two refugees from the 47 Colonies and a third from Earth. We request asylum from the government of Mars and bring an important message for your leaders. Our ship is armed with defensive weapons but is not a threat to your Navy. We await instructions."

They waited for ten long minutes, every second bringing them closer to the massive battleship and the Martian edge of the neutral zone. It was more than enough time for their message to have reached the giant warship and for a response to have come back, even allowing for several minutes of consideration by the ship's captain. When the response finally came, the voice delivering it was terse and cold—as icy a woman's voice as Riggs had ever heard.

"*Blind Monk*, this is the Martian People's Navy Quinquereme *Cassius*. You are not welcome in Martian space. If you enter Martian territory, you will be destroyed. If you do not turnover and accelerate back along your current vector within one minute of receiving this message, you will be destroyed. This is your only warning."

At once, everyone in the *Monk's* cockpit started talking over each other. Riggs started asking what he should do; Toby started babbling about turning back around; even Tyrus started to give the order to turn over and decelerate to buy them some time.

Then one voice rose above the tumult. "Everyone quiet! Now!" The commanding tone of Corey O'Leary's voice instantly shut all of them up, even Tyrus, and gave Riggs an insight into just how this man had become one of the most powerful elected officials on humanity's homeworld.

"Thank you," Corey said in a softer yet still authoritative tone once they'd all stopped talking and gaped at him anxiously. He continued quickly before they could start up again. "Captain Riggs, please open a channel to the Martian ship once again. And please don't change course or velocity."

Riggs opened the channel again. The words had been spoken as a request, but he could understand an order when he heard one.

O'Leary didn't hesitate but launched right into his message again. "*MPNS Cassius*, we understand your instructions but cannot comply. I ask that you check your ship's computer for a set of sealed orders labeled 'Serpico 427'. The password to access them will be 'Atticus'. We await your response."

He chopped his hand, and Riggs stopped the recording.

"What the—?" he started to ask, but Corey held up a hand, and he choked off the question.

"Mr. Riggs, it would take too long to explain. I just ask that you all trust me for another few minutes. Once that Martian captain sees what I've directed her to, she will stand down and let us pass. She may even give us an escort to Mars herself."

Riggs wasn't convinced. "You seem awfully sure of yourself. How can we know if this will work?"

"I guarantee it will, but you'll just need to trust me. This *is* why you brought me along."

They waited in silence, this time for eight minutes. Riggs said nothing more but made his doubts known by putting a large countdown timer zoomed in on the holo in front of him for all to see. It showed their time to Martian space at the end of the neutral zone— just five and a half minutes. The Martian captain's deadline for them to turn around had already passed, and the captain would see that by now, with O'Leary's message arriving just a few seconds afterward.

They waited, and they sweated even in the climate-controlled cockpit. The response could come in several ways, but the most likely, to Riggs' mind, was a flurry of missiles that would surely catch and destroy them.

But when the response finally came, it was a simple comm message. The same female voice, still cold but with just a hint of concerned bewilderment, spoke from the cockpit speakers. *"Blind Monk, we have been ordered to escort you to Phobos Station. You will follow the path we are transmitting to you exactly, or I will give the order to have you destroyed... no matter what those sealed orders say or who wrote them. Cassius out."*

Riggs raised an eyebrow and looked back at O'Leary with a new estimation. Even the nervous Toby grinned a little at the Martian captain's sudden about-face. But before anyone could ask the congressman any questions, he stood from the rear seat. "Well, I imagine we have quite a few hours of flight to Phobos, so I plan to get some sleep. Please wake me when we are 30 minutes out." He strode out the cockpit door, leaving the rest of them with mouths agape. Though Riggs thought he detected a tremor in the man's hands and legs as he left, it could have been his imagination.

---

Landon Hartman was grateful for the stealth shuttle's excellent handling characteristics. The shuttle had been designed, in part, to land marines from an orbiting warship into a warzone on planetary soil, where hostiles would be watching and attempting to blow it and the marines out of the sky.

That meant it was expressly designed to do exactly what Landon was doing with it now: flying nape-of-the-earth, below the scanning floor of virtually all of United Earth's sensors, on its way to the Australian continent.

The space and atmosphere directly above Australia were some of the most heavily scanned and patrolled skies in all of United Earth;

there was an irrational but no-less-real fear of what might happen if the enhanced were allowed to escape their island nation and mingle with the rest of human society. Landon agreed with the concerns in principle but had always thought that the methods were overkill.

So, needless to say, even with the stealth shuttle, he hadn't wanted to brave a direct insertion. Rather, he'd brought the shuttle down over Earth's south pole. From there, he'd flown a white-knuckle approach, first over the ice floes and mountains of Antarctica, then barely a few meters over the choppy waves of the Southern Ocean, to approach Perth, on Australia's southwest coast, where the readers lived.

In his final meeting with her at the Earthside jail, Jordan Archer had asked Jinny Ambrosa to write a series of random numbers on a sheet of paper as a pretense to use the poison pen. Instead, she had written a name and a comm code with a Perth prefix. The blender had kept that piece of paper. And as they approached the southernmost part of the Australian continent, Archer called the comm code, almost holding his breath in anticipation, which hadn't given Landon the utmost confidence in their plan.

Landon could only hear one side of the conversation, but it was clear the person on the other end doubted Archer's story at first. But when the blender detailed the desperate state of Reader Ambrosa in her medical capsule stowed in the back of the shuttle, the other person finally relented. They gave Archer coordinates on the outskirts of the city and promised to meet them there shortly.

The shuttle made landfall a hundred kilometers south of Perth. Then Landon circled the craft around to the eastern outskirts of the city, finding a small, abandoned landing field at the coordinates that had been provided to them. The shuttle's advanced military sensor suite tagged the two aircars that sat at the field with their engines still warm when they were a full klick out. He hoped that was their welcoming committee and not the Federal Police waiting to take them all into custody.

He set the shuttle down and powered down the turbines but left all the systems on standby in case they needed to beat a hasty retreat. Then he strapped on the pistol Tyrus Tyne had insisted he take with him and slowly followed Archer down the shuttle's boarding ramp.

The stealth shuttle's fourth passenger, the hacker oddly named Neon Mouse, stayed nervously behind in the shuttle's troop compartment.

A solitary figure was already waiting for Landon and Archer at the bottom of the ramp, shrouded in darkness; none of the landing field's lights were on, nor were the two cars giving off any external light. Even Luna was only a sliver of dim light in the sky as though giving its silent approval to the clandestine meeting.

"Archer?" the man asked.

"That's me. Mattingly?"

The man nodded. "You're a long way from Brisbane, Blender. Where's Jinny?"

*OK, good. Straight to business,* Landon thought hopefully. He wasn't used to this cloak-and-dagger stuff and was content to let Archer do all the talking.

"Her med capsule is in the troop compartment," the blender answered, waving up the ramp. "There's another girl up there with her; please don't shoot her."

Mattingly nodded and motioned with one of his hands. Two other men appeared from either side, seeming to melt out of the darkness. Both had assault rifles that were lowered, though Landon had the suspicion that they'd been pointed at him and Archer a few moments prior.

The three men wordlessly followed Landon and Archer back up the shuttle's ramp. Inside, the troop compartment was lit only with a dim red light so as not to announce their presence or ruin their night vision. In the ghastly glow, Jinny Ambrosa looked more like a corpse than a living human being, and Charles Mattingly could not contain a gasp when he saw her.

"Can you help her?" Landon asked, speaking for the first time after the other man had examined the readouts on the med capsule for a few moments.

Mattingly shook his head. "I don't know. I'm no doctor, and whatever is wrong in her head may be beyond even our capabilities. But you brought her to the right place; no one else on Earth knows more about Reader physiology and psychology than our medical experts. If anyone can help her, they can."

Archer nodded solemnly. "Tyrus Tyne told me to give you this." He handed the other man a pad. Mattingly pecked at it for a moment and then frowned.

"Well, this is equal parts imploring us to help her and threatening us if we don't. Still, there is, perhaps, some useful information here." He stopped and pecked at his hand implant for a second. He also glanced once toward the Neon Mouse but said nothing to or about her.

Moments later, the sound of multiple steps echoed up the boarding ramp. Two women and a man wearing the uniforms of paramedics entered the shuttle. They proceeded to grab the capsule, activate its built-in grav coil, and carefully move it across the troop compartment and down the ramp, all the while whispering to each other in words that Landon identified as medical jargon but didn't understand.

When they were gone, Mattingly turned back to Archer and Landon and placed a hand on Landon's shoulder. "Listen, let's get this shuttle moved under cover, and then we'll take you two to the same place we're taking her. We'll get you cleaned up and fed, and the doctors will get started helping Jinny. Do you know her well?"

Landon shook his head. "Only met her once when I took her and Congressman O'Leary up to the Lagrange Point One naval shipyards on a tour. I'm afraid I'm just the pilot; I'm not all that important."

Archer said nothing but shook his head as well.

Charles gave them a wry smile and lifted his hand to pat Landon twice on the same shoulder. "Compared to her, I'm not sure any of us are all that important. If we *can* help her, we will. And even if we can't, we won't stop trying. She's the key to everything."

With that cryptic comment, Mattingly turned and left the shuttle. Archer hung back but followed a few moments later.

*The key to everything?* Landon thought. *And what happens if she never wakes up?* He didn't know what was wrong with the pretty young reader or what had been done to her in the Luna prison, but he knew she looked terrible in the medical capsule and had shown no change in vital signs or indications of waking up during the long flight back to Earth.

He shoved the thought aside and turned to the lone passenger still inside the shuttle. "You ready to go?" he asked the girl.

Neon Mouse shrugged and gathered up her things. "Do you have a way to get a message to Congressman O'Leary?" she asked him as they walked down the ramp together.

He turned to her in confusion and shrugged. "Not right now, but he might make contact later. Why?"

The girl frowned, and in the spare light that reached the bottom of the ramp from the dimly lit troop compartment, her purple hair gleamed slightly. She was pretty, he thought, in the same way a brightly colored tropical fish is attractive; Landon never thought that would appeal to him, but something about the girl made him very much want to get to know her better. He'd had a few short exchanges with her while in transit, and he had to admit that she was intriguing.

"If you do hear from him," she said, her voice so soft he had to strain to hear. "Can you tell him something for me?"

"Sure, I guess."

"Tell him I accessed and forwarded along that file to the address he told me to."

"OK?" Landon replied, drawing the word out to make a question. He had no idea what she was talking about.

"But tell him it wasn't from Pereira's personal files. It was a set of military plans on the Government House servers. I assume he knows that." She paused. "But maybe you can tell him just in case?"

"Sure. I guess. If he reaches out, that is."

Her message delivered, the Neon Mouse said nothing more. She walked slowly toward the waiting cars, leaving Landon alone with his confused thoughts.

---

The unnamed captain of the *MPNS Cassius* said nothing more to the crew of the *Blind Monk* for the three hours they spent in transit to Phobos. About an hour out, the massive battleship silently turned and headed back out to her sojourn of the demilitarized zone. In her place, a relatively small destroyer, still more than powerful enough to obliterate the *Monk* with little effort, took up escort duty. Its captain sent a message that was even terser than that from the *Cassius*' captain—the destroyer captain didn't even mention his ship's name; he simply commanded them to follow him in without deviating more than a few meters from the set course.

Corey O'Leary had tried to sleep on the flight inward, but after finding a cabin with an empty bed—Rigg's from the clothing on the floor and the spartan decorations—he lay awake for the entirety of their journey. In his head, a thousand different scenarios played out of how the *Monk* and its passengers would be received at Phobos Station.

He had been to Mars only once before, as a student on an exchange program, so long ago that it didn't even show up in his official bio, several years even before the Six-Month War. He'd spent a grand total of nine standard months studying at the University of Olympus Mons, the campus nestled at the base of its gigantic namesake mountain. That had been when relations between Earth and Mars had thawed for a short period, just long enough that the two planets had started a few exchange programs like the one he'd joined, seeking opportunities to build bridges between the two radically different cultures.

He had met someone on that long-ago trip—someone who had almost made him *stay* on Mars. Now, he only hoped she still had enough residual feelings for him not to have him immediately executed along with his companions. The way they'd ended things, he worried that was unlikely. Either way, he and Gorsky both knew that the only way Earth could survive the coming invasion was to somehow convince Mars to stand with them. He hoped that the big Russian was even now using the information and recordings Corey had sent him after Jinny's rescue to fulfill the vital parts of their plan back on Earth.

He made his way back to the *Monk's* small cockpit, watching in nervous anticipation as they neared a massive space station orbiting one of Mars' moons.

"*Blind Monk*, you are cleared to dock in bay 717 on the moon side of Phobos Station." The voice of the MPN destroyer's captain was all business, without a trace of friendliness or hatred. It was only the second time he'd spoken to them, and Corey couldn't tell from the voice if the man was bored or just hiding his emotion well. Given the state of cold war that existed between the UE and Mars, he guessed the latter.

He knew Tyrus wanted to brace him and force him to tell what the code phrase he'd used meant and what kind of reception they could expect on Phobos Station, but Corey purposefully avoided the big man's questioning gaze.

He only had to do so for a few minutes while Riggs docked the ship.

"*Blind Monk*, this is Phobos Station Control. We show you have successfully docked. Please remain in your ship until your escort arrives. To ensure compliance, the docking bay remains in hard vacuum. Control out."

"Well, so much for the welcome wagon," Riggs said grimly from the pilot's seat. He powered down the primary systems but left the ship on standby in case they needed to beat a hasty retreat.

The approach to the large space station orbiting one of Mars' two moons had been uneventful, and the small bay they'd landed in was just large enough for the *Monk* to fit inside.

"Assume they're listening to everything we say," Tyrus warned from the copilot's seat.

Riggs turned and regarded him with skepticism. It was the first time Corey had seen the pilot meet the big man's gaze since leaving the Crater. "You really think they can listen to us through a *vacuum* and the *Monk's* hull? They're not magic."

"No, Tyrus is right," Corey said from his standing position at the back of the cramped cockpit; now that they were here, he was too nervous to remain seated. "Even when I was here before, as a guest, I always got the feeling they were purposefully hiding from me the extent of their technology. Martians are extremely secretive. They don't trust outsiders, and they fear war above all else. It wouldn't surprise me to find that they invest more than half their GDP in defense and related technologies."

"G D what?" Toby asked.

"Sorry," Corey replied with a half-smile—the solemn mood in the cockpit didn't feel like it could stand his usual politician's grin. "Gross

Domestic Product: the sum total of their economy's output in any year."

Toby raised an eyebrow. "That's a lot of money. But why? The only people they have to worry about are on Earth… and Earth would never attack Mars first, right?"

Corey found himself surprised at the uncharacteristically astute political observation from the boy and reminded himself that of all the crew members, he knew the least about the average-looking young man who had obviously been complex enough to catch Jynx's eye. "You're quite right, Toby. But Mars is a special case, and they've always been paranoid—much more so than the populations on Earth or Europa."

"And why is that?" Riggs asked quietly, peering out the cockpit window and around the hanger like he was trying to detect the listening apparatus Tyrus had warned might be there.

"In truth, it mostly has to do with gravity," Corey admitted.

"Gravity?" Toby eyed him skeptically.

"Yes, gravity," he confirmed, settling easily into the same tone he used when speaking in front of the cameras on Earth. "Mars has just over a third of the gravitational pull of Earth. In fact, it's about as light of gravity as mankind can live in without long-term health problems—and even so, they have to exercise frequently and follow a high-vitamin diet to avoid losing muscle and bone mass below critical levels.

"In the colonies, every world is near the mass and the gravitational pull of Earth, usually plus or minus twenty percent. It was a hard requirement the early terraformers put on finding new worlds to settle. But Mars and Europa were settled before terraforming was invented or the Path through the Rift was discovered. At that time, humans had a limited choice of semi-habitable planets within our own home solar system.

"Europa only has about 13 percent Earth's gravity, requiring its pre-terraforming settlers to spend most of their time in orbiting stations spun up to provide near-Earth gravity—even after terraforming, they had to stay in the stations most of each year until artificial gravity technology advanced enough for them to build it into all of their planet-side settlements. But the Martians were more stubborn. They viewed it as a personal challenge to live full-time on the planet's surface from the start. The history books suggest they accepted and even welcomed the changes to their anatomy that resulted over generations of life in the lower gravity. It was akin to the old Viking tradition of burning their ships to show those they came to conquer that they would never retreat."

"Vikings? What?" Riggs asked, confused.

"In other words, they blatantly wanted to show that they would *never* return to Earth once they'd come to Mars. That is what has, in part, made them so warlike but conversely fearful of war. They literally have *nowhere* else to go. There isn't a single colonized planet, outside of the non-urban areas of Europa, that they can live on for long without the gravity crushing them. It's why emissaries from Mars to Earth—back when the two planets actually spoke to each other—have almost never stepped foot on the homeworld's surface. Instead, in the few times of thawed relations between the planets, they've met with our ambassadors in orbital stations with the artificial gravity dialed down to accommodate their anatomy.

"So, to them, aggressively defending their home planet, even taking a continuous posture of war, is the only way they can ensure they will *always* have somewhere to live. And the fact that early in Martian history, the Council waged a surprise attack that subjugated Mars until the Four Worlds Rebellion and the schism hasn't made them any less paranoid about defending the red planet.

"Therefore, I'm afraid Tyrus is right," he nodded to the big man. "We just don't know what technology they do or don't have. We must assume, despite the pigheaded refusal to acknowledge it by certain of my colleagues in Earth's government, that the Martians are likely ahead of the UE in defense and spy technologies."

"You are absolutely correct, Congressman Corey O'Leary," a mocking voice said suddenly from the air right behind him. It *hadn't* come from the *Monk's* comm but from inside the doorway to the cockpit itself.

Tyrus was much faster in the realization of what was happening and had already leapt to his feet and turned to face the open cockpit door. Together with the rest of them, he stared as the empty air shimmered in the doorway for a fraction of a second before coalescing into the form of an impossibly tall and thin man fully ensconced head-to-toe in a gunmetal gray suit with a metallic sheen. It reminded him of the stealth suit he'd worn at the Crater, only of a smoother texture.

Tyrus reacted out of instinct, throwing a fist toward the newly appeared man's head, instantly calculating that the interloper could mean them no goodwill if he'd failed to even announce his presence before violating the sanctity of their ship.

But he almost cried out in pain when his fist met something solid and unyielding, like an invisible wall of steel, just centimeters in front of the figure's helmeted face. Still, he hadn't been an alpha for so long without learning how to react to the unexpected. Before he'd even retracted his now-broken right fist, he had used the other hand to shove O'Leary out of his way and lifted a leg to deliver a swift kick to the suited man's kneecap, only to again find an invisible barrier protecting the intruder.

"Come now, Mr. Tyne!" the man said, his voice still mocking. "Surely I can at least announce myself before you start trying to kill me?"

"Riggs!" Tyrus cried out, reaching his left hand back toward the pilot without taking his eyes off the intruder, who continued to stand calmly as if he hadn't been attacked at all. He was gratified to feel the pistol pressed into his left hand, grip first, as the pilot understood what he was after. Tyrus quickly raised the gun and pointed it at the intruder's head, holding it in his unbroken left hand.

The figure in front of him didn't react other than to shake his head. Then, slowly, he reached one hand up and pressed on the side of his helmet. For a moment, nothing happened. But then the helmet didn't so much retract as *disintegrate* in full view of everyone in the cockpit, revealing the swarthy complexion, thin and long face, and jet-black hair of a man who looked like he could have blood from Earth's Indian subcontinent in his ancestry.

The man frowned at Tyrus and then shook his head again, clearly continuing to mock his adversary. "I see that our lost colonial brethren are no smarter than the dullards we left behind on Earth," he said with a hint of a sneer.

"Who are you, and what are you doing on my ship?!" Riggs shouted from behind Tyrus before he could open his mouth to reply to the man's insult.

The answer came not from the intruder but from O'Leary. "He's a Praetorian Guard," the congressman said with a solemnity that suggested deep meaning behind that title. "And if we manage to shoot him, we'll start a blood feud with the rest of the Guard that will only end when we're all dead."

Tyrus looked over at Corey in shock but kept the suited man in his peripheral vision to allow him to react if the intruder made another move.

Corey continued. "They never travel alone, so even if you get through whatever shielding he has, there's no doubt a team of his comrades hidden in the corridor behind him. But at least, if he's here, it means someone quite high up in the Martian government knows we're on the station and has taken an interest in us."

The man's sneer widened into an almost smile as Tyrus turned back to focus on him. "That is the first semi-intelligent thing I have heard any of you say," he said in the same mocking tone. "And it is correct. The Praetor herself wishes to speak with you and is even now here on Phobos Station. I am to take you to her, though I cannot imagine the meeting will end well for any of you. So please," he looked into Tyrus' eyes and grinned wickedly, "feel free to resist more so we can all save some time, and I can have an excuse to kill each one of you."

Corey again spoke before Tyrus could respond, which was probably a good thing, given what Tyrus *wanted* to say to the smug man. "I had always heard stories of the professionalism of the Praetorian Guard," he said with clear and thick disappointment coloring his voice. "I'm afraid to say it looks to me like you have more in common with schoolyard bullies than with the elite bodyguards of legend. Have the legions of Mars fallen so far without a proper war to hone their edge?"

The man's mocking countenance instantly disappeared at these words, and he turned an angry glance at O'Leary. The congressman's insult had obviously struck a nerve. When the Martian replied, he almost spat the words, but the mocking tone was also gone. "I should challenge you to a duel for your insolence. Your position on Earth carries no weight here, Corey O'Leary." It was obvious he was now purposefully omitting the congressman's title.

Corey didn't shrink but stepped forward and even lightly pushed Tyrus back, standing between him and the suited man without blocking the pointed pistol. He looked up at the taller intruder, who stood several centimeters above even Tyrus' two-meter height. "And if you were to challenge me to a duel," O'Leary replied, "as the challenged party, I would be free to choose the weapons, place, and conditions. And I would choose tungsten sledgehammers in the UOM commons with gravity dialed up to Earth standard and no augmentations allowed."

In any other situation, Tyrus would be tempted to laugh out loud at Corey's ridiculous suggestion, but the man facing them obviously did not see a joke in the words. In fact, his face took on an even more venomous expression for a second, and Tyrus finally understood. By suggesting they fight with heavy weapons in a high gravity environment and without any augmentation—which meant without the help of the stealth suit that was clearly also supporting the man's strength to allow him to even stand in the *Monk's* near-Earth gravity—Corey had made it clear that the Praetorian guardsman would be at a distinct disadvantage in any duel. In fact, even with Corey's advanced age, his greater muscle and bone density would make him preternaturally fast and strong compared to the unaugmented Martian, even in the low gravity of the red planet. It would be such an advantage that the swarthy man's undoubtedly elite training would only go so far, and the outcome would be in question.

Tyrus was ready to push Corey aside and reengage the unruly interloper when the Martian's expression abruptly changed again. Gone was the mockery, the anger, or any sign of antagonism. What replaced it was a calm indifference as the man nodded to Corey and seemed to relax a little in the metallic suit.

"Forgive me my impudence," he said in an even tone that likewise carried none of the prior mocking sneer or anger. He briefly diverted his gaze and nodded to Tyrus before fixing his view again on O'Leary. "But I had to be sure that you were indeed the Corey O'Leary that came to Mars so many years ago. Facial recognition suggested you were, though that is easy to fake after so many decades have passed. Voiceprint was also positive but likewise could have been faked, especially if you were a blender. But an... acquaintance of yours from your time on Mars suggested exactly how you would respond if challenged to a duel."

To Tyrus' further surprise, Corey smiled lightly. "And you worded the duel as a hypothetical instead of a direct challenge so that I could refuse you without losing my honor. I commend you for your tact, Praetorian Guard."

The man returned the light smile but otherwise kept a mask of professional disinterest. "You worded your response in like manner so I can leave with my honor intact as well. You are as politically astute as your file suggests and have also clearly spent time with the people of Mars. Tell me, the official file bears no record of actual challenges to any duel being issued to you while you were studying here. Is that true?"

Corey shook his head. "Not entirely. I was challenged on my second day, but it was graciously withdrawn before I could respond when the challenger was made aware I was new to your planet. I was challenged once more after that and fought the duel and won, but it was stricken from the official record for reasons I will not go into."

The man's slight smile widened just a bit. Obviously, O'Leary had answered the question well, choosing the path of honesty over subterfuge. "I am Centurion Parn. I will not say I am honored to make any of your acquaintances. Your presence on our world is a threat to all we hold dear. However," he turned and swept his eyes across Tyrus and the others in the cockpit, "I will acknowledge that you came not under false pretenses and directly shared your intentions with our Navy when challenged. So, you have comported yourselves honorably thus far, and I will take you to meet with the Praetor as she has requested."

His smile disappeared completely at his next words. "But, be warned, men of the colonies and of Earth. If at any time I feel your presence is a threat to my charge, I will dispatch each and every one of you with swiftness and prejudice, as will every man and woman under my command. You will never see the blade that ends your life." The way he said the last part, it clearly held a much deeper import than the words suggested. Tyrus made a mental note to ask O'Leary about it later.

"Now," the centurion's gaze centered on Tyrus, meeting his eyes and somehow ignoring the gun still pointed at his face, "you will surrender all weapons to the Guard, or we will be forced to assume your intentions are hostile."

Reading the room quickly, Tyrus flipped the pistol around so that he held it by the barrel and offered the grip end to Parn. The man nodded in acknowledgment and reached out one hand to take the gun away.

"That includes the hideaway pistol that the boy has and the knife in your pilot's boot."

Tyrus looked in narrow-eyed suspicion as Toby begrudgingly crouched down and removed a small pistol from a holster on his ankle just under his pant leg. *How did he hide that without me noticing? And why* does *he even have it?* he thought. Another mystery he would have to attack once their situation on Mars settled, but he resolved to watch the boy more closely moving forward. It seemed there was more to Toby Haight than he'd initially believed.

Ten minutes later, the landing bay having been pressurized, Parn and three other members of the Praetorian Guard in their metallic yet strangely able-to-disintegrate suits—these were *far* more advanced than the stealth suit Corey had procured for Tyrus to use at the Crater—led the four crew and passengers of the *Monk* out of the ship.

Parn led the procession in silence, another guard next to him and the final two taking up the rear. They walked together across the landing bay and into an open hallway toward what looked like a dead end. At first, Toby and O'Leary both found themselves struggling with the low gravity, launching themselves too high with each step. But they quickly adapted to a clumsy gait. Riggs and Tyrus had spent enough time in space that they both fell into the habits of low-gravity movement without a second thought.

They approached the blank wall at the end of the corridor, but before any of them worked up the courage to ask any of the Guard where they were going, Parn gestured, and the wall miraculously disintegrated before their eyes—just as the man's helmet had done—revealing another stark corridor beyond.

"Nanotechnology," Tyrus noted in a matter-of-fact voice. It wasn't a question, and he got no answer other than a sideways glance from Parn. For a moment, he wished he had Jinny along to read the man, but quickly discarded the idea. Even had she been able to get through the mysterious shield surrounding the centurion, she would have balked at the idea of reading anyone unwillingly. She'd been oddly reluctant to read anyone at all since they'd arrived in the Sol system. Unfortunately, thoughts of her brought with them the melancholy that the excitement around the *Monk's* arrival at Mars had momentarily pushed to the back of his mind.

"Did they have this kind of technology when you were here before?" Riggs asked Corey, loud enough for the Martians to hear. Hidden in the question, Tyrus knew, was also the question of exactly *when* the congressman had been on Mars and just *what* he'd been doing there, as he'd neglected to give the details of any prior travels to the planet.

O'Leary caught all the meaning behind his question and answered simply, "Not that I saw. But I was just a young exchange student at a planet-side university. I never got near a military installation of any kind. And as I said, I always got the impression they were hiding much of their technology from me while I was here. I definitely saw nothing that suggested this level of nanotech."

None of them spoke again for several minutes. Parn led them to a lift, though this time, the door simply slid open instead of magically disintegrating. After a descent of several levels, they emerged in a corridor that was as sparse as the previous one, except that it was floored in a spongy gray substance reminiscent of carpet rather than plain deck metal.

After another minute in the new corridor, Parn stopped in front of a nondescript portion of the bulkhead and faced it. He spoke but engaged a privacy field that blocked the sound of his voice from reaching Tyrus and his companions. A moment later, a section of the bulkhead in front of the centurion disintegrated, and the man stepped through without hesitation.

Tyrus followed him and was surprised to find himself in a lush garden, completely at odds with the spartan nature of the rest of the station. The path they walked on changed from the nondescript spongy surface to what looked like real wooden planks. Planters on either side of the walkway were full of ferns and other jungle plants. The ceiling of the room soared overhead, obviously taking up several levels within the station, and Tyrus could even hear birds chirping above them in the canopies of tall trees that grew throughout the room. For all the thick vegetation, and the way the wooden walkway curved out of sight, he couldn't get a feel for the size of the garden space, but his instincts told him it was quite large.

Behind him, Toby gasped. Tyrus turned and regarded his companions, unsurprised to see Riggs wearing his usual bored expression, though the pilot's eyes were moving quickly to take in the sight. When his gaze got to O'Leary, it disconcerted him to find the congressman's expression was thoughtful but grim. It was as if he had learned something the instant they'd stepped inside the garden space but was uncertain how to process it. Tyrus tried to catch the man's eye, but Corey stared ahead in a way that made it clear he was avoiding his gaze.

"The Praetor will meet you 50 meters along this path. We will be watching," Parn said in the same tone a man might relate the weather. At this, he and his companion in front of the group stepped to either side of the path, and Parn nodded for the group to continue. After a few steps, Tyrus turned and glanced behind them to see that the man and his three companions had either engaged their suits' cloaking devices or had melted into the trees and bushes themselves. None of the four were visible any longer.

Tyrus turned and looked again at Corey, who now met his gaze briefly and then shrugged. By unspoken agreement, the congressman took the lead, and the rest of the party followed behind. They moved slowly along the path as if they all shared Corey's obvious trepidation of what they might find at the end with the mysterious Praetor.

Tyrus had heard the term 'Praetor' a handful of times in his briefings with the United Earth Navy. Little was known on Earth of the current governmental structure of Mars, but the term was one in common historical usage on the red planet, even as governments changed. A Praetor usually referred to the patriarch or matriarch of one of Mars' founding families. At various times, those family leaders had formed an oligarchy that directly ruled the planet, a legislative house that passed laws under the authority of Martian emperors, or feudal lords who had independently ruled parts of the planet when no strong central government existed.

Regardless of what government currently ruled the red planet, it was likely that the person they were on their way to meet was one of the dozen most powerful people on Mars. It shocked Tyrus that they'd gotten to such a high-ranking leader right out of the gate; he'd rather expected to be passed between lower-level bureaucrats or naval officers for days, if not weeks, before speaking to anyone of real authority, like had happened on Earth. It made him wonder what Corey wasn't telling them and what the man's mysterious exchange with the first Martian battleship had meant. Wondering about those things kept his mind off Jinny and Jynx, so he worried over them aggressively as they walked the short distance.

Despite knowing what the title might mean, nothing prepared Tyrus for the person they eventually found standing at the side of the trail, nonchalantly smelling a flower that grew on the path's border. The woman was tall and regal, her overly thin Martian frame taking a backseat to the intensity of her eyes that suggested a power that went beyond the physical when she looked up at them. Her hair was almost white, offsetting brown skin a shade darker than Centurion Parn's. She was taller than everyone in their group except for Tyrus himself and only fell a few centimeters short of even him. The woman looked to be roughly the same advanced age as Corey, but in the days of modern medicine and longevity treatments, that could mean an age difference of plus or minus 20 years versus the congressman. Her skin was largely unwrinkled, and she had startling blue eyes that looked unnatural in both their color and intensity. And she was dressed in a white dress that hugged her torso before flaring out at her calves, its folds rippling oddly around her feet in the low gravity as if she were underwater.

In front of him, O'Leary came to an abrupt stop at the sight of her and whispered a word that Tyrus couldn't make out. When Corey finally started walking toward the woman again, who had given no acknowledgment of their presence other than a steady gaze, he did so with shorter steps but with such a sense of constrained excitement and trepidation that it seemed to Tyrus he might break out in a sprint toward or perhaps away from the woman at any moment.

When they'd closed to within two meters of the Praetor, they stopped, and Corey hesitated only a moment before bowing to her deeply. "Praetor Starshadow, it is a pleasure to see you again after these many years. I trust you are well?"

The woman regarded O'Leary and his companions with her cool and direct gaze for several moments before she responded. When she spoke, her voice was that of a much younger woman, a strange mix of authority and liveliness. "Congressman Corey O'Leary of Earth. Indeed, it has been quite some time. I am well. How do you fare? And how is Debra O'Leary?"

Corey couldn't hide the wince when the Praetor asked after his wife. Suddenly it dawned on Tyrus that Corey must have had a very *personal* history with the woman, and he felt a sinking in his stomach that the interaction they were beginning was going to be far more complicated than he'd counted on.

"Debra is well, as am I. Despite the circumstances, I find it pleasing to see you again," Corey said, caution clear in his voice. "But I'm afraid that our visit is neither social nor without a sense of urgency." He turned and indicated his companions. "May I present Tyrus—"

"Tyrus Tyne and Cal Riggs, and a third man I do not know," the tall woman interrupted, turning her icy gaze to each one of them as she spoke their names, her eyes resting on Toby at the end before she turned back to Corey. "You bring war to our planet, Congressman. Do not presume I am not fully aware of why you have come and whom you have brought with you.

"The thing I am trying to decide now is whether I should listen to you for another moment, have you taken back to your ship and delivered to that fool Pereira for judgment back on Earth, or have you all killed here where you stand so that your blood may water my garden."

The woman's voice did not rise nor take on any different tone as she calmly laid out the options before her. Toby's audible gasp came a full count later than it should have as they all digested the impact of the words delivered with almost no inflection or feeling. Only Corey seemed nonplussed as he fell back into his role as a government leader.

"All three are viable options, Praetor," he replied with calm, visibly drawing from some internal wellspring of strength and even appearing to stand up straighter in Tyrus' eyes. "But only the first will ensure the security of Mars in the conflict to come—a conflict that I am sorry to say would come to Mars inevitably with or *without* our visit." He stopped and waited for her to make the next move.

She regarded him with the same cool expression, appearing to look down her perfectly formed nose at him. When she spoke again, it was in the same matter-of-fact tone. "Very well. I will grant you an audience to tell me how you think you can help Mars. But be warned. If I sense even the slightest duplicity or obfuscation of the truth from you or any of your companions, you will never see the weapon that ends your lives." Her wording, so similar to the earlier warning from Centurion Parn, seemed to Tyrus to carry a specific import. He felt like he was part of an inside joke he didn't understand, but that carried far greater consequences than he could know.

To Tyrus' continued surprise, O'Leary smiled. "Yes, we've met your Centurion Parn and his guards. Though the Aphrodite Starshadow that I once knew would hold the knife that kills me herself and not trust it to, nor pass the responsibility to, those that serve her."

The garden went abruptly silent for a long moment; even the birds seemed to hold in their song, awaiting the woman's response to Corey's arguably inflammatory words. When she finally spoke, her voice had taken on a hint of softness that hadn't been there before.

"You remember well, formerly my Corey, but the knife that pierces you shall be no less sharp than that with which you once pierced me. I will hear you, as I said. However, you must set aside now any hopes that our former standing will help you in the conversation to come. It is what got you here to my presence, but it will get you no further. Facts and honesty only will suffice from this moment forward. Or, as Jupiter is my witness, you will see just how sharp a knife in my own hand can be before this day is through."

O'Leary did not shrink from her words but instead smiled a little. When he replied, gone was any challenge in his tone, replaced by solemnity. "I did not come here hoping to deceive nor to hold any sway over you other than that justified by the message and information I bear. I am not here for you, Praetor, but for all the Four Worlds. I am… grateful to see you again after so long, but the nature of my visit is to save Mars *and* Earth from the coming tide. You will be given no duplicity or lies from me nor anyone in my party, or I will gladly bear the knife myself that pierces my heart and theirs. You have my solemn word on my name and my lineage as an O'Leary. Our lives are in your hands, but you would be a fool to throw them away cheaply."

If anything, the garden fell even quieter, and the tension ratcheted up almost noticeably behind Tyrus as he sensed Riggs and even Toby prepping themselves to run at the woman's command. Then, to all of their astonishment, the regal Praetor's face abruptly softened again, and hints even of a smile graced her aged but beautiful features.

"Well said, my former love. I hope that this day does not end with your blood painting my hands, but if it does, I shall add that blood to the honor painting of my house and remember you fondly for the man that you were before you so grievously wounded me long ago.

"Now, let us retire to an area where we can speak together and learn just what troubles you have brought with you to Mars."

# EPILOGUE

### TWO WEEKS LATER; SEPTEMBER 19, 731 P.D.

The black aircar pulled to the curb on the dark desert road. The driver rushed out his own door and around the car to open the rear passenger door, allowing the car's single other occupant to emerge into the warm night air. The big passenger took in a breath and moved his head from side to side to loosen the muscles of his thick neck. The ride hadn't been short, but no Loop station serviced this unpopulated area near the border of Nevada and Utah. And a shuttle would have been too conspicuous for his purposes this evening.

Wordlessly, the driver got back in the car. He would not be accompanying his passenger on the next leg of the journey, which upset him greatly because his job wasn't just to be a driver but also a discrete bodyguard. It was irregular enough for the large man now standing outside the car to travel *anywhere* without the rest of his security detail, but to insist on going on from here without *any* protection defied centuries of law and tradition.

Still, the driver knew better than to argue. That pleased the big man, who left his bodyguard behind and walked to a worn-looking chain-link fence, where he pressed a button on an old intercom set on a post next to the solitary gate. A voice answered, and the man said a single word that satisfied the person on the other end. The gate swung open.

The man walked with confidence across the dusty ground toward the lot's sole structure, an old water tank—a large cylinder that rose from the ground and that was covered in realistic-looking graffiti. A door cut into the side of the water tank opened at his approach, and the man was lost from his driver's view as the door shut behind him.

Inside, rusty, rickety metal stairs led down into the water tank's depths. After a short descent, he came to a landing and another door and looked at the camera situated above it. Without any sign from him or other indication from the person or persons watching, the inner door swung open, and he stepped through.

On the other side of the door, the rust and dust of the outer world gave way to a lushly appointed waiting room with thick carpet and expensive artwork on the finished walls. A single desk occupied the small room, and at it sat a striking woman in her mid-forties, wearing a smart pantsuit, who rose to greet the man.

"He is waiting for you on sub-level six, sir," she said, smiling warmly and motioning toward an open elevator door at the far end of the waiting room.

The man only grunted in reply and walked into the elevator, which promptly closed and descended with no input from him. There weren't even any buttons on the inside or any indication of the floors the lift passed. After a brief ride, the elevator stopped, and the door opened to reveal an antechamber even more ornately decorated than the one above. Its reception desk was empty, but a single heavy wooden door stood open at the far end, and he walked briskly across the antechamber, through the open door, and into the large office beyond.

The man sitting behind the desk looked up as his guest entered, smiling only briefly before resuming the frown he habitually wore. He was a tall man with carefully slicked-back dark hair that was treated to remove any traces of the gray his age would normally impart. Likewise, his tan was just a little too perfect to be natural.

Not waiting for an invitation, the large man sat down at one of the two chairs facing the desk and clasped his hands in front of him, regarding the man he'd come to see.

"Well?" he asked.

The slick man behind the desk frowned more deeply. "You already know what happened. She got away. So did Tyne. We're fairly sure she's on Mars now. And we still didn't get the information we needed." He stopped, eying his guest and raising an eyebrow.

They sat in silence for several moments as the large man digested what the other had said. When he finally spoke, his voice was calm and controlled, which he knew made it far more intimidating than if he'd yelled or screamed. "He will not be pleased," he said simply.

The man behind the desk fought to keep a twitch from his left eye. Few things in life and fewer people could disturb Joseph Blackmont—you didn't own the Sol system's largest mercenary outfit without being confident in your own abilities—but the man across from him now *and* the other man he spoke of were exceptions. "There was no way we could have anticipated what happened. And *you* let the alpha escape, not us. I mean, you practically *helped* him." He clearly meant the words to come out with self-assurance, but they sounded like a whine to the big man across from him.

The visitor shook his head. "All you had to do was get a few simple pieces of information from her; I gave you a *month* to do that, and you could not manage it. Then you just had to let her escape but kill the alpha in the process. But you got arrogant, even when I tried to warn you of just how dangerous Tyne was. Four men. Bah! You should have sent a dozen." He let the accusation hang in the air. He was rewarded by seeing Blackmont squirm in his chair.

"That... man," the mercenary leader said in an almost whisper. "I've seen the recordings. He was like a one-man army. No one could have defended against *that*. So many of my people, just dead."

The big man said nothing in response but kept his steely gaze on the mercenary without blinking. The silence stretched out, and once again, it was Blackmont who got uncomfortable first and broke it. He spoke quickly now.

"Listen, I need you to back me up when we speak with him. We're too close. We learned a lot just from studying the woman's blood. Phase 2 will still happen on schedule. I will personally guarantee it."

"Even though you learned nothing of her actual abilities?" the large man asked, his hard expression belying his casual tone.

Blackmont couldn't stop his eye from twitching this time, and he vainly tried to cover it up by looking away and down at something on his desk. "Yes," he snapped, "our geneticists are confident they can unravel whatever the girl's father did to her. It would have been… *preferable* to have her tell us openly. It would have saved us time. With that said, I am sure her DNA will tell us all we need to know."

The big man's silent frown made it clear he did not share the mercenary leader's optimism.

"I suppose it's time to call him, then?" Blackmont asked, clearly resigned to his fate.

The other man nodded. Both stood, and a door behind Blackmont's desk slid open, revealing a room full of blinking lights and holo displays. The technology the room contained was unknown in the Sol system and even to most citizens of the 47 Colonies. It represented a massive expense, which Blackmont had funded from his own budget with the promise of extreme riches when his new master ultimately arrived. It also took up a lot of space, filling most of the fake water tank and the sub-levels above them.

Blackmont himself didn't understand the technology, nor did his guest. Scientists in his employ had taken the plans they'd been given and followed them exactly, never knowing for sure if the device would work or simply end up being a black hole for the organization's money.

In the end, it *had* worked, with the first successful test taking place just two months before, just a couple of weeks before the Council Navy had staged its false invasion. Joseph had confided in his guest in an unguarded moment that he almost regretted the fact that it *had* worked. Conversations like the one they were about to have were never pleasant.

As he and his guest entered the room and the door shut and locked securely behind them, Blackmont manipulated one of the holo fields to establish a connection. The image of a third man abruptly appeared in the center of the room—or part of him, at least. The disembodied head of Ian Petrov, Keeper and ruler of the 47 Colonies of humanity, glared at the two men who had contacted him.

"Well?" he asked without pleasantries, perfectly echoing the tone of the large man's identical question to Blackmont just moments before.

The large man said nothing but nodded toward the mercenary leader, throwing him to the wolves.

"Your Excellency," Blackmont sputtered, all his normal confidence gone. "We were able to secure the reader's blood samples and are in the process of mapping her DNA. My people are confident that they can unravel the source of her aberration and replicate it in our test subjects in the agreed-upon timeline."

He stopped, afraid to speak what he needed to say next.

"And the reader? She lives?" the Keeper asked.

Taking a deep breath, Blackmont answered in a small voice. "She lives, as you ordered, but there were… complications. She escaped as planned, but Tyrus Tyne also lived through it. And we believe Ambrosa is now on Mars, out of our reach." He shrank back as he spoke, knowing the man on the other end would not react well to the news.

He didn't. The holo of the man's face twisted in anger. "How could you let that happen?!" he shouted, and Blackmont leaned away from the holo as if the man could reach out across the lightyears and grasp him by the neck.

"S-sorry, sir," he stammered. "We put her in our most secure facility and even spread a false story of her death. Then we laid some careful breadcrumbs and opened up gaps in our security for her friends. We even had a special team in the facility waiting for Tyne. But that *man*. He's like a devil. We never stood a chance."

"Of course, he's difficult!" Petrov snapped. "We trained him that way. You *knew* he would present problems and failed to take care of him anyway. The error is yours alone, Mr. Blackmont." The way he said Joseph's name made it sound like a curse word.

"Y-yes, Sir. I'm sorry, Your Excellency."

The Keeper didn't acknowledge Blackmont's lame apology. Instead, he turned and looked at the larger man in the small room. "And your part of the plan?" he asked, his tone making it clear he would tolerate no more unwelcome news.

Mikael Gorsky smiled thinly. "All proceeds well, Your Excellency. President Pereira was removed from office two days ago. When we released the vids of the reader's broken but alive body and the carefully planted evidence tying Pereira and Givens to her fake death and real torture, it was too much for him to overcome. We had enough votes to force a declaration of no confidence."

"Go on," the Keeper prompted.

Gorsky's smile widened. "O'Leary himself would have been the natural replacement, but his treasonous defection to Mars destroyed his and the Red Party's chances of grasping power. I was the... convenient alternative for the moderates."

Left unsaid was the significant amount of leverage Gorsky had gathered, using a variety of hackers and fixers over the last several years, on enough members of Congress and their top financial supporters to virtually guarantee the outcome of the vote on Pereira's replacement. As a result, United Earth President Mikael Gorsky was in the position he had coveted and schemed to attain for decades, even before he knew of the Council's imminent invasion.

The Keeper nodded, the first positive signal from the man. "At least one thing has gone right then. And the Martian situation?"

The big Russian nodded. "Your message pushed many of the moderates firmly into the pro-war camp. O'Leary fleeing there with Tyne and Ambrosa gave us even more of a boost; for many, it now looks as if the Martians were in league with them all along. Right now, I am playing the voice of reason, urging circumspection about the Martian threat and proposing we build up our military instead to counter the Council Navy when it arrives. When the time comes, I will play the reluctant wartime leader and throw my weight behind the anti-Martian movement at the ideal moment to maximize the instability when your fleet attacks."

The Keeper nodded again, and Gorsky continued.

"I am pleased to report I also tricked O'Leary into having his hired hacker access the latest military plans for the defense of Earth. I'm forwarding those along to you after this call. The trail of the breach will lead back to him, and we will eventually disclose it if we need to discredit him any further."

The Keeper smiled now for the first time, showing his teeth in a grin reminiscent of a lion Gorsky had once illegally hunted on the African continent. "Good. But know that I will accept no further setbacks. When my fleet arrives, I will expect all to be as we agreed. Remember that I have other agents on Earth, and you will not like it if it becomes necessary for one of them to visit either of you."

He let the open threat hang in the air and turned his hard gaze between the two men. Neither spoke, but Blackmont squirmed again under the Keeper's scrutiny.

"We will speak again in one month," Petrov continued. "At that point, I will share more about the timing of the invasion. I expect that the two of you can keep things progressing in the meantime without my direct oversight, but I *will* be watching."

The holo of Ian Petrov's head abruptly disappeared as the man cut the connection on his end. Blackmont let out an audible sigh of relief, and even Gorsky released the tension in his shoulders. The two men looked at each other in the now-silent room with its flashing lights and spinning holos, and both wondered for the hundredth time or more what they were truly unleashing on the Four Worlds.

But the time for second thoughts had long passed, and by wordless agreement, they turned back to the door leading out to Blackmont's office to discuss the plans for the next several weeks. After all, one did not betray one's world and all the people on it without planning every step with excruciating precision.

One thing was certain to both of them: the Four Worlds would fall. All that was left to decide—all that had *ever* really been in question—was who would survive and even rise to the top as the dust settled.

Back in the outer office, another man now sat waiting. He had plain features and was of average height and weight. He stood as Gorsky entered, nodding to the new UE president respectfully. "Boss," he said simply.

Gorsky turned to Blackmont. "Joseph, do you mind?" It was neither question nor request.

Blackmont briefly glared in return but obediently left his own office to afford the two other men some privacy. Once he was gone, Gorsky turned to the plain man. He held up a hand while he pulled a device from his pocket and swept the room for any left-behind listening devices. Surprisingly, there were none; Blackmont obviously felt a false sense of security in his underground office.

"Did they suspect anything?" Gorsky asked, turning to face the blender.

"Not a thing," Jordan Archer replied to the man he had once known only as Iasonas. "They think I'm O'Leary's man." He shrugged. "Even O'Leary thinks I'm his man. I mean, *I* thought I was O'Leary's man before you revealed your identity."

"The reader made it safely to Perth?" Let Blackmont and the Keeper think she was safely out of reach on Mars for the time being. Gorsky didn't intend to do *everything* by the Keeper's playbook. Even his instructions to Archer that it did not matter if Ambrosa survived the attack went directly against Petrov's orders; Gorsky had only needed the *body* to prove she hadn't died in the cell on Earth as the Pereira administration had claimed.

Part of rising to the top after the Council invasion would be in having his own cards to play rather than relying only on the mercurial Keeper's goodwill and gratitude for helping him take over the Four Worlds.

Archer nodded, frowning. "If by safely, you mean in a comatose state she might never wake up from, then sure."

Gorsky frowned in equal parts at the message and the flippant way in which the blender delivered it. The man seemed to think he had some kind of power now that he knew his employer's true identity, but his insolent nature would have to change, especially now that Mikael held the highest office in the UE. Still, he pushed aside his annoyance for the time being. He had far more leverage on the blender than the man could ever have on him.

"Good. I have every confidence that the Majko and her people will figure out how to wake her up."

Archer cocked an eyebrow. "Aren't you worried the Majko will teach her to unlock her full abilities, whatever those may be? That could make her into a larger threat, couldn't it? You heard what that other reader told her in Perth. They think she's some sort of savior or destroyer."

Gorsky looked hard at the man, debating whether to answer the ridiculous question. Archer didn't flinch but did finally look away and pretend to study the fingernails on his left hand. Gorsky smiled at the man's subtle surrender and decided to answer him. "I am *counting* on the Majko teaching her. It will keep Ambrosa right where we can find her whenever we need to. And once she is fully trained, we can capture her again and then get what we need out of her and possibly even use her to our own benefit. As long as that nekulturny O'Leary thinks I am still his friend, she is likely to trust me on his word alone."

Archer considered this. When he spoke again, he did so slowly and carefully. "When you do use her, will it be to help the Council get what they want or to stop them and keep the UE free?"

Gorsky scowled. The man knew far too much, and if he hadn't already decided that the blender would need to die after he was done with him, Archer's question would have clinched the decision. "Get back to Perth," he said coldly. "Keep me appraised of Ambrosa's progress and be ready to help us apprehend her when the time is right."

Archer stood and nodded. "Of course, Mr. President." He started out of the room but then turned back. "Is Cecily all right?" His voice broke from its normal calm, and Gorsky frowned.

"She will be," he replied. "As long as you continue to do your job. You have been very useful to me, Archer, and I have compensated you extremely well for it, not to mention the money that my *friend* Corey Ivanovich paid you on top of that. But do not forget what will happen if you fail. She is such a lovely girl. It would be a tragedy for her to meet with an unfortunate end."

"When can I see her?" Archer pressed, not backing down as he should have.

Gorsky regarded the man coldly. He pulled out an envelope from his pocket and threw it down on the desk. The blender did nothing but look at it for a moment, then moved slowly back toward Gorsky and picked it up. Opening it carefully and peering inside, he shuddered, and tears sprang to his eyes.

"You failed me in the Crater," Gorsky said to the man, his voice low with menace. "This time, I only took a finger. Next time, it may be something she cannot live without."

Jordan Archer said nothing, staring forlornly into the envelope at the index finger of the only person he loved in the galaxy. Gorsky left him there, walking toward the exit that would take him to the lone elevator, but right before he left the room, he paused and looked back. "Now, get back to Perth," he repeated. "I will send for you when you are needed."

The big Russian continued on without waiting for a reply, crossing the antechamber to the lift. As the elevator doors closed, Mikael Gorsky allowed himself a broad smile.

---

Octavio Nowak settled wearily onto the small couch in his family's tiny apartment on Greater York and sighed loudly. His mother had just left after staying the day to watch Geneva while he worked his shift at the textile shop just a few blocks away. Now that she was gone and the baby was asleep, he no longer had to pretend to be OK.

He held an open but untasted beer in front of himself as he stared at nothing, lost in his thoughts of a beautiful auburn-haired woman who had been his best friend, his soulmate, and now his greatest source of pain. Sarah's death had left a gigantic hole in his heart, one he was sure he would never fill; even these months later the pain remained unabated.

He was spiraling deeper into his thoughts of her when someone knocked on the apartment's front door.

Octavio looked up in confusion. It was ten o'clock at night, and usually when someone came to the door, at any hour, the apartment's rudimentary AI would immediately show him who it was on whichever viewscreen was closest to him. But all the viewscreens in sight were dormant.

Slowly, he got to his feet, setting the still-full beer on the small coffee table and making his way to the door. Once there, he tried to pull up the camera feed manually on the door's integrated viewscreen, but it stayed stubbornly blank. *Odd*.

Cautiously, he opened the door a crack and peered out. "Who's there?" he asked but received no answer. Nor did he see any sign of anyone; whoever had knocked must have already left. He opened the door wider and peered down the length of the hallway, but it was empty.

Octavio started to shut the door, and it was almost from the merest chance that he glanced down and saw the folded sheet of paper on the doormat. Curious and confused, he crouched to pick it up and then once again looked up and down the hall but saw no indication of the mysterious visitor who had dropped it off.

He went back inside the apartment and shut the door. He stared in confusion again at the folded sheet. It had been years since he'd held a piece of actual paper. Everything was done digitally in the colonies, and paper was an anachronism and novelty.

Making his way back to sit in the same spot on the couch, he slowly unfolded the sheet and looked in astonishment at the typed words on the inner fold.

**Octavio,**

**This is from your little sister, who was with Sarah at the end. Read this letter as many times as you need tonight, but burn it before you go to bed; your life and Geneva's depend on it.**

*Chu Hua?* he thought in confusion. She was the only one of Sarah's mech drivers he had ever referred to as 'little sister'. Why would she be sending him a note in such a strange manner? Then the second part of the message sank in, and he leapt to his feet, dropping the letter and rushing into his bedroom. There, he looked down at nine-month-old Geneva, sleeping safe and sound next to the bed in her cradle, which was rapidly growing too small for the baby to comfortably fit in.

Reassured that his child was OK, he walked back out to the couch and picked up the letter, standing now to read the rest.

**First, know that Sarah's last thoughts were of you and Geneva. I was there right after she died, and I have the recording from her mech. Her last words were to ask you and Geneva to forgive her for what she was about to do.**

*She didn't die from enemy fire, as the Guard no doubt told you. Instead, she did something extraordinary. She disobeyed an order! And not just any order, but one that was morally reprehensible. She killed herself so that she wouldn't have to kill innocents, including a young baby.*

*It's too dangerous for me to tell you, even like this, everything that happened afterward. But it's enough to say that Sarah's decision—her sacrifice—opened the floodgates. Many of us are now in direct rebellion against the Council and the Guard. We're doing our best to do the right thing instead of what we're ordered to do.*

*All because of Sarah.*

*Because she did what was right. She made a choice, and it was one you and Geneva can be proud of.*

*Now I'm offering you a choice like the one Sarah made possible for me. You can stay on Greater York, keep working there, and hope that Geneva doesn't exhibit the enacter gene so she can stay with you past the age of five. That would be the simplest and safest choice. Pretend you never got this letter and move on with your life, taking a small amount of comfort that your wife died for something greater than mere obedience to orders.*

*But I also offer an alternative, though a dangerous one. I have friends who have agreed to help you in recognition of what Sarah did. If you choose to accept their help, they will get you off Greater York and set you up with a new life elsewhere, under a new identity, where no one will know Geneva is the daughter of an enacter. It will be a simple life, with hard work to maintain it, but it gives you the greatest chance of keeping your precious daughter with you, even if she is an enacter like her mother.*

*But it requires leaving everything and everyone else you know behind and never looking back.*

*Time is short. If you choose the first option, do nothing. If you choose the second option, leave one of your work boots outside your apartment door <u>tonight</u>, and someone will be there before morning to take you and Geneva to your new life. Pack light.*

*I will almost certainly never see you again, but I am so grateful for* the love and friendship you and Sarah showed me. It has changed my life forever, and only for the better.

Love,

**Little Sister**

Octavio sat back, stunned. He stared out the apartment's small window into the brightly lit city night and mulled over the contents of the letter. His thoughts went back to the last time he had held his wife in his arms and asked her: 'What would you do if they ordered you to do something you *knew* was wrong?'

Her answer then had been dissatisfying, but he had accepted it because he loved her. But now... Now, Feng Chu Hua had told him that Sarah had once again answered that question in the greatest way possible, even if it had taken her from him and their daughter.

He read through the letter several more times and then dutifully burned it in the kitchen sink with a match, washing the ashes down the drain. Then he went back into the bedroom and stared down at the sleeping Geneva for a long time—his daughter, the last piece of Sarah that he still had.

After several minutes, Octavio Nowak calmly went back to the front door and opened it a crack. Poking his head out and staring up and down the empty hallway, he set one of his work boots on the doormat.

**THE END OF BOOK TWO**

Read the full story of Sarah Nowak, Feng Chu Hua, and the rebellion on Panamar in...

**Revolution: A Four Worlds Story**

And the main story continues in...

**The Four Worlds: Wrath of Mars**

Don't ever miss a new release!

Sign up now for Skyler's newsletter and get access to new release updates, free content, and great deals.

Just go to
**www.skylerramirez.com**

# BOOKS BY SKYLER RAMIREZ

## DUMB LUCK AND DEAD HEROES

The Worst Ship in the Fleet

The Worst Spies in the Sector

The Worst Pirate Hunters in the Fringe

The Worst Rescuers in the Republic

The Worst Detectives in the Federation

The Worst Traitors in the Confederacy

The Worst Fugitives in the Star Nation

The Worst Mercenaries in the Border Systems

The Worst Admiral in the Star Cluster (Coming Soon)

## A STAR NATION IN PERIL

*Set in the same universe as Dumb Luck and Dead Heroes*

Rogue Agent

Suicide Mission

Assassin's Flight

## THE GALAXY'S WORST MERCENARIES

*Set in the same universe as Dumb Luck and Dead Heroes*

The Kaelen Extraction: A Billy Firebrand Adventure

The Calypso Enigma: A Billy Firebrand Adventure (Coming Soon)

## THE BRAD MENDOZA CHRONICLES

*Short stories in the same universe as Dumb Luck and Dead Heroes*

Saving the Academy

Battle for Poe

Siege of Jalisco

Death Station

Bells and Bullets

---

## THE FOUR WORLDS

The Four Worlds: The Truth

The Four Worlds: Subversion

The Four Worlds: Wrath of Mars

Ascension (Working Title; Coming 2026)

Revolution: A Four Worlds Story

## BLACK SKY CLUB (WITH STEPHEN GAY)

Awakening

## STANDALONE SHORT STORIES

Serena

## TRANSLATIONS

Select books also available in:

German

French

Italian

Spanish

Japanese

Simplified Chinese

Hindi

# ABOUT THE AUTHOR

I just love writing. My goal is to write books that my readers enjoy and that celebrate everyday imperfect heroes. I want to show that everyone, no matter how life has dealt with them or how they've dealt with life, deserves a second chance and can go on to do amazing things. Just look at Brad and Jessica in Dumb Luck and Dead Heroes or Jinny Ambrosa and Tyrus Tyne in The Four Worlds.

It's important to me that everyone be able to read my books, including my teenage children, so I purposefully leave out any swearing or graphic scenes, though I don't shy away from serious topics. In this, I follow a tradition set by many (far better) writers before me, most notably in my life, Louis L'Amour.

As for the personal side, I live in Texas with my wife and four children (and often a revolving door of exchange students), and I work for a major tech company in my spare time. But writing is my passion, and

I often toil into the early hours of morning, especially on the weekends, and it's all worth it when I see people enjoy my books.

Thanks for reading!

Skyler Ramirez

Visit me at www.skylerramirez.com

amazon.com/stores/author/B0BLM4MML2
facebook.com/skylerramirezauthor
instagram.com/skyler.ramirez.author
tiktok.com/@skylerramirez_author

Printed in Dunstable, United Kingdom